The Complete Fyodor Dostoevsky Collection (Vol. 1)

Crime and Punishment, Notes from the Underground & His Iconic Exploration of Sin and Redemption

A Modern Translation

Adapted for the Contemporary Reader

Fyodor Dostoevsky

Translated by Tim Zengerink

Table of Contents

Preface - Message to the Reader

What If You Could Help Rebuild the Greatest Library in Human History?

Thousands of years ago, the Library of Alexandria stood as the crown jewel of human achievement — a sanctuary where the collected wisdom of every known civilization was gathered, preserved, and shared freely.

And then, it was lost.

Through fire, conquest, and the slow erosion of time, humanity lost not just books — but ideas, dreams, discoveries, and stories that could have changed the world forever.

Today, the Library of Alexandria lives again — and you are invited to be a part of its restoration.

Our mission is simple yet profound:

To rebuild the greatest library the world has ever known, and to translate all timeless works into every language and dialect, so that no seeker of knowledge is ever left behind again.

By joining our movement to rebuild the modern Library of Alexandria, you become part of an unprecedented mission:

- **Unlimited Access to the Greatest Audiobooks & eBooks Ever Written:**

  Instantly explore thousands of legendary works—Plato, Shakespeare, Jane Austen, Leo Tolstoy, and countless more. All instantly available to read or listen, placing a complete literary universe at your fingertips.

- **Beautiful Paperback & Deluxe Editions at Printing Cost**

  Own any title as an elegant paperback, deluxe hardcover, or stunning collectible boxset—offered to you at true printing cost, delivered straight to your door. Build your personal Library of Alexandria, crafted for beauty, built for durability, and worthy of proud display.

- **Fresh Translations for Modern Readers—in Every Language & Dialect**

  Enjoy timeless masterpieces reimagined in clear, contemporary language—no more outdated phrases or obscure references. Alongside the original versions, we're tirelessly translating these classics into every language and dialect imaginable, ensuring accessibility and understanding across cultures and generations.

- **Join a Global Renaissance of Literature & Knowledge**

  You directly support expanding our library, publishing deluxe editions at true cost, translating works into all global languages, and bringing humanity's greatest stories to people everywhere. By joining today, you're not just preserving a legacy of masterpieces; you set in motion a powerful wave of literary accessibility.

Become a Torchbearer of Knowledge.

Join us for free now at **LibraryofAlexandria.com**

Together, we will ensure that the light of human wisdom never fades again.

With gratitude and a shared love of knowledge,
The Modern Library of Alexandria Team

Visit:

www.libraryofalexandria.com

Or scan the code below:

Introduction

Into the Abyss:
Guilt, Conscience, and the Search for Redemption

Few writers have ever penetrated the human soul with the depth, nuance, and force of Fyodor Dostoevsky. With Crime and Punishment and Notes from the Underground, he created psychological landscapes as arresting as any battlefield, as dangerous as any revolution. These are not just novels; they are explorations of sin and redemption, freedom and suffering, and the terror and ecstasy of confronting one's own moral abyss.

In The Complete Fyodor Dostoevsky Collection (Vol. 1), we begin with two of his most iconic and formative works—texts that set the stage for the vast philosophical drama of his later masterpieces. Crime and Punishment (1866) is the novel that made Dostoevsky's name immortal. It is a profound study of crime not as a legal event but as a spiritual rupture. Notes from the Underground (1864), though smaller in size, may be even more significant in its philosophical impact. It marks the birth of the antihero in modern literature, a figure who rebels not only against society but against reason, morality, and even the self.

Dostoevsky's power lies not in offering answers but in dramatizing the inner storm of the human condition. He brings his characters—and his readers—face to face with the consequences of ideas, with the weight of freedom, and with the possibility that suffering may be the very doorway to salvation. His writing is not for the faint of heart. It is fevered, ecstatic, full of contradictions and violent truths. But for those willing to enter his world, Dostoevsky offers a mirror unlike any other: one that shows not who we appear to be, but who we are at the core, trembling before good and evil.

This introduction will explore the philosophical and narrative architecture of these two works, the historical context that shaped them, and the central themes that define Dostoevsky's vision: the burden of freedom, the sickness of pride, the possibility of redemption, and the mystery of grace.

Crime and Punishment: The Trial of the Soul

Crime and Punishment tells the story of Rodion Romanovich Raskolnikov, a destitute former student in St. Petersburg who murders a pawnbroker, convinced that such an act is justified in the name of a higher moral logic. Raskolnikov believes in the theory of extraordinary individuals—people like Napoleon—who are allowed to transgress moral laws if their actions serve a greater purpose. His murder is a test of this theory. What follows is a descent into guilt, paranoia, confession, and ultimately spiritual reawakening.

But this plot summary barely touches the novel's true power. Dostoevsky is not interested in detective fiction. He is interested in conscience. The novel is an extended interrogation of what happens when man, armed with abstract logic and cut off from faith, attempts to play God.

Raskolnikov's name—derived from the Russian word "raskol," meaning "schism"—signals his inner fracture. He is torn between cold, utilitarian reasoning and a buried instinct for love, mercy, and humility. His inner torment is rendered with excruciating psychological precision. He is not hunted by the police—he is hunted by his own soul.

The novel's supporting characters reflect different responses to suffering and morality. Sonia, a poor young woman forced into prostitution to support her family, embodies Christian self-sacrifice and spiritual resilience. Porfiry, the cunning detective, engages Raskolnikov in philosophical debates that are as much theological as criminal. Even Svidrigailov, a hedonistic nihilist, becomes a mirror to Raskolnikov's potential fate.

Ultimately, Crime and Punishment is not about punishment by the state. It is about the punishment one cannot escape: the judgment of conscience. Raskolnikov's redemption comes not through ideology but through suffering—the crucible through which he discovers humility, love, and the transcendent mystery of grace.

Dostoevsky believed that modernity had created a crisis of meaning. In rejecting God, society had lost not only its moral compass but its very soul. Crime and Punishment is his prophetic warning— and his plea—for the recovery of faith, not as dogma but as a lived encounter with mercy and truth.

Notes from the Underground: The War Against Reason

If Crime and Punishment dramatizes the consequences of pride and abstraction, Notes from the Underground is the manifesto of that sickness. It is a fevered, fragmented monologue delivered by a man who has withdrawn entirely from society, choosing instead to dwell in the acidic realm of irony, resentment, and self-loathing.

This Underground Man is one of the most revolutionary voices in literature. He is a man without illusions—yet consumed by them. He mocks rationalism, utopianism, utilitarianism—all the optimistic ideologies of his time. He hates the idea that man is merely a rational being who seeks pleasure and avoids pain. He insists that man is deeper, darker, and more contradictory.

"Man needs only to act as he chooses," he writes, "but he wants to choose freely, even if it means choosing self-destruction."

This is the core of Dostoevsky's philosophical revolt. Against the emerging worldview of scientific determinism, he asserts that human freedom includes the freedom to err, to suffer, and to rebel. The Underground Man deliberately humiliates himself, rejects love, sabotages connection—not because he is evil, but because he cannot bear to live a life that is pre-programmed.

The second part of Notes from the Underground offers a narrative episode—awkward, painful, and cruel—in which the narrator attempts to reconnect with people, only to end in self-inflicted failure. This section reinforces the first: the cost of freedom is alienation, but the cost of its denial is death of the soul.

For the warrior of conscience, Notes from the Underground is essential. It teaches that the war for meaning is not waged on battlefields but in the interior landscape of the will. It reveals the danger of becoming too clever to believe, too ironic to love, too proud to be healed. And it reminds us that no revolution—political or personal—will succeed unless it begins with an honest reckoning with the self.

Sin, Freedom, and the Long Path to Redemption

Dostoevsky's moral universe is not black and white. It is full of ambiguity, temptation, and the constant possibility of change. What unites these two works is not a moral doctrine but a spiritual anthropology. Dostoevsky writes from the conviction that man is a mystery—not merely a product of environment or ideology, but a soul torn between divine longing and destructive pride.

Both Crime and Punishment and Notes from the Underground confront the modern condition with prophetic urgency. They expose the failures of rationalism, the dangers of egoism, and the consequences of a world without transcendent truth. But they also offer a way forward—a path not of perfection, but of transformation.

That path begins in suffering. For Dostoevsky, suffering is not a flaw in the human experience—it is the furnace in which false selves are burned away. It is through suffering that Raskolnikov finds peace. It is through suffering that the Underground Man glimpses, if only faintly, the possibility of love.

This is Dostoevsky's ultimate gift to the warrior-mind: the understanding that courage is not mere defiance, but the willingness to face one's own moral nakedness. That strength is not hardness, but the endurance to hope in the face of despair. That freedom is not license, but the power to choose humility, responsibility, and the hard-won joy of redemption.

Welcome to The Complete Fyodor Dostoevsky Collection (Vol. 1). May these works challenge you, disturb you, and ultimately change you—not by offering answers, but by inviting you into the terrifying, luminous mystery of the human soul.

Crime and Punishment

(1866)

Fyodor Dostoyevsky

Preface

Dostoevsky was the son of a doctor. His parents worked hard and were deeply religious, but they were so poor that they had to live with their five children in just two rooms. In the evenings, the father and mother would read serious books to their children.

Even though he was always sick and fragile, Dostoevsky graduated third in his class from the Petersburg school of Engineering. While there, he had already started writing his first work, Poor Folk. When the poet Nekrassov published it in his review, it was met with great excitement. The shy, unknown young man quickly became somewhat famous. It seemed like he had a bright and successful future ahead, but those hopes were soon crushed. In 1849, he was arrested.

Although Dostoevsky wasn't a revolutionary by nature or belief, he was part of a small group of young men who gathered to read works by Fourier and Proudhon. He was accused of "speaking out against censorship, reading a letter from Byelinsky to Gogol, and knowing about plans to set up a printing press." Under the rule of Nicholas I (whom Maurice Baring called "a stern and just man"), this was enough to be sentenced to death. After eight months in prison, Dostoevsky and twenty-one others were taken to Semyonovsky Square to be executed. In a letter to his brother Mihail, Dostoevsky wrote: "They snapped words over our heads and made us wear the white shirts of those condemned to die. We were tied in groups of three to stakes, ready for execution. Since I was third in line, I thought I only had a few minutes left to live. I thought of you and your loved ones. I managed to kiss Plestcheiev and Dourov, who were next to me, and say goodbye. Suddenly, the soldiers beat a drum, and we were untied. We were told that the Tsar had spared our lives." The death sentence was changed to hard labor.

One of the prisoners, Grigoryev, went mad after being untied and never regained his sanity.

The terrible suffering from this experience left a lasting mark on Dostoevsky. His religious beliefs eventually led him to accept his suffering and see it as a blessing in his case, but he often wrote about it. He described the intense agony of those condemned to die and criticized the cruelty of such punishment. Afterward, he spent four years in a Siberian labor camp with common criminals, where he began writing The Dead House. He also spent time in a disciplinary battalion.

Before his arrest, he had shown signs of a mysterious nervous condition, which later developed into severe epilepsy. He suffered from this condition for the rest of his life, with seizures happening three or four times a year, more frequently during stressful times. In 1859, he was allowed to return to Russia. He started a journal called Vremya, which was shut down by the Censorship due to a misunderstanding. In 1864, he lost both his first wife and his brother Mihail. Despite being in terrible poverty, Dostoevsky took on his brother's debts. He started another journal, The Epoch, but it was also banned within a few months. He was overwhelmed by debt, responsible for his brother's family, and forced to write at an exhausting pace, reportedly never revising his work. However, the later years of his life were made much easier thanks to the love and devotion of his second wife.

In June 1880, Dostoevsky gave his famous speech at the unveiling of a monument to Pushkin in Moscow. He was welcomed with an outpouring of love and admiration. A few months later, he passed away. His funeral was attended by a huge crowd of mourners, and he was given a sendoff fit for a king. Even today, he remains one of the most widely read authors in Russia.

As a Russian critic once said to explain why Dostoevsky is so beloved: "He was one of us, a man made from the same blood and bones, but he suffered and saw things more deeply than the rest of us. His insight feels like wisdom... that wisdom of the heart that we seek, hoping to learn how to live. His other talents were gifts from nature, but this wisdom he earned for himself, and it is what made him great."

Part 1

Chapter 1

On an exceptionally hot evening early in July, a young man came out of the garret in which he lodged in S. Place and walked slowly, as though in hesitation, towards K. Bridge. He had successfully avoided meeting his landlady on the staircase. His garret was under the roof of a high, five-story house and was more like a cupboard than a room. The landlady who provided him with garret, dinners, and attendance, lived on the floor below, and every time he went out, he was obliged to pass her kitchen, the door of which invariably stood open. And each time he passed, the young man had a sick, frightened feeling, which made him scowl and feel ashamed. He was hopelessly in debt to his landlady and was afraid of meeting her.

This was not because he was cowardly and abject, quite the contrary; but for some time past he had been in an overstrained, irritable condition, verging on hypochondria. He had become so completely absorbed in himself, and isolated from his fellows, that he dreaded meeting, not only his landlady but anyone at all. He was crushed by poverty, but the anxieties of his position had of late ceased to weigh upon him. He had given up attending to matters of practical importance; he had lost all desire to do so. Nothing that any landlady could do had a real terror for him. But to be stopped on the stairs, to be forced to listen to her trivial, irrelevant gossip, to pestering demands for payment, threats and complaints, and to rack his brains for excuses, to prevaricate, to lie—no, rather than that, he would creep down the stairs like a cat and slip out unseen.

This evening, however, on coming out into the street, he became acutely aware of his fears. "I want to attempt a thing like that and am frightened by these trifles," he thought, with an odd smile. "Hmm... yes, all is in a man's hands and he lets it all slip from cowardice; that's an axiom. It would be interesting to know what it is men are most afraid of. Taking a new step, uttering a new word is what they fear most.... But I am talking too much. It's because I chatter that I do nothing. Or perhaps it is that I chatter because I do nothing. I've learned to chatter this last month, lying for days together in my den thinking... of Jack the Giant-killer. Why am I going there now? Am I capable of that? Is that serious? It is not serious at all. It's simply a fantasy to amuse myself; a plaything! Yes, maybe it is a plaything."

The heat in the street was terrible: and the airlessness, the bustle, and the plaster, scaffolding, bricks, and dust all about him, and that special Petersburg stench, so familiar to all who are unable to get out of town in summer—all worked painfully upon the young man's already overwrought nerves. The insufferable stench from the pot-houses, which are particularly numerous in that part of the town, and the drunken men whom he met continually, although it was a working day, completed the revolting misery of the picture. An expression of the profoundest disgust gleamed for a moment in the young man's refined face. He was, by the way, exceptionally handsome, above the average in height, slim, well-built, with beautiful dark eyes and dark brown hair. Soon he sank into deep thought, or more accurately speaking into a complete blankness of mind; he walked along not observing what was about him and not caring to observe it. From time to time, he would mutter something, from the habit of talking to himself, to which he had just confessed. At these moments, he would become conscious that his ideas were sometimes in a tangle and that he was very weak; for two days he had scarcely tasted food.

He was so badly dressed that even a man accustomed to shabbiness would have been ashamed to be seen in the street in such rags. In that quarter of the town, however, scarcely any shortcoming in dress would have created surprise. Owing to the proximity of the Hay Market, the number of establishments of bad character, the preponderance of the trading and working-class population crowded in these streets and alleys in the heart of Petersburg, types so various were to be seen in the streets that no figure, however queer, would have caused surprise. But there was such accumulated bitterness and contempt in the young man's heart, that, in spite of all the fastidiousness of youth, he minded his rags least of all in the street. It was a different matter when he met with acquaintances or with former fellow students, whom, indeed, he disliked meeting at any time. And yet when a drunken man, who, for some unknown reason, was being taken somewhere in a huge wagon dragged by a heavy dray horse, suddenly shouted at him as he drove past: "Hey there, German hatter," bawling at the top of his voice and pointing at him—the young man stopped suddenly and clutched tremulously at his hat. It was a tall round hat from Zimmerman's, but completely worn out, rusty with age, all torn and bespattered, brimless and bent on one side in a most unseemly fashion. Not shame, however, but quite another feeling akin to terror had overtaken him.

"I knew it," he muttered in confusion, "I thought so! That's the worst of all! Why, a stupid thing like this, the most trivial detail might spoil the whole plan. Yes, my hat is too noticeable... It looks absurd and that makes it noticeable. With my rags, I ought to wear a cap, any sort of old pancake, but not this grotesque thing. Nobody wears such a hat, it would be noticed a mile off, it would be remembered. What matters is that people would remember it, and that would give them a clue. For this business, one should be as little conspicuous as possible. Trifles, trifles are what matter! Why, it's just such trifles that always ruin everything...."

He had not far to go; he knew indeed how many steps it was from the gate of his lodging house: exactly seven hundred and thirty. He had counted them once when he had been lost in dreams. At the time, he had put no faith in those dreams and was only tantalizing himself by their hideous but daring recklessness. Now, a month later, he had begun to look upon them differently, and, in spite of the monologues in which he jeered at his own impotence and indecision, he had involuntarily come to regard this "hideous" dream as an exploit to be attempted, although he still did not realize this himself. He was positively going now for a "rehearsal" of his project, and at every step, his excitement grew more and more violent.

With a sinking heart and a nervous tremor, he went up to a huge house which on one side looked on to the canal and on the other into the street. This house was let out in tiny tenements and was inhabited by working people of all kinds—tailors, locksmiths, cooks, Germans of sorts, girls picking up a living as best they could, petty clerks, etc. There was a continual coming and going through the two gates and in the two courtyards of the house. Three or four door-keepers were employed on the building. The young man was very glad to meet none of them and at once slipped unnoticed through the door on the right, and up the staircase. It was a back staircase, dark and narrow, but he was familiar with it already and knew his way, and he liked all these surroundings: in such darkness even the most inquisitive eyes were not to be dreaded.

"If I am so scared now, what would it be if it somehow came to pass that I were really going to do it?" he could not help asking himself as he reached the fourth storey. There his progress was barred by some porters who were engaged in moving furniture out of a flat. He knew that the flat had been occupied by a German clerk in the civil service, and his family. This German was moving out then, and so the fourth floor on this staircase would be untenanted except by the old woman. "That's a good thing anyway," he thought to himself, as he rang the bell of the old woman's flat. The bell gave a faint tinkle as though it were made of tin and not of copper. The little flats in such houses always have bells that ring like that. He had forgotten the note of that bell, and now its peculiar tinkle seemed to remind him of something and to bring it clearly before him... He started, his nerves were terribly overstrained by now. In a little while, the door was opened a tiny crack: the old woman eyed her visitor with evident distrust through the crack, and nothing could be seen but her little eyes, glittering in the darkness. But, seeing a number of people on the landing, she grew bolder and opened the door wide. The young man stepped into the dark entry, which was partitioned off from the tiny kitchen. The old woman stood facing him in silence and looking inquiringly at him. She was a diminutive, withered up old woman of sixty, with sharp malignant eyes and a sharp little nose. Her colorless, somewhat grizzled hair was thickly smeared with oil, and she wore no kerchief over it. Round her thin long neck, which looked like a hen's leg, was knotted some sort of flannel rag, and, in spite of the heat, there hung flapping on her shoulders, a mangy fur cape, yellow with age. The old woman coughed and groaned at every instant. The young man must have looked at her with a rather peculiar expression, for a gleam of mistrust came into her eyes again.

"Raskolnikov, a student, I came here a month ago," the young man made haste to mutter, with a half bow, remembering that he ought to be more polite.

"I remember, my good sir, I remember quite well your coming here," the old woman said distinctly, still keeping her inquiring eyes on his face.

"And here... I am again on the same errand," Raskolnikov continued, feeling a bit unsettled and surprised by the old woman's suspicion. "Maybe she's always like this, and I just didn't notice last time," he thought uneasily.

The old woman hesitated for a moment, then stepped aside and pointed to the door of the room, saying as she let her visitor go ahead of her:

"Step in, my good sir."

The small room that the young man entered had yellow wallpaper, geraniums, and muslin curtains in the windows. At that moment, the setting sun brightly lit up the room.

"So, the sun will shine like this then too!" the thought flashed through Raskolnikov's mind, and with a quick glance, he looked over everything in the room, trying to take in and remember how it was arranged. But there was nothing particularly special about the room. The furniture, which was all very old and made of yellow wood, included a sofa with a large bent wooden back, an oval table in front of the sofa, a dressing table with a mirror between the windows, chairs lined up against the walls, and two or three cheap prints in yellow frames showing German women holding birds in their hands. That was all. In the corner, a small lamp burned in front of an icon. Everything was spotlessly clean; the floors and furniture gleamed with polish, and everything shone.

"That must be Lizaveta's work," the young man thought. There wasn't a single speck of dust to be seen in the entire apartment.

"It's always in the homes of mean old widows that you find such cleanliness," Raskolnikov thought again. He glanced curiously at the cotton curtain over the door that led to another tiny room, which held the old woman's bed and chest of drawers, a room he had never seen before. These two rooms made up the entire apartment.

"What do you want?" the old woman asked sharply, stepping into the room and, as before, standing directly in front of him so she could look him straight in the face.

"I've brought something to pawn," he said, pulling out an old-fashioned flat silver watch from his pocket, with a globe engraved on the back and a steel chain attached to it.

"But your time is up for the last pledge. The month ended the day before yesterday."

"I'll bring you the interest for another month, just give me a little time."

"But that's for me to decide, my good sir, whether to wait or sell your pledge right away."

"How much will you give me for the watch, Alyona Ivanovna?"

"You come with such trifles, my good sir. It's hardly worth anything. Last time, I gave you two roubles for your ring, and you could easily buy a brand-new one at the jeweler's for a rouble and a half."

"Give me four roubles for this. I'll redeem it. It belonged to my father. I'll be getting some money soon."

"A rouble and a half, and interest in advance, if you want."

"A rouble and a half!" the young man exclaimed.

"Suit yourself," the old woman said, handing the watch back to him. The young man took it and was so angry that he almost walked out. But he stopped himself, remembering he had no other options and had come for another reason as well.

"Fine, give it here," he said gruffly.

The old woman fumbled in her pocket for her keys and then disappeared behind the curtain into the other room. Left alone in the middle of the room, the young man listened intently, thinking. He heard her unlocking the chest of drawers.

"It must be the top drawer," he thought. "So, she keeps the keys in her right pocket. They're all on one steel ring... And there's one key, three times bigger than the others, with deep notches. That can't be for the chest of drawers... there must be another chest or a strongbox. That's useful to know. Strongboxes always have keys like that... But how humiliating this all is."

The old woman returned.

"Here, sir: since we charge ten kopecks per rouble a month, I need to take fifteen kopecks from a rouble and a half as interest in advance. And for the two roubles I lent you before, you now owe me twenty kopecks, also in advance. That makes thirty-five kopecks altogether. So, I'll give you a rouble and fifteen kopecks for the watch. Here it is."

"What! Only a rouble and fifteen kopecks?"

"Exactly."

The young man didn't argue and took the money. He looked at the old woman and didn't hurry to leave, as though there was still something he wanted to say or do, but he wasn't sure what.

"I might bring you something else in a day or two, Alyona Ivanovna—something valuable—silver—a cigarette case, as soon as I get it back from a friend..." He trailed off awkwardly.

"We'll talk about it then, sir."

"Goodbye—are you always here alone? Your sister isn't with you?" He asked as casually as he could as he headed out to the hallway.

"What business is that of yours, my good sir?"

"Oh, nothing, I just asked. You're so quick to react... Goodbye, Alyona Ivanovna."

Raskolnikov left, feeling utterly confused. His confusion only grew stronger. As he made his way down the stairs, he stopped a few times, as though struck by a sudden thought. Once he reached the street, he cried out, "Oh, God, how disgusting this all is! How could I possibly... No, it's nonsense, it's absurd!" he added firmly. "And how could such a horrible idea have even crossed my mind? What disgusting, filthy thoughts I'm capable of. Yes, filthy, that's the worst part. Disgusting, revolting, disgusting! And for a whole month, I've been..." But no words or outbursts could express his agitation. The intense feeling of disgust, which had begun to weigh on his heart as he made his way to the old woman's apartment, had now reached such a peak and taken such a clear form that he didn't know what to do with himself to escape the misery. He stumbled along the street like a drunken man, bumping into people without noticing them. He only regained his senses when he found himself in the next street. Looking around, he realized he was standing near a tavern, which had steps leading down from the sidewalk to the basement entrance. At that moment, two drunk men staggered out of the door, cursing and holding each other up as they climbed the steps. Without thinking, Raskolnikov immediately went down the steps. Until that moment, he had never entered a tavern, but now he felt dizzy and was tormented by a burning thirst. He desperately wanted a cold beer and blamed his sudden weakness on hunger. He sat down at a sticky little table in a dark and dirty corner, ordered some beer, and eagerly drank the first glass. Right away, he felt better, and his thoughts became clearer.

"All of this is nonsense," he said to himself with renewed hope, "there's nothing to worry about! It's just physical exhaustion. One glass of beer, a piece of bread, and suddenly, your brain works better, your mind clears up, and your will becomes stronger! Ugh, how trivial it all is!"

But even as he reflected on this with scorn, he already felt happier, as though a terrible weight had been lifted from him. He looked around the room cheerfully at the other people there. Yet, even in that moment, a vague feeling crept in, hinting that this sudden shift to a happier mood wasn't quite right either.

The tavern was almost empty. Apart from the two drunken men Raskolnikov had encountered on the steps, a group of five men and a girl with a concertina had just left, making the room quiet and sparsely populated. Of those who remained, one was a man who seemed to be a craftsman. He was drunk, though not completely out of control, and sat in front of a pot of beer. Beside him sat his companion, a large, stout man with a grey beard, dressed in a short, wide coat. This man was far more intoxicated and had fallen asleep on the bench. From time to time, he stirred, cracking his fingers in his sleep, his arms spread wide as his upper body rocked about on the bench. He would hum fragments of a song, struggling to remember the lyrics:

"His wife a year he fondly loved,

His wife a—a year he—fondly loved..."

Then he would suddenly wake up again and sing:

"Walking along the crowded row,

He met the one he used to know."

But none of the other patrons joined in his singing or found it amusing. His silent companion sat beside him, looking at these outbursts with hostility and suspicion, as if disapproving of the whole display.

Another man in the room sat apart from the others. He had the appearance of a retired government clerk. From time to time, he sipped from his beer and glanced around at the other patrons. He seemed restless, as if something was troubling him.

Chapter 2

Raskolnikov wasn't accustomed to crowds, and as mentioned before, he had been avoiding people lately. But suddenly, he felt the need to be around others. Something new seemed to be stirring inside him, and with it came a sort of thirst for company. He was so exhausted from a month of intense misery and brooding that he craved a break, even if it was just for a moment, in some different environment. And despite the filth and unpleasantness of the tavern, he was glad to stay there now.

The tavern owner was in another room, but he would occasionally come down some steps into the main room. Each time, his tarred boots with red tops were visible before the rest of him. He wore a full coat and a disgustingly greasy black satin waistcoat without a cravat, and his entire face seemed to shine with oil, like a rusty metal lock. A boy, about fourteen, stood at the counter, and another younger boy helped with serving. On the counter were some sliced cucumbers, pieces of dried black bread, and small chunks of fish, all of which smelled awful. The air was stifling and thick with the smell of alcohol, enough to make someone drunk in just five minutes from the fumes alone.

There are times when meeting a stranger leaves a strong impression, even before a single word is exchanged. Such was the case for Raskolnikov when he noticed a man sitting a short distance away, who looked like a retired clerk. The young man often thought back to this moment later, attributing it to a sense of premonition. He kept glancing at the man, partly because the man was staring at him persistently, clearly eager to start a conversation. The clerk seemed familiar with the other people in the room, including the tavern keeper, but looked at them with a kind of weary disdain, as though he saw them as beneath him in both status and culture, and not worth his time. He was a man over fifty, balding, with gray hair, of medium height, and stout. His face, bloated from constant drinking, had a yellowish, almost greenish tint, with swollen eyelids from which sharp reddish eyes peered out like narrow slits. There was something strange about him; his eyes showed signs of deep emotion—maybe even thoughtfulness and intelligence—but there was also a hint of madness. He wore an old, tattered black dress coat, missing all but one button, which he had fastened, clinging to this last shred of dignity. His wrinkled shirtfront was stained and protruded from his canvas waistcoat. Like a typical clerk, he was clean-shaven, though he hadn't shaved in so long that his chin had become a stiff grayish stubble. His manner also carried a certain respectability, like that of an official. But he was restless, occasionally ruffling his hair and dropping his head into his hands as he rested his ragged elbows on the sticky, stained table. Finally, he looked straight at Raskolnikov and spoke loudly and firmly:

"May I dare, honored sir, to engage you in a polite conversation? For, although your appearance may not command respect, my experience tells me that you are an educated man, unaccustomed to heavy drinking. I have always respected education when combined with true feelings, and besides, I am a titular counselor by rank. Marmeladov—that is my name; titular counselor. May I ask, have you ever served in the government?"

"No, I'm a student," the young man replied, somewhat taken aback by the speaker's pompous tone and the directness of being addressed. Despite the fleeting desire he had felt for company, now that someone was actually speaking to him, he immediately felt his usual irritation and unease toward strangers who tried to approach him.

"A student, or perhaps a former student," exclaimed the clerk. "I knew it! I am a man of great experience, sir," and he tapped his forehead with his fingers as if congratulating himself. "You've been a student or attended some academic institution... But please, allow me..." He got up, swayed a little, grabbed his jug and glass, and sat down beside Raskolnikov, slightly sideways. He was drunk, but he spoke confidently and smoothly, only occasionally losing track of his sentences and dragging out his words. He latched onto Raskolnikov as eagerly as if he, too, hadn't spoken to anyone for a month.

"Honored sir," he began with a kind of solemnity, "poverty is not a sin—that's a well-known truth. But I also know that drunkenness is not a virtue, and that is even more true. However, beggary, honored sir, beggary is a sin. In poverty, one can still hold onto their inner nobility, but in beggary—never—no one can. A beggar isn't driven out of society with a stick; no, he's swept away with a broom, humiliated in the worst possible way—and rightly so. For when you're begging, you are the first to humiliate yourself. Hence, the tavern! Honored sir, just a month ago, Mr. Lebeziatnikov beat my wife, and let me tell you, my wife is a very different matter than me! Do you understand? Allow me to ask you out of sheer curiosity—have you ever spent a night on a hay barge, on the Neva?"

"No, I haven't," Raskolnikov replied. "What do you mean?"

"Well, I've just come from one, and it's the fifth night I've slept there..." He poured himself a glass, drank it down, and paused. Bits of hay were clinging to his clothes and sticking to his hair. It seemed likely he hadn't changed or washed for the past five days. His hands were filthy, red and swollen, with black nails.

His conversation sparked some mild interest from the others in the room. The boys behind the counter began to snicker. The tavern owner came down from the upper room, apparently just to hear what the "funny fellow" had to say, and sat down a little distance away, yawning but doing so with a certain dignity. It seemed Marmeladov was a familiar figure here, and he had likely developed his grand way of speaking from frequent conversations with strangers in the tavern. Some drunks, especially those who are controlled strictly at home, develop this habit of justifying themselves when in the company of other drinkers, hoping to gain some understanding or sympathy.

"Funny fellow!" the tavern keeper remarked. "Why don't you work? Why aren't you doing your duty, if you're still employed?"

"Why am I not at work, honored sir?" Marmeladov continued, directing his response solely to Raskolnikov, as if it had been him who asked. "Why am I not doing my duty? Do you think my heart doesn't ache, knowing I'm a useless worm? Just a month ago, when Mr. Lebeziatnikov hit my wife, and I lay there drunk, do you think I didn't suffer? Tell me, young man, have you ever... well, begged hopelessly for a loan?"

"Yes, I have. But what do you mean by hopelessly?"

"Hopelessly, in the truest sense, when you know in advance that you'll get nothing. You know, without a doubt, that the man—this most respectable and upstanding citizen—won't give you a single kopeck. And why should he? He knows I won't repay him. Why would he give it to me out of pity? Mr. Lebeziatnikov, who keeps up with modern ideas, explained the other day that science itself now forbids pity—that's the way things are in England, where they have political economy. So, why would he give me anything? And yet, even knowing he won't, I still go to him and…"

"Why do you go?" asked Raskolnikov.

"Well, when you have nowhere else to go, what else can you do? Every person needs somewhere to go, for there are times when you simply must go somewhere! When my daughter first got her yellow passport, I had no choice but to go… (because my daughter has a yellow passport)," he added uneasily, glancing at Raskolnikov. "No matter, sir, no matter!" he continued hurriedly and with apparent composure when the boys behind the counter burst into laughter, and even the innkeeper smiled. "No matter! I am not embarrassed by their laughter, for everyone already knows all about it, and what is secret has been made public. I accept it all, not with contempt, but with humility. So be it! So be it! 'Behold the man!' Excuse me, young man, can you… no, let me say it more strongly and clearly: do you dare, while looking at me, deny that I am a pig?"

Raskolnikov did not say a word in response.

"Well," the speaker began again, even more resolutely, after waiting for the laughter in the room to fade. "Well, then, I am a pig, but she is a lady! I may look like a beast, but Katerina Ivanovna, my wife, is a person of education and the daughter of an officer. Granted, I am a scoundrel, but she is a woman with a noble heart, full of feelings, refined by education. And yet… oh, if only she could feel for me! Honored sir, you must understand, every person needs at least one place where they are understood, where someone feels for them! But Katerina Ivanovna, despite her noble heart, is unjust… although I know that when she pulls my hair, she does it out of pity—yes, I repeat without shame, she pulls my hair, young man," he declared with even more dignity when he heard the boys snickering again. "But, my God, if only... if only once... But no, no! It's all in vain! There's no use talking! No use talking! For more than once, my wish has come true, and more than once she has felt for me, but... such is my fate, and I am a beast by nature!"

"Rather!" yawned the innkeeper.

Marmeladov resolutely struck his fist on the table. "Such is my fate! Do you know, sir, do you know, I have sold her very stockings for drink? Not her shoes—that would be understandable—but her stockings! I sold her mohair shawl for drink too, a gift to her long ago, her own property, not mine. And we live in a cold room, and this winter she caught a cold and has begun coughing and spitting blood. We have three little children, and Katerina Ivanovna works from morning until night. She scrubs, cleans, and washes the children because she has been used to cleanliness since childhood. But her chest is weak, and she has a tendency toward consumption. Do you think I don't feel it? The more I drink, the more I feel it. And that is why I drink—so I can suffer twice as much!" With that, he laid his head down on the table in despair.

"Young man," he continued, raising his head again, "when you walked in, I could see that something was troubling you. That is why I spoke to you. By sharing my story, I am not making a fool of myself in front of these idle onlookers, for they already know everything about me. Instead, I am seeking out a man of feeling and education. You should know that my wife was educated in a prestigious school for the daughters of noblemen, and when she left, she danced the shawl dance in front of the governor and other dignitaries. For this, she was awarded a gold medal and a certificate of merit. The medal... well, the medal has long since been sold, of course, but the certificate is still in her trunk, and recently she showed it to our landlady. Though she constantly quarrels with the landlady, she felt compelled to show someone her past honors and the happy days that are gone. I don't blame her for this, not at all, for her memories are all she has left, and everything else has turned to dust. Yes, she is a proud and spirited woman. She scrubs the floors herself and eats nothing but black bread, but she won't allow anyone to treat her with disrespect. That is why she could not stand Mr. Lebeziatnikov's rudeness, and when he beat her, it was the insult that hurt her more than the blows. She was a widow when I married her, with three young children. She had married her first husband, an infantry officer, for love and had run away from her father's house to be with him. She was deeply in love with him, but he gambled, got into debt, and eventually died. By the end, he used to beat her, and although she fought back—I have documents to prove it—she still speaks of him with tears and often compares me to him, which I don't mind. I'm even glad that she feels she was happy once, even if only in her imagination.

She was left a widow with three children in desperate poverty, in a remote area where I happened to be at the time. Her relatives had abandoned her, and her pride made it even worse. Then I, a widower with a fourteen-year-old daughter from my first marriage, offered her my hand because I couldn't bear to see her suffer any longer. You can imagine how desperate she was, that a woman of education and culture, from a noble family, would marry someone like me. But she did, sobbing and wringing her hands, for she had nowhere else to turn. Do you understand, sir? Do you understand what it means to have nowhere else to turn? No, you can't understand that yet. For a whole year, I worked faithfully and didn't touch this," he said, tapping the jug with his finger, "because I have feelings. But even then, I couldn't please her, and then I lost my job—not through any fault of my own, but because of changes in the office. And after that, I did turn to drink.

It will soon be a year and a half since we arrived here in this magnificent capital, with its many monuments, after wandering and facing many hardships. I found a job... and then lost it again. This time, it was my fault because my weakness got the better of me. Now, we rent part of a room at Amalia Fyodorovna Lippevechsel's, along with many others. It's chaos—filth and disorder, like Bedlam. And during all of this, my daughter from my first marriage has grown up. What she has had to endure from her stepmother, I won't speak of. Katerina

Ivanovna is full of noble feelings, but she is proud, short-tempered, and often irritable. But there's no point dwelling on that now.

Sonia, my daughter, has received no proper education. Four years ago, I tried to teach her geography and universal history, but I wasn't knowledgeable enough, and we didn't have the right books, so we stopped. We only got as far as Cyrus of Persia. Since then, Sonia has read a few romantic novels, and lately, she has been reading a book on physiology by Lewes, which she got from Mr. Lebeziatnikov. She even shared some passages with us. That's the entirety of her education. Now, sir, let me ask you something: do you think a respectable poor girl can earn much through honest work? Not even fifteen farthings a day, if she is respectable and has no special talents. What's more, Ivan Ivanitch Klopstock, the civil counselor—have you heard of him?—hasn't paid her for the six shirts she made for him. He threw her out, saying the collars weren't stitched properly, and she came home without a kopeck. And all this while, the little ones are crying from hunger, and Katerina Ivanovna is pacing back and forth, wringing her hands, her cheeks flushed red from her illness. 'You live with us,' she tells Sonia, 'you eat and drink and stay warm, but you do nothing to help.' And what does Sonia eat and drink when there isn't even a crumb for the children?

I was lying there drunk, and I heard Sonia's soft voice. She has a gentle little voice, and her face is pale and thin. She asked, 'Katerina Ivanovna, do you really want me to do this?' And Darya Frantsovna, a woman of ill repute and known to the police, had tried to get at her through the landlady several times. 'Why not?' Katerina Ivanovna replied mockingly, 'You think you're too good for that?' But don't judge her, sir. Don't blame her! She wasn't herself when she said it—her illness and the children's cries had driven her mad. That's just her nature. When the children cry, even from hunger, she hits them. At six o'clock, I saw Sonia put on her kerchief and cape and leave the room. At nine o'clock, she came back. She walked straight over to Katerina Ivanovna and silently placed thirty roubles on the table. She didn't say a word, didn't even look at her. She simply picked up our old green shawl, covered her head, and lay down on the bed, facing the wall. Only her little shoulders were shaking. And I... I just lay there, still drunk. But then I saw Katerina Ivanovna silently walk over to Sonia's bed. She knelt by her side all evening, kissing her feet, and wouldn't get up. They both fell asleep in each other's arms... together, together... And I... I lay there, drunk."

Marmeladov stopped suddenly, as if his voice had failed him. Then he quickly filled his glass, drank, and cleared his throat.

"Since then, sir," he continued after a brief pause, "since then, because of an unfortunate event and because of information given by bad-hearted people—among whom Darya Frantsovna played a leading role, claiming she was disrespected—since then, my daughter Sofya Semyonovna has been forced to take a yellow ticket, and because of that, she cannot live with us anymore. Our landlady, Amalia Fyodorovna, won't allow it, even though she had previously supported Darya Frantsovna. And Mr. Lebeziatnikov too... hm.... All the trouble between him and Katerina Ivanovna started because of Sonia. At first, he was interested in Sonia himself, and then all of a sudden, he became very proud: 'How,' he said, 'can a well-educated man like me live in the same place as a girl like that?' And Katerina Ivanovna wouldn't let it go, she defended Sonia... and that's how it all happened. Now Sonia only comes to see us after dark; she comforts Katerina Ivanovna and gives her everything she can. She lives with the Kapernaumovs, the tailors, in a small room partitioned off from the rest of their family. Kapernaumov is a lame man with a cleft palate, and all of his family members have cleft palates too, even his wife. They're all very poor, and they all live in one room, but Sonia has her own small space. Hm... yes... very poor people, all of them with cleft palates... yes. Then, in the morning, I got up, put on my rags, raised my hands to heaven, and went to see His Excellency, Ivan Afanasyvitch. Do you know him? No? Well, then you don't know a true man of God. He's soft as wax... wax before the face of the Lord, melting like wax!... His eyes filled with tears when he heard my story. 'Marmeladov,' he said, 'once already you have disappointed me... but I'll take you back, just this once, on my own responsibility.' That's what he said. 'Remember,' he said, 'and now you may go.' I kissed the ground at his feet—in my mind, of course, because in reality, he wouldn't have let me do that, being a statesman and a man with modern, enlightened ideas. I went home, and when I told them I'd been taken back to work and would be getting a salary—oh, what a celebration there was!"

Marmeladov stopped again, trembling with excitement. At that moment, a group of drunk partygoers entered from the street, and the sound of a hired concertina and the cracked voice of a seven-year-old child singing "The Hamlet" filled the room. The tavern-keeper and the boys were busy serving the newcomers. Marmeladov, ignoring the new arrivals, continued his story. He seemed weaker now, but the more drunk he became, the more he talked. The memory of his recent success seemed to energize him, and a glow appeared on his face. Raskolnikov listened intently.

"That was five weeks ago, sir. Yes... As soon as Katerina Ivanovna and Sonia heard the news—oh, it was like stepping into Heaven. Before, I could lie around like an animal, and they would only shout at me. But now they walked on tiptoe, quieting the children. 'Semyon Zaharovitch is tired from his work at the office, he needs his rest, shh!' They made me coffee before I left for work and even boiled cream for me! They started buying real cream for me, do you hear that? And how they managed to get the money for a decent outfit—eleven roubles, fifty copecks—I'll never know. Boots, cotton shirt-fronts— all magnificent, a uniform, everything perfect, and all for eleven roubles and fifty copecks. The first morning I came home from the office, Katerina Ivanovna had prepared two dishes for dinner—soup and salted meat with horseradish, which we had never even dreamed of before. She didn't have any proper dresses, none at all, but she still managed to dress up as if she were going out. Not that she had much to work with, but she did her hair nicely, put on a clean collar and cuffs, and she looked like a completely different person, younger and more beautiful. Sonia, my little darling, had only helped us with money 'for now,' she said, 'because it wouldn't be proper for me to visit you too often. I'll come after dark when no one can see.' Do you hear that? Do you hear it? After dinner, I took a nap, and what do you think happened? Even though Katerina Ivanovna had had a terrible argument with our landlady, Amalia Fyodorovna, just a week before, she still invited her in for coffee. They sat whispering together for two hours. 'Semyon Zaharovitch is back at work now, and he's receiving a salary,' Katerina Ivanovna said, 'and he went himself to His Excellency, and His Excellency came out to meet him, made everyone else wait, and took Semyon Zaharovitch by the hand and led him into his office.' Do you hear that? 'Yes,' she said, 'Semyon Zaharovitch, remembering your past service,' he said, 'and despite your weakness for that foolish habit, since you've made a promise now, and since we've struggled without you,' he said, 'I trust your word as a gentleman.' And all of that, let me tell you, Katerina Ivanovna completely made up in her head! Not just because she wanted to brag—no, she actually believes it herself! She entertains herself with these fantasies, I swear she does! And I don't blame her for it, no, I don't blame her! Six days ago, when I brought her my first salary— twenty-three roubles and forty copecks—she called me her little poppet: 'Poppet,' she said, 'my little poppet.' And when we were alone, you know? You wouldn't think much of me as a husband, would you? But she pinched my cheek, 'my little poppet,' she said."

Marmeladov stopped, tried to smile, but his chin began to tremble. He controlled himself, however. The tavern, his ragged appearance, the five nights he'd spent sleeping in a hay barge, the bottle of alcohol, and yet his deep love for his wife and children—it all confused Raskolnikov. He listened intently but with a growing sense of unease. He was annoyed that he had come here.

"Honored sir, honored sir," Marmeladov suddenly cried, recovering himself—"Oh, sir, maybe all of this seems like a joke to you, just like it does to others, and maybe I'm just bothering you with the ridiculous little details of my life, but to me, it's no joke. I feel it all deeply... And that whole heavenly day of my life, that whole evening, I spent dreaming of how I would fix everything, how I would dress the children, how I would let her rest, how I would save my daughter from disgrace and bring her back into the family... and so much more... It was all so excusable, sir. But then, sir" (Marmeladov suddenly sat up straight, raised his head, and looked intently at his listener), "well, the very next day after all those dreams, that is to say, exactly five days ago, in the evening, I stole the key to Katerina Ivanovna's chest like a thief in the night, took out what was left of my salary—I can't even remember how much it was—and look at me now! It's been five days since I left home, they're looking for me, I've lost my job, and my uniform is lying in a tavern on the Egyptian Bridge. I traded it for the rags I'm wearing now... and it's all over!"

Marmeladov struck his forehead with his fist, clenched his teeth, closed his eyes, and leaned heavily on the table with his elbow. But a moment later, his face suddenly changed, and with a sly, fake smile, he glanced at Raskolnikov, laughed, and said, "This morning I went to see Sonia. I went to ask her for a little help! Ha-ha-ha!"

"You don't mean she gave it to you?" one of the newcomers shouted, bursting into laughter.

"She gave me this very quart," Marmeladov said, speaking directly to Raskolnikov. "She gave me thirty copecks, her last, all she had. I saw it with my own eyes. She didn't say a word, just looked at me without speaking... Up there, in Heaven, they grieve over men, they weep, but they don't blame them! They don't blame them! But it hurts more, it hurts more when they don't blame you! Thirty copecks, yes! And maybe she needs it herself now, huh? What do you think, sir? Because now she has to look nice. That costs money, that smart appearance, you know? Do you understand, sir? And there's pomade, too, you see. She needs things: petticoats, starched ones, shoes, real pretty ones so she can show off her foot when she steps over a puddle. Do you understand, sir? Do you understand what all that 'smartness' means? And here I am, her own father, taking thirty copecks of her money for a drink! And I'm drinking it! And I've already drunk it! Tell me, who would have pity on a man like me, huh? Do you feel sorry for me, sir, or not? Tell me, sir, do you feel sorry or not? Ha-ha-ha!"

He tried to pour himself another drink, but the pot was empty.

"What are you to be pitied for?" yelled the tavern-keeper, who was now standing near them again.

Laughter and even some cursing followed. The noise came from those who were listening, as well as from people who hadn't heard anything but were just staring at the figure of the dismissed government clerk.

"To be pitied! Why should I be pitied?" Marmeladov suddenly shouted, standing up with his arm stretched out, as if he had been waiting for that very question.

"Why should I be pitied, you ask? Yes! There's no reason to pity me! I should be crucified, nailed to a cross, not pitied! Crucify me, oh judge, crucify me, but have mercy on me! And then I will go willingly to be crucified, for I'm not looking for joy but for tears and suffering! Do you think," he said, turning to the bartender, "that this pint of yours has been sweet to me? No, it's suffering I sought at the bottom of it, tears and suffering, and I found it, and I've tasted it. But He will have mercy on us, the One who has had mercy on all men, who has understood all men and all things. He is the One, He is also the judge. He will come one day, and He will ask, 'Where is the daughter who gave herself for her cross, for her sick stepmother and for the little children of another? Where is the daughter who had pity on the filthy drunk, her earthly father, and wasn't scared away by his beastliness?' And He will say, 'Come to me! I've already forgiven you once.... I have forgiven you once. Your many sins are forgiven, because you loved much....' And He will forgive my Sonia. He will forgive her, I know it... I felt it in my heart when I saw her just now! And He will judge and forgive everyone, the good and the evil, the wise and the humble.... And when He's done with everyone, then He will call us. 'You too, come forth,' He will say, 'Come forth, you drunkards, come forth, you weak ones, come forth, you children of shame!' And we will all come forth, without shame, and stand before Him. And He will say to us, 'You are swine, made in the image of the Beast and with his mark, but come also!' And the wise men and those with understanding will ask, 'Oh Lord, why do you accept these people?' And He will say, 'This is why I accept them, oh wise ones, this is why I accept them, oh you with understanding—because not one of them thought he deserved it.' And He will hold out His hands to us, and we will fall at His feet...

and we will cry... and we will understand everything! Then we will understand everything!... and everyone will understand, even Katerina Ivanovna... she will understand.... Lord, let Your kingdom come!"

And he collapsed onto the bench, exhausted and helpless, looking at no one, completely lost in thought. His words had made an impression; there was a moment of silence, but soon the laughter and swearing began again.

"That's his idea!"

"He talked himself crazy!"

"A fine clerk he is!"

And so on, and so on.

"Let's go, sir," said Marmeladov suddenly, raising his head and speaking to Raskolnikov, "come with me... to Kozel's house, in the yard. I'm going to see Katerina Ivanovna—it's time."

Raskolnikov had been wanting to leave for some time, and he had planned to help Marmeladov. Marmeladov was much shakier on his feet than in his speech and leaned heavily on the young man. They had to walk two or three hundred paces. The drunk man became more and more distressed as they got closer to the house.

"It's not Katerina Ivanovna that I'm afraid of now," he muttered anxiously, "and not that she'll pull my hair. What does my hair matter? Forget my hair! That's what I say! In fact, it would be better if she did pull it. That's not what I'm scared of... it's her eyes I'm scared of... yes, her eyes... and the redness on her cheeks scares me, too... and her breathing.... Have you ever noticed how people with that disease breathe when they get upset? I'm also scared of the children crying.... If Sonia hasn't brought them food... I don't know what will happen! I don't know! But I'm not afraid of getting hit.... Know this, sir, such blows don't hurt me—they even give me a strange satisfaction. I can't live without them.... It's better this way. Let her hit me, it'll make her feel better... it's better this way.... There's the house. Kozel's house, the cabinetmaker... a German, well-off. Lead the way!"

They went through the yard and up to the fourth floor. The staircase grew darker and darker as they climbed. It was almost eleven o'clock, and although in the summer there's no real night in Petersburg, it was quite dark at the top of the stairs.

A dirty little door at the very top of the stairs stood slightly open. A shabby room about ten paces long was dimly lit by the end of a candle; the entire room was visible from the entrance. It was a mess, littered with all kinds of rags, especially children's clothes. A torn sheet was stretched across the far corner, probably hiding a bed. There was almost no furniture in the room except for two chairs and a sofa covered in worn-out American leather, full of holes. In front of the sofa stood an old kitchen table, unpainted and bare. On the edge of the table was a smoking tallow candle in an iron holder. It looked like the family had their own room, not just a section of one, but their room was more like a passageway. The door leading to the other rooms, or rather closets, in Amalia Lippevechsel's flat was half open, and there was shouting, noise, and laughter coming from within. It sounded like people were playing cards and drinking tea. Rude words occasionally came flying out.

Raskolnikov immediately recognized Katerina Ivanovna. She was a rather tall, slim, and graceful woman, terribly thin, with beautiful dark brown hair and a feverish blush in her cheeks. She was pacing back and forth in the small room, clutching her chest; her lips were dry, and she was breathing in nervous, broken gasps. Her eyes glittered feverishly and stared fixedly ahead. That sickly, frantic face, with the last flicker of candlelight playing on it, left a disturbing impression. To Raskolnikov, she looked around thirty years old, and she seemed a strange wife for Marmeladov. She hadn't noticed them enter and didn't hear them either. She seemed lost in her own thoughts, not seeing or hearing anything around her. The room was stuffy, but she hadn't opened the window; a foul smell rose from the staircase, but she hadn't closed the door. Clouds of tobacco smoke drifted in from the other rooms, and she kept coughing, but didn't shut the door. The youngest child, a girl of six, was asleep, curled up on the floor with her head on the sofa. A boy, a year older, stood crying and trembling in the corner, probably after just being beaten. Beside him stood a nine-year-old girl, tall and thin, wearing a tattered chemise and an old cashmere shawl draped over her bare shoulders, much too small for her and barely reaching her knees. Her arm, as thin as a stick, was around her brother's neck. She was trying to comfort him, whispering something and doing everything she could to stop him from crying again. At the same time, her large dark eyes, which seemed even larger because of how thin her face was, were watching her mother with fear.

Marmeladov didn't enter the room but dropped to his knees in the doorway, pushing Raskolnikov in front of him. The woman, seeing a stranger, stopped and looked at him with confusion for a moment, seeming to come to her senses. She seemed to wonder what he was doing there but then seemed to assume he was just passing through to the next room. Without paying him any more attention, she walked towards the door to close it, and suddenly screamed when she saw her husband kneeling in the doorway.

"Ah!" she screamed in a rage, "He's back! The criminal! The monster!... Where's the money? What's in your pocket, show me! And why are your clothes different? Where are your clothes? Where is the money? Speak!"

And she began searching him. Marmeladov, submissive and obedient, raised both arms to help her with the search. There wasn't a single coin.

"Where is the money?" she cried. "Dear God, has he drunk it all? There were twelve silver roubles left in the chest!" In a rage, she grabbed him by the hair and dragged him into the room. Marmeladov, meekly, helped her by crawling on his knees.

"And this is a comfort to me! This doesn't hurt me; it's an absolute con-so-la-tion, honored sir," he called out, being shaken by his hair, even hitting his head on the ground once. The child sleeping on the floor woke up and started crying. The boy in the corner lost control and began trembling and screaming, running to his sister in a panic, almost having a fit. The oldest girl was shaking like a leaf.

"He's drunk it! He's drunk it all!" the poor woman screamed in despair. "And his clothes are gone! And they're hungry, starving!" She wrung her hands and pointed at the children. "Oh, cursed life! And you, aren't you ashamed?"—she suddenly lashed out at Raskolnikov—"coming from the tavern! Have you been drinking with him? You've been drinking with him too! Get out!"

The young man hurried to leave without saying a word. The inner door was flung open, and curious faces peered in. Coarse, laughing faces with pipes and cigarettes and heads covered with caps poked through the doorway. Further in, figures could be seen wearing loose dressing gowns, with very little clothing underneath, some holding cards in their hands. They found it especially funny when Marmeladov, being dragged around by his hair, shouted that it was a comfort to him. They even began stepping into the room. Finally, a sharp, shrill voice was heard. It came from Amalia Lippevechsel herself, pushing her way through the crowd and trying to restore order in her own way. Once again, for what seemed like the hundredth time, she threatened the poor woman with coarse insults, ordering her to clear out of the room by the next day.

As Raskolnikov was leaving, he managed to reach into his pocket, grab the few coppers he had received in change from his rouble at the tavern, and quietly place them on the windowsill. On the stairs, he second-guessed himself and almost went back.

"What a stupid thing I've done," he thought to himself. "They have Sonia, and I need that money myself." But realizing it would be impossible to take it back now, and that even if he could, he wouldn't, he dismissed the thought with a wave of his hand and headed back to his lodging. "Sonia needs pomade, too," he muttered as he walked along the street, laughing bitterly. "All that 'smartness' costs money... Hm! And maybe Sonia herself will end up penniless today because there's always a risk when chasing after big game... digging for gold... Then they'd all be starving tomorrow, except for my few coins. Hurrah for Sonia! What a gold mine they've found there! And they're getting the most out of it! Yes, they are! They've cried over it and gotten used to it. Man can get used to anything, the wretch!"

He sank into thought.

"And what if I'm wrong?" he suddenly cried out after thinking for a moment. "What if man isn't really a scoundrel, I mean mankind as a whole? Then all the rest is just fear, made-up fears, and there are no barriers, and everything is as it should be."

Chapter 3

He woke up late the next day after a restless sleep. But his sleep hadn't refreshed him; he woke up feeling bilious, irritable, and in a foul mood. He looked around his room with hatred. It was a tiny room, more like a cupboard, about six paces long. The room looked pitiful with its peeling, dusty yellow wallpaper, and it was so low that anyone taller than average would feel uncomfortable, always thinking they might hit their head on the ceiling. The furniture matched the room's poverty: three old, rickety chairs; a painted table in the corner, on which lay a few manuscripts and books. The thick layer of dust covering them showed they hadn't been touched in a long time. A large, clumsy sofa took up almost the entire wall and half of the room's floor space. It had once been covered with chintz, but now it was in tatters and served as Raskolnikov's bed. He often fell asleep on it just as he was, without undressing, without sheets, wrapped in his old student overcoat. His head rested on a small pillow, under which he stuffed all his linen, clean and dirty, to use as a bolster. A little table stood in front of the sofa.

It would have been hard to sink to a lower level of disorder, but for Raskolnikov, in his current state of mind, this was strangely comforting. He had completely withdrawn from everyone, like a tortoise in its shell. Even the sight of the servant girl who had to bring him food and sometimes peeked into his room made him writhe in nervous irritation. He was obsessed with a single thought, as some monomaniacs are. His landlady had stopped sending him meals for the last two weeks, and he hadn't yet bothered to complain, even though he was going without dinner. Nastasya, the cook and only servant, seemed pleased with his behavior and had stopped cleaning his room. She only wandered in with a broom about once a week. She was the one who woke him that morning.

"Get up, why are you still asleep?" she called to him. "It's past nine. I brought you some tea; do you want a cup? You must be starving."

Raskolnikov opened his eyes, startled, and recognized Nastasya.

"From the landlady?" he asked slowly, sitting up on the sofa with a sickly look on his face.

"From the landlady? Hardly!"

She placed her own cracked teapot in front of him, filled with weak and stale tea, and laid two yellow lumps of sugar beside it.

"Here, Nastasya, take this," he said, fumbling in his pocket, still dressed in his clothes from the night before, and pulling out a handful of coins. "Run and buy me a loaf of bread. And get me some sausage, the cheapest kind, from the pork butcher."

"I'll get you the bread right away, but wouldn't you rather have some cabbage soup instead of sausage? It's great soup, from yesterday. I saved it for you, but you came in too late. It's really good soup."

When she brought the soup, and he had started eating, Nastasya sat down beside him on the sofa and began to chat. She was a country peasant woman, and very talkative.

"Praskovya Pavlovna is thinking about reporting you to the police," she said.

He scowled.

"The police? What for?"

"You don't pay her rent, and you won't leave the room. That's what she wants, obviously."

"The devil! That's the last thing I need," he muttered, grinding his teeth. "No, that won't work for me... not right now. She's a fool," he added aloud. "I'll go talk to her today."

"She's a fool, all right, just like I am. But if you're so clever, why do you just lie here like a sack, with nothing to show for it? You used to go out and tutor children. So why don't you do anything now?"

"I am doing something..." Raskolnikov said gruffly and reluctantly.

"What are you doing?"

"Work..."

"What kind of work?"

"I'm thinking," he said seriously after a pause.

Nastasya was overcome with laughter. She had a habit of laughing silently, quivering and shaking all over until it made her feel sick.

"And have you made much money from your thinking?" she managed to say through her giggles.

"You can't go out to give lessons without boots. And I'm tired of it."

"Don't turn up your nose at what feeds you."

"They pay so little for lessons. What's the point of a few coins?" he replied, unwillingly, as if speaking more to himself than to her.

"And you want to make a fortune all at once?"

He looked at her strangely.

"Yes, I want a fortune," he said firmly after a short pause.

"Don't rush, you're scaring me! Should I get the loaf or not?"

"As you like."

"Oh, I almost forgot! A letter came for you yesterday while you were out."

"A letter? For me? From who?"

"I don't know. I gave the postman three copecks of my own for it. Will you pay me back?"

"Then bring it to me, for God's sake, bring it!" Raskolnikov cried out, suddenly very excited. "Good God!"

A minute later, the letter was brought to him. That was it— from his mother, from the province of R———. He turned pale as he took it. It had been a long time since he'd received a letter, but another feeling also suddenly pierced his heart.

"Nastasya, leave me alone, please. Here's your three copecks, but for goodness' sake, hurry and go!"

The letter trembled in his hand; he didn't want to open it in front of her. He wanted to be alone with it. Once Nastasya had left, he quickly lifted the letter to his lips and kissed it. Then he stared at the address—the small, slanted handwriting that was so dear and familiar, from the mother who had taught him to read and write. He hesitated; it seemed like he was afraid of something. Finally, he opened it. It was a thick, heavy letter, weighing over two ounces. Two large sheets of note paper were covered with very small handwriting.

"My dear Rodya," his mother wrote, "it's been two months since I last wrote to you, and the delay has caused me great distress, keeping me awake at night with worry. But I hope you won't blame me for not writing sooner—it wasn't something I could avoid. You know how much I love you; you are everything to me and Dounia—our only hope, our only support. When I heard that you had to leave the university some months ago because you couldn't afford to stay and that you lost your lessons and other work, it filled me with sadness. How could I help you with my small pension of only 120 roubles a year? You know the 15 roubles I sent you four months ago—I had to borrow that money, using my pension as collateral, from Vassily Ivanovitch Vahrushin, a kind-hearted merchant who was also a friend of your father's. But since he had the right to collect my pension until the debt was fully paid off, I couldn't send you anything until now. Thank God, that debt is now cleared, and I hope I'll be able to send you more soon. And, dear Rodya, we have some good news to share—something to lift our spirits.

Would you believe it? Dounia has been living with me for the last six weeks, and we won't have to be apart again. Thank God her suffering has come to an end. But let me tell you everything from the beginning, so you understand how it all happened and what we kept hidden from you until now.

When you wrote to me two months ago saying that you'd heard Dounia was struggling at the Svidrigailov household and asked me to tell you the truth, I didn't know how to respond. If I had told you the whole truth, I'm sure you would have dropped everything to come to us, even if you had to walk the entire way. I know your heart, Rodya, and I know you wouldn't allow your sister to be mistreated. I was in despair myself, but what could I do? Besides, at the time, I didn't know the full truth.

The situation was complicated because Dounia had accepted 100 roubles in advance when she started as their governess, with part of her salary to be deducted each month to repay it. That made it impossible for her to leave without paying back the money. Now I can tell you, my dear Rodya, that she accepted that advance mainly so she could send you 60 roubles, which you so desperately needed. We told you at the time that the money came from her savings, but that wasn't true. I want you to know this now, so you understand just how much Dounia loves you and what a kind heart she has.

At first, Mr. Svidrigailov treated her very badly, making cruel and mocking remarks at the dinner table. But I don't want to dwell on those painful details, especially now that it's all over. Despite the kindness of his wife, Marfa Petrovna, and the rest of the household, Dounia had a very difficult time, especially when Svidrigailov reverted to his old military ways and drank too much. And do you know what we later discovered? It turns out that from the very beginning, he was infatuated with Dounia, but he hid his feelings under a mask of rudeness and contempt. Perhaps he was ashamed of his thoughts, considering his age and the fact that he was a married man with children, and that made him angry at her. Or maybe he hoped that by acting coldly, he could conceal his feelings from others.

But in the end, he lost control and made a disgraceful proposal to Dounia, offering her all sorts of promises. He even suggested that he would leave everything behind and take her to another estate or even abroad. Imagine what she must have gone through! Leaving her job immediately wasn't an option—not only because of the money but also to protect Marfa Petrovna's feelings, since her suspicions would have been raised. If she left, it would have caused a terrible scandal for Dounia, and she would have been blamed for breaking up the family. There were many reasons why she couldn't escape that horrible household for six more weeks.

You know Dounia, Rodya—she's clever, determined, and has a strong will. Even in the worst situations, she knows how to hold herself together. She didn't tell me everything at first, worried that it would upset me, even though we stayed in regular contact.

In the end, everything came to light unexpectedly. Marfa Petrovna overheard her husband pleading with Dounia in the garden, but she misunderstood the situation and placed all the blame on her. There was a terrible scene right there in the garden. Marfa even hit Dounia, refused to listen to any explanation, and shouted at her for over an hour. Then she ordered that Dounia be sent back to me immediately. They threw all her things into a peasant's cart, without even folding them properly. And to make things worse, it started pouring rain, and Dounia, humiliated and ashamed, had to ride in that open cart all seventeen versts back to town.

Now imagine, Rodya—how could I have written to you about this two months ago? If I had told you everything, you would have been furious and heartbroken, but what could you have done? You might have ruined yourself trying to help, and Dounia would never have allowed that. And I couldn't fill a letter with meaningless small talk when my heart was breaking.

For a whole month, the scandal was the talk of the town. We didn't even dare go to church because of the stares, whispers, and rude remarks. People we knew avoided us, and no one greeted us on the street. I even heard that some clerks and shopkeepers planned to smear pitch on our gate as a public insult, and the landlord began pressuring us to leave. Marfa Petrovna spread rumors about Dounia everywhere, telling her version of the story to everyone she knew—and she knew a lot of people. She would visit the town frequently, complaining about her husband and gossiping about their problems, and in no time, the whole district knew what had happened.

The stress made me ill, but Dounia remained calm and strong. She comforted me and tried to lift my spirits—she truly is an angel! But, by God's mercy, our suffering didn't last long. Mr. Svidrigaïlov finally came to his senses and admitted the truth. To prove Dounia's innocence, he gave Marfa Petrovna a letter Dounia had written to him, refusing further private meetings and scolding him for his disgraceful behavior.

That letter was written with such strength and dignity that I cried when I read it, and even now, I can't read it without tears. The servants also testified in Dounia's favor, revealing things Svidrigaïlov hadn't realized they knew. Marfa was stunned and fully convinced of Dounia's innocence. The next day, she went to the Cathedral, knelt before the icon of Our Lady, and prayed for strength. Afterward, she came straight to us, weeping, and begged Dounia for forgiveness.

Over the following days, she visited every house in town, publicly clearing Dounia's name and even reading her letter aloud. Some people took copies of the letter, though I thought that was unnecessary. But Marfa wouldn't stop until Dounia's reputation was restored. In the end, Dounia was completely vindicated, and the disgrace fell entirely on Svidrigaïlov. I almost felt sorry for him—it seemed too harsh.

Soon after, Dounia received several offers to teach, but she refused them all. Suddenly, everyone treated her with the greatest respect, and this change played a major role in the event that has now transformed our lives.

Dounia has a suitor, Rodya, and she has accepted his proposal. I want to tell you everything, even though we didn't wait for your consent. The man is Pyotr Petrovitch Luzhin, a government official distantly related to Marfa Petrovna. She introduced him to us, and he visited us, drank coffee, and the very next day, he sent a letter proposing marriage. He asked for a quick answer, as he is very busy and must leave for Petersburg soon.

At first, we were surprised by how quickly everything happened. Luzhin is well-off, holds two government positions, and has already made his fortune. He's 45 years old but still respectable and not unattractive.

Dounia and I talked it over thoroughly. You know how sensible she is—there may not be deep love between them, but Dounia has a kind heart and is determined to make her husband happy. I believe Luzhin will do the same for her. Of course, there will be challenges, but Dounia is prepared to face them with patience and strength."

"I have already mentioned that Pyotr Petrovitch is heading to Petersburg, where he has a lot of business to handle. He plans to open a legal bureau there. For years, he has been involved in civil and commercial litigation, and just recently, he won an important case. He needs to be in Petersburg now because he has a significant case before the Senate. So, Rodya dear, he might be of great help to you in many ways. Dounia and I have already agreed that you could start building your career right away, and we believe that your future is now mapped out and secure. Oh, if only everything falls into place! It would be such a blessing, something we could only see as a gift from Providence. Dounia has been dreaming of nothing else.

We've even cautiously hinted to Pyotr Petrovitch about this possibility. His response was careful. He said that since he can't manage without a secretary, it would be preferable to hire a relative rather than a stranger—if that relative is suitable for the job (as if there's any doubt about your qualifications!). However, he wondered if your university studies would leave you with enough time to work in his office. We left the matter there for now, but Dounia hasn't

44

stopped thinking about it. She's been restless these past few days, full of excitement, and she's even come up with a plan: she envisions you becoming not just an employee, but eventually a partner in Pyotr Petrovitch's business. Given that you're studying law, this seems entirely possible.

I completely agree with Dounia, Rodya. I share all her hopes and plans, and I truly believe they are achievable. Although Pyotr Petrovitch may seem hesitant now—it's natural, since he hasn't met you yet—Dounia is confident that her influence over her future husband will help make everything happen just as we hope. However, we've been careful not to discuss our long-term plans with him, especially the idea of you becoming his partner. He's a practical man and might dismiss these ideas as mere daydreams. We haven't mentioned the possibility of him helping to cover your university expenses either. We believe it's better to wait for the right moment; he will probably offer to help on his own. After all, how could he refuse Dounia anything? And since you'll be earning a salary by working with him, the help wouldn't feel like charity but well-deserved compensation.

Dounia wants everything arranged this way, and I agree with her completely. Another reason we haven't spoken about this to Pyotr Petrovitch is that I want you to feel confident and on equal footing when you first meet him. When Dounia spoke warmly about you, he responded by saying that one can't judge a man without meeting him face-to-face and that he looks forward to forming his own opinion of you once you meet.

My dear Rodya, I've also been thinking—although this has nothing to do with Pyotr Petrovitch, just my own thoughts—that it might be better if I live independently after Dounia's marriage rather than with them. I believe Pyotr Petrovitch will be kind and considerate enough to invite me to stay with them, and I'm sure he would want me to stay with Dounia. If he hasn't mentioned it yet, it's probably because he assumes it's understood. But I think it would be better for me to live on my own. I've often noticed that husbands and mothers-in-law don't always get along well, and I wouldn't want to be in anyone's way. I also prefer to be independent as long as I have my own little piece of bread—and as long as I have children like you and Dounia, I'll be content. If possible, I would like to live somewhere nearby, close to both of you.

And now, Rodya, I've saved the most joyful news for the end of my letter: we may soon all be together again! After almost three years apart, we'll finally be able to embrace one another. It's been decided that Dounia and I will leave for Petersburg very soon—perhaps in a week! The exact date depends on when Pyotr Petrovitch can settle in there and let us know he's ready. He is eager to have the wedding as soon as possible—either before the fast of Our Lady or immediately after, if that's too soon to prepare.

Oh, how happy I'll be to hold you in my arms again! Dounia is just as excited at the thought of seeing you. She even joked that she would marry Pyotr Petrovitch just for the chance to be with you sooner. She truly is an angel! She isn't writing to you now but has asked me to send her love and countless kisses. She says she has so much to tell you that she can't even start writing now, as a few lines wouldn't do it justice and would only upset her.

Even though we'll be seeing each other soon, I'm thinking of sending you some money in the next couple of days. Now that everyone knows about Dounia's engagement to Pyotr Petrovitch, my credit has improved. I believe Afanasy Ivanovitch will lend me up to 75 roubles on the security of my pension, so I might be able to send you 25 or even 30 roubles. I would send more, but I'm a bit worried about our travel expenses. Although Pyotr Petrovitch has generously offered to cover part of the costs—he's arranged for our luggage and big trunk to be transported through some of his acquaintances—we still need some money for our arrival in Petersburg. We can't arrive with nothing, at least for the first few days.

But Dounia and I have calculated everything down to the last penny, and the trip shouldn't cost too much. It's only 90 versts from here to the railway, and we've arranged with a driver we know to take us there. From the station, Dounia and I will travel comfortably in third class. So, I may be able to send you not just 25 but 30 roubles.

But that's enough for now—I've filled two whole sheets and have no more space! So much has happened, and there's so much to tell. My dear Rodya, I send you my warmest embrace and a mother's blessing until we meet again. Love Dounia as she loves you—more than herself. She is an angel, and you, Rodya, are everything to us. You are our one hope, our one joy. If you are happy, we will be happy too.

Do you still say your prayers, Rodya? Do you still believe in the mercy of our Creator and Redeemer? I fear that the new spirit of doubt in the world today may have reached you. If it has, I pray for you. Remember how, when you were little and your father was still alive, you used to kneel at my side and say your prayers? How happy we were back then!

Goodbye for now, until we meet again. I embrace you warmly, warmly, and send you many kisses.

Yours forever,

Pulcheria Raskolnikov."

As he read the letter, tears ran down Raskolnikov's face. By the time he finished, his face had grown pale and twisted, and a bitter, angry smile curled his lips. He laid his head down on the dirty, threadbare pillow and thought for a long time. His heart was pounding, and his thoughts swirled in confusion.

After a while, the tiny yellow room, cramped like a cupboard or a box, became unbearable. His mind and eyes craved space. He grabbed his hat and left the room, no longer worried about running into anyone—he had forgotten his fear. He walked toward Vassilyevsky Ostrov along Vassilyevsky Prospect, as if on urgent business, but his thoughts were so scattered that he didn't pay attention to where he was going. He muttered to himself, sometimes speaking aloud, startling passersby, who thought he was drunk.

Chapter 4

His mother's letter had been pure torment for him, but when it came to the most important part, he hadn't felt a moment's hesitation, even as he read it. In his mind, the matter was settled—completely and without question: "As long as I'm alive, this marriage will never happen, and to hell with Mr. Luzhin!" he muttered to himself, a malicious smile spreading across his face as he savored the idea of defeating this arrangement. "It's perfectly clear," he whispered. "No, mother, no, Dounia—you won't fool me! And they apologize for not asking my opinion, for making a decision without me! As if that changes anything! They think it's all set and can't be undone, but we'll see about that! What a brilliant excuse: 'Pyotr Petrovitch is such a busy man, even his wedding has to be rushed.' No, Dounia, I see right through all of this. I know exactly what you want to tell me. I know what you were thinking that night you paced the room and what kind of prayers you whispered before the icon of the Holy Mother of Kazan in mother's room. The path to Golgotha is steep and bitter… Hm, so you've decided to marry a sensible businessman, Avdotya Romanovna. One who's already made his fortune—how solid and respectable! A man who holds two government posts, shares the progressive views of the younger generation, and seems kind, as Dounia says. That word, 'seems'—how that explains everything! And it's for that very 'seems' that Dounia is marrying him! Wonderful! Just wonderful!"

He paused for a moment, lost in thought. "But why did mother mention 'our most rising generation'? Was it just a detail to make the letter sound polished? Or was it meant to sway me in Mr. Luzhin's favor? Oh, how clever they are! I'd love to know how much they've really talked about this. Did they discuss everything openly, or did they simply understand each other without words, knowing it was best left unsaid? I bet it's a bit of both. It's clear from mother's letter—he seemed a little rude to her, and she, in her innocence, told Dounia what she thought. Of course, Dounia would have been annoyed and snapped back at her. Who wouldn't be angry? Everything was perfectly clear without mother's questions, and they both knew it was pointless to talk about it.

"And why does she tell me, 'Love Dounia, Rodya—she loves you more than herself? Does she feel guilty for sacrificing her daughter for her son's sake? 'You are everything to us, our only comfort, our only hope.' Oh, mother!"

His bitterness grew sharper with every thought. If he had crossed paths with Luzhin in that moment, he might have killed him.

"Yes, it's true," he went on, chasing his spiraling thoughts. "It takes time to understand a person, but I already know enough about Mr. Luzhin. The most important thing is that he's a businessman and 'seems kind.' And just look at his generosity—he's sending their bags and big trunk ahead! What a kind man, no doubt about that! But meanwhile, his fiancée and her mother are expected to ride in a peasant's cart covered with sacking. I know that cart—I've ridden in it myself. But no matter! It's only ninety versts to the station, and then they'll travel 'comfortably, third class,' for a thousand versts! How fitting! 'Cut your coat according to your cloth,' as the saying goes. But what about you, Mr. Luzhin? She's your bride! And you know perfectly well that her mother had to borrow money on her pension for the trip. This is business, a partnership for mutual benefit—each pays their share. Food and drink are provided, but you buy your own tobacco. The businessman has already come out on top. The luggage will probably cost less than their fares, maybe even nothing at all.

"How is it that neither of them sees this, or do they just not want to see? And yet they're pleased, so pleased! And this is just the beginning—what bitter fruit awaits them later! But it's not the stinginess or the pettiness that bothers me—it's the tone of the whole arrangement. That tone will set the pattern for their entire marriage. This is just a preview of what's to come.

"And mother—why should she be so generous? What will she have left when she gets to Petersburg? Three silver roubles, or maybe two paper ones, as she says. That poor woman… What does she plan to live on once she's there? She already suspects she won't be able to stay with Dounia and her husband, not even for the first few months. I'm sure Luzhin let something slip about it, though mother would never admit it. 'I'll refuse,' she says. But who is she counting on? What's left of her 120-rouble pension after paying off Afanasy Ivanovitch's loan? She knits woolen shawls and embroiders cuffs, ruining her eyes for an extra twenty roubles a year. I know that. And she's putting all her hopes on Luzhin's generosity—'He'll offer help on his own, he'll insist on it.' Yes, keep waiting for that!

"That's how it always is with these sentimental, idealistic people. To them, every goose is a swan until the very last moment. They cling to their hopes, refusing to see the truth until it slaps them in the face. Even when they suspect the truth, they push it away with both hands, trembling at the thought of it. And then, the very person they dressed in shining colors will put a fool's cap on their heads himself.

"I wonder if Mr. Luzhin has any awards. I'd bet he has the Order of St. Anna pinned to his coat and wears it when he dines with contractors or merchants. No doubt he'll wear it at his wedding, too! Enough about him—damn him!"

He stopped talking, his anger boiling over.

"Well... it's not surprising from mother—God bless her—but Dounia? Dounia, my darling, as if I don't know you! You were nearly twenty the last time I saw you, and I understood you even then. Mother writes that 'Dounia can endure a lot.' I know that all too well. I knew it two and a half years ago, and I've thought about it constantly ever since—how much Dounia can endure. If she could put up with Mr. Svidrigaïlov and everything that happened there, she can endure a great deal. And now, mother and Dounia believe she can endure Mr. Luzhin, a man who openly preaches that wives raised out of poverty owe everything to their husbands—a theory he shared almost as soon as he met them!

"Yes, maybe he 'let it slip,' but even if he's a sensible man, it's just as likely that he wanted to make himself perfectly clear from the start. But Dounia—Dounia! She knows exactly what kind of man he is, yet she'll have to live with him. Why, she'd survive on nothing but black bread and water before she'd sell her soul. She would never trade her moral freedom for comfort—not for all of Schleswig-Holstein, much less for Luzhin's money! That's not the kind of person she was when I last knew her, and I know she hasn't changed. Yes, the Svidrigaïlovs were a bitter trial for her, and it's hard to spend your life as a governess for a mere 200 roubles. But I know she'd rather be a slave on a plantation or a peasant under a German master than sacrifice her soul and dignity by binding herself to a man she doesn't respect—especially for her own benefit. Even if Mr. Luzhin were pure gold or a giant diamond, she would never agree to be his legal concubine.

"So why is she agreeing to marry him? What's the point? What's the reason? It's clear enough—she's not doing it for herself, not for her own comfort or survival. No, Dounia is doing it for someone else. For someone she loves, someone she adores—she's doing it for us. For me and mother. She will give up everything for us! For those she loves, she will sacrifice everything—her freedom, her peace, even her conscience if necessary. All of it—she'll put it all on the line. 'Let my life be ruined if only my loved ones can be happy!' And in such cases, we become moral casuists, convincing ourselves it's the right thing to do. We learn to justify it, even persuade ourselves that this sacrifice is our duty for the greater good.

"That's exactly what's happening here—it's as clear as day. This whole situation revolves around one person: Rodion Romanovitch Raskolnikov. I'm the center of it all, no one else. Oh yes, Dounia thinks she can ensure my happiness—keep me in university, make me Luzhin's partner, secure my future. She imagines I'll become rich, respected, and perhaps even famous one day! And mother? All her hopes rest on me, her precious Rodya, her firstborn! Who wouldn't sacrifice a daughter for a son like that? Oh, these loving, overindulgent hearts! For my sake, they'd even endure a fate like Sonia's. Sonia Marmeladov, the eternal victim—there will always be people like her in this world.

"But do you two really understand what you're sacrificing? Can you bear it? Is it worth it? Does it make any sense? And let me tell you,

Dounia—Sonia's life might not be any worse than what you'll have with Luzhin. Mother says there's 'no question of love,' but what if there's no respect either? What if you feel nothing but disgust and contempt for him? What then? And you'll have to 'keep up appearances' too, won't you? Do you even understand what that means? That 'Luzhin smartness' is no better than Sonia's—and it might be worse, because at least Sonia sells herself out of desperation, just to survive. But you? You'll be doing it for luxuries.

"And what if you can't endure it, Dounia? What if, later on, you regret everything? What then? You'll be left with bitterness, misery, tears—tears you'll hide from the world, because you're not a Marfa Petrovna. And how will mother feel when she realizes the truth? She's already uneasy about all of this, worried deep down. And what about me? What do you take me for? I won't accept your sacrifice, Dounia! I won't! I won't allow it, mother! It won't happen—not while I'm alive! It won't, it won't, it won't!"

He suddenly stopped in his tracks, his thoughts spinning out of control.

"Won't happen? And how exactly are you going to stop it? Will you forbid it? And what right do you have to do that? What can you offer them in return to justify such a demand? Your whole life? Your future? You'll devote yourself to them after you finish your studies and find a job? We've heard all that before—it's just talk. But what about now? What are you doing now? You're living off them, relying on money they don't have—money they had to borrow. They're borrowing against a 120-rouble pension, borrowing from the Svidrigaïlovs. How are you going to save them from people like that? From Afanasy Ivanovitch Vahrushin? Oh, you future millionaire Zeus, what will you do to rescue them?

"In ten years? By then, mother will be blind from knitting shawls and maybe from crying too. She'll be nothing but skin and bones, worn down by hunger. And what about Dounia? What might become of her in those ten years? Can you even imagine?"

He tortured himself with these thoughts, finding a strange satisfaction in the agony. Yet these weren't new worries—they had been gnawing at him for a long time. This anguish had taken root deep within him, growing and festering until it became a monstrous question, one that demanded an answer. Now, his mother's letter had hit him like a thunderclap. It was clear—he couldn't sit idly by, tormented by unanswered questions. He had to act, and he had to act now.

"Or else... give up on life altogether!" he suddenly cried out in a frenzy. "Accept everything as it is, surrender to it, and smother every hope, every desire for love and life!"

Marmeladov's words echoed in his mind: 'Do you understand, sir, what it means when there's nowhere left to turn? Every man must have somewhere to turn.'

Raskolnikov started as another thought slipped into his mind—a thought he'd had the day before. But this time, he wasn't startled by its return. He had known it would come back—he had expected it. And it wasn't just yesterday's thought; it had been lurking in the shadows of his mind for much longer.

The difference now was that what had once seemed like a distant, half-formed idea had taken on a new, ominous shape. It no longer felt like a dream—it had become something real, something dangerous. And in that moment, Raskolnikov realized it himself.

His head throbbed painfully, and a dark haze clouded his vision.

He looked around anxiously, as if searching for something. He needed to sit down and was looking for a bench. He was walking along K—— Boulevard when he spotted one about a hundred paces ahead. He quickened his pace, heading toward it. But just before he reached the bench, something caught his attention, drawing him away from his original goal.

He had noticed a young woman walking about twenty paces in front of him but, at first, paid her no more mind than any other passerby. It was not unusual for him to walk home without noticing where he was going, lost in his thoughts, a habit he had developed over time. But something about this girl began to strike him as odd, and gradually, his attention became fixed on her. At first, he observed her reluctantly, almost annoyed by the distraction. Yet with every step, his curiosity deepened. He suddenly felt compelled to understand what it was about her that seemed so strange.

The girl appeared to be quite young. She walked in the sweltering heat, bareheaded, without a parasol or gloves, and was waving her arms oddly. She wore a dress made of a light, silky material, but it was disheveled—crookedly fastened and torn at the top, with a large piece hanging loose near her waist. A small scarf was draped carelessly around her bare neck, slipping to one side. She stumbled as she walked, swaying from side to side, almost tripping over herself.

Raskolnikov could not look away. He reached the bench just as she collapsed onto it, slumping into the corner and letting her head fall against the backrest, closing her eyes in utter exhaustion. He leaned in to study her more closely and immediately realized she was completely drunk. The sight was shocking. He could hardly believe what he saw—a young, fair-haired girl, no older than sixteen, maybe even younger. Her flushed, swollen face looked almost childlike, though clouded by intoxication. She sat carelessly, crossing one leg over the other, unaware of how improper it was, oblivious to the fact that she was on a public street.

Raskolnikov didn't sit down. He hesitated, unsure whether to leave her there. The boulevard was usually quiet, and at this hour, under the oppressive heat of the afternoon, it was nearly deserted. Yet, about fifteen paces away, on the other side of the boulevard, a man stood at the edge of the pavement, watching the scene.

The man was a plump, well-dressed fellow in his thirties, with a ruddy complexion, red lips, and a neatly groomed mustache. Raskolnikov immediately knew what the man was thinking. The stranger had probably followed the girl from a distance and now found Raskolnikov blocking his way. He stood impatiently, glaring at him, clearly hoping he would leave. His intentions were obvious.

A wave of fury swept over Raskolnikov. He felt an overwhelming urge to insult the man, to humiliate him somehow. Abandoning the girl for a moment, he strode toward the stranger.

"Hey! You Svidrigaïlov! What are you doing here?" he shouted, clenching his fists and laughing with rage.

"What do you mean?" the man responded coldly, scowling in disbelief.

"Get lost! That's what I mean," Raskolnikov snarled.

"How dare you, you filthy scoundrel!" the man snapped, raising his cane.

Without a second thought, Raskolnikov charged at him, fists raised, despite knowing the man could easily overpower him. But just as he was about to strike, a strong hand grabbed him from behind—a police constable had stepped between them.

"That's enough, gentlemen," the officer said firmly. "No fighting in public. What's going on here?" He glanced suspiciously at Raskolnikov's ragged clothes.

Raskolnikov turned to the constable, studying his sensible, straightforward face, framed by gray whiskers and a mustache.

"You're exactly the person I need," Raskolnikov exclaimed, gripping the constable's arm. "I'm a student—Raskolnikov is my name," he added, shooting a contemptuous glance at the gentleman. "Come with me, I'll show you something."

He pulled the policeman toward the bench.

"Look here," he said, pointing at the girl. "She's hopelessly drunk. I saw her walking along the boulevard, staggering like this. She can't be more than fifteen or sixteen. I'm certain this isn't normal—someone gave her too much to drink and took advantage of her. Look at her clothes. They're all out of place—clearly not put on by her. A man dressed her, clumsily. Someone used her and dumped her here."

He glanced toward the well-dressed man, who was now pretending to light a cigarette a short distance away. "And that man over there? He saw her too—he's been following her, hoping to take advantage of her in this state. He's just waiting for me to leave."

The policeman quickly grasped the situation. He looked over at the gentleman, then bent down to examine the girl. His face twisted with sympathy and anger.

"Poor child," he murmured, shaking his head. "She's just a kid—clearly someone took advantage of her. Miss, where do you live?" he asked softly, leaning closer to the girl.

She opened her dazed, heavy-lidded eyes, looked at him blankly, and waved her hand dismissively.

Raskolnikov rummaged in his pocket and pulled out twenty copecks. "Here," he said, handing the money to the officer. "Find a cab and take her home. We just need to figure out where she lives."

The constable nodded, pocketing the coins. "Miss, let me help you get home," he said gently. "Where do you live?"

"Go away... leave me alone," the girl muttered, waving her hand again.

"Ach, what a disgrace!" the policeman sighed, shaking his head. "It's shameful, truly shameful."

He turned to Raskolnikov. "It's going to be difficult. She won't tell us her address."

"I saw her just ahead of me," Raskolnikov explained. "She only made it to that bench before collapsing."

The constable sighed again. "It's disgraceful," he muttered. "A child like that, treated this way... And she looks refined too, like she might come from a respectable family." He bent down once more, as if seeing in the girl's face a glimpse of his own daughters, and shook his head sadly.

"The main thing," Raskolnikov said urgently, "is to keep her away from that scoundrel." He gestured toward the dandy. "It's obvious what he's after. He's not even hiding it!"

The gentleman, hearing Raskolnikov's words, shot him a look of contempt but held back his anger, merely moving a few more paces away.

"We can keep her safe from him," the policeman assured Raskolnikov, "if only we knew where to take her."

Just then, the girl stirred. She opened her eyes fully, seemed to realize something, and suddenly stood up. Without a word, she began to walk back the way she had come, staggering as before.

"They won't leave me alone," she muttered bitterly, waving her hand once more as she stumbled away.

The dandy immediately followed, though this time he took a parallel path, keeping his distance but watching her closely.

"Don't worry, I won't let him get to her," the constable promised, setting off after them. "What a vile world this is!" he muttered under his breath, sighing deeply.

At that moment, something shifted inside Raskolnikov—a sudden, inexplicable change of heart.

"Wait!" he called after the officer.

The policeman stopped and turned, confused.

"Let them be," Raskolnikov said with a bitter laugh. "What does it matter? Let him have his fun. What's it to you?" He pointed toward the dandy. "What's it to anyone?"

The constable stared at Raskolnikov in disbelief, bewildered by his sudden change of tone.

Raskolnikov threw his head back and laughed, a strange, hollow sound echoing across the deserted boulevard.

"Well!" muttered the policeman with a dismissive gesture as he walked off after the dandy and the girl, probably thinking Raskolnikov was either mad or worse.

"He took my twenty copecks," Raskolnikov grumbled bitterly as he stood alone. "Fine, let him take more from the other fellow to let him have the girl, and let that be the end of it. But why did I even interfere? What right do I have to help? Let them tear each other apart—what does it matter to me? And where did I get the nerve to hand over those twenty copecks? Were they even mine to give?"

Despite his angry words, a deep sense of wretchedness gnawed at him. He sat down on the deserted bench, his thoughts wandering aimlessly. He found it impossible to focus on anything. All he wanted was to lose himself completely, to forget everything, and then to wake up in a new life, as if starting fresh.

"Poor girl," he whispered, glancing at the empty corner of the bench where she had been sitting. "She'll wake up and cry, and when her mother finds out, she'll probably beat her—beat her terribly, in a humiliating way. And maybe she'll throw her out of the house altogether. Even if she doesn't, Darya Frantsovna and others like her will hear about it soon enough. And then the girl will start sneaking out, little by little, and soon she'll end up in the hospital—that's always how it goes for girls with respectable mothers who try to keep their shame hidden. Then it's back to the taverns, back to drinking, and back to the hospital again, until, by eighteen or nineteen, she's completely ruined—a wreck of a person, her life already over.

"Haven't I seen enough of that? Haven't they all ended up the same way? That's how they all come to it. And yet, they tell us it's just how things are supposed to be. Every year, a certain percentage of people have to end up like that, they say, so the rest can stay pure and untouched. A percentage! What a word—it sounds so scientific, so reassuring. Say 'percentage,' and there's no need to feel bad about anything. If we didn't have that word, maybe we'd feel worse about it all. But what if Dounia were part of that percentage? Or if not that one, then some other one?"

He stopped abruptly, shaken by the thought.

"Where was I going?" he suddenly asked himself, confused. "Strange... I came out for a reason. As soon as I read the letter, I left. Oh, yes! I was heading to Vassilyevsky Ostrov, to see Razumihin. That's it... now I remember. But why did I think of going to Razumihin just now? How did that idea pop into my head?"

He was puzzled by his own thoughts. Razumihin had been one of his university friends—one of the few. In truth, Raskolnikov had kept to himself throughout his time at university. He rarely visited anyone, and soon enough, people stopped visiting him. He avoided the usual student gatherings, parties, and discussions. He threw himself into his studies with relentless intensity, earning respect for his dedication, but not friendship. Most of his peers found him cold and distant, as though he carried some secret burden. Some thought he looked down on them, as if their interests and beliefs were beneath him.

But with Razumihin, things had been different—at least a little. He had been more open, more willing to talk. It was hard to be otherwise with Razumihin. He was good-natured to the point of simplicity, though beneath that simplicity lay both depth and dignity. His peers appreciated this and were fond of him. Razumihin was also clever, though at times a bit foolish.

He was striking in appearance—tall, thin, with unruly black hair and a face that was always poorly shaved. He was known for his physical strength, and once, during a wild night out, he knocked a giant policeman flat with a single punch. He could drink like a fish, yet go without alcohol for months if needed. He indulged in pranks at times, but could live just as easily without them. And no matter what hardships life threw at him, nothing seemed to crush his spirit. He could live anywhere, endure any cold or hunger. He scraped by on whatever work he could find. One winter, he didn't light his stove at all, insisting he slept better in the cold.

Though he had recently left the university, it was only temporary. He was working tirelessly to save enough money to return.

Raskolnikov hadn't visited Razumihin in four months. In fact, Razumihin didn't even know where Raskolnikov lived. About two months ago, they had crossed paths on the street, but Raskolnikov had deliberately avoided him, crossing to the other side to avoid being seen. Razumihin had noticed but didn't press him, understanding that Raskolnikov didn't want to be bothered.

And now, here he was, for some reason thinking of Razumihin, wondering why he felt drawn to him after all this time.

Chapter 5

"Of course, I've been meaning to go see Razumihin and ask him for work, maybe get some tutoring jobs," Raskolnikov thought. "But what can he really do for me now? Even if he finds me some lessons and shares whatever little money he has, just enough to buy boots and make myself presentable... and then what? What will a few miserable coins get me? That's not what I need now. It's absurd to go to Razumihin..."

The thought of going to Razumihin began to trouble him more than he expected. He felt as if this simple, everyday decision held some deeper, darker meaning.

"Did I really think I could fix everything by going to Razumihin?" he asked himself, confused.

He rubbed his forehead, trying to clear his thoughts, but then, without warning, a strange, irrational idea crept into his mind.

"To Razumihin's," he muttered quietly, almost with calm certainty, as though he'd come to a final decision. "Yes... I'll go to Razumihin's, but... not now. I'll go to him the day after It happens—when everything is over, and life can begin anew."

Suddenly, the weight of his own words hit him like a blow.

"After It?" he whispered, horrified, jumping to his feet. "So, it's really going to happen? Is it possible that I'm truly going to do it?"

He left the bench abruptly and began walking, almost running, in the direction of home. But just the thought of returning to that tiny, suffocating room filled him with disgust. That miserable little cupboard of a room—it was there that these thoughts had festered inside him for weeks. Unable to bear it, he kept walking aimlessly.

His body shook with a nervous chill that deepened into a fever, even though the afternoon was stiflingly hot. He felt cold, as if the chill were coming from within. In a restless, half-conscious attempt to distract himself, he began staring at everything around him, grasping at any sight or detail that might pull him out of his spiraling thoughts. But nothing helped; his mind kept dragging him back into brooding.

He wandered across Vassilyevsky Ostrov, reaching the Lesser Neva. Crossing the bridge, he headed toward the islands. The greenery and fresh air were a welcome relief after the dust and oppressive buildings of the city. Here, there were no taverns, no suffocating heat, no stench of filth. For a moment, the beauty of the place soothed him.

But the fleeting sense of peace soon gave way to an irritated restlessness. As he walked past brightly painted summer villas nestled among the trees, he stopped now and then to peer through the fences. On the verandas and balconies, elegantly dressed women sipped drinks, while children ran and played in the gardens. The sight of flowers held his attention longer than anything else, as if their color and life offered some strange comfort.

Now and then, he passed carriages and people riding on horseback. He watched them with vague curiosity but forgot them the moment they disappeared from view. Once, he stopped and counted his money: thirty copecks.

"Twenty to the policeman, three to Nastasya for the letter... so I must have given forty-seven or fifty to the Marmeladovs yesterday," he thought, though he wasn't sure why he was bothering to calculate it. Soon, the reason slipped from his mind entirely. He only remembered it again when he passed a tavern and realized how hungry he was.

He went inside, ordered a glass of vodka, and bought a pie. He ate the pie as he walked out, chewing without thinking. It had been a long time since he'd had vodka, and the effect was immediate. His legs grew heavy, and a wave of drowsiness overcame him.

He tried heading home but didn't get far. Exhausted, he veered off the road into a patch of bushes on Petrovsky Ostrov, sank down onto the grass, and fell asleep almost instantly.

In dreams, especially in states of mental distress, the mind can conjure visions so vivid and realistic that they seem more lifelike than waking reality. Sometimes, the dreams are grotesque, filled with strange images, but the details are so finely crafted, so coherent, that even the most gifted artist—like Pushkin or Turgenev—could not invent them while awake. These kinds of dreams linger in the memory, haunting the mind long after waking.

Raskolnikov had one of those dreams—a terrifying dream that gripped him with the force of a nightmare.

In the dream, he was a child again, about seven years old, walking with his father in the countryside on the evening of a holiday. The sky was gray and heavy, just as he remembered it. The small town of his childhood stretched out flat and barren, without a single tree in sight, except for a distant copse on the horizon—a dark blur at the edge of the earth.

A few paces beyond the last vegetable garden stood a tavern, large and grim. Even as a child, Raskolnikov had felt an instinctive fear and revulsion whenever they passed it. The place was always filled with noisy, drunken crowds—peasants, townspeople, and all sorts of riff-raff. There was always shouting, swearing, and crude singing, and sometimes fights broke out. Drunken, sinister figures loitered around the entrance. As a child, he would cling to his father, trembling with fear as they passed by.

The road beyond the tavern turned into a dusty track, always coated with black dust. About a hundred paces further, it curved toward the graveyard. In the center of the graveyard stood a stone church with a green dome. Raskolnikov had been there two or three times a year with his parents, whenever they held a service in memory of his grandmother.

He remembered how they used to bring a special dish—rice pudding with raisins arranged in the shape of a cross—wrapped in a white napkin. He had loved that old church, with its plain icons and the elderly priest, whose head always trembled slightly. Near his grandmother's grave stood a smaller grave—his baby brother's. The child had died at just six months old, long before Raskolnikov could remember him, but he had been told about him often. Whenever they visited the grave, Raskolnikov would cross himself and bow, touching the little stone marker with reverence.

In the dream, he was walking hand-in-hand with his father past the tavern on their way to the graveyard. He glanced nervously at the tavern, just as he used to as a child. Something strange was happening there—it seemed like a celebration of some sort. Crowds of people in colorful clothes—peasants, townsfolk, and drunks—were gathered outside, singing, laughing, and swaying unsteadily.

Near the entrance stood a large cart, the kind usually pulled by powerful draft horses. As a boy, Raskolnikov had always admired those massive animals with their thick legs and flowing manes, pulling heavy loads with ease. But in the dream, the cart was not drawn by a strong horse. Instead, a frail little sorrel nag—one of those skinny peasant horses often beaten mercilessly by their owners—stood between the shafts.

He had seen such pitiful creatures before, straining with all their might to pull heavy loads through mud or deep ruts. He remembered how cruelly the peasants would beat them, even striking their noses and eyes, and how deeply it had hurt him to watch. His mother had always pulled him away from the window whenever he cried over the sight.

Now, in the dream, a loud commotion erupted outside the tavern. A group of drunken peasants, dressed in bright red and blue shirts with coats thrown over their shoulders, staggered out, shouting and laughing. Someone was playing a balalaika, adding to the noisy chaos.

"Get in, get in!" shouted one of the peasants—a thick-necked young man with a face as red as a carrot. "I'll take you all! Get in!"

At this, the crowd burst into laughter, shouting and jeering.

"Take us all with a nag like that?"

"Mikolka, have you lost your mind? Hitching that poor thing to such a cart!"

"That mare's at least twenty years old if she's a day!"

But Mikolka wasn't deterred. "Get in, I said! I'll take you all!" he shouted again, jumping into the cart himself. He seized the reins and stood proudly at the front. "The bay's off with Matvey!" he called out from the cart. "And this miserable thing here—she's been eating her head off! It's driving me mad! I'll kill her, I swear! Get in, and I'll make her gallop!" He cracked the whip with relish, preparing to flog the little mare mercilessly.

"Get in! Come on!"

The crowd roared with laughter. "Hear that? He's going to make her gallop!"

"Gallop? She hasn't galloped in ten years!"

"She'll do well to shuffle along!"

"Don't worry about her, mates. Grab your whips and get ready!"

"All right, give it to her good!"

The men climbed into the cart, still laughing and joking. Six of them squeezed in, with room left for more. They even hoisted up a plump, rosy-cheeked woman dressed in red cotton, with a beaded headdress and thick leather shoes. She cracked nuts between her teeth, laughing along with everyone else. The crowd around them laughed too. How could they not? It was absurd—the poor nag was supposed to drag all of them at a gallop!

Two young men in the cart took out their own whips, ready to join Mikolka.

"Now!" someone cried.

The little mare strained with all her might, but instead of galloping, she could barely move forward. Her legs shook as she gasped for breath, shrinking under the hail of blows from the three whips. The laughter only grew louder. But Mikolka's fury boiled over, and he whipped the mare even harder, as if determined to make her run.

"Let me in too!" a young man from the crowd called, eager to join the chaos.

"Everyone in! She'll pull us all! I'll beat her to death if I have to!" shouted Mikolka, thrashing the mare wildly, lost in a frenzy.

"Father, Father!" a child's voice cried. "They're beating the poor horse! They're killing her!"

"Come away now, don't look," his father said gently, trying to pull him away. "They're drunk and foolish; it's just a game."

But the boy tore free from his father's grasp and ran to the horse, his heart breaking at the sight. The mare gasped, struggling to move, then stumbled, nearly collapsing.

"Kill her! Finish her off!" screamed Mikolka, his rage consuming him.

"Are you even human? What kind of Christian does this?" shouted an old man in the crowd.

"Look at her—how is that poor beast supposed to pull all that?" cried another.

"You'll kill her!" yelled a third.

"Mind your own business!" Mikolka roared. "She's mine! I'll do what I want with her! Everyone in—get in! I'll make her gallop, even if it kills her!"

The crowd's laughter reached a deafening roar as the mare, driven mad with pain, tried feebly to kick. Even the old man couldn't help but smile at the pathetic sight of the tiny nag kicking weakly.

Two young men from the crowd ran to the mare, whipping her sides.

"Hit her in the eyes! Right in the eyes!" Mikolka shouted with glee.

The cart erupted into drunken singing. Someone banged a tambourine, while the men whistled and shouted. The woman in red kept cracking her nuts, laughing all the while.

The boy ran alongside the mare, screaming and sobbing as he watched her get whipped across the eyes. His face was streaked with tears, and he felt as though he couldn't breathe. One of the men lashed him across the face with a whip, but the boy didn't even notice. Wringing his hands in despair, he ran to an old man with a gray beard who stood shaking his head disapprovingly. A woman tried to grab the boy and lead him away, but he broke free and ran back to the mare.

The poor animal was gasping her last breaths, but somehow, she kicked again.

"I'll teach you to kick!" Mikolka bellowed, throwing down his whip. He bent over, grabbed a thick wooden shaft from the bottom of the cart, and raised it high above his head.

"He's going to crush her!" someone shouted.

"He'll kill her for sure!"

"She's mine!" Mikolka shouted, his eyes wild with fury. With all his strength, he brought the shaft down with a sickening thud on the mare's back.

"Keep hitting her! Don't stop!" voices cried from the crowd.

Mikolka struck the mare again, harder this time. She sank to her haunches, then staggered forward, trying desperately to move the cart. But more whips lashed at her from every direction, and the heavy shaft came down on her again and again.

"She's a tough one!" someone yelled admiringly.

"She'll drop any minute now!" another called out.

"Someone get an axe and finish her off!"

"Stand back!" Mikolka screamed. He threw down the shaft, reached into the cart, and pulled out an iron crowbar. "Watch this!" he shouted, and with a terrifying swing, he brought the bar crashing down on the mare's back.

The blow sent her staggering. She tried one last time to pull the cart, but Mikolka struck her again, and she crumpled to the ground like a felled tree.

"Finish her off!" someone shouted.

Mikolka, now beyond reason, jumped out of the cart. A group of drunken men, equally crazed, grabbed whatever they could—sticks, poles, whips—and rushed to the mare, beating her without mercy.

Mikolka stood off to the side, swinging the crowbar wildly. The mare stretched her neck one final time, drew a long, shuddering breath, and lay still.

"You killed her, you butcher!" someone yelled from the crowd.

"Why didn't she gallop, then?" Mikolka snarled, his bloodshot eyes burning with rage. "She's mine! I'll do what I want with her!"

He stood there, gripping the crowbar, as if frustrated that there was nothing left to hit.

"No doubt about it, you're no Christian!" many voices in the crowd shouted angrily.

But the poor boy, consumed with grief, forced his way through the throng. He threw his arms around the dead sorrel mare's bloodied head, kissing her eyes and lips in a frenzy of sorrow. Then, in a burst of rage, he sprang at Mikolka with his small fists raised. Just at that moment, his father, who had been chasing after him, grabbed him and carried him out of the crowd.

"Come now, let's go home," his father said gently.

"Father! Why... why did they kill the poor horse?" the boy sobbed, his voice breaking into desperate cries as he gasped for breath.

"They were drunk... just brutes... it's not for us to meddle," his father muttered, holding him tightly. But the boy's little chest heaved, and he clung to his father, suffocating with grief. He tried to cry out again—and suddenly, he woke up.

He jolted awake, gasping for air, his hair soaked with sweat. For a moment, he sat upright, staring into the darkness, trembling with fear.

"Thank God, it was just a dream," he whispered, sitting under the tree and taking deep breaths to calm himself. "But what a terrible dream... is it some fever coming on?"

He felt utterly drained. A fog of confusion and darkness clouded his mind. He rested his elbows on his knees, burying his face in his hands.

"Good God!" he whispered. "Can it really be? Will I take an axe... strike her on the head... split her skull? Will I walk through sticky, warm blood, steal, break the lock, and run... covered in blood... with the axe in my hand? Dear God, can it really happen?"

He shuddered violently as he whispered these words.

"But why am I torturing myself like this?" he muttered, sitting up in astonishment. "I already know I could never do it—so why do I keep torturing myself? Just yesterday, I knew for certain that I wasn't capable of it. Why can't I let it go? Why do I keep going over it again and again? When I came down the stairs yesterday, I told myself it was vile, disgusting, repulsive... even the thought of it made me feel sick."

He shook his head, as if trying to shake off the nightmare.

"No, I can't do it! I can't! Even if everything I've reasoned is perfectly logical, even if it's as clear as arithmetic... I still can't bring myself to do it. I can't, I can't!"

He stood up slowly, bewildered to find himself in the park. For a moment, he didn't even recognize where he was. Then, as though released from some invisible burden, he began to walk toward the bridge. His limbs were heavy with exhaustion, his face pale, and his eyes burning with an unsettling glow, but he felt lighter inside. It was as if a great weight had been lifted from his soul. A strange sense of peace washed over him, as though he had made a final decision.

"Lord," he whispered as he walked, "show me my path. I renounce that cursed dream."

Crossing the bridge, he gazed out at the Neva River, watching the sun sink low in the red-streaked sky. For the first time in weeks, he felt at ease. The abscess in his heart, which had festered for so long, seemed to have burst at last, releasing him from its poisonous grip.

"Freedom," he thought. "I'm free... free from that cursed obsession."

Later, when he looked back on these moments, he would always remember how strange it was that he had taken a different route home that night—a path through the Hay Market, which was not the shortest or most direct way. Though he had often wandered aimlessly through the streets, he would always wonder why, on that particular night, he had taken that specific path. It seemed to him later that fate had been waiting for him there, lying in ambush at just the right moment, ready to change his life forever.

It was around nine o'clock when he reached the Hay Market. The vendors and stall owners were packing up their goods, ready to head home for the night. Rag pickers and petty traders crowded around the nearby taverns, their laughter and chatter filling the dirty, foul-smelling courtyards. Raskolnikov liked this part of the city. Here, no one gave a second glance to his ragged clothes; here, he could walk unnoticed, blending into the crowd.

At the corner of an alley, a peddler and his wife were lingering at their two little tables, covered with spools of thread, cotton handkerchiefs, and other small goods. They had already packed most of their wares but stayed behind to chat with a friend who had just arrived. That friend was Lizaveta Ivanovna—the younger sister of

Alyona Ivanovna, the old pawnbroker whom Raskolnikov had visited the day before.

Raskolnikov knew of Lizaveta. She was a single woman, around thirty-five years old, tall and awkward, with a timid, almost foolish demeanor. She lived in fear of her sister, who treated her harshly and made her work tirelessly. Alyona even beat her on occasion. Lizaveta stood at the stall with a bundle in her arms, listening intently to the peddler and his wife, though she seemed unsure of herself.

"You need to make up your mind, Lizaveta Ivanovna," the peddler was saying loudly. "Come by tomorrow at seven. They'll be here then."

"Tomorrow?" Lizaveta repeated slowly, as if uncertain.

"Honestly, you act like such a child," the peddler's wife chimed in with a laugh. "You're scared of Alyona Ivanovna, but she's not even your real sister—just your step-sister. And what a life she gives you!"

"Don't say anything to Alyona about it," the peddler added. "Just come over quietly. Trust me, it'll be worth it. Maybe even your sister will come around to the idea later."

"Should I come?" Lizaveta asked hesitantly.

"Yes, at seven o'clock tomorrow," the peddler urged. "They'll be here, and you can decide for yourself."

"We'll have some tea, too," his wife added cheerfully.

"All right, I'll come," Lizaveta said after a moment, still lost in thought, and began walking away slowly.

Raskolnikov, who had passed by unnoticed, overheard everything. He walked on, trying not to draw attention, but every word echoed in his mind. A chill ran down his spine. His heart raced with a mixture of shock and horror. In that moment, something clicked in his mind—something dreadful and final. He had learned, quite by accident, that the next day at seven o'clock, Lizaveta would not be at home. Alyona Ivanovna, the old pawnbroker, would be alone.

He was only a few steps from his apartment when he stopped, feeling as though he had just received a death sentence. His thoughts swirled in confusion, and he couldn't think clearly. Yet somehow, deep within him, he knew that his fate had been sealed. There was no turning back.

It was as if all his doubts and uncertainties had suddenly been swept away, leaving only cold, unchangeable certainty. Even if he had waited years for the perfect opportunity, he could not have hoped for a better chance than this—one that had fallen into his lap without any effort or planning. He now knew, without question, that tomorrow at seven o'clock, the old woman would be home, alone, and vulnerable.

Chapter 6

Later on, Raskolnikov learned why the huckster and his wife had asked Lizaveta to meet them. It turned out to be something completely ordinary, with nothing mysterious about it. A family, having recently fallen into poverty, was trying to sell off their household goods and clothing—all women's things. Since these items wouldn't fetch much in the market, the family needed someone to sell them, and that was Lizaveta's line of work. She often took on jobs like this and was known for being honest, always offering a fair price without haggling. Lizaveta didn't speak much, and, as already mentioned, she was submissive and timid.

However, Raskolnikov had become quite superstitious lately, and even after these events, traces of that superstition stayed with him, deeply ingrained and difficult to get rid of. As he reflected on it later, he saw strange significance in these coincidences, as if some hidden force were at work. During the previous winter, a fellow student named Pokorev, who had left for Harkov, had casually given him the address of Alyona Ivanovna, the old pawnbroker, suggesting that Raskolnikov could pawn something there if needed. For a long time, he hadn't used the address because he was getting by with lessons and other small jobs. But six weeks ago, the idea came back to him. He had two things of value: his father's old silver watch and a small gold ring with three red stones, a gift from his sister when they parted ways. He decided to pawn the ring.

When he met Alyona Ivanovna, he instantly felt an overwhelming sense of revulsion toward her, even though she had done nothing in particular to provoke it. She gave him two roubles for the ring, and on his way home, he stopped by a miserable little tavern, ordered some tea, and sank into deep thought. A strange idea began forming in his mind, like a chick slowly pecking its way out of an egg, occupying his thoughts entirely.

At the next table, two men—a student and a young officer—were sitting together, drinking tea after a game of billiards. Raskolnikov didn't know them, but as he sat there, he overheard their conversation. To his surprise, the student mentioned Alyona Ivanovna by name and gave her address to the officer. The coincidence struck Raskolnikov as eerie. He had just come from the old woman's apartment, and now, here he was, hearing someone else talking about her. It felt like more than chance, as if these words were meant for him to hear.

"She's perfect," the student said. "You can always get cash from her. She's rolling in it—richer than any Jew—and she'll lend you five thousand roubles if you need it. But she'll also take a pledge for just a rouble. Lots of students deal with her, but she's a real witch."

The student went on to describe Alyona's cruelty and stinginess in vivid detail. "If you're even a day late with the interest, she keeps your pledge. She offers maybe a quarter of what something's worth and charges five, sometimes even seven percent interest every month. And you know what? She has a sister, Lizaveta, who's practically her slave. That poor woman does everything—cooks, cleans, even works as a charwoman—and the old hag still beats her."

The student laughed, clearly enjoying the story. "Imagine that—Lizaveta's six feet tall, but she's scared of that little old witch!"

"She sounds like quite a character," the officer said, intrigued.

"Oh, she is! And here's the funny part: Lizaveta's always pregnant. Can you believe it?"

"But isn't she hideous?" the officer asked, puzzled.

"Yeah, she looks like a soldier in a dress—dark-skinned and awkward. But there's something about her... Her face is so kind, and her eyes—there's a sweetness in them. People are drawn to her somehow. She's gentle and patient, always willing to help anyone with anything. And her smile—it's really sweet, in a weird way."

The officer chuckled. "Sounds like you're a bit smitten yourself."

The student grinned. "Not at all. But I'll tell you this: I could kill that old woman and take all her money without feeling the slightest bit of guilt."

The officer laughed again, but Raskolnikov shuddered. The conversation was hitting far too close to the thoughts swirling in his own mind.

The student leaned forward, speaking with more intensity. "Look, I'm joking... kind of. But think about it. That old woman is worthless. She's cruel, greedy, and practically on her deathbed already. On the other hand, her money could do so much good. With just a fraction of it, hundreds of people could be saved from poverty. Families wouldn't have to starve. People could be pulled back from the brink. And instead, all that money will end up in some monastery, wasted. Isn't it obvious? One little crime for the sake of countless good deeds. One death to save a hundred lives. It's simple math."

The officer considered this. "Sure, she doesn't deserve to live... but still, that's just the way life is."

"Yeah, but isn't it our job to correct life's injustices?" the student argued. "Without people willing to challenge the rules, the world would drown in prejudice. Great men—real leaders—don't sit around worrying about rules and morality. They do what needs to be done. People talk about conscience and duty, but what do those words even mean?"

The officer smirked. "So, tell me, would you do it? Would you kill her yourself?"

"Of course not!" the student replied quickly. "I'm just talking. It's not my problem."

"Then it's just talk. If you wouldn't do it yourself, there's no justice in it." The officer laughed and suggested another game of billiards.

Raskolnikov sat frozen, overwhelmed by what he had just heard. It was just idle talk between two young men, the kind of conversation he had heard many times before. But the timing—it was unsettling. Why had he overheard this conversation right after leaving Alyona Ivanovna's apartment? Why had these exact thoughts, which had already begun forming in his mind, been spoken aloud by someone else at that precise moment?

It didn't feel like a coincidence. It was as if fate had arranged for him to hear these words—as if the universe itself were nudging him toward a decision he hadn't yet made. That trivial conversation in the tavern left a lasting impression on him, planting a seed in his mind that would continue to grow. Even later, when he looked back on it, he couldn't shake the feeling that some invisible force had been guiding him toward the path he now feared.

When he got back from the Hay Market, he threw himself onto the couch and sat there for a whole hour without moving. It got dark during that time; he had no candle and didn't even think to light one. He couldn't remember if he had been thinking about anything. Eventually, he started feeling the fever and chills again, and with some relief, realized he could lie down on the couch. Soon, a heavy, almost crushing sleep overtook him.

He slept for an incredibly long time and didn't have any dreams. Nastasya came into his room at ten o'clock the next morning and struggled to wake him up. She brought him tea and bread. The tea was, once again, the second brew and made in her teapot.

"Oh my goodness, how much he sleeps!" she said angrily. "He's always sleeping."

He got up slowly. His head hurt. He stood up, walked around his little room, and then collapsed back onto the couch.

"Are you going to sleep again?" Nastasya shouted. "Are you sick or what?"

He didn't answer.

"Do you want some tea?"

"Later," he said weakly, closing his eyes again and turning to face the wall.

Nastasya stood over him.

"Maybe he really is sick," she said, then left. She came back at two o'clock with soup. He was lying in the same position. The tea was still untouched. Nastasya felt insulted and angrily tried to wake him up.

"Why are you lying there like a log?" she yelled, looking at him with disgust.

He sat up and looked at the floor, still not saying a word.

"Are you sick or not?" Nastasya asked again, but got no response. "You should go outside and get some fresh air," she suggested after a pause. "Are you going to eat this or not?"

"Later," he said weakly. "You can go."

He waved her away. She stood there a bit longer, looked at him with pity, and left.

A few minutes later, he opened his eyes and stared at the tea and soup for a long time. Then he grabbed the bread, picked up the spoon, and started eating. He ate a little, three or four spoonfuls, without any appetite, as if it was just a routine. His headache wasn't as bad. After eating, he stretched out on the couch again, but now he couldn't sleep. He lay still, his face buried in the pillow. Strange daydreams kept popping into his head. One dream, in particular, kept repeating itself: he imagined being in Africa, in Egypt, somewhere in an oasis. The caravan had stopped to rest. The camels were lying peacefully, and there were palm trees all around in a perfect circle. The group was having dinner, but he was drinking water from a nearby spring that bubbled close by. The water was so cool, clear, and wonderful, flowing over colorful stones and sparkling sand that looked like gold in some places.

Suddenly, he heard a clock strike. He jolted awake, lifted his head, and looked out the window. Realizing how late it was, he jumped up like someone had pulled him off the couch. Quietly, he tiptoed to the door, opened it just a crack, and started listening to the stairs. His heart was pounding hard. But everything was quiet, as if everyone was asleep. It felt strange and awful to him that he could have slept so deeply, wasting the whole day, and had done nothing, hadn't prepared anything yet. And meanwhile, maybe it was already six o'clock. His sleepiness and foggy mind suddenly turned into a frantic, feverish rush. But there wasn't much left to do. He focused all his energy on remembering everything and not forgetting anything, while his heart pounded so hard it was hard to breathe. First, he had to make a noose and sew it into his coat—it wouldn't take long. He rummaged under his pillow and pulled out a worn, old shirt that had been stuffed under his bed linens. From its rags, he tore a long strip, about two inches wide and sixteen inches long. He folded it in half, took off his wide, sturdy summer coat made from thick cotton (the only outerwear he owned), and started sewing the two ends of the strip inside the coat, just under the left armhole. His hands were shaking as he sewed, but he managed to do it in a way that nothing showed when he put the coat back on. He had prepared the needle and thread long before; they were wrapped in a piece of paper on his table. The noose was a clever design of his own, made to hold the axe. He couldn't walk down the street carrying the axe in his hands. Even if he hid it under his coat, he would still have to hold it with one hand, which would look suspicious. Now, he could just put the axe's head into the noose, and it would hang quietly under his arm, on the inside of his coat. He could hold the end of the handle by putting his hand in his pocket, making sure it didn't swing, and since the coat was very baggy—more like a sack—it wouldn't look like he was holding anything at all. He had designed the noose two weeks ago.

When he finished, he reached into the small gap between his couch and the floor, felt around in the corner, and pulled out the pledge he had hidden there long ago. This pledge was just a smooth piece of wood, about the size and thickness of a silver cigarette case. He had found it during one of his walks through a courtyard where there was a workshop. Later, he had added a thin piece of iron, which he had also picked up off the street. He had placed the iron, which was slightly smaller, on the piece of wood and wrapped them tightly together with thread. Then he wrapped it carefully in clean white paper and tied it into a neat little package, making it hard to untie. This was meant to distract the old woman for a while as she tried to open it, giving him a moment to act. The iron was added to give the package some weight, so the woman wouldn't immediately realize it was just wood. He had stashed it all under the couch beforehand. He had only just pulled the pledge out when he heard someone outside in the yard.

"It's been six o'clock for a while now."

"For a while! Oh God!"

He rushed to the door, listened, grabbed his hat, and started quietly descending the thirteen steps, as silently as a cat. He still had the most important task left—to steal the axe from the kitchen. He had decided long ago that the deed had to be done with an axe. He also had a pocketknife, but he didn't trust the knife or his own strength, so he finally settled on the axe. One peculiar thing about all his final decisions was that the more he settled on them, the more disgusting and ridiculous they seemed to him. Despite all his mental torment, he couldn't fully believe in his plans for even a second.

And if there had ever been a time when everything was planned out perfectly, with no doubts left, he probably would have abandoned the whole thing as absurd, monstrous, and impossible. But a lot of uncertainties remained. As for getting the axe, that small task didn't worry him at all. Nothing could be easier. Nastasya was often out of the house, especially in the evenings. She would visit neighbors or run errands and always left the door ajar, which the landlady scolded her for constantly. So, when the time came, he only had to quietly sneak into the kitchen, take the axe, and then, an hour later (after everything was done), go back and return it. But there were still uncertainties.

What if he came back in an hour and Nastasya had already returned and was there? He would have to wait for her to leave again. But what if, in the meantime, she noticed the missing axe, started looking for it, and raised the alarm? That would be enough to make her suspicious, or at least give her reason to be.

But those were small worries he hadn't even started to think about, and really, he didn't have time. He was focused on the main task and pushed aside the small details until he could fully believe in it all. But that felt completely out of reach. At least, that's what he thought. He couldn't even imagine that he would stop thinking about it, get up, and just go do it. Even his recent visit, meant as a final check of the place, was more like an experiment, not the real thing. It was as if he told himself, "Come on, let's go try it—why keep dreaming about it?"—and right away he panicked and ran away, cursing himself in frustration.

At the same time, it seemed like he had thought through the moral side of it completely; his arguments were sharp, and he couldn't find any good reasons against it in himself. But in the end, he just stopped believing in himself and stubbornly, desperately looked for reasons in every direction, as if someone was pushing and pulling him toward the act.

At first, long ago even, he had been obsessed with one question: why are almost all crimes so badly hidden and so easily discovered, and why do almost all criminals leave such obvious evidence? He gradually came to many strange and curious conclusions. In his opinion, the main reason wasn't that it was physically impossible to hide the crime, but rather it was the criminal himself. Almost every criminal loses control of their will and their ability to reason with a childlike and remarkable carelessness right when they need to be the most cautious. He believed this loss of control and failure of will affected a person like an illness, growing slowly and peaking just before the crime, continuing with the same intensity during the crime and for a while afterward, depending on the person, then fading away like any other sickness. He wasn't yet sure whether the illness caused the crime or if the crime always came with something like a sickness by its nature.

When he reached these conclusions, he decided that he wouldn't suffer from such a mental breakdown, that his will and reason would stay sharp when the time came, simply because what he was planning wasn't really a crime. We'll skip over how he arrived at this final thought—we've already gone too far ahead. We can add, though, that the practical, physical difficulties of the situation were less important in his mind. "All you need to do is keep your willpower and reason in control, and you can handle them all when the time comes, once you've gotten familiar with every tiny detail of the job." But that preparation never began. His final decisions were what he trusted the least, and when the time came, everything happened differently, almost by accident and surprise.

One small thing ruined his plan before he even left the staircase. When he reached the landlady's kitchen, where the door was open as usual, he peeked in carefully to see if, in Nastasya's absence, the landlady was there, or if the door to her room was closed so she wouldn't see him taking the axe. But to his shock, Nastasya wasn't just home—she was busy in the kitchen, pulling laundry out of a basket and hanging it up. When she saw him, she stopped hanging the clothes and stared at him the whole time he walked by. He looked away and kept walking as if he hadn't noticed. But that was the end of it all—he didn't have the axe! He was devastated.

"What made me think," he thought as he walked through the gateway, "what made me so sure she wouldn't be home at that moment? Why, why, why did I assume that?"

He felt crushed and even humiliated. He could've laughed at himself in anger. A dull, animal-like rage bubbled up inside him. He stood hesitating in the gateway. Going out into the street for a walk just for show felt disgusting; going back to his room was even worse. "What a chance I've lost forever!" he muttered, standing aimlessly in the gateway, right across from the porter's small, dark room, which was also open. Suddenly, something shiny under the bench in the porter's room caught his eye. He looked around—no one was there. He tiptoed over, went down two steps into the room, and in a faint voice called for the porter. "Not here! But nearby, in the yard, since the door's wide open." He rushed to the axe (it was an axe) and pulled it out from under the bench, where it was lying between two chunks of wood. Right away, before stepping out, he attached it to the noose under his coat, put his hands in his pockets, and walked out of the room—no one had seen him! "When reason fails, the devil lends a hand!" he thought with a strange grin. This stroke of luck lifted his spirits.

He walked along slowly and calmly, without rushing, to avoid drawing attention. He barely glanced at the people passing by, trying not to look at their faces and hoping to go unnoticed. Suddenly, he thought of his hat. "Good heavens! I had money two days ago, and I didn't buy a proper cap to wear instead of this!" A curse rose up from deep within him.

Peeking into a shop out of the corner of his eye, he saw a clock on the wall that read ten minutes past seven. He had to hurry but still needed to take a roundabout way to approach the house from the other side.

When he had imagined all this beforehand, he sometimes thought he would be terrified. But now, he wasn't scared at all. In fact, his mind was wandering to random thoughts, though none of them stuck for long. As he passed the Yusupov garden, he found himself thinking about the construction of large fountains and how refreshing they would be in all the city squares. He even started imagining how wonderful it would be if the Summer Garden were extended all the way to the Field of Mars, maybe even connected to the garden of the Mikhailovsky Palace. It would be a great improvement for the city. Then, he started thinking about why people in big cities tend to live in the dirtiest, smelliest, most miserable parts of town, even when they could live near gardens and fountains. Then, his own walks through the Hay Market came to mind, and for a moment, he snapped back to reality. "What nonsense!" he thought. "It's better to think about nothing at all."

"So maybe men being led to their executions cling mentally to every little thing they see on the way," flashed through his mind like lightning, but he quickly shook off the thought. And now, he was close. Here was the house, here was the gate. Suddenly, somewhere nearby, a clock struck once. "What! Could it be half-past seven? No way, it must be fast!"

Luckily for him, things worked out well again at the gate. At that exact moment, as if perfectly timed for him, a huge wagon full of hay drove in, completely blocking him from view as he passed through the gateway. The wagon had barely driven into the yard when he slipped quickly to the right. On the other side of the wagon, he could hear shouting and arguing, but no one noticed him, and no one crossed his path. Many windows overlooking the large courtyard were open at that time, but he didn't lift his head—he didn't have the strength to. The staircase leading to the old woman's room was right there, just to the right of the gateway. He was already on the stairs.

Taking a deep breath, clutching his pounding heart, and once again adjusting the axe in its place, he started creeping up the stairs quietly and cautiously, listening carefully with each step. But the stairs were completely deserted. All the doors were closed. He didn't meet anyone. One apartment on the first floor was wide open, and painters were working inside, but they didn't even look his way. He paused, thought for a moment, and continued. "It would've been better if they weren't here, but... it's two floors above them."

And there was the fourth floor, and there was the door, with the empty apartment opposite. The flat underneath the old woman's seemed empty too—the nameplate on the door had been torn off, so they must've moved out. He was out of breath. For a moment, the thought crossed his mind: "Should I turn back?" But he didn't answer himself and began listening at the old woman's door—dead silence. He listened again on the staircase, long and carefully, then looked around one last time, straightened himself up, checked the axe one more time. "Am I very pale?" he wondered. "Do I look nervous? She's suspicious... Should I wait a little longer until my heart stops pounding?"

But his heart wouldn't calm down. On the contrary, it pounded harder and harder, as if in defiance. He couldn't bear it anymore. Slowly, he stretched out his hand toward the bell and gave it a ring. After waiting half a minute with no response, he rang again, this time louder.

Still, there was no answer. He knew that ringing a third time would seem suspicious and pointless. The old woman had to be at home— he was certain of that. She lived alone and was always cautious. He knew a bit about her routines. Pressing his ear against the door again, he strained to listen. Whether his senses were sharper than usual or the sound was genuinely clear, he couldn't tell. But suddenly, he heard the faintest noise—like the soft touch of a hand on the lock, followed by the subtle rustle of a skirt brushing against the door.

Someone was standing silently on the other side, right next to the lock, just as he was doing on the outside. It felt like she was listening through the door, pressing her ear against it, just as he had.

He shifted his position slightly and muttered something under his breath to make it seem as though he wasn't sneaking around. Then, he rang a third time—this time calmly, without rushing, and without impatience.

Looking back on that moment later, he remembered it with absolute clarity. It stood out in his memory, vivid and unforgettable. What puzzled him was how he had managed to be so calculating when his mind had felt clouded, as though he wasn't fully aware of his own actions.

An instant later, he heard the click of the latch being undone.

Chapter 7

The door, like before, opened just a crack, and again two sharp, suspicious eyes stared at him out of the darkness. Then, Raskolnikov panicked and nearly made a serious mistake. Afraid that the old woman would be alarmed by their being alone, and not trusting that his appearance would calm her suspicions, he grabbed the door and pulled it toward him to stop her from closing it again. Seeing this, she didn't try to pull it back, but she didn't let go of the handle either, so he almost dragged her out onto the stairs. Realizing that she was standing in the doorway, blocking his path, he stepped straight toward her. She backed away in fear, tried to say something, but no words came out, and she just stared at him with wide eyes.

"Good evening, Alyona Ivanovna," he began, trying to speak casually, but his voice wouldn't cooperate. It cracked and trembled. "I've come... I brought something... but it's better if we go inside... where there's light."

Without waiting for her, he walked straight into the room uninvited. The old woman ran after him, and finally, her voice returned.

"Heavens! What is it? Who are you? What do you want?"

"Why, Alyona Ivanovna, you know me... Raskolnikov... I brought the pledge I promised you the other day..." He held out the pledge.

The old woman glanced at the pledge for a moment but quickly shifted her gaze to his face. She looked at him intensely, with malice and suspicion. A minute passed. He even thought he saw a sneer in her eyes, as if she had already figured everything out. He felt his mind slipping, almost overtaken by fear. He thought that if she kept staring at him like that and didn't speak for another half-minute, he would have run away.

"Why are you looking at me like you don't know me?" he said suddenly, with a touch of bitterness. "Take it if you want, if not, I'll go elsewhere. I'm in a hurry."

He hadn't planned on saying that, but the words came out on their own. The old woman seemed to relax a little, and the determined tone in his voice apparently restored her confidence.

"But why so suddenly... What is it?" she asked, looking at the pledge.

"The silver cigarette case; I mentioned it last time, remember?"

She held out her hand to take it.

"But my goodness, how pale you are... and your hands are shaking too? Have you been bathing or something?"

"Fever," he replied abruptly. "You can't help being pale... when you've got nothing to eat," he added, struggling to get the words out.

He was weakening again, but his response seemed believable enough. The old woman took the pledge.

"What is it?" she asked again, still examining Raskolnikov closely and weighing the pledge in her hand.

"A cigarette case... silver... take a look."

"It doesn't look like silver... and how tightly it's wrapped!"

She started to untie the string and turned toward the window for better light (all her windows were closed, despite the stifling heat), leaving him alone for a few seconds with her back turned. He unbuttoned his coat and freed the axe from the noose, but didn't pull it out all the way, just held it in his right hand under his coat. His hands felt weak, growing more numb and stiff by the second. He was afraid he might drop the axe. A sudden wave of dizziness hit him.

"But why has he tied it up like this?" the old woman muttered in frustration as she moved toward him.

He had no time left. He pulled out the axe, swung it with both hands, barely aware of what he was doing, and almost mechanically brought the blunt side down on her head. It felt like he hadn't used any of his own strength. But as soon as the axe hit her, his strength returned.

The old woman, as usual, wasn't wearing a headscarf. Her thin, light hair, streaked with grey and greasy, was braided into a rat's tail and held in place by a broken horn comb sticking out from the back of her neck. Since she was short, the blow landed on the very top of her skull. She let out a faint cry and collapsed onto the floor, raising her hands to her head. In one hand, she still clutched the pledge. Raskolnikov struck her again, and then once more, on the same spot. Blood spurted out like from an overturned glass, and her body fell back. He stepped away, letting her fall, then immediately bent over her face; she was dead. Her eyes bulged from their sockets, and her brow and face were twisted in a final convulsion.

He laid the axe on the floor beside the body and quickly reached into her pocket (trying to avoid the blood). It was the same pocket from which she had taken the keys on his last visit. His mind was clear, and he wasn't dizzy or confused, but his hands were still trembling. Later, he would remember how calm and careful he had been, making sure not to get any blood on himself. He pulled out the keys right away; they were all still together on a steel ring. He rushed into the bedroom with them.

It was a tiny room, filled with religious icons. Against one wall was a large, clean bed covered with a silk quilt. Against another wall was a chest of drawers. Oddly enough, as soon as he started trying the keys in the lock, as soon as he heard them jingling, a violent shudder ran through him. He suddenly had the urge to abandon everything and leave. But that feeling only lasted a moment; it was too late to turn back now. He even smiled at himself, but then another terrifying thought struck him. What if the old woman wasn't really dead? What if she regained consciousness? Leaving the keys in the chest, he ran back to the body, grabbed the axe, and raised it over her again, but didn't bring it down. There was no doubt now that she was dead. Leaning in and looking closer, he could see that her skull was cracked, even crushed, on one side. He started to touch it with his finger but pulled his hand back, realizing it was obvious without needing to check.

There was a pool of blood spreading out beneath her. Suddenly, he noticed a string around her neck. He pulled at it, but it was strong and wouldn't snap, and besides, it was soaked in blood. He tried to pull it out from under her dress, but something was holding it in place. Growing impatient, he raised the axe again to cut the string off the body but didn't dare to. After a couple of minutes of hurried effort, smearing his hands and the axe with blood, he finally managed to cut the string without touching the body with the axe. He had been right—it was a purse. On the string were two crosses, one made of Cyprus wood and the other of copper, along with a silver filigree icon, and a small, greasy leather purse with a steel rim. The purse was stuffed full. Raskolnikov shoved it into his pocket without looking inside, threw the crosses onto the old woman's body, and rushed back into the bedroom, this time taking the axe with him.

He was in a frantic rush. Grabbing the keys, he began trying them again, but with no success. They wouldn't fit the locks. It wasn't so much that his hands were shaking, but he kept making mistakes. Even when he saw that a key wasn't the right one, he still tried to force it in. Suddenly, he remembered that the big key with deep notches, hanging with the smaller ones, couldn't belong to the chest of drawers (this had struck him during his last visit). It must belong to a strongbox, and everything was probably hidden there. He left the chest of drawers and immediately felt under the bed, knowing old women often kept boxes there. Sure enough, there was a large box, about a yard long, with a curved lid covered in red leather and studded with steel nails. The notched key fit perfectly and unlocked it.

At the top, under a white sheet, was a red brocade coat lined with hareskin. Underneath that was a silk dress, then a shawl. It seemed like nothing was there but clothes. The first thing he did was wipe his blood-stained hands on the red brocade. "It's red, so the blood won't show as much," passed through his mind. Then, suddenly, he snapped back to reality. "Good God, am I losing my mind?" he thought, horrified.

But just as he touched the clothes, a gold watch slipped out from under the fur coat. He hurriedly turned everything over. There were various gold items hidden among the clothes—likely all unclaimed pledges or things waiting to be redeemed—bracelets, chains, earrings, pins, and similar items. Some were in cases, others simply wrapped in newspaper, carefully folded and tied with string. Without wasting time, he began stuffing his pockets, both in his trousers and overcoat, without bothering to open the cases or untie the parcels. But he didn't have time to take much.

Suddenly, he heard footsteps in the room where the old woman's body lay. He froze, perfectly still. But everything was quiet again. Maybe it was just his imagination. Then, distinctly, he heard a faint, broken moan. Then, silence for a minute or two. He crouched by the box, holding his breath, waiting. Suddenly, he jumped up, grabbed the axe, and ran out of the bedroom.

In the middle of the room stood Lizaveta, holding a large bundle in her arms. She was staring in shock at her murdered sister, white as a sheet, too stunned to scream. When she saw him run out of the bedroom, she began trembling all over, like a leaf in the wind. A shudder passed over her face; she lifted her hand, opened her mouth, but still couldn't scream. Slowly, she began backing away into the corner, never taking her eyes off him, but still not making a sound, as though she couldn't catch her breath to scream.

He rushed at her with the axe. Her mouth twitched pitifully, like a baby's when they're about to cry, staring at whatever scares them. This poor, helpless Lizaveta was so simple, so crushed with fear that she didn't even raise her hands to protect her face, though that would have been the natural thing to do since the axe was coming right at her. She only raised her empty left hand slowly, not to shield herself, but as if trying to push him away. The axe struck her head, splitting the top of her skull in one blow. She fell heavily to the floor.

Raskolnikov completely lost his senses. He snatched up the bundle she had been holding, but then dropped it again and ran toward the entryway. Fear overwhelmed him, especially after this second, unexpected murder. He was desperate to get away as fast as possible. If at that moment he had been thinking clearly, if he had fully understood the impossibility, horror, and absurdity of his situation—how many obstacles he still had to overcome, how many more crimes he might have to commit just to escape—he probably would have thrown everything aside and gone to turn himself in, not out of fear, but from sheer disgust and horror at what he had done. The feeling of loathing inside him grew stronger with every passing moment. Now, there was no way he would have gone back to the box or even into that room again for anything in the world.

But a kind of blankness, almost dreaminess, was starting to take over. At times, he seemed to forget himself, or at least forget what was important, and became distracted by trivial things. Glancing into the kitchen, he saw a bucket half-filled with water on a bench. He suddenly thought about washing his hands and the axe. His hands were sticky with blood. He dropped the axe into the water, blade first, grabbed a piece of soap from a broken saucer on the windowsill, and started washing his hands in the bucket. When his hands were clean, he pulled out the axe and washed the blade. He spent about three minutes scrubbing the wood handle, trying to remove the bloodstains with soap. Then he wiped it all down with some linen hanging to dry on a line in the kitchen. After that, he carefully inspected the axe in the dim light by the window. There was no trace of blood left on it, except that the wood was still damp. He tucked the axe back into the noose under his coat.

As much as he could in the poor light, he checked over his overcoat, trousers, and boots. At first glance, it seemed like there was nothing, except for a few stains on his boots. He wetted the rag and scrubbed the boots, but he knew he wasn't being thorough. There could be something obvious he was overlooking. He stood in the middle of the room, lost in thought. Dark, agonizing thoughts filled his mind—the idea that he was going mad, that at that moment, he couldn't think straight, couldn't protect himself. Maybe he should be doing something entirely different from what he was doing now. "Good God!" he muttered. "I need to go, now!" And he rushed toward the entryway.

But as soon as he got there, a shock of terror struck him like never before. He stood there, staring in disbelief: the outer door leading to the staircase, the same door he had waited at and rung the bell not long ago, was standing ajar, at least six inches open. No lock, no bolt—all that time! The old woman hadn't closed it after him, maybe as a precaution. But how could that be? He had seen Lizaveta afterward! How had he not realized that she must have come in through that door? She couldn't have walked through the wall!

He dashed to the door and fastened the latch.

"No, that's wrong! I need to get out of here... now!"

He unlatched the door, opened it, and listened intently on the staircase.

He listened for a long time. Somewhere far off, maybe in the gateway, two voices were shouting loudly, arguing and scolding each other. "What are they doing?" he thought. He waited patiently. Finally, everything went quiet, as if the shouting had been suddenly cut off; they must have gone their separate ways. He was just about to step out when, all of a sudden, a door on the floor below opened with a loud noise, and someone began walking downstairs, humming a tune. "Why are they all making so much noise?" flashed through his mind. Once again, he closed the door and waited. At last, there was silence again—no one in sight, not a sound to be heard. He was just about to take a step toward the stairs when fresh footsteps echoed nearby.

The footsteps echoed faintly from the bottom of the stairwell, but from the very first sound, Raskolnikov felt an eerie certainty—they were coming up to the fourth floor, to the old woman's flat. Why did he think that? Was there something strange or significant about the way the steps sounded? They were heavy, slow, and deliberate, each step landing firmly on the wood. He listened as they climbed, steadily moving higher—past the first floor, then the second. His breath became shallow as the sound grew louder, approaching his floor. Now they had reached the third floor. Closer... and closer...

It felt exactly like a nightmare. He stood frozen in place, paralyzed, as though he were trapped in one of those dreams where something terrible is chasing you, and you are moments away from being caught, but you can't move, not even enough to lift an arm.

At the very moment the unknown visitor arrived on the fourth-floor landing, Raskolnikov snapped into motion. He slipped silently back inside the old woman's flat and closed the door behind him with the utmost care, carefully fitting the hook into the latch. His hands moved almost on their own, as if instinct guided them. Once the door was securely hooked, he crouched down by it, pressing his ear against the wood, and held his breath.

The visitor was just on the other side of the door now. They stood separated only by the thin wooden panel, just as Raskolnikov had stood moments ago with the old woman, listening. He could hear the man's heavy breathing. "He must be a big, heavy man," Raskolnikov thought as he squeezed the axe in his hand, feeling its cold metal press into his palm. The surreal nature of the moment overwhelmed him; it was as if none of this could be real.

Then the visitor grabbed the bell and gave it a loud, forceful ring.

The tinny jangle echoed through the quiet, and at that very moment, Raskolnikov thought he heard something stir inside the flat. For a few seconds, he listened with his entire being, straining to catch every sound. The visitor rang the bell again, waited a moment, and then yanked impatiently at the door handle.

Raskolnikov stared in horror as the hook on the latch trembled under the strain. With each pull, it shook more violently, and for a moment, he thought it might give way. He fought the desperate urge to press the latch down himself, afraid the man outside might notice any resistance.

Dizziness swept over him like a wave. "I'll collapse," flashed through his mind. Then, just as his legs threatened to give out beneath him, the visitor spoke, breaking the dreadful silence.

"What the hell? Are they asleep or dead in there?" the man bellowed in a thick, gruff voice. "Damn it! Open up! Alyona Ivanovna, you old witch! Lizaveta Ivanovna, hey, my beauty, where are you? Open the door!"

The man cursed again, shaking the door handle furiously. He seemed familiar with the women inside, speaking with the authority of someone who knew them well.

Just then, quick, light footsteps echoed from the stairs below. A second person was climbing up, though Raskolnikov had not heard him before.

"Don't tell me no one's home!" the newcomer called out in a lively, cheerful voice. His tone was lighthearted, almost casual—a stark contrast to the first man's frustration. "Good evening, Koch!"

From the sound of his voice alone, Raskolnikov could tell the newcomer was young.

"How the hell do you know me?" Koch demanded, still jerking at the bell in irritation.

"We played billiards the other night at Gambrinus. I beat you three times straight!" the younger man answered with a laugh.

"Oh... right," Koch muttered. "Well, it looks like no one's home. Strange... I had business with the old woman."

"So did I," the younger man added. "This is really annoying. Where could she have gone?"

Koch let out an exasperated sigh. "She told me to come at this exact time. It's out of my way too. Where the hell could she have gone? The old hag never leaves her flat!"

"Maybe we should ask the porter," the younger man suggested.

"Yeah, we could ask... but she never goes anywhere," Koch grumbled, giving the door one last tug.

"Damn it, let's just leave."

"Wait a second!" the younger man interrupted. "Do you see how the door rattles when you pull it?"

"So what?" Koch asked impatiently.

"It's fastened with the hook from the inside!" the younger man exclaimed. "Don't you see? If they were all out, they'd have locked it with the key from the outside. But the hook is on the inside! That means someone must be in there."

"Damn it, you're right," Koch said, astonished. "What the hell are they doing in there?" He shook the door violently once more.

"Wait, stop shaking it!" the younger man warned. "Something's not right. We've been ringing the bell and yanking on the handle, but they still aren't opening the door. What if they've both fainted? Or... worse?"

"Worse? What do you mean?"

"I'll tell you what—let's go get the porter. He can wake them up."

"Alright."

"You stay here while I run down for him."

"Why me?"

"Just stay put—I'll be right back. I'm studying law, you know! Something fishy is going on here!" The young man's voice brimmed with self-importance as he hurried down the stairs, his footsteps echoing in the stairwell.

Koch stayed behind, shifting his weight from one foot to the other. He pressed the bell again, softly this time, as though trying to make sense of the situation. Then he gave the door handle a few experimental pulls, testing it to confirm that it was indeed fastened by the hook. With a frustrated sigh, he leaned down to peer through the keyhole.

But the key was still inside the lock, blocking his view entirely.

On the other side of the door, Raskolnikov gripped the axe so tightly that his knuckles turned white. His mind swirled with feverish thoughts, and he felt on the verge of madness. Part of him even considered throwing the door open and confronting them directly.

Several times, the idea crossed his mind to scream at them, to mock them while they stood helpless outside. He could picture himself jeering at them, reveling in their confusion as they banged futilely against the locked door.

"Just hurry up and leave!" he whispered under his breath.

Each second dragged on, stretching into eternity. Time seemed to slow, and the silence grew suffocating. He could feel his heart pounding in his chest, the sound of it echoing in his ears.

Then Koch's impatience got the better of him. "What the hell is taking him so long?" he muttered angrily. Unable to bear the waiting any longer, he abandoned his post and stomped heavily down the stairs, his boots thudding against the wood.

As the sound of Koch's footsteps faded away, Raskolnikov stood rooted in place, the axe still clutched in his trembling hands. His heart raced wildly in his chest, and his mind spiraled with panic.

What do I do now?

Raskolnikov unhooked the latch, pushed the door open, and stepped outside without making a sound. His mind was blank as he shut the door carefully behind him. He headed down the stairs, moving cautiously but quickly. He had made it down three flights when a loud voice suddenly echoed from below—there was nowhere to run. He thought briefly about turning back to the flat, but it was already too late.

"Hey! Catch that scoundrel!" someone yelled from a floor beneath him. A door slammed open, and a man came tumbling out, more falling than running, his voice booming up the stairwell.

"Mitka! Mitka! Mitka! Damn him!"

The shouting grew more frantic and trailed off as the man reached the courtyard. Silence followed—only for an instant. Then, from below, the clamor of several men's voices erupted. They were climbing the stairs now, talking loudly and rapidly. There were at least three or four of them, maybe more. The sharp, clear voice of the young man carried up to him: "Hey!"

Raskolnikov's chest tightened with fear. What now? He felt a cold wave of despair. If they saw him, if they even looked his way—everything would be over. But if they let him pass, it would be just as bad—they'd remember him for sure.

They were only a flight of stairs away from him now, getting closer every second. Suddenly, salvation appeared—just a few steps to his right: an open door to an empty flat. It was the second-floor apartment where the painters had been working earlier. The door gaped open as if inviting him in. It had to be the same men who'd run down the stairs shouting just moments before, leaving the flat empty.

Without a second thought, Raskolnikov slipped inside, flattening himself against the wall. His heart pounded in his chest. He could hear the men reach the landing just as he ducked out of sight. They paused briefly, chatting, before continuing up to the fourth floor.

As soon as their footsteps faded, he crept back out of the flat, moving silently on tiptoe. Once in the stairwell, he bolted down the stairs. He reached the ground floor, crossed the gateway without encountering anyone, and turned left onto the street.

He knew. He knew perfectly well that by now, the men would have reached the old woman's apartment. They would find the door unlocked—though it had been latched moments ago—and would soon discover the bodies. It wouldn't take them long to realize the killer had been there just moments before, hiding nearby, and had managed to slip past them unseen. Most likely, they would guess he had hidden in the empty flat while they were climbing the stairs.

But for now, he had to keep moving. He dared not quicken his pace too much, as that would draw attention. The nearest turn was still almost a hundred yards away. Should I duck into a gateway and hide? he wondered. But that was no good—there were too many unknown streets. Should I throw the axe away? Take a cab? No... no, it was all hopeless.

At last, he reached the turn. He made it around the corner, feeling as though he was half-dead already. Relief washed over him—he was closer to safety now. This street was busier, with plenty of people coming and going. He blended into the crowd like a grain of sand in the desert. But the ordeal had drained him. His body was weak, trembling with exhaustion. Sweat trickled down his face and soaked the back of his neck. His clothes clung to his damp skin.

"My God, look at him! He's been running like mad!" someone shouted as Raskolnikov stumbled past them near the canal.

His mind was clouded, and the farther he went, the more distant everything seemed. The world blurred around him. He vaguely remembered feeling uneasy when he reached the canal, noticing how few people were there. He worried that being alone would make him stand out. Though he was close to collapse, he forced himself to take a longer route home to avoid suspicion.

By the time he reached his building, he was barely conscious. He passed through the gateway on instinct, the familiar surroundings guiding him. Halfway up the stairs, he remembered—the axe!

The thought hit him like a jolt. He had to put it back without being noticed. The situation required careful thought and planning, but he was far beyond that now—his mind refused to cooperate. Perhaps it would have been wiser to throw the axe away somewhere, but the thought didn't even occur to him.

As luck would have it, the door to the porter's room was closed but not locked, which likely meant the porter was inside. Raskolnikov was too dazed to think clearly. He walked straight to the door and pushed it open. If the porter had been there and asked, "What do you want?" Raskolnikov might have handed him the axe without a word.

But the room was empty. Seizing the opportunity, he quickly slipped the axe back under the bench, covering it with the same piece of wood as before. He made it back to his room without encountering a single person. The landlady's door was closed. No one saw him. No one stopped him.

The moment he entered his room, he collapsed onto the sofa, not even bothering to take off his coat. He didn't sleep—his mind drifted into a dark, dreamless void. If anyone had opened the door just then, he would have leapt up with a scream. His thoughts swirled chaotically, fragments and half-formed ideas buzzing through his brain like a swarm of insects. But he couldn't hold on to a single thought—couldn't find any meaning or rest, no matter how hard he tried...

Part 2

Chapter 1

He lay there for a very long time. Every now and then, he seemed to wake up, and during those moments, he noticed it was already late at night. Still, it never crossed his mind to get up. Eventually, he realized the sky was beginning to lighten. He was lying on his back, still groggy from being unconscious for so long. Terrified, desperate cries rang out from the street—noises he heard every night outside his window after two o'clock. This time, they woke him completely.

"Ah, it's the drunks coming out of the taverns," he thought. "It must be past two o'clock." Suddenly, he jumped to his feet, as if someone had yanked him off the sofa.

"What? Past two o'clock?"

He sat back down on the sofa—and in an instant, it all came rushing back to him. Everything! All at once, in a single moment, he remembered everything.

At first, he thought he was losing his mind. A horrible chill crept over him, but it wasn't just fear—it was a fever that had started during his sleep. Now it hit him full force, shaking him violently until his teeth chattered and his whole body trembled. He got up and opened the door, listening carefully—everything in the house was quiet. Everyone was asleep.

He stared at himself and the room around him in shock, confused about how he'd managed to come in the night before, leave the door unlocked, and collapse on the sofa without even taking off his hat. His hat had fallen off and was lying on the floor near the pillow.

"If anyone had come in, what would they have thought? That I was drunk, but…"

He ran to the window. There was enough light now for him to see, and he began frantically checking himself from head to toe. Were there any signs left behind? Any clues? But he couldn't be sure, not like this. Shivering with cold, he started taking off all his clothes and examining them more closely. He searched every piece, down to the smallest thread, turning everything over three times, still doubting himself as he went.

But there didn't seem to be anything else, no trace at all, except for one spot. Thick drops of dried blood were stuck to the frayed edge of his trousers. Grabbing a large clasp knife, he quickly cut off the frayed threads. That seemed to be all.

Suddenly, he remembered that the purse and the items he had taken from the old woman's box were still in his pockets! He hadn't even thought to take them out or hide them! Not even while he was checking his clothes! What should he do now? In a panic, he pulled everything out and threw it all onto the table. Once he had emptied his pockets and turned them inside out to make sure nothing was left, he gathered the pile of things and carried them to the corner. The wallpaper at the bottom of the wall had peeled away and hung in torn strips. He began cramming the items into the hole beneath the paper. "There, it's all hidden! Even the purse!" he thought, feeling a brief surge of relief as he stood back and stared at the bulging hole. But then, out of nowhere, a wave of horror swept over him.

"My God!" he whispered in despair. "What's wrong with me? Is that hiding? Is that how you hide things?"

He hadn't thought about hiding anything other than money, so he hadn't planned for this. Trinkets were harder to conceal.

"And now, why am I even relieved?" he asked himself. "Is this what hiding looks like? My mind… it's falling apart!"

He collapsed onto the sofa, completely drained, and immediately felt another intense wave of shivering. Without thinking, he grabbed an old, tattered student coat from a chair nearby. The coat was still warm, though nearly falling apart. He wrapped it around himself and slipped into a fitful mix of sleep and feverish delirium. He lost all sense of time.

But no more than five minutes passed before he jerked awake again. This time, panic hit him like a lightning bolt. He leapt up and began frantically tearing through his clothes once more.

"How could I have fallen asleep without finishing this? Of course, I forgot something—the loop on the armhole! I didn't take it off! How could I forget something so obvious? Such clear evidence!"

He ripped off the loop, hurriedly cut it into pieces, and shoved the scraps into his pile of linen under the pillow.

"No one would suspect anything from bits of torn cloth. At least, I hope not. I think not. No, they can't," he muttered, standing frozen in the middle of the room. His thoughts spun in a painful cycle as his eyes darted around the space. He scanned the floor, the walls, and every corner, desperate to make sure he hadn't overlooked anything. The realization that his mind—his memory, even his ability to think clearly—was slipping away became an unbearable weight.

"Is it starting already?" he thought with dread. "Is this my punishment? Yes... it is!"

His gaze landed on the frayed threads from his trousers. They were still lying in the center of the room, out in the open where anyone who entered could see them.

"What is wrong with me?" he cried out, his voice filled with desperation.

Then a strange thought crossed his mind. What if all his clothes were covered in blood? What if there were stains everywhere, and he just couldn't see them? Maybe his senses were failing him. Maybe his mind was unraveling. His reasoning felt clouded. Suddenly, he remembered—there had been blood on the purse too.

"Wait! Then there must be blood in my pocket too, since I put the wet purse in there!"

In an instant, he turned the pocket inside out, and there it was—stains, faint but visible, on the pocket lining.

"So I haven't completely lost my mind. I still have some sense left, and my memory's intact enough to figure this out," he thought, feeling a surge of relief as he let out a deep sigh. "It's just the fever, making me weak and delirious," he reassured himself. Without hesitation, he tore out the entire lining of the left pocket of his trousers.

Just then, sunlight fell on his left boot. His eyes caught something—on the sock sticking out of the boot, there seemed to be marks. He ripped off his boots. "Marks, yes! The tip of the sock is soaked in blood!" he realized. He must have stepped carelessly into the pool of blood earlier.

"What am I supposed to do with this now? Where can I hide the sock, the rags, and the pocket lining?"

He gathered the pieces into his hands and stood frozen in the middle of the room.

"In the stove? But no, they'd search the stove first. Burn them? But how? I don't even have matches. No, it's better to go out and throw it all away somewhere. Yes, I'll throw it away," he repeated to himself, collapsing onto the sofa. "I need to do it immediately, right now, without wasting time..."

But instead of acting, his head sank onto the pillow. The unbearable coldness overtook him again, and he pulled the coat over himself once more.

For what felt like hours, he was consumed by the urge to get up, to go somewhere and get rid of the evidence—right then, without delay. Several times, he tried to rise from the sofa, but his body refused to cooperate.

At last, a loud, violent knock at his door jolted him awake.

"Open up! Are you alive in there or not? He just sleeps in there all day!" shouted Nastasya, pounding on the door with her fist. "Days on end, snoring like a dog! He's nothing but a dog. Open up, I'm telling you. It's already past ten!"

"Maybe he's not home," said a man's voice from behind her.

"Ah, that's the porter," he thought, his heart pounding painfully in his chest. "What does he want?"

"Then who could have latched the door?" Nastasya shot back. "He's taken to locking himself in! As if anyone would bother stealing from him. Open up, you idiot! Wake up!"

"What do they want? Why is the porter here? It's all been discovered! Should I resist? Or just open the door? Whatever happens..."

He half sat up, leaned forward, and unlatched the door. His room was so small that he didn't even have to get out of bed to do it. Sure enough, the porter and Nastasya were standing there.

Nastasya looked at him with an odd expression. He gave the porter a defiant and desperate glare, but the man said nothing, only handed him a folded grey paper sealed with red wax.

"It's a notice from the office," the porter said, holding it out.

"Which office?"

"A summons from the police station, obviously. You know the one."

"The police? What for?"

"How should I know? They sent for you, so you have to go."

The porter studied him closely, glanced around the room, and then turned to leave.

"He's really sick," Nastasya said, her eyes still fixed on him. The porter paused and looked back for a moment. "He's had a fever since yesterday," she added.

Raskolnikov didn't answer. He just held the paper in his hands without opening it. Nastasya noticed him lowering his legs from the sofa and said, with some pity in her voice, "Don't get up. You're unwell. You don't have to rush. What's that you've got there?"

He looked down and saw that in his right hand, he was clutching the scraps of fabric he had cut from his trousers, the sock, and the torn pocket lining. He had fallen asleep holding them. Later, when he thought about it, he realized that during one of his fevered half-wakings, he must have gripped them tightly and drifted back to sleep.

"Look at the trash he's hoarding, sleeping with it like it's some kind of treasure…" Nastasya burst into one of her fits of hysterical laughter.

Immediately, he stuffed the scraps under his coat and stared at her intently. He wasn't thinking clearly, but he felt certain that no one would act like this toward someone about to be arrested. Still, the thought nagged him: "But… the police?"

"You should have some tea. I'll bring you some—it's still hot," she offered.

"No… I'll go. I'll go right now," he mumbled as he stood up.

"You'll never make it down the stairs like that."

"I'll go," he insisted.

"Suit yourself," she said, following the porter out.

The moment they left, he rushed to the light to inspect the sock and scraps.

"There are stains, but they're faint. They're dirty and smudged, already faded. No one who wasn't suspicious would notice anything. Nastasya couldn't have seen it from a distance, thank God!"

With trembling hands, he broke the seal on the notice and began to read. It took him a long time to make sense of it. Finally, he understood. It was a standard summons from the district police station, requiring him to appear at the superintendent's office that day at half-past nine.

"But how could this happen? I've never had anything to do with the police before! And why today of all days?" he wondered, his mind racing with confusion and fear. "God, let it be over quickly!"

He dropped to his knees as though to pray but stopped and broke into a sudden, bitter laugh—not at the idea of prayer itself, but at the absurdity of his actions. What was he doing? He shook his head and began hurriedly dressing.

"If I'm doomed, then so be it. It doesn't matter anymore!" he thought, trembling. Then his eyes fell on the sock, and he hesitated. "Should I put it on? If I wear it, the dirt and dust will make the traces harder to see."

He slipped the sock onto his foot but was immediately filled with revulsion. The thought of it made his stomach churn. In a surge of disgust, he pulled it off again. Yet, after a moment of reflection—realizing he had no other socks—he picked it up and put it back on. Once more, a hollow laugh escaped his lips.

"It's all relative... all a matter of perception," he muttered to himself, but the thought barely scratched the surface of his mind. His body trembled as he tried to suppress the creeping dread. "There, it's on. I've done it. It's on now."

His fleeting amusement quickly gave way to despair.

"No, I can't take this anymore," he thought, feeling his legs tremble under him. "This is fear, nothing but fear," he whispered. His head pounded with fever, spinning uncontrollably. "It's a trap! They're calling me there just to confront me with everything, to catch me off guard!" The thought churned in his mind as he stepped out onto the stairs. "And the worst part is, I feel lightheaded... I might say something stupid."

Suddenly, he froze. He had left everything—the rags, the sock, the torn lining—just as they were, stuffed into the hole in the wall. "They'll search the room while I'm gone," he realized with a sinking feeling. But his despair overwhelmed him, and he gave a bitter wave of his hand. "Just let it be over already!"

The street was unbearably hot. Days had passed without a drop of rain. The same choking dust hung in the air, mixed with the smell of bricks, mortar, and the stench of rotting waste from the shops and taverns. Drunken men staggered about, Finnish peddlers shouted their wares, and dilapidated cabs rattled by. The sun burned so brightly that he had to shield his eyes, and even then, his head throbbed as if it might burst. The heat pressed down on him, relentless, and his fevered body felt as though it might collapse under the weight of it.

When he reached the corner of the street leading to the station, his heart pounded with dread. He couldn't bear to look directly at the building. Instead, his eyes darted away, as if avoiding it might delay the inevitable.

"If they start questioning me, maybe I'll just confess everything," he thought in a daze as he drew closer to the police station.

The station itself was about a quarter of a mile away. It had recently been moved to new offices on the fourth floor of a newly constructed building. The old police office was a faint memory from years ago, but he hardly recognized this new place. As he entered through the gateway, he noticed a set of stairs to his right. A peasant was slowly climbing them, holding a book in his hand.

"A house porter, most likely," Raskolnikov thought. "The office must be up there." Without stopping to ask for directions, he began climbing the stairs. He wanted to avoid any interaction if possible.

"I'll just walk in, fall on my knees, and confess everything," he thought grimly as he reached the fourth floor.

The staircase was narrow, steep, and filthy, the air thick with the smell of damp and decay. Kitchens from the surrounding apartments opened onto the stairs, their doors left ajar. The oppressive heat and rank odors from the kitchens made it nearly unbearable to breathe. The staircase was crowded with people—porters carrying books, policemen, and others coming and going. The door to the office itself stood wide open, and peasants were gathered inside, waiting their turn. The heat inside was even worse, made stifling by the heavy smell of fresh paint and stale oil from the newly decorated rooms.

Raskolnikov hesitated for a moment but finally forced himself to move deeper into the building. Each room he entered felt smaller, darker, and lower than the last, yet no one paid him any attention. His anxiety clawed at him, driving him further and further in.

In one of the rooms, a group of clerks sat at their desks, scribbling notes. Their clothing was no better than his own, and they struck him as a peculiar bunch. He walked up to one of them, holding out the notice.

"What do you want?" the clerk asked flatly.

He handed over the paper. "I received this."

"You're a student?" the man asked, glancing briefly at the document.

"I used to be," Raskolnikov replied.

The clerk gave him a quick, indifferent look before turning his attention elsewhere. His disheveled appearance and vacant expression suggested a man preoccupied with his own thoughts, entirely uninterested in the world around him.

"There's no use trying to get anything out of him," Raskolnikov thought. "He doesn't care about anything."

"Go into the next room and see the head clerk," the man said, pointing toward the far end of the hallway.

The next room was the fourth he had entered. It was slightly larger but just as cramped, filled with people who were dressed a little better than those outside. Among them were two women. One was poorly dressed and in mourning; she sat at a table across from the head clerk, writing something as he dictated to her. The other was a heavyset woman with a blotchy, purplish-red face, dressed in garishly bright clothing. She wore a brooch on her chest the size of a saucer and stood waiting impatiently for something.

Raskolnikov approached the head clerk and handed him the notice. The clerk glanced at it briefly and said, "Wait a moment," before turning back to the woman in mourning.

For the first time since entering the station, Raskolnikov felt a small sense of relief. "It can't be about that," he thought, his breathing steadying just slightly.

Gradually, he began to regain a bit of confidence. "I just need to stay calm and keep my wits about me," he told himself, though a deep unease lingered beneath the surface. "A single careless word could ruin everything."

But the air was stifling. The lack of ventilation, combined with the heavy smells, made his head spin even more. His thoughts swirled chaotically, and he struggled to focus. His gaze kept drifting toward the head clerk, desperate to read something—anything—from the man's face.

The young man was no more than twenty-two, though his face seemed older, with sharp, expressive features that shifted easily with emotion. His appearance was carefully styled, bordering on foppish. His hair was parted neatly in the middle, combed and shining with pomade. A gold chain hung across his waistcoat, and his fingers, clean and meticulously scrubbed, were adorned with several rings. He spoke a few words in French to a foreigner in the room, and though his accent wasn't perfect, his pronunciation was competent enough to draw attention.

"Luise Ivanovna, you can take a seat," he said in an offhanded tone to a brightly dressed woman with a flushed, purplish face. She stood hesitantly, though there was an empty chair beside her.

"Thank you," she replied in German, her voice soft and tinged with deference. With a rustle of silk, she sank into the chair. Her pale blue dress, elaborately trimmed with white lace, billowed out like an inflated balloon, seeming to fill half the room. The strong scent of perfume surrounded her, clinging to the air. Despite her bold smile, there was an obvious awkwardness in her manner, a nervousness that contradicted her flashy appearance. She seemed acutely aware of how much space she took up and how overpowering her perfume was.

The woman in mourning finished her task and rose from her seat. Just then, the room stirred as a man entered. He was an officer, striding in confidently with a jaunty swing of his shoulders. Tossing his cockaded cap onto the table, he claimed an armchair with an air of entitlement. The brightly dressed woman practically leaped from her seat at the sight of him, curtseying repeatedly in a near frenzy of admiration. Yet, the officer ignored her entirely, not even sparing her a glance. She didn't dare to sit again in his presence.

This man was the assistant superintendent. His reddish mustache flared horizontally from his face, giving him a distinct, almost theatrical appearance. His small features carried a look of insolent self-importance, but little else. His eyes turned toward Raskolnikov, narrowing slightly with disapproval. Raskolnikov's threadbare clothing and the stubborn, unyielding posture he maintained seemed to irritate the officer. Without realizing it, Raskolnikov had fixed a direct, unflinching stare on the man, which only added to the tension.

"What do you want?" the officer barked, as though shocked that someone so poorly dressed would dare meet his gaze so boldly.

"I received a summons…" Raskolnikov began, his voice faltering under the weight of the man's hostility.

"For unpaid debts, from the student," the head clerk interjected abruptly, barely looking up from his work. He shoved a document toward Raskolnikov, pointing impatiently. "Read it!"

"Debts? What debts?" Raskolnikov thought, his mind racing. But then, as realization dawned, a wave of immense relief swept over him. "So it's not… it's not that." He felt as though a crushing weight had been lifted from his shoulders, and his chest heaved with an involuntary sigh of joy.

"And what time were you instructed to appear, sir?" the assistant superintendent suddenly shouted, his tone growing more agitated with every word. "You were told to come at nine! It's already twelve!"

"The notice was delivered to me only fifteen minutes ago," Raskolnikov replied loudly, turning slightly as he spoke. To his own surprise, anger surged within him, and he found a strange satisfaction in letting it show. "And isn't it enough that I came here at all, given that I'm ill and feverish?"

"Stop shouting!" the officer snapped.

"I'm not shouting," Raskolnikov countered coldly. "I'm speaking clearly. It's you who's shouting at me. I'm a student, and I won't allow anyone to yell at me."

The officer's face turned crimson. He stood abruptly, spluttering in rage, but for a moment he seemed too furious to form coherent words.

"Be silent! This is a government office. Don't you dare show such disrespect!" he finally managed, his voice shaking with anger.

"This is a government office," Raskolnikov shot back, his voice rising slightly. "And yet you're standing there smoking a cigarette while yelling at people. That's disrespectful to everyone here!"

Raskolnikov felt a strange, almost exhilarating sense of satisfaction as the words left his mouth. The head clerk, who had been quietly observing the exchange, allowed himself a faint smile. The assistant superintendent, however, looked utterly thrown, his composure slipping further with each passing moment.

"That's none of your business!" the officer shouted, his voice unnaturally loud. "Now, make your declaration as required. Alexandr Grigorievitch, show him the document! There's a formal complaint against him! He doesn't pay his debts. A fine example he is!"

But Raskolnikov was no longer listening. He had seized the document eagerly, desperate to understand its contents. He read it once, then again, but the words refused to settle in his fevered mind.

"What does this mean?" he asked the head clerk, his voice tight with confusion.

"It's an official writ for the recovery of money owed. You must either pay the sum in full, including all associated costs, or provide a written statement detailing when you'll be able to pay. You'll also need to promise not to leave the city or sell or hide any of your belongings. If you don't comply, the creditor has the right to sell your property and take further legal action," the clerk explained with practiced indifference.

"But I don't owe anyone money!" Raskolnikov protested, his voice rising slightly in frustration.

"That's not for us to decide. This document is based on an IOU for one hundred and fifteen roubles, legally verified and overdue. It was issued by you to the widow of the assessor Zarnitsyn nine months ago. The widow later transferred it to one Mr. Tchebarov. Hence, we're required to summon you."

"But she's my landlady!" Raskolnikov exclaimed.

"And what of it if she is?" the clerk replied dryly.

The head clerk regarded Raskolnikov with a condescending smirk, a look that mingled faint pity with the smug satisfaction of someone watching a novice face a trial for the first time. His expression seemed to say, "Well, how do you feel now?" But Raskolnikov hardly noticed. What did he care about an I.O.U. or a writ for debt collection? Such trivialities seemed laughably insignificant compared to the crushing weight he had feared only moments ago. He stood there reading, listening, responding, and even asking a few questions—but all of it was done mechanically, without thought or focus. His mind was utterly consumed by the triumphant sense of escape, the overwhelming relief of having avoided a greater danger. This feeling filled his soul completely, leaving no room for analysis, doubt, or even thoughts of the future. It was pure, instinctive joy, fleeting but absolute.

Just as he was basking in this strange reprieve, the atmosphere in the office shifted abruptly, like the onset of a sudden storm. The assistant superintendent, still simmering with indignation over

Raskolnikov's earlier insolence, decided to vent his anger on a new target. His gaze landed on the brightly dressed lady, Luise Ivanovna, who had been sitting stiffly, her face stretched into a simpering, foolish smile since his arrival.

"You disgraceful hussy!" he bellowed, his voice echoing through the room and startling everyone present. (By now, the woman in mourning had already left.) "What kind of behavior was going on in your house last night? Again with the drunken brawling and scandal! I've warned you ten times already that I wouldn't tolerate an eleventh! And here you are—yet again—dragging the whole street into disrepute with your disgraceful antics!"

As his tirade escalated, Raskolnikov stood frozen, his document slipping from his fingers. His wild eyes flicked to Luise Ivanovna, who was now the unfortunate object of the assistant's wrath. At first, he was shocked by the unceremonious treatment she was receiving, but soon he began to find the situation oddly entertaining. There was something almost absurd about the spectacle, and a nervous desire to laugh bubbled up within him. His frayed nerves made the scene feel exaggerated, almost surreal, and he couldn't help but take perverse pleasure in the chaos.

"Ilya Petrovitch!" the head clerk interjected cautiously, his tone laced with an undertone of concern. But he quickly fell silent, knowing that once the assistant superintendent began shouting, there was little hope of stopping him.

Meanwhile, Luise Ivanovna seemed to shrink before the storm, trembling at first under the onslaught of insults. Strangely, though, as the abuse grew louder and more colorful, her demeanor shifted. Instead of recoiling, she began to beam at the assistant with increasingly ingratiating smiles. Her curtsies became more frequent, her movements more fidgety, as though she were trying to find an opening to defend herself. Finally, she seized her chance.

"There was no sort of scandal or fighting in my house last night, Mr. Captain," she began rapidly, her words spilling out in a jumble. Though her Russian was fluent, it was heavily accented with German.

"It is all untrue, I assure you, Mr. Captain. His honor came in quite drunk, and that is the whole truth. Mine is an honorable house, and I am always respectful of good behavior. But he—he came tipsy, demanded three bottles of wine, and then he—oh, what a disgrace—he put one foot on the piano and started playing it with his toes! Can you imagine, Mr. Captain? Playing the piano with his foot in an honorable house!"

Her voice quickened as she detailed the chaos that had unfolded. "Then he broke the piano, completely smashed it! I told him it was bad manners, and he picked up a bottle and started swinging it at everyone. When I called Karl—the porter—he hit Karl in the eye, then hit Henriette in the eye, and then he gave me five slaps on the cheek! Such ungentlemanly behavior in an honorable house, Mr. Captain!"

Her voice rose as she continued. "And if that wasn't enough, he opened the window over the canal and began squealing like a little pig! A little pig, Mr. Captain! Right there, out into the street! Karl had to pull him back from the window, and in the process, his coat was torn. He demanded fifteen roubles in damages for the coat, and I—I even paid him five roubles! And then he threatened to write to the papers and ruin my reputation!"

"So he was an author?" the assistant asked dryly, his eyebrows arching.

"Yes, Mr. Captain! And what an ungentlemanly visitor for an honorable house!"

"Enough of this nonsense!" the assistant snapped. "I've warned you before, Luise Ivanovna, and I'm warning you for the last time. If there's another scandal in your 'honorable house,' I'll have you locked up, do you understand? Imagine—an author demanding five roubles for a torn coat! What a disgrace."

He cast a disdainful glance at Raskolnikov, as if lumping him in with this chaotic narrative. "These authors and students are all the same. One of them caused a scene in a restaurant the other day, ate a meal, and refused to pay. Said he'd write a satire instead. Another one insulted a civil servant's family on a steamer last week. And one more was thrown out of a confectioner's shop for using foul language. What a fine group! Authors, students, literary types... town criers!"

Luise Ivanovna, bowing and curtsying repeatedly, backed toward the door. At the threshold, she collided with a tall, handsome officer with a cheerful face and thick blond whiskers. This was the district superintendent, Nikodim Fomitch. Luise Ivanovna made a deep curtsy, nearly to the floor, and hurried out with small, fluttering steps.

"Another storm, I see," Nikodim Fomitch said with a genial smile, addressing the assistant. "You're at it again, Ilya Petrovitch. I heard you all the way from the stairs!"

"Well, what's the matter now?" Ilya Petrovitch drawled with an air of practiced indifference, his tone dripping with a kind of exaggerated courtesy. He picked up some papers from the desk and walked to another table, his shoulders swaying jauntily with every step. "Here we have, if you please, an author—or perhaps just a student, at least he was one once—who doesn't pay his debts, refuses to vacate his room, and is constantly the subject of complaints. And now he's been so gracious as to protest against me smoking in his presence! A fine gentleman, isn't he? Just look at him! Quite the picture."

Nikodim Fomitch, who had been watching the scene unfold with a faint smile, addressed Raskolnikov in a more amiable tone. "Poverty is no disgrace, my friend, though I daresay tempers can flare when people feel slighted. I wouldn't be surprised if you took something the wrong way and things got a bit out of hand. But you must understand, Ilya Petrovitch here is an excellent fellow, truly he is, but he's got a bit of a temper—explosive, even. When he gets heated, there's no stopping him. Fires up like gunpowder, and then it's all over in a flash! Underneath it all, though, he's got a heart of gold. Back in the regiment, they used to call him the Explosive Lieutenant."

Ilya Petrovitch, though still visibly irritable, couldn't help but perk up at the mention of his old nickname. "And what a regiment that was!" he exclaimed, his mood softening as he recalled the past.

The tension in the room began to ease, and Raskolnikov felt a sudden, almost desperate urge to ingratiate himself. He wanted to say something pleasant, something that would lighten the atmosphere further. "Excuse me, Captain," he began, addressing Nikodim Fomitch with a tone of measured deference, "but I would ask you to consider my situation. If I have been rude, I apologize for it. I am a poor student, sick and utterly worn down—shattered, really—by poverty. I am not studying now because I can't afford to support myself, but I have family—my mother and sister live in the provinces. They will send me money soon, and I will pay what I owe. My landlady, she's a kind woman at heart, but she's at her wit's end because I haven't paid her in four months. She's so frustrated that she's even stopped sending up my meals. And now she's pressing me about this I.O.U., which I still don't fully understand. How am I to pay it? Judge for yourselves."

"That's not our concern, you know," the head clerk interjected curtly, without looking up from his papers.

"Yes, yes, I completely understand," Raskolnikov replied quickly, his voice rising slightly as he continued. "But please, let me explain..." He directed his plea toward Nikodim Fomitch but kept glancing at Ilya Petrovitch, hoping for some acknowledgment. The latter, however, appeared engrossed in shuffling through his papers, his expression deliberately dismissive.

Raskolnikov pressed on. "I have been living with my landlady for nearly three years. At first—well, I suppose there's no harm in admitting it now—I promised to marry her daughter. It was a verbal promise, freely given. She was a sweet girl, and though I wasn't in love with her, I did like her. It was... youthful foolishness, I suppose. During that time, my landlady was very generous with me, giving me credit without hesitation. But I was careless, reckless even, and I lived beyond my means."

"Nobody asked for your life story," Ilya Petrovitch cut in sharply, his tone laced with triumph. "We don't have time for this."

"Please, allow me to finish," Raskolnikov shot back, his voice tinged with frustration. He hesitated, struggling to organize his thoughts as his words became more halting. "I... I know it's unnecessary to go into such detail, but I feel it's important to explain how it all came to this. You see, about a year ago, the girl—my landlady's daughter—died of typhus. After that, I stayed on in the same lodgings, and when my landlady moved to her current apartment, she approached me with a request. She said, in the friendliest way, that while she trusted me completely, she would feel more secure if I gave her an I.O.U. for the total amount I owed her—one hundred and fifteen roubles. She assured me, even swore to me, that she would never use it against me, not unless I chose to pay of my own accord. 'I'll trust you with credit again, as much as you need,' she said, 'but just give me this for my peace of mind.'"

He paused for a moment, his voice trembling with indignation. "And now, when I have lost my teaching work, when I don't even have enough to eat, she brings this action against me. How can I explain that? What am I supposed to do?"

"All these sentimental details are none of our concern," Ilya Petrovitch interrupted brusquely, his tone sharp and dismissive. "You need to write a formal undertaking, but as for your love affairs and all these dramatic tales, they don't concern us in the slightest."

"Come now, don't be so harsh," muttered Nikodim Fomitch, lowering himself into a chair at the table and beginning to write. There was a faint flush of discomfort on his face, as though he felt a trace of guilt for his colleague's rudeness.

"Write," the head clerk said flatly, gesturing toward Raskolnikov.

"Write what?" Raskolnikov replied in a rough voice.

"I'll dictate it to you," the clerk said, his tone dripping with condescension.

Raskolnikov thought he detected a change in the clerk's demeanor—he seemed colder, more dismissive, as if the speech Raskolnikov had just delivered had reduced him in the man's estimation. But strangely, Raskolnikov found that he no longer cared in the slightest. This indifference swept over him suddenly, like a wave that wiped his emotions clean in an instant. If he had paused to reflect on it, he would have been astonished at his own transformation. How had he found the energy only moments ago to lay bare his feelings, forcing his words on these indifferent people? And what had inspired him to do so?

Now, he was certain that even if the room were filled with his closest family and dearest friends, he would have no words for them either. His heart felt hollow, as though stripped of all connection to others. A deep and painful awareness of his isolation took hold, not as a mere thought but as an overwhelming, physical sensation. It was not just the humiliation of baring himself before Ilya Petrovitch, nor the clerk's thinly veiled disdain that caused this change. No, this was something deeper—a realization that his life, his struggles, and his very existence had become irreparably separate from those around him. He felt, with piercing clarity, that even if these men were his brothers or friends, it would be impossible to appeal to them for understanding or support. The sheer strangeness of the sensation unsettled him, and its intensity was the most agonizing feeling he had ever experienced.

"Write the usual declaration," the head clerk began, dictating in a monotone. "State that you cannot pay, that you agree to do so at a later date, that you will not leave town, and that you will refrain from selling or hiding your property."

Raskolnikov took the pen, his hands trembling slightly. "You can barely hold it," observed the head clerk, eyeing him curiously. "Are you unwell?"

"Yes, I feel dizzy. Just keep going," Raskolnikov replied shortly.

"That's all. Sign it," the clerk said, handing him the paper. Once Raskolnikov had scrawled his signature, the clerk took the document without a second glance and moved on to the next task.

Raskolnikov returned the pen but didn't rise from his chair. Instead, he leaned forward, pressing his elbows onto the table and burying his head in his hands. His skull throbbed as though a nail were being hammered into it. A sudden, wild impulse seized him—to stand up, walk directly to Nikodim Fomitch, and confess everything. He could lead the officer to his room, show him the items hidden in the wall, and lay it all bare. The urge was so strong that he began to rise, but halfway to his feet, another thought flickered through his mind: Shouldn't I stop and think for just a moment? No, he decided instantly. Better to cast off the weight of it all without thinking further.

But just as he resolved to act, he froze. His body remained rooted to the spot, unable to move. Across the room, Nikodim Fomitch was speaking animatedly to Ilya Petrovitch, and fragments of their conversation reached Raskolnikov's ears.

"It's impossible; they'll both have to be released. The whole story contradicts itself," Nikodim Fomitch was saying. "Why would they have called the porter if they were guilty? To incriminate themselves? That would be too clever. Besides, Pestryakov—the student—was seen at the gate with three friends. They left him there, and he even asked the porters for directions. Would he have done that if he had been planning something? As for Koch, he spent half an hour at the silversmith's downstairs before he even went up to the old woman. And he left precisely at a quarter to eight. Now think about it..."

"But what about the contradiction?" Ilya Petrovitch cut in sharply. "They said they knocked and the door was locked, yet when they came back with the porter, it was unfastened."

"Exactly! That's where the murderer comes in," Nikodim Fomitch replied, leaning forward eagerly. "He must have been inside and bolted the door. Koch, being a fool, went to find the porter instead of waiting. That gave the killer just enough time to slip past them on the stairs. Koch keeps saying, 'If I'd been there, he would have jumped out and killed me with his axe!' He's even planning a thanksgiving service—ha!"

"And no one saw the murderer?" asked another voice from the room.

"It's not surprising they didn't. That building is a madhouse," the head clerk interjected from his desk.

"It's perfectly clear," Nikodim Fomitch said with conviction.

"No, it's anything but clear," Ilya Petrovitch shot back, his tone tinged with frustration.

Raskolnikov stood still, his earlier impulse completely forgotten. The fragments of their discussion swirled in his mind, filling him with an eerie, detached curiosity. He felt as though he were floating above the scene, watching it all unfold from a distance, yet unable to fully grasp its implications.

Raskolnikov grabbed his hat and started walking toward the door, but he never made it there.

When he regained consciousness, he found himself sitting in a chair. Someone was supporting him on his right side, while another person stood on his left, holding a yellowish glass filled with yellow-tinted water. In front of him, Nikodim Fomitch was standing, looking at him closely. Slowly, Raskolnikov got up from the chair.

"What's this? Are you feeling sick?" Nikodim Fomitch asked sharply, his voice edged with concern.

"He could barely hold the pen when he signed the paper," the head clerk added from his seat. He had already returned to his work, his tone indifferent as he resumed shuffling through documents.

"Have you been unwell for long?" Ilya Petrovitch called out from across the room. He, too, had come over to check on Raskolnikov when he fainted but had returned to his place the moment it became clear the young man was recovering.

"Since yesterday," Raskolnikov muttered, his voice low and shaky.

"Did you leave your home yesterday?"

"Yes."

"Even though you were sick?"

"Yes."

"What time did you go out?"

"Around seven."

"And where did you go, if I may ask?"

"Along the street," Raskolnikov answered curtly.

"Short and to the point," Ilya Petrovitch remarked, his tone cool and tinged with sarcasm.

Raskolnikov, pale as a sheet, responded with clipped, jerky answers, his feverish black eyes never wavering as they locked onto Ilya Petrovitch's stare. His defiance seemed to hang in the air, heavy and electric.

"He can hardly stay on his feet. And you..." Nikodim Fomitch began, his words trailing off.

"It doesn't matter," Ilya Petrovitch interrupted, his voice carrying a peculiar finality.

Nikodim Fomitch opened his mouth as though to argue, but then he glanced at the head clerk, who was watching him intently. Whatever he had planned to say was left unsaid. The room fell into a strange, heavy silence.

"Very well," Ilya Petrovitch concluded after a pause. "We won't keep you any longer."

Without another word, Raskolnikov turned and left the room. As he stepped into the corridor, he could hear the eager murmur of voices rising behind him. Above the others, Nikodim Fomitch's questioning tone stood out, sharp and persistent.

Once Raskolnikov was outside, the faintness that had overwhelmed him inside the office faded completely. His head cleared, but a new terror quickly gripped him.

"A search. They're going to search my room immediately," he muttered to himself as he hurried through the streets. "Those bastards—they're onto me."

The fear he thought he'd shaken off earlier came rushing back, stronger than ever, wrapping around him like a suffocating weight.

Chapter 2

"What if they've already searched my room? What if I find them waiting there?" he thought, his panic mounting with every step.

When he reached his door, he found the room exactly as he had left it. No one had been inside—not even Nastasya had entered or touched anything. But the realization struck him like a thunderclap: how could he have been so careless as to leave everything in the hole? His chest tightened with dread as he rushed to the corner, pulled back the loose wallpaper, and retrieved the items hidden there. Without taking the time to examine them closely, he quickly stuffed them into his pockets.

There were eight items in total: two small boxes, each holding earrings or some other type of jewelry—he didn't bother to check; four small leather cases; a chain wrapped in newspaper; and another object also wrapped in newspaper, which looked like some kind of medal or decoration. He divided them between the pockets of his overcoat and the last pocket in his trousers, arranging them as discreetly as he could. Lastly, he grabbed the purse.

Without waiting another moment, he left the room, leaving the door ajar behind him. His movements were swift and deliberate, though his body felt like it was running on fumes. He was terrified that at any moment, perhaps in the next half hour or even sooner, an order might be issued for his arrest. He had to act before that happened. He needed to eliminate every trace of evidence while he still had the strength and presence of mind to do so.

But where could he go?

The plan had already been decided in the haze of his fevered delirium the night before. He would throw everything into the canal—let the water swallow it up, and the matter would be over. The thought had given him a strange, fleeting sense of clarity during the night when he had been seized by the urge to get up and rid himself of the burden. But now, as he walked along the banks of the Ekaterininsky Canal, he realized how complicated this task truly was. For over half an hour, he wandered aimlessly, glancing repeatedly at the steps leading down to the water. Each time, he hesitated.

Rafts were tied up along the edge, and women knelt on them, scrubbing laundry in the water. Boats were moored nearby, and people moved constantly along the banks. It seemed impossible to act without drawing attention. Even the idea of descending the steps, stopping, and throwing something into the water felt conspicuous. And what if the boxes floated instead of sinking? Surely, they would rise to the surface, betraying him.

The feeling of being watched was suffocating. Every passerby seemed to glance at him, their gazes sharp and questioning. Was it his imagination, or did everyone know what he was planning? The thought clawed at his mind. "Why do they keep looking at me? Or am I imagining it?" he wondered.

At last, a new idea occurred to him. The Neva. There would be fewer people there, less chance of being observed, and the open waters would make it far easier to dispose of the items discreetly. It was farther away, but in every other way, it seemed a better option. He cursed himself for wasting so much time wandering by the canal, following a plan born out of feverish delusions. The realization that he had squandered half an hour on an ill-conceived idea left him frustrated and acutely aware of how scattered and forgetful he had become. He needed to hurry.

As he made his way toward the Neva along V—— Prospect, another thought struck him. Why stop at the Neva? Wouldn't it be better to go farther out, perhaps to the Islands? He could find a secluded spot, bury the items under a bush or in a thicket, and even mark the location for later. It seemed like a sound plan, though he doubted his ability to think clearly at the moment.

But fate had other ideas. Just as he was nearing the square at the end of V—— Prospect, he noticed a passageway on his left. It led between two blank walls into a courtyard. On one side, the rough, unpainted wall of a four-story building stretched into the distance, while a wooden fence ran parallel to it, enclosing part of the courtyard. The fence turned sharply to the left, and beyond it, piles of rubbish were scattered across the ground. At the far end of the yard, the corner of a low, grimy stone shed poked out from behind the fence, its surface blackened with coal dust. It was likely part of a carpenter's or carriage-builder's workshop.

The courtyard was deserted, the perfect place for his purposes. Near the entrance, he noticed a large stone sink, the kind commonly found in yards frequented by cab drivers or workmen. Above it, someone had scrawled the familiar chalk warning: "Standing here strictly forbidden." That was even better; the sign gave him an excuse to be there without suspicion.

"Yes, this will do," he thought. "I'll toss everything here in a heap and leave."

Glancing around one last time to ensure he was alone, Raskolnikov reached into his pocket but stopped abruptly. Against the wall near the sink, he spotted a massive, uncut stone that must have weighed at least sixty pounds. On the other side of the wall, he could hear the muffled sounds of people passing by on the street, though no one could see him from there unless they entered the courtyard. Knowing the possibility was real, he worked quickly.

He crouched down and grabbed the top of the stone with both hands, straining as he rolled it to one side. Beneath it was a shallow depression in the dirt. Without hesitation, he emptied his pockets into the hollow, placing the purse on top. Even then, the hole wasn't quite full. He pushed the stone back into place with a final effort, leaving it just slightly higher than before. To conceal the difference, he kicked at the dirt around the edges, smoothing it with his foot until it looked untouched.

When he stepped back to survey his work, the hiding spot was invisible. Satisfied, he straightened up, took a breath, and walked away, not daring to look back.

He stepped out into the square, his steps steady but quick. As he crossed it, an intense, almost unbearable wave of joy washed over him, just as it had back in the police office. "I've covered my tracks! No one could ever think to look under that stone," he told himself, his thoughts racing triumphantly. "That rock has probably been there since the house was built and will stay there for decades. Even if it's found, who would suspect me? It's over. No clues!" He laughed—a thin, nervous laugh that barely made a sound. The laughter carried him across the square, filling the empty space around him.

But as he turned onto K—— Boulevard, the very place where he had encountered that girl two days before, his laughter abruptly ceased. His triumph crumbled, and other thoughts began to creep into his mind. He felt an overwhelming loathing at the idea of passing by the bench where he had sat after the girl had left, brooding and reflecting on his own misery. The thought of seeing that whiskered policeman— the one he had given twenty copecks to—made him shudder with disgust. "Damn him," he muttered under his breath.

He walked on, his eyes darting about restlessly. A sense of anger and confusion churned inside him. His thoughts felt as though they were circling a single point, drawing closer and closer, and now he felt as though he was finally standing face-to-face with it for the first time in months. The realization filled him with fury.

"Damn it all!" he thought, the rage bubbling up uncontrollably. "If it's begun, then so be it. To hell with this new life! God, how absurd it all is! And the lies I told today! Groveling like that to that pathetic Ilya Petrovitch! But what does it matter? What do I care about them or how I acted around them? That's not what matters. It's not about that at all!"

He came to an abrupt halt, as though struck by a new and utterly unexpected thought. It was a simple question, yet it hit him with staggering force.

"If I planned all this deliberately—if I had a clear, definite purpose in mind—then why didn't I even look inside the purse? I don't even know what was in it! Why did I go through all this suffering, stoop to such disgusting, degrading actions, only to immediately want to throw the purse and everything else into the water without even checking? How does that make any sense?"

Yes, that was true. It was all true. Yet this question was not new to him. He had known it all along, even at the moment he had decided in the dead of night, without hesitation or thought, that it must be done. He had known it when he bent over the box and pulled the jewel cases out of it. It wasn't a revelation, but now the question loomed larger, its simplicity cutting deeper.

"It's because I'm ill," he concluded grimly. "I've been tormenting myself, exhausting myself, not even aware of what I've been doing. I've been sick for days—for weeks. Once I'm better, I'll stop worrying like this. I'll stop..." He hesitated, a chilling thought creeping into his mind. "But what if I don't get better? God, I'm so tired of all this. So tired."

He kept walking, unable to rest. A terrible, gnawing desire for distraction clawed at him, but he couldn't figure out what to do or where to go. Each passing moment, a new, overwhelming sensation took hold of him—a visceral, almost physical hatred for everything around him. The faces of the people he passed on the street disgusted him; their movements, their expressions, their very existence seemed intolerable. If anyone had dared to speak to him, he felt certain he would have spat at them or lashed out.

He stopped abruptly when he reached the bank of the Little Neva near the bridge to Vassilyevsky Ostrov. "He lives here," Raskolnikov thought suddenly. "In that house." He realized, with a mix of surprise and irritation, that he had unconsciously walked to Razumihin's building. "Why did I come here? Did I mean to? Or did I just end up here by accident?" He shook his head and sighed. "Never mind. I told myself two days ago that I'd visit him today, so I might as well. Besides, I can't go any further. I have no strength left."

He climbed the stairs to Razumihin's garret on the fifth floor. Razumihin was home, hunched over a desk, busy writing. He opened the door himself, clearly surprised by the unexpected visit. It had been four months since they had last seen each other.

"Is it really you?" Razumihin exclaimed, taking in Raskolnikov's disheveled appearance. He whistled after a moment's pause. "Down on your luck, huh? Looks like you've outdone even me!" He gestured at Raskolnikov's tattered clothes. "Come in, sit down. You look like you're about to collapse."

Raskolnikov sat down heavily on the worn-out leather sofa, which was in even worse condition than Razumihin's own shabby dressing gown and slippers. Razumihin immediately noticed how ill he looked.

"You're seriously sick. Do you realize that?" Razumihin said, leaning closer to feel Raskolnikov's pulse. Raskolnikov pulled his hand away abruptly.

"Never mind that," he muttered. "I only came because... I don't have any lessons. I thought I might..." He trailed off. "But no, I don't really want lessons."

"You're delirious," Razumihin said, watching him carefully.

"No, I'm not," Raskolnikov replied sharply. He stood up from the sofa. As he had climbed the stairs, he hadn't fully realized what it would mean to face Razumihin. Now, it hit him like a blow. The last thing he wanted was to sit across from anyone—friend or stranger—and talk. His frustration boiled over.

"Goodbye," he said abruptly, turning toward the door.

"Wait! Hold on! What's wrong with you?" Razumihin exclaimed, grabbing his arm.

"I don't want to stay," Raskolnikov said, jerking his hand free.

"Then why the hell did you come? Are you insane or what? This is... insulting! You can't just leave like this."

"Fine," Raskolnikov snapped. "I came because I don't know anyone else who could help me. You're the only one I thought of, because you're kinder and smarter than most. But now I see I don't want anything from anyone. Do you hear me? Nothing. No help. No sympathy. I'm alone. Leave me alone."

"Wait a moment, you madman! What's the matter with you? As you like, go if you want to—I don't care!" Razumihin exclaimed, throwing up his hands in exasperation. "Look here, I have no lessons right now, not a single one, but there's this bookseller, Heruvimov. He's worth more than five lessons! He's getting into publishing—natural science manuals, if you can believe it—and they're selling like crazy. Just the titles alone are enough to pull in buyers! You always said I was a fool, but let me tell you, there are bigger fools than me out there!

"Take Heruvimov, for example. He's trying to pass himself off as an intellectual progressive, though he doesn't have the faintest idea what he's talking about. Naturally, I encourage him—it's good business! He's having me translate this German text, crude nonsense if you ask me. It's called, 'Is Woman a Human Being?' Can you imagine? And of course, it triumphantly concludes that she is. Heruvimov plans to market it as some great contribution to the 'woman question.' I've already started translating; it's just two and a half signatures long, but he's going to stretch it into six by adding fluff. We'll slap a flashy title on it, make it half a rouble a copy, and it'll sell like hotcakes! He's paying me six roubles a signature—fifteen roubles in total—and I've already received six in advance.

"When we finish this, we're moving on to a translation about whales—can you believe it?—and then we'll tackle the juiciest scandals from the second part of Les Confessions. Apparently, someone told Heruvimov that Rousseau is like our Radishchev, and the fool believes it! You can bet I won't correct him, though. Why should I? Anyway, here's the deal: if you want, you can take the second signature of 'Is Woman a Human Being?' I'll give you the German text, pens, paper—everything you need—and three roubles as your share since I've already received an advance. Finish it, and there'll be another three roubles waiting for you. Don't think I'm doing you a favor, either. I've been struggling with this—my spelling is awful, and my German? Half the time, I make it up as I go. At least with you, there's a chance it might turn out better. Or worse—who knows? So, will you take it?"

Raskolnikov silently took the German manuscript, the pens, and the three roubles without a word. He turned and left the room as Razumihin watched him, astonished. But before Razumihin could even process what had happened, Raskolnikov returned, climbed the stairs again, and wordlessly placed the manuscript and the money back on the table. Then, without so much as a glance at Razumihin, he walked out again.

"Are you out of your mind?" Razumihin shouted, his voice rising in fury as Raskolnikov descended the stairs. "What kind of nonsense is this? You're going to drive me insane! What did you even come here for, you lunatic?"

"I don't want... the translation," Raskolnikov muttered, barely audible as he continued down the stairs.

"Then what the hell do you want?" Razumihin shouted after him, leaning over the banister. Raskolnikov didn't answer and disappeared onto the street.

"Well, to hell with you then!" Razumihin muttered, slamming the door.

Out on the Nikolaevsky Bridge, Raskolnikov was jolted back to full awareness by an unpleasant incident. A coachman, frustrated by Raskolnikov wandering into traffic, shouted at him several times before finally lashing him across the back with his whip. The blow sent him stumbling toward the railing, his teeth clenched in fury. He could hear laughter and jeering from the people around him.

"Serves him right!" someone sneered.

"Probably a pickpocket," another voice chimed in.

"Pretending to be drunk to get under the wheels—these types are always looking to make trouble."

Raskolnikov leaned against the railing, still fuming, and rubbed his back where the whip had struck him. As he stood there, glaring at the retreating carriage, he suddenly felt someone press something into his hand. He looked down and saw a twenty-copeck piece. Turning, he saw an elderly woman in a kerchief, accompanied by a young girl with a green parasol.

"Take it, my good man, in Christ's name," the woman said kindly before walking away.

He stared at the coin, his face blank. They had mistaken him for a beggar, moved to pity by his shabby appearance and the blow from the whip. He clenched the coin tightly in his fist, walked a few paces, and turned to face the Neva. The sky was clear, and the river's surface gleamed with a rare blue hue. The golden dome of the cathedral glittered in the sunlight, every detail sharp and vivid in the pure air.

The pain in his back faded as he stood there, but another sensation crept in, filling his mind. He gazed at the scene, one he had admired countless times during his university days, always stopping on this very bridge to marvel at its beauty. Yet, back then, it had always left him cold. The grandeur stirred no warmth in him, only a strange, somber detachment. And now, standing there again, he felt it all over again—perhaps even more acutely. The familiar sights and memories seemed alien, as though they belonged to a different person, a different life.

He opened his hand, stared at the coin once more, and then, with a sudden flick of his wrist, flung it into the water. The coin disappeared into the blue depths, and he turned away, walking home. As he did, he felt a deep, cutting sense of finality. It was as if, in that single moment, he had severed himself from everyone and everything.

By the time he reached his apartment, evening was falling. He realized he must have been wandering the city for hours but couldn't remember how or where. Exhausted, he collapsed onto the sofa, pulled his coat over himself, and sank into a deep, dreamless oblivion.

He woke to a piercing scream, so raw and unnatural that it jolted him upright. The sound was like nothing he had ever heard before—howls, sobs, curses, and a frantic clamor of blows. He sat frozen, his heart pounding, as the chaos grew louder and more violent. And then, to his horror, he recognized one of the voices. It was his landlady. She was screaming, begging for mercy as someone beat her mercilessly on the stairs.

The other voice, hoarse with rage and spite, made his blood run cold. It was Ilya Petrovitch. He was bellowing threats, his words garbled and furious, as he slammed her against the steps. Raskolnikov's mind reeled. Was the world falling apart? He could hear the thudding blows, the cries, and the sound of neighbors rushing to their doors, shouting and knocking. Doors slammed, feet pounded on the stairs, voices rose and fell in alarm.

He couldn't move. His terror was paralyzing, and his thoughts spiraled into panic. Surely, this was all connected to him, to what he had done. Surely, they would come for him next. His hands trembled as he tried to reach for the latch on his door but couldn't summon the strength to move it.

The chaos continued for what felt like an eternity, though it was likely no more than ten minutes. Finally, the noise began to subside. He could still hear his landlady sobbing and moaning, and Ilya Petrovitch's voice trailing off as he muttered curses. Then, silence. The landlady's door slammed shut, and the neighbors returned to their rooms, their muffled voices fading into the distance.

Raskolnikov sat motionless, his mind racing. What had just happened? Why had Ilya Petrovitch come here? What did it mean? The questions swirled, but no answers came. All he felt was a gnawing dread, like a cold hand gripping his heart.

Raskolnikov collapsed onto the sofa, utterly drained, but no matter how hard he tried, he couldn't shut his eyes. He lay there for half an hour, overcome by a torment so unbearable, a terror so vast, that it felt unlike anything he had ever experienced before. Suddenly, a bright light pierced the room. Nastasya walked in, carrying a candle and a plate of soup. She paused to study him closely, making sure he wasn't asleep, then placed the candle on the table and began setting out what she had brought—bread, salt, a plate, and a spoon.

"You haven't eaten a thing since yesterday, have you? You've been out and about all day, and now you're shaking with fever," she said.

"Nastasya..." Raskolnikov began weakly, "why were they beating the landlady?"

She froze and turned her full attention to him, her gaze sharp and searching.

"Who was beating the landlady?" she asked.

"Just now... about half an hour ago. Ilya Petrovitch, the assistant superintendent. He was on the stairs, attacking her. Why was he doing that? Why was he even here?"

Nastasya stared at him, her expression unreadable. She didn't answer immediately, but her silence only made her scrutiny more unsettling. Her frown deepened as she studied him, her eyes locked onto his face for what felt like an eternity. The intensity of her stare filled him with unease, and he felt a flicker of fear rise in his chest.

"Nastasya, why don't you say something?" he asked, his voice weak and uncertain.

At last, she spoke, but it was softly, almost as though she were speaking to herself. "It's the blood," she said.

"Blood? What blood?" he asked, his face going pale as he instinctively turned toward the wall.

She didn't answer right away, her gaze still fixed on him with a strange, quiet intensity. Finally, she shook her head and spoke in a firm, decisive tone.

"No one's been beating the landlady," she said.

He looked at her, his breath catching in his throat. He could hardly believe what he was hearing.

"But I heard it... I wasn't dreaming. I wasn't asleep. I was sitting up," he insisted, his voice barely above a whisper. "I listened for a long time. The assistant superintendent came... and everyone ran out onto the stairs from their flats."

"No one's been here," she repeated firmly. "That's just the blood crying in your ears. When it doesn't have anywhere to go, when it clots, you start imagining things.... Will you eat something?"

Raskolnikov didn't respond. He lay still, staring at nothing, as Nastasya continued to stand over him, watching him carefully.

"Bring me something to drink... Nastasya," he said at last, his voice hoarse and barely audible.

Without a word, she left the room. A short while later, she returned carrying a white earthenware jug filled with water. He barely remembered taking it from her. He managed one sip, the cold water spilling from his trembling hands onto his neck. After that, everything faded into darkness, and he sank into complete oblivion.

Chapter 3

Raskolnikov wasn't completely unconscious during the time he was ill; he drifted in and out of a feverish haze. Sometimes he was delirious, and other times he was half-conscious, aware of his surroundings but unable to make sense of them. Later, he would recall certain moments clearly. At times, it felt like there were many people around him. They argued, discussed him as though he weren't there, and seemed to be planning to take him somewhere. Then, just as suddenly, he would find himself alone in the room. It was as if they had all left in fear, occasionally peeking through the door to check on him. He imagined they were threatening him, conspiring together, laughing, and mocking him.

He remembered seeing Nastasya by his bedside often, her presence a strange mix of comforting and unsettling. He also remembered another figure—a person he felt he knew well, though he couldn't recall who it was. This uncertainty gnawed at him, making him so agitated at times that he even wept. Hours and days blurred together. Sometimes it seemed he had been lying there for a month; other times, it all felt like one endless day. But there was a strange gap in his memory, something he felt he should remember but couldn't. The constant struggle to grasp this missing piece tormented him, driving him into fits of frustration, anger, or moments of sheer terror. He tried to get out of bed, to run away, but each time someone held him down, forcing him back into his feverish stupor.

Finally, the haze lifted, and he regained full consciousness.

It happened at ten in the morning. The sunlight was streaming through the window, casting a bright streak of light on the right-hand wall and the corner near the door. Nastasya stood beside him, and with her was a stranger—a young man with a short beard, wearing a fitted, short-waisted coat. He looked inquisitively at Raskolnikov, his expression a mix of curiosity and intent. Behind them, the landlady was peeking nervously through the half-open door.

Raskolnikov sat up. "Who is this, Nastasya?" he asked, pointing to the young man.

"Ah, so you're yourself again!" Nastasya exclaimed, relief evident in her voice.

"He's himself," echoed the young man, a faint smile on his face.

Satisfied that Raskolnikov was alert and coherent, the landlady quickly shut the door and disappeared. She was always shy and seemed to avoid conversations, especially in tense situations. She was a plump woman of about forty, with striking black eyes and eyebrows. Though her round figure and lazy nature made her appear good-natured, she was absurdly bashful.

"And who are you?" Raskolnikov asked the young man. But before he could answer, the door flew open, and Razumihin stepped inside, stooping slightly to avoid hitting his head on the low frame.

"What a hole this place is!" Razumihin exclaimed. "I'm always bumping my head in here. You call this a lodging? So, you're conscious again, brother? I just heard from Pashenka that you'd come to."

"He just regained consciousness," Nastasya added.

"Just now," the young man echoed, still smiling.

Razumihin turned to the stranger. "And who are you?" he asked bluntly. "The name's Vrazumihin, by the way—not Razumihin, as people always say, but Vrazumihin. I'm a student and a gentleman. He's my friend. Now, who are you?"

"I'm a messenger from the merchant Shelopaev's office," the man replied. "I've come on business."

"Please, take a seat," Razumihin said, gesturing to the table before sitting down himself. Turning to Raskolnikov, he continued, "It's good to see you awake, brother. You've barely eaten or drunk anything these past four days. We had to spoon-feed you tea to keep you going. I brought Zossimov here to check on you twice. Do you remember Zossimov? He examined you thoroughly and said it wasn't anything serious. Just something affecting your nerves—a result of poor nutrition, he said. According to him, you need more beer and radishes! He says you'll recover soon. Zossimov's a brilliant guy, by the way. He's making quite a name for himself."

Then Razumihin turned back to the messenger. "Now, let's get down to business. What do you need? By the way, Rodya, this is the second time they've sent someone from the office. The last guy came two days ago. I spoke with him myself. Who was it last time?"

"That was Alexey Semyonovitch, sir," the messenger replied. "He's also from our office."

Razumihin nodded thoughtfully, then grinned. "He was smarter than you, wasn't he?"

"Yes, indeed, sir," the messenger admitted with a slight bow. "He's much more capable than I am."

"Exactly, go on."

"At your mother's request, through Afanasy Ivanovitch Vahrushin—you've probably heard of him before—a remittance has been sent to you from our office," the man said, addressing Raskolnikov. "If you're in a fit state to understand, I have thirty-five roubles to deliver to you. Semyon Semyonovitch received instructions from Afanasy Ivanovitch, as per your mother's request, just like before. Do you know him, sir?"

"Yes, I remember... Vahrushin," Raskolnikov answered dreamily.

"You see? He knows Vahrushin!" Razumihin exclaimed. "He's in his right mind, and you're a sharp fellow for noticing it. It's always nice to hear something sensible."

"That's the man, Vahrushin, Afanasy Ivanovitch," the messenger continued. "At your mother's request, he's sent remittances before, and he hasn't refused this time either. A few days ago, he instructed Semyon Semyonovitch to hand you thirty-five roubles, hoping for better things ahead."

"That 'hoping for better things ahead' is the best part of your speech, though 'your mother' wasn't bad either. So, what do you think? Is he fully aware of what's happening?" Razumihin asked.

"He seems fine. He just needs to sign this little paper," the man replied.

"He can scribble his name. Do you have the ledger?"

"Yes, here it is."

"Give it here. Now, Rodya, sit up. I'll hold you. Take the pen and write 'Raskolnikov.' Money is sweeter than honey to us right now, brother."

"I don't want it," Raskolnikov said, pushing the pen away.

"What do you mean, you don't want it?"

"I won't sign it."

"Why not? How can you refuse to sign?"

"I don't want... the money."

"Don't want the money? Come on, brother, that's ridiculous. Don't worry, he's just wandering in his thoughts again—it's pretty common for him. Don't mind him; I'll help him sign. We'll take his hand and make him write it. Here."

"But I can come back later," the messenger suggested.

"No need for that! You're a sensible man, and we won't trouble you more than necessary. Now, Rodya, stop delaying. The man's waiting." Razumihin got ready to guide Raskolnikov's hand.

"Stop, I'll do it myself," Raskolnikov said suddenly. He took the pen and signed his name.

The messenger handed over the money and left.

"Well done! Now, brother, are you hungry?" Razumihin asked.

"Yes," Raskolnikov answered quietly.

"Is there any soup?" Razumihin asked, turning to Nastasya.

"Some leftover from yesterday," she replied.

"Does it have potatoes and rice in it?"

"Yes."

"I know that soup well. Bring it here and make us some tea."

"All right," Nastasya said and left the room.

Raskolnikov watched everything with a mixture of astonishment and unease. He didn't understand what was happening but decided to stay quiet and see where it led. "This is real, isn't it? I'm not imagining it," he thought.

A couple of minutes later, Nastasya returned with the soup and announced the tea would be ready soon. She brought two plates, two spoons, salt, pepper, mustard, and everything else needed for the meal. The table looked cleaner and more neatly set than it had in a long time.

"Nastasya, tell Praskovya Pavlovna to send up two bottles of beer. We'll finish them off," Razumihin said.

"You're shameless," muttered Nastasya as she left to carry out his request.

Raskolnikov sat in silence, watching everything unfold with strained attention. Razumihin clumsily sat beside him on the sofa, putting his left arm around Raskolnikov's shoulders to support him. With his right hand, Razumihin scooped up a spoonful of soup, blowing on it to cool it before offering it to Raskolnikov. The soup was warm but not hot. Raskolnikov greedily swallowed the first spoonful, then the second and third. After a few more bites, Razumihin paused.

"I should ask Zossimov if you can eat more," he said.

Nastasya returned with two bottles of beer. "What about tea?" she asked.

"Yes, bring it. Tea's safe enough without needing Zossimov's approval. But here's the beer!" Razumihin moved back to his chair, pulled the soup and meat toward him, and began eating like a starving man.

"I have to tell you, Rodya, I eat like this every day now," Razumihin said between bites of beef. "And it's all thanks to Pashenka, your dear landlady. She loves doing things for me. I never ask, but I certainly don't object."

Nastasya entered with the tea. "She's quick, this one. Nastasya, would you like some beer?" Razumihin asked.

"Stop talking nonsense."

"How about a cup of tea, then?"

"Maybe I'll have tea."

"Let me pour it. Sit down." Razumihin poured two cups of tea, left his food, and sat back on the sofa. Once again, he put his arm around Raskolnikov to support him and fed him the tea in small spoonfuls, carefully blowing on each spoonful before giving it to him, as if this act were vital to his recovery.

Raskolnikov made no effort to resist. Although he felt strong enough to sit upright, hold a cup, and even walk around if necessary, he chose to hide his strength. Some instinct, almost animal-like, made him feign weakness. He wanted to observe silently and figure out what was happening around him. Still, the situation filled him with an overwhelming sense of discomfort.

After sipping several spoonfuls of tea, he abruptly pulled his head away, pushed the spoon aside, and sank back onto the pillows. He noticed for the first time that they were real pillows—clean, down-filled, and neatly covered. He made a mental note of it.

"Pashenka should get us some raspberry jam today so we can make raspberry tea," Razumihin said as he returned to his chair and resumed eating his soup and drinking his beer.

"And where is she supposed to find raspberries for you?" Nastasya retorted, balancing a saucer on her fingers and sipping tea through a lump of sugar.

"She'll buy it from the shop, my dear. You see, Rodya, a lot has been happening while you've been stuck here sick. When you ran off without leaving your address, I got so angry that I decided I'd track you down and give you a piece of my mind. I started looking for you the very same day. I ran all over, asking questions, trying to find you. I couldn't remember this lodging of yours at all—I mean, I never really knew it to begin with. I could only remember your old place at the Five Corners, Harlamov's house. I searched for that house, but guess what? It wasn't Harlamov's house at all—it was Buch's. How easy it is to mix up names sometimes! That got me frustrated, so the next day, on a whim, I went to the address bureau. Can you believe it? In just two minutes, they found you! Your name is written down there."

"My name?" Raskolnikov asked.

"Of course! Meanwhile, they couldn't even find a General Kobelev while I was there. That's a whole story in itself. Anyway, once I found this place, it didn't take me long to figure out everything about you. Everything, brother—I know it all now. Nastasya here can back me up. I've gotten to know Nikodim Fomitch, Ilya Petrovitch, the house porter, Mr. Zametov, Alexandr Grigorievitch, who's the head clerk at the police station, and even Pashenka! Nastasya knows."

"He's won her over," Nastasya muttered, smiling slyly.

"Why don't you put some sugar in your tea, Nastasya Nikiforovna?" Razumihin teased.

"You're impossible!" Nastasya burst out laughing. "It's not Nikiforovna—it's Petrovna," she corrected, still chuckling.

"I'll make a note of it. Anyway, brother, to sum it up, I was ready to cause a big scene here, to root out all the troublemakers in the area. But guess what? Pashenka got the better of me. Honestly, I didn't expect her to be so... charming. What do you think?"

Raskolnikov said nothing, but his eyes, filled with worry, remained fixed on Razumihin.

"And she's quite admirable, really, in every sense," Razumihin continued, unbothered by Raskolnikov's silence.

"Oh, you sly devil!" Nastasya shrieked with laughter again. The conversation seemed to delight her endlessly.

"Brother, it's a shame you didn't handle things properly from the start. You should have approached her differently. She's a very peculiar character, you know. But we'll talk about her personality later. How could you let things get so bad that she stopped sending you meals? And that I.O.U.? You must have lost your mind to sign it. Not to mention that promise of marriage to her daughter, Natalya Yegorovna, when she was still alive. I know all about it! But I see now that's a sensitive topic, and I'm being a fool. Forgive me. Still, I have to say, Praskovya Pavlovna isn't as foolish as she might seem at first."

"No," Raskolnikov muttered, looking away but deciding it was better to keep the conversation going.

"Exactly! She isn't, is she?" Razumihin said enthusiastically, thrilled to get a response. "But she's not exactly brilliant either, is she? She's... unpredictable. I don't know how else to describe her. Sometimes she baffles me. I swear, she's at least forty, though she claims to be thirty-six—and who's going to argue with that? But I look at her from a purely intellectual perspective, almost metaphysical. It's like there's some strange connection between us, like algebra, or something equally incomprehensible. I don't get it myself.

"But putting all that aside, since you're no longer a student and have lost your lessons and clothes, and with her daughter gone, she doesn't see any reason to treat you like family. You isolated yourself, cut ties with her, and holed up in this room. So, she decided to get rid of you altogether. She's been planning it for some time, though she hesitated because of that I.O.U. You made her believe your mother would pay it off."

"It was wrong of me to say that," Raskolnikov said loudly and clearly. "My mother's barely getting by herself. I lied to keep my room and to get fed."

"Yes, you handled it sensibly enough. But the trouble was, that's when Mr. Tchebarov stepped in—a real businessman. Pashenka would never have thought to do anything about it herself; she's far too shy. But Tchebarov? He's anything but shy. The first thing he asks is, 'Can anything be done with this I.O.U.?' The answer? Yes, there's hope—because you've got a mother who would starve herself to save you with her one-hundred-and-twenty-five-rouble pension, and a sister who would sacrifice everything for you. That's what he was counting on. Why are you reacting like that? I know all about your situation now, brother. You were very open with Pashenka when you were practically her son-in-law, and I say this as your friend. But let me tell you something—an honest man is open, but a businessman listens and takes advantage of you while you're distracted.

"So Pashenka handed over the I.O.U. to Tchebarov as payment, and he wasted no time demanding the money. When I heard about it, I wanted to give him a piece of my mind, just to clear my conscience. But by that point, Pashenka and I were on good terms, and I managed to put a stop to the whole thing. I promised her you'd pay and even vouched for you myself. Do you get it? I stood up for you. We called Tchebarov, handed him ten roubles, and got the I.O.U. back. Now she trusts your word again. Here, take it—see, I tore it up."

Razumihin placed the torn note on the table. Raskolnikov glanced at him briefly, then turned his face toward the wall, saying nothing. Even Razumihin seemed a bit uneasy.

"I see now, brother," he said after a moment, "that I've been making a fool of myself again. I thought my chatter might amuse you, but it looks like I've only annoyed you."

"Was it you I didn't recognize when I was delirious?" Raskolnikov asked after a pause, still not turning his head.

"Yes, and you got angry about it—especially when I brought Zametov over one day."

"Zametov? The head clerk? Why did you bring him here?" Raskolnikov turned quickly, fixing his eyes on Razumihin.

"What's the matter? What's upset you? He just wanted to meet you because I'd been talking about you a lot. How else do you think I learned so much about you? He's a decent guy, really—first-rate, in his way. We've become friends. I see him almost every day now. I've even moved to this part of town. I've been with him to Luise Ivanovna's place a couple of times. Do you remember Luise Ivanovna?"

"Did I say anything while I was delirious?"

"Did you ever! You were completely out of it."

"What did I say?"

"What do people usually say when they're raving? Well, brother, I don't have time to go into it now. I need to get to work." He stood up, grabbing his cap.

"What did I say?" Raskolnikov pressed.

"Oh, how persistent! Are you worried you spilled some big secret? Don't stress over it. You didn't say anything about a countess, if that's what you're worried about. But you did go on about a bulldog, some earrings and chains, Krestovsky Island, a porter, and Nikodim Fomitch and Ilya Petrovitch, the assistant superintendent. Oh, and your sock—that seemed particularly important to you. You kept whining, 'Give me my sock.' Zametov searched all over your room and finally found it. He handed it to you himself, with his fancy, ring-covered fingers. You wouldn't let go of that ragged thing for twenty-four hours. It's probably still under your quilt. And then you kept asking for fringe for your trousers. We couldn't figure out what you meant. Anyway, enough of that! Here's thirty-five roubles. I'm taking ten for now and will give you an account of it later. I'll let Zossimov know what's going on too—he should have been here by now; it's nearly noon. And Nastasya, check in on him while I'm gone. See if he needs a drink or anything else. I'll speak to Pashenka myself. Goodbye!"

As Razumihin left, Nastasya muttered, "He calls her Pashenka! What a smooth operator!" She opened the door slightly to listen but couldn't resist running downstairs after him, eager to overhear his conversation with the landlady. She seemed entirely taken with Razumihin.

The moment they were gone, Raskolnikov threw off the covers and leapt out of bed like a man possessed. His impatience, burning and uncontrollable, had been building as he waited for them to leave. But as soon as he stood there, ready to act, he froze.

"What now?" he muttered to himself, his thoughts swirling chaotically. "Do they already know everything? Are they just playing games with me, pretending they don't, only to mock me later? What if they've discovered it all and are just waiting for the right moment to confront me? And what am I supposed to do now? What was it I needed to remember? I knew it just a minute ago—how could I forget?"

He stood in the middle of the room, looking around in miserable confusion. He walked over to the door, opened it, and listened, but that didn't seem to help. Suddenly, as though remembering something, he rushed to the corner where there was a hole under the wallpaper. He crouched down and began inspecting it, reaching his hand into the hole and fumbling around—but it wasn't what he was looking for. Next, he went to the stove, opened it, and rummaged through the ashes. The frayed edges of his trousers and the scraps from his pocket were still there, exactly as he had left them. No one had checked! Then he remembered the sock Razumihin had mentioned. He turned to the sofa, pulled back the quilt, and there it was, lying underneath. It was so dirty and dusty that it was no wonder Zametov hadn't noticed anything unusual about it.

"Zametov! The police office!" he muttered. "And why was I summoned to the police office? Where is the notice? Wait—I'm confusing everything. That was before. I looked at my sock back then, but now... now I've been sick. But why did Zametov come? Why did Razumihin bring him here?" He sank helplessly onto the sofa. "What does it all mean? Am I still delirious, or is this real? No, it's real... Ah, I remember—I have to escape! Yes, I must get away immediately. But where? And where are my clothes? My boots—they've taken them! They've hidden them! I understand now! Ah, here's my coat—they let me keep that. And there's money on the table, thank God! And the I.O.U. is still here too. I'll take the money and find a new place to stay. They won't be able to track me! But wait, the address bureau—Razumihin will find me. No, I need to disappear completely... far away... maybe to America. Let them do what they want! And I'll take the I.O.U. It might be useful over there. What else do I need to bring? They think I'm too sick to move! They don't know I can walk just fine, ha-ha-ha! I could tell by their eyes—they know everything! If only I could get downstairs. But what if they've stationed policemen there to watch me? What's this? Tea? And half a bottle of beer, cold!"

He grabbed the bottle, which still had about a glass of beer in it, and drank it all in one go, as though trying to extinguish a fire inside him. For a moment, the beer seemed to calm him. A faint, pleasant shiver ran down his spine, and his head felt light. He lay back down, pulling the quilt over himself. His thoughts, already incoherent, grew even more disjointed. A soft drowsiness crept over him, and he felt a strange sense of comfort as he rested his head on the pillow. The warm quilt, so much softer than his old, ragged coat, enveloped him. With a sigh, he drifted into a deep, restful sleep.

He woke up to the sound of someone entering the room. Opening his eyes, he saw Razumihin standing hesitantly in the doorway, as though unsure whether to come in.

"Ah, you're awake! Good!" Razumihin exclaimed. Turning toward the stairs, he shouted, "Nastasya, bring the parcel! I'll explain everything in a minute."

"What time is it?" Raskolnikov asked, glancing around uneasily.

"You had quite the nap, brother. It's nearly six in the evening. You've been asleep for more than six hours."

"Six hours? Really?"

"Why not? You needed it. What's the rush? Got an appointment? Don't worry, we have plenty of time. I've been waiting for hours for you to wake up. I came by twice and found you fast asleep. I even went to see Zossimov twice, but he wasn't home. Can you imagine? Anyway, he'll turn up eventually. I also ran some errands. You know I've been moving today, right? My uncle is moving in with me. But never mind that—let's get to business. Bring the parcel, Nastasya. Let's open it up. How are you feeling now, brother?"

"I'm fine. I'm not sick. Razumihin, have you been here long?"

"I told you, I've been waiting three hours."

"No, I mean before today."

"What are you talking about?"

"How long have you been visiting me?"

"I explained it all this morning. Don't you remember?"

Raskolnikov frowned. The events of the morning felt like a blurry dream. He couldn't piece it together and looked questioningly at Razumihin.

"Hm," Razumihin said, watching him closely. "I thought you weren't quite yourself earlier. That sleep seems to have helped, though. You really do look better now. Much better! Alright, let's get started. Look at this, my dear boy."

He began untying the bundle he had brought, clearly excited about its contents.

"Believe me, this is something I really care about. We need to make a proper man out of you. Let's start from the top. Look at this cap!" He pulled out a simple but decent-looking cap from the bundle. "Try it on!"

"Not now. Later," Raskolnikov said, waving him off impatiently.

"Come on, Rodya, don't fight it. Later will be too late, and I won't sleep a wink tonight because I bought it all by guesswork without measurements. Perfect fit!" Razumihin exclaimed triumphantly, placing the cap on Raskolnikov's head. "A proper hat is the first step to dressing well, and it makes a good impression on its own. Take my friend Tolstyakov—he always has to take off his ridiculous pudding-shaped hat when he goes somewhere public. People think it's out of politeness, but really, he's just embarrassed by how shabby it looks. Look, Nastasya, two fine examples of headwear: this masterpiece," he said, picking up Raskolnikov's battered old hat, which he oddly referred to as a 'Palmerston,' "and this beauty! Guess how much I paid for it, Rodya? Or what do you think, Nastasya?"

"Twenty copecks at most," Nastasya replied.

"Twenty copecks! Nonsense!" Razumihin shouted, clearly offended. "Nowadays, even you would cost more than that—eighty copecks! And that's only because it's second-hand. Plus, I bought it with the condition that if it wears out, they'll replace it next year. Yes, that's the deal! Now let's move on to the United States of America— what they used to call trousers back at school. Look at these!" He proudly displayed a pair of lightweight, gray woolen pants. "No holes, no stains, and still respectable, though a bit worn. And here's a matching waistcoat, quite fashionable. Actually, being pre-worn makes them softer and more comfortable.

"You see, Rodya, in my opinion, the secret to success is living within the seasons. If you don't demand asparagus in January, you save your money. It's the same with clothes. It's summer now, so I bought summer clothes. You'll need warmer ones for autumn anyway, so you'll probably toss these by then. They'll likely fall apart by then, even if your fashion standards don't ruin them first. Guess the price—two roubles and twenty-five copecks! And remember, the deal includes a free replacement if they wear out. Only Fedyaev's offers deals like that. If you buy from them once, you're set for life—mainly because you'd never willingly go back! Now, for the boots—take a look. Yes, they're a little worn, but they'll last a couple of months at least. They're made of foreign leather, proper quality! I got them from the secretary of the English Embassy. He sold them after wearing them just six days because he needed cash. Price? One rouble and fifty copecks. A bargain, right?"

"But what if they don't fit?" Nastasya pointed out.

"Not fit? Just watch!" Razumihin pulled Raskolnikov's old, broken boot from his pocket, caked in dried mud. "I didn't go unprepared— I had them take the size from this monstrosity. We thought of everything. And as for your shirts, your landlady took care of that. Here, three of them to start with—plain, but with stylish fronts.

"Alright, let's add it up: eighty copecks for the cap, two roubles twenty-five copecks for the suit, one rouble fifty copecks for the boots—that's four roubles and fifty-five copecks. Five roubles for the shirts, bought as a bundle, makes it nine roubles and fifty-five copecks. Forty-five copecks left over in small change. So, Rodya, you've got a complete outfit. Your overcoat will do just fine; it even has a bit of flair to it. That's Sharmer's work! As for socks and other things, you can take care of those. We've still got twenty-five roubles left. Don't worry about paying Pashenka for your room. Trust me—she'll let you owe her. Now, let's change your shirt. A fresh shirt will help you shake off this illness."

"Leave me alone! I don't want to!" Raskolnikov said, waving him off. He listened with irritation as Razumihin enthusiastically detailed his purchases.

"Come on, brother. Don't tell me all my running around was for nothing," Razumihin insisted. "Nastasya, don't just stand there—help me. That's it." Despite Raskolnikov's protests, Razumihin managed to change his shirt. Raskolnikov sank back onto the pillows, silent for a moment.

"I'll never get rid of them," he thought to himself. Then, after a pause, he asked aloud, "What money paid for all this?"

"Money? Your own, of course—the remittance from Vahrushin that your mother sent. Did you forget that, too?"

"I remember now," Raskolnikov said quietly after a long pause. Razumihin looked at him, frowning, concern written on his face.

The door opened, and a tall, stout man stepped inside. Something about him seemed familiar to Raskolnikov.

Chapter 4

Zossimov was a tall, hefty man with a pale, puffed-up face, clean-shaven and framed by straight, light-colored hair. He wore glasses and had a thick gold ring on one of his plump fingers. He was twenty-seven years old, dressed in a fashionable loose grey coat and light summer trousers. Everything about him—from his clothes to his demeanor—was stylish, neat, and deliberately casual. His linen was spotless, and his heavy watch-chain gleamed impressively. Though he carried himself in an easygoing manner, there was an air of self-importance he couldn't fully hide, no matter how hard he tried. People often found him dull company, but they admitted he was good at his profession.

"I've been here twice today, brother. Look, he's awake!" Razumihin exclaimed excitedly.

"I see, I see. How are you feeling now?" Zossimov asked Raskolnikov, watching him closely. Sitting at the foot of the sofa, he adjusted himself to sit as comfortably as possible.

"He's still down," Razumihin answered. "We just changed his shirt, and it nearly made him cry."

"That's perfectly normal. You could've waited if he didn't want it." Zossimov checked Raskolnikov's pulse. "His pulse is fine. Does your head still hurt?"

"I'm fine! I'm perfectly fine!" Raskolnikov declared irritably. He pushed himself upright on the sofa, his eyes glinting feverishly, but immediately collapsed back onto the pillow and turned his face to the wall. Zossimov observed him intently.

"All right... seems like he's doing okay," Zossimov said lazily. "Has he eaten anything?"

Razumihin and Nastasya filled him in and asked what Raskolnikov could eat.

"He can have soup, tea... but no mushrooms or cucumbers. Probably best to skip meat, too. You don't need me to tell you the rest," he said with a knowing glance at Razumihin. "No need for any more medicine either. I'll check on him again tomorrow—or maybe even later today. We'll see."

"I'll take him for a walk tomorrow evening," Razumihin chimed in. "We'll go to the Yusupov Garden and then to the Palais de Cristal."

"I wouldn't take him out tomorrow, but maybe just a short one... we'll see."

"Ah, what a nuisance! I've got a housewarming party tonight, just around the corner. Couldn't he come along? He could rest on the sofa there. You're coming, right?" Razumihin turned to Zossimov. "You promised."

"All right, but I'll come later. What's on the menu?"

"Oh, nothing fancy—tea, vodka, herrings. There'll be a pie... just a gathering of friends."

"And who's coming?"

"All local folks, mostly new friends, except for my uncle—though he's new, too. He just got to Petersburg yesterday for some business. We only see each other once every five years."

"What does he do?"

"He's been a district postmaster all his life. Lives on a small pension. He's sixty-five now—nothing remarkable—but I like him. Then there's Porfiry Petrovitch, head of the Investigation Department. You know him."

"Is he related to you?"

"Very distantly. But why the scowl? Because you've quarreled with him before? Is that why you won't come?"

"I don't care about him."

"All the better. There'll be some students, a teacher, a government clerk, a musician, an officer, and Zametov."

"Zametov? What on earth could you or he"—Zossimov nodded at Raskolnikov—"have in common with someone like Zametov?"

"Oh, don't be so particular! Always clinging to your principles like a clockwork toy. If someone's a decent fellow, that's all that matters to me. And Zametov is all right."

"Even though he takes bribes?"

"Well, he does—so what? I'm not saying I admire him for it, but he's a good guy in his own way. If you judged everyone on their flaws, there wouldn't be many good people left, would there? I'd probably barely be worth a baked onion myself."

"And you'd throw me in with the onion, I suppose?"

"Maybe, but not more than that. Enough joking! You don't change people by pushing them away, especially someone young like Zametov. You need to be careful with him. You 'progressive thinkers' don't get it. You harm yourselves by tearing others down. Besides, we do have something in common."

"Oh? What's that?"

"It's about a house-painter. We're helping him out of a tight spot. Not that there's much to worry about anymore—it's all pretty clear. We just need to push a little to get it resolved."

"A painter?"

"Haven't I told you? It's about that old pawnbroker who was murdered. The painter got tangled up in it."

"Oh, yes, I heard about that murder. I was interested in it... for a reason. I read about it in the papers, too."

Lizaveta was killed too," Nastasya suddenly exclaimed, addressing Raskolnikov. She had been standing by the door the entire time, listening closely.

"Lizaveta," Raskolnikov muttered, his voice barely audible.

"Yes, Lizaveta, the one who sold old clothes. Don't you remember her? She used to come here sometimes. She even mended a shirt for you once."

Raskolnikov turned his face to the wall. He focused intently on a single clumsy white flower with brown lines printed on the dirty yellow wallpaper. He began counting the petals, tracing the scalloped edges, and noting the number of lines on each petal. His arms and legs felt as though they had been drained of all life, like useless weights hanging from his body. He didn't even attempt to move. Instead, he kept staring at the flower with a grim fixation.

"But what about the painter?" Zossimov interrupted sharply, clearly displeased with Nastasya's chatter. She sighed and fell silent.

"Oh, he was accused of the murder," Razumihin said heatedly.

"Was there actual evidence against him?" Zossimov asked skeptically.

"Evidence? Hardly! It was the flimsiest nonsense imaginable. That's exactly what we're trying to clear up," Razumihin replied, his voice rising with frustration. "It's just like when they initially went after those other two—Koch and Pestryakov. The whole investigation is a joke! It's enough to make you sick, even though it's not our problem. By the way, Pestryakov might stop by tonight. Rodya, you've already heard about this case, haven't you? It happened right before you fainted at the police station. They were discussing it then."

Zossimov glanced curiously at Raskolnikov, who remained perfectly still and silent.

"Razumihin, I'm amazed at you," Zossimov remarked with a trace of irritation. "You've got your nose in everything, don't you?"

"Maybe I do, but we're going to clear his name regardless," Razumihin declared, slamming his fist on the table for emphasis. "What really gets under my skin isn't just their lying—though that's bad enough. I can forgive lies because, at least, lies can sometimes lead to the truth. But what's infuriating is when people lie and then worship their own lies as though they were sacred. That's what I can't stand. Take Porfiry, for example—I respect the man, but even he…"

"What exactly tripped them up in the first place?" Zossimov interjected.

"The door," Razumihin said with a wave of his hand. "It was locked when they first checked it, and then, when they came back with the porter, it was open. So naturally, the bright minds at the station concluded that Koch and Pestryakov must be the murderers. That's the kind of brilliant logic they're working with!"

"Calm down, Razumihin. They only detained them because they had to," Zossimov said, attempting to soothe him. "By the way, I've met this Koch before. He used to buy unredeemed pledges from the old woman, didn't he?"

"Yes, he's a crook. Buys up bad debts too—it's practically his profession. But let's not waste time on him. What really enrages me is the system itself—their outdated, bureaucratic nonsense. This case could be an opportunity to bring in fresh methods. It's all about interpretation. Facts aren't everything; half the work lies in how you interpret those facts!"

"And can you interpret them any better?" Zossimov asked skeptically.

"Maybe I can, or maybe I can't. But it's impossible to stay silent when you have a gut feeling—when you sense you might actually be able to help if only you had the chance. Anyway, do you know the details of the case?"

"I'm waiting to hear about the painter," Zossimov replied.

"Oh, right. Here's the story," Razumihin began, leaning forward. "Three days after the murder, when they were still wasting time questioning Koch and Pestryakov—despite their airtight alibis—something unexpected surfaced. A peasant named Dushkin, who owns a bar across from the building, walked into the police station with a jeweler's box containing gold earrings. He gave this long-winded account about how he'd come across them.

"Dushkin said that the day after the murder, just after eight in the morning, a journeyman painter named Nikolay came into his bar. Nikolay, who'd already stopped by earlier that day, had the box with him and asked Dushkin for two roubles in exchange. When Dushkin asked where he got the box, Nikolay claimed he'd found it in the street. Dushkin didn't press him further, but gave him a single rouble anyway, thinking, 'If I don't take it, someone else will, and he'll just spend it on booze anyway.' Supposedly, Dushkin intended to turn it over to the police if he heard anything suspicious. But that's all nonsense. Dushkin is a known pawnbroker and a receiver of stolen goods. He must've realized the trinket was worth at least thirty roubles. He only went to the police out of fear.

"Anyway, Dushkin claims he's known Nikolay since they were kids—they're from the same village in the Ryazan district. Nikolay isn't a full-blown drunk, but he does drink, and Dushkin knew he was working on a painting job in the same building where the murders happened. When Nikolay got his rouble, he had a couple of drinks, took his change, and left. The next day, Dushkin heard about the murders of Alyona Ivanovna and her sister Lizaveta. Feeling suspicious, he went to the building to ask around. He found out from Nikolay's coworker Dmitri that Nikolay had been out drinking all night, came home briefly at dawn, and then disappeared again. Dmitri was finishing the job alone, right on the same floor as the murder scene.

"That's when Dushkin got really suspicious. The next morning, he saw Nikolay again—this time in his bar, looking nervous. When Dushkin asked him about the earrings, Nikolay repeated that he'd found them in the street, but his behavior was odd—he wouldn't meet Dushkin's eyes. Then, when Dushkin told him about the murders and asked where he'd been that night, Nikolay panicked and bolted out the door. Dushkin hasn't seen him since. And that's where we are now."

"I should think so," Zossimov said calmly.

"Wait, let me finish. Naturally, they started looking for Nikolay everywhere. They detained Dushkin and searched his house, then they arrested Dmitri. They even questioned the Kolomensky men and left no stone unturned. Finally, two days ago, they caught Nikolay at a tavern on the edge of town. He had gone there, taken the silver cross from around his neck, and traded it for a drink. The tavern keeper gave it to him, but then, only a short while later, the woman who worked there went out to the cowshed. Through a crack in the wall, she saw Nikolay in the adjacent stable. He had tied his sash to a beam, stood on a block of wood, and was trying to put his neck into the noose. The woman screamed at the top of her lungs. People ran in. 'What are you up to?' they yelled. Nikolay said, 'Take me to the police officer. I'll confess everything.' So, they took him to the station here, under guard.

"They began questioning him—how old he was, 'twenty-two,' and so on. When they asked, 'When you were working with Dmitri, did you see anyone on the staircase at that time?' Nikolay answered, 'People might have gone up and down, but I didn't notice.' Then they asked, 'Did you hear anything—any noises, anything unusual?' He replied, 'Nothing special.' 'Did you hear about the murder of Widow So-and-so and her sister on the same day?' 'I didn't know anything about it until Afanasy Pavlovitch told me the day before yesterday.' Then they asked, 'Where did you find the earrings?' 'I found them on the pavement,' he said. 'Why didn't you go to work with Dmitri that day?' 'I was drinking.' 'Where were you drinking?' 'Oh, at such-and-such a place.' 'Why did you run away from Dushkin's bar?' 'I was scared.' 'What were you scared of?' 'That I'd be accused.' 'Why would you be scared if you were innocent?' Zossimov, can you believe it? They actually asked him that—word for word! I know because it was repeated to me exactly. What do you make of that?"

"Well, there's evidence, at least," Zossimov replied thoughtfully.

"I'm not talking about evidence right now," Razumihin snapped. "I'm talking about how they think. Anyway, they kept pressuring him, and eventually, Nikolay confessed: 'I didn't find the earrings on the street. I found them in the flat where Dmitri and I were painting.' 'How did that happen?' they asked. 'Well,' Nikolay explained, 'we had been painting all day and were getting ready to leave. Dmitri took a brush and smeared paint on my face. Then he ran off, and I chased after him. I was shouting and laughing as I went. At the bottom of the stairs, I bumped into the porter and some gentlemen. I can't remember how many. The porter yelled at me, then his wife came out and started yelling too. A man with a lady on his arm also started scolding us. Meanwhile, Dmitri and I had fallen to the ground, rolling around and laughing like kids. I pulled Dmitri's hair; he grabbed mine. Then Dmitri escaped into the street, and I went back upstairs to pack up our things. That's when I saw a box wrapped in paper lying in the corner near the door. I opened it and found the earrings inside.'"

"Behind the door? The box was lying behind the door?" Raskolnikov suddenly interjected, sitting up abruptly on the sofa and staring at Razumihin with wide, terrified eyes.

"Yes, behind the door. Why? What's wrong?" Razumihin asked, startled, standing up.

"Nothing," Raskolnikov replied faintly, turning his face back to the wall. The room fell silent.

"Must've been a dream," Razumihin muttered, glancing uneasily at Zossimov. The doctor gave a slight shake of his head.

"Go on," Zossimov prompted. "What happened next?"

"What happened next?" Razumihin echoed, calming down. "Well, Nikolay took the box to Dushkin and got a rouble for it. He lied, saying he'd found it in the street, then went off drinking. But he keeps insisting he knows nothing about the murders. 'I didn't hear about it until the day before yesterday,' he says. 'Why didn't you come forward sooner?' they asked him. 'I was scared,' he said. 'Why did you try to hang yourself?' 'Because of anxiety.' 'What were you anxious about?' 'That I'd be accused of the crime.' That's his story. Now, guess what conclusion they've drawn from all this?"

"They've decided he's the murderer, haven't they?" Zossimov said flatly.

"Exactly! They're completely convinced now," Razumihin replied, throwing up his hands. "It's ridiculous!"

"But what about the earrings?" Zossimov countered. "If the earrings from the murdered woman's box ended up in Nikolay's hands on the very same day, that's significant. There's no denying that."

"How did they get there? That's what I want to know," Razumihin shot back. "You're a doctor, someone who studies human behavior, someone who should be better at reading people than most. Can't you see Nikolay is telling the truth? His story about finding the box is entirely plausible."

"But didn't he admit to lying at first?"

"Sure, but listen carefully," Razumihin pressed. "The porter, Koch, Pestryakov, the other porter, his wife, the woman in the porter's lodge, and even Kryukov, who came in with a lady—at least eight witnesses—all agree that Nikolay and Dmitri were scuffling like children at the gate. They were rolling on the ground, pulling each other's hair, and laughing. Now consider this: the bodies upstairs were still warm when they were found. If Nikolay or Dmitri—or both—had killed those women, do you think they'd be rolling around, giggling and drawing attention to themselves right afterward? And they left the flat open, with the bodies inside? It doesn't add up."

"It's strange, I'll admit that. Impossible, even," Zossimov conceded, though he still seemed skeptical.

"No, my friend, no 'buts' here," Razumihin said firmly. "If finding the earrings in Nikolay's possession on the same day and hour as the murder forms a significant piece of circumstantial evidence against him, then the explanation he gave—which makes sense—cannot be ignored. It means this evidence doesn't hold the weight they claim it does. But here's what gets me worked up: the legal system won't care about the facts that prove his innocence, even though those facts are undeniable. They won't accept the psychological impossibility of his guilt as an irrefutable argument to dismantle the case against him. No, they'll cling to the circumstantial evidence—the jewel case and the fact that he tried to hang himself. To them, it's simple: 'If he wasn't guilty, why would he try to kill himself?' That's their entire argument, and it drives me crazy! Do you understand why this frustrates me?"

"Yes, I see you're worked up," Zossimov said, trying to calm him. "But let's focus for a moment. I forgot to ask—what solid proof is there that the jewel case came from the old woman?"

"That's already been proven," Razumihin admitted reluctantly, frowning. "Koch recognized the case and identified its owner. The owner confirmed it beyond doubt."

"That's a problem," Zossimov remarked thoughtfully. "Another question: was there anyone who saw Nikolay around the time Koch and Pestryakov were going upstairs? Is there any evidence to place him there?"

"No one saw him," Razumihin replied, his frustration growing. "That's the biggest issue. Even Koch and Pestryakov didn't notice them on their way up. They only said the flat was open and assumed there was work being done inside. But they didn't pay attention, so they can't confirm whether or not anyone was actually there."

"Hm... so the defense hinges entirely on the idea that Nikolay and Dmitri were seen scuffling and laughing. It's a strong argument, but not definitive. How do you interpret the situation yourself?"

"What's there to interpret? It's obvious," Razumihin said, leaning forward with intensity. "At least, it's clear where we need to look for answers. The jewel case gives us a direction. The real murderer must have dropped the earrings. Here's what I think happened: the murderer was hiding upstairs, locked inside the flat, when Koch and Pestryakov knocked on the door. Koch, being a fool, didn't wait at the door. That gave the murderer the chance to slip out and run downstairs—he had no other way to escape.

"The murderer hid in the flat Dmitri and Nikolay had just left. While the porter and others were going upstairs, he stayed hidden until the coast was clear. Then, at just the right moment, when the staircase was empty and Dmitri and Nikolay had run outside, he calmly walked down. Maybe someone saw him, but no one paid attention—there's always a crowd coming and going. While hiding behind the door, he must have dropped the earrings without realizing it because he was focused on escaping. The jewel case proves he was standing right there. That's my explanation."

"Too clever by half," Zossimov replied skeptically. "No, my friend, you're overthinking this. It's too perfect. Everything ties up too neatly—it feels like something out of a melodrama."

"Too perfect? Too perfect?" Razumihin exclaimed in frustration. But before he could say more, the door opened, and a stranger walked in, interrupting their conversation.

Chapter 5

The man who entered was middle-aged, with a stiff posture and a cautious, sour expression. He paused in the doorway, staring around the room with open astonishment, as if questioning what kind of place he had stumbled upon. His eyes swept over Raskolnikov's small, dingy quarters with a look of disdain and mistrust. His gaze settled on Raskolnikov himself, sprawled on the dirty, disordered sofa, unwashed and disheveled, staring back at him blankly. Then, with equal scrutiny, he examined Razumihin, whose scruffy, unkempt appearance was met with a bold, steady glare.

An awkward silence lingered for several moments. The visitor seemed to realize that attempting to intimidate these men in such a setting would get him nowhere. Adjusting his demeanor, he softened slightly and spoke civilly, though each word was carefully measured and enunciated.

"Rodion Romanovitch Raskolnikov, a student—or perhaps formerly a student?" he asked, directing his question toward Zossimov.

Zossimov shifted slightly, as if preparing to respond, but Razumihin interjected before he could.

"He's right here on the sofa! What do you want?" Razumihin's casual tone undercut the man's pompous air, leaving him momentarily at a loss. He turned as if to address Razumihin but quickly reconsidered and refocused on Zossimov.

"This is Raskolnikov," Zossimov confirmed with a nod toward the figure on the sofa. Then, as if bored, he let out a loud yawn, stretched, and slowly retrieved a gold pocket watch from his waistcoat, examined the time, and returned it just as lazily.

Raskolnikov, still lying flat, stared at the stranger with an unfocused gaze. His face, pale and strained, bore the look of someone who had just endured intense physical suffering. Yet, as the man's presence began to sink in, a flicker of awareness crossed his expression. He sat up suddenly, his voice weak but defiant.

"Yes, I am Raskolnikov. What do you want?"

The visitor regarded him with an air of self-importance before declaring in a deliberate tone, "Pyotr Petrovitch Luzhin. I believe my name may not be entirely unfamiliar to you?"

But Raskolnikov, caught off guard, simply stared at him as if hearing the name for the first time. His silence unsettled Luzhin, who hesitated and then asked, "Is it possible you haven't received any news?"

Instead of answering, Raskolnikov sank back against the pillows, crossed his hands behind his head, and stared blankly at the ceiling. Luzhin's confidence faltered further. Both Razumihin and Zossimov watched him with growing curiosity, and his discomfort became increasingly evident.

"I had assumed," Luzhin began hesitantly, "that a letter sent over ten days ago—perhaps even two weeks ago—would have arrived by now…"

"Why are you standing there like that?" Razumihin suddenly interrupted. "If you've got something to say, sit down. There's enough crowding with Nastasya here already. Nastasya, move aside. Here, take this chair and squeeze in!"

Razumihin shuffled back to create a narrow space between himself and the table, clearly intending to make the visitor comply. Trapped by the awkwardness of the moment, Luzhin stumbled his way to the chair, eventually sitting down with a look of unease.

"No need to be nervous," Razumihin said brusquely. "Rodya's been sick for five days, delirious for three, but he's improving now. This is his doctor," he nodded toward Zossimov, "and I'm a friend, a former student like him, helping out. Don't mind us; go ahead with your business."

"Thank you," Luzhin replied stiffly, turning to Zossimov. "But am I not disturbing the patient with my presence and conversation?"

"Not at all," Zossimov muttered, suppressing another yawn. "He might even find it entertaining."

"He's been conscious since this morning," Razumihin added cheerfully. His casual attitude began to thaw Luzhin's reserve, though he still regarded Razumihin with a mix of suspicion and curiosity.

"Your mother," Luzhin began, only to be interrupted by Razumihin's loud throat-clearing.

"Go on," Razumihin prompted. Luzhin, visibly irritated, shrugged and continued.

"Your mother started a letter to you while I was staying near her. After arriving here, I delayed visiting for a few days, thinking you would have received her news by now. But to my surprise—"

"I know, I know!" Raskolnikov snapped impatiently. "So you're the fiancé? I get it—that's enough!"

This abrupt response clearly offended Luzhin, though he struggled to conceal it. He sat stiffly, attempting to make sense of Raskolnikov's hostility. The room fell silent, thick with tension.

Raskolnikov, who had shifted slightly toward Pyotr Petrovitch during his initial response, now began to examine him with renewed interest, as though seeing him for the first time or noticing something entirely new. With purpose, he lifted himself from the pillow to get a better look, his gaze sharp and inquisitive. There was undeniably something striking about Pyotr Petrovitch's appearance that lent a certain credibility to the title of "fiancé," a label Razumihin had thrown out so casually.

Pyotr Petrovitch's attire revealed much about him. It was clear he had spent his brief time in the capital preparing meticulously for his role as an engaged man. This eagerness to impress was innocent enough, even understandable, yet it was impossible not to notice how overtly he flaunted his efforts. His freshly tailored clothes, though impeccably made, were too new, their appropriateness almost exaggerated. His stylish round hat, carried with an air of reverence, and the lavender gloves—real Louvain, no less—were not worn but held conspicuously in hand, as if for display. Light, youthful colors dominated his outfit: a charming fawn-colored summer jacket, delicate trousers, and a matching waistcoat, paired with fine new linen and a cravat of light cambric with subtle pink stripes.

Despite the ostentation, the ensemble suited him. Pyotr Petrovitch's face, fresh and well-kept, appeared younger than his forty-five years. His thick, dark mutton-chop whiskers framed his clean-shaven chin neatly, lending him an air of distinction. Even his hair, though showing hints of gray and carefully styled by a hairdresser, avoided the foolishness often associated with overly groomed appearances. There was, however, an undercurrent of something less pleasant in his otherwise handsome and commanding demeanor, a quality that hinted at deeper flaws.

After scrutinizing him thoroughly, Raskolnikov smiled—a thin, sardonic expression—and sank back onto the pillow. His eyes returned to the ceiling, as though dismissing the visitor entirely.

Pyotr Petrovitch, undeterred by this apparent indifference, composed himself and chose to ignore the peculiarities of his audience. He seemed determined to push forward with his purpose.

"I deeply regret finding you in such circumstances," he began with effort, his tone polished but strained. "Had I known of your illness sooner, I would have come earlier. However, as you are aware, business demands much of one's time. I have, in fact, been consumed with a pressing legal matter in the Senate, along with other obligations you might easily imagine. Your mother and sister should arrive at any moment now."

Raskolnikov stirred slightly at this, his face betraying a flicker of interest. It seemed he wanted to speak, but he stopped short, and Luzhin, after a brief pause, continued.

"I have arranged accommodations for them upon their arrival," he added.

"Where?" Raskolnikov asked faintly, his voice barely audible.

"In Bakaleyev's house, not far from here," Pyotr Petrovitch replied.

Razumihin perked up. "Oh, that's in Voskresensky. I know it well. Yushin, a merchant, rents out the rooms there. I've been to the place."

"Yes, rooms..." Luzhin started but was interrupted.

"Filthy hole!" Razumihin declared bluntly. "It reeks, the place is shady, and the people living there—well, let's just say they're not respectable. I only went there once to settle a nasty business. Sure, it's cheap, but—"

"As a newcomer to Petersburg," Luzhin retorted stiffly, "I could not be expected to know every detail of the local lodging houses. However, I can assure you the two rooms I secured are clean and perfectly suitable, given the short duration of their stay. Meanwhile, I have secured a more permanent residence for our future needs," he added, turning to Raskolnikov. "It's currently being prepared."

"And where are you staying now?" Razumihin asked with a raised eyebrow.

"I am temporarily sharing quarters with a friend, Andrey Semyonovitch Lebeziatnikov, in Madame Lippevechsel's flat. He was also the one who suggested Bakaleyev's house," Luzhin explained.

"Lebeziatnikov?" Raskolnikov repeated slowly, as if trying to place the name.

"Yes, Andrey Semyonovitch Lebeziatnikov, a clerk in the Ministry. Do you know him?" Luzhin asked with a hint of curiosity.

"Perhaps... no," Raskolnikov replied, uncertain.

"I thought as much," Luzhin said, appearing slightly disappointed. "I was once his guardian—a promising young man, quite advanced in his thinking. I appreciate engaging with younger minds. One can learn much from them."

"What do you mean by 'advanced'?" Razumihin interjected, his curiosity piqued.

"I mean progressive in thought and critical in perspective," Luzhin elaborated, his face lighting up with enthusiasm. "It's been a decade since I was last in Petersburg. While we hear of reforms and innovations in the provinces, seeing them firsthand in the capital is enlightening. Observing the younger generation offers a glimpse into the future, and I confess I find it invigorating."

"And what precisely do you find so invigorating?" Razumihin pressed.

"Ah, your question touches on a broad topic," Luzhin replied, visibly pleased to elaborate. "But, in short, I notice sharper insights, more critical thinking, and a focus on practicality among them."

Razumihin shot back at Zossimov with a wave of frustration, clearly unimpressed by the assertion. "Practicality? There's no practicality to be found," he declared emphatically. "Practicality isn't something that just falls into your lap; it's rare and hard-earned. For the past two hundred years, we've been severed from the realities of practical life. Sure, ideas are bubbling up," he said, now turning to Pyotr Petrovitch, "and there's a childish kind of desire for good. Honesty exists, though it's often overshadowed by the sheer number of scoundrels around. But practicality? That's a different beast entirely. Practicality always comes well-prepared, well-equipped—it doesn't stumble in bare-footed."

"I beg to differ," Pyotr Petrovitch replied with an air of patient indulgence, his words measured but his pleasure at the debate evident. "Certainly, people make mistakes, and enthusiasm sometimes leads them astray, but isn't that evidence of progress in itself? These missteps arise from a genuine passion for improvement and the unfavorable conditions in which they work. True, not much has been achieved yet, but the time has been short. And let's not ignore the means available—or rather, the lack thereof. Still, I maintain that there's been significant progress. Fresh ideas and works of substance are circulating now, replacing the old dreamy, sentimental authors of yore. Literature has matured, outdated prejudices have been challenged and mocked. In essence, we've severed ties with a past that was holding us back. And, in my view, that alone is an achievement of no small importance."

Before anyone could respond, Raskolnikov's voice cut through the conversation. Though weak, it carried a sharpness that could not be ignored. "He's memorized all that to show off," he muttered suddenly, a faint smirk playing on his lips.

"What was that?" Pyotr Petrovitch asked, slightly taken aback, though it was clear he had not fully caught the remark. Raskolnikov, however, offered no clarification, returning to his reclined position and staring at the ceiling as though bored by the discussion.

Zossimov interjected smoothly, eager to restore civility. "There's truth in what you've said."

"Precisely," Pyotr Petrovitch resumed, encouraged by Zossimov's agreement and now addressing Razumihin with a faintly superior air. "You cannot deny, sir, that we are witnessing progress—what some might even call a forward leap in the name of science and economic truth."

"That's a cliché," Razumihin shot back without hesitation.

"It's far from a cliché!" Luzhin protested, his words spilling out faster now, as though his thoughts demanded immediate expression. "Consider this: in the past, when someone said, 'Love thy neighbor,' what was the result? One might tear their own coat in half to share, leaving both parties shivering and poorly dressed. The Russian proverb sums it up: 'If you chase two hares, you'll catch neither.' Modern science, however, teaches us something far wiser—love yourself first and foremost, for the stability of society depends on self-interest. Manage your affairs well, and your coat remains intact. And as economic truth adds, the stronger private enterprise becomes, the sturdier society's foundation grows. When I acquire wealth for myself, I am, in a sense, contributing to the prosperity of all. My neighbor may then afford more than scraps, not through my charity but as a byproduct of collective progress. It's a simple concept, yet sentimentality and outdated idealism have obscured it for far too long."

Razumihin had been listening with increasing irritation, and now he cut in sharply. "Pardon me, but I have little wit to spare for such theories, so let's end this here. I started this discussion to gauge the kind of man you are, but I've grown utterly sick of these same empty arguments, repeated endlessly for amusement. It's tiresome, and frankly, embarrassing. Forgive me for saying so, but your eagerness to parade your knowledge is all too obvious, though understandable. What's less forgivable is how so many unscrupulous people have hijacked progressive ideals for their gain, dragging them through the mud in the process. That's enough from me."

Pyotr Petrovitch's expression hardened. His tone grew formal and cold. "Am I to understand that you are including me in this category of unscrupulous people?"

Razumihin gave a dismissive wave. "Come now, sir, don't take it personally. I merely spoke in general terms. Let's drop it." With that, he turned deliberately to Zossimov, signaling an end to the discussion.

Luzhin, though visibly affronted, had enough self-control to let it go. He adjusted his posture, signaling his intent to take leave. "I trust that as your health improves, Mr. Raskolnikov, we might develop a closer acquaintance, given the circumstances. Above all, I wish you a swift recovery."

Raskolnikov didn't move or acknowledge the sentiment, staring blankly upward. Luzhin began to rise from his chair.

"One of her clients must have done it," Zossimov said suddenly, breaking the awkward silence.

"No question about it," Razumihin agreed, his tone resolute. "Porfiry is investigating everyone who had dealings with her."

"He's questioning them?" Raskolnikov asked aloud, his voice sharper than before.

"Yes, why?" Razumihin replied, glancing at him curiously.

"Nothing," Raskolnikov murmured, his face unreadable as he turned away once more.

Zossimov leaned forward slightly, his expression one of genuine curiosity. "How exactly does he track them down?" he asked.

Razumihin answered without hesitation. "Koch provided the names of some. Others were identified by the labels on the pledges, and a few even came forward on their own."

"A bold and cunning criminal, to say the least!" Zossimov remarked, his voice tinged with admiration. "The audacity! The composure!"

"But that's just it—it wasn't boldness or cunning," Razumihin countered, his voice rising passionately. "That's precisely what throws everyone off. I'm convinced he wasn't cunning or experienced. In fact, this must have been his first crime. The idea that it was a carefully planned act by a seasoned criminal doesn't hold up. Look at the facts—he bungled it completely and was saved by sheer luck. He probably didn't anticipate obstacles and acted impulsively. Think about it: he snatched jewels worth only ten or twenty roubles, filled his pockets with junk, rummaged through an old woman's chest full of rags, and left behind fifteen hundred roubles in cash in the top drawer! He didn't even know how to steal—he only knew how to kill. I'm telling you, it was his first crime. He panicked, lost his head, and escaped purely by chance, not skill."

At this moment, Pyotr Petrovitch, who had been preparing to leave but couldn't resist inserting himself into the discussion, addressed Zossimov with a faintly self-satisfied air. "I take it you're speaking about the murder of the old pawnbroker?"

Zossimov nodded slightly. "Yes, of course. You've heard about it?"

"Oh, certainly," Luzhin replied, clearly eager to contribute. "Being in the vicinity, it's hard not to hear of such a shocking event."

"Do you know any of the details?" Zossimov asked.

"Not extensively," Luzhin admitted, pausing as though to choose his words carefully. "But the case intrigues me—not merely because of its specifics, but because of the broader implications. Have you noticed how crime, not just among the lower classes but even within the higher echelons of society, has been increasing dramatically over the past five years? We hear of students robbing mail coaches, respectable citizens forging banknotes, and, more recently, a historian implicated in counterfeiting lottery tickets. Even a government secretary abroad was recently murdered over financial gain. If this pawnbroker was indeed killed by someone of a higher social standing—for after all, peasants don't typically pawn gold trinkets—what does this suggest about the moral decay of our so-called 'civilized' society?"

"There are many economic factors at play," Zossimov offered, attempting to steer the conversation into less speculative territory.

"Indeed," Razumihin interjected, his tone growing sharper. "But perhaps the root cause lies in our chronic impracticality."

"In what sense?" Luzhin asked, clearly intrigued.

"Take, for example, the historian involved in that forgery ring in Moscow," Razumihin continued. "When asked why he forged notes, his response was something along the lines of, 'Everyone else is getting rich by one method or another, so why shouldn't I?' That attitude sums it up. People have grown used to shortcuts—ready-made solutions, walking on crutches, having their food pre-chewed for them. When the era of serfdom ended, and freedom was thrust upon us, everyone's true nature came to light."

"But what about morality? Principles?" Luzhin asked, raising an eyebrow.

"Why do you concern yourself with such questions?" Raskolnikov cut in suddenly, his voice low but laced with biting sarcasm. "Aren't these developments perfectly aligned with the theory you were advocating just a moment ago?"

"Aligned with my theory?" Luzhin asked, visibly startled.

"Why not?" Raskolnikov pressed, a mocking smile tugging at his lips. "If you follow your logic to its conclusion, doesn't it suggest that killing for personal gain is not only permissible but inevitable?"

"That is a gross misrepresentation!" Luzhin exclaimed, his voice rising defensively.

Zossimov interjected calmly. "No, no, I don't believe that's the conclusion to be drawn."

But Raskolnikov ignored the interruption. His pale face twisted with a mixture of fury and dark amusement. "Tell me, is it true," he asked suddenly, his voice trembling with intensity, "that you told your fiancée, within an hour of her accepting you, that what pleased you most about her was her poverty? That it was better to marry a woman from nothing so you could dominate her entirely and constantly remind her of your so-called generosity?"

Luzhin turned a deep shade of crimson, clearly caught off guard. "That's absurd!" he sputtered. "Allow me to clarify—such claims are pure distortion. They stem from... from a misunderstanding. Your mother, though well-meaning and admirable, appears to have misinterpreted my words. I would never imply such a thing—"

"Listen to me," Raskolnikov interrupted, sitting upright on the bed, his piercing gaze fixed on Luzhin. His voice, though quiet, was laced with menace. "If you ever again dare to say anything about my mother, I will throw you down the stairs myself."

Razumihin sprang to his feet. "What's wrong with you?" he cried.

But Luzhin's face had turned pale. He was visibly shaken but struggled to maintain his composure. "I see now," he said slowly, breathing heavily, "that you have been prejudiced against me from the very beginning. I had hoped to find common ground, but clearly, that is impossible. This will be my last attempt at civility."

"I'm not ill!" Raskolnikov shouted suddenly, his voice echoing through the room.

"All the worse for you," Luzhin retorted, his voice icy. Without waiting for further provocation, he turned sharply and made his way to the door, his movements stiff and formal. As he exited, he carefully lifted his hat, ensuring it wouldn't be crushed as he stooped through the doorway. Even the curve of his back as he departed seemed to radiate indignation at the insult he had endured.

"How could you—how could you!" Razumihin exclaimed, shaking his head in bewilderment.

"Leave me alone—leave me alone, all of you!" Raskolnikov shouted, his voice filled with desperation. "Why won't you stop tormenting me? I'm not afraid of you! I'm not afraid of anyone—anyone at all! Get out! I just want to be left alone—completely alone!"

"Come on, let's go," Zossimov said firmly, nodding to Razumihin.

"But we can't leave him like this!" Razumihin protested.

"I said, come on," Zossimov repeated, more insistent this time, as he stepped out. Razumihin hesitated for a moment, then quickly ran to catch up with him.

"It could be worse if we don't listen to him," Zossimov remarked as they descended the stairs. "We shouldn't irritate him any further."

"What's wrong with him?" Razumihin asked, his face creased with concern.

"If only he could experience some sort of positive shock—that might help! At first, he seemed to be improving... but you can tell he's got something weighing heavily on him. Some fixed idea he can't shake. I'm really worried about that."

"Could it have something to do with that man, Pyotr Petrovitch?" Razumihin mused. "From what I overheard, he's planning to marry

Raskolnikov's sister, and it sounds like Raskolnikov got a letter about it just before he fell ill."

"Yes, damn that man! He could have thrown the whole situation off balance. Have you noticed, though? Raskolnikov doesn't seem to care about anything—nothing at all—except for one thing: the murder."

"Exactly," Razumihin agreed. "I've noticed that, too. He seems interested but also terrified. When it was brought up in the police station, he fainted—it really shook him."

"Tell me more about that later tonight," Zossimov said thoughtfully. "I'll share something with you as well. He's fascinating— there's a lot going on with him. I'll stop by to check on him again in half an hour... though I don't think there's any risk of inflammation."

"Thanks," Razumihin replied. "I'll stay with Pashenka for now and keep an eye on him through Nastasya."

Raskolnikov, now alone in the room, looked at Nastasya with frustration and weariness. Her presence clearly bothered him, but she didn't leave right away.

"Do you want some tea now?" she asked, her voice soft.

"Later!" he snapped. "I'm tired. Just go."

He turned sharply to face the wall, signaling the conversation was over. Taking the hint, Nastasya quietly left the room.

Chapter 6

As soon as Nastasya left the room, Raskolnikov got up, latched the door, and untied the bundle Razumihin had brought earlier. He carefully rewrapped it after looking inside and began dressing himself. Strangely enough, he suddenly felt calm, as if the feverish panic that had plagued him recently had vanished completely. His movements were deliberate and focused, as though he were driven by a clear and unwavering purpose. "Today... it must be today," he muttered under his breath. Though he realized he was still physically weak, his intense mental focus seemed to give him strength. He was determined not to collapse in the street.

Once he was fully dressed in the new clothes, he glanced at the money left on the table. After a brief moment of thought, he pocketed it—twenty-five roubles in all—along with the remaining small change from the money Razumihin had spent. Quietly, he unlatched the door, stepped out, and crept downstairs. As he passed the open kitchen door, he saw Nastasya standing with her back to him, fanning the landlady's samovar. She didn't hear him leave. Who could have imagined he'd be going out? Moments later, he was outside on the street.

It was close to eight in the evening, and the sun was setting. The air was still stifling, but he eagerly breathed in the dirty, dusty atmosphere of the city. His head swam slightly, and his face was pale and gaunt, but his eyes burned with a wild energy. He didn't know exactly where he was headed; he didn't even care. All that filled his mind was the unshakable thought: "It must all end today. Everything. Right now. I won't go back home without it being done because I can't go on living like this anymore." How he would achieve this or what exactly he meant by "ending it," he had no idea. He didn't want to think about it. Thinking hurt too much. All he knew was that something had to change, and he repeated it to himself with an almost reckless certainty.

By force of habit, his feet carried him toward the Hay Market. In front of a small general shop, a dark-haired young man with a barrel organ stood playing a sentimental tune. A young girl, about fifteen years old, sang along as she stood on the pavement. She was dressed in an old crinoline skirt, a worn-out mantle, and a straw hat with a bright, tattered feather. Despite her shabby appearance, her voice was strong and pleasant, though roughened from her street performances. She sang in hopes of earning a few coins from passersby. Raskolnikov joined the small group of listeners and pulled a five-copeck coin from his pocket, placing it in her hand. She abruptly stopped mid-note, called out sharply to the organ grinder, "Let's go," and the two of them moved on to the next shop.

"Do you like street music?" Raskolnikov asked a middle-aged man who was standing nearby, watching the scene unfold. The man turned to him with a startled and puzzled expression.

"I enjoy listening to a street organ," Raskolnikov continued, his tone oddly intense. "Especially on cold, damp autumn nights—don't you think? Nights when everything is wet and heavy, and the streetlamps cast a faint, misty glow through the falling snow... but it has to be the kind of snow that falls straight down, without any wind. You know what I mean?"

"I... I don't know. Excuse me," the man stammered, visibly unnerved by Raskolnikov's strange manner. Without another word, he crossed to the other side of the street.

Raskolnikov continued walking, his steps bringing him to the corner of the Hay Market where the huckster and his wife had once stood talking with Lizaveta. The couple wasn't there now, but recognizing the spot, he paused. Looking around, he spotted a young man in a red shirt idly standing outside a corn chandler's shop.

"Isn't there a man who runs a booth here with his wife?" Raskolnikov asked.

As Raskolnikov approached, he asked a young man nearby, "Doesn't a man keep a booth here with his wife?"

The young man glanced at him dismissively and replied, "A lot of people keep booths here."

"What's his name?"

"Whatever he was christened," the young man said mockingly.

"Aren't you from Zaraïsk, too? What district?"

The young man stared at him again, clearly unimpressed. "It's not a province, your excellency, it's a district. Pardon me, your excellency!" he added sarcastically.

"Is that a tavern up there?" Raskolnikov asked, pointing.

"Yes, it's an eating-house with a billiard room. You'll even find 'princesses' there, too," the man sneered before humming a mocking tune.

Raskolnikov crossed the square and entered a crowded area filled with peasants. They were gathered in tight groups, loudly talking and shouting amongst themselves. He pushed through the crowd, searching their faces as though he needed to speak with someone. He felt an inexplicable urge to strike up a conversation, to connect with these people. Yet the peasants ignored him entirely, preoccupied with their animated discussions.

After standing there for a moment, Raskolnikov turned down a small street leading away from the market. He often wandered through this area when he felt particularly despondent, as if the gloomy atmosphere mirrored his own mood and made him feel even worse. The street was lined with old buildings housing taverns and cheap eateries. Women hurried in and out of these establishments, some bareheaded and still dressed in their indoor clothes. They often gathered in groups by the entrances, chatting loudly. From one of the lower floors, the clamor of laughter, music, and singing spilled into the street. Someone was strumming a guitar, and a high-pitched, somewhat raspy voice sang a playful tune.

Outside one door, a small crowd of women had formed. Some sat on the steps, others squatted on the pavement, and a few leaned casually against the doorway, deep in conversation. A drunken soldier, cigarette in hand, stumbled nearby, cursing loudly as though trying to remember where he was going. Further down the street, two beggars were having an argument, while another man, completely intoxicated, lay sprawled across the road.

Raskolnikov stopped near the women. They wore simple cotton dresses and goatskin shoes, their hair uncovered. Most were older, though a few seemed barely seventeen. Nearly all of them bore marks of hard lives—bruises, puffy faces, and blackened eyes. Yet he found himself oddly drawn to the noise, the singing, and the chaos of the saloon below. He leaned closer to the doorway, listening intently.

From inside came the sound of someone stomping their feet in time to the music, their frantic dancing keeping pace with the high-pitched singing.

"Oh, my handsome soldier,

Don't beat me for nothing,"

the voice sang.

Raskolnikov strained to catch the words, as though understanding the lyrics might somehow clarify his own thoughts. "Should I go in?" he wondered. "They're laughing, probably drunk. Maybe I should get drunk, too."

"Why don't you come inside?" one of the women asked him. Her voice, unlike the others, was still youthful and sweet, and her face had a softness to it that stood out in the group.

"She's actually pretty," Raskolnikov said aloud, standing straighter to take a better look at her.

The woman smiled, pleased by his attention. "You're good-looking yourself," she said.

"Thin, though," another woman chimed in, her voice deep and husky. "Have you just come out of the hospital?"

"Generals' daughters, all of them," joked a drunken peasant standing nearby. He wore a loose coat and had a sly grin on his face. "But they've all got snub noses. Look how cheerful they are!"

"Go away, you pest!" one of the women shouted, but the peasant only laughed.

"I'm going, sweetheart!" he called as he staggered off toward the saloon. Raskolnikov began to move on as well, but the young woman called after him.

"Hey, sir!"

"What is it?" he asked, turning back.

She hesitated for a moment before smiling shyly. "I'd be happy to spend an hour with you, kind sir, but I'm feeling a bit bashful. Could you give me six copecks for a drink? You're such a nice man."

Without thinking, Raskolnikov pulled out a coin and handed her fifteen copecks. "Ah, what a generous gentleman!" she exclaimed.

"What's your name?" he asked.

"Just ask for Duclida," she replied with a playful smile.

"That's a bit much," muttered one of the other women, shaking her head disapprovingly. "I don't know how you can beg like that. I'd die of shame."

Raskolnikov glanced at the speaker. She was older, her face pockmarked and bruised, with a swollen upper lip. She seemed genuinely embarrassed by Duclida's boldness, and her comment was made with quiet sincerity.

He turned away, lost in thought. "Where have I read about this?" he wondered. "Someone condemned to death who says, or thinks, just an hour before their execution, that if they could live on a tiny ledge, surrounded by a vast ocean, with storms and darkness all around, they'd choose to live there for a thousand years, eternity even, rather than die. Just to live—no matter what the conditions. How true that is! Life, no matter how terrible, is worth holding onto. And yet, how vile a creature man must be to think that way... and how vile it is to judge him for it."

He shook his head and wandered into another street. "The Palais de Cristal," he murmured, recalling Razumihin mentioning it earlier. "What was it I came here for? Oh, right, the newspapers... Zossimov said something about the papers."

He entered a restaurant that was surprisingly clean and spacious, with several empty rooms. A few patrons sat drinking tea, while further inside, a group of four men were drinking champagne. Raskolnikov thought he recognized Zametov among them, though he couldn't be sure at such a distance. "And what if it is him?" he muttered.

When the waiter approached, he asked, "Would you like some vodka?"

"No, bring me tea and the newspapers from the last five days. I'll tip you for it," Raskolnikov replied.

"Right away, sir. Here's today's paper. Still no vodka?"

The waiter brought the tea and a stack of old newspapers. Raskolnikov sat down, flipping through them impatiently.

"Accidents, fires, and more fires... what a mess," he muttered to himself. "Ah, here it is." Finally, he found what he had been searching for and began to read. The words seemed to blur before his tired eyes, but he forced himself to focus, scanning eagerly for updates in later editions. His hands trembled slightly as he turned the pages, growing more agitated by the second.

Suddenly, someone sat down beside him. Startled, Raskolnikov looked up and saw Zametov, the head clerk, sitting there. He was as sharply dressed as ever, with rings on his fingers and a chain across his vest. His dark curly hair was neatly styled, though his coat looked a bit worn. His face was flushed, likely from champagne, but he was smiling cheerfully.

"What a surprise to see you here!" Zametov exclaimed. "I heard from Razumihin yesterday that you were still unconscious. How odd! Did you know I came to visit you?"

Raskolnikov had anticipated this encounter. He set the papers aside and turned toward Zametov, a slight, irritated smile playing on his lips.

"Yes, I know. I heard about it," Raskolnikov said calmly. "You were looking for my sock, weren't you? And by the way, Razumihin seems quite taken with you. He said you've been hanging around Luise Ivanovna's place—the woman you tried to help by signaling that 'Explosive Lieutenant.' But he didn't understand you, did he? How could he not? It was so obvious."

"What a fiery temper Razumihin has," Zametov remarked with a chuckle.

"Who, the lieutenant?"

"No, Razumihin, your friend."

"Well, you must have quite the life, Zametov—access to all the best places. Who's been filling you with champagne today?"

"We just had a little gathering," Zametov replied lightly. "You talk as if I drink it all the time!"

"Call it a fee for services rendered," Raskolnikov said, laughing abruptly and slapping Zametov's shoulder. "Don't take it personally; I'm just teasing, like that worker in the case with Dmitri and the old woman."

"How do you even know about that?"

"Maybe I know more than you think," Raskolnikov said with a sly grin.

"You're acting strange... Are you sure you should be out? You don't seem well."

"Strange? Do I seem strange to you?"

"Yes, very."

"What are you reading?" Zametov asked, glancing at the stack of newspapers.

"Just the papers."

"There's been a lot about the fires recently."

"I'm not reading about fires," Raskolnikov said, his tone suddenly secretive. He leaned closer to Zametov, his lips twisting into a mocking smile. "But you're dying to know what I am reading about, aren't you?"

"Not really. But why are you being so cryptic?"

"Tell me, Zametov, you're an educated man, right?"

"I made it to the sixth grade at the gymnasium," Zametov replied with a touch of pride.

"Ah, a man of sophistication!" Raskolnikov teased. "With your rings and your stylish part, you must be a true gentleman. How charming!" He burst into a nervous laugh, startling Zametov, who instinctively leaned back.

"Are you delirious?" Zametov asked, more perplexed than offended.

"Delirious? You think so? You really find me strange?"

"Very strange."

"Would you like to know what I've been reading about?" Raskolnikov asked suddenly, gesturing to the pile of papers. "Come on, admit it—you're curious."

"Not particularly."

"Liar," Raskolnikov shot back. He paused dramatically before leaning in close, his voice dropping to a near-whisper. "I came here specifically to read about the murder of the old pawnbroker."

Zametov froze, staring at him in shock. For a full minute, neither spoke. They simply sat there, gazing at one another in silence.

"And what if you were reading about it?" Zametov finally asked, his voice impatient and confused. "What's that to me?"

Raskolnikov leaned forward slightly, his voice dropping to a whisper as he continued, "The same old woman... the one you were talking about in the police station when I fainted. Do you remember that? Well, do you understand now?"

"What are you talking about? Understand what?" Zametov asked, his tone uneasy, almost alarmed.

Raskolnikov's face, previously serious and intense, suddenly changed, breaking into a strange, nervous laugh that seemed beyond his control. A vivid memory flashed through his mind—the moment he stood behind the door with the axe, the latch trembling as the men outside cursed and tried to get in. He had felt a wild urge to yell at them, to taunt them, to stick out his tongue, to laugh uncontrollably. And now, the memory brought that same laughter bubbling up again.

"You're either insane or..." Zametov began, but then stopped abruptly, as if struck by a sudden realization.

"Or what? Come on, say it. What?" Raskolnikov demanded, his eyes narrowing.

"Nothing," Zametov replied sharply, his irritation evident. "This is nonsense."

They sat in silence after that. Raskolnikov's sudden burst of laughter had passed, replaced by a heavy, somber mood. He propped his elbow on the table and rested his head in his hand, staring off into space as if he had forgotten Zametov was even there. The quiet stretched on for several minutes.

"You're letting your tea get cold," Zametov said at last.

"What? Tea? Oh, yes..." Raskolnikov muttered absently. He picked up the glass, took a sip, and nibbled on a piece of bread. As he turned his gaze back to Zametov, it was as if he snapped out of a trance. His face took on its earlier mocking expression, and he began drinking his tea more purposefully.

"There have been a lot of crimes like this lately," Zametov remarked. "Just the other day, I read in the Moscow News about a gang of counterfeiters. A whole organization! They were making fake lottery tickets."

"Oh, that? I read about that weeks ago," Raskolnikov replied casually. Then, with a smirk, he added, "And you call them criminals?"

"Of course they're criminals," Zametov said, puzzled.

"They're idiots, not criminals!" Raskolnikov shot back. "Half a hundred people working together for something like that? Ridiculous! Even three people would be too many. And they trusted strangers to exchange the fake notes? Fools! All it took was one of them to slip up, and the whole operation fell apart. Imagine making a fortune like that, only to spend the rest of your life looking over your shoulder, depending on others to keep quiet. They might as well have hanged themselves right away."

Zametov raised an eyebrow. "Do you think it's that simple? That a person's hands wouldn't tremble in such a situation? I'm sure they would."

"Could you do it?" Raskolnikov asked, a strange intensity in his voice.

"No, I couldn't. Risking all that for a little money? Walking into a bank with fake notes where they're trained to spot forgeries? No, I wouldn't have the nerve. Would you?"

Raskolnikov shivered slightly but smiled. "I'd do it differently," he said with a hint of mischief. "I'd count each thousand carefully, over and over, and make a show of examining the notes, holding them to the light. I'd tell a long story about someone I knew losing money to a fake bill. I'd confuse the clerk so much, they'd want to get rid of me just to have peace. Then I'd leave, come back, ask more questions, and drive them to the brink of madness. That's how I'd do it."

Zametov laughed, though he looked uneasy. "You're full of wild ideas, but I doubt you'd pull it off. Even the most experienced criminal slips up. Take the old pawnbroker's murder, for example. That was a desperate man who got lucky, but even he lost his nerve and botched the robbery."

Raskolnikov's smile vanished, replaced by a sharp glare. "If it's so clear, why haven't you caught him?" he snapped.

"They will," Zametov replied confidently.

"Who? You? Don't make me laugh. Your idea of catching someone is watching to see if they start spending money. Any child could fool you with that logic."

"Well, it's how most criminals get caught," Zametov countered. "They can't resist spending their loot. Not everyone's as clever as you seem to think you are."

Raskolnikov stared at him, his expression dark. "You really want to know how I'd handle it, don't you?" he asked, his voice low and unsettling.

"I do," Zametov replied, his tone serious, almost eager.

"How badly?" Raskolnikov pressed, leaning closer.

"Very much," Zametov admitted, meeting his gaze.

Raskolnikov leaned in closer to Zametov, his face inches away, his voice dropping to an eerie whisper. "All right then," he began, his words slow and deliberate, "this is exactly how I would have done it. I would have taken the money and jewels, walked calmly out of there, and gone straight to some hidden, deserted spot. It would need to be a place where no one goes—a fenced-off yard, a neglected garden, or something like that. I'd have picked a spot beforehand, somewhere with a big stone, maybe one that's been sitting there since the house was built. It would need to weigh at least a hundredweight. Then I'd lift that stone. There's always a hollow underneath. I'd bury the loot there, cover it back up so it looked untouched, press it down firmly with my foot, and walk away like nothing happened."

He paused, his glittering eyes fixed on Zametov, whose face had gone pale. "And then," Raskolnikov continued, "I wouldn't touch it. Not for a year, maybe two or three. I'd leave it there, completely untouched. Let them search all they want—there wouldn't be a trace."

Zametov shuddered involuntarily, his voice dropping to a whisper as well. "You're insane," he said, leaning back slightly to put some distance between them.

Raskolnikov didn't seem to hear him. His pale face twitched, his upper lip trembling uncontrollably. His mouth moved as if he were about to speak but couldn't quite get the words out. For several tense moments, he hovered on the brink, the confession trembling on his lips like a door latch about to snap.

Then, in a sudden, almost reckless burst, he said, "And what if it was I who killed the old woman and Lizaveta?"

The words hung in the air like a thunderclap. Zametov froze, his eyes wide with shock, his face draining of color. A strained, awkward smile twisted his features. "That's not possible," he stammered faintly.

Raskolnikov's gaze hardened. "Admit it—you believed me just now, didn't you?"

"No! Of course not!" Zametov replied hastily, but his embarrassment betrayed him.

"I've got you now," Raskolnikov sneered, his voice sharp. "You believed it before, didn't you? And now you're trying to convince yourself otherwise."

"Not at all!" Zametov insisted, flustered. "Were you just trying to scare me into thinking that?"

"Do you deny it? Then why were you whispering behind my back at the police station? Why did that explosive lieutenant interrogate me after I fainted?" Raskolnikov shouted suddenly, standing up. "Hey, waiter! How much do I owe?"

"Thirty copecks," the waiter answered, rushing over.

"Here's twenty more for vodka," Raskolnikov said, his hand shaking as he held out the coins. "See how much money I've got!" He waved a handful of notes at Zametov. "Red ones, blue ones, twenty-five roubles. Where did I get them, huh? And where did these new clothes come from? I didn't have a single copeck before. You've probably questioned my landlady by now, haven't you? Well, that's enough. Assez causé! See you later!"

He stormed out, trembling with a wild mix of emotions—part elation, part rage, and part exhaustion. His face twisted as if he'd just endured a seizure. The surge of adrenaline that had carried him out of the restaurant faded quickly, leaving him weak and drained.

Inside, Zametov remained seated, his mind racing. The conversation had shaken him deeply, reshaping his understanding of the situation. "Ilya Petrovitch is an idiot," he muttered to himself.

Outside, Raskolnikov barely made it out the door before running into Razumihin on the steps. Neither saw the other until they almost collided. They stopped, staring at each other in astonishment. Razumihin's surprise quickly turned to anger, his eyes blazing.

"So here you are!" he bellowed. "You ran off from your bed, and I've been turning the place upside down looking for you! I even searched under the sofa! I almost thrashed Nastasya because of you, and here you are, wandering around! What's the meaning of this? Speak up! Confess!"

Raskolnikov looked at him with a calm, weary expression. "It means I'm sick of all of you," he said. "I want to be alone."

"Alone? When you can barely stand? When your face is white as a sheet, and you're gasping for air? You idiot! What were you doing at the Palais de Cristal? Tell me now!"

"Let me pass," Raskolnikov said quietly, attempting to move around him.

That was the last straw for Razumihin. He grabbed Raskolnikov by the shoulder, holding him firmly. "Let you pass? Not a chance! Do you know what I'll do? I'll pick you up, carry you home, and lock you in like a child!"

"Razumihin," Raskolnikov began, his voice steady but icy, "don't you understand that I don't want your help? Why do you insist on forcing your so-called kindness on someone who doesn't want it? Can't you see it's making me worse? Even Zossimov left to avoid upsetting me. Why can't you leave me alone, too?"

He stepped closer, his voice rising. "I told you before—you're suffocating me! Your constant interference is hindering my recovery. Why can't you respect that? I may be ungrateful. I may be selfish. But I'm asking—no, begging—you to let me be. Just let me be!"

He began his tirade slowly, savoring the venom in his words as though each phrase were a finely crafted insult. His calm at the start only made the biting edge of his words more cutting, but as he continued, his control slipped, and by the end, his voice was hoarse, trembling with the same frenzied anger he had shown toward Luzhin.

Razumihin stood motionless, watching Raskolnikov with a mixture of frustration and sadness. For a moment, he seemed to consider grabbing his friend by the shoulders and shaking him into sense, but instead, he let his hand drop and sighed deeply. "Well, go to hell, then," he said quietly, though his tone carried a strange weight of resignation. Then, as if unable to let the matter rest, he suddenly shouted, "Wait a minute!"

Raskolnikov froze but did not turn back.

"Listen to me!" Razumihin demanded, his voice rising. "You're all the same, you brood over your miseries like hens over eggs. You can't even come up with anything original! No, you just copy each other's misery like it's some kind of art form. There's no independence in you—none of you! You're all made of wax, soft and lifeless, and instead of blood, you've got lukewarm water running through your veins. Do you even know what it means to be human anymore?"

Raskolnikov made a slight movement as if to walk away, but Razumihin raised his voice even louder, his frustration boiling over. "Stop! Just stop! You know I'm having a housewarming tonight. My guests are probably already there, and my poor uncle is playing host for me while I'm out here chasing after you. But no, I had to come running like a fool! And why? Because I care about you, you idiot!"

Razumihin stepped closer, his voice softer but no less intense. "If you weren't such a stubborn fool—such a ridiculous, self-destructive fool—you'd come to my place tonight. You'd sit in a comfortable chair, drink some tea, maybe even stretch out on the sofa. You'd be surrounded by people who care about you. Zossimov will be there, too. But no! You'd rather wander aimlessly, wasting your strength and your boots on the streets. So tell me, will you come?"

"No," Raskolnikov replied flatly, his face devoid of emotion.

"Rubbish!" Razumihin exploded. "How do you even know what you want? You're so wrapped up in your own misery that you can't see straight. People fight, they argue, and then they go back to each other. It's human nature! You'll come to your senses eventually—mark my words. And when you do, remember: Potchinkov's house, third floor, flat 47, Babushkin's place."

Raskolnikov, unmoved, turned to leave. "I won't come," he said simply.

"I bet you will," Razumihin yelled after him. "If you don't, I'll refuse to know you! Oh, and hey—did you see Zametov in there?"

"Yes," Raskolnikov answered without stopping.

"Did you talk to him?"

"Yes."

"What about?" Razumihin pressed, but Raskolnikov ignored him and continued walking.

"Fine, don't tell me!" Razumihin shouted. "But remember: Potchinkov's house, third floor, flat 47!"

Raskolnikov turned the corner and disappeared onto Sadovy Street, leaving Razumihin standing there, shaking his head. For a moment, Razumihin stood lost in thought, muttering to himself. Then, with an irritated wave of his hand, he stormed back toward the Palais de Cristal but stopped abruptly at the stairs.

"Damn it," he muttered aloud. "He sounded sane enough, but who's to say madmen can't sound sane? What if...?" He tapped his forehead with his finger as a grim thought struck him. "What if he does something reckless? What if he—?" The possibility was too much to bear. Without another word, Razumihin turned on his heel and rushed back to the street, hoping to catch up with Raskolnikov. But his friend was already gone. With a muttered curse, he headed for the Palais de Cristal to confront Zametov.

Meanwhile, Raskolnikov made his way to X—— Bridge. His body felt so heavy, his legs so weak, that he doubted he could take another step. He longed to collapse on the ground and let the world fade away. Reaching the middle of the bridge, he leaned over the railing, both elbows pressed against the cool iron, and stared out over the water. The last rays of the setting sun cast a pinkish glow on the horizon, while shadows deepened along the rows of darkening buildings. A single attic window on the far bank caught the light, burning like a tiny flame against the growing gloom.

For a while, he stood there, hypnotized by the murky waters below. The rippling current seemed to hold a strange power over him. He felt the world around him blur; the buildings, the carriages, and the people on the street all seemed to sway and dissolve into one chaotic whirl. Suddenly, he was snapped out of his trance by a horrifying sight.

A tall woman stood nearby, her face gaunt, her eyes hollow and bloodshot. Without a word or a glance at anyone, she climbed onto the railing and leapt into the canal. The filthy water swallowed her instantly, but a moment later, her body resurfaced, bobbing lifelessly with the current. Her skirt puffed up around her like a grotesque balloon.

"A woman's drowning!" voices cried out in alarm. People rushed to the bridge, their shouts filling the air.

"Mercy! It's our Afrosinya!" wailed a woman nearby. "Someone save her! Please, kind people, help her!"

A policeman dashed down the embankment steps, tearing off his coat and boots as he ran. Without hesitation, he plunged into the water and grabbed the drowning woman by her clothes. A comrade held out a pole, and together they hauled her onto the pavement. She coughed and sputtered, slowly regaining consciousness, her hands fumbling clumsily at her soaked dress.

"She's drunk out of her mind," another woman lamented tearfully. "It's not the first time, either! Just the other day, she tried to hang herself. We had to cut her down! I only stepped out to the shop for a minute, left my little girl to watch her, and now this!"

The woman gestured frantically toward a nearby house, her voice cracking with despair. "We're neighbors, sir. Second house from the end, right over there...."

The crowd began to disperse, though a few onlookers lingered. The police gathered around the drenched woman, and someone muttered about taking her to the station. Raskolnikov stood at the edge of the scene, feeling an odd mix of detachment and disgust. His face was expressionless, but inside, he felt a deep repulsion. "No, that's revolting," he murmured under his breath, "drowning in water... it's not enough. It's no way to end things."

His thoughts drifted as he stood there. "Nothing will come of this," he whispered again. "What about the police station? Why isn't Zametov there? It's open until ten, isn't it?" He turned his back on the commotion and scanned his surroundings with hollow eyes, his mind made up.

"Alright then!" he said aloud, as if reaching a decision. He set off toward the police station, his steps slow and unsteady. His heart felt empty, almost weightless. He wasn't thinking clearly—or rather, he wasn't thinking at all. Even the despair that had driven him to act earlier seemed to have faded. Now, there was only a dull void, a strange, apathetic calm.

"Well, it's a way out," he muttered as he trudged along the canal bank. "At least it's an end, which is what I want. But is it really an end? Does it matter? No. There'll be that square yard of space... ha! But what a stupid end it is. Should I tell them everything? Or not? Damn it, I'm so tired. I just want to sit somewhere, anywhere. I'm so ashamed, but even that doesn't matter now. What ridiculous thoughts are these?"

The police station was only a short walk away—straight ahead and a left turn. But when he reached the first corner, he stopped abruptly. Without thinking, he veered into a side street and wandered two blocks out of his way. There was no real purpose to it. Perhaps he just wanted to delay the inevitable. His gaze remained fixed on the ground as he walked, his mind blank. Suddenly, he felt a strange sensation, as though someone had whispered in his ear. He lifted his head and found himself standing at the gate of that house—the house he hadn't dared approach since that fateful night.

An inexplicable force seemed to pull him forward. Without hesitation, he stepped through the gateway and entered the first stairwell on the right. Slowly, deliberately, he climbed the narrow, steep staircase. It was dark, and he paused on each landing, looking around as if trying to remember something. On the first landing, he noticed the window frame had been removed. "That wasn't like that before," he thought absently. On the second floor, he saw the door to the flat where Nikolay and Dmitri had worked. It was shut and newly painted. "So it's for rent now," he mused.

He continued upward, past the third floor, until he reached the fourth. He stopped, staring at the familiar door. To his surprise, it was wide open. Inside, he could hear voices. Workmen. This was unexpected; he had somehow imagined the flat would be exactly as he had left it, untouched, frozen in time. For a moment, he hesitated, but then he stepped inside.

The flat was unrecognizable. Bare walls, no furniture—just an empty shell. The workmen were busy pasting new wallpaper, a bright pattern of lilac flowers replacing the dingy yellow paper he remembered. The sight irritated him. He stared at the new wallpaper with an inexplicable sense of loss, as if something precious had been stolen from him.

Two young workmen were there, one older than the other. They were hurriedly rolling up their tools, clearly staying late to finish their work. They paid no attention to Raskolnikov, continuing their conversation as they worked. Raskolnikov folded his arms and listened.

"She came to see me this morning, all dolled up," said the older one. "All dressed to the nines. 'Why are you all done up?' I asked her. And she says, 'I just wanted to please you, Tit Vassilitch!' Imagine that! Dressed like something out of a fashion magazine."

"What's a fashion magazine?" the younger one asked, wide-eyed, clearly looking up to his companion.

"It's a book full of pictures," the older man explained. "They come every Saturday by post from abroad. Tailors use them to show folks how to dress—both men and women. The men are always wearing fur coats, and the women, well, their clothes are beyond imagination."

"Petersburg has everything," the younger man said with admiration. "Everything but parents."

"That's right," the older man agreed sagely. "Everything but father and mother."

Raskolnikov turned and walked into the adjoining room, where the strongbox, the bed, and the chest of drawers had once stood. Without furniture, the space seemed cramped, almost suffocating. The wallpaper in the corner bore faint marks where the icon case had been. He stared at it for a long moment, then moved to the window.

The elder workman noticed him for the first time and asked sharply, "What do you want?"

Raskolnikov ignored the question and walked back into the hallway. He pulled the bell cord, hearing the familiar cracked tone. He rang it again, then a third time, each ring bringing back the gut-wrenching fear he had felt that night. The sensation was almost unbearable, yet strangely satisfying.

"What are you doing? Who are you?" the workman shouted, stepping toward him. Raskolnikov re-entered the flat, standing calmly in the middle of the room.

"I'm looking for a flat," he said. "Just inspecting the place."

"This isn't the time for that! You should have come with the porter," the workman replied, clearly uneasy.

"Will the floors be painted?" Raskolnikov asked, ignoring him. "And is there no blood?"

"What blood?" the man stammered.

"The blood of the old woman and her sister," Raskolnikov said, his voice eerily calm. "There was a pool of it right here."

"Who are you?" the workman demanded, his voice rising.

"Who am I?" Raskolnikov echoed, his lips curling into a strange smile. "Come to the police station, and I'll tell you."

The workmen exchanged puzzled glances, their expressions shifting from confusion to irritation.

"It's late. Time for us to lock up," said the elder workman, gathering his tools. "Come on, Alyoshka, let's go."

"Alright, let's go," Raskolnikov said absently, stepping out ahead of them. He descended the stairs slowly, as if each step required great effort. As he reached the gateway, he raised his voice. "Hey, porter!"

At the entrance, a small group had gathered—a couple of porters, a peasant woman, a man wearing a long coat, and a few idlers, all watching the passersby. Raskolnikov approached them with deliberate steps.

"What do you want?" one of the porters asked, narrowing his eyes.

"Have you been to the police station?" Raskolnikov inquired, his tone detached.

"I've just come from there. What about it?"

"Is it open?"

"Of course."

"Is the assistant there?"

"He was earlier. Why? What's this about?"

Raskolnikov didn't answer. Instead, he stood silently among them, staring into the distance as though deep in thought.

"He's been up to the flat," the elder workman chimed in, stepping closer.

"What flat?" the porter asked, his tone suspicious.

"The one we're working on," the workman explained, his voice tinged with annoyance. "He asked why we washed away the blood, said there'd been a murder there, and that he'd come to 'take it.' Then he started yanking on the bell like a madman, ringing it over and over. Said we should all go to the police station and that he'd tell everything there. He wouldn't leave us alone."

The porter's gaze shifted sharply to Raskolnikov, his frown deepening. "Who are you?" he barked, his tone carrying a mixture of irritation and authority.

Raskolnikov finally turned his head slightly, speaking in a slow, almost languid voice. "I'm Rodion Romanovitch Raskolnikov, formerly a student. I live nearby, in Shil's house, flat number fourteen. Ask the porter there; he knows me."

"Why did you go to the flat?" the porter demanded.

"To look at it," Raskolnikov replied without emotion.

"What's there to look at?"

"Take him to the police station," interjected the man in the long coat, his voice firm and authoritative.

Raskolnikov turned his gaze toward the man, studying him for a moment before responding in the same slow, detached tone. "Alright. Let's go."

"Yes, take him," the man repeated, his confidence growing. "What's he up to, poking around like that? Something's not right."

"He's not drunk," muttered the workman, glancing nervously at Raskolnikov, "but who knows what's wrong with him."

The porter's patience finally snapped. "What do you want?" he shouted. "Why are you hanging around here?"

"Afraid to go to the police station?" Raskolnikov taunted, his lips curling into a faint, mocking smile.

"Afraid? What's that supposed to mean? Why are you loitering?"

"He's a scoundrel!" the peasant woman exclaimed, clutching her shawl tighter around her shoulders.

"Enough talking!" bellowed the second porter, a burly man with a ring of keys jingling at his waist. "Get out of here, you rogue!"

Without waiting for a reply, the porter grabbed Raskolnikov's shoulder and shoved him into the street. Raskolnikov stumbled but quickly regained his balance. He turned to look at the group, his expression unreadable, before walking away in silence.

"Strange fellow," muttered the elder workman, shaking his head.

"There are plenty of strange ones about these days," added the peasant woman, still clutching her shawl.

"You should've taken him to the police station anyway," the man in the long coat insisted, his voice stern.

"It's better to leave him be," the burly porter countered with a dismissive wave. "He's trouble, that one. Once you take him in, you'll never get rid of him. I've seen his kind before."

Meanwhile, Raskolnikov had stopped in the middle of the street, standing at a crossroads. He looked around as though waiting for someone—or something—to give him a sign. The world around him felt utterly lifeless, as though it existed only in a dream. The streets, the stones beneath his feet, the very air itself seemed indifferent to his presence.

At that moment, a commotion caught his attention. Two hundred yards away, at the end of the street, a small crowd had gathered. Their voices rose in shouts and murmurs, and in the middle of the throng, he glimpsed the outline of a carriage, its lantern casting flickering light into the growing dusk.

"What's happening there?" he murmured, his interest piqued. Without hesitation, he turned toward the crowd, his steps deliberate but unsteady. A cold, bitter smile played on his lips as he approached, as if he were mocking himself for his own curiosity. Yet he knew, with absolute certainty, that he was still headed for the police station. It was only a matter of time now, and soon, everything would be over.

Chapter 7

An elegant carriage stood stationary in the middle of the street, its polished surface gleaming faintly in the lantern light. Two spirited grey horses, their manes tossing impatiently, were held tightly by the bridle. The coachman, visibly agitated, had climbed down from his seat and now stood wringing his hands beside the vehicle. A crowd had gathered, their faces alight with curiosity and concern. At the center of the commotion, one of the police officers stood holding a lantern, its beam trained on something crumpled on the ground near the carriage wheels.

"What a terrible misfortune! Oh, dear God, what a misfortune!" the coachman kept repeating, his voice trembling.

Raskolnikov pushed through the throng with difficulty, his thin frame navigating the tight spaces as he elbowed his way forward. At last, he managed to get close enough to see what everyone was staring at. Lying in a twisted heap on the pavement was a man, unconscious and smeared with blood. His clothes were shabby, though they didn't quite mark him as a laborer. Blood trickled from a deep wound on his head, pooling beneath his crushed, disfigured face. His injuries were grave, leaving little hope for survival.

"Mercy, what else could I have done?" wailed the coachman, his hands moving as if to illustrate his plight. "If I'd been driving recklessly or hadn't shouted to him—but I wasn't! I was moving slowly, carefully. Everyone could see that. He was stumbling across the street, drunk as a skunk, could barely stand upright. I shouted once, twice, three times! Then I tried to pull the horses back, but he went down right under their feet! Either he was too drunk or he did it on purpose. And the horses—they're young, they got spooked. He screamed, and that made it worse! That's how it happened!"

"That's exactly how it was," confirmed someone from the crowd.

"True, he shouted three times," echoed another voice.

"Yes, we all heard it," agreed a third.

Despite his apparent distress, the coachman's concern seemed more for the potential consequences than for the injured man. It was clear the carriage belonged to someone wealthy and influential, someone who would not appreciate delays caused by such an incident. The police appeared anxious to manage the situation quickly, their priority being to transport the injured man to a hospital or police station. No one seemed to know his identity.

Raskolnikov, now close enough to kneel down, peered intently at the man's bloodied face. The lantern light fell directly on it, and recognition struck him like a blow.

"I know him! I know him!" Raskolnikov cried, his voice rising above the noise. "It's Marmeladov, a former government clerk. He lives nearby in Kozel's house. Quickly, fetch a doctor! I'll pay for it— do you hear?" He reached into his pocket and pulled out some money, waving it urgently.

His sudden agitation spurred the police into action. Relieved to have identified the man, they began to organize help. Raskolnikov provided his own name and address, speaking with an urgency that suggested he was advocating for a close family member.

"Take him home, not to the hospital," Raskolnikov pleaded. "His house is only a few steps away—three doors down, in Kozel's building. He has a family there—a wife, children, and a daughter. He's a drunkard, yes, but they'll know how to care for him. A doctor in the house can help immediately; he won't survive the trip to the hospital!"

He pressed something discreetly into the policeman's hand, ensuring his suggestion carried weight. The policemen, seeing the sense in his plea, agreed. Marmeladov was gently lifted by willing hands from the crowd.

"This way, follow me," Raskolnikov directed, his voice still trembling with urgency. He walked alongside the makeshift stretcher, supporting Marmeladov's head with great care. "Turn here—careful! Upstairs, head first. I'll make it worth your while," he murmured to those helping.

Inside Kozel's house, Katerina Ivanovna was pacing back and forth in her cramped room, her thin arms folded across her chest. She muttered to herself in quick, half-formed sentences, pausing occasionally to cough into her sleeve. Her eldest daughter, Polenka, was busy undressing her younger brother, who sat stiffly on a chair, waiting patiently for his shirt to be removed so it could be washed. The boy, serious and silent, stretched his legs out straight, his heels together, and his toes pointing outward, as though he were at a military inspection.

A younger girl, clad in rags, stood quietly by the makeshift screen, waiting for her turn. The door to the stairwell was ajar, allowing some relief from the tobacco smoke wafting in from the adjoining rooms. The smoke made Katerina Ivanovna's coughing fits worse, her thin frame trembling with each spasm. Her cheeks were flushed, the vivid color contrasting sharply with her pale, gaunt face, which seemed even thinner than before.

Polenka, perceptive beyond her years, watched her mother carefully, nodding in all the right places even when she didn't fully grasp the words. She knew her mother needed her, and her big, intelligent eyes reflected an unwavering determination to understand and help.

The sudden commotion on the stairs—the shuffle of hurried footsteps and the sound of anxious voices—broke the monotony of the tiny, smoke-filled room.

"You can't even imagine, Polenka," Katerina Ivanovna began, pacing the cramped room with her arms crossed over her chest, her voice wavering between bitterness and despair. "What a grand, luxurious life we had in my father's house before this wretched drunkard ruined me—and is now dragging you all down with him! My father was a civil colonel, just one step away from becoming a governor. Everyone who visited him used to say, 'We already see you, Ivan Mihailovitch, as our governor!' And when I..." She paused, breaking into a violent fit of coughing, pressing her trembling hands against her chest. "Oh, cursed life!" she exclaimed with a hoarse cry before trying to clear her throat and continue. "When I was at the marshal's last ball, Princess Bezzemelny saw me—she's the one who gave me her blessing when your father and I married. 'Isn't that the charming girl who danced the shawl dance at the academy's break-up?' she asked immediately."

She stopped and gestured toward a tear in Polenka's clothes. "You need to mend that tear. Use your needle, the way I showed you. If you don't fix it, he'll make it worse tomorrow." Her voice grew weaker, interrupted by another bout of coughing, but she forced herself to keep speaking. "Prince Schegolskoy had just returned from Petersburg back then—a kammerjunker, no less. He danced the mazurka with me and wanted to propose the very next day. But I turned him down, politely of course, and told him my heart already belonged to someone else. That someone was your father, Polya. Papa was furious, of course."

"Is the water ready yet?" she asked abruptly, glancing at the children. "Give me his shirt and the stockings! Lida," she called to the youngest child, "you'll have to go without your chemise tonight, and leave your stockings out as well. I'll wash them all together. I might as well, since that miserable drunkard has torn his shirt to rags—it's no better than a dishcloth now. I'll do it all at once, so I don't have to stay up two nights in a row."

She stopped mid-rant, coughing again, just as a commotion erupted in the hallway. Men were pushing their way into the room, carrying a heavy burden. Her voice broke as she stared at them, her face draining of color. "What is it? What are they bringing in? Mercy on us!" she cried out.

"Where should we put him?" asked one of the policemen, glancing around the cramped room as they carried Marmeladov, unconscious and bloodied, into the center of the space.

"On the sofa—put him on the sofa, with his head this way," Raskolnikov directed hurriedly, his voice sharp with urgency.

"Run over in the street! Drunk!" someone shouted from the passage.

Katerina Ivanovna stood frozen, gasping for breath, her face pale as chalk. The children clung to one another in terror. Little Lida screamed and ran to Polenka, burying her face in her sister's skirt.

"For God's sake, calm down!" Raskolnikov exclaimed, rushing toward Katerina Ivanovna. "Don't be frightened! He was crossing the road and got run over by a carriage, but he's still alive. I told them to bring him here. I've been here before, you remember? He'll come to, I promise. I'll pay for everything, I swear!"

"He's done it this time," Katerina Ivanovna said with a choked cry, rushing to her husband's side. But even in her despair, she kept her composure. She immediately placed a pillow under Marmeladov's head and began to undress him, her trembling fingers checking his injuries with a grim determination. Her lips quivered, but she bit them to keep herself from screaming.

Raskolnikov, meanwhile, persuaded someone to fetch a doctor. "There's a doctor just two doors down," someone muttered, and the message was quickly relayed.

"I've already sent for a doctor," Raskolnikov reassured Katerina Ivanovna. "Please, don't worry. He's injured, yes, but not dead. We'll see what the doctor says. Do you have water? A towel or a napkin—anything will do!"

Katerina Ivanovna rushed to a corner where a large basin of water stood on a broken chair. She had prepared it earlier for washing her family's few pieces of clothing that night. She tried to lift the heavy basin, but her frail body almost gave out under its weight. Raskolnikov stepped in quickly, finding a towel, soaking it in the water, and beginning to wipe the blood from Marmeladov's battered face.

Breathing heavily and clutching her chest, Katerina Ivanovna stood watching, her own physical state growing increasingly precarious. Raskolnikov began to doubt whether bringing Marmeladov here had been the right decision. The room was filling with people—neighbors, lodgers, even strangers peering in from the doorway.

"Polenka!" Katerina Ivanovna cried suddenly. "Run to Sonia's lodging. Tell her what's happened and bring her here immediately. If she's not there, leave word for her to come as soon as she gets back. Hurry, Polenka! Take the shawl, don't forget."

"Run fast!" piped up the little boy on the chair, his voice unexpectedly sharp. Then he returned to his rigid posture, legs outstretched and toes splayed, his wide eyes fixed ahead.

The room grew more crowded by the second. The police had left, except for one who lingered to try to control the throng. Almost all of Madame Lippevechsel's lodgers had squeezed into the room, jostling to get a look. Their curiosity outweighed their consideration, and the noise became unbearable.

"Have you no decency?" Katerina Ivanovna shrieked at the gawking crowd. "Can't you let a man die in peace? Smoking cigarettes in here, of all places! And you—take your hat off! Show some respect for the dead, if not for the living!"

Her coughing fit returned, but her words seemed to have some effect. The crowd began to back away, though their reluctance was clear. Some lingered in the doorway, craning their necks for a last glimpse, their faces alight with the grim satisfaction that often accompanies witnessing tragedy from a safe distance. Outside, voices murmured about sending the injured man to the hospital and questioned the wisdom of bringing him here in the first place.

"No business to die!" Katerina Ivanovna cried out, her voice breaking with frustration and despair. She stormed toward the door, ready to lash out at the growing crowd outside, but as she reached the threshold, she came face-to-face with Madame Lippevechsel. The landlady had just learned about the commotion and hurried over to assert her authority. Madame Lippevechsel was a notoriously quarrelsome and erratic German woman.

"Oh, my God!" she exclaimed, clasping her hands together dramatically. "Your husband—trampled by drunken horses! To the hospital with him! I am the landlady, and I command it!"

"Amalia Ludwigovna, I must insist that you watch your tone," Katerina Ivanovna replied, adopting a haughty, imperious manner. Despite the dire situation, she could not resist taking the opportunity to remind Madame Lippevechsel of her perceived place. "Amalia Ludwigovna," she repeated with deliberate emphasis.

"I have told you before!" the landlady snapped, her accent thick with indignation. "You may not dare to call me Amalia Ludwigovna. I am Amalia Ivanovna!"

"No, you are not Amalia Ivanovna," Katerina Ivanovna retorted with sharp defiance. "You are Amalia Ludwigovna, and I will always call you so. Unlike your sycophantic admirer, Mr. Lebeziatnikov, who is undoubtedly snickering behind the door right now," she added, raising her voice just as a muffled laugh and a muttered "they're at it again" came from the hallway.

"And let me tell you, Amalia Ludwigovna," she continued with increasing speed and fervor, "Semyon Zaharovitch is dying! I demand that you close this door at once and admit no one else! Let him have peace in his final moments, or I will make certain the Governor-General hears of your conduct tomorrow! The prince himself knew me as a young girl, and he remembers Semyon Zaharovitch well. The prince was often a benefactor to him, though my husband abandoned his many friends and supporters out of a sense of honorable pride, knowing his unfortunate weakness."

She gestured toward Raskolnikov. "Now, thanks to this generous young man—a man of means and connections, who has known Semyon Zaharovitch since childhood—we have some help. So, Amalia Ludwigovna, rest assured that—"

Her rapid tirade came to an abrupt halt as a violent coughing fit overtook her. At that very moment, Marmeladov stirred and let out a weak groan. Katerina Ivanovna rushed to his side, her tirade forgotten.

The injured man's eyes fluttered open. He gazed blankly at Raskolnikov, who leaned over him anxiously. His breathing was labored, deep, and rattling. Blood seeped from the corners of his mouth, and beads of sweat dotted his forehead. Marmeladov's eyes darted around, searching the room without recognition, his confusion palpable.

Katerina Ivanovna looked at him with a mix of sorrow and stern resolve. Tears streamed down her face, but her expression remained composed. "Dear God, his whole chest is crushed," she murmured in despair. "Look at the blood—how much he's bleeding. We need to take his clothes off. Semyon Zaharovitch, try to turn, just a little, if you can," she urged him softly.

Marmeladov's gaze finally settled on her, and recognition flickered in his dimming eyes. "A priest," he rasped faintly, his voice barely audible.

Katerina Ivanovna turned abruptly and leaned her head against the window frame, her composure cracking. "Oh, cursed life!" she cried out in despair.

"A priest," Marmeladov repeated after a moment, his voice trembling.

"They've already gone for one," Katerina Ivanovna shouted, her tone both commanding and desperate. Her words seemed to calm him, and he grew quiet, his eyes searching timidly for her. She returned to his side and stood by his pillow, her presence steadying him momentarily.

His eyes landed on little Lida, huddled in a corner. The girl trembled violently, her tiny frame wracked with silent sobs as she stared at her father with wide, frightened eyes. Marmeladov's expression twisted with anguish as he struggled to focus on her.

"A-ah," he sighed weakly, gesturing toward her with trembling fingers. He tried to speak, his lips forming silent words.

"What is it now?" Katerina Ivanovna demanded, her voice sharp with irritation.

"Barefoot... barefoot!" he muttered, his bloodshot eyes darting toward Lida's bare feet.

"Be silent!" Katerina Ivanovna snapped, her tone cutting. "You know perfectly well why she's barefoot!"

At that moment, Raskolnikov let out a sigh of relief. "Thank God, the doctor!" he exclaimed as an elderly German doctor entered the room. The man moved with careful precision, his gaze sweeping the chaotic scene with thinly veiled mistrust.

The doctor approached Marmeladov, taking his pulse with a practiced hand. With Katerina Ivanovna's help, he unbuttoned the bloodstained shirt to examine the injuries. The sight was gruesome: Marmeladov's chest was a mass of crushed ribs, deep gashes, and livid bruises. Over his heart, a large, dark bruise revealed the devastating force of a horse's hoof. The doctor's brow furrowed deeply.

"He was caught in the wheel," a policeman explained quietly. "Spun around for thirty yards before we could stop the carriage."

"It's a miracle he regained consciousness," the doctor murmured to Raskolnikov, his voice low. "What do you think?" Raskolnikov asked anxiously.

The doctor shook his head grimly. "He will die any moment now. There's no hope—not even the faintest."

"Nothing at all? Can't something be done?"

"His injuries are fatal. His head is severely injured as well," the doctor replied. "I could bleed him, but it would be futile. He has mere minutes left."

Raskolnikov hesitated but nodded. "Do it. At least try."

The doctor sighed and prepared to proceed, his expression resigned. The room fell silent, save for Marmeladov's labored breathing and Katerina Ivanovna's barely suppressed sobs.

At that moment, the sound of approaching footsteps echoed from the passageway. The crowd of onlookers parted, and a small, elderly priest with a gray beard entered the room, carrying the sacrament. He had been summoned by the policeman shortly after the accident. The doctor moved aside to make room for him, and the two exchanged a brief glance. Raskolnikov asked the doctor to stay for a while longer, and though the doctor shrugged as if to say there was little more he could do, he remained.

The room fell silent as everyone stepped back. The priest began administering the last rites. The confession was brief, for Marmeladov was too weak to say much. His words came out as faint, broken murmurs that were almost incomprehensible. Katerina Ivanovna gathered little Lida and the boy from the chair, guiding them to kneel beside her in a corner near the stove. Lida trembled uncontrollably, while the boy knelt on his small, bare knees with a serious expression. Carefully and rhythmically, he crossed himself and bowed low, his forehead touching the floor. It seemed to give him a solemn sense of purpose. Katerina Ivanovna, holding back her tears, prayed as well, occasionally adjusting the boy's shirt or pulling a kerchief over Lida's bare shoulders. She moved swiftly, her hands trembling but precise, as though her prayers were the only thing keeping her from falling apart.

The door to the inner rooms creaked open again, and curious faces peeked out. In the hallway, the crowd from the other flats pressed closer, but they hesitated to step into the room. A single stub of a candle burned weakly, casting flickering shadows across the somber scene.

Suddenly, Polenka burst into the room, breathless from running. She tore off her kerchief, scanning the crowded space until she found her mother. Rushing to her side, she exclaimed, "She's coming! I met her on the way!" Katerina Ivanovna quickly pulled Polenka down to kneel with the others.

Just then, a timid figure slipped through the doorway, her presence startlingly out of place in the grim setting. It was Sonia, and her entrance drew every eye. She wore a garish silk dress, clearly secondhand, with a clumsy, exaggerated train and an enormous crinoline. Her light-colored shoes, utterly impractical for the circumstances, and her absurd straw hat with its bright flame-colored feather, added to her incongruous appearance. She even clutched a parasol, though it served no purpose in the dim room. Beneath the ridiculous attire was a pale, frightened face, her lips parted and her large blue eyes wide with distress. Her delicate features, marred by anxiety, made her look even younger than her eighteen years.

Sonia froze just inside the doorway, her breath uneven from running. She glanced at the priest and the bed, taking in the scene with a mix of horror and helplessness. Whispers from the crowd eventually seemed to register, and she lowered her eyes, stepping hesitantly into the room while clinging to the wall for support.

The service concluded, and the priest stepped back, turning to offer words of solace to Katerina Ivanovna. She, however, cut him off with sharp irritation, pointing toward the children. "What am I supposed to do with these?" she demanded.

"God is merciful," the priest began gently. "Look to Him for help and guidance."

"Merciful?" she snapped bitterly. "Not to us."

"That is a sin, madam," the priest cautioned, shaking his head. "You must not speak so."

"And isn't this a sin?" Katerina Ivanovna retorted, gesturing toward her dying husband. Her voice rose with mounting anger. "Will they compensate me for this? For what? He threw himself under the horses! He was drunk! What earnings did he bring us? He only brought misery! He drank away every penny, ruined our lives, ruined theirs!" Her voice cracked as she motioned to the children. "Thank God he's dying! One less burden!"

"Madam, in these moments, you must forgive. It is a sin to harbor such feelings now."

"Forgive?" Katerina Ivanovna cried, her voice a mix of anguish and fury. "What good is forgiveness? If he hadn't been run over, he'd have come home drunk, filthy, and useless! I'd spend the entire night washing his rags, scrubbing these children's clothes, only to start mending them at dawn. I've forgiven him a thousand times already!" She coughed violently, pressing a bloodied handkerchief to her lips. Silently, the priest bowed his head, unable to reply.

Marmeladov stirred faintly, his eyes locked on Katerina Ivanovna as though trying to say something. His lips moved, forming indistinct shapes, and she seemed to understand his intention. "Be silent!" she commanded, her voice cracking. "There's no need to say it. I know."

Obediently, he fell silent, but his gaze shifted toward the doorway. There, standing quietly, was Sonia. He had not noticed her before. Now, he stared at her with growing alarm, struggling to prop himself up on one elbow. "Who's that? Who's there?" he gasped, his voice hoarse with desperation.

"Lie down! Stay still!" Katerina Ivanovna cried, trying to push him back.

He ignored her, his eyes fixed on Sonia's face. His expression twisted in a mix of recognition and torment. He had never seen her dressed this way—humiliated and adorned in garish finery. His face contorted with unbearable shame and grief.

"Sonia! Daughter! Forgive me!" he choked out, reaching a trembling hand toward her. But his strength gave out, and he collapsed, falling face-first onto the floor.

A cry of alarm broke through the room. They rushed to lift him and lay him back on the sofa. His body sagged lifelessly, his breathing stilled. Sonia let out a faint, heartbreaking cry as she knelt beside him, her arms wrapping tightly around his lifeless form. She did not move, even as the room filled with a heavy, suffocating silence. Marmeladov had died in her embrace.

Katerina Ivanovna looked down at her husband's lifeless body, her face pale but her eyes blazing with despair and fury. "So, he's finally gotten what he wanted!" she cried out, her voice shaking. "But what do I do now? How am I supposed to bury him? And what am I supposed to feed the children tomorrow?" Her words were raw, charged with pain and anger, and they hung heavy in the room.

Raskolnikov stepped forward, his movements hesitant yet purposeful. "Katerina Ivanovna," he began softly, his tone filled with a mix of sorrow and urgency, "last week, your husband spoke to me about his life... and about you. He told me everything. Believe me, he held you in the highest regard. He spoke of you with so much love and respect, even in the face of his own... weakness. It was clear how deeply devoted he was to you and the children."

He paused, his gaze lowering as though searching for the right words. "From that evening, I felt I owed him something. He considered me a friend, and now... please, let me help. I don't have much, but here... take this." He reached into his pocket and placed twenty roubles into her trembling hands. "It's not much, but if it can help in any way, then it's yours. I will come back—I promise I'll come back tomorrow. Please, take care of yourself and the children." His voice broke slightly as he turned to leave.

As Raskolnikov moved toward the door, the crowd in the passage parted to let him through. Just as he reached the stairs, he collided with Nikodim Fomitch, who had arrived to oversee the situation. They hadn't seen each other since the tense encounter at the police station, but Nikodim Fomitch recognized him immediately.

"Oh, it's you," he said, his expression a mixture of curiosity and concern.

"Yes," Raskolnikov replied, his voice quiet but firm. "He's gone. The priest and doctor have both been here. Everything was done as it should be. But please," he added, his tone softening, "try not to trouble her too much. She's ill, very ill. She needs kindness now." Raskolnikov gave him a faint, weary smile.

Nikodim Fomitch frowned slightly, his eyes catching on something. "You're covered in blood," he remarked, pointing to the stains on Raskolnikov's clothes.

Raskolnikov glanced down at himself and then back at the officer. "Yes," he said simply, his tone peculiar, almost detached. Then, with a faint nod and a half-smile, he turned and descended the stairs.

As he walked down, his steps were slow but deliberate. His mind was swirling with a strange, overpowering sensation—an intense rush of vitality and clarity, as though he had been pulled back from the brink of despair. It felt like a man condemned to die who had suddenly been granted a pardon. About halfway down the staircase, he heard footsteps behind him. Turning, he saw the priest descending, and they exchanged a brief, silent nod before parting ways.

When Raskolnikov reached the last few steps, he heard a small, hurried voice calling out, "Wait! Please wait!" He turned and saw Polenka running after him, her little face flushed with excitement. She stopped a step above him, catching her breath. Even in the dim light of the stairwell, her bright, hopeful smile shone through.

"What is your name? Where do you live?" she asked eagerly, her words tumbling out all at once.

Raskolnikov crouched slightly, placing his hands gently on her thin shoulders. He gazed at her with a sudden, inexplicable joy. "Who sent you, Polenka?" he asked softly, his voice filled with wonder.

"Sister Sonia," she replied, smiling even wider. "She told me to run after you, and then Mama said, 'Go quickly, Polenka!'"

"Do you love your sister Sonia?" he asked, his tone tender but serious.

"I love her more than anyone in the world," Polenka answered earnestly, her smile fading slightly as her expression grew more solemn.

"And will you love me?" he asked quietly.

Without hesitation, Polenka leaned forward and kissed him on the cheek, her small arms wrapping tightly around his neck. Her head rested on his shoulder as she began to cry softly. "I'm so sorry for Papa," she whispered through her tears. "Everything is so hard now. It's all just... misfortunes."

Raskolnikov felt his throat tighten. "Did your father love you?" he asked gently.

She pulled back, wiping her face with her hands. "He loved Lida the most," she said with the seriousness of a child trying to sound grown-up. "She's the youngest and always sick. He used to bring her little presents. But he taught me things, too—grammar and scripture. And Mama liked that, even though she didn't say so."

"Do you know your prayers?" Raskolnikov asked after a moment.

"Of course!" Polenka said proudly. "I say mine by myself because I'm big now. But Kolya and Lida say theirs with Mama."

"Polenka, my name is Rodion. Will you pray for me, too? Just say, 'And Thy servant Rodion.' Nothing more."

"I'll pray for you always," she declared fervently. Her smile returned as she hugged him tightly once more. Raskolnikov gave her his address and promised he would visit the next day. She ran back up the stairs, her steps lighter than before.

Raskolnikov stepped out into the night. The air was cool and sharp, and the streets were quiet. He made his way to the bridge, pausing at the spot where the woman had jumped into the canal. The memory seemed distant now, like a ghost fading into the mist.

"Enough," he said aloud, his voice firm and resolute. "No more fears, no more illusions. Life is real—it's here and now. My life didn't end with that old woman's. It's only beginning. Let the past bury itself. Now, it's time for reason, for strength, for action. Let's see what I can do—what I'm capable of!" His words rang out like a challenge, echoing into the night. A cold determination settled over him as he turned and walked away, his steps purposeful, his head held high.

Raskolnikov's steps faltered slightly as he walked away from the bridge, his body weak, but his spirit strangely fortified. "I feel so feeble right now," he murmured to himself, "but I know my illness has passed. I could feel it the moment I stepped outside. And Potchinkov's house is only a short distance from here. I really must visit Razumihin. Even if it weren't so close, I would still go. Let him win his bet! It's only fair to give him that satisfaction. Why not?" His voice gained a note of conviction. "Strength—that's the key! Without it, nothing can be achieved. And strength isn't handed to you; it's earned, forged through effort. That's what most people fail to grasp," he added, his tone swelling with a mix of pride and self-assurance.

Each step seemed to reshape him, filling him with a confidence he hadn't known in a long time. It was as if a sudden transformation was taking place within him. He couldn't quite comprehend the cause of this inner revolution. It felt as though, like a drowning man grasping at a lifeline, he had rediscovered a reason to live. "I'm alive," he thought, almost in disbelief. "There is still life for me, after all. My life didn't end with that old woman's death." He knew he might be jumping to conclusions, but he couldn't bring himself to care.

The thought of Polenka's promise flickered across his mind. "I asked her to pray for 'Thy servant Rodion,'" he mused. "Well, that was... just in case." A faint laugh escaped his lips, and he shook his head at his own whimsy, feeling strangely buoyant.

When he arrived at Potchinkov's house, finding Razumihin proved effortless. The new lodger had already become well-known, and the porter pointed Raskolnikov up the stairs without hesitation. As he ascended, the sound of animated voices and bursts of laughter grew louder. The door was wide open, spilling light and noise into the stairwell. Inside, Razumihin's room was lively with the chatter of at least fifteen people, filling the space with a chaotic energy.

Raskolnikov paused in the entryway. Behind a modest screen, two of the landlady's servants bustled about, tending to samovars and an array of dishes brought up from the kitchen. He sent word to Razumihin, who came rushing out the moment he heard. His face lit up with joy, but it was clear from his flushed cheeks and slightly unsteady movements that he had indulged in more than a little drink. Razumihin had always been one to hold his liquor well, but tonight, even he was showing the effects.

"Rodya! You're here!" Razumihin exclaimed, his delight genuine and unrestrained.

Raskolnikov cut him off before he could say more. "I only came to tell you that you've won your bet," he said quickly. "And to remind you that no one knows what might happen to them. That's all. I'm too weak to stay. I'll collapse if I try to go in. So, good evening, and goodbye. Come see me tomorrow."

Razumihin frowned. "If you're that weak, I'm walking you home," he declared.

"And what about your guests?" Raskolnikov asked, glancing toward the open door. "Who was that curly-haired fellow who just peeked out?"

"Him?" Razumihin waved dismissively. "Probably some friend of my uncle's, or maybe he just wandered in uninvited. Doesn't matter. My uncle's more than capable of keeping them entertained. Honestly, I needed a break. You've saved me! I was seconds away from knocking someone out—they were spouting such nonsense, you wouldn't believe it."

Raskolnikov chuckled faintly. "Why not? We're all guilty of talking nonsense sometimes."

"True," Razumihin admitted, "but at least we learn from it, or we should. Wait here. I'll grab Zossimov."

Zossimov greeted Raskolnikov with a mixture of professional curiosity and relief. He examined him briefly, his face softening. "You need rest, immediately," he said firmly. "And I have a powder for you—it's already prepared. Will you take it?"

"Two, if you like," Raskolnikov replied dryly.

After taking the powder, Raskolnikov allowed Razumihin to lead him out. As they walked through the night, Razumihin couldn't hold back. "You'll never guess what Zossimov whispered to me," he began, clearly eager to share. "He wanted me to get you talking on the way home and then report back to him. He's convinced you're—wait for it—mad! Can you believe that?"

Raskolnikov's brow furrowed. "Did Zametov tell him about our conversation earlier?" he asked.

"Of course he did," Razumihin replied. "Zossimov thinks that chat of yours is all the proof he needs. But don't let it get to you, brother. You've got twice his brains, at least. Still, I have to admit, the idea of him diagnosing you based on a single conversation—it's almost funny."

Raskolnikov said nothing, his expression unreadable, as they continued down the quiet, moonlit street.

"Yes, and Zametov made the right move telling me about it," Razumihin continued, his words slurring slightly under the influence of drink. "Now I finally get what's going on, and so does he. But listen, Rodya, the truth is… well, I've had a bit to drink, you see… but never mind that. The thing is, this idea—do you understand me?—this ridiculous idea, was just beginning to form in their minds. No one dared say it outright, though. It was too absurd, especially now that the painter's been arrested. That whole theory has burst like a soap bubble. But oh, how foolish they are! I gave Zametov a bit of a thrashing over it—just between us, brother, keep that to yourself. He's a sensitive one, that Zametov, and I gave it to him at Luise Ivanovna's. But today, things have cleared up. Ilya Petrovitch—he's the one behind all this! Took advantage of you fainting at the station, but you know what? I think he's embarrassed about it now."

Raskolnikov, though exhausted, listened intently. Razumihin's loosened tongue was revealing more than usual.

"I fainted because of the heat, the smell of paint," Raskolnikov interjected weakly.

"Oh, you don't need to explain that!" Razumihin waved dismissively. "It wasn't just the paint—it's that fever you've had brewing for weeks. Zossimov said so himself! But you should've seen Zametov earlier—he's absolutely crushed. He actually said, 'I'm not worth his little finger.' By 'his,' he meant you. He has these bouts of decency, you know. And today, the way you toyed with him at the

Palais de Cristal—brilliant! At first, you terrified him; he nearly had a fit. You almost convinced him of all that dreadful nonsense again, only to throw it back in his face like, 'There you go, what now?' Perfect! He's annihilated, completely deflated. Oh, how I wish I'd been there to see it! And Porfiry—he wants to meet you."

"Porfiry?" Raskolnikov murmured, his curiosity piqued. "But why do they think I'm mad?"

"Oh, they don't really think that. It's just Zossimov—he's a fanatic about mental illnesses. I may have said too much, brother. But you know what tipped him off? Your focus on… well, that topic. It got under his skin because of all the circumstances. Don't pay him any mind."

They fell silent for a moment, the street quiet save for the occasional distant sound of life in the city.

"Razumihin," Raskolnikov began, his voice heavy. "I was just at a deathbed—a clerk's. Gave away all my money. And… someone kissed me, someone who'd still kiss me even if… even if I'd done something unspeakable. And I saw another person there, too—a woman with a flame-colored feather. But I'm talking nonsense. I feel so weak. Help me; we're almost at the stairs."

"What's wrong? Are you all right?" Razumihin asked, alarmed.

"I'm dizzy, but it's more than that," Raskolnikov confessed. "I feel so sad, so overwhelmed, like… like a woman. Look! Do you see it?"

"See what?"

"That light! In my room, do you see it through the crack?"

They had reached the base of the staircase, and indeed, a faint light was visible from Raskolnikov's garret.

"Strange. Maybe it's Nastasya," Razumihin suggested.

"She'd never be there this late. She's long since gone to bed. No matter. Goodbye, Razumihin."

"What do you mean, goodbye? I'm coming with you."

"I know you're coming. But let me shake your hand and say goodbye here, at this spot."

"Rodya, what's going on?"

"Nothing. Let's go. You'll be my witness."

As they climbed the stairs, Razumihin couldn't help but feel uneasy. "Could Zossimov be right after all?" he muttered to himself. "Maybe I upset him with all my chatter."

At the top of the stairs, muffled voices could be heard coming from Raskolnikov's room.

"What's this?" Razumihin exclaimed.

Raskolnikov pushed the door open and froze in the doorway. Sitting on the sofa, waiting for him, were his mother and sister.

For a moment, he stood paralyzed. Though he'd been told they were on their way and would arrive soon, he had somehow managed to forget. They had been there for over an hour, questioning Nastasya, who had relayed everything she knew, including his mysterious disappearance that day. Pulcheria Alexandrovna and Dounia were frantic with worry, imagining the worst.

When they saw him, their cries of joy and relief filled the room. They rushed to him, embracing him, kissing him, laughing and crying all at once. But Raskolnikov didn't respond. A wave of emotion, too intense to bear, crashed over him. His body swayed; his knees buckled. Before anyone could catch him, he collapsed onto the floor in a dead faint.

Panic erupted. Razumihin darted forward, scooping Raskolnikov up with ease and placing him on the sofa. "It's nothing!" he assured the terrified women. "Just a faint, that's all. The doctor said earlier he's much better. He'll be fine!" He grabbed Dounia's arm, nearly pulling it out of its socket, and urged her to see for herself. "Look! He's already coming around."

Pulcheria Alexandrovna and Dounia clung to Razumihin with tearful gratitude. In that moment, they regarded him as nothing less than a savior. Nastasya had already sung his praises, recounting how this "very capable young man" had been instrumental in caring for their beloved Rodya during his illness. Pulcheria Alexandrovna later confided to Dounia that she couldn't imagine what they would have done without him.

Part 3

Chapter 1

Raskolnikov pushed himself up from the floor and sank back onto the sofa. He gestured weakly for Razumihin to stop his effusive attempts to comfort his mother and sister. Then, with a trembling hand, he took Pulcheria Alexandrovna's and Dounia's hands in his own. For a long, silent moment, he studied their faces. His expression, fraught with overwhelming emotion, seemed to grip his mother with dread. It was a look of almost unbearable anguish, coupled with a steely, unyielding resolve that bordered on madness. Pulcheria Alexandrovna's tears began to flow.

Dounia, pale and clearly shaken, felt her brother's hand tremble in hers. His grasp was weak but desperate, as though clinging to something slipping away.

"Go home... with him," Raskolnikov finally said, his voice low and uneven as he gestured toward Razumihin. "Goodbye till tomorrow. Tomorrow... everything. When did you arrive?"

"This evening, Rodya," Pulcheria Alexandrovna replied softly. "The train was dreadfully late. But, Rodya, nothing on earth will make me leave you now. I'll stay here tonight, right by your side."

"Don't torture me!" Raskolnikov snapped, irritation flashing across his face as he waved her words away.

"I'll stay with him," Razumihin interjected with fervor, stepping forward. "I won't leave him for a single moment. Forget my visitors! Let them squabble and drink without me. My uncle can handle them."

"How... how can I ever thank you!" Pulcheria Alexandrovna exclaimed, pressing Razumihin's hands in gratitude. But Raskolnikov cut her off sharply.

"No! I won't have it!" he barked, his tone raw and agitated. "Don't bother me with this. Enough! Leave me alone. I can't... I can't bear it!"

"Mama, let's step out for a moment," Dounia urged, her voice low and anxious. "We're only upsetting him more."

"How can I leave him?" Pulcheria Alexandrovna cried through her tears. "After three years—how can I not look at him?"

"Stay," Raskolnikov murmured suddenly, halting their movements as they tried to retreat. His tone had softened slightly, but his words came slowly, as though weighed down by conflicting thoughts. "You keep interrupting me... My ideas get muddled." He paused and frowned deeply. "Have you seen Luzhin?"

"No, Rodya," Pulcheria Alexandrovna answered hesitantly, "but he already knows we've arrived. We heard he was kind enough to visit you today."

"Yes... so kind," Raskolnikov replied with a bitter twist to his lips. He shifted his gaze to Dounia. "I promised Luzhin I'd throw him down the stairs and told him to go to hell."

"Rodya! What are you saying?" Pulcheria Alexandrovna gasped, her voice trembling. "You can't mean that..."

She faltered, her words trailing off as she exchanged a concerned glance with Dounia. Dounia, however, kept her eyes fixed on her brother. Her expression was calm but deeply intent, as though trying to read the storm brewing behind his weary gaze. Both women had already heard bits of the confrontation from Nastasya, though her fragmented account left them full of anxious questions.

"Dounia," Raskolnikov continued with visible strain, "I don't want this marriage. Tomorrow, at the first chance you get, you must refuse Luzhin. Make it final, so we never have to hear his name again."

"Good heavens!" Pulcheria Alexandrovna exclaimed, clutching her chest as if the words had struck her physically.

"Brother, please consider what you're saying!" Dounia burst out, her voice sharp but quickly tempered by restraint. "You're not well. You're exhausted. Maybe this isn't the time to discuss such things," she added gently.

"You think I'm delirious? I'm not," Raskolnikov retorted with a grim determination. "You're marrying Luzhin because of me. But I won't let you make that sacrifice. Tomorrow, you will write a letter refusing him. Let me read it in the morning, and that will be the end of it."

"That's not something I can do!" Dounia replied, her voice tinged with both offense and defiance. "What gives you the right—"

"Dounia, you're too quick to anger," Raskolnikov interrupted. His voice was firmer now, though his exhaustion was evident in every word. "Wait until tomorrow. You'll understand then."

"Can't we talk about this later?" Pulcheria Alexandrovna pleaded, her voice cracking under the strain. "Come, let's leave him to rest. We're only upsetting him more."

Her words hung in the air as Dounia hesitated, torn between her loyalty to her brother and her rising frustration with his demands.

Razumihin, clearly tipsy but fiercely determined, exclaimed, "He's raving—how else could he dare say all that? By tomorrow, all this nonsense will be over. Today, though, he really did drive Luzhin away, that's true. Luzhin got all puffed up, trying to show off his knowledge, but left here looking thoroughly humiliated."

"Then it's true?" Pulcheria Alexandrovna cried, her voice trembling with disbelief.

"Goodbye until tomorrow, brother," Dounia said softly, her tone full of compassion. She turned to her mother, taking her hand. "Let's go, Mama... Goodbye, Rodya."

"Wait," Raskolnikov called after them, his voice strained with the effort of forcing out the words. "Do you hear me, sister? I'm not raving. This marriage—this marriage is nothing but disgrace. If I am a scoundrel, fine, but you won't be one, too. One scoundrel is enough. If you go through with this, then you're no sister of mine. It's me or Luzhin. Now go."

Razumihin, both alarmed and indignant, shouted, "You're out of your mind! You tyrant!" But Raskolnikov didn't respond, nor did it seem he could. He collapsed onto the sofa and turned his face to the wall, utterly spent.

Avdotya Romanovna cast a sharp glance at Razumihin, her dark eyes flashing with something between curiosity and disapproval. The intensity of her gaze startled him so much that he flinched slightly. Pulcheria Alexandrovna, meanwhile, stood frozen, overwhelmed by the scene unfolding before her.

"I can't leave him like this," she whispered desperately to Razumihin. "I'll stay somewhere close by. Please, just take Dounia home."

"You'll ruin everything if you stay," Razumihin replied in a low voice, his frustration barely contained. "At least step out onto the stairs for now. Nastasya, bring a light!"

On the landing, Razumihin continued in an urgent whisper, "He was nearly ready to attack the doctor and me earlier today! Even the doctor gave up and left to avoid aggravating him further. I stayed downstairs to keep an eye on him, but he dressed himself and slipped out anyway. If you upset him again tonight, there's no telling what he might do—or where he might go."

"What are you saying?" Pulcheria Alexandrovna gasped, her voice rising with panic.

"And Dounia can't possibly stay in those lodgings without you," Razumihin continued. "Think about where you're staying! That wretch Luzhin couldn't have found a worse place for you. But forgive me—I've had a little too much to drink, and that's why I'm being so blunt. Please don't take it the wrong way."

"But I'll speak to the landlady here," Pulcheria Alexandrovna insisted. "I'll beg her to let Dounia and me stay somewhere in this building. I can't just leave him!"

Razumihin, now in a feverish state of excitement, seized both women's hands in his enormous grip as he pleaded with them. He spoke with a wild, almost manic clarity, squeezing their hands with such force that they occasionally had to pull away. Oblivious to his lack of decorum, he stared directly at Dounia, his eyes alight with an intensity that was both unsettling and captivating. Pulcheria Alexandrovna was too consumed by worry for her son to notice or care about these eccentricities, but Dounia, though equally concerned, found herself wondering whether this strange young man could truly be trusted.

"You can't go to the landlady!" Razumihin cried. "That's absurd! If you stay here, you'll only make things worse for him. He'll be beside himself, and who knows what might happen! Listen, here's what we'll do: Nastasya will stay with him tonight. I'll take you both home myself. You can't be walking the streets alone at this hour—this is Petersburg! Then I'll come straight back here, and in fifteen minutes, I swear, I'll bring you news about him—whether he's asleep or not, how he's doing, everything."

He paused, catching his breath but still gripping their hands tightly. "Then I'll run home and fetch Zossimov—the doctor, you know. He's not drunk, I promise. I'll drag him back here to check on Rodya, and then to you, so you'll get a proper report from him. If something's wrong, I'll bring you back here myself. If everything's fine, you can go to bed knowing he's in good hands. I'll stay here in the hallway all night to keep an eye on him. And Zossimov can sleep at the landlady's so he'll be nearby. Now, tell me: would you rather stay here and make things worse, or trust me and let the doctor handle it?"

Pulcheria Alexandrovna hesitated, glancing at Dounia for reassurance. Razumihin, his fervor undiminished, added, "The landlady's out of the question, anyway. She's—well, she's impossible. She'd be jealous of Avdotya Romanovna, for heaven's sake! Jealous! Of you, too, probably. She's utterly ridiculous, but that's beside the point. The important thing is, you can't stay here. So, do you trust me or not?"

Pulcheria Alexandrovna and Dounia exchanged a look, their shared concern evident. Finally, Pulcheria Alexandrovna sighed deeply and nodded, though her worry was far from alleviated.

"Let's go, Mother," said Avdotya Romanovna with quiet firmness. "He will do exactly what he has promised, I'm sure of it. He's already done so much to help Rodya. And if the doctor stays the night here, what could be better?"

"You understand me, you wonderful angel!" Razumihin exclaimed, his voice overflowing with gratitude and excitement. "Let's go! Nastasya, hurry upstairs and stay with him. Keep a light on. I'll be back in fifteen minutes."

Though Pulcheria Alexandrovna was still uneasy, she offered no further objections. Razumihin, brimming with energy, took an arm from each lady and began to guide them down the stairs. Yet as he spoke with increasing animation, his fervent state only heightened Pulcheria Alexandrovna's lingering doubts. She couldn't help but question whether he, even with all his good intentions, was capable of fulfilling his promises. His current condition was troubling to her.

"Ah, I can see what you're thinking!" Razumihin suddenly interrupted her thoughts as if reading her mind. "You're worried I'm not in the right state for this. Well, you're mistaken!" His voice rose with a blend of pride and exasperation as they walked briskly along the pavement. His long strides made it difficult for the two women to keep up with him, though he didn't seem to notice. "Yes, I've had some wine, but that's not why I'm like this! No, it's seeing you two that's gone to my head! Don't mind me, though! Don't take offense— I'm talking nonsense, I know. I'm not worthy of either of you. No, not even close. But as soon as I see you both safely home, I'll pour a couple of buckets of water over my head, right here in the street if I must, and that will set me straight."

He paused for a moment, then continued, almost breathless, "If only you could understand how deeply I care for both of you! Don't laugh at me, and don't be angry. Be angry with anyone else, but not with me! I'm Rodya's friend, and because of that, I want to be your friend, too. It feels like fate—like I've been waiting for this moment for so long. I can't explain it! Last year, I had a strange feeling, like a premonition, but now I see it wasn't that at all. You're like a miracle, falling straight out of heaven. I won't sleep a wink tonight, I'm sure of it."

Razumihin's voice softened momentarily, but his words still spilled out in a rush. "Zossimov was worried earlier—he even said Rodya might lose his mind if he's not careful. That's why we can't risk upsetting him."

"What did you just say?" Pulcheria Alexandrovna asked sharply, her tone full of alarm.

"Did the doctor really say that?" Dounia echoed, her concern evident.

"Yes, but don't let it trouble you!" Razumihin answered quickly, attempting to reassure them. "It's not as bad as it sounds, I promise. Zossimov gave him some medicine—a powder of some kind. And your arrival here... well, it's shaken him, but not in a bad way. In fact, it's for the best that we left when we did. In just an hour, Zossimov will come to you and explain everything himself. He's not the sort to drink himself silly. And I'll be back as well—completely sober! I only had too much because those fools at the gathering dragged me into an argument. I swore I wouldn't argue anymore, but they provoked me! You wouldn't believe the ridiculous things they say. It nearly came to blows! I had to leave my uncle there to deal with it all."

Pulcheria Alexandrovna opened her mouth to speak, but Razumihin barreled on, his fervor only increasing. "Do you think I'm angry because of their nonsense? Not at all! I actually enjoy when people talk nonsense—it's one of humanity's greatest privileges! We make mistakes, we stumble into errors, but through those errors, we uncover the truth. That's what it means to be human! And even our mistakes should be our own. To make a mistake in your own way is infinitely better than being right in someone else's way. That's what makes life worth living!"

Razumihin's voice had risen to a near-shout, and in his passion, he clasped the hands of both women tightly, his grip almost painful. Pulcheria Alexandrovna winced, but her maternal concern for her son kept her from pulling away. Dounia, though composed, glanced at him with a mix of astonishment and unease.

"Please, you're hurting me," Dounia finally said, her calm voice cutting through his tirade.

Razumihin immediately let go of her hand and dropped to his knees on the pavement, his face a picture of remorse and admiration. "Forgive me! I'm a fool—a drunken fool! But I can't help it. Let me pay my respects, at least! You deserve so much more than this."

"Get up!" Dounia said, laughing despite herself. "What are you doing?"

Pulcheria Alexandrovna, meanwhile, was horrified. "Please, Mr. Razumihin, this is too much! Get up at once!"

Razumihin stood, brushing himself off but still brimming with energy. "You're right, both of you. I am a fool, but I swear I'll make this right. We're almost there now—here are your lodgings. And may I just say, it's outrageous that Luzhin put you here! That man is unfit to breathe the same air as you."

"Mr. Razumihin, you're forgetting yourself," Pulcheria Alexandrovna said, trying to restore some semblance of order.

"You're absolutely right again, madam, and I apologize," Razumihin replied earnestly. "But I'll say one last thing before I go: Luzhin is a scoundrel, and Rodya was right to send him packing. Now lock yourselves in and don't open the door for anyone but me or

Zossimov. I'll be back in a quarter of an hour with news, and half an hour after that, I'll bring the doctor himself. Good night!"

With that, he turned and bounded away, leaving the two women standing in stunned silence.

"Heavens, Dounia, what is going to happen to us now?" Pulcheria Alexandrovna asked, her voice filled with worry and her eyes darting anxiously toward her daughter. The fear and confusion on her face made her look even more fragile.

"Please don't torment yourself, mother," Dounia replied gently, removing her hat and cape with a calm grace that belied the turmoil of the evening. "We are not alone in this. God has sent us a friend in Mr. Razumihin, though he may have come straight from a lively drinking party. I truly believe we can rely on him. Look at all he's done for Rodya already."

Pulcheria Alexandrovna clasped her hands together, her lips trembling as her doubts bubbled to the surface. "Ah, Dounia, but what if he doesn't come back as he promised? What if something happens? And how could I bear to leave Rodya there alone like that? Oh, my heart breaks just thinking about it! And then... how different everything was from what I had imagined. I thought our reunion would be joyful, filled with warmth, but he—he seemed so sullen, almost resentful of our presence."

Tears welled up in her eyes, her voice breaking as she spoke.

"No, mother," Dounia said firmly, taking her mother's trembling hands in her own. "You didn't see clearly—you were crying too much to notice. It's not that he's unhappy to see us. He's gravely ill, that's all. It's his illness making him this way. You mustn't think the worst."

"Ah, this wretched illness!" Pulcheria Alexandrovna cried despairingly, clutching at her chest as though to steady her racing heart. "What will become of him? Of us? And how sharp he was with you, Dounia! The way he spoke to you—so cold, so unkind! It frightened me."

She glanced timidly at her daughter, trying to gauge her thoughts, searching for reassurance. But when she noticed the calm resolve in Dounia's expression, her own panic subsided slightly. Dounia's quiet defense of her brother was a balm to her mother's heart; it meant she had already forgiven him, and that alone gave Pulcheria Alexandrovna a small measure of hope.

"I am certain he'll see things differently in the morning," she added tentatively, almost pleading, as if urging her daughter to confirm it.

But Avdotya Romanovna was unmoved, her tone steady and definitive. "No, mother. He will hold the same view tomorrow— about that matter. I am sure of it."

Her words brought an uneasy silence between them, as Pulcheria Alexandrovna dared not press the subject further. It was clear from Dounia's demeanor that this was not a topic for discussion, not now. Resigned, Pulcheria Alexandrovna let out a soft sigh and reached out to her daughter. Dounia bent down and kissed her mother gently on the cheek, and in return, Pulcheria Alexandrovna embraced her warmly, holding her close as though to absorb some of her quiet strength.

When they broke apart, Pulcheria Alexandrovna sat down in her chair, her hands nervously clutching the fabric of her dress. Her gaze shifted restlessly to the door as she waited anxiously for Razumihin's return. Every passing moment stretched unbearably long, her mind cycling through a whirlwind of fears.

Meanwhile, Dounia began pacing slowly back and forth across the room, her arms crossed tightly over her chest. Her steps were measured, deliberate, as though each turn of the room gave her a moment to sort through her thoughts. This habit of hers—walking while deep in contemplation—was familiar to Pulcheria Alexandrovna, but it never failed to unnerve her. She always hesitated to interrupt her daughter when she was in such a mood, afraid that even the smallest word might break the delicate thread of her concentration.

Pulcheria Alexandrovna watched Dounia silently, her own emotions swinging between pride in her daughter's composure and an aching maternal worry for what lay ahead.

Razumihin's sudden and impassioned infatuation with Avdotya Romanovna might have seemed absurd to some, especially given his drunken state, but anyone who had seen Avdotya Romanovna in that moment would have found it understandable, even inevitable. As she walked back and forth across the room, her arms folded, her expression thoughtful and touched with melancholy, her striking beauty seemed to radiate even more powerfully. Avdotya Romanovna was not just beautiful; she was commanding, statuesque, and gracefully poised. She moved with a natural elegance that suggested both strength and refinement.

Her resemblance to her brother, Raskolnikov, was unmistakable, but her features were more finely chiseled. Her dark brown hair, lighter than Raskolnikov's, framed a face that combined pride and softness in a way that was uniquely her own. Her large, nearly black eyes carried a proud light, but there was also an unmistakable warmth and kindness in their depths. Her complexion was pale, yet vibrant with a youthful vigor. Her small, delicate mouth was accentuated by a full, slightly projecting lower lip and a prominent chin—features that lent her an air of determination and individuality, though some might see in them a touch of haughtiness.

Her natural demeanor was serious and contemplative, but when she smiled, or better yet, laughed, her face seemed transformed. Her rare moments of lightheartedness revealed a youthful charm that made her beauty even more captivating. It was no wonder that Razumihin, with his open-hearted nature and lack of experience with women of her caliber, was immediately smitten. The sight of her, animated by her love and concern for her brother, combined with the fire of indignation she displayed at Raskolnikov's harsh words, sealed Razumihin's fate.

His drunken ramblings earlier about Praskovya Pavlovna, Raskolnikov's peculiar landlady, being jealous of both Pulcheria

Alexandrovna and Avdotya Romanovna on his account had a grain of truth. Despite her forty-three years, Pulcheria Alexandrovna retained a delicate beauty that hinted at her youth. Time and sorrow had left their marks—her hair was greying and thinning, and faint crow's feet framed her expressive eyes—but her face still bore traces of the charm and vitality she must have radiated as a young woman. Her cheeks, though slightly sunken from worry, retained a graceful contour. Her inner warmth and sincere, loving heart shone through her every expression, a trait that had preserved her attractiveness even as the years took their toll.

Pulcheria Alexandrovna and her daughter shared many similarities, though the mother lacked the distinctive projection of the lower lip that gave Dounia her unique and striking profile. Pulcheria Alexandrovna was emotional but not overly sentimental. Her timidity and inclination to yield were tempered by a core of unshakable principles. There were boundaries she would not cross, no matter the cost, guided as she was by her deeply held convictions.

Exactly twenty minutes after Razumihin had dashed off, two hurried yet subdued knocks sounded at the door. Pulcheria Alexandrovna and Dounia both looked up, hearts leaping with anticipation. When the door opened, there stood Razumihin, still breathless from his errand.

"I won't come in; I haven't time," he announced quickly. "He's sleeping soundly, like a log. Nastasya is with him, and I told her not to leave until I return. Now I'm off to fetch Zossimov. He'll come and give you the full report. Then you must rest—you look absolutely worn out."

Without waiting for a response, he turned and disappeared down the corridor.

"What a devoted and capable young man!" Pulcheria Alexandrovna exclaimed, her relief and gratitude evident.

"A remarkable man," Dounia agreed with uncharacteristic warmth, though her pacing resumed as she tried to sort her thoughts.

Almost an hour passed before they heard footsteps and another knock at the door. Both women waited in hopeful silence. This time, Razumihin had succeeded in bringing Zossimov, the doctor. Though Razumihin's obvious intoxication had initially made Zossimov skeptical, the doctor was reassured when he saw how earnestly the two women awaited his arrival.

Zossimov was a young man, serious and self-assured, and he conducted himself with the dignity of a professional at an important consultation. He greeted them with a polite but reserved demeanor, addressing himself primarily to Pulcheria Alexandrovna, though he could not help but notice Dounia's stunning beauty. He deliberately avoided looking at her too much, focusing instead on his role as a physician. This restraint only seemed to heighten the women's impression of his competence and reliability.

In his concise yet sympathetic report, Zossimov assured them that Raskolnikov's condition was stable. He explained that the illness had both physical and psychological roots—stemming from material hardships as well as emotional strain. While he noted the presence of a "fixed idea" or obsession that bordered on monomania, he emphasized that the family's presence would likely aid in his recovery, provided he was shielded from further shocks or stresses.

By the time Zossimov took his leave, Pulcheria Alexandrovna was visibly comforted. She showered him with gratitude, and Dounia, with her characteristic grace, offered him her hand in thanks. The doctor departed with an air of satisfaction, clearly pleased with his visit and the impression he had made.

Razumihin escorted Zossimov to the door and turned back to the women. "Go to bed now; there's nothing more to worry about for tonight," he said earnestly. "I'll come by first thing in the morning with news."

With that, he left them to their rest, the echo of his hurried footsteps fading into the night.

As they stepped out into the cool night air, Zossimov couldn't help but let out a remark, his voice laced with a mix of appreciation and something almost smug. "That's quite the fetching young woman, your Avdotya Romanovna," he said, practically savoring the words as if they were a delicacy.

Razumihin turned on him like a storm. "Fetching? You dare call her fetching?" he roared, his voice echoing in the empty street. Before Zossimov could react, Razumihin had him by the collar, slamming him against the wall with a force that startled even himself. "Listen here, and listen well," Razumihin bellowed, his face inches from Zossimov's, his hands trembling with barely restrained fury. "If you ever, ever dare to speak of her in that way again... do you understand me? Do you?"

"Let go, you drunken fool!" Zossimov gasped, struggling against Razumihin's iron grip. When Razumihin finally released him, Zossimov staggered back, his surprise quickly giving way to laughter—loud, uncontrollable laughter.

Razumihin stood there, brooding, his brow furrowed deeply. "I'm an idiot," he muttered, almost to himself, his tone dark and reflective. "But you're no better."

Zossimov, wiping tears of laughter from his eyes, regained his composure. "No, my friend, I'm not the same kind of idiot as you," he said, his voice tinged with amusement. "Don't worry, I'm not about to do anything foolish."

They walked in silence for a while, the only sound their footsteps on the quiet street. Razumihin's earlier outburst seemed to weigh heavily on him, and by the time they neared Raskolnikov's lodgings, he spoke again, his tone tinged with concern.

"Look," he began, turning to Zossimov, "you're a good fellow, I know that. But let's not beat around the bush—you've got your flaws. You're a bit of a libertine, aren't you? Indulgent, lazy, always taking the easy way out. You're not the worst of them, but still, you've let yourself go in some ways. It's not just the wine or the comforts; it's the way you let these things take hold of you. You're a doctor, and a decent one, but what happens in a few years when you're too comfortable to get up in the middle of the night for your patients? What happens then?"

Zossimov raised an eyebrow, caught off guard by the sudden lecture. "I'm still here, aren't I?" he countered.

"Yeah, for now," Razumihin shot back. "But mark my words, complacency is a slippery slope. Anyway, none of that is the point right now." He sighed and waved a hand as if brushing the thought away. "You're staying here tonight, in the landlady's flat. Don't argue; I had to bend over backward to arrange it. Meanwhile, I'll crash in the kitchen. It's all settled."

Zossimov's confusion only deepened. "And why, exactly, do I need to stay?"

Razumihin leaned in conspiratorially, his voice dropping to a whisper. "To keep her company."

Zossimov stared at him. "Her? Who?"

"The landlady," Razumihin said dramatically. "She's... well, she's taken a liking to me. It's unbearable. I need you to distract her."

Zossimov laughed so hard he nearly doubled over. "And how do you propose I do that?"

"Talk to her, anything! Recite the integral calculus if you must! She'll hang on your every word as long as you're there. She's bashful to the point of hysteria, but trust me, she's melting like wax."

Zossimov shook his head, incredulous. "And you've promised her... what? Marriage? Eternal devotion?"

"Nothing of the sort!" Razumihin declared indignantly. "She's not the type. She doesn't need promises—just attention. Look, it's not what you think, brother. It's just... she's lonely, and she needs someone to talk to. Anyone, really. It doesn't even matter who."

Zossimov gave him a long, scrutinizing look. "You've really gotten yourself into a mess, haven't you?"

Razumihin threw up his hands. "I don't deny it. But I'm asking for your help. Is that so much? I'll owe you, big time. Just keep her occupied, will you?"

Shaking his head, Zossimov finally relented. "Fine. But only for tonight. And only because I want to see how this ridiculous situation unfolds."

"Thank you, my friend. You won't regret it," Razumihin said, clapping him on the back. Then, as if remembering something important, he added, "Oh, and about Raskolnikov—keep an eye on him tonight, just in case. If he shows any signs of fever or delirium, wake me immediately."

They parted ways at the door, Razumihin offering one last dramatic plea before disappearing into the kitchen. Zossimov shook his head, chuckling softly to himself. "What an absurd night," he muttered as he headed toward the landlady's flat, bracing himself for whatever peculiarities awaited him inside.

Chapter 2

Razumihin woke the next morning feeling heavy, as though the weight of the previous day had seeped into his very bones. It wasn't just the wine—it was everything that had transpired, everything he had said, and everything he had felt. He sat on the edge of his bed, running his hands through his hair, which was still unkempt from sleep. The memories of the day before came back to him with painful clarity, and for the first time in years, he felt a pang of shame that he couldn't shake off.

He recalled how he had behaved, the drunken bravado that had made him loud and foolish, and worse, the way he had criticized Pyotr Petrovitch Luzhin in front of Avdotya Romanovna. What right had he, Razumihin, to interfere in her affairs? What did he even know about Luzhin, their relationship, or the circumstances that had brought them together? Nothing. He had judged and spoken rashly, not out of concern but out of jealousy. It was an ugly realization, and he couldn't deny it.

And then there was the most humiliating memory: his audacious remark about the landlady being jealous of Dounia. That wasn't just clumsy—it was disgraceful. He clenched his fists, furious at himself. He slammed his hand down on the kitchen stove in frustration, sending a loose brick tumbling to the floor.

"What kind of fool am I?" he muttered, pacing back and forth. "Drunk or not, it's no excuse. The truth came out in my drunken state, and that truth shows just how coarse and envious I am. How could someone like me ever even dream—dream—of someone like her?"

He stopped abruptly, staring into space. The very thought of his foolish daydreams, of imagining himself as a worthy match for Avdotya Romanovna, made his face burn with shame. What was he compared to her? A loud, unruly brute, good for nothing but shouting and stumbling about like a common tavern drunkard. He swore under his breath and resolved, at the very least, to carry himself with dignity that day.

With renewed determination, he began to prepare for the morning. He inspected his clothes critically; they were clean but threadbare. He brushed them carefully, even though he felt a perverse urge to wear them as they were, as if to say, "This is who I am—take it or leave it." But he couldn't bring himself to be so careless. His linen was spotless, as always; he prided himself on that. He washed thoroughly, borrowing a bar of soap from Nastasya, and scrubbed his hands and face with more vigor than usual, as if trying to wash away his shame.

When it came time to decide whether to shave, he hesitated. The razors left behind by Praskovya Pavlovna's late husband were sharp enough, and he considered using one. But then he shook his head violently. "No," he said aloud. "If I shave, they'll think I did it just to impress them." He tossed the razor aside. "Let it be. I'll go as I am."

Still, a gnawing unease persisted. He remembered his raucous, pothouse manners and felt disgusted with himself. "What a contrast," he thought bitterly. "Her dignity, her grace—set against my coarse behavior and clumsy words. I'm nothing but a blundering fool."

His self-recrimination was interrupted by Zossimov's arrival. The doctor looked rested but impatient, clearly eager to check on Raskolnikov before attending to his other duties.

"How is he?" Zossimov asked briskly as he entered the room.

"Sleeping like a log," Razumihin replied, gesturing toward the closed door. "I told them not to wake him. He needs the rest."

"Good. Let him sleep," Zossimov said, nodding approvingly. "I'll check on him around eleven. If he's still at home, that is. Who knows? He might wander off again."

Razumihin frowned. "Do you think he's likely to go to them, or will they come here?"

Zossimov shrugged. "They'll probably come here. Family matters to discuss, no doubt."

Razumihin sighed heavily. "In that case, I'll clear out. You're the doctor; you've got more right to be here than I do."

"I'm no family counselor," Zossimov muttered. "I'll check on him, give my opinion, and leave. I've got enough patients as it is without adding family drama to the list."

Before Zossimov could leave, Razumihin hesitated, rubbing the back of his neck awkwardly. "Listen," he began, "there's something I need to tell you. Last night... I said some things. To him, to them. I was drunk and talked a lot of nonsense. Including... well, I mentioned your thoughts about his mental state."

Zossimov raised an eyebrow. "You told them that?"

Razumihin winced. "Yeah. I know—it was stupid. I wasn't thinking. I probably made everything worse."

The doctor sighed, rubbing his temples. "Did you at least clarify that it's just a hypothesis? Something to keep an eye on?"

"I... didn't exactly put it that way."

"Fantastic," Zossimov said dryly. "You may as well have told them he's a certified lunatic. Well done."

Razumihin groaned and buried his face in his hands. "I'll make it right," he vowed. "Somehow, I'll fix this. Just tell me—did you really think he might lose his mind?"

Zossimov gave him a long, measured look. "It's too early to say," he admitted. "But he's under a lot of strain. Let's hope today is calmer than yesterday—for everyone's sake."

With that, Zossimov left, leaving Razumihin alone with his thoughts, his regrets, and a determination to face whatever the day might bring, no matter how humiliating.

"That's nonsense, I tell you—how could I have thought it seriously?" Razumihin exclaimed, throwing his arms up in exasperation. "You yourself were the one who called him a monomaniac when you dragged me over to see him! And yesterday, instead of helping, we just added fuel to the fire—you did, that is— with your story about that painter. What a conversation to have had, especially when he might have been already unhinged on that very topic! If I'd known then about what happened at the police station, and how some fool dared to insult him with this absurd suspicion, I'd never have let that talk happen. These monomaniacs—they latch onto something small, a speck, and blow it up into something monumental, something solid in their minds. It becomes their entire reality."

He paced a few steps, clearly agitated, then spun back toward Zossimov. "I swear, it was Zametov's big mouth that cleared half the mystery for me, but also managed to make things worse in the process. Do you know, I once read about a hypochondriac—some guy in his forties—who slashed the throat of an eight-year-old boy at dinner, all because he couldn't handle the kid's jokes anymore? Think about that for a second. And here we have Rodya, dealing with his poverty, that damned police officer, a raging fever, and now this ludicrous suspicion hanging over him like a noose. Can't you see how all of that could twist him into this state? It's enough to drive anyone to the edge!"

He groaned in frustration, running a hand through his hair. "And then there's Zametov. Sure, he's a decent enough guy in some ways, but he talks too much. He's a walking disaster when it comes to keeping things private. He shouldn't have let half of what he did slip out last night."

Zossimov gave him a dry look. "Who did he talk to? Just you and me, right?"

"And Porfiry."

"So what?"

"It matters! It's like giving a match to a pyromaniac. And for God's sake, if you have any sway with Rodya's family—his mother, his sister—tell them to be careful with him today. He's fragile right now, even if he doesn't look it."

Razumihin sighed reluctantly. "They'll manage," he said, though his tone lacked confidence.

Zossimov raised an eyebrow. "What's his deal with this Luzhin fellow? The man's got money, and from what I can tell, she doesn't seem to hate him. They don't exactly have a pile of cash themselves, do they?"

"What business is it of yours?" Razumihin snapped. "Do I look like their accountant? Go ask them yourself if you're so curious."

Zossimov chuckled, shaking his head. "You're a bit of an ass when you're hungover. Well, goodbye for now. And thank your landlady for the night's stay. She didn't even bother to answer my 'good morning.' Locked herself in and acted like I was the plague. And here I thought I might at least get some tea."

By the time Razumihin arrived at Bakaleyev's house at nine sharp, Pulcheria Alexandrovna and Dounia had been anxiously awaiting him for hours, having risen at the crack of dawn. As soon as he entered, Pulcheria Alexandrovna rushed to greet him, seizing his hands in gratitude, nearly pulling him into an embrace. Razumihin, unused to such displays, flushed deeply and stammered out a greeting, avoiding eye contact with Dounia, whose composed and unexpectedly warm expression caught him off guard. He had prepared himself for disdain or coldness, but her gratitude and respect unnerved him even more than outright hostility would have.

Pulcheria Alexandrovna, relieved by the news that Raskolnikov was still resting, quickly ushered Razumihin inside. "You must stay for breakfast! We waited for you. We have so much to discuss," she said, her words tumbling out in her eagerness.

Dounia rang the bell for tea, though the service left much to be desired. The waiter brought the tea in a state of disarray that embarrassed the ladies, and Razumihin, though tempted to rant about the conditions, held back, aware of Luzhin's connection to their lodgings. Instead, he launched into a detailed account of Raskolnikov's recent troubles, filling in as much as he could without delving into sensitive or alarming details.

For three-quarters of an hour, he spoke earnestly, only pausing to field a flurry of questions from Pulcheria Alexandrovna, who was desperate for every scrap of information. He tactfully omitted the more unsavory incidents, like the confrontation at the police station, but gave a clear picture of Raskolnikov's declining health and financial struggles.

When he finally paused, thinking he'd covered everything, Pulcheria Alexandrovna leaned forward, her eyes wide with concern. "Dmitri Prokofitch," she said earnestly, "tell me, what do you think of his state of mind? His hopes, his fears? Is he always so... irritable? What does he dream of? What drives him now?"

Razumihin was momentarily taken aback by the breadth of her question. "Good heavens, mother," Dounia interjected gently, "he can't possibly answer all of that at once."

Pulcheria Alexandrovna clasped her hands, her face a mix of desperation and maternal love. "I just didn't expect him to be like this," she murmured. "Not like this at all."

Razumihin, moved by her distress, leaned forward and tried his best to reassure her, though even he wasn't entirely sure of what to say.

"Naturally," Razumihin began thoughtfully, his voice steady but marked with a tinge of hesitation. "I have no mother myself, but I do have an uncle who visits me once a year. Almost every time he comes, he struggles to recognize me, even by appearance, though he's a clever man. A three-year separation, like yours from Rodion, means a great deal—it changes everything. What can I tell you about him? I've known him for a year and a half. Rodion is... complicated. He is morose, gloomy, and proud, with a haughtiness that can push people away. Lately—and maybe for longer than I've known—he's been suspicious, even fanciful. But he has a noble nature, and his heart is kind.

"At the same time," Razumihin continued, a trace of sorrow in his tone, "he's not the type to show his feelings. He would rather commit a cruel act than open his heart freely. And sometimes... well, sometimes he isn't morbid at all. Instead, he can become cold, detached, even inhumanly callous. It's like watching him switch between two entirely different characters. He's also incredibly reserved at times. He claims he's overwhelmed with work and that everything distracts him, yet I've seen him spend whole days lying in bed, doing absolutely nothing. He doesn't mock others—not because he lacks wit, but because he thinks it beneath him, a waste of time. He often seems indifferent to what interests other people."

Razumihin paused for a moment, his brows knitting together in thought. "And yet, he thinks highly of himself—maybe too highly. Then again, perhaps he's right to, in some ways. He is brilliant, after all. Still, I can't help but think your arrival will do him good, more good than anything else could."

"God grant it may," Pulcheria Alexandrovna replied, her voice trembling with a mixture of hope and unease. Razumihin's candid description of her son, though honest, left her distressed.

Meanwhile, Razumihin dared to glance more boldly at Avdotya Romanovna, whose quiet dignity both unnerved and captivated him. Her presence was formidable: she had risen from her seat and was pacing the small room, her arms folded tightly across her chest and her lips pressed in a thoughtful line. Her movements carried an elegance that seemed at odds with the poverty suggested by her surroundings. Razumihin noticed the thin, dark material of her dress and the simple, transparent scarf draped around her neck. The signs of hardship were evident in every detail of their belongings, but instead of feeling pity, he was struck with a profound respect that only deepened his self-consciousness.

"You've spoken about my brother with remarkable impartiality," Dounia said at last, pausing in her pacing to face Razumihin. Her expression was calm but inquisitive. "I admit, I was afraid you might be too blindly loyal to him to see his flaws clearly. But I think you're right—he does need someone to care for him, someone who can reach him."

Razumihin hesitated, his heart thudding loudly in his chest. "I didn't say that," he murmured, his words stumbling. "But perhaps... you might be right."

"And why not?" she pressed, her tone suddenly sharp with curiosity. "What stops him from being capable of love?"

Razumihin, feeling cornered by the question, blurted out without thinking, "You're so much like him, Avdotya Romanovna! In almost every way!"

He froze, realizing too late how his words sounded, especially given his earlier criticisms of Rodion. His face flushed a deep red, and he struggled to form an apology. Dounia, however, burst into a soft laugh, her eyes sparkling with genuine amusement at his flustered state.

Pulcheria Alexandrovna, though slightly offended on her son's behalf, seemed more concerned about other matters. "You may both be mistaken about Rodya," she interjected. "I'm not saying that his recent behavior hasn't been troubling, but you must understand—he has always been so... unpredictable. Even as a boy, I could never be sure what he might do next."

She hesitated, as if wrestling with an unpleasant memory, before continuing. "Do you remember, Dounia, how he nearly married that girl—what was her name? His landlady's daughter?"

Dounia nodded, her expression growing serious. "Yes, I remember."

Razumihin looked surprised. "I'd heard a little about it," he admitted cautiously. "But nothing in detail. What happened?"

Pulcheria Alexandrovna sighed deeply. "She was no great beauty, and her health was so poor. But she must have had some admirable qualities—there's no other explanation for why Rodya would have cared for her. Still, it was such a shock! The idea of him marrying her, despite our poverty, my illness, my tears—it was unbearable! And yet, I believe he would have gone through with it if she hadn't passed away."

Razumihin frowned, deeply puzzled. "It's hard to understand, but perhaps he saw something in her that others couldn't. Rodya is like that."

Pulcheria Alexandrovna nodded but said no more. Instead, she turned the conversation toward the events of the previous day, particularly the altercation with Luzhin. Though hesitant to speak directly, she probed Razumihin for his opinion, clearly uneasy about the entire situation.

Razumihin recounted the incident again, this time with more careful consideration of his words. While he criticized Raskolnikov for being deliberately provocative, he also subtly hinted at his belief that Pyotr Petrovitch had been equally at fault.

"So, this is your opinion of Pyotr Petrovitch?" Pulcheria Alexandrovna finally asked, her voice tinged with disappointment.

Razumihin hesitated, glancing at Dounia before answering. "I think... there's more to consider before passing judgment on him," he said carefully. But inwardly, he couldn't help but wonder how someone like Dounia could ever tolerate such a man, let alone marry him.

Razumihin listened intently as Pulcheria Alexandrovna poured out her anxieties, his face reflecting a deep seriousness. He let her finish before speaking, his voice steady yet warm. "Madam, I can have no opinion other than respect for the man your daughter has chosen to marry. My opinions from yesterday were those of a drunken fool, and for that, I deeply apologize. I let my irritation and madness at the moment cloud my judgment, and I said things that were not only disrespectful but entirely unjustified."

He paused, visibly uncomfortable, and glanced briefly at Dounia, who stood silent but composed, her face unreadable. The silence that followed Razumihin's confession seemed to weigh heavily on the room. Pulcheria Alexandrovna fidgeted, looking from her daughter to Razumihin with an expression torn between relief and lingering concern.

Finally, Pulcheria Alexandrovna spoke, her words coming out in a rush as though she feared losing the chance to say them. "Dmitri Prokofitch, I must confess there is something in this entire situation that troubles me greatly. I don't know what to do, and I hoped you might help me decide."

"Of course, madam," Razumihin said, his tone softening. "Please, tell me what's on your mind."

Pulcheria Alexandrovna hesitated, glancing at her daughter, who gave a slight nod of encouragement. Taking a deep breath, she began again, this time with more conviction. "This morning, we received a note from Pyotr Petrovitch. It came in response to the letter we sent him about our arrival. He promised to meet us at the station but instead sent a servant with directions to these lodgings. And now this!" She pulled out the letter with a trembling hand and passed it to Razumihin. "Please, read it. There's something in it that... deeply disturbs me."

Razumihin unfolded the letter and read it carefully. As his eyes scanned the page, his expression grew darker. By the time he finished, his brow was furrowed, and he let out a heavy sigh.

"Well?" Pulcheria Alexandrovna prompted anxiously, her voice almost a whisper. "What do you make of it? What should we do?"

Razumihin was silent for a moment, thinking deeply. Finally, he spoke with measured calm. "It's clear that Pyotr Petrovitch wants to dictate the terms of this meeting. His request to exclude Rodion Romanovitch from the conversation is, frankly, presumptuous. But beyond that, the tone of this letter is troubling. He's already making accusations and assumptions without understanding the full context. That suggests a lack of trust, and trust is the foundation of any relationship."

Pulcheria Alexandrovna wrung her hands in distress. "But how can I prevent Rodya from coming if he insists? He was so adamant yesterday that we should reject Pyotr Petrovitch entirely. If he knows about this meeting, he will certainly come!"

"You must decide based on Avdotya Romanovna's wishes," Razumihin replied, glancing at Dounia, who had remained silent throughout the exchange.

Dounia, standing tall and composed, finally spoke. Her voice was calm but carried an unmistakable resolve. "Mother, I've already told you my decision. Rodya must come. He has the right to be present, regardless of Pyotr Petrovitch's wishes. If Pyotr Petrovitch cannot handle such a meeting, then perhaps that tells us everything we need to know about him."

"But, Dounia, my dear!" Pulcheria Alexandrovna cried, clearly torn. "What if this causes an irreparable conflict? What if things escalate?"

"Better to have clarity now than regret later," Dounia replied firmly. "If Pyotr Petrovitch truly respects me, he will respect my family as well."

Razumihin felt a swell of admiration for Dounia's strength and conviction. "She's right, madam," he said, his tone resolute. "The truth will come out, one way or another. Let's not avoid it. Besides, it's nearly time. We should go to Rodion Romanovitch ourselves. That way, we'll know how to proceed."

Pulcheria Alexandrovna nodded reluctantly, still visibly anxious. "Yes, yes, you're right. We mustn't delay any longer. But oh, how my heart aches at the thought of facing him after everything that's happened. I barely slept last night!"

Razumihin gave her an encouraging smile. "Don't worry, madam. Rodya may be irritable, but he loves you deeply. He'll understand, in time."

As the three of them prepared to leave, Razumihin couldn't help but notice the shabbiness of the ladies' attire, the frayed edges of Dounia's gloves, and the well-worn look of their cloaks. Yet, despite their evident poverty, both women carried themselves with a dignity that was almost regal. Dounia, in particular, struck him as a figure of grace and strength, and he felt an almost overwhelming pride at the thought of accompanying her.

Stepping out into the street, Pulcheria Alexandrovna took a deep breath. "I never thought I'd feel fear at the thought of seeing my own son," she murmured, her voice filled with sorrow.

"Have faith in him, mother," Dounia said, taking her arm gently. "He's still the Rodya we love, no matter what has happened."

Razumihin walked beside them, silent but determined. Whatever lay ahead, he resolved to stand by them, come what may.

"Do you know, Dounia, this morning I dozed off for a bit and had a dream about Marfa Petrovna. She was dressed all in white. She came up to me, took my hand, and shook her head at me—but so sternly, as if she were scolding me. What do you think? Is that a good sign? Oh, my goodness! Dmitri Prokofitch, you probably don't know— Marfa Petrovna has passed away!"

"No, I didn't know. Who is Marfa Petrovna?"

"She died very suddenly. And you won't believe what happened..."

"Later, Mother," Dounia interrupted. "He doesn't even know who Marfa Petrovna is."

"Oh, you don't know? And here I was thinking you already knew everything about us! Forgive me, Dmitri Prokofitch, I've been so scatterbrained these past few days. I truly think of you as a blessing sent to us, so I just assumed you knew all about us. Honestly, I feel like you're family already. I hope you won't be offended by me saying so. Oh, dear, what happened to your hand? Did you hurt it?"

"Yes, I bruised it," Razumihin mumbled, clearly thrilled.

"I tend to speak straight from the heart sometimes, and Dounia always scolds me for it. But, goodness, what a tiny room he lives in! How can anyone call this a proper living space? Do you think he's awake yet? And that landlady of his—does she seriously call this a room? Tell me, since you say he doesn't like showing his feelings, do you think I'll irritate him with my... emotional ways? Please, Dmitri Prokofitch, tell me how I should act around him. I feel so out of sorts."

"Try not to ask him too many questions if he starts to frown. And don't bring up his health too often; it annoys him."

"Oh, Dmitri Prokofitch, being a mother is so hard! But, look, here are the stairs. What a dreadful staircase this is!"

"Mother, you've gone pale. Please don't upset yourself so much," Dounia said softly, putting a comforting arm around her. Then, with a flash of determination in her eyes, she added, "He should be happy to see you, not the other way around. You're worrying for no reason."

"Wait, let me peek in and see if he's awake," Razumihin said.

The women trailed behind Razumihin as he led the way upstairs. When they reached the fourth floor and came to the landlady's door, they noticed it was slightly ajar. From the darkness inside, a pair of sharp black eyes watched them intently. As soon as their gazes met, the door slammed shut with such force that Pulcheria Alexandrovna nearly let out a scream.

Chapter 3

"He is doing well, quite well!" Zossimov announced cheerfully as they entered the room.

He had arrived about ten minutes earlier and was seated in his usual spot on the sofa. Raskolnikov, fully dressed, washed, and combed—a rarity for him of late—was sitting in the opposite corner. The room quickly became crowded as Nastasya followed the visitors inside, staying to eavesdrop.

Compared to the day before, Raskolnikov did appear almost recovered, though he remained pale, withdrawn, and grim. His face bore the look of someone who had endured immense physical or emotional suffering. His eyebrows were furrowed, his lips tightly pressed together, and his eyes had a feverish gleam. He spoke sparingly and reluctantly, as though each word were a chore, and his movements carried a nervous energy.

He seemed like a man nursing a painful injury; a sling or a bandage might have completed the image. When his mother and sister entered, his somber face momentarily brightened, but the fleeting light only deepened the impression of his suffering, replacing apathy with a sharper, more visible anguish. That fleeting brightness faded almost immediately, leaving behind the same strained expression.

Zossimov, keenly observing his patient with the enthusiastic curiosity of a young doctor, noted a lack of joy in Raskolnikov at seeing his family. Instead, there was a grim resolve, as though he were steeling himself to endure the inevitable discomfort of the visit. Almost every comment in the ensuing conversation seemed to strike a nerve, agitating rather than soothing him. And yet, Zossimov couldn't help but admire the self-control Raskolnikov displayed—a stark contrast to the unrestrained frenzy he had shown the day before.

"Yes, I can see I am almost well now," Raskolnikov said as he greeted his mother and sister with a brief but heartfelt kiss. Pulcheria Alexandrovna's face lit up instantly. "And I don't say this as I did yesterday," he added, directing a friendly handshake toward Razumihin.

"I must admit, I'm amazed by his progress today," Zossimov chimed in, clearly pleased with the ladies' presence, which seemed to encourage conversation. "If this continues, in three or four days he'll be as good as new—or at least as he was a month ago, or two... maybe even three. This must have been building for quite some time, wouldn't you say? Perhaps, to some extent, it's your own doing?" he ventured with a cautious smile, wary of provoking his patient.

"That's very possible," Raskolnikov replied coolly.

"I would even go so far as to say," Zossimov pressed on, clearly enjoying his role as an advisor, "that your full recovery depends entirely on you. Now that we can talk openly, let me stress that avoiding the underlying causes of your condition is absolutely critical. If you address those causes, you'll recover fully; if not, the situation will deteriorate. While I can't pinpoint those causes, I imagine you are well aware of them. You're an intelligent man, and I assume you've noticed the patterns yourself. I suspect your troubles began around the time you left university. Having a purpose and staying occupied— something concrete to work toward—would be immensely beneficial."

"Yes, you're absolutely right," Raskolnikov agreed with a faint, unreadable smile. "I'll hurry back to university. Once I'm back, everything will sort itself out."

Zossimov, who had been partially showing off for the ladies with his advice, paused. Something in Raskolnikov's expression—a fleeting look of mocking amusement—gave him pause. The moment passed quickly, but it left Zossimov slightly perplexed.

Pulcheria Alexandrovna, seizing the opportunity, began effusively thanking Zossimov, especially for his visit to their lodgings the previous evening.

"What? You saw them last night?" Raskolnikov interjected, his tone sharp with surprise. "Then you haven't slept at all after your journey."

"Oh, Rodya, it wasn't so late—only until two o'clock. Dounia and I never go to bed before two when we're at home."

"I truly don't know how to thank him either," Raskolnikov said suddenly, his brow darkening as he looked down at the floor. "Setting aside the question of payment—forgive me for bringing it up," he added, addressing Zossimov directly. "I honestly don't understand why you've shown me such extraordinary attention. It puzzles me... and, to be frank, it feels burdensome because I don't know how to make sense of it. I'm telling you this honestly."

"Don't get annoyed," Zossimov said, forcing a light chuckle. "Think of it this way: you're practically my first patient, and we young doctors tend to get attached to our first patients as if they were family. Some of us even grow sentimental about it. Besides, I don't exactly have a crowd of patients to distract me."

"I won't even start on him," Raskolnikov added, motioning to Razumihin, "though all I've done is burden him with insults and trouble."

"What nonsense are you spouting now? Feeling sentimental today, are you?" Razumihin exclaimed, almost laughing.

If he had been paying closer attention, he might have noticed that Raskolnikov's tone was far from sentimental. It was, in fact, marked by something entirely opposite—something distant and controlled. Avdotya Romanovna, however, caught it immediately. She had been watching her brother closely, her eyes filled with quiet unease.

"And as for you, mother," Raskolnikov continued, his voice more measured now, as if he were reciting a rehearsed line, "I hardly dare to speak. Only today have I begun to grasp how much you must have gone through yesterday, waiting for me."

After saying this, he unexpectedly extended his hand to his sister, a small smile appearing on his face. The smile was brief but genuine—a flicker of unguarded feeling. Avdotya Romanovna recognized it instantly and clasped his hand warmly, her heart lightened by the gesture. It was the first sign of reconciliation since their argument the previous day. Pulcheria Alexandrovna's face lit up, a wave of joy washing over her as she saw her children silently make peace.

"Yes, this is what I admire in him," Razumihin murmured to himself, shifting energetically in his chair. "He has these sudden, genuine moments."

"And how beautifully he handles it all," Pulcheria Alexandrovna thought, watching him intently. "What a generous heart he has, and how delicately he ended the misunderstanding with Dounia—just by extending his hand and looking at her that way. His eyes, his whole face... they're finer than I remembered. He's even more handsome than Dounia. But, oh dear, look at that suit—so shabby, so terribly worn! Even the messenger boy at Afanasy Ivanitch's shop is better dressed. I just want to hug him, weep over him... but I'm afraid. Why am I afraid when he's being so kind? What is it that frightens me?"

"Oh, Rodya, you have no idea," she began suddenly, her words spilling out in a rush. "You can't imagine how upset Dounia and I were yesterday! Now that it's all behind us and we're together again, I can tell you. We rushed straight here from the train to see you, and then that woman—oh, here she is! Good morning, Nastasya!" She paused to acknowledge the housemaid before continuing. "She told us you were burning with fever, that you had run out in delirium, and that they were searching for you in the streets. You can't imagine how it felt! I couldn't stop thinking of Lieutenant Potanchikov—your father's friend, though you wouldn't remember him—how he wandered out in a fever, fell into a well, and wasn't found until the next day. We were so frightened, Rodya! We even considered going to Pyotr Petrovitch for help. We were so alone, completely alone!" Her voice trembled, and then she stopped, realizing it might still be unwise to bring up Pyotr Petrovitch, even in passing, despite the current semblance of harmony.

"Yes, yes, of course... it must have been very troubling for you," Raskolnikov muttered, though his tone was distracted, his gaze distant. This unsettled Dounia, who observed him carefully, her confusion growing.

"What else was I going to say?" he murmured, as if trying to gather his scattered thoughts. "Ah, yes—Mother, Dounia, please don't think that I was deliberately avoiding you today or waiting for you to come to me first. That wasn't the case."

"What are you talking about, Rodya?" Pulcheria Alexandrovna exclaimed, startled. She looked at him with a mixture of surprise and concern, unable to make sense of his words.

"Is he speaking to us as if it's just something he has to do?" Dounia wondered to herself. "Is he trying to reconcile and ask forgiveness as though he's performing some kind of ritual or reciting a memorized lesson?"

"I only just woke up and was about to go to you, but I was delayed because of my clothes," Raskolnikov began, sounding detached. "I forgot yesterday to ask Nastasya to wash the blood out of them. I've only just managed to dress."

"Blood? What blood?" Pulcheria Alexandrovna asked sharply, her alarm rising.

"Oh, it's nothing—don't worry," Raskolnikov replied quickly. "Yesterday, while wandering around deliriously, I came across a man who had been run over—a clerk."

"Delirious? But you remember everything!" Razumihin interjected, looking at him closely.

"That's true," Raskolnikov acknowledged, choosing his words carefully. "I remember everything—down to the smallest detail. Yet, why I did those things, why I went there, why I said those words... I can't explain it clearly now."

"That's a common phenomenon," Zossimov cut in, eager to display his knowledge. "Sometimes, people can perform actions with incredible precision, yet their intentions and reasoning are completely clouded by some underlying disorder. It's much like a dream."

"Perhaps it's just as well if they think I'm nearly mad," Raskolnikov thought to himself, listening but keeping his expression neutral.

"Even perfectly healthy people act like that sometimes," Dounia said, glancing uneasily at Zossimov.

"There's some truth in what you say," Zossimov agreed, leaning forward. "In that sense, none of us is entirely sane. But with the mentally ill, the difference is just a matter of degree—they cross that line where most of us stop. Truthfully, a perfectly normal person doesn't exist. Among thousands, you might not find a single one."

At Zossimov's mention of "madness," a shadow fell over everyone's expressions. The word seemed to linger uncomfortably in the air. Raskolnikov, however, sat in apparent detachment, staring at nothing with a faint, inscrutable smile. His mind seemed to be elsewhere, focused on thoughts he didn't share.

"What about the man who was run over? I interrupted you!" Razumihin blurted, desperate to redirect the conversation.

"What?" Raskolnikov seemed startled back to the moment. "Oh... I got blood on me while helping to carry him to his lodging. By the way, mother, I did something completely unforgivable yesterday. I was practically out of my mind and gave away all the money you sent me—to his wife for the funeral. She's a widow now, with consumption. A poor woman, with three starving children... and nothing in the house. There's a daughter too. If you had seen them, you might have done the same. But I had no right to do it. I know that. To help others, one must first have the right. Otherwise... well, Crevez, chiens, si vous n'êtes pas contents." He laughed bitterly and turned to his sister. "Isn't that correct, Dounia?"

"No, it's not," Dounia replied firmly, her voice steady.

"Ah, so you too have your ideals," he said, his tone shifting to something colder, almost resentful. His smile twisted into something bitter. "I should have considered that. Yes, yes, it's admirable. It's better for you to have limits—lines you won't cross. But if you reach them, you'll be unhappy. And if you cross them, maybe you'll be even unhappier. Still, all this talk is pointless," he snapped, growing irritable. "What I mean to say is... I apologize, mother," he concluded abruptly, almost harshly.

"That's enough, Rodya," Pulcheria Alexandrovna said eagerly, her voice filled with relief. "I'm sure whatever you do is for the best."

"Don't be so sure," he replied, his mouth curling into a sardonic smile.

A tense silence settled over the room. There was a stiffness in their conversation, a strained undercurrent in their reconciliation and the apologies. Everyone could feel it but seemed powerless to address it.

"They're afraid of me," Raskolnikov thought, stealing a glance at his mother and sister. Pulcheria Alexandrovna, in particular, grew more hesitant the longer the silence stretched. "But when they weren't here, I thought I loved them so much," he mused to himself.

"Rodya, did you know Marfa Petrovna is dead?" Pulcheria Alexandrovna suddenly blurted, breaking the quiet.

"Marfa Petrovna? Who is that?"

"Oh, dear—Marfa Petrovna Svidrigailov! I wrote you so much about her."

"A-ah, yes, I remember now... So she's dead? Really?" He seemed to wake up a little, his interest piqued. "What did she die of?"

"Quite suddenly," his mother answered quickly, encouraged by his curiosity. "On the very day I sent you that letter! Can you imagine? They say that dreadful man—her husband—was the cause of it. It's said he beat her horribly."

"Were they on such bad terms?" Raskolnikov asked, turning to Dounia.

"Not at all," Dounia replied, her tone calm but firm. "In fact, he was usually very patient and considerate with her. For seven years of marriage, he indulged her every whim. But suddenly, it seems he lost his temper."

"Then he couldn't have been so terrible if he managed to control himself for seven years. Are you defending him, Dounia?" Raskolnikov asked, his tone sharper than he intended.

"No, no, he's a dreadful man! I can't imagine anyone worse!" Dounia replied, almost shuddering as she frowned deeply, her expression darkening as though the thought itself was unbearable. She seemed to sink into a troubled silence.

"That incident happened in the morning," Pulcheria Alexandrovna said hastily, eager to explain. "And right afterward, she ordered the horses to be harnessed so she could drive to town right after dinner. That's what she always did in such cases—she would go to town. I heard she ate a very good dinner that day, too...."

"After the beating?" Raskolnikov interrupted, his tone tinged with disbelief.

"Yes, that was her habit," his mother continued, nodding earnestly. "And as soon as she had finished dinner, not wanting to delay her trip, she went to the bathhouse. You see, she had been undergoing some kind of treatment there, bathing regularly in a cold spring. But as soon as she got into the water, she had a stroke!"

"Well, I should think so," Zossimov muttered, his professional curiosity piqued.

"And did he beat her badly?" Raskolnikov pressed, though his voice lacked genuine interest.

"What does that matter!" Dounia interjected sharply, her voice firm, almost reproachful.

"Hm! But I don't understand why you're telling us all this gossip, mother," Raskolnikov said irritably, though he seemed more annoyed at himself than at her.

"Ah, my dear, I don't know what else to talk about," Pulcheria Alexandrovna admitted, her voice breaking slightly, as if she felt defeated by her own inadequacy to please.

"Why? Are you all afraid of me?" Raskolnikov asked suddenly, forcing a constrained smile that seemed more like a grimace.

"That's true," Dounia replied without hesitation, meeting his gaze with a stern and unflinching look. "Mother was crossing herself in fear while coming up the stairs."

Her words struck him like a blow. His face twitched, almost as if in pain.

"Ach, Dounia! What are you saying? Don't upset him, please, Rodya, don't take it to heart!" Pulcheria Alexandrovna exclaimed, overwhelmed by her daughter's bluntness. "You must forgive her; she didn't mean it that way. You see, Rodya, on the train ride here, I spent the whole time dreaming about our reunion—about how we'd sit and talk, how we'd share everything. I didn't even notice the length of the journey because I was so happy. But what am I saying now? I am happy! Just seeing you makes me happy, Rodya. That's enough for me...."

"Hush, mother," he murmured, his voice low and unsteady as he avoided her gaze. He reached out and squeezed her hand gently. "We'll have time to talk about everything. Let's not rush."

But even as he spoke, a pallor crept across his face. A wave of cold dread washed over him—a familiar, chilling sensation that had plagued him lately. It struck him with terrible clarity that he had just uttered a monstrous lie. He realized with crushing certainty that he would never be able to talk freely about everything. He would never again be able to speak honestly about anything to anyone. The thought was so suffocatingly painful that, for a moment, he almost forgot where he was.

Suddenly, he stood up from his seat, his movements stiff and disconnected, and began walking toward the door without looking at anyone.

"What are you doing?" Razumihin cried, grabbing him by the arm, alarmed at his abrupt departure.

Raskolnikov paused, then slowly turned back and sat down again, his movements mechanical and his gaze distant. He looked around the room in silence, as if seeing the others for the first time.

"What's the matter with you all? Why are you so gloomy?" he burst out suddenly, his voice sharp and unexpected. "Say something! What's the use of sitting here like this in silence? Come on, talk about something! Anything! We meet after so long, and then we just sit here like statues. Let's have a conversation!"

Pulcheria Alexandrovna let out a sigh of relief and crossed herself. "Thank God. I was so afraid it was going to be like yesterday all over again."

"What's wrong, Rodya?" Dounia asked warily, her eyes searching his face for some sign of what was troubling him.

"Oh, nothing! I just remembered something," Raskolnikov replied suddenly and, out of nowhere, laughed.

"Well, as long as it's just a memory, that's fine," Zossimov muttered as he rose from the sofa, glancing at his patient with faint curiosity. "I was beginning to worry. Anyway, it's time for me to go. I might drop by again later—if I can." He nodded politely and made his way out of the room.

"What a fine man!" Pulcheria Alexandrovna observed warmly as the door closed behind him.

"Yes, excellent, educated, intelligent," Raskolnikov said quickly, his voice unusually animated, as though a sudden surge of energy had overtaken him. "I can't quite recall where I met him before I got sick. I think I must have run into him somewhere.... And this one here," he nodded toward Razumihin, "is a good man, too. What do you think, Dounia? Do you like him?" He turned to his sister and, for some inexplicable reason, burst into laughter.

"I do, very much," Dounia replied with a calm sincerity.

"Ha! What a boor you are!" Razumihin exclaimed, his face flushing a deep red as he shot up from his chair in embarrassment. Pulcheria Alexandrovna allowed herself a faint smile, but Raskolnikov laughed more loudly this time, his mirth bordering on mockery.

"Where are you going?" he asked Razumihin, watching his flustered friend.

"I need to leave," Razumihin mumbled awkwardly.

"No, you don't. Stay. Zossimov has gone, so you must stay. What's the time? Is it already noon? Dounia, what a beautiful watch you have! Why are you all so silent again? I'm doing all the talking here."

"It was a gift from Marfa Petrovna," Dounia explained simply.

"And an expensive one at that!" Pulcheria Alexandrovna chimed in, eager to add her approval.

"Aha, quite large for a lady's watch," Raskolnikov remarked, examining it with interest.

"I like this style," Dounia said, brushing off the remark lightly.

"So, it wasn't from her fiancé," Razumihin thought to himself, feeling an inexplicable wave of relief wash over him.

"I thought it was from Luzhin," Raskolnikov said aloud, his tone unreadable.

"No, he hasn't given Dounia anything yet," Pulcheria Alexandrovna replied quickly.

"Aha! And do you remember, mother, I once fell in love and wanted to get married?" Raskolnikov said suddenly, shifting the subject so abruptly that Pulcheria Alexandrovna was taken aback.

"Yes, my dear, I remember," she said cautiously, exchanging uncertain glances with Dounia and Razumihin.

"Hm, yes... what can I say? I don't remember much now. She was a very sickly girl," Raskolnikov said, his voice softening as he seemed to drift into a reverie. "Always unwell, often talking about charity and dreaming of becoming a nun. Once, she cried while discussing it with me. Yes, yes, I remember her now. She wasn't beautiful—rather plain, to be honest. I can't even say why I was drawn to her. Perhaps it was because she was so ill. If she'd been lame or hunchbacked, I think I'd have liked her even more," he added with a dreamy smile. "It was a kind of spring fever, I suppose."

"No, it wasn't just spring fever," Dounia said firmly, her tone filled with warmth and quiet conviction.

Raskolnikov looked at her sharply, his expression strained, but it seemed her words didn't fully register. Instead, he rose from his chair, walked over to his mother, kissed her gently, and then returned to his seat without saying another word.

"Do you still love her?" Pulcheria Alexandrovna asked, her voice filled with tender curiosity.

"Her? Now? Oh, no.... That's all so far away now, like it happened in another life," he replied, his gaze distant. "Everything here feels so far away. Even you both—I feel as though I'm looking at you from a thousand miles away. But why are we talking about this? It's pointless," he said abruptly, irritation creeping into his tone. He bit his nails distractedly and fell into silence once more.

"This place you're living in, Rodya—it's dreadful!" Pulcheria Alexandrovna exclaimed, breaking the tense quiet. "It's like a tomb. I'm sure it's part of what's made you so unhappy."

"My lodging," he muttered with a lifeless laugh. "Yes, the room has a lot to do with it.... Funny, though, what a strange thing you've just said, mother."

Their reunion—his mother and sister by his side after three years apart—felt oddly suffocating, the kind of intimacy that he could barely endure. He realized with relief that there was something pressing he needed to address, something that gave him an escape from this unbearable closeness.

"Dounia, listen," he began with an abrupt seriousness that stilled the room. "I owe you an apology for yesterday, but let me make one thing clear: I haven't changed my position. It's either me or Luzhin. If

I'm a scoundrel, you mustn't become one. One scoundrel in the family is enough. If you marry Luzhin, I will stop considering you my sister."

"Rodya, Rodya! You're saying the same thing as yesterday," Pulcheria Alexandrovna cried mournfully, her voice quivering. "And why do you call yourself a scoundrel? I can't bear to hear you say that. You said it yesterday, too!"

"Brother," Dounia responded with firmness and the same restrained tone as before. "You are mistaken about all this. I spent the night thinking it over, and I see now where the misunderstanding lies. You seem to believe that I am sacrificing myself to someone or for someone else. That is not the case at all. I am marrying purely for my own sake because my situation is difficult. Of course, I will be glad if I can also help my family by doing so, but that is not my main reason."

"She's lying," Raskolnikov thought bitterly, biting his nails with an almost vindictive intensity. "So proud, so stubborn! She refuses to admit she's doing this out of charity. Too arrogant to confess! Oh, these hypocritical souls—they even love as though they hate. Oh, how I despise them all!"

Dounia continued without a pause, her voice steady. "In truth, I am marrying Pyotr Petrovitch because, out of two evils, I've chosen the lesser. I intend to fulfill honestly all the expectations he has of me. I am not deceiving him in any way.... Why did you smile just now?" Her cheeks flushed slightly, and a glint of anger appeared in her eyes.

"All of them?" Raskolnikov asked with a twisted grin.

"Within reasonable limits. His manner and the way he courted me made it clear from the start what he wanted. Perhaps he thinks too highly of himself, but I also believe he respects me. Why are you laughing again?" she demanded, her voice rising slightly.

"And why are you blushing again?" he retorted, his grin becoming more malicious. "You're lying, Dounia. You're deliberately lying, purely out of some feminine stubbornness, just to stand your ground against me. You can't respect Luzhin—I've seen him, spoken with him. No, you're selling yourself for his money, and in doing so, you're behaving despicably. At least you can still blush about it."

"That's not true! I am not lying!" Dounia cried, her composure cracking for the first time. "I would never marry him if I weren't convinced that he esteems me and thinks highly of me. I would never marry him if I didn't believe I could respect him in return. And such a marriage is not the vile thing you make it out to be! But even if it were, even if I were deciding to do something truly base, is it not cruel of you to speak to me like this? Why do you demand a kind of heroism from me that you yourself may not possess? This is tyranny, Rodya— it's despotism! If I ruin anyone, it will only be myself. I am not committing a crime. Why are you staring at me like that? Why are you so pale? Rodya, my dear, what's wrong?"

"Good heavens! You've made him faint!" Pulcheria Alexandrovna exclaimed in a panic.

"No, no, nonsense! I'm fine—it's just a bit of dizziness, not fainting. You've got fainting stuck in your head," Raskolnikov muttered irritably. "Hm, yes, what was I saying? Oh, right. How exactly do you intend to get this 'convincing proof' today that you can respect him, and that he esteems you, as you put it? You said today?"

"Mother, show Rodya Pyotr Petrovitch's letter," Dounia said decisively.

With trembling hands, Pulcheria Alexandrovna handed him the letter. He took it with evident interest but paused before opening it, studying his sister with a strange expression.

"How peculiar," he murmured slowly, as though a new thought had struck him. "Why am I making such a fuss? What's the point of all this? Marry whoever you like."

He spoke as if to himself, but his words were audible. He stared at Dounia for a moment, puzzled, before finally opening the letter. His face retained the same strange look of wonder as he read it, slowly and carefully, not once but twice. Pulcheria Alexandrovna watched him with visible anxiety, while everyone else in the room seemed to brace for his reaction.

"What strikes me most," he said at last, handing the letter back to his mother, "is that for a man who prides himself on being a businessperson and a lawyer, his writing is remarkably unpolished."

Everyone started; they had expected something entirely different.

"But isn't that how they all write?" Razumihin interjected abruptly.

"Have you read it?" Raskolnikov asked, narrowing his eyes.

"Yes, they showed it to me earlier," Razumihin admitted.

"That's just the jargon of legal documents," Razumihin added. "They're still written that way today."

"Yes, legal jargon. A peculiar blend—not entirely illiterate, but certainly not refined. Just business language," Raskolnikov agreed.

"Pyotr Petrovitch doesn't hide the fact that he had a modest education. In fact, he's proud of having made his own way in life," Dounia said, her tone revealing a hint of irritation at her brother's criticism.

"Well, if he's proud of it, then perhaps he has reason to be," Raskolnikov replied. "But you seem offended, sister, as if my critique of his style is a deliberate attempt to annoy you. It's not—it's simply an observation. And actually, the style of this letter is very relevant to the matter at hand. There's one phrase in particular—'blame yourselves'—that is very pointed. And then there's the threat to leave if I'm present, which really means he's threatening to abandon you both if you disobey him. After summoning you to Petersburg, no less. Now, what do you make of that? Can we be outraged by such a phrase coming from Luzhin, in the same way we might if Razumihin or Zossimov had written it?"

"No," Dounia admitted with a new energy in her voice. "I noticed that it was clumsily expressed—perhaps because he isn't skilled at writing. That's a fair criticism, Rodya. I hadn't expected it, but I think you're right."

"It is phrased in the formal, detached style of legal jargon, and as a result, it comes across harsher than he likely intended. However, I must open your eyes to something. There is a particular expression in the letter, a slander aimed at me, and a rather shameful one at that. Last night, I gave the money to a widow—a woman gravely ill with consumption, overwhelmed by misfortune. It was not, as he puts it, 'on the pretext of the funeral,' but explicitly to cover the actual expenses of the burial. Moreover, it wasn't given to the daughter—a young woman of alleged 'notorious behavior,' as he claims, someone I saw for the first time in my life last night—but to the widow herself.

This misrepresentation reveals a haste to discredit me and stir up division between us. The slander is couched in that same legalese, with a transparent eagerness to achieve its purpose, almost laughably so. Pyotr Petrovitch is undoubtedly intelligent, but intelligence alone does not ensure sound judgment. His approach reveals more about his character than he probably realizes, and frankly, it doesn't suggest any particular respect for you. I'm telling you this not to hurt you but to warn you, because I genuinely want what's best for you."

Dounia didn't respond. Her expression was firm, her mind clearly made up. She was merely awaiting the evening to act on her decision.

"And what about you, Rodya? What's your decision?" Pulcheria Alexandrovna asked, her voice tinged with anxiety. The sudden shift in his tone to a more calculated, detached manner only heightened her unease.

"My decision?" he asked, almost absently.

"Yes, my dear," she pressed. "Pyotr Petrovitch has written that you're not to attend this evening's meeting and that he will leave if you show up. So, will you come?"

"That's not really for me to decide," he replied in a measured, deliberate tone. "First, it's up to you—if you're not insulted by such a condition. And second, it depends on Dounia—whether or not she feels offended by it. I'll abide by what you both think is best," he concluded, his words carrying a faint chill.

"Dounia has already made her decision, and I completely support her," Pulcheria Alexandrovna quickly interjected, eager to ease the growing tension.

Dounia turned to her brother, her voice steady but firm. "I've decided to ask you, Rodya, to attend the meeting without fail. I believe your presence is necessary. Will you come?"

"Yes," he replied, simply but decisively.

"And I'd like to extend the same request to you, Razumihin," Dounia added, turning toward him. "I would like you to join us at eight o'clock this evening. Mother, I'm inviting him as well."

Pulcheria Alexandrovna nodded approvingly. "That's absolutely the right thing to do, Dounia. I feel the same way. Since this is the decision you've made, so be it. At least this way, everything will be in the open, and I won't have to carry the weight of secrecy. Whatever happens, let it happen now, whether Pyotr Petrovitch is angry or not!"

Chapter 4

At that moment, the door opened softly, and a young girl entered, her demeanor hesitant and shy. The room turned as one to face her, surprise and curiosity evident on every face. Raskolnikov himself did not immediately recognize her. It was Sofya Semyonovna Marmeladov. Though he had met her only the night before, the circumstances and her appearance then were so entirely different that her current image felt like an entirely different person. Today, she was plainly dressed, modestly so, with a simple indoor outfit and a worn, old-fashioned hat. She carried a parasol, an accessory that seemed oddly out of place. She looked very young, almost childlike, with a delicate, timid face that bore traces of fear. Overwhelmed by the number of people in the room, she hesitated near the doorway, her shyness almost compelling her to retreat.

"Oh... it's you!" Raskolnikov exclaimed, his surprise evident. He, too, was caught off guard. His immediate thoughts leapt to his mother and sister, who were aware—thanks to Luzhin's letter—of the existence of "a young woman of notorious behavior." He had just vehemently refuted Luzhin's accusations, insisting he had only met Sonia the previous night, and now here she was, appearing unexpectedly. He also recalled, uncomfortably, that he had not protested Luzhin's description of her as "notorious." These thoughts raced through his mind in disjointed fragments. However, as he observed Sonia more closely, her humble demeanor and visible humiliation struck him deeply, and his irritation gave way to pity. When she instinctively stepped back toward the door in fear, the sight of it pierced his heart.

"I wasn't expecting you," he said hurriedly, his tone softening as his expression compelled her to stay. "Please, come in and sit down. You must have come from Katerina Ivanovna? Allow me—not there. Sit here."

Razumihin, who had been occupying one of the room's sparse chairs near the door, immediately stood to make space for Sonia. Raskolnikov initially motioned toward the sofa where Zossimov had been sitting, but realizing it doubled as his bed, he quickly changed his mind. He gestured for her to take Razumihin's chair instead.

"You sit here," he directed Razumihin, guiding him toward the sofa.

Sonia, visibly nervous, sat down tentatively in the chair, her hands trembling slightly. She cast timid glances at the two ladies, unable to mask her self-consciousness. The thought of sitting among them seemed so unthinkable that she rose almost immediately, flustered and unsure of herself.

"I... I... only came for a moment," she stammered, her voice faltering. "I didn't mean to disturb you. I've come from Katerina Ivanovna. She asked me to... to beg you... to be at the service tomorrow morning... at Mitrofanievsky... and afterward to join us at her home... to honor her request. She asked me to beg you especially..." Her voice trailed off as she struggled to get the words out.

"I'll try, of course," Raskolnikov replied, standing now as well. He stumbled over his words, clearly affected by her presence. "Most certainly, I will try. Please, sit down again. I want to talk to you. I know you may be in a hurry, but grant me just two minutes of your time." He pulled a chair closer for her, his tone unexpectedly earnest.

Sonia hesitated but finally sat down once more, her eyes flitting nervously toward the two women in the room. Their presence seemed to unnerve her, and she quickly dropped her gaze. Meanwhile, Raskolnikov's pallid face grew flushed, his emotions betraying themselves in the intensity of his eyes.

"Mother," he said with a determined edge to his voice, "this is Sofya Semyonovna Marmeladov, the daughter of Mr. Marmeladov, who was tragically run over yesterday. I was just telling you about him."

Pulcheria Alexandrovna glanced at Sonia, her expression tightening slightly, though her curiosity was evident. Despite Raskolnikov's firm and almost challenging tone, she couldn't resist the urge to scrutinize the young woman. Dounia, in contrast, gazed at Sonia with quiet gravity, her penetrating look betraying a mixture of thoughtfulness and concern. Sonia, hearing herself introduced, tried to lift her eyes but was overwhelmed by embarrassment and quickly looked down again.

"I wanted to ask," Raskolnikov began, his words coming more quickly now, "how things were handled yesterday. Were there any complications? The police didn't trouble you, did they?"

"No, everything was straightforward," Sonia replied, her voice low but steady. "The cause of death was obvious. They didn't bother us. But... the other lodgers are upset."

"Why are they upset?"

"They're angry that the body has been kept in the house for so long. You see, it's quite warm now, and... Katerina Ivanovna has finally agreed that it must be moved. It will be taken to the cemetery chapel today and remain there until tomorrow."

"So, today then?"

"Yes," Sonia confirmed. "She also asked me to invite you to the service tomorrow and to join us for the funeral meal afterward."

"She's hosting a funeral meal?" Raskolnikov asked, surprised.

"Yes, though it will be modest," Sonia answered, her voice trembling slightly as her emotions threatened to overcome her. She continued quickly, "She asked me to thank you, as well. Without your help yesterday, we wouldn't have been able to afford anything for the funeral." Her lips quivered, and she fought to maintain her composure.

Throughout the conversation, Raskolnikov watched her closely. Her face was thin and pale, with delicate, angular features—a sharp nose and a pointed chin. She wasn't conventionally beautiful, but her striking blue eyes held an undeniable warmth and simplicity. When they lit up, her entire expression became so kind and sincere that it was impossible not to feel drawn to her. Her figure and gestures had a peculiar quality; despite being eighteen, she seemed almost childlike, and her mannerisms only heightened this impression.

"But how has Katerina Ivanovna managed all this with so little?" Raskolnikov asked, pressing gently. "Can she even afford a funeral meal?"

"The coffin and everything else will be very simple, very plain," Sonia explained quickly. "We've calculated it all carefully. There will be just enough left for a small meal. It brings her some comfort, you see. She's... well, she's like that."

"I understand. I do," Raskolnikov said softly. His gaze fell on Sonia again, his expression unreadable. "Why do you keep glancing around my room like that? My mother just remarked that it looks like a tomb."

Sonia, caught off guard, responded in a rapid whisper. "You gave us everything yesterday." Her words were rushed, almost blurted out, and she immediately looked down, her face coloring in embarrassment.

A brief silence fell over the room. Dounia's eyes shone with a quiet intensity, while Pulcheria Alexandrovna softened, her own expression growing gentler as she regarded Sonia.

"Rodya," Pulcheria Alexandrovna said as she rose from her seat, "we'll all have dinner together, of course. Come, Dounia. And you, Rodya, you should take a little walk and rest for a while before joining us. I'm afraid we've tired you out."

"Yes, yes, I'll come," Raskolnikov replied, standing up quickly, his movements fussy and distracted. "But I have something I need to attend to first."

"What? You're not having dinner with us?" Razumihin interjected, staring at Raskolnikov in surprise. "What do you mean?"

"No, no, I'll be there," Raskolnikov assured him, almost stammering. "Of course, of course, I'll come. And you stay here for a moment. Mother, you don't need him right now, do you? Or am I keeping him from you?"

"Oh, no, no," Pulcheria Alexandrovna said hurriedly. "And Dmitri Prokofitch, would you do us the honor of joining us for dinner?"

"Please do," Dounia added, her tone warm.

Razumihin bowed deeply, a radiant smile lighting up his face. For a brief moment, an odd awkwardness settled over everyone, as if they were all unsure of what to say next.

"Goodbye, Rodya, or rather, see you later. I don't like saying goodbye," Pulcheria Alexandrovna said as she prepared to leave. "Goodbye, Nastasya... Oh, there I go again, saying goodbye."

Pulcheria Alexandrovna appeared to hesitate as if meaning to say something to Sonia but ultimately left without doing so, flustered and overwhelmed. However, Dounia paused in the doorway, turning back to Sonia with a polite, attentive bow. Sonia, startled by this unexpected courtesy, quickly curtsied in return, her discomfort palpable. Her face betrayed a poignant unease, as though Dounia's kindness only heightened her feelings of humiliation.

"Dounia, wait," Raskolnikov called after her from the passage. "Give me your hand."

"Why, I already did," Dounia replied, turning toward him with a slightly awkward yet affectionate smile. "Did you forget?"

"Never mind. Give it to me again." He took her hand and squeezed it warmly.

Dounia smiled, her cheeks flushing as she gently withdrew her hand and left, clearly buoyed by the exchange.

"Well, that's better," Raskolnikov said, turning back to Sonia with a sudden brightness in his expression. "The dead deserve peace, but the living have to go on living. Isn't that right?"

Sonia looked at him, startled by the sudden shift in his demeanor. He studied her for a long moment in silence, as though seeing not just her, but the entire tragic story of her father's life and death.

Meanwhile, outside on the street, Pulcheria Alexandrovna turned to her daughter, her voice tinged with unexpected relief. "You know, Dounia, I actually feel better now that we've left. I can't believe I'm saying this, but I feel a bit more at ease. If someone had told me that yesterday on the train, I wouldn't have believed them."

"Mother," Dounia replied earnestly, "you must see that he's still unwell. His health and everything he's endured recently have made him like this. It's probably our arrival that unsettled him further. We need to be patient with him. Much can be forgiven."

Pulcheria Alexandrovna bristled slightly. "Well, you weren't exactly overflowing with patience yourself," she said, a touch defensively. "I was watching you two. You're so much alike—not just in appearance but in spirit. Both of you are intense, proud, and sensitive, with those fiery tempers and generous hearts. He can't possibly be selfish, can he, Dounia? When I think of what's to come this evening, my heart just sinks!"

"Don't worry so much, mother," Dounia replied firmly. "What will happen, will happen."

Pulcheria Alexandrovna sighed deeply, her anxiety spilling over. "Oh, Dounia, just imagine what a position we're in. What if Pyotr Petrovitch decides to break everything off?"

"If he does, then he won't be worth much," Dounia answered sharply, her voice laced with contempt.

"You're right, of course," Pulcheria Alexandrovna said quickly, as though trying to soothe herself. "But it was good we left when we did. He needed time alone. The room was so stuffy, so suffocating. I hope he goes out for some air—it's desperately needed in a place like this. But even the streets here feel like closed-in rooms! What a strange and oppressive city. Watch out, dear, they're carrying something. A piano, I think. Look how they push! It's a wonder people don't get crushed."

She paused, her thoughts shifting abruptly. "I'm also worried about that young woman."

"What young woman, mother?" Dounia asked, puzzled.

"Sofya Semyonovna," Pulcheria Alexandrovna said in a low, hesitant voice. "The one who was just there."

"Why are you worried about her?"

"I have a... a feeling, Dounia. Call it a mother's intuition if you like. But as soon as she walked in, I felt that she was at the heart of all this trouble."

"Nonsense, mother!" Dounia exclaimed in frustration. "Your 'feelings' are completely unfounded. He only just met her the evening before. He didn't even know who she was until she walked into the room."

"You'll see," Pulcheria Alexandrovna insisted. "She unsettles me. There's something about her eyes. And then he introduced her to us, Dounia, as if she were someone very important. I could barely sit still in my chair. And think about what Pyotr Petrovitch wrote in that letter! Yet Rodya brings her into the conversation as if she were..." She trailed off, shaking her head.

"People write all sorts of things, mother. Have you forgotten how we were once talked about and written about? I am certain Sonia is a good girl, and all that nonsense is just slander."

"God grant you're right."

"And Pyotr Petrovitch is a contemptible slanderer," Dounia added sharply, her voice cutting through the tension.

Pulcheria Alexandrovna fell silent, subdued by her daughter's firmness. The conversation faded, leaving them both deep in their own thoughts.

"I'll explain what I need from you," Raskolnikov said, pulling Razumihin toward the window with a firm but hurried gesture.

Sonia, sensing the conversation might not involve her, quickly said, "Then I'll let Katerina Ivanovna know you'll be coming," and began gathering herself to leave.

"Wait a moment, Sofya Semyonovna," Raskolnikov interjected, stopping her mid-step. "We don't have any secrets here, and you're not in the way. I want to have a word or two with you as well." He turned back to Razumihin. "Listen, you know that man... Porfiry Petrovitch?"

"Of course I know him! He's a relative of mine," Razumihin replied with interest. "Why do you ask?"

"Isn't he in charge of that investigation—about that murder? You mentioned it yesterday."

"Yes, that's right. What about it?" Razumihin's eyes widened in surprise, clearly curious where this was heading.

"Well," Raskolnikov continued, lowering his voice slightly, "he's been looking into people who pawned items with the old woman. I've got some things there too—trivial stuff. A ring my sister gave me as a keepsake before I left home and my father's silver watch. Together they're worth no more than five or six roubles, but they're priceless to me. I can't lose them. Especially the watch—it's the only thing of my father's that we have left. Mother would be devastated if it were gone.

You know how women are. She might ask about it before dinner, especially after we spoke of Dounia's watch. What should I do? Should I go straight to Porfiry about it? Would that be better than going to the police station? What do you think?"

"Absolutely not to the police station! Go straight to Porfiry," Razumihin said, his excitement rising. "It's the best course of action, and besides, we're bound to find him if we go now—it's just a short walk from here."

"All right, let's go."

"He'll be thrilled to meet you! I've spoken about you to him many times, especially yesterday. Let's go immediately. Wait—so you knew the old pawnbroker? That's what this is about, isn't it? Everything's starting to fall into place now... Oh, and Sofya Semyonovna—"

"Semyonovna," Raskolnikov corrected with a quick glance at Sonia. "This is my good friend Razumihin. He's someone you can trust."

"If you need to go, I won't hold you up," Sonia began timidly, avoiding Razumihin's gaze and looking even more flustered.

"We're going," Raskolnikov said firmly, cutting her off. "But I'll visit you today, Sofya Semyonovna. Just tell me where you live."

She hesitated before quietly giving her address, her face turning a deep shade of red. All three of them stepped out of the room together.

"Don't you ever lock your door?" Razumihin asked, noticing the absent lock as they walked out.

"Never," Raskolnikov answered nonchalantly. "I've been meaning to get one for two years, but it never seemed important. People who don't need locks are the lucky ones," he added with a small laugh, glancing at Sonia. They paused for a moment in the gateway.

"You turn to the right, don't you, Sofya Semyonovna?" Raskolnikov asked, as if to confirm her direction. Then, almost as an afterthought, he added, "By the way, how did you find me?"

"You gave your address to Polenka yesterday."

"Polenka? Oh, yes, the little girl. She's your sister, isn't she? Did I give her the address?"

"Yes. Had you forgotten?"

"No... I remember now," he replied, looking thoughtful.

"I had heard my father mention you before, but he didn't know your name. When I learned it yesterday, I asked around for 'Mr. Raskolnikov,' and that's how I found you."

"Ah, I see," Raskolnikov muttered distractedly. "Goodbye for now, then. I'll let you get back to Katerina Ivanovna."

Sonia gave a quick nod, clearly eager to leave, and walked away, her eyes downcast. She hurried around the corner and disappeared from view, moving quickly as though she couldn't wait to be alone. Her thoughts were swirling as she replayed every word, every glance, every moment. A strange, unfamiliar feeling was building within her— a sensation of a world opening before her, vast and unknown.

Yet, as she moved further away, a wave of anxiety washed over her. "Not today, please not today," she whispered under her breath, almost pleading with herself like a frightened child. "To me... in that room... oh no, he'll see. What will he think? Oh dear!" Her steps quickened as her mind raced, her heart pounding with apprehension.

Sonia didn't notice the man who had been watching her since she left the gateway. He had lingered near the entrance when she, Raskolnikov, and Razumihin stood talking. At the mention of Raskolnikov's name, his interest had been piqued. He had turned, watching them intently as though studying the group, and then focused on Sonia as she left. Now, maintaining a discreet distance, he followed her silently, his intent unclear.

"Home? Where is home? I've seen that face before somewhere," the man mused, his curiosity deepening. "I must figure out who she is."

At the next corner, he crossed the street, keeping his eyes discreetly on Sonia. She continued walking, utterly unaware of his presence, her thoughts evidently far away. He followed her from a distance, carefully measuring his steps to avoid drawing her attention. After about fifty paces, he crossed the street again, catching up to her until he was only a few yards behind.

The man was around fifty, tall and solidly built, with broad, high shoulders that gave him a slightly stooped appearance. His attire was fashionable and of fine quality, befitting a man of apparent wealth and standing. He carried an elegant cane, which he tapped rhythmically against the pavement with each step, and his immaculate gloves completed the image of a well-kept gentleman. His face was broad, with high cheekbones and a fresh, ruddy complexion that was uncommon in the city. His light flaxen hair, slightly streaked with grey, was thick and well-maintained, while his square-cut beard was a shade lighter. His blue eyes held a cold and calculating gaze, and his crimson lips hinted at a vitality that made him appear younger than his years.

When Sonia reached the canal bank, the pair were the only ones walking along the pavement. The man studied her, noting her absorbed expression and the heavy preoccupation that seemed to weigh on her. He watched her turn into a gateway leading to her lodging, then followed, his curiosity now mingled with a tinge of surprise.

Inside the courtyard, Sonia headed toward a corner of the building. "Bah!" he muttered under his breath, as though this development was unexpected, and began climbing the stairs after her. It wasn't until she reached the third floor and turned down a narrow passage that Sonia finally noticed his presence. She paused before a door marked in chalk with the words "Kapernaumov, Tailor," and rang the bell. The man stopped a few steps behind her and muttered again, "Bah!" as though amused by the coincidence. He moved to the door next to hers, just a few feet away, and rang the bell at No. 8.

"So, you lodge at Kapernaumov's," he said with a laugh, addressing Sonia. "What a coincidence. He altered a waistcoat for me just yesterday. I'm staying nearby, at Madame Resslich's. What a small world!" His tone was cheerful, even friendly, but Sonia only managed a fleeting glance at him before the door opened and she slipped inside without a word, her unease evident. For some reason, his presence left her feeling ashamed and uncomfortable.

As Raskolnikov and Razumihin made their way toward Porfiry's office, Razumihin's mood seemed unusually buoyant, his excitement bubbling over.

"That's great, brother, just great," he exclaimed more than once. "I'm really glad—so glad!"

"Glad about what exactly?" Raskolnikov wondered silently, casting a skeptical glance at his companion.

"I didn't know you had pawned things at the old woman's place," Razumihin went on. "When was that? A long time ago?"

"What a simpleton," Raskolnikov thought, his irritation rising. He stopped abruptly, as though trying to remember. "It must have been two or three days before her death," he said at last. "But I'm not planning to redeem them now," he added hurriedly, as if anxious to dismiss the subject. "I've got barely a silver rouble left after yesterday's infernal delirium." He emphasized the word "delirium" with a noticeable sharpness.

"Yes, yes, of course," Razumihin agreed eagerly, though it wasn't clear what he was agreeing to. "That explains it... partially, at least. You were mumbling about rings and chains in your delirium yesterday— now it all makes sense!"

"So, the idea has taken root in their minds," Raskolnikov mused grimly. "Here's this fool, ready to defend me to the bitter end, and yet he's delighted to have some trivial nonsense about rings cleared up. The hold that idea has on them all—it's suffocating."

"Will we find him, do you think?" Raskolnikov asked abruptly, shifting the topic.

"Oh, definitely," Razumihin assured him. "Porfiry's a good man—you'll see. He can be a bit... clumsy, though. Not socially, mind you; he's actually quite polished. But there's a sort of calculated awkwardness in the way he deals with people. He's sharp, very sharp, but he enjoys toying with others, testing them. He cleared up a murder case last year when the police had no leads at all. I've told him a lot about you, and he's very eager to meet you."

"Eager? Why?"

"Well," Razumihin began hesitantly, "I mentioned you a few times, especially since you've been unwell. He seemed intrigued. I think he felt... pity for you, in a way. He even said, 'What a waste,' about you leaving the university. And then, of course, there was Zametov—" Razumihin broke off suddenly. "Oh, Rodya, I may have talked some nonsense yesterday... I was drunk, you know."

"What? You mean they think I'm mad?" Raskolnikov asked with a strained smile.

"No, no... not exactly. It's just... whatever I said—it was all rubbish, drunken rambling."

"If you're so ashamed, stop apologizing," Raskolnikov snapped, his irritation now barely disguised.

Silence fell between them after that. Razumihin's exuberance grated on Raskolnikov, filling him with both revulsion and unease. His mind churned over what Razumihin had said about Porfiry, and he felt the weight of an invisible noose tightening.

"I'll have to put on a convincing act," he thought, his heart racing. "But not too convincing—that would seem unnatural. What's the best course of action? Do nothing? No, that's suspicious too... Oh, we'll see soon enough."

As they reached the building, Raskolnikov turned to Razumihin with a sly smile. "You've been acting strangely all day. Excited, fidgety... it's obvious."

"Me? Not at all!" Razumihin bristled, clearly embarrassed.

"Yes, you have. You've been sitting on the edge of your chair, blushing over nothing. Especially when Dounia invited you to dinner—you nearly turned purple!"

"What nonsense!" Razumihin sputtered. "You're imagining things."

"Ah, the blush again! You're hopeless, Romeo," Raskolnikov teased with a laugh.

They reached Porfiry's flat still laughing, their voices echoing in the hallway. Just before they entered, Razumihin grabbed Raskolnikov's shoulder and hissed furiously, "Not one more word, or I'll strangle you!"

Chapter 5

Raskolnikov stepped into the room, his face betraying the enormous effort it took to suppress his laughter. He looked as though he might burst out at any moment. Razumihin followed, towering awkwardly in the doorway, his face glowing red with embarrassment and irritation, his expression caught somewhere between indignation and utter defeat. His awkward demeanor, coupled with his flushed, comical appearance, was enough to justify Raskolnikov's amusement, which he struggled valiantly to contain.

Without waiting for formalities, Raskolnikov moved forward and bowed slightly to Porfiry Petrovitch, who stood in the center of the room, observing them with an expression of curiosity. Extending his hand, Raskolnikov greeted him, attempting to maintain a veneer of seriousness. However, no sooner had he begun speaking than his eyes inadvertently flicked to Razumihin, whose exasperated and furious demeanor proved too much for his composure. Stifled laughter bubbled up uncontrollably, breaking free despite his efforts to suppress it. The harder he tried to regain control, the more impossible it became, and soon his laughter erupted in earnest.

Razumihin's reaction—a mix of visible humiliation and exaggerated outrage—only added to the absurdity of the moment. His dramatic fury gave the impression that this scene was entirely spontaneous and natural, making Raskolnikov's laughter seem all the more infectious. Razumihin, as though determined to escalate the absurdity, swung his arm wildly in a gesture of frustration, accidentally knocking over a small round table. A tea-glass resting on it shattered on the floor.

"For heaven's sake, why break furniture?" Porfiry Petrovitch interjected jovially, quoting a popular saying with a grin. "You know the loss is to the Crown!"

Raskolnikov continued to laugh, though he carefully tempered his amusement, aiming to let it die down naturally. Meanwhile, Razumihin, thoroughly flustered by his clumsiness and the resulting mess, stood brooding over the shards of glass. He muttered curses under his breath and turned sharply toward the window, his back to the room, as though determined to detach himself from the situation entirely.

Porfiry Petrovitch, though clearly entertained by the spectacle, looked expectantly toward Raskolnikov, as though waiting for an explanation. Seated in the corner, Zametov had risen at the visitors' entrance and now stood watching the scene unfold. His expression betrayed a mix of amusement and incredulity, and his attention seemed fixed on Raskolnikov, whose behavior left him slightly unsettled.

The sight of Zametov caught Raskolnikov off guard, an unpleasant jolt passing through him. His mind raced, considering the implications. Nevertheless, he pressed forward.

"Please excuse the disruption," Raskolnikov began, his voice tinged with feigned embarrassment as he introduced himself. "My name is Raskolnikov."

"Not at all, not at all! A pleasure to meet you. And quite an entrance!" Porfiry Petrovitch replied warmly, nodding toward Razumihin. "Though your friend seems to be in quite a mood. Won't he even say good morning?"

"I don't know why he's so furious," Raskolnikov said, half-smiling. "All I did was joke with him on the way here, calling him Romeo and offering proof of it. That was it, I think!"

"Pig!" Razumihin growled, refusing to turn around.

"Well, whatever it was, it must have struck a nerve!" Porfiry laughed. "Sharp wit, sharp tongue, eh?"

"Oh, sharp lawyer, more like!" Razumihin spat, but then, as if a switch had flipped, he burst into laughter himself. The sudden shift in his demeanor was almost comical in its own right. "All right, all right. Let's move on. This is my friend, Rodion Romanovitch Raskolnikov. He wanted to meet you and has a matter to discuss with you. But wait—Zametov? What brings you here?"

Zametov seemed momentarily startled but quickly recovered. "We met yesterday, at your lodgings," he replied smoothly.

"So I'm saved the trouble of introducing you," Razumihin said, grinning. "Looks like Porfiry sniffed you out without my help. Now, where's the tobacco?"

Porfiry Petrovitch was dressed casually in a neat dressing gown and spotless linen, though his worn slippers betrayed a certain domestic informality. He was a stocky man in his mid-thirties, his large, round head and closely cropped hair giving him a distinctive appearance. His pale, slightly jaundiced face carried a playful yet piercing expression. The ironic glint in his watery blue eyes, framed by nearly white lashes, seemed oddly at odds with his otherwise soft and almost feminine features. It was this contrast that lent him an air of disconcerting depth.

Once it became clear that Raskolnikov had business to discuss, Porfiry invited him to sit on the sofa, taking a seat at the other end himself. His demeanor became strikingly formal and overly attentive, as though every word were of critical importance. The intensity of his focus, combined with the trivial nature of the matter at hand, made the atmosphere feel oddly stifling.

Raskolnikov, however, laid out his concerns succinctly and confidently, explaining his situation with measured clarity. The success of his delivery emboldened him, allowing him to observe Porfiry more closely. Throughout the explanation, Porfiry's gaze never wavered from Raskolnikov, his interest unwavering. Across the table, Razumihin followed the exchange with almost excessive enthusiasm, his eyes darting between the two men.

"Idiot," Raskolnikov cursed inwardly, irritated by Razumihin's conspicuous eagerness.

"You'll need to file a report with the police," Porfiry finally said, his tone crisp and businesslike. "Simply state that, upon learning of the incident—the murder, I mean—you wish to reclaim your belongings. They'll draft the necessary documents and notify you accordingly."

"That's just the point," Raskolnikov began, making every effort to appear genuinely embarrassed, "at the moment, my finances are in poor shape... and even a small sum is beyond my means. My intention was simply to declare that the items are mine and, once I have the money... well, you understand."

"That's irrelevant," Porfiry Petrovitch replied coolly, showing little interest in Raskolnikov's financial difficulties. "You can, if you prefer, write directly to me. State in the letter that, having been informed of the matter, you are claiming such and such items as your property and intend to redeem them in due course."

"On a plain sheet of paper?" Raskolnikov asked eagerly, his interest in the financial details betraying a bit too much enthusiasm.

"Oh, the plainest," Porfiry replied, suddenly fixing Raskolnikov with a peculiar look. His eyes narrowed, and for a fleeting moment, it seemed as though he winked. But the expression was so brief and subtle that Raskolnikov questioned whether it was real or imagined. Still, the impression left him unsettled.

"He knows," the thought flashed through Raskolnikov's mind like a jolt of electricity.

"Forgive me for troubling you over such trifles," Raskolnikov continued, trying to regain his composure. "The items are worth little—five roubles at most—but they hold sentimental value for me. They belonged to my father and sister, and when I heard about the inquiries, I was concerned..."

"That's why you reacted so strongly when I mentioned Porfiry was investigating pledges!" Razumihin interjected, his tone pointed and suggestive.

Raskolnikov's patience strained. A flash of anger lit up his dark eyes, but he quickly masked it, turning to Razumihin with feigned irritation.

"Are you mocking me, brother?" he asked, attempting a convincing tone of annoyance. "I might seem absurdly worried about trivial things to you, but these items are far from trivial to me. That silver watch, though worthless in value, is the last thing we have from my father. If my mother found out it was lost, she'd be devastated. You know how women are!"

"Not at all! I didn't mean it that way," Razumihin stammered, clearly distressed by the misunderstanding.

"Was that too much? Too theatrical?" Raskolnikov wondered, his mind racing. "Why did I mention women? Was it a mistake?"

"Oh, your mother is with you?" Porfiry asked, redirecting the conversation smoothly.

"Yes," Raskolnikov replied, his voice steady.

"When did she arrive?"

"Last night."

Porfiry paused, as if mulling something over. "Your belongings wouldn't have been lost in any case," he said nonchalantly. "I've been expecting you here for some time."

The casual comment felt like a blow to Raskolnikov, who instinctively tensed. Porfiry, however, appeared utterly indifferent, focusing instead on offering Razumihin an ashtray to prevent further damage to the carpet from his haphazardly scattered cigarette ash.

"What? Expecting him? Did you know he had pledges there?" Razumihin asked, his surprise evident.

Porfiry turned to Raskolnikov with calm precision. "Your items—the ring and the watch—were wrapped together. The paper they were in had your name written clearly in pencil, along with the date you left them."

"How observant of you," Raskolnikov said, forcing an awkward smile as he fought to meet Porfiry's gaze. His effort to appear composed faltered, and he hurriedly added, "I mean, considering there must be so many pledges, it's impressive you recall mine so clearly."

"Foolish. Why did I say that?" he scolded himself internally.

"It's standard," Porfiry replied, his voice carrying a faint note of irony. "We know everyone who left pledges. You're the only one who hasn't come forward yet."

"I haven't been well," Raskolnikov muttered curtly.

"Yes, I heard about that. I was told you were in considerable distress. You still look unwell."

"I'm not pale at all," Raskolnikov snapped, his tone abruptly shifting to anger. His frustration was rising uncontrollably, and he knew it. "Why are they tormenting me?" he thought, panic creeping into his mind.

"Not well!" Razumihin exclaimed. "He was delirious yesterday, completely out of his mind! He even slipped away, dressed himself, and wandered off, all while still feverish! Would you believe it, Porfiry? He was gone till midnight!"

"Delirious, you say?" Porfiry asked, tilting his head and looking almost amused.

"Nonsense!" Raskolnikov barked. "And you don't believe it anyway," he added impulsively, realizing too late how strange his outburst sounded. Porfiry, however, seemed not to notice.

"Then why go out if you weren't delirious?" Razumihin pressed, his voice rising with agitation. "What was so important? Why sneak off? Were you even in your senses?"

"Now that the danger has passed, we can speak plainly," Razumihin finished, his tone laced with exasperation.

"I was thoroughly fed up with them yesterday," Raskolnikov said suddenly to Porfiry Petrovitch, a smile of insolent defiance crossing his face. "I ran away from them, found myself a place to stay where they wouldn't track me down, and even took a good amount of money with me. Mr. Zametov there can confirm it. I say, Mr. Zametov, tell me—was I sensible or delirious yesterday? Let's settle this debate."

He could have throttled Zametov at that moment. The man's expression, his silence, everything about him was unbearable.

"In my opinion," Zametov said coolly, "you spoke quite sensibly, even craftily, but you were highly irritable."

"And Nikodim Fomitch told me today," Porfiry Petrovitch interjected, "that he saw you late last night at the lodgings of a man who had been run over."

"And there you have it!" Razumihin added triumphantly. "Weren't you mad then? You gave every last coin you had to the widow for the funeral! If you wanted to help, you could have given fifteen or twenty roubles and kept a few for yourself. But no, you had to fling away all twenty-five!"

"Maybe I stumbled upon a hidden treasure somewhere," Raskolnikov retorted, his lips trembling slightly. "Maybe that's why I felt so generous yesterday. Mr. Zametov here surely knows all about my newfound wealth!" He turned to Porfiry Petrovitch with an overly polite tone, masking his growing irritation. "Forgive us, please, for wasting your time with such trivialities. Surely we're boring you."

"Not at all, not at all!" Porfiry replied with a cheerfulness that felt almost mocking. "If only you knew how much I'm enjoying this! It's fascinating to watch and listen. And, honestly, I'm glad you've finally come forward."

"Well, then, how about some tea?" Razumihin interjected. "My throat feels like sandpaper."

"Excellent idea! Perhaps we could even have something stronger before tea?" Porfiry suggested with a grin.

"Get on with you!" Razumihin waved him off, half-laughing.

Porfiry excused himself to order the tea, leaving Raskolnikov to wrestle with his seething thoughts. His mind churned, his anger bubbling just beneath the surface.

"They don't even bother hiding it," he thought furiously. "They aren't standing on ceremony. If you know so much about me, why not be upfront about it? Instead, they're playing these games, treating me like a mouse they can toy with. Well, maybe I won't allow it! Maybe I'll stand up right now and throw the truth in their faces. Let them see how little I care for their tricks."

The intensity of his rage made it difficult for him to breathe. He shook slightly, uncertain whether he could maintain his facade.

"And what if I'm wrong? What if it's all just paranoia? Maybe I'm imagining it, letting my nerves get the better of me. Their words could all be perfectly ordinary... but their tone—there's something in the tone. Why did Porfiry casually say 'with her'? Why did Zametov emphasize that I spoke 'artfully'? What's behind their words?"

He glanced at Razumihin, sitting obliviously nearby. "And this simpleton doesn't notice a thing! The blockhead sees nothing, hears nothing. Feverish! Am I feverish again? Did Porfiry wink at me earlier? Was that real? Or are they just trying to rattle me, tease me like a child? Either they know something, or it's all in my head."

He shot a sharp look at Zametov. "Even he's being rude. Has he switched sides? Of course he has! He feels at home here, unlike me on my first visit. Porfiry doesn't even treat him as a guest. They're thick as thieves, no doubt whispering about me before I arrived. Do they know about the flat? They must! But they have no proof—just suspicions. I'll outlast them."

His thoughts turned to his own anger. "And yet, here I am, visibly irritated. Maybe they'll take that as a sign. Am I overplaying it? Acting the invalid might be the safer move. He's trying to feel me out, catch me in something. But why did I even come here?"

His eyes darted to the door as Porfiry returned, carrying the tea tray. Raskolnikov steeled himself, his fury barely contained, yet he forced a brittle smile.

All of this raced through Raskolnikov's mind like a flash of lightning as Porfiry Petrovitch returned quickly, exuding an air of joviality that hadn't been there before.

"Yesterday's gathering, brother, has left my head spinning a bit... and honestly, I'm feeling out of sorts altogether," Porfiry began with a hearty laugh, addressing Razumihin in a markedly different tone.

"Was it interesting? I left just as it was getting good. Who had the upper hand?" Razumihin asked eagerly.

"Oh, no one, of course! They went off on endless tangents, debating eternal questions, floating away into the abstract," Porfiry replied with amusement.

"Just imagine, Rodya," Razumihin said, turning to Raskolnikov with a burst of enthusiasm, "we ended up discussing whether crime even exists as a concept! It turned into a full-blown philosophical debate. I told you we talked ourselves hoarse."

"What's strange about that? It's a typical social question," Raskolnikov answered casually, brushing off the apparent significance.

"Ah, but the question wasn't framed quite like that," Porfiry observed, his tone carrying a subtle edge of interest.

"True," Razumihin admitted, immediately warming to the topic. "Listen, Rodion, I want to hear your opinion on this. I was arguing with them like a madman, and I kept wishing you were there to back me up. The conversation started with the socialist idea—this notion that crime is nothing more than a protest against the abnormality of the social order. They claim it all boils down to environment and nothing else, absolutely nothing!"

"You've got that wrong," Porfiry interjected, clearly energized, his laughter adding a spark to the exchange as he turned his amused gaze toward Razumihin.

"No, I haven't!" Razumihin retorted, his voice rising in heat. "I'll show you their pamphlets—they're filled with that nonsense. Everything is blamed on 'the influence of environment,' as though there are no other factors at play! Their favorite mantra is that once society is perfectly organized, crime will vanish overnight because there will be nothing left to rebel against. Everyone will suddenly become virtuous and righteous, as if by magic!"

Porfiry's laughter deepened, but Razumihin pressed on, undeterred.

"They act as though human nature doesn't exist! They ignore that humanity evolves through a historical, living process. Instead, they believe some grand, mathematically derived social plan will instantly transform society into a perfect utopia. That's why they detest history—it's messy, full of so-called stupidity. They'd rather reject the complexities of life and replace the living soul with some lifeless, obedient construct."

"Now he's really off, beating the drum!" Porfiry chuckled, addressing Raskolnikov. "Can you imagine six people going on like this in one room, with punch fueling the fire?"

"You're wrong, Porfiry," Razumihin shot back, undeterred. "Environment can't explain everything! Take this, for example: a man of forty violates a child of ten—are you seriously going to blame his environment?"

"Strictly speaking, you could," Porfiry replied, his tone now serious and measured. "A crime like that could very well be tied to environmental factors."

Razumihin exploded. "Oh, come on! If you want, I'll prove that your white eyelashes are caused by the Church of Ivan the Great being two hundred and fifty feet high—and I'll do it with precision, logic, and even a Liberal twist! Care to bet on it?"

"Done!" Porfiry replied, laughing heartily. "Let's hear this theory of yours."

"You see?" Razumihin exclaimed, throwing up his hands in exasperation. "He does this on purpose! Rodion, you don't know him yet—he loves taking people for a ride. Yesterday, he took their side just to make fools of them, and they lapped it up!"

"And what about your stunts last year?" Porfiry teased. "Pretending you were joining a monastery? That lasted for two months!"

"Are you really such a good dissembler?" Raskolnikov asked casually, masking his growing irritation.

"You wouldn't believe it, would you? But wait, I'll have you fooled too!" Porfiry declared, bursting into laughter.

Then his tone shifted. "Speaking of which, all this talk reminds me of an article you wrote, Rodion. Something about crime, wasn't it? I read it a couple of months ago in the Periodical Review. Quite intriguing!"

"My article? In the Periodical Review?" Raskolnikov repeated in surprise. "I did write something about a book when I left the university, but I sent it to the Weekly Review."

"But it appeared in the Periodical," Porfiry insisted, leaning forward slightly.

"And the Weekly Review ceased to exist, which is why it wasn't published at the time," added Razumihin, piecing things together aloud.

"That's correct," Porfiry nodded. "When the Weekly Review folded, it was absorbed into the Periodical, so your article ended up being published there about two months ago. Didn't you know?"

Raskolnikov blinked in surprise. He had not known.

"You might even be owed some payment for it! What a strange fellow you are, living so shut off from the world that you're unaware of things that directly affect you. I assure you, it's true," Porfiry added, with a bemused smile.

"Bravo, Rodya!" Razumihin exclaimed, genuinely astonished. "I didn't know about it either! I'll go to the reading room today and look up the issue. Two months ago, was it? What date? No matter—I'll find it. And you didn't even think to tell us?"

"How did you know the article was mine? It's only signed with an initial," Raskolnikov asked, now genuinely curious.

"I found out by chance," Porfiry replied with a casual wave of his hand. "The editor mentioned it to me—he's an acquaintance of mine. I was intrigued, of course."

"I recall analyzing the psychology of a criminal, both before and after committing a crime," Raskolnikov said thoughtfully.

"Yes," Porfiry nodded eagerly, "and you argued that the act of committing a crime is often accompanied by a kind of illness or derangement. That part of your article was quite original. But what fascinated me more wasn't that—it was an idea you introduced near the end. Unfortunately, you only hinted at it without developing it fully. You suggested there are certain individuals who—well, not exactly have the ability, but perhaps the right—to commit crimes, even transgressing moral laws. And that the law doesn't entirely apply to them. Is that correct?"

Raskolnikov gave a faint smile, detecting the deliberate exaggeration in Porfiry's interpretation. It was clear the man was twisting his words to draw him out.

"What? What are you talking about?" Razumihin interjected, looking alarmed. "A right to commit crimes? Surely not because of environmental factors?"

"No, not because of environmental factors," Porfiry replied smoothly. "In Rodya's article, humanity is divided into two categories: the 'ordinary' and the 'extraordinary.' The ordinary people, he argues, must live in submission. They have no right to break the law, precisely because they are ordinary. But the extraordinary individuals, according to his idea, have a right to commit any crime, to step over moral and legal boundaries, simply by virtue of being extraordinary. That's what you wrote, isn't it?" Porfiry asked, his tone both inquisitive and faintly provocative.

"That can't be right," Razumihin muttered, his face a mixture of disbelief and bewilderment.

Raskolnikov's smile widened slightly. He saw through the game immediately and recognized where Porfiry was trying to lead him. A challenge had been presented, and he resolved to meet it head-on.

"That wasn't quite my argument," he began, his tone measured and unassuming. "But I do admit, you've almost captured its essence—perhaps even perfectly. If there's a difference, it's this: I don't claim that extraordinary individuals are invariably compelled to commit breaches of morality, as you term them. Frankly, I doubt anyone could publish such an assertion without it being dismissed outright. What I suggested, rather, was that an 'extraordinary' individual possesses a kind of right—not an official or legal one, but an internal, personal right—to decide for themselves, in their conscience, whether to overstep certain boundaries. And this would only be in circumstances where such an action is essential to achieve their vision or fulfill an idea, one that might potentially benefit all of humanity."

He paused briefly, gauging his audience, and continued with more clarity. "You've said my article wasn't definitive enough, so let me try to be as explicit as possible. Consider this hypothetical: if the discoveries of Kepler or Newton could not have been brought to light without sacrificing the lives of a few individuals—one, a dozen, perhaps even a hundred or more—then Newton would not only have had the right but might even have been morally obligated to eliminate those lives for the greater good of humanity. But this does not mean that Newton—or anyone else—has the right to go about murdering indiscriminately or stealing daily in the marketplace. That distinction is crucial."

His expression grew more thoughtful as he pressed on. "In the article, I also posited that all great leaders and lawmakers—Lycurgus, Solon, Muhammad, Napoleon, and others—were, in a sense, criminals. By creating new laws, they necessarily violated the old ones, those handed down from their ancestors and considered sacred by the people. And they didn't hesitate to shed blood to achieve their goals—often innocent blood, spilled by those who defended the old laws with courage. It's a striking historical pattern: the majority of these figures, whom humanity later reveres as benefactors and visionaries, were guilty of immense bloodshed. In essence, my point was this: all great men—or even those who deviate slightly from the ordinary—are, by nature, transgressors to some degree. They have to be, because breaking free from the confines of convention is inherent to their nature. To remain within those confines is something they can neither accept nor endure."

He leaned back slightly, his voice steady but infused with a subtle undercurrent of conviction. "There's nothing particularly revolutionary about these ideas; similar thoughts have been expressed countless times before. As for my division of people into the 'ordinary' and the 'extraordinary,' I concede it's somewhat arbitrary. I don't claim to have pinned down exact categories or numbers. What I do believe—firmly—is that, by some natural law, humanity tends to divide itself into two groups. The first, the 'ordinary,' consists of those who act as the material foundation of society. They exist primarily to perpetuate their kind, living within established norms, and often find satisfaction in being governed. In fact, I argue it is their duty to submit to governance, as this aligns with their role and nature. There's nothing degrading in that—it's simply their calling."

He shifted slightly in his seat, his voice gaining a subtle intensity. "The second group, the 'extraordinary,' are those who defy the laws of their time. They are disruptors, destroyers even, though the extent and nature of their disruptions vary widely. Their actions—sometimes deemed crimes—are relative and depend entirely on the scope and necessity of their ideas. Often, they work to dismantle the present for the sake of building something better. And if, for the sake of their vision, they find themselves compelled to step over a corpse or wade through blood, they may discover within themselves a moral justification for doing so. Again, I emphasize, this depends entirely on the idea and its magnitude."

He met their gazes firmly now, speaking with quiet resolve. "This, and only this, was the sense in which I spoke of their 'right' to crime in my article. It's worth noting, though, that the masses rarely, if ever, recognize this right at the time. They punish such individuals, sometimes executing them, fulfilling their own conservative role in the process. Yet, in the generations that follow, these same masses are often the ones to elevate these so-called criminals onto pedestals, venerating them as heroes or visionaries."

Raskolnikov's voice softened slightly as he concluded. "The first category of people—the ordinary—are the custodians of the present, maintaining and propagating life as it is. The second category—the extraordinary—are the architects of the future, the ones who propel the world toward its ultimate goals. Both categories, in my view, have an equal right to exist, and neither diminishes the value of the other. And so, life continues in this eternal conflict—vive la guerre éternelle—until, perhaps, we arrive at the New Jerusalem."

"Then you genuinely believe in the New Jerusalem?" Porfiry asked, his tone slightly edged with curiosity.

"I do," Raskolnikov replied firmly, his voice steady. Throughout the preceding conversation and now, his gaze remained fixed on a specific spot on the carpet, as though anchoring himself.

"And... do you believe in God? Forgive my curiosity."

"I do," Raskolnikov repeated, this time raising his eyes to meet Porfiry's, his expression unwavering.

"And what about Lazarus—do you believe in his resurrection?"

"I... I do," Raskolnikov answered, a hint of confusion creeping into his voice. "Why are you asking me this?"

"Do you believe it literally?" Porfiry pressed, his gaze sharpening.

"Literally," Raskolnikov affirmed.

"You don't say so.... I only asked out of curiosity. Excuse me," Porfiry said, waving a hand dismissively before steering the conversation back. "But let us return to the point. Those extraordinary individuals you mentioned—they are not always executed, are they? Some manage to..."

"To triumph in their lifetime? Oh yes, some do," Raskolnikov interjected with a faint smile. "And then—"

"And then they begin executing others?" Porfiry finished the thought with an arched brow.

"If it's necessary. Yes, often they do," Raskolnikov replied dryly. "Your remark is quite astute."

"Thank you," Porfiry said, inclining his head with mock politeness. "But tell me this—how do you distinguish these extraordinary individuals from the ordinary ones? Are there any signs at birth? Surely, for practical, law-abiding citizens like myself, it would be useful if they had some clear mark, don't you think? Perhaps they could wear a distinctive uniform or bear a visible brand to avoid confusion. After all, what if someone mistakenly imagines themselves extraordinary and starts... 'eliminating obstacles,' as you so eloquently put it?"

"Oh, that happens quite often," Raskolnikov said with a faint smirk. "That observation is even sharper than your last."

"Why, thank you again."

"But take note," Raskolnikov continued, "this confusion only arises within the first category—among the so-called ordinary people.

Despite their innate tendency toward obedience, many of them—perhaps as a kind of capricious whim, almost like a cow trying to jump a fence—imagine themselves advanced thinkers or destroyers of the old order. They throw themselves into 'new movements' quite sincerely. Yet, ironically, the truly innovative thinkers often remain unnoticed or, worse, are dismissed by these same would-be reformers as reactionary. But don't worry yourself too much; these pretenders rarely go far. At most, they might deserve a bit of a thrashing to set them straight, though even that's often unnecessary—they're quite adept at punishing themselves. They invent public acts of penitence, grand and dramatic displays of remorse, and some even inflict their own punishments. It's all quite orderly, really—a law of nature, you might say."

"Well, that's a relief," Porfiry replied, chuckling softly. "But let me ask you another thing. Are there many of these extraordinary people who have the right to... well, you know, eliminate others? I'm ready to bow down to them, of course, but it's rather unsettling to think they might be numerous, don't you agree?"

"Oh, you can rest easy," Raskolnikov assured him with a faintly sardonic smile. "They are extremely rare. People capable of conceiving new ideas—truly groundbreaking ones—are few and far between. The emergence of such individuals follows a law, though we have yet to understand it fully. Most of humanity is mere raw material, existing only to sustain life until, through some mysterious process, one independent thinker is born among thousands—perhaps one in ten thousand. A man with true genius? He is one in millions. And the truly great geniuses—the crowning achievements of humanity—may appear only once in many millions. I can't claim to understand the precise mechanism by which this happens, but it's certainly no accident. There must be a definite law at work."

"Are you two serious?" Razumihin finally burst out, looking between them with incredulous frustration. "You're sitting here, talking as though this is a joke. Rodya, are you honestly serious?"

Raskolnikov raised his pale face, his expression solemn and introspective, offering no immediate reply. The quiet, almost mournful look on his face starkly contrasted with Porfiry's persistent, sardonic amusement.

Razumihin continued, undeterred. "If you're serious about this, then you're right—it's not a new idea. We've all read and heard it before, countless times. But what's truly disturbing, and undeniably your own twist, is the notion that you justify bloodshed—sanction it, even—in the name of conscience. And you do it with such... such chilling conviction."

"You're correct," Porfiry chimed in with a nod. "It is more terrifying when sanctioned by conscience than when justified by law."

Razumihin shook his head, visibly unsettled. "You must have exaggerated in your article. There's some misunderstanding. I'll read it myself—I need to see for myself what you wrote."

"That part isn't in the article," Raskolnikov said quietly. "It's only hinted at."

"Ah, but now I see where you stand on crime," Porfiry remarked, leaning forward with a strange blend of curiosity and amusement. "Still, forgive my persistence; there's a practical concern I can't shake. Suppose some young man fancies himself a Lycurgus or a future Muhammad—what then? What if he starts removing obstacles, as you put it, for some grand enterprise of his and, say, needs money to fund it?"

At this, Zametov let out a sharp laugh from his corner, but Raskolnikov didn't so much as glance at him.

"I'll admit," Raskolnikov said calmly, "cases like that are bound to happen. The vain and the foolish are particularly prone to such delusions—especially the young."

"Yes, you see," Porfiry continued with a slight shrug, his tone light but probing. "Well then?"

"What then?" Raskolnikov replied with a faint smile, his expression calm but tinged with a subtle defiance. "That's not my fault. That's the way things are, and that's the way they always will be. Razumihin said a moment ago"—he nodded toward his friend—"that I sanction bloodshed. But society is well-protected, don't you think? We have prisons, banishment, criminal investigators, penal servitude—there's no real need for concern. All you need to do is catch the thief."

"And what if we do catch him?" Porfiry asked, his tone sharpening slightly.

"Then he gets what he deserves," Raskolnikov answered coolly.

"You are certainly logical," Porfiry remarked, his voice carrying a faint, almost teasing undertone. "But what about his conscience? What of that?"

"Why should that matter to you?" Raskolnikov countered, his tone almost dismissive.

"Simply out of humanity," Porfiry replied with a sly smile.

"If he has a conscience," Raskolnikov said evenly, "he will suffer for his mistake. That will be his punishment—on top of the prison sentence, of course."

"But the real geniuses," Razumihin suddenly interjected, his brow furrowed deeply, "those extraordinary individuals who you say have the 'right' to kill—shouldn't they suffer too? Even for the blood they shed?"

"Why use the word 'ought'?" Raskolnikov asked, his voice softening into a contemplative tone. "It isn't about permission or prohibition. They will suffer if they feel remorse for their victims. Pain and suffering are always unavoidable for those with large intellects and deep hearts. The truly great men of this world must, I think, carry great sadness with them throughout their lives." His voice grew quieter, almost dreamlike, as though he were speaking to himself rather than to the others.

He raised his eyes, scanning the faces of those around him with a strange, almost melancholy intensity. A faint smile appeared on his lips as he reached for his cap, his movements slow and deliberate. Compared to the energy he had shown upon entering the room, his demeanor now was almost unnervingly subdued. It was as if he had retreated inward, leaving the others to puzzle over the change.

Everyone stood up, their movements almost synchronized, as though guided by an unspoken cue.

"Well, you're free to abuse me or be angry with me if you wish," Porfiry began again, his tone once more sliding into that of a man pretending to apologize while deliberately pressing a point. "But I simply cannot resist! Allow me one small question—just one little notion that's been troubling me. Humor me; it's nothing, really."

"Very well," Raskolnikov said, his voice cold and steady. He stood in front of Porfiry, pale and rigid, his expression betraying nothing. "Tell me your little notion."

"You see..." Porfiry hesitated, rubbing his hands together as though warming up for a speech. "I don't quite know how to put it properly—it's more of a playful, psychological thought, if you will. When you were writing your article, surely you couldn't have helped, just for a moment, imagining yourself as... oh, I don't know... one of those 'extraordinary' men, uttering a new word in the way you describe. Isn't that so?"

"Quite possibly," Raskolnikov replied with a scornful smile. "Perhaps you're even perfectly correct."

Razumihin shifted uncomfortably but said nothing.

"And if that's the case," Porfiry continued, his voice laced with a peculiar kind of amusement, "could you—purely hypothetically, of course—bring yourself, if faced with worldly difficulties or the chance to serve humanity, to, shall we say, step over certain obstacles? For example, could you rob or even kill?"

As he spoke, Porfiry gave an exaggerated wink with his left eye and chuckled softly, his laughter oddly soundless.

"If I could," Raskolnikov replied, his tone cutting and disdainful, "I certainly wouldn't tell you."

"No, of course not," Porfiry said with mock earnestness, spreading his hands as though to concede the point. "I only meant it as a question of literary interest, nothing more."

"How crude and transparent," Raskolnikov thought, a wave of revulsion washing over him.

"Allow me to clarify," Raskolnikov said aloud, his voice now sharper and more deliberate. "I don't consider myself a Mahomet or a Napoleon—or any figure of that sort. Not being one, I can't possibly tell you how I would act in their place."

"Oh, come now," Porfiry said with disarming familiarity, his tone taking on an almost playful lilt. "Doesn't everyone in Russia fancy themselves a Napoleon these days?"

There was something unsettling in his tone, a subtle yet unmistakable edge.

"Perhaps," Porfiry added, his voice dropping slightly, "it was one of these aspiring Napoleons who dealt with Alyona Ivanovna last week?"

Zametov, standing in the corner, suddenly blurted out a laugh, the sound sharp and jarring against the tension that had been building in the room.

Raskolnikov said nothing. He stood perfectly still, his gaze fixed firmly on Porfiry, his expression hard and unyielding. Razumihin, who had been watching the exchange closely, was now scowling deeply. He seemed to have noticed something—though what, exactly, he couldn't yet articulate.

A heavy silence fell over the room, the air thick with unspoken thoughts. At last, Raskolnikov turned toward the door, his movements slow but resolute, as if signaling the end of the conversation without uttering another word.

"Are you leaving already?" Porfiry asked with a tone of amiable surprise, extending his hand with a politeness that felt almost exaggerated. "It was truly a pleasure to make your acquaintance. As for your little request, don't trouble yourself; just write as I instructed—or better yet, come to see me personally in a day or two. Tomorrow, in fact, would be perfect. I'll be at my office at eleven o'clock sharp. We'll sort everything out then; have a proper discussion. Being one of the last to visit her, you might be able to shed some light on something for us," he added with an expression so genial it almost seemed too studied.

"You mean to officially cross-examine me?" Raskolnikov retorted sharply, his eyes narrowing as if to catch the slightest shift in Porfiry's demeanor.

"Oh, no, no, not at all," Porfiry replied with an air of mock surprise. "That's not necessary for now. You misunderstand me entirely. I simply like to leave no stone unturned, you see. I've spoken with everyone who had dealings with her—those who left pledges, that is. I even managed to collect a bit of evidence from some of them. You're simply the last on my list.... Oh, wait," he exclaimed, as if a sudden thought had struck him, and turned toward Razumihin with a light of mock delight in his eyes. "You know, you've been going on about that Nikolay fellow! Of course, I understand—yes, yes, I know quite well he's innocent." He then turned back to Raskolnikov, his smile broadening. "But what can one do? We had to question Dmitri as well. These things must be thorough. Anyway, this is what I wanted to ask: when you went upstairs that day, it was past seven, wasn't it?"

"Yes," Raskolnikov replied, feeling a strange and immediate sense of unease, as though he had just taken a misstep. Why had he answered so readily?

"Good, good," Porfiry continued, nodding as though everything was falling into place. "Now, when you went up between seven and eight, did you happen to notice an open flat on the second floor? Perhaps you saw two workmen—or at least one—inside? They were painters. Does that ring a bell? It's a matter of great importance for them."

"Painters?" Raskolnikov repeated, his voice measured and deliberate as though rifling through his memory. Simultaneously, his mind raced, analyzing every word, every intonation, trying desperately to spot the trap that he was certain lay hidden. He felt a suffocating wave of anxiety crash over him, but he kept his composure. "No," he said slowly, as if pondering deeply. "I don't remember seeing any painters, nor do I recall noticing an open flat on the second floor. But on the fourth floor"—he paused deliberately, as though the memory had just surfaced—"now that you mention it, I do recall something. Someone was moving out of the flat opposite Alyona Ivanovna's. Yes, I remember it quite clearly now—there were porters carrying out a sofa, and I was squeezed up against the wall as they passed. But painters? No, I don't recall seeing any painters or any flat open elsewhere. No, I'm quite certain of that."

"What do you mean?" Razumihin suddenly burst out, his voice sharp as though a realization had just dawned on him. "Hold on! The painters were working there on the day of the murder! And he was there three days before that. Why on earth are you asking about this?"

"Ah, confound it! I've gotten myself completely muddled!" Porfiry exclaimed, slapping his forehead with a theatrical gesture. "The devil take this case—it's enough to drive anyone mad!" He turned back to Raskolnikov, now speaking in a tone of mild apology. "I'm terribly sorry about that. It's just that it would be such a help if we could find anyone who might have seen those painters between seven and eight that evening. I suppose I got my dates mixed up and thought you might remember something useful. My mistake entirely."

"You should really be more careful," Razumihin muttered grimly, his tone heavy with disapproval.

Porfiry escorted them to the door with a degree of politeness that bordered on the obsequious. His manner, though outwardly pleasant, felt almost oppressive.

Once they stepped out onto the street, an uncomfortable silence settled over them, heavy and suffocating. They walked several paces in this oppressive quiet before Raskolnikov suddenly drew a deep breath, as though trying to expel the tension that had knotted itself within him.

Chapter 6

"I don't believe it, I simply can't believe it!" Razumihin repeated emphatically, shaking his head in perplexity, as if trying to fend off the unsettling arguments Raskolnikov had just laid out. His tone was charged with a mixture of frustration and confusion, his face flushed with the intensity of their exchange.

By now, they were nearing Bakaleyev's lodgings, where Pulcheria Alexandrovna and Dounia had been anxiously waiting for their arrival. Razumihin, however, was too caught up in the conversation to walk steadily. He kept stopping abruptly along the way, his excitement growing as they delved further into the topic. For the first time, they were discussing it openly, and that alone seemed to thrill and unsettle him in equal measure.

"Don't believe it, then," Raskolnikov retorted, his voice cutting and tinged with cold amusement. A faint, detached smile lingered on his lips as he glanced at his friend. "As usual, you notice nothing, but I was weighing every word, every nuance."

"You're suspicious, that's why you were analyzing every word so closely," Razumihin countered, almost pleadingly. "Still... I admit, Porfiry's tone did seem odd, and that wretch Zametov! There's something there, you're right—but why? What's their angle?"

"He's changed his mind since last night," Raskolnikov said dismissively, his voice steady but edged with disdain.

"On the contrary! If they truly believed that brainless theory, they'd be hiding it better, playing their cards close to their chest. They'd wait, wouldn't they? They'd try to catch you off guard later. But this... this was just impudence—carelessness even."

"If they had solid facts—real, undeniable facts—or even reasonable grounds for suspicion, they'd be playing a subtler game," Raskolnikov explained, his tone sharpening as if speaking to a slow student. "They would have made a move long ago, conducted a search, something. But they don't have facts—not a single one. It's all conjecture, mirages, ambiguous insinuations. Since they have nothing concrete, they try to provoke me, to throw me off balance with their arrogance. Porfiry, for instance—maybe he was irritated at his lack of evidence and let something slip in frustration. Or maybe he's working on a plan. He's clever, that one. I can't say for sure. It's revolting even to talk about it. Enough."

"And it's insulting! Insulting beyond measure!" Razumihin erupted, stopping short and throwing up his hands. "I get it, Rodya, I do. It's maddening. But, you know, now that we've laid it all out—and I'm glad we have, finally—I'll admit I've noticed it, too. That insinuation, that barely concealed suspicion—it's been there all along. But on what basis? None! How dare they? Just think of it—a poor, half-starved student, stricken by poverty and hypochondria, about to be consumed by fever and delirium. He collapses in front of a few arrogant policemen, subjected to their insolence. Add to that the sudden confrontation with Tchebarov and his debt, the oppressive heat, thirty degrees Reaumur, and the suffocating crowd. He's already faint with hunger, and to top it all off, there's talk of a murder committed nearby. Anyone might have a fainting spell under such conditions! And this... this is what they're basing everything on? It's absurd! Damn them!" Razumihin's voice rose in anger, and he began pacing. "If I were in your place, Rodya, I'd laugh in their faces. No, better yet—I'd spit on them. Spit on them all, I say!"

Raskolnikov's lips curled faintly into a sardonic smile. "He really does put it well," he thought, though the bitterness in his expression remained.

"But that interrogation tomorrow..." Raskolnikov muttered, his voice dropping. "Do I really have to go and endure their questioning again? I'm already irritated enough that I lowered myself to talk to Zametov yesterday."

"Damn it!" Razumihin cried, striking his palm with his fist. "I'll go to Porfiry myself. I'll get the truth out of him. He's practically family; he can't brush me off. And Zametov? That scoundrel..."

"At last, he's starting to see through them," Raskolnikov mused silently, his eyes narrowing slightly.

"Wait a moment!" Razumihin grabbed him by the shoulder, stopping him mid-step. "Listen, you're wrong. I've thought it through. You're wrong! That question about the workmen—it wasn't a trap, not the way you think. If you had done... well, that, would you really have said you'd seen them painting the flat? On the contrary, you'd have claimed to have seen nothing! Who would incriminate themselves like that?"

"If I had done that," Raskolnikov said slowly, his words heavy with reluctance and distaste, "I'd have said I saw the workmen and the flat."

"But why would you admit that?" Razumihin demanded, baffled.

"Because," Raskolnikov replied, his tone sharp and almost cutting, "only peasants or absolute novices deny everything outright during an interrogation. Anyone with even a little experience knows that. They admit to the unavoidable facts—those that can't be denied—and then they provide an alternative explanation. They spin it in a way that changes its significance, recasts it in a new light. Porfiry knows this. He might have counted on me answering as I did, just to make it seem more truthful, and then he'd have tried to twist it against me."

Razumihin stared at him, stunned, as though a new realization had just dawned. But he said nothing, and they resumed walking, the air between them charged with unspoken tension.

"But he would have told you immediately that the workmen couldn't have been there two days before, which means you must have been there on the day of the murder at eight o'clock. That's how he would have caught you in a detail," Razumihin exclaimed, his words tumbling out in a rush as if he had solved a puzzle.

"Exactly," Raskolnikov replied, his voice cold yet deliberate. "That's precisely what he was counting on—that I wouldn't have enough time to think it through, that I'd rush to give the most plausible answer and forget that the workmen couldn't have been there two days before."

"But how could you forget such a simple thing?" Razumihin asked, his brow furrowing in frustration.

"Nothing could be easier," Raskolnikov said with a faint, grim smile. "It's in precisely those stupid little details that clever people are most easily trapped. The more cunning a man is, the less likely he is to suspect that he'll be undone by something so small. The more intricate his plans, the simpler the trap needs to be to ensnare him. Porfiry isn't as foolish as you seem to think."

"Then he's a scoundrel if that's true!" Razumihin burst out angrily.

Raskolnikov couldn't help but laugh, though the sound was dry and humorless. Yet, even as he laughed, he felt a sudden unease. It struck him how openly he was explaining his thoughts, how eagerly he was clarifying, despite the tension that had marked their entire conversation up to this point. The frankness of his response surprised even himself.

"Why am I explaining all this?" he wondered, his unease deepening as the thought hit him. The conversation, once a mere necessity, now seemed to spark something within him—a disturbing mixture of engagement and alarm.

His discomfort grew until it became almost unbearable. They had just reached the entrance to Bakaleyev's lodgings when Raskolnikov suddenly stopped. "Go in without me," he said abruptly, his voice tight. "I'll be back shortly."

"Where are you going? We're already here," Razumihin said, looking at him with a mix of concern and confusion.

"I need to go," Raskolnikov said sharply. "I'll only be a half-hour. Tell them I'll be back."

"What's going on? I'll come with you," Razumihin insisted, taking a step forward.

"You want to torment me, too, don't you?" Raskolnikov suddenly shouted, his voice filled with such bitterness and despair that Razumihin froze in place, his hands falling limply to his sides. For a moment, he stood there on the steps, watching Raskolnikov stride off in the direction of his lodging, his expression dark and brooding.

Grinding his teeth in frustration, Razumihin clenched his fists. "I'll get to the bottom of this," he muttered to himself. "I'll wring the truth out of Porfiry if it's the last thing I do." Resolute, he turned and headed upstairs to reassure Pulcheria Alexandrovna, who by now must have been growing anxious over their delay.

Meanwhile, Raskolnikov reached his room, his face pale and his hair damp with sweat. His breath came in short, ragged gasps as he rushed up the stairs. Once inside, he latched the door immediately and moved directly to the corner where he had hidden the stolen items. His hands trembled as he dug into the hole under the wallpaper, his fingers probing every crease and crack.

Nothing.

He straightened up, his breath catching as relief flooded him. Yet the very act of checking had unsettled him further. A thought had struck him like a lightning bolt as he had approached Bakaleyev's—a horrifying, insidious thought: what if something—a chain, a stud, even a scrap of paper with the old woman's handwriting—had fallen out unnoticed and was waiting to betray him?

For a moment, he stood there, lost in thought, a faint, bitter smile tugging at his lips. It was a smile that betrayed his humiliation and mounting dread. Finally, he grabbed his cap, smoothed back his damp hair, and left the room quietly, his mind a tangled mess of conflicting ideas.

As he passed through the gateway, a loud voice suddenly called out, "Here he is himself!"

Raskolnikov stopped and looked up. A porter stood at the entrance to his room, pointing him out to a short, stout man standing nearby. The man wore a long coat and greasy cap, his posture stooped and his face flabby, with little eyes that seemed to glint maliciously beneath heavy lids. He had a curiously androgynous appearance, his features almost doll-like, yet his expression was anything but soft—it was grim and discontented.

"What is it?" Raskolnikov asked, stepping forward.

The man glanced at him briefly, his gaze cold and deliberate, before turning and walking away without a word.

"What is it?" Raskolnikov repeated, his voice rising slightly as he addressed the porter.

"He was asking if a student lived here," the porter replied, his tone casual yet puzzled. "Mentioned your name and asked who you were staying with. I saw you coming and pointed you out, so he left. Strange fellow."

Raskolnikov frowned but didn't respond. Without a word, he ran after the stranger, catching sight of him walking slowly along the opposite side of the street. His pace was deliberate, his gaze fixed on the ground as though lost in thought. Raskolnikov followed him at a distance, his steps quickening until he was level with the man.

"You were asking for me at the porter's?" Raskolnikov asked, his voice calm but edged with tension.

The man didn't reply, nor did he look at him. They walked side by side in silence for a moment before Raskolnikov spoke again, his tone sharper this time. "Why did you ask for me and then say nothing? What is the meaning of this?"

The man stopped walking and finally turned to look at Raskolnikov. His expression was grim, his small eyes narrowing as he spoke a single word in a quiet, deliberate tone: "Murderer."

Raskolnikov kept walking beside the man, his legs suddenly feeling like they had turned to water. A cold shiver coursed down his back, and for a moment it felt as though his heart had stopped entirely, only to begin hammering wildly as if it had been set free from some restraint. Neither spoke as they continued side by side for what felt like an eternity, though it was barely a hundred paces. The silence between them was oppressive, like a weight pressing down on Raskolnikov's chest.

The man didn't glance at him, keeping his gaze fixed ahead.

"What... what do you mean?" Raskolnikov muttered at last, his voice barely audible. "Who are you talking about? Who's a murderer?"

"You are a murderer," the man replied, his voice clear and deliberate. The words were like ice, sharp and cutting, as if he were savoring the moment. He turned to face Raskolnikov then, his eyes burning with triumphant hatred, a cold, mocking smile twisting his lips.

They had reached a crossroad, and without another word, the man turned left, not bothering to look back. Raskolnikov stood frozen in place, staring after him, his feet seemingly rooted to the ground. When the man was about fifty paces away, he turned his head and glanced back. Even at that distance, Raskolnikov thought he could see the same icy smile still lingering on the man's face, as though he were relishing some private, malevolent joke.

With unsteady steps and knees that felt as though they might buckle beneath him, Raskolnikov finally turned and headed back toward his garret. A chill seemed to seep into his very bones, and his hands trembled as he reached for the latch to his door. Once inside, he set his cap on the table with a mechanical motion and stood motionless for several minutes, staring at nothing, his mind blank.

Eventually, he staggered to the sofa and collapsed onto it, releasing a low, weak moan of pain. Exhaustion washed over him like a wave, and he lay there for what might have been half an hour, utterly motionless. His mind refused to focus; instead, fragments of thoughts and disjointed images flitted before him, like leaves caught in a whirlwind.

He saw faces—faces he hadn't thought of in years, faces of people from his childhood, fleeting acquaintances he barely remembered, or strangers he had passed once in the street. He saw the belfry of the old church in his hometown, the green felt of a billiard table in some smoky tavern, and the stern faces of officers playing billiards nearby. The sharp, acrid smell of cigars from an underground tobacco shop suddenly filled his memory, mingling with the muddy water of a dark, slippery back staircase scattered with broken eggshells. Somewhere in the distance, he thought he could hear the sound of Sunday church bells, faint and echoing.

The images swirled and shifted, one blending into the next with dizzying speed. Some he clung to, finding a strange, fleeting comfort in them, while others faded before he could grasp them fully. All the while, a strange sense of oppression hung over him, but it wasn't entirely unbearable. At times, it was even oddly soothing, a peculiar kind of numbness that dulled his thoughts.

The faint sound of hurried footsteps reached him, snapping him out of his haze. Recognizing them, he quickly shut his eyes and feigned sleep. The door opened softly, and Razumihin stood in the doorway, hesitating. After a moment, he stepped quietly into the room, his footsteps careful and deliberate.

"Don't disturb him. Let him sleep," whispered Nastasya from behind him. "He can eat later."

"Yes, yes, you're right," Razumihin replied softly. The two retreated, shutting the door behind them with a gentle click.

Raskolnikov remained still for another half hour before opening his eyes. He turned onto his back, clasping his hands behind his head, his expression dark and brooding.

"Who was he?" he muttered aloud. "Who was that man? Where did he come from? What did he see? He must have seen something— he knows. That's certain. But how? Where was he? How could he have seen? And why now? Why has he only just appeared, as if springing out of the earth?"

He shivered, the chill returning as the questions pounded in his mind. "And the jewel case—Nikolay found it behind the door. Is that possible? Could it really be a clue? It takes the slightest line—just a thread—and they can weave a whole web of evidence from it. A fly buzzing past might have seen it, and that could be enough. Is it possible?"

His thoughts spiraled, and he felt the sickening weight of his physical weakness pressing down on him. "I should have known," he whispered bitterly. "I should have known this would happen. How could I, of all people, take up an axe? How could I have dared to shed blood? I should have known better—no, I did know," he added, his voice trembling with despair.

He lay there, staring at the ceiling as one last thought took shape. "No, real great men don't crumble like this. The true masters—the Napoleons, the conquerors—they storm through life. They massacre cities, leave armies to die, sacrifice millions, and they laugh about it later. Altars are built in their honor after their deaths. They aren't made of flesh and blood—they're forged from bronze."

A sudden, absurd idea brought a faint, humorless smile to his lips. "Napoleon, the pyramids, Waterloo," he thought, "and me—hiding under an old woman's bed with an axe, hunting for a red trunk. What a joke for Porfiry Petrovitch! How could he possibly digest such a ridiculous hash? It's too grotesque. A Napoleon creeping under a bed! Disgusting, revolting!"

And yet, despite his grim smile, he could feel the cold weight of his fear settling deeper into his chest.

At moments, Raskolnikov felt as though he were losing his grip on reality. His thoughts twisted and turned feverishly, feeding his agitation. "The old woman... she doesn't matter," he muttered, his mind racing incoherently. "She was a mistake, yes, but she's not what's important! She was merely an illness... a hurdle. I wanted to overstep, but I stumbled. I didn't kill a person; I killed a principle! Yet I didn't even cross the boundary—I stopped short. All I could do was kill, and even that I couldn't manage properly. Principle? Ha! What nonsense! Why was Razumihin ranting about the socialists? Industrious people, they are. Practical. 'Happiness for all'—isn't that their motto? But life comes only once, and I refuse to wait for this grand 'happiness for all.' I need to live now. I can't stand by and watch my mother starve while clinging to my meager rouble, hoping for a future utopia."

He laughed suddenly, the sound harsh and strange. "I'm just another louse, an aesthetic louse, nothing more!" His laughter deepened, turning almost manic. "Yes, a louse! First, because I can reason myself into that label. Second, because for weeks I've been deluding myself, troubling fate, justifying my actions by invoking some grand, noble purpose. And third—because I tried to carry it out with some twisted sense of justice, weighing and measuring every detail. Out of all the vermin, I picked the most useless one to snuff out, and I only planned to take what I needed—no more, no less. And yet... here I am, vilifying myself, knowing full well I'm even more loathsome than the one I killed!"

Grinding his teeth, he continued, his voice filled with venom. "The real horror of it all? I knew I'd feel this way afterward, yet I did it anyway. And for what? The vulgarity of it! The abjectness of it! The old woman—she's just a symbol of my failure. I hate her. I hate her so much I'd kill her all over again if she somehow came back. And Lizaveta... poor Lizaveta. Why did she have to walk in? Strange how I rarely think of her—almost as if I didn't kill her. Sonia... Lizaveta... gentle creatures, both of them. Soft, kind eyes... women who give everything without complaint. And Sonia... gentle Sonia!"

He groaned as his fevered thoughts spiraled. At some point, he lost track of time, and when he came to, he found himself on the street. The day had slipped into twilight, and the moon hung high in the sky, casting an eerie glow over the bustling street. The air felt heavy, suffocating, and there was a faint scent of mortar and stagnant water. People bustled about—workmen heading home, others out for an evening stroll—but Raskolnikov barely registered them. He moved as if in a trance, aware only that he had set out with some purpose, though he couldn't remember what it was.

Then he saw him—a man standing on the other side of the street, beckoning. Raskolnikov crossed over, but as soon as he approached, the man turned and began walking away, his head bowed. "Did he really beckon?" Raskolnikov wondered, his pulse quickening. He followed the man, his steps faltering but insistent. The stranger never looked back.

At last, they reached the courtyard of a large building. The man entered without a glance behind, and Raskolnikov hurried after him, his heart pounding. Inside the courtyard, the man turned briefly, appearing to beckon once more before vanishing into a stairwell. Raskolnikov hesitated, then rushed after him, his footsteps echoing ominously. The staircase seemed oddly familiar, and with each step, a growing dread filled him. By the time he reached the third floor, the stillness was suffocating, and the darkness seemed alive with menace.

The door to a flat stood ajar. He hesitated again but stepped inside. The room was bathed in cold, coppery moonlight. Everything was as it had been before—the yellow sofa, the mirror, the chairs. But now it felt otherworldly, as if time itself had frozen. He stood in silence, his heartbeat thundering in his ears. Suddenly, a sharp crack echoed in the stillness, then silence again.

Then he saw it—a cloak draped in the corner. It hadn't been there before. His breath caught as he crept toward it. He pulled it aside, and there, hunched on a chair, was the old woman. She was bent double, her face hidden.

He stood frozen, staring at her. Slowly, he reached for the axe, struck her once, then again. But she didn't move, didn't react, as though she were made of wood. Panic surged within him as he bent down to peer into her face. What he saw made his blood run cold. The old woman was shaking with silent laughter, her face contorted in grotesque mirth.

From the bedroom came faint whispering and laughter. Overwhelmed, Raskolnikov struck again and again, but the laughter only grew louder. He turned to flee, but the passageway was filled with people—silent, watching, their faces a sea of unreadable expressions. He tried to scream, but no sound came. He woke with a start.

He drew a shaky breath, but the nightmare lingered. His door creaked open, and a stranger stepped inside. Tall, stout, with a fair beard and a calm demeanor, the man closed the door quietly and sat, cane in hand, watching Raskolnikov intently.

For ten unbearable minutes, silence filled the room. At last, Raskolnikov sat up and demanded, "Who are you? What do you want?"

The man smiled faintly. "Arkady Ivanovitch Svidrigaïlov," he said, leaning forward slightly. "Allow me to introduce myself."

Part 4

Chapter 1

"Could this still be a dream?" Raskolnikov wondered, his thoughts twisting and turning with doubt and unease. He scrutinized the visitor carefully, his eyes narrowing as though he might unravel some hidden truth in the man's expression.

"Svidrigaïlov? This is absurd—it can't be," he finally muttered aloud, his voice tinged with disbelief and confusion.

The unexpected guest showed no signs of surprise at Raskolnikov's exclamation. His demeanor was calm, almost amiable, as though this encounter were entirely ordinary.

"I've come to see you for two reasons," Svidrigaïlov began, his tone measured and deliberate. "First, I wanted to make your personal acquaintance. I've already heard quite a lot about you—things both interesting and, I might add, flattering. Second, I hold onto the hope that you won't refuse to help me with a matter that directly concerns the welfare of your sister, Avdotya Romanovna. Without your support, she might not even allow me to approach her. You see, she is...

somewhat prejudiced against me. But with your assistance, I believe I could—"

"You believe wrongly," Raskolnikov cut him off sharply, his voice cold and resolute.

Svidrigaïlov raised his eyebrows but showed no sign of offense. "They arrived yesterday, did they not? May I confirm that?"

Raskolnikov remained silent, refusing to answer.

"Ah, yes, it was yesterday—I'm certain of it. I myself arrived the day before," Svidrigaïlov continued smoothly, unfazed by the lack of a response. "Now, Rodion Romanovitch, let me speak plainly. I don't feel the need to justify myself to you, but I would like to ask: what exactly was so criminal about my behavior in all this business? Let's speak without prejudice and with a little common sense, shall we?"

Raskolnikov said nothing, his gaze fixed on the man with an icy intensity.

"Was it that in my own house, I pursued a defenseless girl and 'insulted her with my disgraceful proposals'? Is that it?" Svidrigaïlov asked, leaning forward slightly. "I am anticipating your accusations, of course. But let's consider for a moment: suppose I, too, am merely a man, subject to the same weaknesses, et nihil humanum mihi alienum puto. In other words, that I am capable of feeling attraction, even love—feelings that, I assure you, are beyond anyone's control. Doesn't that explain things naturally enough? The real question is whether I am a monster—or, perhaps, a victim myself? What if, in proposing to the object of my affection that we elope to America or Switzerland, I was motivated by a genuine respect for her and a belief that I was securing both our happiness? After all, reason is often the servant of passion, is it not? And who's to say I wasn't harming myself more than anyone else in this situation?"

"That's not the point," Raskolnikov interrupted him, his voice laced with disgust. "It doesn't matter whether you're right or wrong. The fact is, we dislike you. We want nothing to do with you. You are unwelcome here. Leave."

For a moment, Svidrigaïlov seemed taken aback. Then, suddenly, he threw his head back and laughed—a deep, uninhibited laugh that seemed to echo in the small room.

"You really are... quite something," he said, still chuckling. "There's no getting around you, is there? I had hoped to maneuver around you, but you've taken exactly the right stance from the start!"

"And yet you're still trying to maneuver," Raskolnikov said icily, his glare unwavering.

"What if I am? What if I am?" Svidrigaïlov exclaimed, throwing up his hands in mock surrender. His laughter was unrestrained, almost cheerful. "It's what the French call bonne guerre—a fair game! The most innocent kind of deception, I assure you. But, my dear fellow, you've interrupted me. Let me finish what I was saying. I'll repeat: there would have been no unpleasantness—none whatsoever—if not for that wretched incident in the garden. You know what I mean. It was Marfa Petrovna who..."

He trailed off, a sly smile playing at the corners of his lips, as though inviting Raskolnikov to fill in the rest of the story. But Raskolnikov remained silent, his expression darkening further.

"You've managed to rid yourself of Marfa Petrovna as well, so they say?" Raskolnikov interjected abruptly, his tone sharp and unyielding.

Svidrigaïlov raised his eyebrows slightly, but his demeanor remained composed. "Oh, you've heard about that, too? Naturally, you would have. Still, it's an interesting topic. As for your rather pointed question, I truly don't know what to say. My own conscience is entirely clear on the matter, let me assure you. And no, I'm not the least bit apprehensive about it. Everything was carried out properly and in perfect order. The medical examination concluded that her death resulted from apoplexy, brought on by bathing too soon after a heavy meal and a bottle of wine. The evidence supports nothing else."

He paused for a moment, seemingly reflecting, and then added, "But, you know, on the train here, I couldn't help turning it over in my mind, wondering—did I, in some indirect way, contribute to her untimely demise? Perhaps by irritating her or through some other, subtler influence? But after careful consideration, I've concluded that's simply not the case."

Raskolnikov let out a short, cold laugh. "It's surprising that you bother troubling yourself about it at all."

"But why are you laughing?" Svidrigaïlov asked with a faint smile, tilting his head inquisitively. "Just think about it. I struck her twice with a switch—twice! And not even hard enough to leave a mark. Don't misunderstand me; I am fully aware of how appalling my behavior was. But, ironically, I suspect Marfa Petrovna might even have appreciated it in her own peculiar way. You see, for the past three days, she'd been cooped up at home, unable to show her face in public after exhausting every drop of drama from your sister's letter. She'd bored the entire town with her incessant readings of it. And then, suddenly, those two little switches fell into her lap, so to speak, as though heaven-sent. Her immediate reaction? She ordered the carriage to be prepared."

Svidrigaïlov leaned forward slightly, lowering his voice conspiratorially. "There are, after all, moments when women secretly revel in being insulted, no matter how indignant they might outwardly appear. Don't you think so? It's not unique to Marfa Petrovna; it's a universal truth about human beings, but especially women. Insults and indignities—they're almost like a sport to them. Perhaps even their only form of entertainment at times."

Raskolnikov shifted in his seat, suppressing the urge to rise and leave. His disgust was palpable, but a lingering curiosity—or perhaps an instinct for caution—kept him rooted in place. He asked coolly, "You seem to enjoy fighting?"

"Not particularly," Svidrigaïlov replied with an air of nonchalance. "Marfa Petrovna and I rarely fought, truth be told. Our marriage was mostly harmonious. I only resorted to the whip twice in seven years of marriage—well, three times, if you count an ambiguous incident. The first occasion was shortly after we married, once we'd settled in the countryside. The last time was what we're discussing now. Did you imagine me as some kind of ogre, a tyrant lording over his domain? Ha, ha!"

He leaned back, his laughter sudden and sharp. "Oh, but do you recall, Rodion Romanovitch, how a few years ago, during the golden age of public scandals, some nobleman—his name escapes me—was publicly shamed in every paper for thrashing a German woman on a train? What a spectacle that was! And yet, in hindsight, I can't help but think there are certain 'Germans' so exasperating that even the most progressive individual might find their patience worn thin. Of course, no one considered such a perspective back then, but it's the most humane one, don't you think?"

Raskolnikov studied him intently, noting the deliberate nonchalance with which he veiled his deeper intentions. "You must not have spoken to anyone in days," he observed, his tone carefully neutral.

"Hardly anyone," Svidrigaïlov admitted with a shrug, though his eyes glinted with something sharper than indifference. "You might be marveling at how adaptable I seem, but I assure you, I'm quite used to isolation. Still, I suppose I may come across as too adaptable for your liking?"

"It's not that," Raskolnikov replied flatly. "I'm simply struck by how willing you are to adapt to any situation, regardless of what's thrown at you."

"You mean I don't take offense at your bluntness? But why should I? You ask, I answer. Simple as that," Svidrigaïlov said, with an air of mild amusement. "I find very little in this world that holds my interest these days. And truthfully, I'm quite bored. These past three days especially—it's been unbearable. Meeting you has been a rare delight. Don't be angry, Rodion Romanovitch, but you strike me as quite peculiar yourself. There's something about you that seems... off. I don't mean this moment specifically, but in general."

He held up his hands in mock surrender as Raskolnikov's expression darkened. "Don't scowl; I meant no offense. Believe it or not, I'm not the ogre you seem to think I am."

Raskolnikov regarded Svidrigaïlov with a mixture of suspicion and curiosity, his brow furrowed in an expression of reluctant interest. "You are not much of a bear, perhaps," he said, his voice tinged with sarcasm, "but I daresay you are a man of considerable refinement— or at least you know how to present yourself as such when it suits you."

Svidrigaïlov responded with a dry chuckle, a faint shadow of haughtiness passing over his features. "I cannot say I'm overly concerned with anyone's opinion of me," he remarked coolly. "And given that indifference, why should I not indulge in a touch of vulgarity when it serves my purpose? Vulgarity, after all, can be an excellent disguise, especially in climates such as ours." His smile widened into a laugh. "Not to mention, it happens to suit my natural inclinations."

Raskolnikov's expression did not soften. "But I've heard you are not without connections in this town. You seem to have plenty of acquaintances. So why bother with me? Surely you have some specific aim in mind."

Svidrigaïlov inclined his head slightly, acknowledging the observation without entirely addressing it. "True, I do have acquaintances here," he admitted. "I've encountered some of them already over the past few days. A matter of course, really. I am decently dressed, I give the impression of being well-off, and my estate— forests and water meadows, chiefly—remains profitable despite the emancipation of the serfs. My revenue hasn't suffered. Yet I haven't called on anyone since arriving, despite being here three days. Frankly, I grew tired of them all long ago."

He leaned back, his tone turning reflective. "What a strange town this is. How it came to exist in this form, among us, is beyond me. A city filled with bureaucrats and students of all kinds. It's changed since I was last here eight years ago, when I was kicking up my heels and making a spectacle of myself. Now, I find my only hope lies in anatomy. Truly, that's all that keeps me going."

"Anatomy?" Raskolnikov echoed, bemused by the abrupt shift in topic.

But Svidrigaïlov ignored the question, continuing on his own tangent. "As for the clubs, parades, and whatever else people think constitutes 'progress' these days—well, they can manage perfectly well without me. And really, who wants to end up a card-sharper?"

"Were you a card-sharper, then?" Raskolnikov asked, his tone dry but edged with genuine curiosity.

"How could I not be?" Svidrigaïlov answered with a shrug. "We had quite the circle of such men eight years ago—men of the best breeding, poets even, and men of property. In fact, in Russian society, have you noticed how some of the most polished manners are found among those who've suffered humiliation? I had my share. I even ended up in debtor's prison once, thanks to a swindling Greek from Nezhin. Then Marfa Petrovna came to my rescue. She bargained with the man and bought my freedom for thirty thousand silver roubles, though I owed seventy thousand. And so we were united in lawful matrimony, and she carried me off to the country like a prized possession."

He chuckled at the memory but quickly turned serious. "You know, she was five years my senior and absolutely devoted to me. I spent seven years there, managing her estate. She held an IOU for those thirty thousand roubles over my head the entire time. If I ever dared to step out of line, she would have pounced without hesitation. Women are capable of holding such contradictions without a second thought."

"If it weren't for the IOU, would you have left her?" Raskolnikov asked pointedly.

Svidrigaïlov considered the question, his expression inscrutable. "I can't say for sure. The document wasn't really what kept me there. I didn't feel the need to go elsewhere. In fact, Marfa Petrovna once encouraged me to travel abroad, seeing how restless I was. But I've been abroad before, and I hated it. The sights everyone raves about— the sunrise over the Bay of Naples, the endless sea—they only left me melancholic. Revolting, really, how they stir such sadness without any clear reason. No, it's better here at home. Here, at least, you can blame others for everything and excuse yourself."

He paused, then added with a faint smile, "I might have considered an expedition to the North Pole. Something about the isolation and the challenge appeals to me. But instead, here I am. By the way, is it true that Berg is going up in a balloon from the Yusupov Garden next Sunday, taking passengers for a fee?"

"Would you go?" Raskolnikov asked, not bothering to hide his skepticism.

"I? No, I don't think so," Svidrigaïlov murmured, lapsing into apparent introspection. He remained silent for a moment before resuming. "No, the IOU wasn't what tethered me. About a year ago, Marfa Petrovna gave it back to me, as a gesture of trust—on my name day, no less. She even gifted me a substantial sum of money. 'You see, Arkady Ivanovitch,' she said, 'how much I trust you.' Imagine that!" He chuckled bitterly. "And yet, I stayed. I managed the estate well, too. I even took to ordering books. Marfa Petrovna approved initially but later grew concerned I might be over-studying."

"You seem to miss her," Raskolnikov observed, his tone carefully neutral.

"Miss her?" Svidrigaïlov repeated, his eyes narrowing thoughtfully. "Perhaps I do. By the way, do you believe in ghosts?"

"Ghosts?" Raskolnikov asked, startled by the sudden shift in tone. "What ghosts?"

"The ordinary kind," Svidrigaïlov replied nonchalantly. "Do you believe in them?"

"Do you?" Raskolnikov countered, his suspicion deepening.

"Perhaps not entirely. But I wouldn't rule them out," Svidrigaïlov said, his lips curling into a strange smile. "Marfa Petrovna, for instance, seems to take great pleasure in visiting me."

Raskolnikov stared at him, baffled. "What do you mean, 'she visits you'?"

"I've seen her three times now," Svidrigaïlov said, leaning forward slightly. "The first was an hour after her funeral. The second was just two days ago, at dawn, during my journey here. And the third was earlier today, in my room. I was alone."

"Were you awake?" Raskolnikov asked, unable to hide his unease.

Svidrigaïlov's face took on an odd expression as he spoke, his eyes narrowing slightly as though he were trying to gauge Raskolnikov's reaction. "Yes, I was quite awake, wide awake every time," he said with conviction, leaning back slightly in his chair. "She comes in, speaks to me briefly about the most trivial matters, and then she leaves—always through the door, mind you, as though she were just stepping out for a moment. I can almost hear the sound of her steps as she goes."

Raskolnikov's brow furrowed. Something about Svidrigaïlov's words unsettled him deeply, though he could not have explained why. Then, suddenly, as though the thought had been waiting on the edge of his consciousness, he blurted out, "What made me think something like this must be happening to you?"

The moment the words left his lips, he regretted them. They had come out too impulsively, too revealingly. His own reaction startled him; it was as though he had inadvertently acknowledged some eerie connection between them.

Svidrigaïlov, however, seemed genuinely intrigued. "What!" he exclaimed, leaning forward slightly in his chair. "You thought so? Really thought so? Didn't I say there was something in common between us? Didn't I?"

"You never said anything of the sort!" Raskolnikov retorted sharply, his voice trembling with a mix of irritation and unease. His eyes burned with an almost feverish intensity as they locked on Svidrigaïlov's.

"Didn't I?" Svidrigaïlov repeated, his tone almost absentminded, as though he were speaking to himself. Then, shaking his head slightly, he added with a faint smile, "I thought I had. When I came in and saw you lying there with your eyes closed, pretending to be asleep, I said to myself right away, 'Here's the man.'"

"What do you mean by 'the man'? What nonsense are you talking about?" Raskolnikov demanded, his voice rising in both pitch and intensity.

"I don't know," Svidrigaïlov replied, his tone strangely thoughtful. "I really don't. It just came to me at the moment. Perhaps I meant nothing at all."

The two men sat in tense silence for a moment, their eyes locked in a battle of wills. Svidrigaïlov's expression was unreadable, while Raskolnikov's face betrayed a growing storm of agitation.

Finally, breaking the silence with a tone of exasperation, Raskolnikov burst out, "This is nonsense—utter nonsense! Tell me, what does she say when she comes to you?"

"She?" Svidrigaïlov replied, raising his eyebrows. "You wouldn't believe it. She talks about the most ridiculous, insignificant things. And would you believe it—it infuriates me! The first time she appeared was right after the funeral service. I was in my study, utterly exhausted. There had been the ceremony, the funeral luncheon, all that dreary business. At last, I was alone, smoking a cigar and trying to clear my head. Suddenly, she walked in through the door and said, 'You've been so busy today, Arkady Ivanovitch, you've forgotten to wind the dining-room clock.' Can you imagine? Seven years I wound that clock every week, and if I forgot, she'd always remind me."

He paused, letting out a low, humorless chuckle before continuing. "The next time was at a railway station on my way here. I'd just woken up, half-asleep, drinking some coffee at dawn. I looked up, and there she was, sitting beside me with a pack of cards in her hands. 'Shall I tell your fortune for the journey, Arkady Ivanovitch?' she asked. She always fancied herself a fortune-teller, you know. But instead of asking her to go ahead, I bolted—ran like a fool. The station bell rang, and I used it as an excuse to escape."

He leaned forward slightly, his voice dropping as though confiding a great secret. "And then today, just a couple of hours ago, she came again. I was sitting in my room, miserable after a wretched meal from some cookshop, smoking again. Suddenly, she walked in, dressed to the nines in a green silk gown with a long train. She said, 'Good day, Arkady Ivanovitch. How do you like my dress? Aniska can't make anything like this!' Aniska was a dressmaker we had in the country, a former serf girl trained in Moscow. Pretty thing, but not much of a seamstress. Anyway, Marfa turned around, showing off her dress, and I looked at her face, studying her carefully. Then I said, 'Why trouble yourself coming to me about such trivialities, Marfa Petrovna?' And do you know what she said?"

Raskolnikov shook his head, unwilling but unable to stop himself from listening.

"She said, 'Good gracious, you won't let anyone disturb you about anything!' And to provoke her, I replied, 'I'm thinking of getting married, Marfa Petrovna.' She actually laughed at that and said, 'That's just like you, Arkady Ivanovitch. You've hardly buried your wife, and already you're seeking a bride! And of course, it won't end well—for you or for her. You'll just make yourself a laughing-stock.' Then she turned and left. Her dress rustled as she went."

He leaned back in his chair, a strange smile playing on his lips. "Now tell me, isn't that the most ridiculous thing you've ever heard?"

Raskolnikov's gaze hardened as he stared at Svidrigaïlov. "But perhaps you are lying?" he asked bluntly, his voice tinged with skepticism and hostility.

Svidrigaïlov's expression did not change, as though he had expected such a question. "I rarely lie," he answered, his tone calm and reflective, as though he were discussing a point of philosophy rather than responding to an accusation.

"And in the past, have you ever seen ghosts before?" Raskolnikov pressed, his suspicion undiminished.

Svidrigaïlov seemed to ponder the question for a moment before replying, "Yes, I have seen them, but only once in my life—six years ago. I had a serf named Filka. Shortly after his burial, I called out absentmindedly, 'Filka, my pipe!' And, believe it or not, he came in, walked to the cupboard where my pipes were kept, and began searching for one. I sat there, stunned, thinking he was doing it out of spite because we had quarreled violently just before his death. I even scolded him: 'How dare you come in with a hole in your elbow? Go away, you scamp!' And he left, just like that. He never came back. I didn't tell Marfa Petrovna about it at the time; I thought of having a memorial service sung for him, but I was too ashamed."

Raskolnikov listened in silence, his unease growing with every word. At last, he said curtly, "You should see a doctor."

Svidrigaïlov smirked faintly, as though amused by the suggestion. "I know I am not well. I don't need you to tell me that," he replied with a hint of sarcasm. "But even so, I believe I am five times as strong as you are. And let me clarify—I wasn't asking whether you believe that ghosts are seen. I was asking whether you believe they exist."

"No," Raskolnikov replied sharply, his voice rising in anger. "I won't believe it!"

Svidrigaïlov tilted his head, his expression turning contemplative. "What do people usually say?" he murmured, as though talking to himself. "They say, 'You are ill, so whatever you think you see is nothing but a delusion.' But that argument isn't entirely logical, is it? I admit that ghosts only appear to the sick, but doesn't that prove only that they are incapable of appearing to the healthy? Not that they don't exist."

"That's nonsense," Raskolnikov shot back irritably.

"Is it?" Svidrigaïlov asked, his gaze locking with Raskolnikov's. "Let me propose this thought: ghosts might be fragments of another world—just tiny pieces of it breaking through. A healthy man has no reason to see them because he belongs entirely to this world. His body, his mind, everything about him is tied to this earthly existence. But when someone is ill, the boundary between the two worlds weakens. The sicker a person becomes, the closer they draw to that other world, until death finally carries them over completely. Doesn't that align with the idea of a future life?"

"I don't believe in a future life," Raskolnikov said coldly.

Svidrigaïlov sat back, lost in thought for a moment. Then, with a strange, almost whimsical tone, he added, "And what if the afterlife is nothing but spiders? Or something equally dreadful."

Raskolnikov shuddered internally. "This man is mad," he thought, feeling a cold chill creep over him.

Svidrigaïlov continued, undeterred. "We always imagine eternity as something vast and incomprehensible," he mused, "but why must it be vast? What if it's just one small, dark room—like a grimy bathhouse in the country, with spiders in every corner? That could be eternity, couldn't it?"

Raskolnikov was horrified. "Is that really the best you can imagine?" he demanded, his voice trembling with a mixture of anger and despair. "Isn't there anything more just, more comforting, that you can conceive of?"

Svidrigaïlov smiled faintly, a shadow of amusement in his expression. "And why should it be comforting? Perhaps that is what's just. And to tell you the truth, if I had to design it, that's exactly how I would make it."

Raskolnikov felt the words like a blow. This man's cynicism and the eerie conviction in his tone were unbearable. He stared at Svidrigaïlov in silence, unable to form a response.

Svidrigaïlov, however, broke into sudden laughter. "Imagine that," he said, his voice filled with mockery. "Half an hour ago, we were strangers, practically enemies. There's a matter unresolved between us—serious enough, wouldn't you say? But here we are, debating eternity and ghosts like old friends. Didn't I tell you there's something similar about us?"

Raskolnikov's face darkened, his irritation boiling to the surface. "Can we drop all this nonsense?" he snapped. "I'd like to know why you came to see me. I don't have time to waste."

"By all means," Svidrigaïlov replied, his tone growing serious. "I came to discuss your sister, Avdotya Romanovna. She is planning to marry Pyotr Petrovitch Luzhin, is she not?"

Raskolnikov's jaw tightened. "Don't you dare mention my sister's name," he said, his voice cold and threatening. "How dare you speak of her to me, if you truly are who you claim to be?"

"But that's precisely why I've come," Svidrigaïlov replied, his calm demeanor unshaken. "How can I discuss the matter without mentioning her? I promise I won't waste your time. Shall we proceed?"

Raskolnikov listened with a growing mix of astonishment and irritation as Svidrigaïlov continued speaking. "I am certain you've already formed an opinion of this Mr. Luzhin," Svidrigaïlov began, his voice measured and deliberate. "A connection of mine through my late wife, as you might know. Even if you've only encountered him briefly or gathered some facts, you must see that he is in no way a suitable match for your sister, Avdotya Romanovna. I am convinced she is sacrificing herself, quite recklessly and out of pure altruism, for her family's sake. From all I have heard of you, I fancied you would be eager to see such a match undone, especially if it could be managed without sacrificing worldly advantages. Now that I've met you, I am even more certain of it."

"All this," Raskolnikov interrupted coldly, "is either astonishingly naïve or intolerably presumptuous on your part."

"Ah, you mean to suggest that I have ulterior motives?" Svidrigaïlov replied, his tone still calm. "Rest assured, Rodion Romanovitch, if I were pursuing selfish ends, I would hardly be so blunt. I am not so foolish. Let me admit something to you, however—a psychological oddity, if you will. Just now, as I was explaining my feelings for Avdotya Romanovna, I spoke as though I were still in love with her. But to tell you the truth, I feel nothing now, not even the faintest trace of what I once believed I felt. It's strange to admit it, but it is the truth."

"Depravity and idleness," Raskolnikov said sharply. "That's all there is to it."

"Perhaps I am idle and depraved," Svidrigaïlov admitted with a faint smile. "But your sister's virtues are undeniable. Even a man like me couldn't help being deeply impressed. Yet it's clear to me now that what I felt was nonsense—a passing illusion."

"Have you been aware of this long?" Raskolnikov asked, his voice edged with sarcasm.

"I began to suspect it before, but I was only completely certain of it the day before yesterday—almost as soon as I arrived in Petersburg. Even in Moscow, I had the absurd notion that I might win her hand, that I might outmaneuver Mr. Luzhin." He paused, then added, "But allow me to get to the point. I can see you are impatient."

"Please do," Raskolnikov said curtly, glancing toward the door. "I have no time for long-winded stories."

"With pleasure," Svidrigaïlov said smoothly. "You see, before undertaking a particular journey I have in mind, I wish to settle certain matters. My children are with a relative and well cared for, so there's no concern there. As for my late wife's estate, I've taken nothing more than what she gave me while she was alive. I live modestly enough. However, I am deeply unsettled by Mr. Luzhin. Not because I loathe the man—though I find him thoroughly uninspiring—but because it was through him that I quarreled with Marfa Petrovna. When I learned she was supporting this match, I was incensed. So, I wish to see Avdotya Romanovna, through your mediation if possible, to dissuade her from this marriage. And—if you'll allow me to finish—offer her ten thousand roubles as a gift to help make the separation easier."

Raskolnikov stared at him as though he had lost his mind. "You are insane," he said at last, his voice low but firm. "How dare you suggest such a thing?"

"I expected you to react this way," Svidrigaïlov said with a faint smile. "But let me explain. First, while I am not wealthy, this sum is completely free—money I do not need. If your sister refuses it, I'll only squander it elsewhere, perhaps on something ridiculous. Second, my conscience is clear. This is not a bribe, nor does it come with conditions. I deeply regret the trouble I've caused Avdotya Romanovna in the past, and this is simply my way of expressing that regret. There is no ulterior motive. If there were, I wouldn't be so forthright about my intentions."

Raskolnikov's scowl deepened. "This conversation is over. What you are proposing is an insult."

"Why should it be?" Svidrigaïlov asked calmly. "If I were to die tomorrow and leave this money to her in my will, would she refuse it then? Surely not. What difference does it make whether it comes from me now or later?"

"She would refuse it."

"Oh, I doubt that," Svidrigaïlov said with a faint laugh. "But if you're determined to reject it, so be it. Though ten thousand roubles is no small sum. Regardless, I ask only that you relay my message to her."

"I won't," Raskolnikov replied, standing abruptly. "And if you try to see her, I will stop you."

Svidrigaïlov raised an eyebrow, a trace of amusement in his expression. "Very well," he said, rising to his feet. "But don't be so quick to judge. Perhaps one day you'll find we aren't so different after all. Until then, I'll take my leave."

He stepped toward the door, pausing as though he had remembered something. "Oh, one last thing. Marfa Petrovna left Avdotya Romanovna three thousand roubles in her will. She made the arrangements herself, just a week before her death. Your sister should be able to collect the money within a few weeks."

"Is that true?" Raskolnikov asked sharply.

"Entirely true," Svidrigaïlov said, tipping his hat. "Goodbye, Rodion Romanovitch. We'll meet again, no doubt."

As he opened the door, he nearly collided with Razumihin, who was just entering.

Chapter 2

It was nearly eight o'clock, and the two young men were hurrying through the streets toward Bakaleyev's lodgings, aiming to arrive before Luzhin. The evening was brisk, and a faint sense of urgency seemed to pervade their quick strides, as if they were chasing time itself.

"By the way, who was that man?" Razumihin asked suddenly, breaking the silence as they moved down the dimly lit street.

"That was Svidrigaïlov," Raskolnikov replied, his voice unusually tense. "You remember—the landowner. It was in his house that Dounia was insulted when she worked as a governess. His... attentions toward her led to her being thrown out by his wife, Marfa Petrovna. Later, Marfa Petrovna sought Dounia's forgiveness and reconciled with her. She's the same woman whose sudden death we discussed earlier this morning."

Razumihin frowned, glancing at Raskolnikov. "I see. And what does this Svidrigaïlov want now?"

"I don't know exactly," Raskolnikov muttered, looking ahead as though the cobblestones themselves might hold some answer. "But he's strange, Razumihin—very strange. He came to Petersburg almost immediately after Marfa Petrovna's funeral, and I can't shake the feeling that he's planning something. We need to guard Dounia from him at all costs. That's what I wanted to tell you—do you understand?"

Razumihin straightened his shoulders as if preparing for action. "Guard her? Of course. But what can he do to harm Avdotya Romanovna? Whatever it is, he'll find no opportunity. Thank you, Rodya, for speaking to me about this. We will guard her—I promise. By the way, do you know where he's staying?"

Raskolnikov shook his head. "No, I didn't think to ask."

"What a pity," Razumihin said with a hint of frustration. "Never mind. I'll find out somehow."

There was a brief silence as they walked a few more paces. Then Raskolnikov asked suddenly, "Did you see him clearly? Did you really notice him?"

Razumihin gave him a puzzled look. "Yes, I saw him clearly. Why are you asking?"

Raskolnikov persisted, his voice dropping to an almost conspiratorial tone. "You're sure? You could recognize him if you saw him again?"

"Yes, of course. I have a good memory for faces, you know. I would recognize him in a crowd of thousands. What's this about?"

Raskolnikov seemed to relax slightly, but his expression was still clouded. "Nothing... it's fine," he muttered. "It's just... strange."

Razumihin's frown deepened. "Strange? What do you mean by that?"

Raskolnikov hesitated, then forced a peculiar smile. "I don't know. Sometimes I think... maybe I'm imagining things. You all say I'm not well—that I'm losing my mind. What if he wasn't even real? What if it was just an hallucination?"

Razumihin stopped in his tracks, staring at his friend in disbelief. "What are you saying? How can you think that? You're not making sense."

Raskolnikov shrugged, his smile fading into something colder, more distant. "Who knows? Maybe I really am mad. Maybe everything that's happened these past days is just some elaborate delusion."

Razumihin looked at him with a mix of concern and frustration. "Rodya, stop it. You're overthinking again. What did Svidrigaïlov say to you, anyway? Why did he come?"

Raskolnikov didn't answer immediately, his mind elsewhere. After a moment, Razumihin decided to distract him. "Listen, let me tell you about my day," he began, his tone lightening slightly. "I went to see Porfiry after lunch. Zametov was still hanging around his office, looking as smug as ever. I tried to talk to Porfiry, to get a sense of what he's thinking, but it was useless. He just stared out the window half the time, and when I pressed him, he gave me these vague, irritating answers."

Razumihin gestured animatedly as he spoke, his irritation clearly genuine. "At one point, I got so fed up that I shook my fist at him and told him I'd bash his head in if he didn't start making sense. Of course, he just looked at me like I was an idiot. I cursed him to his face and left. Zametov, that snake, just smirked the whole time—I didn't even bother talking to him."

Raskolnikov smirked faintly, amused despite himself. "And that's supposed to reassure me?"

"Wait, wait, I'm getting to the good part!" Razumihin exclaimed. "As I was walking back down the stairs, it suddenly hit me—why are we even bothering to play along with these fools? What do they really have? Nothing. If they had anything solid, they'd have made their move already. Instead, they're fumbling around, trying to rattle us. You know what I say? Let them. Let's laugh in their faces, Rodya. Let them stew in their own nonsense while we get on with our lives."

Raskolnikov listened quietly, his smirk fading into something more thoughtful. Razumihin's enthusiasm was infectious, but he couldn't shake the gnawing unease that clung to him like a shadow. As they approached Bakaleyev's, the sense of foreboding returned, sharper than ever.

"To be sure," answered Raskolnikov with a faint, detached tone. "But what will you say tomorrow?" he mused inwardly, his thoughts already turning inwards and away from the present moment. Strangely, up until now, it had never truly crossed his mind to wonder how Razumihin might react when he eventually learned everything. The thought lingered like a shadow as he glanced at Razumihin, who continued recounting his day. Raskolnikov barely registered the details. Too much had already transpired, shifting his focus elsewhere.

As they stepped into the corridor, they encountered Pyotr Petrovitch Luzhin, who had arrived with punctuality. Luzhin appeared to be searching for the apartment number, and without exchanging greetings or glances, all three entered the flat together. Raskolnikov and Razumihin walked in first, while Luzhin paused briefly in the hallway, removing his coat with deliberate movements, as if orchestrating his own entrance. His delay seemed intentional, an act of asserting presence rather than courtesy.

Pulcheria Alexandrovna was the first to greet him, stepping forward with a mixture of warmth and apprehension. Meanwhile, Dounia turned to welcome her brother with a quiet smile that held traces of both affection and worry. Luzhin entered shortly after, bowing to the ladies with an air of heightened formality, his demeanor a careful blend of amiability and self-importance. Yet, there was a stiffness to him, as though something had unsettled him on the way over, leaving him slightly off-balance.

Pulcheria Alexandrovna, sensing the tension in the air, hurried to usher everyone toward the round table, where the samovar was already boiling, its steam rising softly. The seating arrangement seemed almost deliberate in its symmetry. Dounia and Luzhin found themselves opposite each other, with Razumihin and Raskolnikov seated across from Pulcheria Alexandrovna. Razumihin sat beside Luzhin, his towering figure slightly imposing, while Raskolnikov placed himself beside his sister, his expression unreadable.

For a moment, silence reigned, heavy and uncomfortable. Luzhin, maintaining his composure, pulled out a scented cambric handkerchief and dabbed at his nose, the gesture exaggerated in its deliberateness. The faint aroma of his cologne seemed to linger unnecessarily, an unspoken declaration of his cultivated refinement. His movements carried an air of wounded dignity, as though he felt slighted but was too magnanimous to make a scene—yet. Moments earlier, while still in the passage, Luzhin had entertained the notion of keeping his coat on and leaving abruptly to deliver a pointed lesson. However, his need for clarity and control over the situation had overridden that impulse. If his instructions had been ignored, there was a deeper matter to uncover, and he was determined to address it.

"I trust your journey was favorable," he began, his tone deliberately neutral as he addressed Pulcheria Alexandrovna.

"Oh yes, Pyotr Petrovitch, thank you," she replied quickly, her voice carrying a note of over-eagerness that betrayed her underlying discomfort.

"And Avdotya Romanovna? I trust the journey was not too fatiguing for her?" he inquired, turning his gaze to Dounia with an air of polished concern.

"I'm young and strong; such things don't tire me," Dounia answered evenly. "But it was a strain for my mother, though she bore it admirably."

"That's quite understandable," Luzhin replied, nodding sagely. "Travel on our national railways is always an ordeal—though, of course, 'Mother Russia,' as they say, is vast beyond measure." He allowed himself a slight chuckle, as though to invite shared amusement. "It is unfortunate that I was unable to meet you upon your arrival yesterday. I hope everything passed without undue inconvenience?"

Pulcheria Alexandrovna leaned forward slightly, her expression brightening at the opportunity to steer the conversation. "Oh, Pyotr Petrovitch, we were terribly disheartened! But, truly, it seemed that God Himself sent Dmitri Prokofitch to our aid! Without him, I don't know what we would have done." She turned, gesturing warmly to Razumihin, who flushed slightly but inclined his head modestly.

"Yes, I had the pleasure of meeting Mr. Razumihin yesterday," Luzhin murmured, his tone suddenly cooler. His eyes flicked toward Razumihin with a glance that bordered on contemptuous. For a moment, his expression darkened, but he quickly composed himself, withdrawing behind his façade of politeness.

Another pause fell over the group. Luzhin, with all his practiced social graces, seemed at a loss for how to proceed. Pulcheria Alexandrovna's earlier energy waned as the silence stretched. Razumihin's usual buoyancy seemed to have deserted him, and even Dounia seemed inclined to let the awkwardness settle. Raskolnikov, for his part, remained silent, his attention drifting elsewhere.

Eventually, Pulcheria Alexandrovna spoke up again, grasping for the only topic she thought might stir conversation. "Have you heard about Marfa Petrovna's sudden death?" she asked, her voice rising slightly as she addressed Luzhin.

"Yes, I was informed immediately," Luzhin replied, his tone measured. "And I must also inform you of another matter: Arkady Ivanovitch Svidrigailov has departed for Petersburg in great haste following her funeral."

"For Petersburg? He's come here?" Dounia exclaimed, her voice tinged with alarm. She exchanged a quick, worried glance with her mother.

"Indeed," Luzhin confirmed, his expression darkening slightly. "Given the speed and circumstances of his departure, I can't help but believe his intentions are not entirely innocent."

Pulcheria Alexandrovna raised her hands in dismay. "Will that man not leave Dounia in peace, even here?"

The words seemed to reverberate through the room, amplifying the tension already present. Raskolnikov sat motionless, his eyes fixed on a distant point as though attempting to see beyond the walls of the room and into the designs of the man they now discussed.

"I imagine that neither you nor Avdotya Romanovna have any grounds for uneasiness unless, of course, you yourselves desire communication with him," Luzhin began with a deliberate and measured tone, his words calculated to project calm authority. "For my part, I am taking steps to remain on guard and am currently investigating where he might be lodging."

Pulcheria Alexandrovna, who had been sitting with a visibly tense expression, let out a small gasp of alarm. "Oh, Pyotr Petrovitch, you can't imagine the fright you've given me," she said, clutching her hands tightly. "I've only seen him twice, but both times I found him utterly terrifying—truly terrible! I am convinced that he must have been the cause of Marfa Petrovna's death."

"It is impossible to state such a thing with certainty," Luzhin replied, his tone a mix of caution and authority. "I have precise information regarding the circumstances of her death. While I wouldn't argue that he didn't, perhaps, accelerate matters by exerting a moral influence—if one could even term it that—it remains speculative. However, when it comes to his general character and behavior, I must confess that I fully agree with your impressions of him. He is, without a doubt, a man of the most depraved and vicious kind."

Pulcheria Alexandrovna gasped again, this time more dramatically, her anxiety visibly heightened. Raskolnikov, who had been listening intently, glanced briefly at his sister. Dounia, although outwardly composed, was leaning forward slightly, her hands clasped tightly in her lap.

"I am not entirely sure of his current financial position or what Marfa Petrovna might have left him," Luzhin continued. "However, I will know soon enough. If he does have any resources at his disposal, it's safe to assume that here, in Petersburg, he will swiftly revert to his old habits. I have no doubt of it. Marfa Petrovna, despite her misfortunes in being ensnared by her misguided affection for him, did much to support him. It was she who paid his debts when they first married, and, I have good reason to believe, she managed to shield him from the consequences of a criminal accusation that might otherwise have landed him in Siberia. This accusation involved a horrific instance of violent brutality—one that, to this day, carries a particularly sordid and fantastical element."

"My God!" Pulcheria Alexandrovna exclaimed, her face pale with shock.

Raskolnikov shifted slightly in his seat but did not speak, while Dounia fixed Luzhin with a penetrating gaze. "Are you certain of this?" she asked, her tone sharp and deliberate, demanding clarification.

"I am merely repeating what Marfa Petrovna confided to me in strictest confidence," Luzhin replied, his demeanor serious. "Legally, the case was never conclusively proven. There is a woman here in Petersburg, a foreigner named Resslich, who lent money at high interest and engaged in other, less respectable dealings. Svidrigaïlov had a long-standing and mysterious association with her. Living with Resslich was her niece, a young girl, barely fourteen or fifteen, who was both deaf and mute. Resslich treated this poor child with unspeakable cruelty—starving her, beating her—and one day, the girl was discovered hanging in the garret. It was ruled a suicide during the inquest, and no further legal actions were taken. However, later whispers suggested something more sinister: that the girl had been horrifically wronged by Svidrigaïlov himself. Although the accusations came from another German woman of questionable reputation, who might not have been trustworthy, the rumors persisted. Thanks to Marfa Petrovna's efforts and her monetary interventions, the matter never reached the authorities. Yet, such stories are hard to dismiss entirely."

Pulcheria Alexandrovna could barely contain her horror. "What a monstrous story!" she cried, her voice trembling.

Dounia, however, remained composed, though her brow furrowed. "When I lived with them, I heard only a vague account of a servant named Philip who died, but the details seemed to vary. Some said he hanged himself," she remarked, her tone cautious.

"That's correct," Luzhin interjected. "The official account was suicide. However, it was said that his death was the direct result of Mr. Svidrigaïlov's relentless persecution and cruelty. It seems the man's nature has always been consistent."

Dounia's tone grew sharper. "I recall the servants saying that Philip was a peculiar man—a sort of amateur philosopher, always reading—and that his death was more the result of Svidrigaïlov's mockery than any physical abuse. Whatever the case, I saw no signs of such cruelty while I was there. The servants even seemed to like him, though they did occasionally grumble about Philip's fate."

"I perceive that you, Avdotya Romanovna, seem inclined to defend Mr. Svidrigaïlov's character," Luzhin said with an insinuating smile, his lips twisting slightly. "But that is precisely his talent—his insidious ability to charm and manipulate. Marfa Petrovna was a prime example of his skill in this regard."

"Enough!" Dounia interrupted firmly, her voice filled with quiet strength. "I have no interest in discussing Mr. Svidrigaïlov further. It brings me nothing but distress."

It was at this moment that Raskolnikov, who had been silent until now, finally spoke, his voice cutting through the tension. "He has just been to see me," he said. The suddenness of his words and the weight they carried brought a sharp silence to the room.

The room was instantly charged with a tense energy as everyone turned their attention to Raskolnikov. Even Pyotr Petrovitch, usually measured in his responses, appeared momentarily ruffled by the unexpected revelation. Pulcheria Alexandrovna's hand trembled as she adjusted her scarf, her expression a mixture of alarm and curiosity.

"An hour and a half ago," Raskolnikov began, his voice calm but tinged with weariness, "Svidrigaïlov came to see me while I was resting. He woke me up, introduced himself as though we were old acquaintances, and proceeded to make himself quite at home. He seemed cheerful—oddly so, given the circumstances—and even expressed hope that we might strike up a friendship." He paused briefly, letting the words settle. "What's more, Dounia, he's particularly eager for an interview with you, one that he's asked me to facilitate. He has some kind of proposal in mind. Oh, and he also mentioned something else—that Marfa Petrovna left you three thousand roubles in her will. Apparently, you'll be able to claim it soon."

Pulcheria Alexandrovna clasped her hands together, exclaiming with genuine relief, "Thank God! Pray for her soul, Dounia! Such kindness even after all that trouble."

"It's true," Luzhin interjected stiffly, as though validating the information lent him authority.

Dounia leaned forward slightly, her composure intact but her voice urgent. "And what else did he say? Tell us everything, Rodya."

Raskolnikov shrugged slightly, avoiding his sister's gaze. "He claimed not to be particularly wealthy. Most of Marfa Petrovna's estate, he said, went to his children, who are now living with an aunt. As for his own lodging, he mentioned it's near mine, but I didn't ask for details."

Pulcheria Alexandrovna's face grew pale as her thoughts raced. "But what does he want with Dounia?" she asked in an alarmed tone. "What kind of proposal did he mention? Did he tell you?"

"Yes, he did," Raskolnikov answered tersely. "But I'll explain later."

Without elaborating further, he turned his attention to his tea, taking a deliberate sip as though to signal that the discussion, at least for him, was over for the moment.

Luzhin, however, was far from satisfied. He pulled out his watch, glancing at it pointedly before speaking. "I am afraid I have a prior engagement that demands my attention," he said with a hint of irritation. "I would rather not intrude further."

"Don't leave, Pyotr Petrovitch," Dounia said firmly. Her tone was calm but carried unmistakable resolve. "You had planned to spend the evening with us. Besides, you wrote in your letter that you wished to discuss something important with Mother."

"Precisely, Avdotya Romanovna," Luzhin replied, sitting back down with a stiff air of wounded dignity but still clutching his hat as though prepared to leave at a moment's notice. "However, given that your brother appears unable to speak openly about Svidrigaïlov's proposals in my presence, I, too, find myself unable to address certain delicate matters while others are present."

Dounia's brows furrowed slightly. "Your request that my brother not be present at this meeting was disregarded at my insistence," she stated plainly. "You wrote that he insulted you, and I feel this matter must be resolved. If my brother truly wronged you, he will offer an apology."

Luzhin leaned back in his chair, his face hardening. "There are insults, Avdotya Romanovna, that no amount of goodwill can erase. Once certain lines are crossed, there is no going back."

"That's not what I'm referring to," Dounia countered, her voice edged with impatience. "Our entire future depends on resolving these misunderstandings today. If you care for me at all, Pyotr Petrovitch, you will address this now. Let me be clear: if Rodya is at fault, he will apologise."

Luzhin's irritation deepened. "I am astonished that you frame the issue this way. I hold you in the highest regard, Avdotya Romanovna, yet I cannot be expected to endure the presence of someone who has treated me with such hostility."

"Do not be so quick to take offense," Dounia replied with a note of warmth. "You are a man of sense and generosity, or so I have always believed. Trust me, and believe that I can judge fairly. If this conflict between you and my brother persists, I will be forced to choose between you. Understand that this is not a decision I take lightly, but I will not allow uncertainty to linger."

Luzhin bristled. "Your words, Avdotya Romanovna, are deeply wounding. To place me on equal footing with someone who has shown me such disdain is offensive, especially considering our relationship."

"What?" Dounia's voice rose slightly, her cheeks flushing. "I am weighing your concerns against what has always been most precious in my life, and yet you find fault in my efforts to resolve this?"

The tension in the room was palpable, each word like a thread pulling the scene tighter. Pulcheria Alexandrovna sat silently, her gaze darting between her daughter and Luzhin, while Raskolnikov remained aloof, his expression unreadable. The unresolved tension promised an explosive conclusion, but for now, the air hung heavy with unsaid thoughts and simmering emotions.

Raskolnikov's lips curled into a sardonic smile, while Razumihin shifted uncomfortably in his seat. Pyotr Petrovitch, however, seemed utterly unfazed by the tension in the room. On the contrary, as if deriving some perverse satisfaction from the escalating conflict, he became more persistent in his tone and sharper in his remarks, his irritation barely masked by a facade of decorum.

"Love for your future husband, the partner of your life, ought to outweigh any misplaced familial loyalty," Luzhin declared pompously, his tone heavy with self-righteousness. "In any case, I must insist that I cannot and will not accept being placed on the same level as your brother. While I initially refrained from addressing certain matters openly in his presence, I now find myself compelled to seek a necessary explanation on an issue that concerns my dignity."

He turned sharply toward Pulcheria Alexandrovna, addressing her in a tone both formal and accusatory. "Madam, your son, in the presence of this gentleman,"—he nodded briefly and dismissively toward Razumihin—"insulted me grievously. He deliberately misrepresented a sentiment I expressed in private conversation with you over coffee. I merely stated that a marriage with a young woman who has experienced hardship could be more advantageous from a conjugal perspective than one with a woman who has been accustomed to luxury, as the former is more beneficial to moral character. This observation, entirely innocent and even considerate in its essence, was distorted by your son, who exaggerated its significance, twisted its meaning into ridicule, and accused me of base intentions. As far as I can discern, this misrepresentation stems directly from the way my remarks were communicated to him in your correspondence. I would consider myself fortunate, Pulcheria Alexandrovna, if you could kindly reassure me by clarifying the exact words in which you conveyed my meaning to Rodion Romanovitch."

Pulcheria Alexandrovna, visibly flustered by the confrontation, faltered as she replied, "I... I don't quite remember. I repeated your words as I understood them. Perhaps I didn't convey them exactly as you intended. And perhaps... Rodya misinterpreted them... or exaggerated."

Luzhin's expression darkened further. "He could not have misinterpreted or exaggerated them except under your instigation," he said, his voice heavy with insinuation.

Pulcheria Alexandrovna drew herself up with quiet dignity, her voice gaining firmness. "Pyotr Petrovitch, the very fact that Dounia and I are here today is proof enough that we did not take your words in the worst possible sense."

"Well said, Mother," Dounia interjected approvingly, her voice calm but resolute.

"And yet, somehow, I find myself being blamed again," Luzhin muttered, feigning wounded pride.

"You accuse Rodya of wrongdoing, Pyotr Petrovitch, but have you considered your own actions?" Pulcheria Alexandrovna countered, her growing courage evident in her tone. "You yourself wrote things in your letter that were simply not true."

"I do not recall writing anything false," Luzhin said stiffly, though the corners of his mouth twitched with suppressed annoyance.

Raskolnikov, who had remained mostly silent until now, suddenly spoke, his tone cutting and precise, though he refused to look at Luzhin. "In your letter, you claimed I gave money yesterday not to the widow of the man who was killed, which is the truth, but to his daughter, whom I had never even met until that very day. You wrote this with the deliberate intention of sowing discord between me and my family, and you added crude insinuations about a young woman you know nothing about. Your words amount to nothing but base slander."

Luzhin's face turned an angry shade of red, and his voice trembled with fury as he responded. "Excuse me, sir, but I mentioned your qualities and conduct in my letter solely in response to inquiries from your sister and mother regarding my impressions of you. As for what you call slander, kindly point out a single falsehood in what I wrote. Demonstrate that you did not throw away your money recklessly, or that the individuals in question are not, in fact, of dubious character—however unfortunate their circumstances."

"To my mind," Raskolnikov shot back icily, "you, with all your self-proclaimed virtues, are not worth the little finger of that unfortunate girl you dare to disparage."

Luzhin's eyes widened in incredulity. "Would you go so far as to let her associate with your mother and sister?" he sneered.

The room fell silent for a moment, the air thick with tension as everyone awaited Raskolnikov's response. His contemptuous gaze seemed to pierce Luzhin, and the sheer weight of his disdain rendered words almost unnecessary. Pulcheria Alexandrovna shifted in her chair, while Dounia's expression hardened with quiet resolve. The confrontation hung precariously, threatening to erupt further, as each word and gesture seemed to etch a deeper rift between Luzhin and the family.

Raskolnikov's declaration struck the room like a thunderclap. "I have done so already, if you care to know. I made her sit down today with mother and Dounia." His words carried an air of calm defiance that only seemed to intensify the brewing tension.

Pulcheria Alexandrovna gasped audibly, shocked by her son's audacity. Dounia's face flushed crimson with embarrassment and anger, while Razumihin knitted his brows, his expression darkening with disbelief. Luzhin, however, remained composed on the surface, his lips curving into a lofty smile that barely concealed his indignation.

"You may see for yourself, Avdotya Romanovna," Luzhin began, addressing her with cold sarcasm, "whether it is possible for us to find any common ground. I trust this matter is now concluded, once and for all. Since I see no benefit in further prolonging this meeting, I shall withdraw to avoid hindering the pleasures of family intimacy or the discussion of your... private secrets." He rose from his chair with exaggerated dignity and reached for his hat, making a show of his displeasure. "However, before I leave, I must request—nay, demand—that I be spared such encounters in the future. I appeal particularly to you, Pulcheria Alexandrovna, as my letter was addressed to you alone and not to anyone else."

Pulcheria Alexandrovna bristled at the implication, her natural kindness momentarily overridden by a surge of indignation. "You seem to think you have complete authority over us, Pyotr Petrovitch," she said, her tone uncharacteristically firm. "Dounia explained why your request was not honored, and it was done with the best of intentions. Besides, your letter came across more like commands than requests. Are we to interpret every wish of yours as law? Let me remind you, Pyotr Petrovitch, that we have given up everything and come here relying on your support. It is you who owe us consideration, not the other way around."

Luzhin's face darkened further. "That is not entirely true, Pulcheria Alexandrovna, especially now that Marfa Petrovna's legacy has come to light," he retorted with a hint of malice. "The timing of that inheritance, I must say, appears to have had a most fortuitous influence on the tone you now adopt toward me."

Dounia's eyes flashed with anger as she intervened. "From your insinuation, it seems clear that you were counting on our helplessness," she said sharply. Her voice carried a cold, cutting edge that made Luzhin visibly flinch.

"But now," Luzhin shot back, his tone icy, "I cannot count on it. And I see you are more interested in discussing the 'proposals' of

Arkady Ivanovitch Svidrigaïlov, which appear to hold great—and possibly agreeable—interest for you."

Pulcheria Alexandrovna, who had been struggling to maintain her composure, let out an anguished exclamation. "Good heavens!"

Razumihin, who had been trying to restrain himself, could no longer sit still. He shifted in his chair, his hands clenched into fists, his body taut with frustration.

"Aren't you ashamed now, sister?" Raskolnikov asked quietly, his voice laced with bitter irony.

"I am ashamed, Rodya," Dounia admitted, her voice trembling with anger. Then, turning to Luzhin, she said resolutely, "Pyotr Petrovitch, leave. I do not want to see you again." Her face was pale, but her eyes burned with an intensity that left no room for doubt.

Luzhin, stunned by this unexpected dismissal, hesitated for a moment. His confidence, so absolute mere moments before, seemed to falter. His lips quivered, and a sickly pallor crept over his face. "Avdotya Romanovna," he began, his voice trembling with disbelief, "if I leave now after such a dismissal, let me assure you, I will not return. You should consider carefully what you are doing. My word is firm, and I do not change it."

"What insolence!" Dounia cried, springing to her feet. "I have no desire for you to return. Leave this instant!"

Luzhin, now completely undone, stared at her in open disbelief. "So, that's how it stands?" he stammered. "But do you realize, Avdotya Romanovna, that I might protest against this treatment?"

Pulcheria Alexandrovna could no longer contain herself. "What right have you to speak to my daughter in such a manner?" she demanded hotly. "What can you possibly protest? What right do you have over her? Should I give my Dounia to a man like you? No, sir! Leave us altogether! We are at fault for even considering such a wrong, and I am most to blame."

"But you have bound me, Pulcheria Alexandrovna!" Luzhin shouted, his composure completely shattered. "By your promises! And now you break them, leaving me... besides, I have incurred expenses on your behalf!"

The absurdity of Luzhin's complaint was so characteristic of him that Raskolnikov, despite his anger, could not suppress a bitter laugh. Pulcheria Alexandrovna, however, was livid.

"Expenses? What expenses? Are you referring to the luggage that the conductor brought for us without charge? Good heavens, Pyotr Petrovitch, it was you who bound us, hand and foot—not the other way around!"

"Enough, Mother, please," Dounia implored, her voice heavy with weariness. "Pyotr Petrovitch, for the last time, I beg you to leave." Her words carried a finality that made it clear there was no point in further argument.

Luzhin stood frozen for a moment, his pride and hopes crushed. Then, with a scornful bow, he turned and walked out, leaving behind him a tension that lingered in the room like an oppressive fog.

"I am going, but before I leave, let me say one last thing," Luzhin declared, his voice trembling with poorly suppressed anger as he stood his ground near the door. He seemed unable to restrain himself, his tone growing more venomous with every word. "It appears to me that your mother has entirely overlooked the fact that, despite the sordid gossip which spread like wildfire throughout the district concerning your reputation, I had the magnanimity to offer my hand to you, Avdotya Romanovna. I chose to disregard the public censure that had attached itself to your name, chose to shield you and restore your position, which, I may add, was precarious at best. Considering the personal risk I undertook for your sake, I believe I was fully entitled to expect some measure of gratitude in return."

His words, each one dripping with spite and self-righteousness, seemed to hang heavily in the air. Dounia's face flushed crimson with indignation, and she clenched her fists tightly at her sides.

"And only now," Luzhin continued, his voice rising, "do I see with startling clarity how reckless and naive I was to disregard the judgment of the community at large. How blind I was to place my trust in you!"

"Does he want his head broken?" Razumihin roared, leaping to his feet in a towering rage. He made a threatening step toward Luzhin, but Raskolnikov's firm hand shot out, gripping his arm tightly.

"Not a word. Not a single movement," Raskolnikov commanded in a low, measured tone that carried the weight of authority. His face, pale and drawn with quiet fury, turned toward Luzhin. He took a step forward, his gaze unwavering as he approached the man who had so grievously insulted his sister.

Dounia, meanwhile, unable to contain herself any longer, spoke through clenched teeth, her voice trembling with fury. "You are a mean and despicable man. There is no other word for you."

But it was Raskolnikov's calm, cold tone that cut through the rising tension like a knife. Standing mere inches from Luzhin, he said with chilling clarity, "You will kindly leave this room at once. Do not speak another word. Just go."

For a moment, the room was still. Luzhin stared at Raskolnikov, his pale face contorted with suppressed rage, his lips quivering as though he might attempt some final retort. But something in Raskolnikov's expression—a quiet menace that promised swift retribution—made him think better of it. With a visible effort, Luzhin turned on his heel and stormed out.

As he descended the stairs, his steps heavy with humiliation and anger, his mind seethed with bitter thoughts. Never before had he been treated with such blatant disregard, such outright dismissal. He blamed Raskolnikov for everything—every word, every failure of the evening, every insult that had wounded his pride. The hatred he bore for the younger man burned so fiercely that it seemed to consume all reason.

Yet, even as he left the building, his bruised ego clinging to shreds of delusion, he allowed himself the faint hope that not all was lost.

"Perhaps," he thought, "this can still be salvaged. Perhaps, in time, the ladies will come to see reason, will regret their rashness, and will reach out to me again."

Such was the depth of his conceit that, even as he carried away the memory of the scornful faces and cutting words he had endured, he could not fully accept the finality of his dismissal.

Chapter 3

Pyotr Petrovitch descended the stairs, his mind a chaotic whirl of indignation, disbelief, and wounded pride. Until the very moment of his dismissal, he had not truly conceived that such an outcome was possible. The thought that two women—destitute, vulnerable, and utterly reliant on him, as he saw it—could extricate themselves from his control was inconceivable to him. This unshakable confidence was a product of his towering vanity, a conceit so deeply ingrained that it bordered on delusion.

Luzhin, who had clawed his way up from insignificance to the relative comfort and prestige he now enjoyed, was morbidly preoccupied with his self-image. He held his intelligence and abilities in the highest regard and often indulged in moments of solitary admiration, sometimes even preening before the mirror. Yet, what he prized most was the fortune he had painstakingly amassed through his relentless efforts and dubious schemes. That wealth, in his eyes, elevated him to an equal footing with those who had once looked down on him. It was his armor, his badge of worthiness.

When he had reminded Dounia of his supposed magnanimity in offering her marriage despite the scandalous rumors surrounding her name, he had spoken from a place of genuine indignation. To him, her failure to appreciate this gesture was nothing short of "black ingratitude." Yet even as he voiced this complaint, he was fully aware that the malicious gossip about her had been thoroughly debunked. Marfa Petrovna herself had publicly defended Dounia, and the townspeople had rallied to her side. Luzhin knew all of this, but he still relished the idea of casting himself as a savior, someone heroic enough to overlook the baseless slander. It was a secret satisfaction he cherished, an image of himself he admired deeply. That others did not share his admiration was a mystery he could not fathom.

He had approached Raskolnikov and his family with the self-satisfaction of a benefactor who expected to bask in their gratitude and submission. Now, as he left, humiliated and rejected, he felt himself wronged, unappreciated, and deeply misunderstood. The sting of the encounter was sharp, but even more painful was the realization that his carefully constructed dream of a life with Dounia was crumbling before his eyes.

For years, Luzhin had nurtured fantasies of marriage, but he had bided his time, waiting until his financial position was secure. In his secret musings, he had envisioned a wife who would embody his ideal: virtuous, young, beautiful, and poor. She had to be poor—her gratitude for his rescue was essential to his vision. This imagined woman would be timid, refined, and deeply impressed by his intelligence and success. She would worship him, depend on him, and never question his authority. In Dounia, he had found the perfect match. Her pride, education, and beauty only heightened her allure, and her vulnerable circumstances made her seem destined for him. She was, in his eyes, a prize, one that he had already claimed in his mind. The thought that she could refuse him, that she could assert her own will, was something he had never seriously considered.

Adding to his bitterness was the fact that he had recently made significant changes in his life to pave the way for this union. He had embarked on new ventures, entered higher circles of business, and relocated to Petersburg with the expectation of climbing the social ladder. He had even calculated how Dounia's charm and refinement could enhance his prospects, imagining how she might attract influential allies and lend him an air of respectability. Now all of those plans lay in ruins. The abruptness of it all struck him like a bolt of lightning—absurd, incomprehensible, and deeply humiliating.

He could not even comprehend how it had come to this. He had barely raised his voice, barely begun to assert his authority, and yet the situation had spiraled out of his control. He had believed himself in love with Dounia, or at least with the idea of her, and the thought of losing her gnawed at him. In his mind, he had already made her his own, and now the loss felt like a robbery, an injustice that demanded redress. By the time he reached the street, he had resolved to set things right. The very next day, he decided, he would mend this situation. He would find a way to restore his position and crush the "conceited milksop" Raskolnikov, whom he blamed for the fiasco. Razumihin crossed his mind as well, but Luzhin dismissed him as a nonentity, beneath serious consideration. The true threat, he decided with a shiver of unease, was Svidrigaïlov. Luzhin could sense that the man harbored intentions of his own, and that thought filled him with dread.

Meanwhile, upstairs, the tension lingered in the air. Dounia clung to her mother, her voice trembling as she spoke. "I was wrong, Mama. More wrong than I can bear to admit. I let myself be tempted by his money, but I swear to you, Rodya, I had no idea what kind of man he was. If I had known, I would never—never—have considered it. Please, don't judge me too harshly."

Pulcheria Alexandrovna held her daughter close, her voice trembling with emotion as she whispered, "God has delivered us, Dounia. He has delivered us. We are free now, and that is all that matters." Yet even as she spoke, it was clear that she was still struggling to fully grasp the enormity of what had just happened. For all of them, the encounter with Luzhin had been a painful but necessary reckoning.

The tension in the room had lifted, replaced by a palpable sense of relief. Within minutes, the group found themselves laughing, as though the confrontation with Luzhin had been nothing more than an unpleasant but necessary ordeal. However, the laughter was tinged with traces of unease; Dounia, for one, occasionally turned pale and furrowed her brow, the memory of Luzhin's words still weighing heavily on her. Pulcheria Alexandrovna, on the other hand, was astonished to realize that she felt glad. Only that morning, the prospect of a falling out with Luzhin had seemed like an unimaginable disaster, yet now it felt as though they had narrowly escaped a catastrophe.

Razumihin was practically beside himself with joy. Though he held back, not daring to express the full extent of his exhilaration, it was evident in his restless movements and the spark in his eyes. The weight of Luzhin's presence, a suffocating burden on his chest, had been lifted, and with it came an overwhelming sense of freedom. Now he could dedicate himself entirely to the family, to Dounia and Pulcheria Alexandrovna, without the shadow of Luzhin looming over them. The possibilities stretched out before him like a vast, open field, though he was too cautious to let his imagination run unchecked.

Raskolnikov, however, seemed impervious to the lightened mood in the room. He remained seated in the same spot, unmoving, his face set in a sullen expression that bordered on indifference. Though he had been the one most adamant about severing ties with Luzhin, he now appeared the least affected by the outcome. Dounia, noticing his brooding silence, could not help but wonder if he was still angry with her. Pulcheria Alexandrovna, too, observed him with a mixture of timidity and concern, as though afraid to provoke him further.

Breaking the silence, Dounia approached her brother with evident hesitation. "What did Svidrigaïlov say to you, Rodya?" she asked softly.

"Yes, tell us!" Pulcheria Alexandrovna echoed, her voice filled with nervous urgency.

Raskolnikov lifted his head slowly, his gaze heavy but focused. "He wants to give you ten thousand roubles as a gift," he said, his tone measured and unemotional. "And he's asked to see you—once—while I'm present."

"See her? Absolutely not!" Pulcheria Alexandrovna exclaimed, her voice trembling with indignation. "And how dare he offer her money! What sort of man is he?"

Raskolnikov recounted his conversation with Svidrigaïlov, though he deliberately left out the unsettling mention of Marfa Petrovna's spectral appearances, deeming it wiser to avoid unnecessary alarm. He spoke plainly, almost mechanically, as if summarizing an event that no longer held any personal significance.

"What did you say to him?" Dounia asked after he had finished.

"At first, I told him I wouldn't deliver any message to you," Raskolnikov replied. "But he insisted that, with or without my help, he would find a way to meet you. He claimed that his so-called passion for you was nothing more than a fleeting infatuation and that he feels nothing for you now. He said he opposes your marriage to Luzhin, but beyond that, his words were muddled and contradictory."

Dounia frowned, her unease deepening. "What do you make of him, Rodya? How did he strike you?"

Raskolnikov considered her question carefully before responding. "I can't quite figure him out," he admitted. "He offers you ten thousand roubles, yet claims he isn't wealthy. He says he's leaving Petersburg, only to forget and contradict himself moments later. He mentions plans to marry someone else, yet seems to have no real focus or direction. It's clear he has some kind of motive, likely a bad one, but he's so clumsy about it that it's hard to tell what he's truly after. Perhaps he's simply mad. Then again, it could all be an act, a façade to mask his true intentions. The death of Marfa Petrovna seems to have unsettled him deeply."

Pulcheria Alexandrovna crossed herself and sighed. "May God rest her soul. I shall pray for her always. And yet, where would we be now, Dounia, without this money she left us? It's as though heaven itself intervened on our behalf. This morning, Rodya, we had just three roubles to our names. Dounia and I were on the verge of pawning her watch just to avoid asking for Luzhin's help."

Dounia remained standing, her expression unreadable as she processed her brother's words. Something about Svidrigaïlov's proposal seemed to haunt her. "He has a terrible plan," she murmured to herself, her voice barely audible. Her body gave an almost imperceptible shudder, as though the mere thought of him cast a shadow over her spirit.

The room grew quiet again, the brief spell of laughter and lightheartedness eclipsed by the lingering unease surrounding Svidrigaïlov's enigmatic intentions. Though they had rid themselves of Luzhin, the family was acutely aware that another, perhaps greater, threat still loomed on the horizon.

Raskolnikov noticed the exaggerated fear in Dounia's demeanor and spoke in a measured tone, almost as though thinking aloud. "I suspect I will have to meet with him again, likely more than once," he said, glancing at Dounia with a hint of unease.

Razumihin, catching the tension in the air, immediately took up the charge with fervent energy. "We will keep an eye on him! I will track him down!" he declared with a determined edge to his voice. "I won't let him out of my sight. Rodya has already given me permission—he told me himself just now, 'Take care of my sister.' Avdotya Romanovna, will you trust me with this responsibility as well?"

Dounia offered him a faint smile, extending her hand in an unspoken gesture of trust, but the lines of worry on her face did not ease. Pulcheria Alexandrovna, observing the exchange, remained silent, her gaze flitting between the two. Still, the assurance of the three thousand roubles seemed to have a calming effect on her, and her earlier anxiety had softened slightly.

In another quarter of an hour, the oppressive atmosphere began to dissipate as the conversation turned livelier. Even Raskolnikov, who had been silent and withdrawn, appeared to listen with more attention, though he contributed little to the discussion. Razumihin, on the other hand, took center stage, his enthusiasm growing with every word.

"And why must you even consider leaving?" he exclaimed passionately, addressing the group but fixing his eyes on Dounia. "What's the point of moving to some small town? Look at the big picture: you're all together here—you need each other! You do, believe me, at least for now. Why not stay? Let me join forces with you! I swear, we can build something incredible together. Just listen to this idea—it hit me like lightning earlier today, even before all this drama started. Let me explain."

He paused dramatically, ensuring everyone's attention was fixed on him. "I have an uncle—an accommodating and respectable man, mind you—who has a thousand roubles sitting idle. He lives off his pension and doesn't really need the money. For two years, he's been pestering me to borrow it from him at a modest six percent interest. I know what that means—it's his way of helping me without making it seem like charity. I didn't need it before, but now, with this opportunity staring us in the face, it's time. You lend me another thousand from your inheritance, and we'll have the capital to start something big. We'll form a partnership, and do you know what we'll do?"

Without waiting for an answer, Razumihin launched into an animated description of his vision. He spoke of how poorly informed most publishers and booksellers were about their own trade and how this incompetence presented an opportunity. Publishing, he argued, could be both profitable and intellectually fulfilling.

"You see," he continued with mounting excitement, "I've been working with publishers for two years now. I know the ins and outs of the business, and I speak three European languages fluently. There's a goldmine of material out there waiting to be translated and published. Some books can turn a profit just by being printed. I even know of a few titles that could earn hundreds of roubles just for the idea of translating them. But publishers—oh, they're such blockheads! They wouldn't recognize a great project if it hit them in the face. That's where we come in. We'll start small, publish a few sure hits, and then expand. It's work, yes, but good, meaningful work—and it'll provide for all of us. What do you think?"

Dounia's eyes lit up with interest, her earlier tension momentarily replaced by genuine curiosity. "I like the sound of it, Dmitri Prokofitch," she said, her tone reflective but warm.

Pulcheria Alexandrovna, however, remained more cautious. "I don't know much about business," she admitted, glancing at

Razumihin and then at her son. "It does sound promising, but it's untested, and we don't have experience with such things. Still, we must stay here for now, at least for a while."

She looked to Raskolnikov for his opinion, clearly valuing his judgment above all. "What do you think, brother?" Dounia asked him directly.

"I think it's an excellent idea," Raskolnikov replied after a brief pause. "Of course, it's too early to think about a full publishing house, but starting small with a few key books could work. I even know of one title myself that would likely sell well. And as for managing it, Razumihin certainly has the experience. We can discuss it in more detail later."

"Hurray!" Razumihin shouted, unable to contain his enthusiasm. "Listen, I even know of a flat in this very building. It's owned by the same landlord, separate from these rooms, and it has three furnished rooms at a reasonable rent. Why don't you take it? You can all live together, and Rodya can stay close by. Everything will be so much easier. I'll even pawn your watch tomorrow to sort out any immediate expenses, and we'll get everything arranged!"

As the group mulled over the suggestion, Raskolnikov suddenly rose from his seat. His abrupt movement caught everyone's attention.

"What? You're leaving already, Rodya?" Pulcheria Alexandrovna asked, her tone tinged with dismay.

Razumihin's voice rang out, thick with disbelief and urgency. "At a time like this?" he exclaimed, his tone a mixture of shock and reproach as he watched Raskolnikov prepare to leave.

Dounia's eyes were fixed on her brother, wide with incredulous worry. Her gaze flickered to the cap he clutched in his pale hand, a signal of his inexplicable determination to go. "What's going on, Rodya?" she asked, her voice trembling slightly.

Raskolnikov stood still for a moment, his expression distant and peculiar. "One might think I was taking leave of you forever," he said in a strained voice, his attempt at a reassuring smile failing miserably.

His lips barely curved, and the expression vanished almost as quickly as it had appeared. Then, almost as though the words escaped him unintentionally, he added, "But who knows... perhaps this is the last time we'll see each other."

The room froze. Pulcheria Alexandrovna gasped audibly, her hands gripping the table in alarm. "What's the matter with you, Rodya? Why would you say such a thing?" she cried, her voice rising with fear.

Dounia stepped forward, her voice low and firm. "Where are you going? What are you doing?" she asked, her worry deepening with each word.

Raskolnikov's eyes darted between them, his jaw tightening as though battling to keep himself composed. "I have to," he began vaguely, struggling to articulate his thoughts. He hesitated, as though searching for the right words, but his face was set with an almost unyielding determination. "I've been meaning to tell you... before now. Mother, Dounia, it's better if we part for a while. I need to be alone. I'm not... at peace. I've decided this already." His voice broke slightly as he spoke, but his tone remained resolute. "I'll come back later. When I'm ready. I'll come of my own accord... if I can. Until then, please... don't inquire about me. Don't follow me. Let me go."

The silence that followed was broken only by Pulcheria Alexandrovna's trembling voice. "Rodya, what are you saying? You can't mean that! What has happened to you, my son?" She was on her feet now, her panic and confusion evident in every line of her face.

"Please," Raskolnikov said, almost pleading now, though his tone carried a weary finality. "If you love me, you'll let me go. Otherwise... I don't know what I'll do. I might start hating you... and I don't want to feel that way. Goodbye."

Pulcheria Alexandrovna's hands flew to her face, a muffled cry escaping her lips. Dounia stared at her brother, frozen in disbelief. "You can't mean this," she said, her voice sharp with indignation. "You're breaking mother's heart. How can you be so cruel?"

Raskolnikov turned away, heading toward the door with a slow, deliberate pace. Dounia rushed after him, grabbing his arm before he could leave. "Brother, stop!" she whispered fiercely. "Do you even see what you're doing to her? To us?"

He turned his face to her, his expression dull and distant, as though her words barely reached him. "I'll come back," he muttered, his voice almost mechanical. "I'm coming... later." Without another word, he slipped out of her grasp and walked out.

"Wicked, heartless egoist!" Dounia cried, trembling with anger and hurt.

Razumihin, who had been silent until now, grabbed her arm gently but firmly. His voice was low, yet intense. "No, Dounia. He's not heartless. Can't you see? He's unwell—he's not in his right mind. Don't you dare say that about him."

He turned back to Pulcheria Alexandrovna, who was on the verge of collapse. "Stay here. I'll bring him back," he promised, his voice shaking with determination as he darted out after Raskolnikov.

In the dimly lit corridor, Razumihin found him near the staircase. Raskolnikov seemed to be waiting, as though he had anticipated this pursuit. "I knew you'd come after me," he said quietly. "But there's no point. Go back. Stay with them—be with them tomorrow and always. They need you more than I do."

"Where are you going? What are you doing to yourself, Rodya?" Razumihin demanded, his voice rising in desperation. "You can't just walk away like this. Let me help you!"

"Don't ask me anything," Raskolnikov interrupted, his voice firm but laden with exhaustion. "I have nothing to tell you. Leave me, Razumihin. Just... don't leave them. Promise me that."

Razumihin stood rooted to the spot, his breath catching as something unspoken passed between them in the dim corridor. For a fleeting moment, it was as though he glimpsed a terrible truth in Raskolnikov's piercing gaze, something that chilled him to the core. His face paled.

"Do you understand now?" Raskolnikov asked, his voice trembling but insistent. Then, before Razumihin could respond, he turned abruptly and disappeared into the shadows, leaving the building without looking back.

Razumihin returned to the women in the room, his face tight with suppressed emotion. He did his best to reassure them, inventing plausible excuses for Raskolnikov's behavior. "He's unwell," he explained, "and needs time to recover. He's overwhelmed, but I'll watch over him—I'll make sure he's all right. We'll get a doctor, the best doctor, and he'll come back soon. I promise."

From that night onward, Razumihin stepped fully into their lives, becoming not just a friend but a steadfast protector. To Pulcheria Alexandrovna and Dounia, he became both a son and a brother, tirelessly ensuring they were safe and cared for, even as his own heart remained heavy with concern for Raskolnikov's increasingly erratic behavior.

Chapter 4

Raskolnikov moved swiftly along the canal bank until he reached the old, green, three-story house where Sonia resided. The building's paint had long faded, and the structure seemed tired and worn, reflecting the lives of its inhabitants. He approached the porter, a weary man lounging near the entrance, and after a brief exchange managed to obtain vague directions to Kapernaumov, the tailor. Following the instructions, he entered a narrow, dimly lit courtyard. The air was heavy with dampness and the faint smell of mildew. In one corner, he found the entrance to a dark, cramped staircase.

With slow and deliberate steps, he ascended to the second floor. The faint creak of the wooden boards beneath his feet was the only sound breaking the oppressive silence. Emerging onto a gallery that encircled the second story, he stopped, disoriented by the maze of identical doors. He hesitated in the dimness, unsure which direction to turn to find Kapernaumov's residence.

Then, as if guided by instinct, he approached a door only a few paces away. Just as he reached for it, the door opened slightly, and a voice, soft yet tinged with unease, called out from within.

"Who is there?" a woman's voice asked, trembling with uncertainty.

"It's me... I've come to see you," Raskolnikov replied, his voice low but steady. Without waiting for an invitation, he stepped into the small entryway.

Inside, the dim light of a single candle flickered weakly atop a broken chair. The copper candlestick was battered and discolored, much like the home it illuminated. Sonia stood just beyond the doorway, frozen in surprise.

"It's you! Good heavens!" she gasped, her voice faltering. She seemed paralyzed, unable to process his unexpected arrival.

"Which is your room? This way?" Raskolnikov asked, deliberately avoiding her gaze as he moved past her into the space beyond.

A moment later, Sonia entered the room behind him, carrying the candle. She set it down on a plain wooden table with a trembling hand. Her face, pale and worn, was suddenly suffused with color, and her eyes filled with tears. She appeared both startled and overwhelmed by emotion—an uneasy blend of fear, shame, and a strange happiness.

Raskolnikov sat heavily on one of the simple chairs by the table, his eyes scanning the room with a deliberate, calculating air.

The room was large, but the low ceiling made it feel oppressive. Its irregular shape gave it a peculiar, almost distorted appearance. One wall slanted at a sharp angle, its three small windows overlooking the canal. The faint light from outside barely penetrated the interior. The opposite corner of the room was wide and obtuse, leaving much of the space shrouded in shadow.

The furniture was sparse and unremarkable. A narrow bed stood in the corner nearest the door, unadorned by even the simplest curtain. Next to it was a chair, worn and unsteady. The table, covered with a faded blue cloth, sat near the adjoining door to the tailor's quarters. Two mismatched rush-bottom chairs were placed haphazardly beside it. Against the far wall, a small chest of drawers stood alone, as though lost in the barren expanse of the room. The walls were papered with yellowing, scratched wallpaper, stained black in the damp corners. The entire space spoke of unrelenting poverty, of a life eked out in quiet suffering.

Sonia stood motionless, her hands clasped tightly before her, watching him with a growing sense of dread. Her wide eyes betrayed her rising terror, as though she were being scrutinized by a judge who might deliver an irreversible verdict.

"I'm late... it must be past eleven, isn't it?" Raskolnikov asked abruptly, his eyes fixed on the floor.

"Yes," Sonia whispered, her voice barely audible. "Oh, yes, it is," she added quickly, grasping at the words as if they might shield her from his silent judgment. "My landlady's clock just struck... I heard it myself."

Raskolnikov sat silent for a moment, his shoulders hunched as though weighed down by unseen burdens. Then, without raising his eyes, he said in a low, somber voice, "I've come to you for the last time."

The words hung in the air, heavy and final. Sonia's lips parted, but no sound came out. She stared at him, her expression one of bewildered sorrow.

"For the last time?" she echoed faintly. "Are you... are you going away?"

"I don't know," he replied, his voice flat and devoid of certainty. "Tomorrow... perhaps."

The room fell into an uneasy silence. Sonia's hands clutched at the edge of the table as though seeking support, her breath shallow and unsteady. Raskolnikov's gaze remained fixed on some indeterminate point beyond the walls, as though he were already far away in mind, if not yet in body.

Sonia's voice trembled as she spoke, her unease unmistakable. "Then you are not coming to Katerina Ivanovna tomorrow?" she asked, her hands clenched tightly in her lap.

Raskolnikov did not answer her immediately. His gaze was distant, as though he were speaking more to himself than to her. "I don't know," he said at last. "I shall know tomorrow morning... Never mind that. I've come to say one word." His tone was abrupt, but then, catching sight of her standing before him while he sat, his expression softened. There was a sudden gentleness in his voice as he added, "Why are you standing? Sit down."

Sonia hesitated for a moment before obediently sitting across from him. Her movements were slow and uncertain, as though she were afraid of disturbing something fragile in the air between them. Raskolnikov turned his gaze to her, studying her closely, and a faint shadow of compassion crossed his face.

"How thin you are," he murmured, reaching out to take her hand. He held it lightly in his own and turned it slightly, as if examining something delicate and breakable. "What a hand! It's almost transparent... like the hand of a dead person."

Sonia smiled faintly, though her face betrayed the weariness she carried. "I have always been like that," she replied softly, almost apologetically.

"Even when you lived at home?" he asked, tilting his head slightly, as though trying to imagine her in a different setting.

"Yes," she said simply.

"Of course, you were," Raskolnikov muttered abruptly. His mood shifted as quickly as it had softened, and his voice turned brusque. His eyes wandered around the room. "You rent this room from the Kapernaumovs?" he asked.

"Yes..." Sonia said, her tone hesitant, as though uncertain where his questions were leading.

"They live just beyond that door?" he asked, gesturing toward the adjacent room.

"Yes... They have another room like this," Sonia answered, her voice growing quieter with each response.

"All in one room?" he asked with a note of incredulity.

"Yes," she replied again.

Raskolnikov frowned, his expression darkening. "I should be afraid to sleep here at night," he remarked gloomily, his voice heavy with unspoken thoughts.

"They are good people," Sonia said hurriedly, as though defending not only the Kapernaumovs but her own fragile existence. "Very kind. And all the furniture... everything... everything in here belongs to them. They are kind, and the children often come to see me."

"They all stammer, don't they?" Raskolnikov asked, his voice sharper than before.

"Yes..." Sonia admitted. "He stammers, and he's lame. His wife... she doesn't exactly stammer, but she can't speak clearly. She's very kind, though. And he was once a house serf. They have seven children, and it's only the eldest who stammers. The others are just ill... but they don't stammer." She paused, looking at him with slight surprise. "But how do you know about them?"

"Your father told me," Raskolnikov said flatly. "He told me everything about you... how you would leave at six in the evening and return by nine, how Katerina Ivanovna would kneel by your bed..."

Sonia's face flushed deeply, and she looked down in confusion. "I... I thought I saw him today," she whispered hesitantly.

"Whom?" Raskolnikov asked sharply.

"My father," she said, her voice trembling. "I was walking on the street... just at the corner, around ten o'clock, and it seemed like he was walking in front of me. It looked so much like him... I was going to see Katerina Ivanovna."

"You were walking the streets at that hour?" he asked, his voice growing sterner.

"Yes..." Sonia admitted, her words faltering. She lowered her eyes again, overwhelmed by an undefinable mix of shame and grief.

"Katerina Ivanovna used to beat you, I suppose?" Raskolnikov asked abruptly.

Sonia's head snapped up, and she stared at him with wide, almost horrified eyes. "Oh, no! What are you saying? No!" she cried, her voice filled with a plaintive urgency.

"You love her, then?" he asked, his tone softer but still probing.

"Love her? Of course!" Sonia exclaimed, her voice rising with emotion. Her hands clasped together tightly as if to contain her distress. "Ah, you don't understand! You don't know her! She's like a child... her mind is not... it's unhinged from so much sorrow. But she used to be so clever, so kind, so generous... If only you knew!" Her voice broke, and she wrung her hands, a visible anguish spreading across her face.

"She is unhappy... so unhappy," Sonia went on, her words spilling out as though they could no longer be contained. "She believes in righteousness; she searches for it everywhere, and when she doesn't find it, it breaks her heart. She's pure, truly pure, and she believes that people can be righteous, that they should be... She's good, but she suffers so much."

"And what will happen to you?" Raskolnikov asked abruptly, cutting through her impassioned plea.

Sonia stared at him, puzzled and uncomprehending.

"They are all left on your hands now," he said grimly. "They were on your hands before, but now... What will happen to you?"

"I... I don't know," Sonia murmured, her voice low and filled with despair. She looked away, her eyes welling with tears, and for a moment, the room was filled with a silence so heavy that it seemed to press down on both of them.

"Will they stay there?" Raskolnikov pressed, his voice low but pointed, as though urging Sonia to confront the inevitable.

"I don't know," Sonia murmured, her hands trembling slightly as they rested in her lap. "They are in debt for the lodging, but the landlady said today that she wants them out. And Katerina Ivanovna—she's so determined—she says she won't stay another minute."

"How is it she can be so bold?" Raskolnikov asked sharply. "Does she rely on you?"

"Oh no! Don't talk like that!" Sonia cried, her voice trembling with emotion. "We are one; we live like one. Don't you see? What else can she do? What could she possibly do?" Her voice rose with a mixture of agitation and anger, as if defending Katerina Ivanovna against an unseen accuser. She seemed so delicate in her distress, like a fragile bird fluttering in a cage. "And how she cried today!" Sonia continued, her words spilling out in a rush. "Her mind is unhinged—haven't you noticed it? One moment, she's worrying like a child, wanting everything to be perfect tomorrow for the lunch and all of that. The next, she's wringing her hands, spitting blood, weeping, and then banging her head against the wall in despair. And then she'll cling to me, kissing me, comforting herself with all these dreams... She says you'll help us now, that we'll borrow some money and go to her native town, start a boarding school for the daughters of gentlemen, and I'll help her run it. She believes it so fully—she has such faith in her fancies that it's impossible to contradict her. And yet... oh, you should see her!"

Sonia's voice broke, her face twisting with emotion. "All day long, she's been working so hard, washing, cleaning, mending. She even dragged a heavy wash tub into the room with those feeble hands of hers, and after that, she collapsed onto the bed, gasping for breath. We went to the shops this morning to buy shoes for Polenka and Lida because theirs are so worn out they can't be fixed anymore. But the money—oh, it wasn't nearly enough! Not even close. She picked out the sweetest little boots—she has such good taste, you know—but in the end, she realized she couldn't afford them. Right there in the shop, she burst into tears in front of everyone." Sonia covered her face with her hands. "It was so sad, so unbearable to see."

Raskolnikov listened in silence, his face a mask of grim contemplation. "Well, after hearing all that, I can understand why you live the way you do," he said at last, his smile bitter and faint.

"But aren't you sorry for them? Aren't you sorry?" Sonia demanded, her voice trembling with a mixture of desperation and defiance. "I know you are. You gave your last penny to them, didn't you? Even though you'd seen nothing of it. And if you had seen everything... oh, dear God!" She broke off, wringing her hands in agony. "And yet, even I—oh, I've been so cruel to her at times!"

"You were cruel to her?" Raskolnikov asked, startled by her words.

"Yes, I was!" Sonia admitted, her voice shaking as she began to sob. "It was only a week before he—before my father—died. He was sitting there with a book he'd borrowed from Lebeziatnikov. He said, 'Read to me, Sonia, my head aches,' but I refused. I'd only come to show Katerina Ivanovna some collars I'd bought from Lizaveta, and I didn't want to stay. Oh, those collars! They were so pretty, embroidered so delicately, and Katerina Ivanovna admired them so much. She tried them on and looked in the mirror—it made her so happy. 'Make me a gift of them, Sonia,' she said. She never asks for anything, you know. She's proud, even when she has nothing. And yet I refused her. I said something harsh, something heartless. I can't even remember my exact words now, but they crushed her. Not because she didn't get the collars—no, it wasn't about that. It was my refusal, my coldness that grieved her."

Sonia's tears flowed freely now. "If only I could take it back! If only I could bring those words back! But what's the use in saying that now? It means nothing to anyone, least of all you."

"Did you know Lizaveta, the pedlar?" Raskolnikov asked suddenly, his tone shifting.

"Yes," Sonia replied hesitantly. "Did you?"

Instead of answering, Raskolnikov said quietly, "Katerina Ivanovna is dying. It's rapid consumption. She won't last long."

Sonia gasped and clutched his hands, her face stricken with terror. "No, no, no! Please, don't say that!" she pleaded, her voice rising in desperation.

"But it would be better if she did," Raskolnikov continued, his voice devoid of comfort.

"No, it wouldn't! Not better at all!" Sonia cried, her face contorting in anguish.

"And the children?" he pressed, relentless. "What can you do for them except take them in yourself?"

"I don't know!" Sonia exclaimed, her voice breaking as she covered her face with trembling hands. The weight of his words crushed her, and it was clear this thought had haunted her before. Now, his merciless questions only brought it back to torment her anew.

"And if you fall ill?" Raskolnikov went on ruthlessly. "What happens then? What happens if you're taken to the hospital? Who will care for them?"

"Don't say that!" Sonia cried, her face pale with horror. Her trembling hands moved to her head as though trying to hold herself together against the tidal wave of despair. It was as though he had forced her to stare into an abyss she could not bear to face.

"Cannot be?" Raskolnikov repeated, his voice low and sharp, as though deliberately cutting into her hopes. His lips twisted into a harsh smile. "You are not insured against it, are you? What will happen to them then? They will be out on the streets, all of them. Katerina Ivanovna will cough and beg, knocking her head against some wall in despair, just as she did today. The children will cry for her, wailing in hunger and fear. And then, when her strength finally gives out, she will collapse—be taken to the police station and then to the hospital, where she will die alone. And the children... what will become of them?"

Sonia gasped, her face paling with horror as her trembling hands clenched into fists. "Oh no... God will not let it be!" she finally burst out, the words ripped from her heart as though they could ward off the nightmare he was painting.

Her gaze clung to him, imploring and desperate, her hands clasped tightly as if he held the power to change their fate. She looked as if she were pleading with him not to make these things true merely by speaking them aloud.

Raskolnikov rose abruptly and began pacing the room, his movements restless, as though he were trying to escape his own words. Minutes passed in strained silence, broken only by the sound of his boots against the floorboards. Sonia stood where she was, head bowed, her shoulders sagging under the weight of terrible dejection.

"And can't you save anything? Put by for a rainy day?" he asked suddenly, stopping in front of her, his tone sharp and biting.

Sonia looked up, her face flushed with humiliation and despair. "No," she whispered.

"Of course not," he said bitterly, as if the very idea was absurd. "Have you even tried?" His voice was almost mocking.

"Yes," she admitted, the word barely audible.

"And it didn't work, did it? Of course not. There's no need to ask," he replied, resuming his pacing as though her answer had been inevitable.

Another tense minute passed. Then he stopped abruptly again. "You don't get money every day, do you?"

Sonia's blush deepened. She looked down, her hands twisting together in her lap. "No," she admitted, the words escaping her with painful difficulty.

"And Polenka," he said suddenly, his voice colder now. "It will be the same for her, no doubt."

The words struck Sonia like a physical blow. Her head snapped up, her wide eyes filling with terror. "No, no! It can't be! No!" she cried out, her voice breaking as though she had been stabbed. "God would never allow something so horrible to happen!"

Raskolnikov's lips curled into a sardonic smile. "He lets others fall into it."

"No, no! God will protect her! God will!" Sonia repeated fervently, as if her conviction alone could shield her little sister from the horrors of the world.

"But what if," Raskolnikov said slowly, his voice soft but tinged with cruel amusement, "there is no God at all?"

Sonia froze, her face crumpling as though he had struck her. A tremor passed over her entire body, and she looked at him with unutterable pain and reproach in her tear-filled eyes. She opened her mouth to speak but no words came. Instead, a deep, wrenching sob broke from her chest, and she hid her face in her hands, her body trembling as she wept bitterly.

"You say Katerina Ivanovna's mind is unhinged," Raskolnikov said quietly after a pause. "But it seems your own mind is unhinged as well."

Five long minutes passed. He continued to pace, silent and brooding, while Sonia's sobs filled the air. At last, he approached her, his eyes glittering with a feverish light. He placed his hands on her thin shoulders and looked into her tear-streaked face. His gaze was intense, piercing, as though he was trying to see into her very soul. His lips twitched as though he wanted to say something but could not.

Then, suddenly, he bent down and dropped to the floor, pressing his lips to her foot in an impulsive, almost violent gesture.

Sonia jerked back, her face pale with shock and confusion. She stared at him as though he had gone mad. "What are you doing?" she whispered, her voice trembling with anguish. "What are you doing to me?"

Raskolnikov stood quickly, his expression wild and unreadable. "I didn't bow to you," he said, his voice almost a shout. "I bowed to all the suffering of humanity!" He turned away abruptly and walked to the window, standing there with his back to her, his shoulders rigid.

After a moment, he spoke again, his tone calmer but still charged with emotion. "Do you know what I said earlier today? I told an insolent man that he wasn't worth your little finger. I told him that I was honoring my sister by making her sit beside you."

Sonia gasped and stepped back, her face filled with horror. "You said that? And in her presence? Why would you say such a thing?" she asked, her voice trembling.

"It wasn't because of your dishonor or your sin," he said, turning to face her, his eyes fierce. "It was because of your great suffering. But you are a great sinner, Sonia. That's the truth. Your worst sin is that you've destroyed yourself and betrayed yourself for nothing. Can't you see how fearful that is? You live in this filth that you loathe, and yet you're not saving anyone by it—not yourself, not anyone else. Wouldn't it be better, a thousand times better, to leap into the water and end it all?"

Sonia's face went white, but her eyes remained locked on his, full of anguish rather than surprise. "What would happen to them?" she asked faintly, as though the question was the only thing keeping her grounded.

Raskolnikov studied her face and saw the truth written there. She had thought of this before—many times, perhaps. Her despair had taken her to the edge of that abyss, and his words had merely echoed thoughts she had already wrestled with. Her pain, her shame, her fear—they were all laid bare before him.

Yet, even in her despair, she had not succumbed. And for the first time, Raskolnikov began to grasp the depth of her suffering, the weight of the burden she bore for others. Sonia stood before him, fragile yet unbroken, a figure of both tragedy and resilience. He stared at her as though seeing her for the first time, and the enormity of her silent strength left him shaken.

"There are three paths ahead of her," Raskolnikov thought grimly, pacing with a nervous energy that matched his dark ruminations. "The canal, the madhouse, or finally, that slow descent into depravity—a depravity that dulls the mind and hardens the heart into stone."

He shuddered, though he could not push the thought away. The last scenario was the most repulsive to him, but it was also, he believed, the most plausible. He was young, cynical, and given to abstraction— qualities that often lent themselves to a peculiar kind of cruelty. It was in his nature to see the darkest possibilities as the most likely outcomes. Yet, despite himself, he recoiled from the image of Sonia, so full of suffering yet so pure of spirit, being swallowed by the filth and iniquity of such a fate.

"Could it really be true?" he wondered aloud, almost despairingly. "Could someone like her, who has held on to the purity of her soul amidst all this horror, be consciously dragged down into that abyss? Could it be happening even now? Could she have endured up to this point only because the horror is becoming familiar—less revolting to her? No, no, that can't be! It's impossible!" he exclaimed, echoing Sonia's earlier desperate cry. "What's kept her away from the canal until now is her belief in sin... and those children. But if she hasn't gone mad already... Wait, who says she hasn't gone mad? Look at her. Can someone who reasons the way she does, who clings so stubbornly to these delusions, truly be sane? Does she think a miracle will save her? No doubt she does. Isn't that madness in itself?"

He latched onto this explanation with a strange, morbid satisfaction, as though finding solace in reducing her suffering to a pathological condition. The thought offered a grim clarity, one he preferred over more complex or ambiguous truths. He began observing her more closely, his gaze penetrating, searching.

"So, you pray to God a great deal, don't you?" he asked abruptly, breaking the silence.

Sonia did not respond at first. She stood still, her frail figure trembling slightly under the weight of his scrutiny. He waited, his question hanging in the air between them like a challenge.

"What would I be without God?" she finally whispered, her voice low but intense. Her eyes flashed with sudden emotion, and she reached out impulsively to squeeze his hand. The touch was brief but forceful, charged with a sincerity that startled him.

"Ah, so that's it," he thought, his mind racing.

"And what does God do for you?" he pressed, his tone sharp and probing.

Sonia hesitated, struggling to find words. Her thin chest heaved as though she were battling an overwhelming wave of emotion. Finally, she burst out, "Be silent! Don't ask! You don't deserve to know!" Her voice was trembling, but it carried an edge of defiance, her eyes meeting his with a fire that startled him.

"Yes, that's it," he murmured to himself, as though confirming a hypothesis.

"He does everything," Sonia whispered at last, her gaze dropping again. The words came quickly, almost defensively, as though she were trying to shield herself from further questioning.

Raskolnikov studied her intently. There was something feverish, almost manic, in the way his eyes darted over her fragile form, her angular features, her wide, soft eyes that seemed capable of flashing with both stern resolve and deep vulnerability. The sight of her filled him with a strange mixture of curiosity, pity, and something darker— an almost perverse fascination.

"She's a religious maniac," he concluded to himself, though the thought brought him no satisfaction, only a deeper unease.

His wandering eyes fell on a book lying on the chest of drawers. It was old, bound in worn leather, and he had noticed it several times while pacing. On an impulse, he picked it up and examined it.

"What's this?" he asked sharply. "The New Testament?"

Sonia, who had been standing motionless a few steps away, seemed to shrink under his gaze. "It was brought to me," she said softly, her reluctance evident.

"Who brought it?"

"Lizaveta. I asked her for it," Sonia admitted, her voice barely above a whisper.

"Lizaveta," he repeated, the name lingering on his tongue like a mystery. His thoughts grew darker. Everything about Sonia seemed to draw him deeper into a strange, inexplicable labyrinth.

He turned the pages of the book idly before stopping suddenly. "Where is the story of Lazarus?" he demanded, his voice sharper now.

Sonia remained silent, her eyes fixed stubbornly on the floor.

"Find it for me," he ordered. "Read it."

At last, she moved, hesitant and visibly uneasy. Her thin fingers closed around the book, and she began flipping through the pages. "You're looking in the wrong place," she said softly but firmly. "It's in the fourth gospel."

"Then read it," he said, sitting down and leaning his head against his hand, his expression sullen. His voice was tinged with a strange mixture of command and despair.

Sonia hesitated, clutching the book tightly. "Haven't you read it before?" she asked, looking up at him with a rare sternness in her eyes.

"Long ago. When I was at school," he said curtly. "Read."

"And haven't you heard it in church?" she pressed.

"I haven't been," he replied, his tone flat. "Do you often go?"

"No," she whispered.

He smiled faintly, a cold, bitter smile. "I see. And you're going to your father's funeral tomorrow, I suppose?"

"Yes," she said simply. "I was at church last week, too. I had a requiem service said."

"For whom?"

"For Lizaveta," she replied, her voice breaking slightly. "She was killed... with an axe."

Her words struck him like a physical blow. His head spun, his nerves fraying under the weight of everything he had heard. As the room seemed to close in around him, Raskolnikov felt himself teetering on the edge of an abyss—a chasm filled with questions, guilt, and the growing fear that there might be no escape for either of them.

"Were you close to Lizaveta?" Raskolnikov asked, his tone sharper than intended.

"Yes... she was kind," Sonia replied softly, her voice catching slightly. "She would visit sometimes... not often; she couldn't... but when she did, we'd read together and talk. She will see God."

The last phrase struck Raskolnikov as peculiar, almost jarring. It hung in the air, a simple declaration imbued with unfathomable depth. A new layer of mystery seemed to surround Sonia—her clandestine friendship with Lizaveta, their shared moments of reading and reflection. It was as if they were bound together by a secret, something both profound and incomprehensible.

And now, the word "maniac" slipped into his thoughts unbidden. "So Lizaveta was a religious maniac," he thought, "and Sonia must be one too. At this rate, I'll become one myself. It's infectious!"

"Read!" he suddenly demanded, his irritation surfacing as an almost instinctual defense against the rising tide of incomprehensible emotions.

Sonia hesitated, clutching the book tightly, her small hands trembling. Her heart pounded so fiercely it seemed to echo in the silence between them. She stared at the pages, as if the mere act of opening them required immense strength.

"Why?" she whispered finally, her voice thin and trembling. "Why do you ask this of me? You don't believe... why should I read to you?"

"Read," he repeated, his tone hard and insistent. "You read to Lizaveta, didn't you? Read to me."

Still trembling, Sonia opened the book. Her hands shook so much that the pages rustled audibly as she searched for the passage. Twice she tried to begin, but her voice faltered, catching on the first word and failing her entirely. It was as though some unseen weight pressed down upon her, silencing her against her will.

"Now a certain man was sick, named Lazarus of Bethany..." she finally managed to begin. Her voice was unsteady, and by the third word, it broke entirely, trembling like a fragile string stretched too far. She drew in a shallow, unsteady breath.

Raskolnikov watched her closely, and his expression grew harder. He understood, perhaps better than he wished to admit, why Sonia found it so agonizing to read to him. These words were not just a recitation; they were a window into her very soul, her private solace in a world filled with suffering. And now, he was forcing her to expose it, to lay it bare before him. Yet, for all her dread and resistance, he could see a flicker of something else in her—a deep, almost desperate need to share this moment with him, as though the act of reading was a plea, an offering of faith she longed for him to accept.

"Keep reading," he commanded, his voice more subdued but no less firm.

Sonia fought to master herself. She drew a long, steadying breath and began again. Slowly, haltingly, she read on:

"Then Martha, as soon as she heard that Jesus was coming, went and met Him: but Mary sat still in the house. Then said Martha unto Jesus, Lord, if Thou hadst been here, my brother had not died."

Her voice quivered with emotion, but she pressed on. As the story unfolded, her trembling diminished, replaced by a new energy, a quiet but growing power that seemed to radiate from her. She read with reverence, with pain, and with an almost otherworldly fervor. Her words carried with them a weight beyond their mere meaning, as if each phrase was imbued with years of sorrow, hope, and unspoken prayers.

Raskolnikov sat motionless, his elbows resting on the table, his face half-turned away. He refused to meet her gaze, as though shielding himself from the intensity of her conviction. Yet, he listened intently, each word striking a chord within him that he could neither ignore nor fully comprehend.

When she reached the words, "I am the resurrection, and the life: he that believeth in Me, though he were dead, yet shall he live," her voice grew steadier, clearer, as if the truth of the passage lent her strength. She paused, took another deep breath, and looked up briefly at Raskolnikov. Her eyes shone with something between defiance and pleading. Then, as though resolving to see it through to the end, she continued, her voice ringing out with a quiet but unyielding determination.

By the time she read the line, "Jesus wept," her voice was trembling again, but now it was with something entirely different—triumph. She was nearing the climax, the moment when disbelief would be swept away by an undeniable miracle. Her anticipation was palpable, as though she were willing the words themselves to work their power upon him.

"He will see it," she thought. "He will understand. He will believe. Yes, he must!" This thought burned within her, giving her courage. She was trembling, her hands clutching the book as if it were the only anchor holding her steady.

Raskolnikov finally turned his gaze toward her. He could see the feverish glow in her cheeks, the light in her eyes, and he felt something shift within him—something he did not understand, something he was not ready to name. For the first time, he found himself truly listening, not just to the words, but to the force behind them, to the spirit that gave them life.

"'Jesus therefore again groaning in Himself cometh to the grave. It was a cave, and a stone lay upon it.

Jesus said, Take ye away the stone. Martha, the sister of him that was dead, saith unto Him, Lord, by this time he stinketh: for he hath been dead four days.'"

Sonia's voice faltered momentarily but then steadied as she laid a delicate but deliberate emphasis on the word "four," as though its weight carried a deeper significance.

"'Jesus saith unto her, Said I not unto thee that if thou wouldest believe, thou shouldest see the glory of God?

Then they took away the stone from the place where the dead was laid. And Jesus lifted up His eyes and said, Father, I thank Thee that Thou hast heard Me.

And I knew that Thou hearest Me always; but because of the people which stand by I said it, that they may believe that Thou hast sent Me.

And when He thus had spoken, He cried with a loud voice, Lazarus, come forth.

And he that was dead came forth.'"

Her voice rose and quivered with an almost otherworldly fervor as she read these lines, trembling visibly as though she were witnessing the miraculous scene herself, as if the very words conjured the sight of the dead man stepping forth, bound in graveclothes.

"'Bound hand and foot with graveclothes; and his face was bound about with a napkin. Jesus saith unto them, Loose him, and let him go.

Then many of the Jews which came to Mary and had seen the things which Jesus did believed on Him.'"

Sonia stopped abruptly. She shut the book with a trembling hand and stood up quickly, her movements sharp, almost defensive, as though she feared further exposure of her soul.

"That is all about the raising of Lazarus," she said quietly but firmly, her voice tinged with an abruptness that hinted at something far deeper. She turned her back to him and stood motionless, her trembling hands clasped tightly together as if in prayer or silent desperation. The air seemed to hang heavy with her raw emotion.

Raskolnikov sat still for a moment, his gaze fixed on her fragile figure as the flickering light of the dying candle cast wavering shadows on the walls of the bare room. The dim glow illuminated the scene of the murderer and the harlot reading from the eternal book, a tableau at once tragic and transcendent. Time seemed to stretch, the silence between them vast and impenetrable.

"I came to speak of something," Raskolnikov said finally, breaking the stillness with a voice that was low but carried the weight of an unspoken burden. He rose from his seat and approached her. Sonia turned to face him, her expression a mix of fear and confusion. His own face bore a grim, determined set, his eyes shadowed with something savage, as though he were wrestling with forces beyond his control.

"I have abandoned my family today," he said, his voice heavy with finality. "My mother and sister—I am not going to see them again. I've broken with them completely."

Sonia stared at him in stunned silence, her breath catching as she absorbed his words. The recent memory of his mother and sister— frail Pulcheria Alexandrovna and resolute Dounia—flashed before her mind, making his declaration all the more incomprehensible.

"What for?" she finally managed to whisper, her voice trembling with alarm and disbelief.

"I have only you now," he continued, his tone relentless, his gaze piercing. "Let us go together. I've come to you because we are both accursed. Let us go our way together."

His eyes shone with an intensity that frightened her. It was as if he were on the edge of madness, consumed by some dark, inscrutable purpose.

"Go where?" Sonia asked, her voice faint and shaky as she instinctively stepped back, her body retreating even as her mind struggled to grasp his meaning.

"I don't know," he admitted, his voice low but fervent. "I only know it's the same road. The same goal. That's all I know."

Sonia continued to stare at him, her wide, imploring eyes searching his face for answers. She saw only profound misery there, a despair so deep that it seemed to radiate from every part of him.

"No one else will understand," he said, his tone softening slightly but losing none of its intensity. "If I told them, they wouldn't understand. But I know you will. I need you. That's why I came to you."

"I... I don't understand," Sonia whispered, her voice breaking under the weight of his words.

"You will," he said with quiet insistence. "Haven't you done the same? Haven't you had the strength to transgress? You've destroyed a life—your own. And now you're trapped. Alone, you'll go mad, just as I am. That's why we must go together."

"What are you saying?" Sonia cried, her voice rising in panic. "What is all this for? What's to be done?"

"To be done?" he echoed, his voice tinged with bitter urgency. "Break what must be broken. Take the suffering on yourself. Freedom, power—over all trembling creation. That's the goal. That's my message to you."

He paused, his face twitching with some inner turmoil, then added ominously, "If I don't come to you tomorrow, you'll hear of it all. Remember my words."

Sonia gasped audibly, her hands clutching her chest. "What do you mean? Do you know—do you know who killed Lizaveta?" she asked, her voice a trembling whisper, her eyes wild with horror.

"I know," he said simply. "I'll tell you tomorrow. Only you. I've chosen you to hear it."

With that, he turned and left. Sonia stood frozen, staring after him as though she had seen a ghost. Her head swam with confusion and terror. The weight of his words, his declarations, and his dark, cryptic promise pressed heavily on her.

"What did he mean? What did he mean?" she whispered to herself, clutching her arms as though to steady herself. "He must be terribly, terribly unhappy. But why? Why has he abandoned his family? What is it that drives him to such despair?"

Her thoughts spiraled, but the answers eluded her. Yet one thing was clear—Raskolnikov's suffering was as boundless as her own, and she, somehow, had become entangled in it.

Sonia spent the entire night in a state of restless delirium, her fragile mind overwhelmed by the turmoil of the day. She would toss and turn in her small, narrow bed, occasionally springing up with a cry, her hands clasped tightly together as though in prayer or despair. She would then fall back, utterly exhausted, into a feverish half-sleep that was haunted by vivid, unsettling dreams. In her mind's eye, she saw Polenka's wide, innocent eyes filled with tears, Katerina Ivanovna's gaunt, fevered face distorted with grief, and Lizaveta's gentle, almost ethereal presence. Over and over, fragments of the gospel she had read that evening seemed to echo in her ears, mingling with the image of Raskolnikov—his pale, haunted face, his burning eyes boring into her, and the shocking memory of him bowing down, kissing her feet, and weeping. The weight of his words, his cryptic declarations, and his grim resolve pressed on her like a suffocating shroud.

Each time she woke, it was as though she were surfacing from some dark and suffocating abyss. She would weep silently, wring her hands, and pace the small, dimly lit room. Then, drained of strength, she would collapse onto the bed again, only for the feverish visions to resume. The candle in the battered candlestick flickered weakly on the chest of drawers, its wavering light casting long, distorted shadows across the barren walls.

In the adjacent flat, separated from Sonia's room by a thin partition wall and a door that had long remained shut, was a space that had stood empty for as long as Sonia could remember. A card had been affixed to the gate below, and a faded notice was visible in the windows overlooking the canal, advertising the room as available for rent. It was a part of her surroundings she had grown so accustomed to that it rarely entered her mind. The emptiness of the room had become as much a part of her reality as her own poverty.

But on this night, unknown to her, Mr. Svidrigaïlov had taken up a peculiar interest in her. He had been standing silently on the other side of that dividing door in the empty room. His ear was pressed against the wooden panel, straining to catch the faintest sounds of her conversation with Raskolnikov earlier in the evening. His curiosity, sparked initially by mere happenstance, had grown into a morbid fascination. There had been something about the tones of their voices, the sharp edges of Raskolnikov's words, and the tremulous, almost pleading quality of Sonia's replies that had gripped him.

When Raskolnikov had finally left, Svidrigaïlov remained in place, his brow furrowed in thought. After a few moments, he tiptoed back into his own room, the one adjacent to the empty flat. He moved quietly, careful not to make a sound that might betray his presence. From the corner of his cluttered room, he retrieved a chair and, with exaggerated caution, carried it back into the empty room. He placed it directly beside the closed door that connected it to Sonia's quarters, arranging it carefully so that it was positioned for maximum comfort. The events of the night, particularly the snippets of conversation he had overheard, had intrigued him more than he cared to admit, and he resolved to prepare for the next opportunity to eavesdrop.

He could not deny the enjoyment he had derived from listening in—a strange, almost perverse pleasure in being privy to such raw and intimate exchanges. The idea of standing for hours again, should there be another such opportunity the following day, was unacceptable to him. The chair, he thought with a sly smile, was a necessary investment in his comfort.

As he settled himself into his room for the night, he was filled with a peculiar sense of anticipation. What secrets might he uncover tomorrow? What desperate or extraordinary words might be exchanged between those two strange, tortured souls? He leaned back, his mind weaving scenarios, each one more dramatic and scandalous than the last, and waited for the dawn with a smirk playing on his lips. Meanwhile, in the next room, Sonia remained lost in her feverish dreams, utterly unaware of the shadow that loomed just beyond the thin partition.

Chapter 5

When Raskolnikov arrived promptly at eleven o'clock the following morning at the department for the investigation of criminal cases, he fully expected to be immediately ushered in or, worse, ambushed in some dramatic fashion. Yet, contrary to his expectations, he was left to wait. The moments stretched into ten long minutes, during which time he stood uneasily in the waiting area, feeling as though he were dangling on the edge of some invisible precipice. People came and went—clerks, functionaries, and others—none of whom seemed to pay him the slightest attention. They passed by without so much as a glance, absorbed in their own petty concerns.

Raskolnikov scrutinized the environment with a mix of suspicion and disbelief. In the adjacent office, clerks sat engrossed in their work, their quills scratching against the paper, their expressions indifferent and detached. No one seemed to recognize him or show any indication that he was a person of interest. It was as if he were invisible to them, a nonentity. He glanced around uneasily, half-expecting to spot some hidden guard or shadowy figure assigned to monitor him. Yet nothing of the sort materialized. The mundanity of the scene clashed violently with the weight of his own paranoia.

The more he waited, the more convinced he became that his fears might be unfounded. If the strange man from the day before—the one who seemed to materialize from nowhere—had truly seen something incriminating, wouldn't the entire machinery of the law have already pounced on him? Surely, they wouldn't have left him standing idly, free to walk away. This line of thought planted a fragile seed of hope in his mind. Perhaps the man had seen nothing, or perhaps he was merely a figment of his overwrought imagination. He had started to entertain such a possibility the previous evening, even amid his darkest despair.

As he brooded over these thoughts, Raskolnikov became abruptly aware that his body was betraying him. He was trembling. The realization ignited a flash of indignation within him—how dare he tremble at the thought of facing Porfiry Petrovitch, a man he loathed with every fiber of his being? The intensity of his hatred for the investigator startled even himself. The idea that his hatred might inadvertently expose him only deepened his resolve to regain control. With a visible effort, he stilled his trembling and straightened his posture. He silently vowed to maintain an air of cold detachment, to limit his words, and to suppress his volatile nerves.

At last, his name was called, and he was ushered into Porfiry Petrovitch's office. The room was modest, neither too large nor too small, furnished with utilitarian government-issued pieces—a large writing desk, a checked-upholstered sofa, a bookcase, and a polished bureau. The yellow-hued furniture gave the room a peculiar cheerfulness that clashed with its purpose. A closed door in the far wall hinted at further rooms beyond, but the two men were alone for the moment. Porfiry, who had personally closed the door behind Raskolnikov, greeted him with a jovial air that seemed calculated to disarm.

"Ah, my dear fellow, welcome to our little domain!" Porfiry exclaimed, extending his hands as though to embrace him but withdrawing them just before any actual contact was made. "Come, come, sit down. Or do you prefer formality? Perhaps I'm being too familiar? Do forgive me." He gestured to the sofa with exaggerated politeness.

Raskolnikov sat down, his expression stony and unreadable, but his mind raced. The phrases "our domain" and "tout court," as well as the insincere warmth, struck him as deliberate flourishes meant to unsettle. Every gesture, every word seemed loaded with double meaning. Even the way Porfiry had offered his hands only to pull them back felt calculated. For a moment, their eyes met, but both men quickly looked away, as though the contact had burned.

Raskolnikov reached into his pocket and handed over a piece of paper. "I brought the statement about the watch," he said evenly. "Is it satisfactory, or should I rewrite it?"

Porfiry took the paper with an almost comical haste. "Ah, yes, yes. Don't trouble yourself; it's perfectly fine," he said, glancing at it briefly before setting it down on the table. His movements were quick, almost impatient, as if the paper itself were of little consequence. A moment later, as though struck by an afterthought, he picked it up again and moved it to his bureau.

"I believe you mentioned yesterday that you wanted to formally question me about my acquaintance with the deceased woman?" Raskolnikov said. His voice was measured, but internally he berated himself for adding the phrase "I believe." Why had he included it? What subtle insecurity had crept into his tone?

"Yes, yes, there's no rush," Porfiry replied, his tone evasive and his movements restless. He paced around the room, seeming to dart from one piece of furniture to another without purpose. At times, he would glance out the window; at others, he appeared to be organizing his desk, only to abandon the task midway. His rotund figure seemed almost comically disproportionate to the frenetic energy he radiated. At intervals, he would stop and meet Raskolnikov's gaze directly, only to break it with an abrupt turn of his head.

Raskolnikov felt his nerves stretch taut. Every movement Porfiry made seemed to poke at his already frayed composure. His hatred surged anew, mingled with the gnawing fear that he might betray himself with a careless word or gesture. The room, with its banal yellow furnishings and the absurd figure of Porfiry bustling about, began to feel oppressive, like the walls were inching closer with every passing second.

Porfiry Petrovitch seemed in no rush, settling into a languid yet deliberate manner that only served to heighten Raskolnikov's irritation.

"We've plenty of time. Do you smoke? Have you your own cigarettes? Here, take one!" he offered, holding out a cigarette from his case. His tone was almost infuriatingly casual, as though this were a social visit and not a meeting fraught with unspoken tension. "You see, I'm receiving you here in the official department, but my own quarters are through there—my government quarters, you know." He gestured vaguely toward a door. "I've been living outside for now, though, because I had to have some repairs done here. It's nearly finished. Government quarters are a capital thing, don't you think?"

"Yes, a capital thing," Raskolnikov replied, his voice dry with sarcasm, his eyes narrowing as he regarded Porfiry with a mixture of contempt and curiosity.

Porfiry echoed the phrase, repeating it absentmindedly, as though chewing over the words for hidden meaning. "A capital thing, indeed. Yes, capital, capital," he said, his tone suddenly shifting into something louder, almost emphatic. He paused abruptly, stopping two steps away from Raskolnikov, and stared at him with an expression that was both probing and inscrutable.

The incongruity of Porfiry's words and his brooding gaze unsettled Raskolnikov, stirring a sharper irritation within him. Unable to suppress his spleen, he decided to meet Porfiry's odd behavior head-on, pushing back with a boldness that teetered on insolence.

"Tell me," he began suddenly, his tone cutting, his eyes locked on Porfiry's face with a challenging gleam. "Is it true, as they say, that it's a sort of tradition among investigators to begin with irrelevant or trivial subjects? To lull their target into a false sense of ease before suddenly springing some fatal question? I've heard it's a sacred rule of your craft, mentioned in all the manuals."

Porfiry's eyes gleamed as he listened, and then he gave a knowing chuckle. "Ah, so that's what you think of us, eh? Do you believe I brought up government quarters just for that purpose? To start from afar and knock you down with a sudden blow?"

Before Raskolnikov could respond, Porfiry's face transformed. His features softened, his forehead smoothed, and a good-humored, almost mischievous smile broke across his face. He squinted slightly, as though letting Raskolnikov in on a private joke, and then burst into laughter—a full-bodied, uncontrollable guffaw that shook his entire frame. The laughter grew louder and more boisterous, until his face flushed crimson.

Raskolnikov forced himself to smile, attempting to mimic the humorless sound of Porfiry's laughter. But the longer Porfiry laughed, the more difficult it became to maintain the pretense. The forced smile dropped from Raskolnikov's face, replaced by a scowl of barely concealed hatred. He stared at Porfiry's convulsing form with growing revulsion, his mind racing with suspicions. Was this laughter genuine, or was it a deliberate provocation? Was it designed to throw him off balance, to test his nerves?

The prolonged laughter grated on Raskolnikov's already frayed composure, and when it finally subsided, Porfiry didn't appear the least bit perturbed by his visitor's obvious displeasure. On the contrary, the investigator seemed almost amused by Raskolnikov's scornful silence.

Feeling trapped and unable to bear the charade any longer, Raskolnikov stood abruptly, grabbing his cap with a sharp, jerking motion. "Porfiry Petrovitch," he began, his voice low but tinged with irritation, "yesterday, you requested that I come here to answer some inquiries." He stressed the word "inquiries" with deliberate force. "Well, here I am. If you have questions to ask, then ask them. If not, allow me to leave. I have no time for this. I have other matters to attend to—such as the funeral of the man who was run over, which I assume you know about."

Even as he spoke, Raskolnikov cursed himself inwardly for bringing up the funeral and exposing his irritation. He clenched his teeth, furious at how easily his anger betrayed him.

Porfiry stopped fidgeting and looked at him with wide-eyed innocence. "Good heavens! What do you mean? What inquiries?

There's no need to disturb yourself!" He adopted a tone of exaggerated concern, moving hurriedly around the room as though to placate his visitor. "Come now, sit down. There's no rush, no rush at all. I assure you, Rodion Romanovitch, my laughter was nothing personal. It's my nerves, you see. Sometimes the most unexpected things set me off. I must apologize if I seemed out of line."

Despite Porfiry's words, Raskolnikov remained standing, his cap still in hand. His frown deepened as he observed the investigator's antics. He felt the conversation twisting into an incomprehensible game, and he struggled to discern Porfiry's true intentions.

"Please, sit, sit," Porfiry implored, his voice insistent yet coaxing. "I assure you, I meant no harm. It's just that your observation about investigative tactics—it struck me as so witty, so sharp. I simply couldn't contain myself. Sometimes I laugh so much I fear I'll have an attack of paralysis!" He laughed nervously at his own remark, then gestured toward Raskolnikov's cap. "Do put that down. It's making me uncomfortable—it looks as though you're about to bolt out the door."

After a moment's hesitation, Raskolnikov set his cap on the table and sat down stiffly, his posture rigid. His expression remained grim as he listened to Porfiry's continued rambling, a stream of seemingly inconsequential chatter about Petersburg society, bachelor life, and the peculiarities of middle-class conversation.

Raskolnikov's mind churned beneath his stony exterior. Was Porfiry trying to distract him with this idle talk, or was it a calculated ploy to study his reactions? Every word, every movement felt loaded with hidden meaning. And yet, the sheer triviality of Porfiry's chatter gnawed at him, making him question his own assumptions. Was he imagining things, or was he truly being toyed with? The room seemed to close in around him as his unease deepened.

Porfiry Petrovitch's voice filled the room, a constant stream of chatter that seemed both aimless and calculated. "I'm sorry I can't offer you coffee here," he said cheerily, "but why not indulge in five minutes of friendly conversation? After all, what's a few minutes among acquaintances? Please, pay no mind to my pacing; it's a necessity for me. My dear fellow, I must confess, I lead such a sedentary life with all these official duties that I'm always eager for a chance to stretch my legs. They say physical exercise is a cure-all. Have you heard about the gymnasiums? Even Privy Councillors are reportedly skipping about like boys these days, thanks to the marvels of modern science!"

He laughed softly to himself, but Raskolnikov merely stared at him, unamused. The investigator's words spilled forth without pause, and the more he spoke, the more Raskolnikov's irritation simmered.

"But enough about me," Porfiry continued, his tone light but his eyes sharp. "These inquiries and interrogations—why, you mentioned them yourself just now!—can be such a muddle. Would you believe me if I said that these so-called interrogations are often more perplexing for the interrogator than the interrogated? You put it quite well earlier, so wittily," he added, though Raskolnikov had said no such thing.

Porfiry's pacing grew more energetic, his words more disjointed, as though his thoughts had run ahead of him and left his sentences to limp after. "It's true, though, that one can get into a regular rut with these formalities—drumming on the same point like a cracked tambourine! Oh, but we're to have reforms soon, new titles, a modern touch. Legal tradition! You hit the nail on the head earlier with your observation about starting an inquiry from afar. Everyone knows the method, even the simplest peasant. First, disarm the man with idle chatter, then deliver a sudden blow. Oh, it's a fine tradition, he-he-he!"

He paused to glance at Raskolnikov, his laughter quick and artificial, as if daring him to respond. When Raskolnikov remained silent, Porfiry pressed on, his tone growing increasingly animated.

"And that's why I laugh, you see, at the so-called psychological techniques some of my colleagues swear by. Why bother with all that? Sometimes a simple, friendly chat yields far more. And formality? Pfft! Formality is a tool, yes, but not a cage. The work of investigation, my dear Rodion Romanovitch, is not merely a science—it's an art! A free art, in its way. He-he-he!"

Porfiry stopped abruptly, catching his breath, his small figure almost quivering with energy. His feet shuffled as he paced the room, his gestures exaggerated and his movements erratic. Raskolnikov, watching him with a mix of suspicion and disdain, noticed something peculiar. Twice, as Porfiry meandered near the door, he seemed to pause, almost imperceptibly, as though listening for something beyond the room.

"What is he expecting?" Raskolnikov thought, his instincts prickling. His unease deepened as Porfiry turned to him again, his expression strangely innocent, his eyes unnervingly direct.

"You're quite right to laugh at our legal forms," Porfiry said suddenly, as though continuing a conversation that hadn't been spoken aloud. "Some of these psychological methods are absurd if you take them too seriously. Yes, yes, forms again! But let me give you an example, purely hypothetical, of course. Suppose I suspect someone of a crime. Why, I ask, should I pounce on him immediately, even if I have evidence? Not every case demands instant action. Why not let him walk free for a time? Let him breathe, let him think. He-he-he! You see the sense in that, don't you?"

"I'm not sure I do," Raskolnikov replied coldly, his voice laced with tension. He crossed his arms, leaning slightly back in his chair as if to put distance between them.

Porfiry's smile widened, his eyes gleaming. "Ah, you don't understand? Well, let me explain more clearly. Arresting a man too soon might offer him... shall we say, moral support. Strange, isn't it? He might even gather strength from the certainty of his predicament. But if he remains free, walking about, he may fall into a kind of internal chaos. You see the brilliance in that, don't you? Or... are you laughing at me?"

The question was posed lightly, but there was a glint in Porfiry's gaze, sharp and probing, like a needle seeking a soft spot. Raskolnikov said nothing, but his jaw tightened. He felt the trap closing around him, though its design remained maddeningly unclear. Porfiry's voice, with its mix of joviality and menace, grated on his nerves, and he resisted the urge to lash out.

Instead, he forced himself to remain still, to listen, and to wait. This, he realized, was no ordinary conversation—it was a battle, fought with words and silences, and the stakes were far higher than either man was willing to admit.

Raskolnikov sat rigid, his lips pressed tightly together, his feverish, burning eyes fixed unwaveringly on Porfiry Petrovitch, who seemed to revel in his monologue. There was no humor in Raskolnikov now, no inclination to laugh, only a growing sense of unease and fury bubbling just beneath the surface.

"Ah, but you see," Porfiry began again, his tone lilting with mock reasonableness, "men are so different, are they not? You mentioned evidence just now. Evidence is a curious thing. It is rarely as solid as twice two equals four. Evidence, my dear fellow, can often be interpreted in two entirely different ways. That is the conundrum for someone in my position. As an examining lawyer, I'm a weak man, I'll admit it—I long for that mathematical certainty, that unbreakable chain of proof that leaves no room for doubt."

He took a step closer to Raskolnikov, his eyes narrowing slightly as if he could see into the younger man's very thoughts. "But suppose I act too soon—let's say I shut up my suspect prematurely. Even if I am personally convinced he's the one, I risk losing the opportunity to gather more evidence. By placing him in a defined, secure position, I might inadvertently grant him peace of mind, and he could retreat into himself, close himself off entirely. No, no! Sometimes it is far better to let him remain free, to let him stew in his own terror."

Raskolnikov's jaw clenched, but he made no move, no reply, as Porfiry continued with exaggerated cheerfulness. "Take the example of Sevastopol after Alma. The clever men there were in such a panic, expecting an open attack to end it all. But when the enemy began a long, drawn-out siege, they were relieved. It gave them time—time to think, time to plan. You see, my friend, time is often the best tool we have. Let a man walk about freely, and his very freedom will become his prison. The constant awareness that he is being watched, the unrelenting weight of suspicion—oh, it works wonders on the nerves!"

Porfiry stopped abruptly, his tone shifting as he eyed Raskolnikov with unsettling precision. "Ah, but it depends on the man, doesn't it? A simple peasant might crumble quickly. But an intelligent man, someone cultivated, someone with... let us say... certain moral sensitivities, well, that's a different story altogether. Such men are like finely tuned instruments, prone to discord if the strings are plucked too harshly. Nerves, my dear Rodion Romanovitch, nerves are the weak point of all intellectuals. And in this city of ours, rife with spleen and irritability, those nerves are a veritable gold mine for us examiners."

Raskolnikov remained silent, his pale face betraying nothing but the intensity of his focus. Porfiry's voice grew more animated as he paced, his small figure darting about the room like a restless sparrow. "Let him wander about the city; where could he possibly go? Escape abroad? Perhaps a Pole might manage it, but here? A modern man cannot hide among peasants. The very thought is laughable! No, my friend, he will stay, bound not by chains, but by his own mind. Like a moth to a flame, he will circle and circle, his freedom losing all meaning, his every step weaving a tighter web of his own making."

He stopped again, his eyes gleaming with a peculiar light as he leaned forward slightly. "And then—flop!—he will fall into my hands. He'll present me with proof, not just evidence, but a mathematical certainty. And I will simply wait for the moment he can resist no longer. It's almost poetic, wouldn't you say? But you, my dear Rodion Romanovitch—you don't seem to agree. You're not laughing."

Raskolnikov's fingers tightened on the armrest of his chair, his breath shallow and rapid. He felt as though a vice were closing around him, every word from Porfiry's mouth tightening its grip.

"This isn't a game," Raskolnikov thought, his pulse pounding in his temples. "This is no idle taunting, no mere display of power. He has a purpose—there's a trap here, but what is it? Does he truly know?

No, he's trying to provoke me, to unnerve me, to push me into making a mistake. But I won't give him the satisfaction. Whatever he's waiting for, he won't get it from me."

He swallowed hard, his throat dry, his resolve hardening as he braced himself against the storm of his own anger. At times, the urge to lash out, to silence Porfiry's maddening voice with force, surged within him, but he quelled it with sheer will. Silence, he knew, was his strongest weapon now—a shield against the probing questions and insinuations that sought to expose him.

And so he sat, a statue of defiance and dread, while Porfiry Petrovitch continued to circle like a hawk, waiting for the moment to strike.

"No, no, I can see you don't believe me. You think I'm just toying with you, indulging in some harmless jest," Porfiry Petrovitch began again, his voice gaining an almost playful liveliness. He chuckled intermittently, pacing back and forth across the room like a man whose thoughts were too restless to let him stand still. "And, of course, why wouldn't you? I mean, look at me! God has given me this figure, this demeanor, that invites only the most comic of interpretations. A buffoon! That's what I must seem to you."

He stopped, tilting his head slightly as though pondering the very absurdity of his own existence. Then, with a sudden change in tone, he leaned forward. "But let me tell you something, Rodion Romanovitch—no, no, allow an old man a moment of indulgence," he added with a wave of his hand, though he was clearly far from old. "You are still young, so terribly young, caught in the thrall of intellect, placing it above all else. It's the folly of youth, isn't it? You revel in wit, in abstract arguments, and you're charmed by clever ideas. It's as if you're a strategist in the Austrian Hofkriegsrath, devising brilliant plans on paper, confidently capturing Napoleon and his armies in your mind. But alas! General Mack surrenders instead, he-he-he! Reality has a way of deflating even the cleverest strategies, doesn't it?"

Raskolnikov's expression tightened. Porfiry's incessant chatter felt like needles pricking at his resolve, but he refused to rise to the bait.

Porfiry, however, was undeterred, his smile broadening as he continued, "Ah, I see that amused you. You're laughing at me, aren't you? A civilian drawing analogies from military history! Well, I can't help it—it's my weakness. I've always had a soft spot for military science, always enjoyed reading the histories. You know, I sometimes think I missed my true calling. I should've been a soldier! No, no, not a Napoleon, of course, but perhaps a respectable major—he-he! But here I am, merely an examining lawyer, my dear Rodion Romanovitch, stuck with cases and calculations, trying to make sense of temperaments and circumstances."

He paused dramatically, his tone shifting to one of apparent sincerity. "And that's the rub, isn't it? Temperament, my dear sir! It's a weighty matter, deceptive even to the sharpest calculations. Actual facts, a man's nature—these are tricky, slippery things. Even the most cunning intellect can falter when temperament comes into play. Take, for instance, the man you so cleverly described yesterday—the one who oversteps all obstacles with wit and cunning. He might lie brilliantly, spin tales with such flair that he dazzles everyone in the room. But then, at the crucial moment, he faints! Aha! He hadn't accounted for his temperament."

Porfiry chuckled again, a laugh so peculiar it seemed to echo in the room. "Yes, yes, he'll faint, or perhaps he'll blush at just the wrong time, or his voice will crack when it shouldn't. Illness? A stuffy room? Oh, perhaps. But the truth, my dear fellow, is that temperament always betrays him. It's a mirror—every action, every slip of the tongue, every subtle shift in expression is reflected back. And if the man is clever, well-read, even a literary type, his temperament might make him all the more transparent. He'll try too hard, overcompensate, speak when he ought to remain silent, or laugh too loudly at something that isn't remotely amusing."

Raskolnikov shifted uncomfortably, his face pale, his hands gripping the edge of the sofa. He could feel the weight of Porfiry's words pressing down on him like a vice.

Porfiry tilted his head, his eyes narrowing slightly. "But you, Rodion Romanovitch, you're looking pale. Is it the room? Shall I open a window?"

"Don't trouble yourself," Raskolnikov cut in sharply, a strained laugh escaping his lips. "Please, don't trouble yourself."

Porfiry stopped pacing and turned to face him, his own laugh suddenly rising to match Raskolnikov's, though it carried a peculiar edge. For a moment, they both stood there, laughing—one from genuine amusement, the other from something far more volatile.

Abruptly, Raskolnikov rose from the sofa, cutting his laughter short as though it had burned him. The room fell silent, save for the sound of his shallow breathing and Porfiry's soft chuckle fading into an unsettling grin.

"Porfiry Petrovitch," Raskolnikov began, raising his voice so it resounded in the room, each syllable spoken with measured clarity, though his legs trembled under him and his body swayed slightly. "I now understand—clearly and without doubt—that you truly suspect me of murdering that old pawnbroker and her sister Lizaveta. Let me tell you, this insinuation, this game of cat and mouse, has gone far enough. I am weary of it, utterly weary. If you have a case against me, if you believe you have the right to arrest me, then do it! Do it now! But this... this treatment, this mockery, this insufferable torment—you will not jeer at me to my face!"

His voice rose, the anger in it raw and unrestrained. His lips quivered, and his eyes burned with such intensity that they seemed almost feverish. Unable to restrain himself further, he brought his fist down heavily on the table, causing a stack of papers to shift.

"I will not tolerate it!" he shouted, his voice cracking with the force of his declaration. "Do you hear me, Porfiry Petrovitch? I will not allow it!"

Porfiry recoiled as if genuinely startled. "My God, what's come over you, Rodion Romanovitch?" he exclaimed, raising his hands in an almost theatrical gesture of alarm. "What on earth is the matter?"

"I will not allow it!" Raskolnikov repeated, his fists clenched tightly, his breath coming in short, heated bursts.

"Hush, hush, my dear man! For goodness' sake, lower your voice! They'll hear us, they'll come in. What on earth would we tell them?" Porfiry hissed, leaning in close, his face a mask of exaggerated horror, his tone one of pleading.

"I will not allow it... I will not..." Raskolnikov repeated, his voice dropping to a whisper, as though his strength had suddenly given out.

Porfiry darted to the window, pulling it open in a swift, almost frantic motion. "Fresh air, we need fresh air! You're ill, my dear fellow, quite ill!" he said hurriedly, before spotting a decanter of water in the corner. "Wait here—here, drink some water. You'll feel better. Just a moment."

Grabbing the decanter, he rushed back to Raskolnikov, pouring water into a glass with trembling hands. His concern seemed genuine, his every movement infused with urgency and care.

"Drink this," he urged softly, pressing the glass into Raskolnikov's hands. "Come, come, my dear Rodion Romanovitch. This will do you good."

Raskolnikov raised the glass mechanically to his lips but set it down without taking a sip, his face curling into an expression of disdain.

"Ah, you've had an episode, haven't you?" Porfiry prattled on, his voice laced with a nervous, almost paternal concern. "This isn't good, not good at all. You'll make yourself ill again, I swear it. Such nerves! You'll end up driving yourself mad, you know. Dmitri Prokofitch was telling me only yesterday about how worried he's been for you... but what am I saying? Here, sit down, sit down, won't you? You'll feel better if you rest."

"I knew Razumihin went to see you," Raskolnikov interjected sharply, cutting through Porfiry's babble. "I knew why he went, too."

Porfiry raised his eyebrows, momentarily taken aback. "Ah, you knew? Well then, what of it?" His tone was deliberately light, though his eyes glittered with something sharper, more calculated.

Raskolnikov leaned forward, his voice steely. "What of it? Everything. I knew."

Porfiry didn't answer directly. Instead, he began to pace the room again, this time with a nervous energy that seemed almost to mirror Raskolnikov's inner turmoil. After a pause, he stopped suddenly and turned to face his guest, his expression a peculiar mixture of concern and sly satisfaction.

"Well, Rodion Romanovitch, I know more about you than you might think," he said finally, his voice soft but cutting. "For example, I know about your little nocturnal visit to the flat, how you rang the bell, inquired about blood... frightened the workmen and the porter half out of their wits. Oh yes, I understand your frame of mind back then—it was all too clear. But, my dear fellow, you'll destroy yourself with behavior like that. You're full of anger and indignation, and that's understandable! But rushing about like this, demanding answers, trying to provoke a confrontation—you'll unravel entirely."

Raskolnikov froze. The words hit him like a blow. How did Porfiry know about the flat? And more importantly, why was he revealing this knowledge now?

"Why tell me this?" Raskolnikov asked, his voice shaking, the heat in his face spreading to his entire body.

Porfiry shrugged, his tone becoming almost jovial again. "Oh, my dear boy, I've seen it before, you know. Cases of... let's say, extreme psychological strain. People convincing themselves of things, acting in ways even they don't fully understand. Sometimes the mind plays tricks, you see. It's fascinating, really." He chuckled softly, but the sound was hollow, unsettling.

Raskolnikov stared at him, every nerve in his body straining as though pulled taut. "Is he playing me for a fool? Testing me? Or worse... does he know everything?" The questions spun through his mind, but he kept silent, clinging to the slim hope that his restraint might yet save him from the abyss.

"I was not delirious. I knew exactly what I was doing," Raskolnikov exclaimed with sudden vehemence, his voice tense and charged, every word deliberately thrown out like a challenge. He leaned forward as though trying to pierce through the murky labyrinth of Porfiry's words, searching desperately for the strategy behind them. "I was completely myself, do you understand?"

Porfiry tilted his head slightly, watching him with that unsettling mixture of interest and amusement that had marked their entire exchange. "Yes, yes, I hear you," he said, his voice smooth yet vaguely teasing. "And I understand, I do. Why, you emphasized it repeatedly just yesterday—insisted on it with such vigor. So emphatic, in fact! I can't help but wonder..." He let the words hang in the air, drawing out the moment deliberately. "If you were a criminal, or in any way involved in this... this damned business, would you really insist so strongly that you weren't delirious but entirely in control of yourself? Persistently? Vehemently? Would that even be possible? To my mind, quite impossible."

Raskolnikov's eyes narrowed. He could sense a trap in the way Porfiry leaned closer as he spoke, his voice tinged with a subtle, almost mocking slyness. "If you were guilty," Porfiry continued, "surely your best course would be to claim you were delirious. Wouldn't it?"

The suggestion hit like a sudden chill, creeping up Raskolnikov's spine. He stiffened, his back pressing harder into the sofa as he stared at Porfiry, bewildered yet alert. The man's words seemed calculated to provoke, to unsettle, and he was succeeding.

"And then," Porfiry went on, "take your Razumihin, for instance. If you had anything to hide, wouldn't it have been wiser to say he acted entirely of his own accord? But no! You've gone and emphasized that he came at your instigation, of all things. Isn't that odd?"

Raskolnikov's breath caught. He hadn't emphasized any such thing, but Porfiry's assertion struck with the weight of certainty. A wave of icy unease swept over him.

"You're lying," he muttered weakly, his lips twisting into a bitter, strained smile. "You're doing it again, pretending you know all my thoughts, all my moves before I even make them." His voice wavered, betraying his inner turmoil. "You're trying to frighten me... or maybe you're just mocking me."

Porfiry met his gaze steadily, his own face calm, almost serene, as if unfazed by the mounting tension. "Lying?" he repeated with a soft chuckle. "Oh, come now. And yet here you are, accusing me of knowing too much, even as you insist you're not frightened."

"You're lying," Raskolnikov said again, his voice firmer this time, though still tinged with the faintest quiver. His eyes burned with a cold, simmering hatred. "You know as well as I do that the smartest thing for a criminal to do is tell the truth, or as close to it as possible, while concealing just enough. You're trying to make me believe otherwise. But I don't believe you. Not a word."

Porfiry's laughter broke out again, soft and infuriating. "Oh, you're a clever one," he said, wagging a finger as though in admiration. "So sharp, so wary. There's no catching you, is there? A true monomaniac! You don't believe me—no, not entirely—but you believe me a little, perhaps just enough. And that's all I need."

Raskolnikov's lips trembled faintly, but he held his composure, staring down Porfiry with an intensity that bordered on feral.

"You must think of your health," Porfiry said, his tone suddenly shifting to one of disarming geniality. He reached out and patted Raskolnikov's arm lightly. "Your mother and sister are here now. Surely you want to care for them, to give them peace. Yet all you do is frighten them, and yourself along with them."

"And what business is that of yours?" Raskolnikov snapped, his voice sharp with suspicion. "Why do you care? You're watching me, aren't you? Trying to make me feel your eyes on me every moment?"

"Good heavens, Rodion Romanovitch, I've learned it all from you!" Porfiry exclaimed, throwing up his hands in mock exasperation. "In your excitement, you tell me and everyone else far more than you realize. Even Razumihin—bless him, he shared such interesting tidbits with me just yesterday!"

Raskolnikov's fists clenched as Porfiry's words sank in. The man's tone, his manner, even his choice of words—it all seemed calculated to tighten the invisible noose.

"And take this business with the bell-ringing," Porfiry continued smoothly. "If I truly suspected you, why would I mention it to you directly? Surely, I'd keep it to myself, disarm your suspicions, and wait for the perfect moment to strike. But I haven't done that, have I? No, I've laid it all out before you, plain as day. What does that tell you?"

"It tells me," Raskolnikov said through gritted teeth, "that you're playing a deeper game."

Porfiry's smile widened. "Or perhaps, my dear Rodion Romanovitch, it simply tells you that I have no reason to suspect you at all. But then again..." He trailed off, leaving the words to hang in the air, heavy with implication.

Raskolnikov leaned back slowly, his chest heaving with suppressed rage and fear, his thoughts a chaotic storm. Porfiry's game was relentless, and every move seemed designed to unbalance him further.

Raskolnikov flinched visibly, his entire body tensing like a coiled spring. Porfiry Petrovitch could not possibly miss the reaction.

"You are lying! Lying the whole time!" Raskolnikov burst out, his voice trembling with fury. "I don't understand your purpose, but you are lying. You didn't speak like that just a moment ago, and I'm certain of it!"

"Am I lying?" Porfiry repeated, his tone laced with mock indignation. He maintained his good-humored, almost jovial demeanor, as though Raskolnikov's accusations were of no consequence to him. "Lying, you say? Well, let's consider how I, as the examining lawyer, treated you just now. Didn't I provide you with every possible excuse for your defense? I spoke of illness, delirium, injuries, melancholy—and even those dreadful police officers you detest so much! He-he-he! Though, of course, all these psychological defenses can cut both ways, can't they? But tell me this—why, in your supposed delirium, were you haunted by just those specific delusions and not others? Eh? Isn't that curious?"

Raskolnikov met his gaze with a sharp, cold glare, his expression brimming with contempt. He stood abruptly, the force of his movement causing Porfiry to take a reflexive step back.

"Enough of this!" Raskolnikov declared, his voice rising in pitch and volume. "I demand to know—am I free from suspicion or not? Speak plainly, Porfiry Petrovitch. Tell me once and for all, and do it quickly!"

Porfiry threw up his hands in mock exasperation, his face still calm and composed, though his eyes glinted with amusement. "What a fuss you make!" he exclaimed, shaking his head. "Why are you so desperate to know, my good man? Why are you forcing yourself upon us like this? He-he-he! You're like a child begging for matches! Why so uneasy?"

"I repeat—I won't tolerate this any longer!" Raskolnikov shouted, his voice raw with frustration.

"Ah, so it's uncertainty you can't bear?" Porfiry interjected smoothly, his tone calm yet needling.

"Don't mock me!" Raskolnikov thundered, his fist slamming down on the table. "I won't have it, do you hear me? I won't tolerate your games any longer! Arrest me if you must, but stop toying with me!"

Porfiry's expression shifted momentarily, his joviality replaced by a fleeting look of sternness. His voice dropped to a warning murmur. "Calm yourself," he said firmly. "Keep your voice down, for heaven's sake. They'll hear us outside. I'm serious—control yourself. This is not a joke."

For an instant, Raskolnikov obeyed, his voice dropping to a whisper though his rage had not abated. "I won't let myself be tormented like this," he hissed, his chest heaving. "If you're going to arrest me, do it formally, according to the law. But don't you dare keep playing these games with me!"

"Don't worry about formalities," Porfiry replied, his smile returning, sly and deliberate. "This isn't an interrogation; I invited you here in good faith, as a friend."

"I want none of your friendship," Raskolnikov spat, venom in his voice. "And I spit on it. Do you hear me? I'm leaving. What will you do now? Arrest me?"

Grabbing his cap, he strode to the door, but Porfiry intercepted him with an infuriatingly light chuckle, placing a hand on his arm. "Ah, but won't you stay for my little surprise?" he said, his voice full of mischievous glee.

"What surprise?" Raskolnikov demanded, his voice sharp with suspicion. He froze mid-step, his eyes narrowing.

Porfiry gestured toward the locked door at the back of the room. "Why, it's sitting right there, waiting for you. My little surprise, locked safely behind that door."

Raskolnikov's heart raced. His gaze darted between Porfiry and the door. "What is it? Who's there?" he asked, his voice tinged with both anger and alarm.

Porfiry produced a key from his pocket, dangling it teasingly. "Shall we see?" he asked, his grin widening. "But perhaps you already know."

"You're lying!" Raskolnikov roared, lunging toward Porfiry. "Lying and mocking me, trying to make me incriminate myself with your infernal tricks!"

Porfiry retreated toward the other door, his demeanor maddeningly calm. "Oh, my dear Rodion Romanovitch," he said lightly. "You're already doing an excellent job of incriminating yourself. There's no need for me to press further."

The words struck Raskolnikov like a blow. "You're lying!" he shouted again. "This is all a ploy to provoke me, to make me betray myself. Produce your evidence, if you have any! Stop hiding behind these cheap theatrics!"

Porfiry raised a finger, a signal for silence. A faint noise came from beyond the door, a muffled shuffling sound. Raskolnikov's pulse quickened.

"They're coming, aren't they?" he said, his voice now laced with a strange mixture of defiance and despair. "Your deputies, your witnesses—bring them all in! Let's finish this now. I'm ready for whatever trap you've set."

But before anything further could happen, something completely unforeseen occurred, derailing the entire encounter in a way neither Raskolnikov nor Porfiry could have anticipated.

Chapter 6

When Raskolnikov thought back on the moment later, this is how he remembered it.

The noise behind the door grew louder, and suddenly the door opened a little.

"What is it?" Porfiry Petrovitch shouted, irritated. "Didn't I give orders...?"

There was no immediate reply, but it was clear that several people were at the door, apparently trying to push someone back.

"What is it?" Porfiry asked again, now sounding uneasy.

"The prisoner Nikolay has been brought," someone replied.

"He's not needed! Take him away! Let him wait! Why is he here? This is so improper!" Porfiry exclaimed, hurrying toward the door.

"But he..." the voice began but abruptly stopped.

In the next two seconds, a brief struggle occurred. Suddenly, there was a strong shove, and a man, pale as a ghost, stepped into the room.

The man's appearance was striking at first glance. He stared straight ahead as if he couldn't see anything. His eyes had a fierce determination, but his face was as pale as death, like someone about to be executed. His thin, colorless lips twitched slightly.

He was dressed like a laborer, about average height, young, and slim. His hair was cut short in a rounded style, and his features were sharp and thin. The man he had pushed aside followed him into the room and grabbed his shoulder—it was a guard—but Nikolay yanked his arm free.

Several others crowded curiously into the doorway, some even trying to enter the room. All of this happened in a matter of seconds.

"Get out! It's not time yet! Wait until you're called!" Porfiry Petrovitch muttered, clearly frustrated and thrown off balance. "Why did you bring him so early?"

But Nikolay suddenly dropped to his knees.

"What's going on?" Porfiry asked in surprise.

"I'm guilty! It's my fault! I'm the murderer," Nikolay said all at once, speaking a little breathlessly but loudly enough for everyone to hear.

For about ten seconds, there was complete silence, as if everyone had been struck speechless. Even the guard stepped back, retreated to the door mechanically, and stood still.

"What's going on?" shouted Porfiry Petrovitch, snapping out of his momentary shock.

"I... am the murderer," Nikolay repeated after a short pause.

"What... you... what... who did you kill?" Porfiry Petrovitch stammered, clearly confused.

Nikolay paused again before replying.

"Alyona Ivanovna and her sister Lizaveta Ivanovna. I... killed them... with an axe. Darkness overtook me," he added suddenly, then fell silent again.

He stayed on his knees as before. Porfiry Petrovitch stood still for a few moments, as though deep in thought. Then, all of a sudden, he snapped out of it and motioned for the onlookers to leave. They quickly disappeared and shut the door behind them.

Porfiry then turned toward Raskolnikov, who was standing in the corner, staring at Nikolay with a wild look in his eyes. Porfiry began to approach Raskolnikov, then stopped, glancing back and forth between Nikolay and Raskolnikov. Unable to hold back, he suddenly rushed toward Nikolay.

"You're in a hurry to confess," he shouted at him, almost angrily. "I didn't ask what overcame you... Speak up, did you really kill them?"

"I'm the murderer... I want to confess," Nikolay said firmly.

"Ah! And how did you kill them?"

"With an axe. I had it ready."

"Ah, you're rushing this! Were you alone?"

Nikolay didn't seem to understand the question at first.

"Did you do it by yourself?" Porfiry repeated.

"Yes, I was alone. Mitka isn't guilty and had nothing to do with it."

"Don't bring up Mitka so quickly! A-ach! Why did you run down the stairs like that at the time? The porters saw both of you!"

"It was to throw them off... I ran after Mitka," Nikolay said quickly, as if he had rehearsed his answer.

"I knew it!" Porfiry exclaimed, frustrated. "This isn't his own story," he muttered to himself. Then his eyes suddenly turned back to Raskolnikov.

For a moment, Porfiry seemed to have forgotten about Raskolnikov, so focused was he on Nikolay. When he looked at him again, he seemed startled.

"My dear Rodion Romanovitch, forgive me!" he said, hurrying over. "This won't work; I'm afraid you have to leave... There's no point in you staying here... You see what an unexpected turn this is! Goodbye!"

Taking Raskolnikov by the arm, Porfiry led him to the door.

"I suppose you didn't see this coming?" Raskolnikov asked. Though he hadn't fully grasped the situation yet, he seemed to have regained some confidence.

"And you didn't expect it either, my friend. Look, your hand is shaking! Ha-ha!" Porfiry replied.

"You're shaking too, Porfiry Petrovitch!"

"Yes, I am surprised; I didn't see it coming."

They were already near the door, and Porfiry was eager for Raskolnikov to leave.

"And what about your little surprise? Aren't you going to show it to me?" Raskolnikov asked with a sarcastic tone.

"Why, your teeth are chattering as you ask that, he-he! You really are quite the sarcastic person! Well, until we meet again!"

"I think we can just say goodbye!"

"That's up to God," Porfiry muttered with an awkward smile.

As Raskolnikov walked through the office, he noticed many people staring at him. Among them, he recognized the two porters from his building, the ones he had asked to come to the police station that night. They stood there waiting. But just as he started down the stairs, he heard Porfiry Petrovitch's voice behind him. Turning around, he saw Porfiry running after him, out of breath.

"Hold on, Rodion Romanovitch. As for everything else, that's in God's hands. But as a matter of procedure, I'll need to ask you a few more questions... so we'll see each other again, won't we?"

Porfiry stopped and smiled at him.

"We will, right?" he repeated.

He seemed like he wanted to say more but couldn't get the words out.

"You'll have to excuse me, Porfiry Petrovitch, for what just happened. I lost my temper," Raskolnikov began, now feeling calm enough to show some composure.

"Don't worry about it, don't worry about it," Porfiry replied almost cheerfully. "I have a bad temper myself, I'll admit it! But we'll meet again. If it's God's will, we might even see a lot of each other."

"And get to know each other completely?" Raskolnikov added.

"Yes, completely," Porfiry agreed, narrowing his eyes as he looked closely at Raskolnikov. "So, are you off to a birthday party now?"

"To a funeral."

"Ah, yes, the funeral! Take care of yourself and get some rest."

"I'm not sure what to wish for you," Raskolnikov said as he started down the stairs but then paused to look back. "I'd like to wish you success, but your job is such a strange one."

"Strange? What do you mean?" Porfiry had turned to leave but seemed intrigued by this comment.

"Well, just think about how you must have been tormenting that poor Nikolay, playing your mind games until he confessed! You must have worked on him day and night, convincing him he was the killer. And now that he's confessed, you'll start tearing his story apart all over again. 'You're lying,' you'll say. 'You're not the killer! This isn't even your story!' You've got to admit, it's a pretty ridiculous line of work!"

"He-he-he! So you noticed when I told Nikolay earlier that it wasn't even his own story he was telling?"

"How could I not notice?"

"He-he! You're sharp. You catch everything! You've got such a lively mind, always noticing the funny side of things... he-he! They say that was Gogol's defining trait as a writer."

"Yes, Gogol had that."

"Yes, Gogol... I look forward to seeing you again."

"So do I."

Raskolnikov walked straight home. His mind was so clouded and confused that when he arrived, he sat on the sofa for fifteen minutes, trying to gather his thoughts. He didn't even try to think about Nikolay. He felt dazed; Nikolay's confession seemed bizarre, unbelievable—completely beyond his understanding. Yet, it was a real confession. That much was undeniable. He understood at once what it meant: the lie would eventually be exposed, and when it was, they'd be after him again. But for now, at least, he was free. He needed to act quickly because the danger was very real.

But how immediate was the threat? His situation slowly became clearer to him. As he recalled bits and pieces of his tense exchange with Porfiry, he couldn't help but shudder in horror. He didn't fully understand Porfiry's intentions or calculations yet. But Porfiry had revealed part of his plan, and Raskolnikov knew better than anyone how dangerous Porfiry's moves had been. Just a little more pressure, and he might have incriminated himself entirely.

Porfiry's strategy had been bold, but it was bound to succeed, especially since he had quickly figured out Raskolnikov's nervous personality. There was no denying that Raskolnikov had put himself in a precarious position, but no concrete evidence had surfaced so far—nothing definitive. But was he seeing things clearly? Could he be mistaken? What exactly had Porfiry been trying to achieve? Did he really have some kind of surprise planned for him? And if so, what was it? Would things have ended differently if Nikolay hadn't appeared when he did?

Porfiry had revealed almost everything he had up his sleeve—he'd clearly taken a risk by doing so. If he'd had anything else, Raskolnikov thought, he would have used it. So, what was this "surprise"? Was it just a trick? Or did it actually mean something? Could it have been a fact, a solid piece of evidence? And what about the man who had visited him yesterday? Where was he now? If Porfiry had any proof, it had to be connected to that man.

Raskolnikov sat on the sofa, his elbows resting on his knees, his face buried in his hands. He was still trembling with nerves. Finally, he stood up, grabbed his cap, thought for a moment, and headed toward the door.

He had a gut feeling that, for today at least, he was safe. For a moment, he felt almost joyful. He decided to hurry to Katerina Ivanovna's. He knew he'd miss the funeral, but he could still make it to the memorial dinner, where he'd see Sonia.

He paused at the door, thinking for a moment, and a sad smile briefly crossed his face.

"Today. It has to be today," he said to himself. "Yes, today. That's the way it has to be..."

But just as he was about to open the door, it started to open on its own. He froze and stepped back. The door creaked open slowly, and standing there was the man who had visited him yesterday—the man from the underground.

The visitor stepped into the room silently, looking straight at Raskolnikov. He looked exactly the same as the day before: same clothes, same posture. But his face had changed. He looked worn down, and he let out a deep sigh. If he had tilted his head to the side and rested his hand on his cheek, he could have passed for a peasant woman.

"What do you want?" Raskolnikov asked, frozen with fear.

The man didn't answer right away. Instead, he suddenly bowed deeply, almost touching the floor with his hand.

"What is this?" Raskolnikov cried out.

"I have sinned," the man said softly.

"How?"

"With wicked thoughts."

They stared at each other.

"I was angry. When you came—maybe drunk—and told the porters to go to the police and ask about the blood, I got angry that they let you leave and assumed you were just drunk. I was so upset I couldn't sleep. That's why we came here yesterday to find you."

"Who came?" Raskolnikov interrupted, his mind racing to piece it all together.

"I did. I wronged you."

"So, you're from that building?"

"I was standing at the gate with them... don't you remember? We've worked in that building for years. We tan and prepare hides; we take work home to do... but most of all, I was upset."

The entire scene from two days ago in the gateway came back vividly to Raskolnikov. He remembered that besides the porters, there had been several others there, including women. He recalled someone suggesting they take him straight to the police station. He couldn't remember the speaker's face, and even now he didn't recognize it, but he distinctly remembered turning and giving that person some sort of reply.

So, this explained the terrifying experience from the day before. The most horrifying thought was that he had almost doomed himself over such a small, insignificant detail. All this man could tell was that he'd asked about the apartment and the bloodstains. That meant Porfiry had nothing solid—just a few vague suspicions and some psychological guesses, which could go either way. There was nothing concrete. As long as no new evidence came to light (and it mustn't, it simply mustn't!), what could they do to him? Even if they arrested him, how could they convict him?

"Was it you who told Porfiry... that I'd been in the building?" he suddenly asked, struck by the thought.

"Porfiry? Who's that?"

"The head of the detective department."

"Yes. The porters didn't go to him, but I did."

"Today?"

"I got there two minutes before you did. I heard everything—how he questioned you."

"Where? What? When?"

"In the next room. I was sitting there the whole time."

"What? So, you were the surprise? But how did that even happen? This is unbelievable!"

"I saw the porters weren't going to act on what I said," the man explained. "They said, 'It's too late now, and he'll just be mad that we didn't go earlier.' That made me angry, and I couldn't sleep. I started asking questions, and yesterday I found out where to go. I went there today. The first time I went, Porfiry wasn't there. An hour later, I came back, but he couldn't see me. I went a third time, and they finally let me in. I told him everything, just as it happened. He started pacing the room and pounding his chest. 'What kind of fools are you?' he shouted. 'If I'd known, I would have arrested him right then!'

"Then he ran out, called someone, and had a conversation in the corner. After that, he turned back to me, scolding and questioning me. He yelled at me a lot, but I told him everything. I told him you didn't say anything back to me yesterday and that you didn't even recognize me. He started pacing and pounding his chest again. When you were announced, he told me to go to the next room. 'Sit there,' he said. 'Don't move, no matter what you hear.' He set up a chair for me and locked me in. 'I might call for you,' he said. When Nikolay was brought in, he let me out as soon as you left. 'I'll call you back later and question you again,' he said."

"And did he question Nikolay while you were there?"

"No, he sent me away, just like he sent you out, before he talked to Nikolay."

The man stood still for a moment, then suddenly bowed low, almost touching the floor with his hand.

"Forgive me for my bad thoughts and for speaking ill of you," he said.

"May God forgive you," Raskolnikov replied.

After hearing this, the man bowed again, though not as deeply, then turned and walked slowly out of the room.

"It cuts both ways now. Everything cuts both ways," Raskolnikov repeated to himself as he left, feeling more confident than before.

"Now we'll fight this," he said with a bitter smile as he descended the stairs. His bitterness was directed at himself. With shame and disgust, he recalled his earlier "cowardice."

Part 5

Chapter 1

The morning after the difficult meeting with Dounia and her mother brought a harsh reality to Pyotr Petrovitch. As unpleasant as it was, he was gradually forced to accept that what had seemed unreal and impossible just the day before was now a fact he couldn't undo. The sting of wounded pride had tormented him all night like a gnawing snake.

When he got out of bed, Pyotr Petrovitch went straight to the mirror. He was worried he might have jaundice. Thankfully, his health seemed fine, and when he looked at his handsome, clear-skinned face—though it had become a little fuller lately—he felt a small comfort. He told himself that he could find another bride, perhaps an even better one. But when his thoughts returned to his current predicament, he turned away and spat forcefully.

This action drew a sarcastic smile from Andrey Semyonovitch Lebeziatnikov, the young man he was staying with. Pyotr Petrovitch noticed the smirk and immediately added it to the growing list of grievances he had against his young friend. Lately, that list had become quite long. His irritation grew as he realized he shouldn't have told Andrey Semyonovitch the details of yesterday's meeting. It was the second mistake he'd made in his frustration and impulsiveness.

That morning only brought more problems. One annoyance followed another. Even a legal case he was working on in the senate hit a snag. He was especially irritated with the landlord of the apartment he had rented for his upcoming marriage. The place was being redecorated at his expense, but now that the wedding was off, the wealthy German landlord refused to cancel the lease. He demanded full payment of the penalty fee, even though the apartment would be returned to him almost fully redecorated.

The furniture sellers also refused to return any of the money he had already paid for items that hadn't even been moved into the apartment yet.

"Am I supposed to get married just to keep the furniture?" Pyotr Petrovitch muttered through clenched teeth. At the same time, a faint glimmer of hope flickered in his mind. "Can this really be the end? Is there no way to try again?"

The thought of Dounia sent a painful longing through his chest. He felt a deep ache in that moment. If he could have destroyed Raskolnikov with a single wish, he wouldn't have hesitated to make it.

"It was my own fault for not giving them money," he thought bitterly as he walked back to Lebeziatnikov's room. "Why was I so stingy? It was a mistake—a false sense of thrift! I wanted to keep them penniless so they'd rely on me completely and see me as their savior. And now look at the result! Foolishness!"

He shook his head at his own miscalculation. "If I'd spent a little—fifteen hundred roubles, maybe—on their trousseau, some gifts, fancy trinkets, jewelry, fabrics, all that nonsense from Knopp's and the English shop, things would've turned out better for me. My position would've been stronger! They wouldn't have been able to turn me down so easily.

"They're the kind of people who would feel obligated to return money and gifts if they broke things off. That would've made it much harder for them to do so. Their consciences would've nagged them—'How can we abandon a man who's been so generous and considerate?' But no! I was too cheap for my own good. What a blunder I've made."

And grinding his teeth once more, Pyotr Petrovitch berated himself as a fool—though he would never say it out loud, of course. His thoughts churned angrily as he made his way home, his irritation and frustration doubling with every step. The funeral dinner preparations for Katerina Ivanovna caught his attention as he passed by, stirring a flicker of curiosity within him. He had heard about the event the previous day and vaguely recalled that he might have been invited. Yet, preoccupied with his own troubles, he had dismissed it as unimportant at the time.

When he stopped to inquire from Madame Lippevechsel, who was bustling about setting the table while Katerina Ivanovna attended the cemetery, he was told that the dinner was planned as quite the grand affair. Apparently, all the lodgers had been invited, even those who hadn't known the deceased. Among the guests was Andrey Semyonovitch Lebeziatnikov, despite his past quarrel with Katerina Ivanovna, and Pyotr Petrovitch himself was not only on the guest list but was, in fact, eagerly anticipated. He was regarded as the most significant of the lodgers, which, though it briefly stroked his ego, only added to his growing internal conflict.

Amalia Ivanovna had also been invited with notable pomp, despite the recent unpleasantness surrounding her. She seemed thrilled with her role in the preparations, bustling about with enthusiasm and proudly showing off her new black silk dress, which she had put on specifically for the occasion. Her excitement and ostentation further underscored the significance of the event. This display sparked an idea in Pyotr Petrovitch's mind as he made his way to his room—or rather, to Lebeziatnikov's room—appearing thoughtful. He had also learned during his inquiry that Raskolnikov would be attending the dinner.

Andrey Semyonovitch had been at home all morning. The relationship between Pyotr Petrovitch and Andrey Semyonovitch was peculiar, though perhaps not unusual. From the moment Pyotr Petrovitch began staying with him, he had harbored a mix of disdain and hatred for the young man. At the same time, he seemed vaguely uneasy around him. Pyotr Petrovitch's choice to stay with Andrey Semyonovitch had not been purely out of stinginess, though that had certainly played a large role. He had heard of Andrey Semyonovitch before arriving in Petersburg, knowing him to be a young, leading progressive involved in some notable intellectual circles. These circles, shrouded in a kind of mysterious prestige, had long been the stuff of whispered rumors in the provinces, and Pyotr Petrovitch had been intrigued, if somewhat apprehensive, about their power and influence.

These legendary circles of "progressives," often referred to as nihilists or radicals, had been exaggerated in his mind to an almost comical extent. Like many others, Pyotr Petrovitch had blown their supposed influence out of proportion, inflating their significance into something nearly absurd. Yet, his fear was genuine. What he dreaded most was being "exposed" or publicly humiliated—an anxiety that had haunted him for years. This fear had been the primary reason behind his hesitation to move his business to Petersburg.

His apprehension wasn't unfounded, either. Years ago, when Pyotr Petrovitch was starting his career, he had witnessed two notable incidents where powerful figures in his province were disgracefully exposed. One case had ended in a major scandal, while the other had come dangerously close to serious legal trouble. These experiences had left a lasting impression on him. He decided early on that if he ever moved to Petersburg, he would make a point to investigate and, if necessary, ingratiate himself with these younger progressives to avoid any potential pitfalls.

This was where Andrey Semyonovitch had initially seemed like a useful connection. Before his visit to Raskolnikov, Pyotr Petrovitch had already tried to familiarize himself with a few popular phrases and ideas to navigate this crowd. However, it didn't take long for him to realize that Andrey Semyonovitch was, at his core, a simpleton. Yet, even this revelation didn't fully ease Pyotr Petrovitch's anxiety. He remained uneasy, reasoning that even if all progressives were as foolish as Andrey Semyonovitch, their collective influence could still pose a threat.

Andrey Semyonovitch's endless chatter about doctrines, systems, and revolutionary ideas bored Pyotr Petrovitch to no end. He had no real interest in any of it. His only concern was practical: to figure out whether these groups had any real power. Were they capable of undermining him or exposing his ventures? What were their goals? Did they currently pose any direct threat to him? If they were influential, could he maneuver around them or even use them to his advantage? Countless questions swirled in his mind, and he had no clear answers. All he knew was that he needed to tread carefully while keeping a sharp eye on Andrey Semyonovitch and others like him.

Andrey Semyonovitch was a frail, pale man, with an unhealthy complexion and a slight frame that seemed almost fragile. He had peculiar, flaxen mutton-chop whiskers, of which he was immensely proud, and he never missed an opportunity to stroke or adjust them as though they were his crowning glory. A clerk by profession, Andrey Semyonovitch was plagued by frequent problems with his eyes, which often appeared red or watery, adding to his overall unwell look. Despite his appearance, he carried himself with a surprising degree of self-assurance and occasionally even arrogance, especially in his speech. This air of confidence often clashed absurdly with his diminutive stature and unimpressive demeanor, creating a comical effect that was hard to ignore.

Amalia Ivanovna held him in high regard compared to most of her lodgers. He didn't drink excessively like many others and was always punctual with his rent payments, qualities that endeared him to her. But beneath his seemingly amiable surface, Andrey Semyonovitch was, in reality, rather foolish. His enthusiasm for progress and his alignment with "our younger generation" were born more out of excitement than understanding. He was one of those many mediocre minds who latch onto fashionable ideas without fully grasping their depth, ultimately trivializing and distorting the causes they claim to serve. Despite his sincerity, his involvement in progressive ideologies often came off as a parody, reducing them to something shallow and ridiculous.

Though Lebeziatnikov was generally kind-hearted, he had begun to harbor a growing dislike for Pyotr Petrovitch. This mutual aversion developed almost unconsciously on both sides. Simple as Andrey Semyonovitch might be, he had started to sense that Pyotr Petrovitch secretly despised him and was, in fact, manipulating him. He was beginning to see that Pyotr Petrovitch was not a trustworthy or admirable man.

In his enthusiasm, Andrey Semyonovitch had attempted to explain to Pyotr Petrovitch the principles of Fourier's system and the theory of evolution as outlined by Darwin. At first, Pyotr Petrovitch had feigned interest, but recently he had grown openly sarcastic and even rude during these discussions. It had dawned on Pyotr Petrovitch that Andrey Semyonovitch wasn't merely a naïve simpleton but might also be something of a fraud. He suspected that Lebeziatnikov had no real connections in the intellectual circles he claimed to be part of and that most of his ideas were second- or third-hand interpretations. Pyotr Petrovitch began to doubt that Andrey Semyonovitch even fully understood the progressive causes he so passionately advocated.

Despite these realizations, Pyotr Petrovitch had, in the past ten days, eagerly accepted the most absurd compliments from Andrey Semyonovitch. For instance, when Andrey Semyonovitch praised him for being willing to support the establishment of a "new commune" or for being open to progressive ideas like refraining from christening future children or allowing his wife to take a lover after marriage, Pyotr Petrovitch didn't protest. Instead, he basked in the praise, no matter how ridiculous or ill-founded it was, because he relished the flattery.

That morning, Pyotr Petrovitch had managed to liquidate some bonds, leaving him with a significant sum of cash. Sitting at the table, he meticulously counted the bundles of notes, the rhythmic clicking of the reckoning frame filling the room. Andrey Semyonovitch, who rarely had any money of his own, wandered around the room, trying to act indifferent to the sight of the money. He even attempted to convince himself that he felt nothing but contempt for it.

Pyotr Petrovitch, however, was entirely convinced that Andrey Semyonovitch couldn't possibly remain unaffected by the sight of so much cash. The idea that Lebeziatnikov might be genuinely unmoved never crossed his mind. Meanwhile, Andrey Semyonovitch was internally fuming, bitterly resenting the way Pyotr Petrovitch seemed to take pleasure in flaunting his wealth. He felt as though Pyotr Petrovitch was using this display to remind him of their vast differences in status and power.

As Andrey Semyonovitch began to speak about his favorite topic—the establishment of a new commune—Pyotr Petrovitch's disinterest was evident. He barely paid attention, only occasionally offering dismissive, sarcastic comments in response. The irritation in his tone was unmistakable. Still, Andrey Semyonovitch, ever "humane" and well-meaning, attributed Pyotr Petrovitch's foul mood to his recent falling out with Dounia. He was eager to share his progressive views on relationships and offer advice that he believed would console his friend and encourage his "growth."

"There's some kind of event being prepared at the widow's place, isn't there?" Pyotr Petrovitch suddenly interrupted, cutting off Andrey Semyonovitch mid-sentence just as he was reaching what he thought was the most interesting part of his argument.

"Don't you know? I told you about it yesterday," Andrey Semyonovitch replied, slightly annoyed but quick to regain his composure. "It's some sort of memorial dinner. She even invited you, didn't she? I saw you speaking with her yesterday..."

"I never expected that poor fool to spend all the money she got from that other fool, Raskolnikov, on such an elaborate feast. I was shocked when I passed through and saw the preparations—there's wine! Several people are invited! It's absolutely outrageous!" Pyotr Petrovitch declared, his tone laced with both disdain and a hint of curiosity, as if he had some ulterior motive for continuing the conversation. "Wait, you said I'm invited too? When was that? I don't recall it. But even if I were, I wouldn't go. Why should I? Yesterday, I merely mentioned in passing the possibility of her getting a year's salary as the destitute widow of a government clerk. That's probably why she invited me, don't you think? He-he-he!"

"I'm not planning to go either," said Lebeziatnikov curtly.

"Not surprising, considering you gave her a thrashing! I imagine you'd hesitate to show your face there, he-he!" Pyotr Petrovitch teased, his laughter sharp and malicious.

"Who thrashed whom?" Lebeziatnikov burst out, clearly flustered and reddening with embarrassment.

"Why, you thrashed Katerina Ivanovna a month ago. I heard all about it yesterday. So much for your lofty convictions and your stance on the 'woman question,' he-he-he!" Pyotr Petrovitch's amusement only grew as he returned to clicking the beads on his reckoning frame.

"That's all slander! Utter nonsense!" Lebeziatnikov protested vehemently, his voice rising. It was evident that this topic made him deeply uncomfortable. "It wasn't like that at all. You've heard the story wrong—it's a complete fabrication! I was merely defending myself. She attacked me first, scratching at me with her nails and even pulling out some of my whiskers! Surely anyone is allowed to defend themselves when attacked. I never permit anyone to use violence against me, on principle, because it's an act of tyranny. What else could I do? I simply pushed her away!"

"He-he-he!" Luzhin continued to laugh maliciously, his mockery relentless.

"You keep laughing because you're in a foul mood yourself. But your taunts are irrelevant and have absolutely nothing to do with the woman question!" Lebeziatnikov retorted, his frustration mounting. "You don't understand. I once thought that if women were truly equal to men in every respect, including strength—which some claim now—then there should also be equality in such matters. But upon reflection, I realized that such issues shouldn't even arise. Fighting should not exist in an enlightened society, and in the future, it won't. Seeking equality through fighting is absurd. Of course, fighting still happens now, but in the future, it won't... Confound it! You've muddled my thoughts again! Anyway, that's not why I'm not going. I'm refusing to attend on principle. I don't want to participate in the disgusting ritual of these memorial dinners. That's the reason. Though, I admit, it might have been amusing to go just to mock it all. It's a shame there won't be any priests there; I'd certainly have gone if there were."

"So, you would go just to sit at someone else's table and insult them and their guests?" Pyotr Petrovitch asked mockingly.

"Not to insult, but to protest! There's a difference. I would have a higher purpose—promoting enlightenment and spreading progressive ideas. That's a duty for any enlightened man. Sometimes, harshness is necessary to make a point. I could plant a seed, introduce an idea, and who knows what might grow from it? They might be offended at first, but later they'd see that I'd done them a favor. Take Terebyeva, for example. She left her family to dedicate herself to the cause, even writing her parents a letter explaining that she was entering a free marriage. People criticized her, saying the letter was too harsh and she should have written more gently. That's nonsense! Harshness is sometimes essential. Another example: Varents. She left her husband and two children after seven years of marriage, writing him a blunt letter that she had discovered a new societal organization through a noble man she had joined. That's how letters should be written!"

"Is Terebyeva the one you said has had three free marriages?"

"No, no. It's only her second. But what if it were her fourth or her fifteenth? That's irrelevant! And if I ever regretted my parents' deaths, it's now. I wish they were alive so I could protest against them! I would've done something to shock them—to astonish them! What a pity I have no one left to protest against."

"To astonish, eh? He-he! Well, suit yourself," Pyotr Petrovitch interjected dismissively. "But tell me this: do you know the deceased's daughter, that frail-looking girl? The rumors about her—are they true?"

"And what of it?" Lebeziatnikov replied, his tone growing defensive. "In my opinion—and this is my personal conviction—what she did is completely understandable. In our current society, it's seen as abnormal because it's forced upon women. But in a future society, it will be voluntary and perfectly normal. She was suffering, and her suffering became her asset—her capital, so to speak. She had every right to use it. In the future, there will be no need for such assets, but her actions will have a different meaning. They'll be rational and harmonious with her environment. As for Sofya Semyonovna herself, I see her as a bold protest against the flaws of society. I respect her for it. In fact, I rejoice when I look at her."

"I heard you were the one who got her thrown out of these lodgings."

"That's another lie!" Lebeziatnikov shouted, his face reddening with anger. "That's entirely untrue! That was all Katerina Ivanovna's misunderstanding. She didn't comprehend the situation. I never tried to seduce Sofya Semyonovna. My intentions were purely intellectual— I was trying to awaken her, to inspire her to protest. It was entirely selfless! She couldn't have stayed here anyway."

"Have you asked her to join your community?"

"You're laughing again, and it's completely inappropriate!" Lebeziatnikov snapped. "You don't understand! There's no such role in a community. Communities are meant to eliminate such roles altogether. What seems irrational in today's society becomes perfectly rational in a community. Everything depends on the environment, and man himself is nothing without it. And for the record, I'm still on good terms with Sofya Semyonovna, which proves she doesn't feel wronged by me. I'm even trying to involve her in the community—but on entirely different terms. She has a beautiful, remarkable character!"

"And you're exploiting that beautiful character, aren't you? He-he!"

"No, not at all! Quite the opposite!" Lebeziatnikov exclaimed, his voice rising in indignation.

"Oh, on the contrary! What a peculiar thing to say! He-he-he!"

"Believe me, why should I hide it? Honestly, I even find it strange myself how timid, proper, and modern she is with me," Lebeziatnikov said earnestly.

"And you, of course, are trying to 'develop' her—he-he! Trying to prove to her that all that modesty is just silly nonsense?" Pyotr Petrovitch retorted, his tone mocking.

"Not at all, not at all! How crude and, if you'll pardon me for saying so, how ignorant your interpretation of 'development' is! My goodness, how outdated your thinking remains! We are striving for the liberation and equality of women, and yet you reduce everything to a single, narrow perspective," Lebeziatnikov countered, clearly irritated. "Let me clarify. Setting aside the broader question of chastity and feminine modesty as prejudices rooted in tradition, I completely respect her modesty as it pertains to me. That's her choice to make. Of course, if she were to express an interest in me, I'd consider myself very fortunate—I like her a lot. But as it stands, no one has treated her with more respect or consideration than I have. I honor her dignity entirely. I wait in hopes, nothing more."

"Why not make her a gift? I'd wager you haven't thought of that," Pyotr Petrovitch suggested slyly.

"You just don't get it, as I've said before! Yes, she's in a difficult situation, but that's not the issue here. It's a completely different matter! You simply dismiss her because of her circumstances. You see something you mistakenly deem contemptible and refuse to see her as a fellow human being. You don't understand what a remarkable character she has. It's a shame that she's stopped borrowing books from me recently; I used to lend them to her. I regret that she has shown such determination in some areas—like when she protested once—but lacks the self-reliance to fully overcome certain outdated notions and prejudices. Still, she has grasped certain ideas very well. For example, she understands that hand-kissing is an insult to women because it signifies inequality. We've had discussions about it, and I explained the concept to her. She even listened attentively when I described the workers' associations in France. Now I'm helping her understand the future societal framework, like the protocols for entering private rooms in a communal living arrangement."

"And what is that supposed to mean?" Pyotr Petrovitch asked with a smirk.

"Recently, we debated whether a member of the community should have the right to enter another member's room at any time, regardless of gender, and we concluded that they should," Lebeziatnikov replied with enthusiasm.

"Sounds inconvenient—he-he!"

Lebeziatnikov's face flushed with anger. "You always twist things into something unpleasant! It's maddening. I regret mentioning the issue of personal privacy prematurely. People like you fixate on it, ridicule it, and misunderstand it completely. Worse, you act proud of your ignorance! Honestly, I've always said that this topic shouldn't even be addressed with someone who hasn't fully embraced the system. It's too easily misinterpreted. And tell me this: why do you find something shameful in manual labor or even in cesspools? I'd be the first to clean out any cesspool if needed—not as an act of sacrifice, but because it's honest, useful work. It's far more valuable than the paintings of Raphael or the poetry of Pushkin, because it serves a practical purpose!"

"And it's more honorable, isn't it? He-he-he!"

"What do you mean by 'more honorable'? I reject such outdated terms for human activity. 'Honorable,' 'noble'—these are all antiquated prejudices. I only recognize one measure: usefulness. Anything that benefits humanity is worthy and important. Laugh all you like, but that's the truth!"

Pyotr Petrovitch laughed heartily, having finished counting the money and now tucking it away. However, he left a few notes lying conspicuously on the table. The so-called "cesspool debate" had long been a point of contention between them, with Lebeziatnikov growing genuinely angry whenever the subject arose, while Luzhin found it endlessly amusing. At the moment, Pyotr Petrovitch seemed particularly eager to provoke his young companion further.

"It's your bad luck from yesterday making you so irritable and unbearable today," Lebeziatnikov snapped, though his tone carried a trace of deference. Despite his claims of independence and protest, he still treated Pyotr Petrovitch with some of the respect ingrained from earlier years.

"Never mind that," Pyotr Petrovitch interrupted coldly. "Tell me, do you happen to know that young woman well enough to ask her to step in here for a moment? I believe they've all returned from the cemetery—I heard footsteps. I'd like to speak with her."

"Why?" Lebeziatnikov asked, surprised.

"That's my business," Pyotr Petrovitch replied curtly. "I'm leaving either today or tomorrow, and I want to have a word with her. However, you're welcome to stay during the conversation—it's probably better that you do. No telling what kind of wild ideas you might otherwise conjure up."

"I wouldn't assume anything of the sort. But if you have something to say to her, it's easy enough to call her in. I'll fetch her now, and you can be sure I won't interfere," Lebeziatnikov said, walking briskly out of the room.

A few minutes later, he returned with Sonia. She entered timidly, her shyness and unease evident, as always. Sonia had always been uncomfortable in unfamiliar situations or around strangers. She had been like this as a child, and her circumstances had only amplified this trait over the years.

Pyotr Petrovitch greeted her with a show of politeness and affability, though his tone carried a faint trace of condescension. He believed this mixture of courtesy and superiority was appropriate for a man of his stature when addressing someone as young and vulnerable as Sonia. He quickly urged her to sit down across from him at the table, making every effort to put her at ease.

Sonia sat cautiously, her eyes darting around the room—first at Lebeziatnikov, then at the scattered banknotes on the table, and finally settling on Pyotr Petrovitch. Her gaze lingered on him, wide-eyed and nervous, as though trying to anticipate his intentions.

As Lebeziatnikov began to retreat toward the door, Pyotr Petrovitch gestured for Sonia to remain seated and motioned for Lebeziatnikov to stay as well. "No need to leave," he said firmly.

"Is Raskolnikov inside? Has he arrived?" Pyotr Petrovitch asked in a low, almost conspiratorial tone.

"Raskolnikov? Yes, he's here. Why do you ask? I saw him come in just now," Lebeziatnikov responded, his curiosity piqued.

"Good, good. Now, I must particularly request that you stay here with us and not leave me alone with this... young woman," Pyotr Petrovitch continued, his voice laced with an undertone of unease. "I only want to exchange a few words with her, but who knows what people might make of it? I wouldn't want Raskolnikov spreading any stories. You understand what I mean?"

"Yes, I understand," Lebeziatnikov replied, nodding in agreement. "You're probably right. Of course, I personally don't think you have anything to worry about, but it's still better to be cautious. I'll stay right here. I'll stand by the window and keep out of the way. Yes, I think you're making the right choice."

Pyotr Petrovitch nodded, satisfied, and returned to the sofa. He sat down opposite Sonia, studying her intently with an air of authority and seriousness, as if silently warning her not to step out of line. Sonia, visibly nervous, averted her gaze, her discomfort apparent in her every movement.

"First of all, Sofya Semyonovna," Pyotr Petrovitch began in a tone that was both formal and condescending, "I must ask you to convey my apologies to your esteemed mother. Or rather, Katerina Ivanovna, who stands in the place of a mother to you. Am I correct?"

"Yes, that's correct," Sonia answered quickly, her voice trembling.

"Good. Please let her know that, due to unavoidable circumstances, I will not be able to attend the dinner, despite her kind invitation."

"Yes... I'll tell her right away," Sonia said, rising hurriedly from her seat.

"Wait, wait, that's not all," Pyotr Petrovitch said, gesturing for her to sit back down, a faint smile playing on his lips. It was the kind of smile that hinted at amusement over her lack of social refinement. "And truly, Sofya Semyonovna, you underestimate me if you think I would trouble you over something so trivial. My absence from the dinner is hardly the most pressing matter. I have something else I wish to discuss."

Sonia hesitated before sitting down again. Her eyes briefly flickered to the colorful notes still lying on the table but quickly shifted away, as though she felt it improper, especially for her, to let her gaze linger on someone else's money. She then focused on Pyotr Petrovitch's gold-rimmed eyeglasses and the ornate ring with its large yellow stone on his finger, but her discomfort made her glance away again. Finally, she settled her gaze on his face, though it was clear she would rather look anywhere else.

Pyotr Petrovitch, seemingly oblivious to her nervousness, paused with exaggerated dignity before continuing. "Yesterday, as I was passing through, I happened to exchange a few words with Katerina Ivanovna. That brief interaction was enough for me to observe that she is in a rather... extraordinary position. If I may use the term, preternatural."

"Yes, preternatural," Sonia murmured in agreement, eager to please.

"Or to put it more plainly—ill," Pyotr Petrovitch corrected himself, his tone suggestive of his own magnanimity in simplifying his language.

"Yes, ill," Sonia repeated, nodding quickly.

"Exactly. Now, out of a sense of humanity and compassion, I would like to offer my assistance, seeing as her situation is clearly dire. If I'm not mistaken, the entire burden of supporting this impoverished family now falls squarely on your shoulders?"

Sonia stood up, her nervousness giving way to a flicker of boldness. "May I ask, sir, did you tell her yesterday that you could secure a pension for her? She mentioned something to that effect—she said you promised to help her obtain one. Was that true?"

"Not at all," Pyotr Petrovitch replied, his voice sharp with annoyance. "That's an absurd notion. I merely suggested the possibility of temporary assistance as the widow of a government official—provided she could secure the necessary patronage. But as it turns out, your late father hadn't completed his term of service and wasn't even in government service toward the end. In such cases, there is no real claim to assistance. Any hope in that regard would be fleeting, to say the least. Yet, she's already dreaming of a pension! He-he-he! A rather ambitious lady, isn't she?"

"She's... she's just very trusting and kind-hearted," Sonia stammered. "She believes what people tell her because of her goodness... and her faith in others. Please don't hold it against her."

"Of course not," Pyotr Petrovitch said, waving a hand dismissively. "But please, sit down; you haven't yet heard what I wish to propose."

Sonia, flustered, sat down for the third time, her anxiety evident in the way she fidgeted with her hands.

"Now, considering her unfortunate circumstances and the plight of her young children, I would be willing, within my limited capacity, to provide some assistance. Perhaps we could arrange a subscription fund or a small lottery—something friends or even benevolent outsiders often organize in such cases. That was what I wished to discuss with you. Such a thing could be done."

"Yes... yes... God will surely bless you for such kindness," Sonia faltered, her wide eyes fixed on Pyotr Petrovitch, a mixture of hope and confusion flickering in her gaze.

"It might be possible, but we'll discuss it later," Pyotr Petrovitch replied thoughtfully. "We could even start today—talk it over this evening and begin laying the groundwork, so to speak. Come to me at seven o'clock. I trust that Mr. Lebeziatnikov will be willing to assist us. But there is one particular matter I feel I must address now, Sofya Semyonovna, and this is why I've troubled you to come here. In my opinion, it would be unwise—dangerous even—to put any money directly into Katerina Ivanovna's hands. Today's dinner is proof enough of that. Despite having nothing for tomorrow—not even a crust of bread, let alone shoes or other necessities—she's gone and bought Jamaica rum, Madeira, and even coffee. I saw it myself when I passed through earlier. Tomorrow, everything will fall on you again. It's absurd, really, and I believe the best course would be to raise a subscription for her, but to ensure that she doesn't know about the money. Instead, it could be entrusted to you. Do you see my point?"

"I... I don't know," Sonia stammered, visibly distressed. "This is just for today, just this one time... She wanted so much to honor his memory, to celebrate it properly. And she is sensible, very sensible, truly... but as you think best. I'll be very, very grateful—so will they all—and God will reward you... and the orphans..."

Her voice broke, and tears began to flow.

"Very well then, keep that in mind," Pyotr Petrovitch said, his tone softening slightly as he watched her distress. "And now, I hope you will accept this small sum from me personally, for the benefit of your family. I must insist, however, that my name not be mentioned in connection with it. Here..." He carefully unfolded a ten-rouble note and held it out to her. "Unfortunately, given my own financial concerns, this is all I can manage at the moment."

Sonia's face flushed bright red as she accepted the note with trembling hands. She jumped to her feet, muttered a few incoherent words of thanks, and began to take her leave.

Pyotr Petrovitch rose ceremoniously and accompanied her to the door, his demeanor both polite and slightly theatrical. Sonia finally managed to leave the room, overwhelmed with confusion and agitation, and made her way back to Katerina Ivanovna, her emotions still in turmoil.

All the while, Lebeziatnikov had been pacing near the window or standing awkwardly, trying not to interrupt the conversation. Once Sonia was gone, he approached Pyotr Petrovitch with an air of solemnity and extended his hand.

"I saw and heard everything," he announced, placing particular emphasis on the last word. "That was an honorable thing to do—humane, even. I could see you were trying to avoid any gratitude, which is commendable. Although, I must admit, I don't entirely agree with private charity in principle. It fails to address the root of the problem and can even perpetuate it. But I have to say, I appreciated what I saw today—yes, I did."

"That's all nonsense," muttered Pyotr Petrovitch, though he looked somewhat flustered as he avoided Lebeziatnikov's earnest gaze.

"No, it's not nonsense!" Lebeziatnikov exclaimed, his voice rising with enthusiasm. "A man who has suffered the sort of annoyance you did yesterday, and yet still manages to show sympathy for the suffering of others—such a man deserves respect, even if his actions reflect a social mistake. Honestly, Pyotr Petrovitch, I didn't expect it from you. Especially considering your usual ideas..."

He trailed off, then suddenly added with a burst of sincerity, "Ah, what a hindrance your ideas are to you! How upset you've been since yesterday—clearly distressed by your misfortune. But tell me, why do you even want a marriage, a legal marriage? My dear, noble Pyotr Petrovitch, why cling to something so outdated? You may not like it, but I'm glad the engagement didn't work out. Truly, I am! I'm glad you're free—you haven't lost your humanity entirely. There, I've said it!"

"I want a legal marriage," Pyotr Petrovitch replied curtly, "because I don't intend to be made a fool of in your so-called free marriages, raising another man's children as my own." His tone was dismissive, and it was clear his thoughts were elsewhere.

"Children? Ah, yes, children!" Lebeziatnikov exclaimed, his enthusiasm reigniting like a spark to dry kindling. "Children are a vital social question, no doubt about it. But the family structure itself is the issue. Some radicals argue against having children at all because it ties people to the outdated institution of the family. We'll discuss children another time, though. Right now, let's talk about the question of honor. That's my weak spot, I confess! Such a dated, military concept! Words like 'honor' have no place in the dictionary of the future. It's absurd, truly! In free marriages, there is no deception. Deception is the byproduct of legal marriage, a reaction to its oppressive nature. Free marriages, on the other hand, are based on honesty and respect."

He paused, then continued with growing fervor. "If I were to marry—legally or not—it would make no difference to me. I'd tell my wife, 'My dear, until now, I've loved you. But from this moment forward, I respect you even more, for you've shown you can protest!' You laugh because you can't free yourself from old prejudices! Damn it all, I sometimes think that if I were married, I'd even present my wife with a lover if she hadn't found one herself. 'My dear,' I'd say, 'I love you, but more than that, I respect you. I want you to be happy.' Am I wrong?"

Pyotr Petrovitch let out a faint snigger but seemed distracted, barely engaging with Lebeziatnikov's tirade. His hands moved restlessly as though he were preoccupied with something far more pressing. Noticing this, Lebeziatnikov stopped and studied him curiously, later reflecting on the peculiar behavior he had observed that day.

Chapter 2

It is difficult to pinpoint precisely what inspired Katerina Ivanovna to conceive the idea of hosting such an elaborate dinner in her chaotic mental state. Nearly half of the twenty roubles given by Raskolnikov for Marmeladov's funeral had been squandered on preparations for this event. Perhaps Katerina Ivanovna felt a pressing need to honor the memory of her late husband in a manner that would prove to all the lodgers—and particularly to Amalia Ivanovna—that he was in no way their inferior, and perhaps even far superior. It might also have been driven by the peculiar "pride of the poor," a sentiment that often compels individuals of limited means to spend their last resources on social ceremonies, simply to maintain the appearance of normalcy and avoid the disdain of others.

Equally likely was her desire to demonstrate to the "wretched, contemptible lodgers" that she knew how to host properly, that she had been raised in a "genteel," nearly aristocratic, household under her colonel father. She wanted to prove that she was never meant for the indignities of scrubbing floors or washing rags late into the night. Even those crushed by circumstances can sometimes experience a burst of pride and vanity so overwhelming that it becomes an uncontrollable, almost irrational compulsion. And while Katerina Ivanovna might have been broken by circumstances, her spirit remained defiant. She was not the type to be intimidated or cowed. Sonia's observation that her mind was unhinged was not without merit. Though Katerina Ivanovna could not be called insane, her intellect had been deeply strained over the past year, and her relentless battle with poverty and illness had left its mark. Doctors often note that the later stages of consumption can affect mental clarity, and Katerina Ivanovna's behavior was certainly indicative of such strain.

The dinner itself lacked variety and extravagance, but there was alcohol: vodka, rum, and Lisbon wine, all of poor quality but in sufficient supply. Alongside the traditional rice and honey, there were three or four dishes, including pancakes, all prepared in Amalia Ivanovna's kitchen. Two samovars were set to boil, ensuring there would be tea and punch after the meal. Katerina Ivanovna personally oversaw the purchase of provisions with the assistance of a hapless Polish lodger. This unfortunate man, stranded at Madame Lippevechsel's boarding house, eagerly volunteered his services to Katerina Ivanovna. For two days, he ran tirelessly at her beck and call, making sure everyone was aware of his efforts. Every trivial task became an opportunity to seek her out, even tracking her down at the bazaar to report on the smallest errands and addressing her with exaggerated politeness as "Pani."

Initially, Katerina Ivanovna declared that she could not have managed without this "noble and magnanimous man," but by the end, she was thoroughly exasperated with him. Her habit of viewing every new acquaintance in an excessively positive light had backfired again. She had a tendency to invent glowing attributes for people, sincerely believing her own fabrications, only to grow disillusioned and dismiss them with scorn and contempt shortly after.

Amalia Ivanovna, for her part, suddenly found herself elevated to a position of great importance in Katerina Ivanovna's eyes. This was likely due to her enthusiastic involvement in the dinner preparations. Amalia had taken responsibility for setting the table, providing linens, crockery, and cutlery, and cooking the food in her kitchen. Katerina Ivanovna left everything in Amalia's hands while she went to the cemetery. To her credit, Amalia executed her duties well: the tablecloth was reasonably clean, and the mismatched crockery and glassware—borrowed from various lodgers—were laid out neatly. By the appointed time, everything was in place.

Feeling proud of her accomplishments, Amalia dressed in her best black silk dress and adorned her cap with new mourning ribbons, greeting the returning party with a sense of satisfaction. However, her evident pride grated on Katerina Ivanovna. The sight of Amalia's ribbons and her attitude seemed to imply that the success of the preparations was entirely due to her efforts, which infuriated Katerina

Ivanovna. "As if the table couldn't have been laid without her!" she thought bitterly.

This perceived arrogance was intolerable to Katerina Ivanovna, who inwardly resolved to put Amalia Ivanovna in her place at a later time. After all, her father, a colonel and nearly a governor, had once hosted dinners for forty guests, during which someone like Amalia would not have even been allowed in the kitchen. For now, however, Katerina Ivanovna masked her irritation with cold politeness, waiting for the right moment to assert her superiority.

Her mood soured further as she noticed that only a few lodgers had attended the funeral, and those who came were the least respectable among them—poor, shabby individuals, some visibly intoxicated. The older and more reputable lodgers, as if by mutual agreement, had stayed away. Even Pyotr Petrovitch Luzhin, whom she had praised the night before as the most distinguished and generous of men, failed to make an appearance.

The absence of Luzhin stung particularly, as she had told everyone—Amalia Ivanovna, Polenka, Sonia, and the Pole—that he was a man of great means and influence, a friend of her first husband, and a former guest in her father's home. She had even boasted that Luzhin had promised to secure her a substantial pension. Katerina Ivanovna's habit of exalting the connections and wealth of others was entirely genuine and without ulterior motive. She derived pleasure simply from elevating those she admired.

To make matters worse, Lebeziatnikov, that "contemptible wretch," had also failed to attend. His absence was particularly insulting, as he had been invited solely out of kindness due to his association with Luzhin. His refusal to attend seemed to highlight the lack of respect she felt she deserved, leaving her fuming over the perceived slight.

Among those who failed to appear at the dinner were the so-called "genteel lady and her old-maidish daughter," a pair who had only been renting rooms in the house for about two weeks. Despite their short stay, they had already made complaints about the noise and commotion coming from Katerina Ivanovna's quarters, especially on nights when Marmeladov returned home drunk. Katerina Ivanovna had learned of their grievances during an earlier quarrel with Amalia Ivanovna, who, in the heat of the argument, had threatened to evict her entire family and declared that they "were not worth the foot" of the more respectable lodgers being disturbed. Deeply insulted, Katerina Ivanovna resolved to invite the haughty woman and her daughter to the dinner.

Her intention was not only to show them that she bore no malice but also to demonstrate that she was far superior in spirit and manners. She wanted them to see that she was accustomed to a higher way of life, far removed from her current circumstances. At dinner, she had planned to weave subtle allusions to her late father's position as a governor and to hint delicately that their snobbish behavior—turning away from her when they crossed paths—was both rude and unnecessary.

Another absentee was the so-called "fat colonel-major," who was, in truth, a discharged officer of low rank. His absence was attributed to his being "not himself" for the past two days.

The guests who did attend, however, hardly met Katerina Ivanovna's expectations. There was the ever-helpful Pole, who had brought with him two additional Polish acquaintances no one had ever seen before. Then there was a pitiful-looking clerk with a blotchy face and a greasy coat who sat silently throughout the meal, exuding an unpleasant odor. Another guest was a deaf and nearly blind old man who had once worked in the post office and had been living off the charity of an unknown benefactor for years.

The most unseemly of the guests included a retired clerk from the commissariat department who arrived visibly drunk, laughed loudly and inappropriately, and, shockingly, was without a waistcoat. Yet another man appeared wearing only a dressing gown, an affront so egregious that Amalia Ivanovna and the Pole managed to usher him out.

All of this irritated Katerina Ivanovna to no end. "For whom have we made all these preparations?" she asked herself bitterly. To accommodate the guests, she had gone so far as to exclude her own children from the table. The younger ones had been given their meal on a box in a far corner of the room, where Polenka, acting as a responsible elder sister, was tasked with feeding them and ensuring they behaved like "proper, well-bred children."

Katerina Ivanovna's frustration only heightened her sense of dignity and pride. She greeted her guests with an exaggerated air of formality, staring down some of them with pointed severity. Convinced that Amalia Ivanovna was to blame for the absence of more respectable attendees, she began to treat her with cold disdain. Amalia, ever sensitive to such treatment, quickly noticed and resented it, setting a tense tone for the evening.

Raskolnikov arrived almost at the same moment the party returned from the cemetery, much to Katerina Ivanovna's delight. His presence lifted her spirits for two reasons: first, he was the only truly educated guest, a man who was expected to achieve a professorship in two years. Second, he immediately apologized for his absence at the funeral, doing so with such respect and decorum that she felt vindicated in her esteem for him.

Practically pouncing on him, she insisted that he sit to her left, with Amalia Ivanovna relegated to her right. Despite her constant fretting over the proper distribution of dishes and her worsening cough, which interrupted her every other sentence, she poured out her pent-up frustrations to Raskolnikov in a hurried whisper. Her indignation at the failures of the dinner mingled with bursts of uncontrollable laughter, mostly directed at her guests and, most pointedly, at Amalia Ivanovna.

"It's all that cuckoo's fault! You know who I mean—her, her!" Katerina Ivanovna said, nodding toward the landlady. "Look at her, sitting there with those ridiculous round eyes. She knows we're talking about her, but she can't figure it out. Pfoo, the owl! Ha-ha-ha! And what is that cap she's wearing? Have you seen it? It's absurd! She puts it on as if she wants everyone to think she's doing me some grand favor by being here. Can you imagine?"

Her voice dropped conspiratorially, though her tone grew sharper. "I asked her, as any sensible person would, to invite people who actually knew my late husband. And who does she bring? Look at them—the spotty-faced one, the miserable Poles! Ha-ha-ha! Not a single one of them has ever been here before, and now they're all sitting here in a row. What do they want? Hey, pan!" she suddenly called out to one of the Poles. "Have you tried the pancakes? Go on, take some more! Have some beer! Or vodka, if you like. Ah, look at him jumping up and bowing! They must be starving, poor things. Well, let them eat. At least they're quiet, though I'm a little worried about the spoons. Amalia Ivanovna!"

She turned abruptly to the landlady, her voice now loud enough for others to hear. "If your silver spoons go missing, I'm warning you, I won't be held responsible! Ha-ha-ha!"

Turning back to Raskolnikov, she nodded toward Amalia Ivanovna, her laughter brimming with mockery. "She doesn't get it. Look at her, sitting there with her mouth open like an owl. An owl in new ribbons, ha-ha-ha!"

Katerina Ivanovna's biting remarks and barely suppressed laughter left her alternately coughing and gasping for breath. Despite the tension of the evening and the chaos around her, she seemed oddly energized, feeding off her indignation and the absurdity of the situation.

Katerina Ivanovna's laughter abruptly gave way to a violent coughing fit that seemed to shake her entire frame, lasting several agonizing minutes. Beads of sweat appeared on her pale forehead, and when she pressed her handkerchief to her lips, it came away stained with blood. Wordlessly, she held it out for Raskolnikov to see, her expression one of both resignation and defiance. As soon as she managed to catch her breath, she resumed her animated whispers, her cheeks flushed with a hectic, feverish glow.

"Do you know," she began, her tone laced with indignation, "I gave Amalia Ivanovna the most precise, delicate instructions on how to invite that lady and her daughter. You know who I mean, don't you? It required tact, an exquisite touch, but what did she do instead? She botched it completely! That foolish, conceited woman—an absolute nobody! She thinks she's someone just because she's the widow of a major and spends her time fluttering about government offices trying to secure a pension, all while dragging around those pitiful, frayed skirts. And imagine—at her age, she paints her face! Everyone knows it. And what happened? She didn't even have the decency to reply to the invitation, let alone show up! The sheer audacity, the nerve!"

She paused for breath, her voice growing more animated. "And why, I ask you, hasn't Pyotr Petrovitch come? I can't understand it. But where is Sonia? Where has she disappeared to? Ah, there she is! Finally! What took you so long, Sonia? Even at your father's funeral, you can't manage to be on time. Rodion Romanovitch, please make room for her beside you. That's where she should sit. Sonia, take anything you like—here, try the cold entrée with jelly. It's the best we have. The pancakes will be brought out shortly. Have the children eaten yet? Polenka, is everything all right? Good. Lida, behave like a proper young lady, and Kolya, stop fidgeting with your feet! Sit still, like a little gentleman. What were you saying, Sonia?"

Sonia, flustered and pale, hurried to deliver Pyotr Petrovitch's apologies. She spoke just loudly enough for the rest of the table to hear, choosing her words with great care. She conveyed, in the most respectful terms, that Pyotr Petrovitch deeply regretted his absence and had instructed her to explain that he would visit as soon as possible to discuss important business matters with Katerina Ivanovna and to determine how he might assist her.

Katerina Ivanovna's expression softened as she listened, and her posture straightened with pride. She glanced around the table as if daring anyone to doubt the respect and regard that a man of Pyotr Petrovitch's stature had for her family. Sonia's tactful message had precisely the desired effect. Katerina Ivanovna inclined her head graciously and inquired with great dignity after Pyotr Petrovitch's health. Then, leaning closer to Raskolnikov, she whispered with an air of triumph, "Of course, it would be difficult, even awkward, for a man of Pyotr Petrovitch's position to find himself in such extraordinary company. Naturally, his devotion to my family and his old friendship with my father are what would compel him to endure it."

She added almost audibly, "That is why I am especially grateful to you, Rodion Romanovitch. You have not scorned my hospitality, even in such surroundings. I know it is out of the special regard you had for my late husband that you have honored us with your presence today."

With renewed pride, she surveyed the room, her sharp gaze falling on the guests one by one. Her attention settled on the deaf old man seated across the table, and she asked in a loud voice whether he would like more meat and whether he had been served wine. The man, however, did not respond and seemed utterly bewildered by her inquiry. His neighbors, finding this amusing, began poking and shaking him to draw his attention, but he only gaped around the room with his mouth open, adding to the general hilarity.

"What an imbecile!" Katerina Ivanovna exclaimed, shaking her head in exasperation. "Why was he even brought here?" She turned back to Raskolnikov, her voice regaining its earlier indignation. "As for Pyotr Petrovitch, I've always had confidence in him. He is, after all, nothing like..."

She abruptly shifted her focus to Amalia Ivanovna, her tone becoming sharp and cutting. "Nothing like the ridiculous, dressed-up nobodies you seem to think worthy of inviting. My father wouldn't have let them set foot in his kitchen, let alone dine at his table. And my late husband—God rest his soul—would have only tolerated them out of the goodness of his heart."

Her remarks were interrupted by the commissariat clerk, who, having consumed his twelfth glass of vodka, blurted out loudly, "Yes, he was fond of drink! Loved it, he did!"

Katerina Ivanovna immediately turned on him, her voice rising in defense of her husband. "That weakness of his is well-known to everyone, and I won't deny it. But he was a kind and honorable man who always loved and respected his family. His only fault was his good nature—it made him too trusting, too generous with people who weren't fit to polish his shoes! Would you believe, Rodion Romanovitch, they found a gingerbread cock in his pocket when he was dead drunk. Even in that state, he didn't forget the children!"

"A cock? Did you say a cock?" the commissariat clerk shouted, his voice slurring.

Katerina Ivanovna didn't bother to respond. Instead, she sighed deeply, her expression softening as her thoughts seemed to drift elsewhere, momentarily lost in memory.

"No doubt you think, as everyone else does, that I was too harsh with him," Katerina Ivanovna began again, addressing Raskolnikov with a tone of defiance mixed with a tinge of sorrow. "But that's not true! He respected me—he respected me deeply! He was a kind-hearted man, and at times I felt such pity for him. Oh, you can't imagine how he'd sit in a corner, watching me with those sad eyes. It would make me want to be tender with him, to show him some kindness. But then I'd think, 'If I'm kind to him, he'll start drinking again.' You see, the only way to keep him under control was through strictness—there was no other way."

"Yes, and he used to get his hair pulled pretty often, too!" bellowed the commissariat clerk, who had just downed another glass of vodka, his voice slurred with drunken amusement.

"Some fools would indeed benefit from a good thrashing as well as a hair-pulling," Katerina Ivanovna retorted sharply, her eyes flashing with anger. "But I'm not talking about my late husband!" She snapped at the clerk with such force that even his drunkenness couldn't mask his discomfort.

Her face was now flushed with indignation, her chest rising and falling with the effort of restraining herself. The tension in the room thickened as many of the guests began to snicker, enjoying the escalating scene. Some of them leaned toward the clerk, whispering provocations to encourage him further, their amusement growing as they watched Katerina Ivanovna's irritation mount.

"What exactly are you trying to say?" the clerk stammered, attempting to sound offended but ultimately dismissing it with a wave of his hand. "Ah, it's nonsense! Widow, I forgive you! Pass!" And with that, he swallowed yet another glass of vodka, his movements unsteady.

Raskolnikov observed the spectacle silently, his face set in a mask of polite composure. He barely touched the food that Katerina Ivanovna insisted on piling onto his plate, tasting only enough to avoid offending her. His attention, however, was fixed on Sonia, who sat beside him, increasingly uneasy. Her distress was palpable as she watched Katerina Ivanovna grow more agitated. Sonia's own discomfort was compounded by the knowledge that she was the reason for the "genteel ladies" snubbing the invitation. Amalia Ivanovna had told her that the mother had been outright offended by the idea of her daughter sitting at the same table as "that young person." Sonia had a sinking feeling that Katerina Ivanovna was already aware of this slight, and she knew that an insult to her would weigh even heavier on Katerina Ivanovna's pride than one directed at herself or her family.

As if to confirm her fears, a plate was passed down the table to Sonia, containing two crude shapes of hearts pierced by an arrow, cut from black bread. The mocking gesture sent Katerina Ivanovna's face into a deep crimson flush. Without hesitation, she announced loudly across the table that the sender was "a drunken ass!" The room momentarily fell silent, the insult hanging in the air, before murmurs and muffled laughter broke out again.

Amalia Ivanovna, sensing the growing tension and eager to restore some semblance of good humor to the gathering, launched into a story. She recounted, apropos of nothing, an incident involving her acquaintance "Karl from the chemist's," who had been in a cab one night when the cabman allegedly tried to kill him. According to her tale, Karl had begged the cabman not to harm him, weeping and clasping his hands in terror, until he fainted from fright, claiming that his heart was pierced.

Although Katerina Ivanovna smiled faintly at the absurdity of the story, she couldn't resist commenting. "Amalia Ivanovna, you really ought not to tell anecdotes in Russian," she said, her tone condescending. The remark stung, and Amalia, deeply offended, replied indignantly that her "Vater aus Berlin was a very important man, who always went with his hands in his pockets."

Katerina Ivanovna burst into laughter, unable to contain herself. "Did you hear that?" she whispered to Raskolnikov, her good humor suddenly restored. "She meant to say he kept his hands in his pockets, but instead she said he put his hands in people's pockets! And look at her sitting there, glaring at us like an owl—ha-ha-ha! (Cough-cough.) And have you noticed, Rodion Romanovitch, how all these Petersburg foreigners, especially the Germans, are so much stupider than we are? Imagine one of us telling such a ridiculous story about fainting from fear while clasping our hands and begging a cabman for mercy. She thinks it's so touching, poor thing, and doesn't realize how foolish it sounds!"

As Katerina Ivanovna regained her composure, she began speaking enthusiastically about her plans for the future. Turning to Raskolnikov, she confided that once she secured her pension, she intended to open a boarding school for the daughters of gentlemen in her hometown. It was the first time she had mentioned this ambitious project to him, and her words were full of energy and hope as she described the peaceful life she envisioned for herself and her children. She elaborated on the teachers she planned to hire, including a respectable old Frenchman named Mangot, who had once taught her and still lived in T——.

As she spoke, she produced a worn but treasured certificate of honor that Marmeladov had mentioned to Raskolnikov in the tavern. This document, which confirmed her late father's rank as a major and his membership in a distinguished order, was a source of great pride. Katerina Ivanovna had brought it to the dinner not only to prove her credentials but also to silence the "two stuck-up draggletails" had they attended.

With the certificate now circulating among the drunken guests, Katerina Ivanovna seemed unbothered, confident in its authenticity. As her excitement grew, she turned to Sonia, announcing that Sonia would join her in T—— to help bring her vision to life. At this, someone at the far end of the table burst into a loud, mocking guffaw, breaking the flow of her speech. Katerina Ivanovna froze, her flushed face darkening as she turned toward the source of the laughter. The mood at the table, already fragile, hung in the balance.

Though Katerina Ivanovna tried her best to appear indifferent to the snickers and whispers around the room, she raised her voice, as though to drown out the mockery, and began speaking passionately about Sonia. She extolled Sonia's virtues with fervor, proclaiming her "gentleness, patience, devotion, generosity, and good education," as though listing her qualities would silence the doubts and scorn of others. With each word, she grew more animated, tapping Sonia affectionately on the cheek and, in a burst of emotion, kissing her warmly twice.

Sonia's face turned scarlet, and her eyes filled with embarrassment as Katerina Ivanovna's voice quivered with a mixture of pride and sorrow. Suddenly, Katerina Ivanovna broke into tears, her hand trembling as she wiped her face. She excused herself almost immediately, muttering that she was "nervous and silly," that everything had upset her too much. With a shaky laugh, she announced it was time to end the dinner and begin serving tea.

At that moment, Amalia Ivanovna, who had been brooding over her exclusion from the conversation and her perceived slight by Katerina Ivanovna, decided to assert herself. She cleared her throat dramatically and, with great effort, ventured an observation she believed to be both deep and practical. "In the future boarding school," she declared, "attention must very much be paid to die Wäsche, the laundry. And also, it is necessary that the young ladies not novels at night read."

Katerina Ivanovna, visibly weary and exasperated, immediately snapped back. "You know nothing about such matters! You're talking absolute nonsense! The laundry is the business of the laundry maid, not the directress of a high-class boarding school. And as for novel-reading—well, that's just rude of you to even mention! Kindly keep your thoughts to yourself."

Amalia Ivanovna's face turned an alarming shade of red as she struggled to defend herself. "But I meant only good!" she protested, her voice rising in frustration. "I only meant very good for you! And it's long since you pay gold for the lodgings!"

This last remark was too much for Katerina Ivanovna. Her voice cut through the room like a whip. "Good? You call it good when you nagged me about the lodgings even yesterday, while my husband's body was still lying on the table? And now you talk to me about goodness?"

Amalia Ivanovna, stung and desperate to regain some dignity, blurted out her ace. "I invited those ladies, but those ladies are real ladies. They cannot come to a lady who is not a lady!"

The room fell silent for a moment as Katerina Ivanovna's face contorted with fury. She drew herself up to her full height and retorted with icy disdain. "And you, a vulgar slut, think you can judge who is or isn't a lady? What do you know about it?"

Amalia Ivanovna's response came quickly, her indignation now bubbling over. "My Vater aus Berlin was a very, very important man! He always with his hands in pockets went and said 'Poof! Poof!'" In an attempt to mimic her father, she puffed out her cheeks, stuck her hands in her pockets, and strutted clumsily around the room, repeating the sound "Poof! Poof!"

This performance drew loud laughter from the guests, many of whom were only too eager to encourage the escalating drama. But Katerina Ivanovna's temper had reached its boiling point. She raised her voice so that everyone could hear. "Your Vater aus Berlin!" she spat contemptuously. "If you even had a father, which I doubt, he was probably some drunken Petersburg Finn, and likely nothing more than a cook—or worse!"

Amalia Ivanovna's face turned as red as a boiled lobster. "And perhaps you never had a father either!" she shrieked, her voice cracking with rage. "But my Vater aus Berlin wore a long coat and always said 'Poof-poof-poof!'"

Katerina Ivanovna stood abruptly, her expression icy yet dangerous. Her voice was calm but cutting as she declared, "If you dare compare that contemptible wretch of a father to my papa—a colonel, a gentleman—I swear I'll tear that ridiculous cap off your head and trample it underfoot!"

Amalia Ivanovna, now beyond reason, began running around the room, screaming that she was the mistress of the house and that Katerina Ivanovna and her family must leave immediately. She darted toward the table and, for reasons known only to her, began frantically gathering the silver spoons.

The room erupted into chaos. Voices rose, the children began crying, and Sonia rushed to Katerina Ivanovna in an attempt to calm her. But when Amalia Ivanovna shrieked something about Sonia's "yellow ticket," Katerina Ivanovna shoved Sonia aside and lunged at the landlady, determined to carry out her threat.

At that moment, the door swung open, and the commotion froze. Standing in the doorway was Pyotr Petrovitch Luzhin, his face stern and his eyes scanning the room with a cold, calculated gaze. The air seemed to shift as Katerina Ivanovna, her rage momentarily forgotten, turned toward him and rushed forward, her voice trembling with a mix of desperation and relief.

Chapter 3

"Pyotr Petrovitch!" Katerina Ivanovna cried out, her voice trembling with desperation. "Protect me, I beg you—protect me and my family! Make this foolish, insolent woman understand that she cannot treat a lady in misfortune like this! There is a law for such things, and I will go to the governor-general himself if I must! She shall answer for her behavior. Think of my father's hospitality, of his noble name! Protect these helpless orphans who have done nothing to deserve such cruelty!"

Pyotr Petrovitch raised his hand dismissively, a gesture that froze her where she stood. "Allow me, madam. Allow me to speak." His tone was cold, almost detached. "Your esteemed papa, as you are well aware, I never had the honor of knowing." A ripple of muffled laughter broke out among the guests at this remark, which only deepened the severity of Luzhin's expression. "And I do not intend to embroil myself in your endless squabbles with Amalia Ivanovna. I have come here on my own affairs, which are far more pressing, and I wish to have a word with your stepdaughter. Sofya Ivanovna, I believe? Now, kindly step aside."

With that, Pyotr Petrovitch brushed past Katerina Ivanovna, ignoring her stunned expression, and made his way toward the corner of the room where Sonia stood. The room fell silent as his commanding presence, so incongruous with the disheveled gathering, made it clear that something of consequence was about to unfold. Even the faint cries of the children ceased.

Katerina Ivanovna stood frozen, her face pale with shock and disbelief. How could he deny knowing her father, a connection she had woven into her narrative so tightly that even she had begun to believe in its authenticity? But worse than the denial was the tone—dry, dismissive, and menacing. The weight of his presence silenced the room. Even the guests, who had moments earlier been snickering at the chaos, now sat rigid, their eyes fixed on Luzhin.

Raskolnikov, who had been standing near Sonia, stepped aside to allow Luzhin to pass but remained close, his sharp gaze following the man's every movement. From the doorway, Andrey Semyonovitch Lebeziatnikov appeared, hesitant to enter but clearly intrigued by the unfolding scene. He lingered there, his face a mixture of curiosity and bewilderment.

Pyotr Petrovitch surveyed the room, his eyes cold and calculating. "I must apologize for the interruption," he began, addressing the assembly with a tone of forced civility, "but I am here on a matter of some importance. I am, however, glad to find an audience present. Amalia Ivanovna, as the mistress of this house, I must ask you to pay particular attention to what I am about to say."

Turning sharply toward Sonia, he continued, his voice now steely. "Sofya Ivanovna," he said, his formal address making her name sound like an accusation in itself. Sonia, who had already been pale, turned nearly as white as the tablecloth. "Immediately following your visit to my quarters today, I discovered that a one-hundred-rouble note was missing from my table. This occurred in the room of my good friend Mr. Lebeziatnikov, who can corroborate the circumstances. Now, if you have any knowledge of its whereabouts and can explain this matter, I give you my word of honor, and in the presence of these witnesses, that I shall let the issue rest here and now. However, should you fail to clarify the situation, I will have no choice but to resort to very serious measures. In such a case, you will have only yourself to blame."

The silence in the room was deafening. Even the children, who had been fidgeting and whining moments before, sat frozen in wide-eyed stillness. All eyes were on Sonia, who stood as though paralyzed, her lips trembling but unable to form words. Her large, frightened eyes stared at Luzhin, trying to comprehend what she had just heard.

"Well?" Luzhin pressed, his gaze unyielding. "What have you to say?"

Sonia finally managed to whisper, her voice barely audible, "I don't know... I know nothing about it."

"No?" Luzhin repeated, his tone icy and measured. He paused deliberately, letting the silence stretch uncomfortably. "Think carefully, mademoiselle," he said, his voice now adopting a tone of false gentleness, as though he were patiently admonishing a child. "Take a moment to reflect. I am prepared to give you that time. Understand, I would not venture to make such a direct accusation, particularly in the presence of witnesses, if I were not entirely convinced of my claim. I know the consequences of a false or mistaken accusation—consequences which would fall upon me. But consider this: this morning I exchanged several securities, five-percent bonds, for the sum of approximately three thousand roubles. The details are noted in my pocketbook. Upon returning home, I counted the money carefully in Mr. Lebeziatnikov's presence. After tallying two thousand three hundred roubles, I placed the remainder, five hundred roubles, on the table, including three notes of one hundred roubles each."

He paused to let the details sink in before continuing. "At that very moment, you arrived—at my invitation, I might add—and throughout our conversation, you were visibly nervous and embarrassed. You rose from your seat no fewer than three times, as if eager to leave. Mr. Lebeziatnikov can attest to this. I invited you solely to discuss the dire situation of your relative, Katerina Ivanovna, and to propose measures for her assistance—subscriptions, perhaps, or a lottery. You even thanked me with tears in your eyes. Am I wrong, mademoiselle? Did I not hand you a ten-rouble note from the table as a first contribution to this cause? Mr. Lebeziatnikov can confirm this as well."

Luzhin's words were slow, deliberate, and laced with an air of authority. "After you left, I spent ten minutes in conversation with Mr. Lebeziatnikov before returning to the table. To my astonishment, one of the one-hundred-rouble notes was missing. I cannot suspect Mr. Lebeziatnikov, of course. Nor can I have made a mistake in my accounting; I had just completed it before your arrival. Considering your unusual behavior, your repeated attempts to leave, and the fact that your hands lingered on the table during our conversation, I was forced—against my will, I assure you—to entertain a suspicion. I found it cruel but unavoidable."

His voice hardened as he delivered the final blow. "You repay my goodwill and my assistance with this act? Such ingratitude cannot be tolerated. Reflect on your actions, mademoiselle. I give you one last chance to speak before I am compelled to proceed. And remember, I am your best friend in this moment. If you wish to spare yourself greater humiliation, speak now. What do you say?"

The room held its collective breath as all eyes shifted to Sonia, who remained frozen, tears welling in her wide, horrified eyes.

"I have taken nothing," Sonia whispered, her voice trembling with terror. Her hands fumbled in her pocket as she pulled out her handkerchief. "You gave me ten roubles; here it is. Take it." Her trembling fingers untied the corner of the handkerchief, revealing the crumpled ten-rouble note, which she held out to Luzhin.

But Luzhin, his expression icy and unrelenting, refused to take it. "And the hundred roubles?" he pressed, his tone low but weighted with reproach. "Do you not confess to taking it?"

Sonia's eyes darted around the room, searching for a shred of understanding, a hint of sympathy, but found none. Every gaze fixed upon her was cold, stern, or filled with disdain. Even those who had seemed indifferent now looked at her with cruel judgment. Her glance fell on Raskolnikov, who leaned against the wall with his arms crossed, his eyes blazing with an intensity that made her heart pound.

"Good God!" Sonia gasped, her voice breaking.

"Amalia Ivanovna," Luzhin said, turning to the landlady with an air of forced civility, "it seems we must send for the police. I humbly request that you call the porter in the meantime."

Amalia Ivanovna clapped her hands together, her face lighting up with vindication. "Gott der Barmherzige! I knew she was the thief all along!" she exclaimed, her shrill voice slicing through the tense atmosphere.

"You knew it?" Luzhin seized on her words, his voice sharpening. "Then you had prior reason to suspect her? Kindly take note of your statement, Amalia Ivanovna. You have uttered this in the presence of witnesses."

A low murmur of conversation began to rise around the room, a buzz of voices as guests leaned toward one another, whispering, speculating. The commotion grew until Katerina Ivanovna, suddenly realizing the gravity of what had been said, let out a cry of outrage.

"What!" she screamed, her voice breaking through the noise. "You accuse Sonia of stealing? Sonia?" She darted toward Luzhin, her frail body trembling with fury. "Ah, you wretched man, you villain!" she cried. Her thin arms wrapped around Sonia in a fierce, protective embrace, as if shielding her from the accusations hurled at her.

"Sonia! How could you even accept ten roubles from him?" Katerina Ivanovna exclaimed, her tone one of heartbreak mixed with anger. "Foolish girl! Hand it to me! Give it to me this instant—here!" She snatched the note from Sonia's hand and, with trembling fingers, crumpled it into a ball. In a flash, she hurled it directly at Luzhin's face. The note struck him squarely in the eye before falling to the floor.

Amalia Ivanovna scurried forward, stooping to retrieve the fallen note, while Luzhin's composure finally broke. His face darkened with fury as he shouted, "Hold that madwoman!"

At that moment, the doorway filled with new arrivals: several people, including two well-dressed women, peered in curiously, their faces a mix of shock and intrigue.

"Mad? You dare call me mad?" Katerina Ivanovna shrieked, her voice rising with each word. "You are the madman, you pettifogging lawyer! You base, contemptible creature! Sonia—my Sonia—a thief? Do you know her heart? Do you know her sacrifices? She would give her last penny to anyone in need!" Her voice turned shrill with hysterical laughter. "And you!" She turned on Amalia Ivanovna, pointing an accusatory finger. "You call her a thief, too? You, a sausage-eating, trashy Prussian hen in a crinoline! She hasn't left this room, not for a second! She's been sitting here beside me the entire time! Search her! Go on, search her! If you find anything, then I'll answer for it! But if you don't—oh, if you don't—you'll regret this, you hear me?"

The room erupted into chaos. Katerina Ivanovna, now completely frenzied, grabbed Luzhin by his coat and shook him violently. "Search her, I said! Do it now!" she screamed.

Luzhin, clearly flustered but attempting to maintain his composure, muttered, "Very well, if it must be done… but let's have calm, madam. We should wait for the authorities—this is no way to handle such matters."

"Authorities? Nonsense! Search her now!" Katerina Ivanovna demanded. "Sonia, empty your pockets! Show them!"

Sonia, trembling and on the verge of collapse, hesitated but finally turned her pockets inside out. "There! Look! See for yourself!" Katerina Ivanovna shouted triumphantly.

But as Sonia pulled her right pocket out, a small folded piece of paper fluttered to the ground, landing at Luzhin's feet. The room collectively gasped. Luzhin bent down, picked it up between two fingers, and held it aloft for all to see. It was a hundred-rouble note, folded meticulously into eighths.

A cacophony of voices erupted around the room. Amalia Ivanovna shrieked, "Thief! Police! Police! To Siberia with them!"

Sonia stood frozen, her face drained of color. The world seemed to close in around her. Then, as if from nowhere, her face turned a deep red, and she let out a heart-wrenching cry. "No! It wasn't me! I didn't take it! I don't know how it got there!" Her voice cracked with anguish as she buried her face in her hands.

Katerina Ivanovna immediately wrapped Sonia in her arms, cradling her like a child. "Sonia! My darling Sonia! I don't believe it, you hear me? I don't believe it!" She rocked Sonia back and forth, her own tears falling unchecked. "These fools don't know you! You'd give the very clothes off your back to help someone in need! How could they think this of you? Fools, all of them!"

Her voice broke as she turned on the room. "And you, all of you, standing there, doing nothing! How dare you accuse her? She sold herself for us—for my children, to save us from starvation! And this is the thanks she gets? This is the justice she deserves?" Her voice rose to a wail. "Oh, husband! See what's happening now? Is this what you left us for? Is this your memorial dinner?"

The raw emotion in Katerina Ivanovna's voice silenced the room. Even Luzhin appeared momentarily taken aback. After a brief pause, he cleared his throat and said, "Madam, this matter does not implicate you. You have shown your innocence by turning out her pockets yourself. I am willing to show compassion, to forgive her in light of her circumstances. However," he turned to Sonia, his tone colder, "this must serve as a lesson. Such behavior cannot go unacknowledged. Let this disgrace be a warning for the future."

But his words only served to deepen the sorrow in the room as Katerina Ivanovna tightened her embrace around Sonia, weeping and shaking her head in disbelief.

Pyotr Petrovitch stole a glance at Raskolnikov, and their eyes locked for a brief, incendiary moment. Raskolnikov's gaze burned with such intensity that it seemed it might physically scorch Luzhin. Though shaken, Luzhin quickly averted his eyes, attempting to mask his discomfort. Meanwhile, Katerina Ivanovna remained oblivious to the tension between the two men, entirely consumed by her frantic embrace of Sonia. She kissed her stepdaughter's pale cheeks repeatedly, her frail frame trembling with equal parts despair and defiance. The children had joined in, clinging to Sonia as though to shield her from the scorn of the room. Polenka, her little face swollen with tears, buried it against Sonia's shoulder, her sobs shaking her tiny body.

The room was heavy with emotion when a loud, resolute voice cut through the charged silence.

"How vile!"

All heads turned toward the doorway, where Lebeziatnikov stood with his short-sighted eyes blazing. His gaze locked onto Luzhin with such ferocity that even the brazen lawyer flinched.

"What vileness!" Lebeziatnikov repeated, his voice trembling with righteous anger as he stepped into the room.

Pyotr Petrovitch visibly started, a reaction noted by everyone present and later remembered with satisfaction. He stammered, his composure faltering. "What... what are you talking about?"

"I mean that you, Pyotr Petrovitch, are a scoundrel—a slanderer! That's what I mean!" Lebeziatnikov declared, his voice rising in pitch and force. His thin frame seemed to quiver with the intensity of his emotions.

Raskolnikov's sharp eyes flickered toward Lebeziatnikov, watching him intently, as though weighing and analyzing each word. The room grew so silent that even the faintest shuffle of feet could be heard. Luzhin appeared momentarily dumbfounded, his usual smugness replaced by a flash of panic.

"Are you mad?" Luzhin finally managed, his voice a mixture of incredulity and anger. "Have you lost your senses? What absurdity are you spouting now?"

"I am in full possession of my senses," Lebeziatnikov shot back, his face flushing with righteous fury. "But you, sir, are a vile liar and a hypocrite! I heard everything—everything! And though it took me a moment to comprehend the full extent of your depravity, I see it clearly now. What you've done defies all logic, all decency."

"What on earth are you accusing me of?" Luzhin demanded, though his voice had lost much of its strength. "This is lunacy! Speak plainly, or are you drunk?"

"Drunk? Me?" Lebeziatnikov's voice quivered with indignation. "Unlike you, I never touch vodka—it's against my convictions. And let me tell you, I saw it all with my own eyes. You, Pyotr Petrovitch, you placed that hundred-rouble note in Sonia's pocket yourself!"

The accusation hit like a thunderclap, sending a wave of shock through the room. Gasps and murmurs rippled among the onlookers.

"You're raving!" Luzhin snapped, though the pallor spreading across his face betrayed his fear. "She herself admitted that I gave her only ten roubles. How could I have possibly slipped her a hundred-rouble note?"

"I saw it with my own eyes," Lebeziatnikov insisted, his voice cracking but resolute. "I was standing nearby when you said goodbye to her. You took her hand with one of yours, and with the other, your left hand, you slipped the folded note into her pocket. I thought at first that you were acting out of generosity, but now I see your true intent!"

"This is madness! Lies!" Luzhin retorted, his voice rising in pitch as he gestured wildly. "You're short-sighted! How could you possibly see such a thing from where you were standing?"

"I may be short-sighted, but I am not blind!" Lebeziatnikov shot back, stepping closer to Luzhin. "I noticed it clearly, even from a distance, because I had already seen you take the note from the table earlier when you handed her the ten roubles. You held onto that hundred-rouble note the entire time, transferring it between your hands like you didn't know what to do with it. And when you escorted her to the door, that's when you slipped it into her pocket. I saw it all!"

His voice rang out with conviction, and the murmurs in the room grew louder. Several guests began to close in on Luzhin, their faces hardening with suspicion. The tide of the room had turned, and even those who had earlier supported Luzhin now eyed him with distrust.

Katerina Ivanovna, who had been silent in shock, suddenly sprang into action. She flung herself at Lebeziatnikov, grabbing his hands. "I was wrong about you!" she cried. "You are her protector! Her savior! God Himself must have sent you to defend her! Protect my Sonia— she is an orphan! She has no one else!"

Her desperate pleas only intensified the crowd's murmurs. Amalia Ivanovna's shrill voice cut through the cacophony, demanding order, but her cries were drowned out by the rising voices of outrage. All eyes were now on Luzhin, who stood frozen, pale, and visibly shaken as the walls seemed to close in around him.

Katerina Ivanovna, trembling and overwhelmed, sank to her knees before Luzhin without realizing the depth of her humiliation. Her voice, faint and choked, carried a desperation that matched her broken posture. Luzhin, however, was unmoved. Instead, he erupted in anger, his voice booming as he gestured wildly to emphasize his words.

"This is sheer nonsense!" he shouted, his face flushing red with fury. "What kind of absurdity are you spouting now? 'You had an idea,' 'you noticed,'—what does all of this amount to? You're suggesting I deliberately slipped the money into her pocket in secret? Why would I? For what purpose? What on earth have I to gain from such a ridiculous act?"

"What purpose?" Lebeziatnikov echoed, his voice rising, fueled by indignation. "That's precisely what I cannot fathom! But I know what I saw. You put that note into her pocket—there's no mistaking it. And yes, I wondered why you did it secretly, but I chalked it up to your discomfort with openly displaying your so-called generosity in front of me, knowing my principles. Perhaps you were ashamed because I disapprove of private charity that offers no real, structural solution to societal problems. Or maybe you were hoping she'd find it later and come back to thank you—another one of those theatrical 'benevolent' acts some people enjoy staging. I even thought, perhaps, you wanted to avoid her gratitude entirely, to ensure, as the saying goes, that your right hand wouldn't know what the left was doing."

Lebeziatnikov's words came in a torrent, almost breathless, his face flushed with passion. "At the time," he continued, "I decided not to embarrass you by acknowledging what I'd seen, but another thought struck me: what if she lost the money before realizing it was there? That's why I planned to pull her aside and tell her what you'd done. But before I could, I got sidetracked, first going to Madame Kobilatnikov's to deliver the 'General Treatise on the Positive Method.' Then I came here, only to find this chaos. Now, I ask you all—could I have formed all these ideas if I hadn't clearly seen him slip that note into her pocket?"

By the time Lebeziatnikov finished, his face was drenched in sweat, his voice hoarse from exertion. Though his phrasing had been clumsy and his sentences tangled, the conviction in his tone left no room for doubt. The room, previously chaotic, was now silent except for the quiet murmurs of those processing his testimony.

Luzhin, visibly flustered, tried to regain his composure. "What rubbish! What utter drivel! You're just imagining things, having these so-called 'ideas' and dreams," he snapped, though his voice lacked its usual confidence. "You're lying! This is nothing but slander, driven by spite because I didn't entertain your foolish, godless, and socially dangerous ideas!"

But this retort fell flat. The onlookers, far from being swayed by his words, began murmuring with disapproval.

"Ah, now you resort to insults and deflection!" Lebeziatnikov retorted sharply. "Well, then, call the police! I'll swear to it before any court. I saw what I saw, and there's no denying it. But what I can't understand is why a man like you would stoop to such a despicable act. It's beyond comprehension—truly pitiful!"

At this point, Raskolnikov, who had remained silent until now, stepped forward with an air of quiet authority. His composed demeanor immediately drew everyone's attention.

"I can explain why he did it," Raskolnikov said firmly, his voice steady. "And I am willing to swear to my explanation if necessary."

His calm yet commanding tone silenced the room. Everyone turned to him, sensing that the mystery was about to be unraveled.

"This entire situation has been suspicious from the start," Raskolnikov began, addressing both Lebeziatnikov and the assembled crowd. "I suspected from the very beginning that there was an ulterior motive behind all of this—a scheme carefully orchestrated by this man here," he gestured toward Luzhin, "to serve his own twisted ends. Allow me to lay out the facts clearly for everyone to understand."

He paused, scanning the room to ensure he had everyone's attention. Then, he began recounting the chain of events with meticulous detail.

"Not long ago, this man, Pyotr Petrovitch Luzhin, was engaged to my sister, Avdotya Romanovna Raskolnikov. When he arrived in Petersburg, we quarreled during our very first meeting. The argument escalated to the point where I forced him to leave my room. There are witnesses who can attest to this. What I didn't know at the time was that he was staying here, in the same lodging. That very day, he saw me give money to Katerina Ivanovna to help cover the costs of her late husband's funeral."

Raskolnikov's voice grew sharper, his words laced with contempt. "Luzhin then wrote a vile note to my mother, accusing me of squandering their money—not on Katerina Ivanovna, but on Sofya Semyonovna. He even made vile insinuations about her character. His intention was clear: to sow discord between me and my family, to make them believe I was wasting their hard-earned savings on 'unworthy' causes."

He turned back to the crowd, his voice growing louder and more impassioned. "Last night, during a confrontation in front of my family, I exposed his lies. I declared, in his presence, that I had given the money to Katerina Ivanovna, not to Sofya Semyonovna, and that I had never even met her before. In his fury, Luzhin insulted my mother and sister and was finally thrown out of the house."

Raskolnikov's piercing gaze fixed on Luzhin, who looked increasingly cornered. "Now, think about this: if he had succeeded today in framing Sofya Semyonovna as a thief, he would have proven his earlier accusations. He would have shown my family that he was justified in condemning her, justified in his suspicions about me. He hoped this would alienate me from my family and restore him to their good graces. And, of course, he wanted revenge against me, knowing how much I value Sofya Semyonovna's dignity and well-being. That's the truth of it. That's why he did it. There is no other explanation!"

The room erupted into murmurs once again, this time tinged with outrage. The tide had definitely turned against Luzhin. He stood frozen, his face pale, his mouth opening and closing as though searching for a rebuttal but finding none. Raskolnikov's revelation had stripped him bare, exposing his malice and deceit for all to see.

Raskolnikov's words were delivered with such clarity and determination that even the frequent interruptions from the agitated audience could not diminish their impact. Every phrase, every argument he laid out, carried weight, and his tone of conviction held the crowd spellbound. His firm demeanor and unyielding gaze left no doubt about his sincerity. The room, electrified by his speech, buzzed with a mixture of astonishment and murmurs of agreement.

"Yes, yes, that's exactly it!" Lebeziatnikov exclaimed with unrestrained excitement, his face alight with the thrill of revelation. "He asked me the moment Sofya Semyonovna came into the room whether you were here—whether I'd seen you among Katerina Ivanovna's guests! He even pulled me aside, whispering at the window. It was critical to him that you were here! That explains everything!"

Pyotr Petrovitch Luzhin, standing pale and stiff, managed a contemptuous smile but said nothing. The color had drained from his face, and it was evident that he was searching for a way to extricate himself from the increasingly hostile situation. Escaping, however, seemed impossible. Admitting defeat would mean confirming the accusations against him. Adding to his predicament was the chaotic fervor of the room—an uproar fueled by drink and indignation.

The commissariat clerk, barely grasping the full scope of the situation, added to the noise with loud, incoherent threats, while the three Polish lodgers, brimming with righteous fury, hurled curses in their native tongue, calling Luzhin a "lajdak" and making threatening gestures.

Sonia stood rooted to the spot, her face pale, her wide eyes fixed on Raskolnikov as though he were her only lifeline. She barely seemed to breathe, her entire being focused on his every word. Katerina Ivanovna, visibly drained and gasping for air, leaned heavily against the wall, while Amalia Ivanovna stood frozen, her mouth agape, struggling to comprehend what was happening. She appeared as confused as she was bewildered by Luzhin's sudden downfall.

Raskolnikov attempted to speak again, his voice rising above the cacophony, but the frenzied crowd surrounding Luzhin drowned him out with jeers and threats. Luzhin, though visibly shaken, quickly resorted to a defiant sneer. His tone turned insolent, his words dripping with venom.

"Step aside, gentlemen!" Luzhin demanded, pushing through the crowd. "Don't obstruct me! I'll not stand for this. Your drunken threats are meaningless, and you're fools to think they'll amount to anything. Mark my words, justice will prevail. The courts will see the truth, unlike you lot, blinded by your idiotic prejudices and inebriated fantasies!"

He straightened his coat with a sharp tug, his pale complexion belying his feigned bravado. "As for you," he spat, glaring at Lebeziatnikov, "don't think I'll forget your slanderous lies. You'll pay for this insolence!"

But as Luzhin shoved his way toward the door, the commissariat clerk, now thoroughly drunk, picked up a glass from the table and hurled it at him. The glass missed its target and instead shattered against Amalia Ivanovna, who let out a piercing scream before retaliating with a torrent of insults. In the chaos, the clerk stumbled and fell heavily under the table, eliciting laughter from some of the spectators.

Luzhin, seizing the opportunity, slipped away to his room. Within half an hour, he had packed his belongings and left the house, his disgrace evident in his hurried departure.

Sonia, meanwhile, was overwhelmed. She had long harbored a belief that her submissive, gentle nature could shield her from life's cruelties, but the events of the day shattered that illusion. Even though her innocence had been proven, the sheer magnitude of the wrong done to her left her shaken to her core. Her first wave of relief was soon replaced by a profound anguish, a reminder of how easily she could be targeted and humiliated.

Tears streamed down her face as she tried to compose herself, but the emotional toll was too great. Overcome with hysteria, she fled the room shortly after Luzhin's departure, seeking the solitude of her own space to process what had just occurred.

The remaining chaos escalated when Amalia Ivanovna, still reeling from the glass incident and emboldened by her rage, turned her fury on Katerina Ivanovna. "Out! Out of my lodgings! Get out this instant!" she shrieked, grabbing whatever belongings of Katerina Ivanovna's she could find and tossing them onto the floor.

Katerina Ivanovna, pale and trembling, struggled to her feet. Though weak and gasping for breath, her indignation gave her a fleeting strength. "What? You dare? On the day of my husband's funeral, you throw us out? After all we've endured? After I shared my bread and salt with you? And with my poor orphans—where will we go?" Her voice cracked with despair, and her thin chest heaved with the effort of speaking.

"Is there no justice left in this world?" she cried, her eyes blazing with a sudden, wild energy. "We'll see! There is law, there is justice, and I'll find it! Just wait, you wretched woman, just wait! Polenka, stay here with the children. I'll return, even if I must throw myself at the Tsar's feet! We'll see whether there's justice on this earth!"

With that, she swept out of the room, leaving the stunned audience behind. The air remained thick with tension, and though laughter and murmurs filled the space, a sense of unease lingered as the fallout from the day's events hung heavy over everyone.

Wrapping herself tightly in the green shawl Marmeladov had once mentioned to Raskolnikov, Katerina Ivanovna pushed through the chaotic crowd of drunken and disorganized lodgers who were still swarming in the room. Her face was pale, streaked with tears, and her movements were frantic, driven by a singular and hazy purpose: to find justice, wherever it might be found. She stumbled onto the street, wailing incoherently, her words merging into the sounds of the bustling city. Her breath came in ragged gasps, and her thin frame seemed barely capable of carrying her forward, but an unyielding determination kept her moving.

Behind her, in the tumultuous room she had fled, Polenka sat trembling on a battered trunk in the corner. The two younger children clung to her desperately, their small arms wound tightly around her neck. Polenka's face was pale, her wide eyes darting nervously between the arguing adults and the door through which her mother had disappeared. She tried to quiet her younger siblings, who were whimpering softly, but her own fear made her voice tremble. She clutched them closer, whispering words of comfort she scarcely believed herself, waiting anxiously for her mother's return.

Amalia Ivanovna, meanwhile, was consumed by her own fury. Her face was flushed, her movements jerky and erratic as she stormed about the room. She screamed insults into the air, lamenting her misfortune and accusing everyone of betrayal. Her anger manifested in a whirlwind of destruction: plates were hurled onto the floor, chairs were knocked over, and anything within her reach became a target for her uncontained rage. Her shrieks mingled with the din of the other lodgers, creating a cacophony that seemed to shake the very walls of the crumbling house.

The lodgers themselves were caught up in the chaos, each reacting in their own way to the spectacle that had just unfolded. Some were trying, in slurred voices, to recount the events to each other, embellishing the details as they saw fit. Others were openly mocking the situation, their laughter cutting through the discord like a blade. Quarrels broke out among a few, the heated words escalating into curses and the occasional shove. Still others, too drunk to comprehend or care about what had happened, began to sing loudly, their off-key voices adding a surreal layer to the already overwhelming noise.

Amid the disorder, Raskolnikov stood silently, observing the pandemonium around him. His expression was inscrutable, though his mind was clearly working. The disarray of the room, the desperation of the children, and the futile rage of Amalia Ivanovna seemed to hold no sway over him. He appeared detached from it all, as though he were already elsewhere, mentally and emotionally.

At last, as if coming to a decision, he turned sharply toward the door. "Now it's time for me to leave," he thought, his lips curling into a faint, almost sardonic smile. "Well, Sofya Semyonovna, let's see what you have to say now."

Without a backward glance, he strode out into the street, his steps purposeful as he made his way toward Sonia's lodgings. Behind him, the chaotic sounds of the house began to fade, replaced by the muffled hum of the city—a sound as indifferent and relentless as the thoughts swirling in his mind.

Chapter 4

Raskolnikov had thrown himself vigorously into defending Sonia against Luzhin, even though his own heart was weighed down by an almost unbearable burden of horror and anguish. The turmoil of the morning had been relentless, but strangely, he found some fleeting relief in the act of championing Sonia, as though the shift in focus allowed him a temporary escape from his own torment. His strong personal connection to Sonia only deepened his resolve, driving him to stand up for her with a passion that surprised even himself. Yet beneath this outward strength, he was acutely aware of the monumental task ahead of him: the impending conversation with Sonia, during which he would have to confess that he was the one who had killed Lizaveta. The thought gnawed at him, and though it loomed heavily, he kept pushing it aside, unable or unwilling to fully confront its weight.

As he left Katerina Ivanovna's chaotic lodgings, triumphant over Luzhin and still caught up in the adrenaline of the confrontation, he called out defiantly, "Well, Sofya Semyonovna, we shall see what you'll say now!" At that moment, his energy was high, his spirit bolstered by the victory. But by the time he reached the familiar threshold of

Sonia's humble lodging, his mood shifted abruptly. A wave of fear and impotence swept over him, and he found himself hesitating, his hand hovering near the door. A strange question formed in his mind: "Must I tell her who killed Lizaveta?" It was absurd, he knew, because the answer was already clear. There was no escaping the need to confess— it was a compulsion he could neither deny nor delay. Yet the inevitability of it filled him with a crushing sense of helplessness.

Desperate to end his turmoil, he pushed the door open and stepped inside. Sonia sat at the table, her elbows propped up and her face buried in her hands. At the sight of him, she rose quickly and moved to meet him, as though she had been waiting for his arrival. Her face was a mixture of anxiety and relief.

"What would have become of me but for you?" she exclaimed, her words tumbling out in a rush. It was clear she had been longing to say this, holding onto it as a lifeline.

Raskolnikov walked to the table and sank into the chair she had just vacated. Sonia stood before him, only a couple of steps away, just as she had the previous day. The moment felt weighted, heavy with unspoken truths.

"Well, Sonia?" he began, his voice trembling despite himself. "Did you understand what Luzhin meant about your 'social position and the habits associated with it'?"

Her face fell, a flicker of distress crossing her features.

"Please," she interrupted, her tone almost pleading. "Don't talk to me like you did yesterday. Not now. There's already so much misery— there's no need to add more."

She attempted a weak smile, as if afraid he might take her words as a reproach, eager to soften them.

"I shouldn't have left there," she added hastily. "What's happening now? I wanted to go back right away, but I thought... I thought you might come."

Raskolnikov told her, with a hint of irritation, that Amalia Ivanovna was evicting Katerina Ivanovna and her children, and that Katerina Ivanovna herself had rushed off somewhere, determined to seek justice.

"My God!" Sonia cried, leaping up and grabbing her cape. "We have to go to her immediately—"

"It's always the same with you!" Raskolnikov snapped, his irritation boiling over. "You never think of yourself—only them! Just sit here for a moment, with me."

"But... Katerina Ivanovna..." Sonia began anxiously.

"You won't lose her," he interrupted curtly. "She'll come looking for you herself when she realizes you're not with her. If you go chasing after her now, you'll only give her another reason to blame you later."

Sonia hesitated, torn between her worry for Katerina Ivanovna and her obedience to Raskolnikov's request. Slowly, she sat back down, her hands twisting in her lap as she waited in tense silence.

Raskolnikov, meanwhile, stared at the floor, lost in thought. The weight of his confession loomed over him, and the room grew heavy with the quiet, each passing second thick with unspoken fears and the anticipation of what was to come.

Raskolnikov began, his tone distant and almost mechanical, as though he were speaking to himself as much as to Sonia. "This time, Luzhin didn't press charges against you," he said without looking directly at her. "But if he had wanted to—if it had suited his plans—he could have sent you to prison. If not for Lebeziatnikov and me, what then? What would have happened?"

Sonia nodded faintly, her voice barely above a whisper. "Yes," she murmured. "I understand... yes."

"But what if I hadn't been there? And it was pure chance that Lebeziatnikov came in at the right moment. A complete accident."

Sonia remained silent, her gaze fixed somewhere distant. The weight of his words pressed down on her, but she didn't respond.

"And if you had gone to prison?" Raskolnikov continued, his tone more insistent. "Do you remember what I said to you yesterday?"

Sonia still did not answer. She seemed lost in thought, her distress written plainly on her face. Raskolnikov waited for her response, but none came.

"I thought you'd shout at me again," he said with a forced laugh. "'Don't speak of it, leave off!' But no, nothing? Silent again?" He waited a moment longer, then added, "We can't just sit here without saying anything. Let's talk about something. I have a question for you, Sonia—a kind of moral puzzle, if you will."

She glanced at him uneasily, sensing an edge in his voice that made her uncomfortable. He went on without waiting for her acknowledgment. "Imagine this, Sonia: suppose you knew all of Luzhin's intentions beforehand. Imagine you knew with absolute certainty that he would destroy Katerina Ivanovna, ruin her children, and even bring you down with them, dragging Polenka into the same abyss. Now imagine it all rested on your decision—Luzhin or Katerina Ivanovna. One of them must die. Who would you choose?"

The question was chilling, and Sonia looked at him with growing unease. There was something strange in the way he approached it, as though circling an idea he dared not name outright.

"I thought you might ask something like that," she said at last, her voice trembling slightly. She studied him closely, trying to understand where his question was leading.

"I'm sure you did," he replied, a faint smile tugging at his lips, though it lacked warmth. "But how would you answer it?"

"Why do you ask about things that could never happen?" Sonia asked, her reluctance evident in her tone. "It's pointless."

"So, you'd let Luzhin live and keep doing his wickedness? You can't even decide that?"

"I don't know the will of God," she protested. "Why do you ask such impossible questions? How could I decide who lives and who dies? Who am I to judge such things?"

"If you bring God into it, then nothing can be done at all," Raskolnikov muttered bitterly. His frustration was evident, but it was directed inward as much as outward.

"Why don't you just tell me what you're trying to say?" Sonia cried, her distress spilling over. "Why do you twist everything into riddles and puzzles? Did you come here just to torment me?"

She couldn't hold back her tears any longer. Her sobs filled the room, and Raskolnikov watched her with a heavy heart, his own emotions a storm of guilt, frustration, and anguish. Five long minutes passed in silence, broken only by her quiet weeping.

"You're right, Sonia," he said finally, his voice soft and subdued. The arrogant defiance that had colored his tone earlier was gone, replaced by a quiet weariness. "You're absolutely right. Yesterday I told you I didn't come to ask for forgiveness, and yet here I am, practically begging for it." He paused, struggling for the right words. "I said what I did about Luzhin and Providence for my own sake, to justify myself... but really, I was asking for forgiveness."

He tried to muster a smile, but it came out weak and broken, more a grimace than an expression of warmth. Lowering his head, he hid his face in his hands, overcome with emotion.

And then, suddenly, an inexplicable feeling coursed through him—a fleeting surge of bitterness, almost hatred, directed at Sonia. It shocked him, like a flash of lightning through his soul. He looked up, startled, his eyes locking with hers. Her gaze met his, full of unease, but also of unwavering love. In an instant, the bitterness melted away, replaced by a hollow ache. He realized the hatred had not been real; it was a phantom of his own turmoil, misinterpreted for something it was not.

Hiding his face in his hands again, he tried to steady himself, but the weight of the moment crushed him. He rose abruptly from his chair, pale and trembling, and crossed the room to sit on Sonia's bed. He moved as though on autopilot, his body responding to impulses he could neither control nor understand.

"What's wrong?" Sonia asked, her voice filled with fear as she moved closer to him. She reached out tentatively, her concern growing with every passing second.

He couldn't answer. Words failed him completely. This was not how he had imagined confessing to her; nothing about this moment resembled the plan he had formed in his mind. Yet here it was, unfolding uncontrollably.

Sonia sat down beside him, her heart pounding in her chest. She waited in silence, her wide, tearful eyes fixed on him, pleading for an explanation. But he could only stare back at her, his lips trembling, unable to form the words.

Finally, he whispered, as if to himself, "Why did I come here? Was it just to torture you? What am I doing, Sonia?"

Sonia's voice quivered as she muttered, "Oh, how you are suffering!" Her eyes were wide with distress as she stared intently at him, trying to grasp the depth of his torment.

"It's all nonsense... meaningless," Raskolnikov said suddenly, his voice brittle. A fleeting smile crossed his lips, pale and fragile, lasting only a moment. "Do you remember what I said yesterday? What I meant to tell you?"

Sonia nodded uneasily, her breath quickening as she waited for him to continue. Her heart pounded in anticipation, and yet she dreaded the answer.

"I told you yesterday," he went on slowly, "that perhaps I was saying goodbye forever, but if I came back today, I'd tell you... tell you who killed Lizaveta."

At his words, Sonia's body began to tremble. She couldn't hide the terror spreading through her as she clutched at the edge of the table for support.

"Well, here I am," he said with a faint, unnatural calmness, "to tell you."

Sonia's lips moved soundlessly for a moment before she managed to whisper, "Then... then you meant it? Yesterday... you really meant it?" Her voice barely carried across the small space between them.

"How do you know?" she asked suddenly, her eyes wide with confusion and fear, as though clinging to one last thread of disbelief.

"I know," he answered, his voice steady but cold.

There was a pause—a long, agonizing pause that seemed to stretch into eternity. Sonia's face turned pale, her breaths becoming shallow and rapid. "Have they found him?" she asked timidly, her voice breaking.

"No."

"Then... how do you know about it?" she repeated, her voice now barely audible, trembling as she spoke.

Raskolnikov turned to her and fixed her with a penetrating stare, his eyes dark and unrelenting. "Guess," he said with that same weak, distorted smile that seemed to mock his own suffering.

A visible shudder passed over her entire body. She stared at him, wide-eyed, unable to comprehend. "But you... why do you frighten me like this?" she murmured, her voice trembling and uncertain, trying to smile as if to dismiss the absurdity of it all. Her attempt at levity only made her terror more evident.

"I must be a close friend of his to know," Raskolnikov continued, his voice quieter but with an eerie intensity. His eyes remained locked on hers, and there was no trace of escape in his gaze. "He... he didn't mean to kill Lizaveta. It wasn't planned. He killed her... by accident. He went there to kill the old woman, to kill her when she was alone, but Lizaveta came in... and so... he killed her too."

The room seemed to freeze as his words hung in the air. The seconds ticked by like hours. Sonia didn't speak. Her lips trembled, but no sound came out. Her gaze never left his, her eyes pleading for him to say something—anything—that would contradict what he had just revealed.

"You can't guess, then?" he asked, the question almost childlike, as though he were throwing himself from a precipice.

"N-no..." Sonia whispered, her voice faltering.

"Take a good look," he urged, his tone pressing her toward the inevitable.

As he said this, Raskolnikov suddenly felt an icy terror grip his heart. He stared at Sonia, and in her frightened, trembling face, he saw another—Lizaveta's. The memory of that moment flashed vividly before him: Lizaveta shrinking against the wall, her hands raised defensively, her eyes filled with a helpless, childlike fear. And now Sonia looked at him the same way—helpless, terrified, her hand instinctively moving forward, pressing faintly against his chest as though to keep him at bay. Slowly, as if in a trance, she rose from the bed, stepping back while keeping her eyes fixed on him, unable to look away.

Her terror was infectious. Raskolnikov felt it creep into his own soul. His face mirrored hers, his expression growing pale and strained, his lips curling into an almost childlike, fearful smile.

"Have you guessed?" he whispered, his voice hoarse and broken.

And then it happened—an awful, guttural wail broke free from Sonia's chest, a sound filled with anguish and disbelief. She collapsed onto the bed, burying her face in the pillows as though she could block out the truth. But almost immediately, she sprang to her feet, moved toward him with startling swiftness, and seized his hands in hers. Her thin fingers gripped him tightly as her tear-filled eyes searched his face for some trace of denial, some fragment of hope that it wasn't true. But there was none. She knew. She could see it plainly.

"Stop, Sonia, enough," he begged miserably, unable to bear the weight of her despair. "Don't torture me."

Sonia staggered back, wringing her hands in anguish. She paced the room for a moment before sinking back onto the bed beside him, her shoulder nearly brushing his. Then, as if struck by lightning, she cried out and fell to her knees before him, clutching at his arms.

"What have you done? What have you done to yourself?" she cried in despair. Her voice cracked with sorrow, and suddenly, without thinking, she threw her arms around his neck and held him as if she could shield him from the world.

Raskolnikov leaned away from her, his face drawn into a mournful smile. "You're a strange girl, Sonia," he said softly. "You kiss me, you embrace me... after I've told you that. You don't even think about what you're doing."

"No one... no one in the world is as unhappy as you!" she cried in a frenzy, her voice raw with emotion. Tears streamed down her face as she clung to him. "Oh, how miserable you are!"

Something stirred in Raskolnikov's heart—a feeling he hadn't experienced in what felt like an eternity. It softened him, washing over his tormented soul like a wave. Tears welled up in his own eyes, hanging on his lashes.

"Then you won't leave me, Sonia?" he asked, his voice trembling with something close to hope.

"Never!" she cried passionately. "No, never! I will follow you anywhere. Oh, my God, why didn't I know you sooner? Why didn't you come to me before?"

"Well, here I am now," he murmured quietly.

"Yes, now... now we're together. What do we do now? Together," she repeated, her voice breaking as she embraced him once more. "Even to Siberia, I'll follow you to Siberia!"

At the mention of Siberia, Raskolnikov recoiled slightly, his expression shifting. A faint, almost mocking smile played on his lips. "Maybe I'm not ready for Siberia just yet, Sonia," he said dryly.

Her eyes widened in confusion, and for a moment, her joy was eclipsed by the shadow of what he had confessed. Again, the enormity of his crime overwhelmed her. Questions she hadn't dared to ask began to surface. How? Why? What had driven him to such an act? The man she saw before her—a tortured soul, yes, but also a man she had come to care for deeply—seemed so at odds with the thought of a cold-blooded murderer.

"Why... why did you do it?" she whispered, her voice trembling as she struggled to comprehend. "What does it mean? How could you... how could you bring yourself to it?"

Raskolnikov turned away, his face weary. "Leave it, Sonia," he muttered. "There's no use in asking why."

Raskolnikov sat with his hands pressed together, his fingers twitching slightly, as though he were trying to grasp some intangible thought. He spoke again, almost to himself, his voice tinged with irony and something deeper, a hollow despair.

"I don't know... I haven't yet decided whether to take that money or not," he said, as if weighing an invisible scale in his mind. Suddenly, he seemed to startle himself out of his musings, giving a brief, sardonic smile. "Ah, what silly things I'm saying, don't you think?"

Sonia watched him with a mixture of worry and confusion. A fleeting thought passed through her mind—could he be mad? But just as quickly, she pushed it aside. No, there was something else here, something she couldn't quite understand. She stayed silent, waiting for him to continue, her heart heavy with foreboding.

"Do you know, Sonia," he said suddenly, his voice carrying a strange conviction, "let me tell you this: if I'd killed just because I was hungry..." He paused, emphasizing each word, his eyes locked on hers with an intensity that made her shiver. "If it were only that, I'd be happy now. You have to believe me!"

He leaned forward suddenly, his tone shifting to one of almost desperate frustration. "What does it matter to you," he cried, "if I were to confess that I've done wrong? What do you gain from such a stupid triumph over me? Is that what you want? Ah, Sonia, was that why I came to you today?"

Sonia opened her mouth to speak, but her voice faltered, and no words came. She shook her head slightly, her eyes brimming with an unbearable sadness.

"I asked you yesterday to go with me because you're all I have left," he continued after a moment, his voice quieter but no less intense.

"Go where?" Sonia whispered timidly, as though afraid of the answer.

"Not to steal and not to murder, don't worry," he replied with a bitter smile. "We're so different, you and I... And you know, Sonia, it's only now—only at this moment—that I understand where I was asking you to go with me yesterday. When I said it then, I didn't even know. I just knew I needed you not to leave me. You won't leave me, will you, Sonia?"

Without hesitation, she reached out and squeezed his hand tightly.

"And why... why did I tell you? Why did I burden you with this?" he cried suddenly, his voice breaking as he looked at her with raw anguish. "You're expecting an explanation, aren't you? I can see it— you're sitting there waiting for me to make sense of it all. But what can I say, Sonia? What can I possibly say that will make you understand and not hurt you even more? You're crying, you're holding me, and why? Because I couldn't bear my own burden, so I've come to throw it onto you! To make you suffer too, so that I might feel some relief. And yet... and yet, you can still love someone as wretched as me?"

"But aren't you suffering too?" Sonia cried out, her voice filled with a mixture of heartbreak and desperation.

Raskolnikov's hardened expression softened briefly as a wave of emotion surged through him. For an instant, his heart seemed to thaw, and he looked at her almost tenderly.

"Sonia, I have a bad heart. That's something you need to know— it explains a lot," he said softly, his tone almost apologetic. "I came here because of that. Because I'm a coward, a selfish, miserable coward. There are men who wouldn't have come... but I did. And now I've dragged you into my darkness. But never mind that, I need to speak now, even though I don't know how to begin."

He fell silent for a moment, his head bowed as if in prayer or despair. Then, almost as if speaking to himself, he muttered, "We're so different, you and I. Why did I come? I'll never forgive myself for coming."

"No, no, it's good that you came," Sonia exclaimed, her voice trembling with emotion. "It's better that I know—it's far better!"

Raskolnikov looked at her, his anguish etched deeply into his face. "What if it really was that?" he murmured, his voice distant. "Yes... that's exactly what it was. I wanted to become a Napoleon. That's why I killed her. Do you understand now?"

"N-no," Sonia stammered, her voice a whisper. "But please, please speak. I'll understand... I'll understand somehow."

"You think you'll understand?" He gave a short, bitter laugh. "Let's see, then." He leaned back and stared at the ceiling for a moment, lost in thought. Finally, he spoke again, his words measured and deliberate.

"It was like this: one day, I asked myself a question—what if Napoleon, instead of his grand wars and heroic deeds, had started his career with something as small and grotesque as murdering an old pawnbroker? What if there was no other way for him to achieve greatness? Would he have done it? Would he have hesitated, even for a moment? Would he have felt shame or guilt? And then, suddenly, I realized—he wouldn't have. He wouldn't have thought twice about it. That realization... it changed everything for me."

He paused, his eyes fixed on hers as though daring her to judge him. "And so I followed his example. I stopped thinking about it, stopped worrying about the morality of it. I just... did it."

He laughed, a hollow, joyless sound. "Do you think it's funny, Sonia? Because that's the funniest part of all. That's exactly how it was."

Sonia's face grew even paler. "You'd better tell me straight," she whispered, her voice trembling. "Without these... examples."

Her words hung in the air between them, a desperate plea for clarity amid the chaos of his confession.

Raskolnikov turned toward Sonia, his face pale and strained, his eyes filled with a strange mixture of sorrow and resolve. He reached for her hands and held them lightly, as though afraid his touch might crush something fragile.

"You're right, Sonia. Of course, you're right again," he began, his voice low and uneven. "All of this, everything I've been saying—it's nonsense, or at least most of it is. Just talk. You see, you know what my mother has been through. She has almost nothing, and my sister, even with her education, was forced into that dreadful existence as a governess. They pinned all their hopes on me. I was supposed to be the one to lift them out of it, but I couldn't even stay at the university. I had to leave because I couldn't support myself. And even if I had stayed—if I had scraped through for another ten or twelve years— what would I have become? A teacher? A clerk? Living on a meager thousand roubles a year? By then, my mother would be worn down completely—crushed by her grief and her sacrifices. And my sister..." He faltered, his voice catching for a moment. "Well, my sister might not have survived it. Maybe she would have suffered even worse."

He paused, his gaze distant, as though watching some grim scene play out in his mind. "How could I accept that fate? To stand by while they suffered and struggled, just to end up burying them? To then carry on, burdening myself with others—taking on a wife, children— only to leave them as destitute as I was? No, Sonia. I couldn't let that happen."

His grip on her hands tightened slightly as he continued, his voice more resolved. "So, I decided to act. I thought, if I could take that old woman's money, I could use it to finish my education. I wouldn't need to rely on my mother anymore. I could support myself and even provide for her and my sister, at least for a while. And then I'd build something new for myself—a career, a life of independence, all on a grander scale. That was my plan. That's what I told myself."

He slumped forward slightly, his head bowing under the weight of his words. "Of course, killing her was wrong. I know that now. I knew it then. But..." His voice trailed off, his exhaustion overtaking him.

Sonia stared at him, her eyes wide with disbelief and anguish. "Oh, but that's not it, that can't be it!" she cried, her voice trembling. "How could anyone think that way? How could you justify—"

"I know, I know," Raskolnikov interrupted, lifting his head to look at her with a hollow smile. "It doesn't make sense, does it? But it's the truth. That's what I thought. That's why I did it."

Sonia shook her head vigorously, as though trying to dispel his words from her mind. "No, no, that's not the truth! It can't be! How could you call a human being... a louse?"

Raskolnikov's smile grew bitter. "I told myself she was nothing but a louse. A useless, loathsome, harmful creature. That's what I told myself to make it easier."

"But she wasn't a louse! She was a person!" Sonia exclaimed, her voice breaking.

"I know that now," he admitted, his tone shifting to one of quiet despair. "I knew it even then. But I tried to make myself believe otherwise. I tried to convince myself it was justified. But it was nonsense, Sonia. All of it. And you're right to say so."

He leaned back, his face contorted with pain. "You see, I haven't spoken to anyone like this in so long. My head—it feels like it's about to split open. I've been locked up with these thoughts for so long, they've turned into something monstrous."

Sonia watched him, her heart breaking as she saw the torment etched into every line of his face. He spoke again, his voice rising slightly as though driven by some newfound urgency.

"Perhaps, Sonia," he said, his tone growing more feverish, "it wasn't about my mother or my sister at all. Maybe it was something else entirely. Maybe I'm vain, or envious, or just plain cruel. Maybe I have a streak of madness running through me. After all, they've hinted at that, haven't they?" He let out a short, mirthless laugh. "I told you I left the university because I couldn't afford it, but that wasn't the whole truth. My mother would have found a way to send me the money. I could have taken on work, like Razumihin does. But I didn't. I refused to."

He paused, his voice dropping to a near whisper. "I stayed in that miserable little room, Sonia. You've seen it. That suffocating garret. It felt like it was crushing my soul. And yet, I wouldn't leave. I wouldn't even try. I just lay there, doing nothing. I wouldn't eat unless it was brought to me. I wouldn't ask for anything. I just... thought."

"What did you think about?" Sonia asked, her voice trembling.

"About how pointless it all was," he said, his eyes fixed on some invisible point in the distance. "About how nothing ever changes, and how people will always be the same. I realized that the only ones who succeed, who truly matter, are the ones who dare to take what they want. The ones who are bold enough to step over the rest. That's the way of the world, Sonia. And I thought... I thought I could be one of them."

He looked at her then, his eyes blazing with a mix of defiance and despair. "I wanted to prove it, Sonia. To prove that I had the courage to step over the line. That's why I did it. Not for my mother, or my sister, or anyone else. Just to prove that I could."

Sonia's tears flowed freely now, her heart aching for the broken man before her. She reached out, placing a trembling hand on his shoulder. "Oh, Raskolnikov," she whispered, her voice thick with emotion. "What have you done to yourself?"

Sonia clasped her hands tightly, her face pale and her voice trembling with desperation. "Oh, hush, hush," she cried out, as though trying to block out his words. "You turned away from God, and now God has smitten you, given you over to the devil!"

Raskolnikov leaned forward, his face shadowed by a grim smile. "Then, Sonia, when I used to lie there in the dark, thinking of all of this, and it began to seem clear to me—was that the devil tempting me?"

"Hush!" she exclaimed again, her voice rising in anguish. "Don't laugh, don't blaspheme! You don't understand, you don't see it! Oh, God, how can he not understand?"

"Sonia, I am not laughing," Raskolnikov said, his tone growing darker, more insistent. "I know it was the devil. I know it now, just as I knew it then. Don't you see? I have thought about this endlessly, turned it over and over in my mind, whispered it to myself, argued every single point. Lying there in the dark, I dissected it all, piece by piece, until I was sick of it, sick of myself. I wanted to stop thinking, Sonia! I wanted to forget and start anew. But I couldn't. And don't think for a moment that I went into this blindly or like some fool. No, Sonia, I went into it with my eyes wide open, deliberately, like a so-called wise man. And that—" his voice broke, trembling—"that was my true destruction."

Sonia stood frozen, her wide eyes locked on his as he continued. "I knew from the start, Sonia, that if I had to ask myself whether I had the right to seize power, it meant I didn't have it. And if I had to question whether a human being could be reduced to a louse, then for me, it was already false—though perhaps for someone else, someone who could march toward their goal without hesitation, it might have been different. That wasn't me, Sonia! I knew it then, and I know it now. But still, I went on. I wanted to kill—not with justifications, not with excuses—I wanted to kill purely for myself, for the sake of killing. I didn't even want to lie to myself about it."

Sonia shook her head, her lips moving as though to speak, but no sound came out.

"I didn't do it for money, Sonia!" he went on with rising agitation. "It wasn't about helping my mother or gaining power, or any of the other things I tried to tell myself. I killed her for myself, to see if I could. To find out, once and for all, whether I was just like everyone else, just a trembling creature—or whether I had the right to step over, the right to take what I wanted. Do you see? That's all it was—just to see if I had the right."

"To kill? To have the right to kill?" Sonia gasped, her voice barely audible, her hands clasped tightly in front of her chest.

"Ah, Sonia!" he snapped impatiently, his face contorting in anguish. He opened his mouth as if to retort but fell into a bitter silence instead. Finally, after a long pause, he spoke again, his voice hollow. "It wasn't about the old woman. It was never about her. I killed myself, Sonia, not her. I destroyed myself that day. Crushed myself completely, forever. And it wasn't me who killed her—it was the devil. The devil killed her through me." He suddenly buried his face in his hands and let out a groan that seemed to echo with the weight of his torment. "Enough, Sonia, enough! Let me be!"

Sonia let out a wail of anguish, her hands trembling. "What suffering!" she cried, her voice breaking. "What terrible, terrible suffering! What will you do now? What's left for you?"

Raskolnikov lifted his head, his face a mask of despair. "What am I to do now?" he asked, his voice devoid of hope. "Tell me, Sonia, what am I to do?"

She jumped to her feet, her eyes burning with a sudden intensity. "Stand up!" she commanded, her voice trembling but resolute. She grabbed his shoulders and pulled him to his feet. "Go at once, right now, to the crossroads. Bow down, kiss the earth that you have defiled, and then bow to the world, to every man, and cry out, 'I am a murderer!' Only then will God send you life again. Will you go? Will you?"

He stared at her, his face a mixture of astonishment and confusion. "You mean Siberia, Sonia?" he asked, his tone dull. "You're telling me I should give myself up?"

"Suffer and atone for your sin," she replied, her voice firm and full of conviction. "That's what you must do."

"No, Sonia. I'm not going to them," he said flatly, shaking his head.

"But how will you live now?" she cried, her voice breaking again. "What will you live for? How can you go on like this? How can you even speak to your mother? What will happen to her now? What will become of you?"

He shook his head again, his voice soft but resolute. "Don't be a child, Sonia. What wrong have I done to them? Why should I go to them? What can I possibly say to them?" He gave a bitter smile. "That I killed her but didn't even dare to take the money? That I hid it under a stone like some fool? They'd laugh at me, Sonia. Call me a coward and a fool. They wouldn't understand. They don't deserve to understand."

He looked at her, his eyes filled with a strange mixture of pity and defiance. "Why should I go to them? I won't. Don't be a child, Sonia."

"It will be too much for you to bear, far too much!" Sonia repeated, her voice trembling with despair as she extended her hands toward him in a plea. Her eyes, red from weeping, searched his face for any sign of hope or resolve.

"Perhaps I've been unfair to myself," Raskolnikov muttered gloomily, his gaze fixed on the floor. He seemed to be arguing internally, his tone laced with self-reproach yet tinged with defiance. "Perhaps, after all, I am a man and not merely a louse, and maybe I've been too hasty in condemning myself. I'll make another fight for it."

A faint, almost mocking smile crept onto his lips, a flicker of haughty determination that seemed to defy both himself and the world.

"What a burden to bear!" Sonia whispered, her voice breaking with sorrow. "And for your whole life—your entire life!"

"I'll get used to it," he replied grimly, his tone sharp with finality. He spoke as if resigning himself to a bitter truth. After a pause, his face hardened, and he began again, his voice lower but steadier. "Listen," he said, "stop crying now. It's time to talk about the facts. I came here to tell you something important—the police are on my trail."

"Ach!" Sonia gasped, her hands flying to her mouth as her face paled in terror.

"Why do you cry out like that?" he asked irritably, his expression darkening. "You wanted me to go to Siberia, didn't you? And now you're frightened? Let me explain: I am not giving myself up. I've decided to fight, and they won't catch me. They don't have any solid evidence. Yesterday, I thought I was finished, that it was all over for me—but today, things look better. Every fact they have against me can be explained in more than one way. I've learned my lesson, Sonia, and I'll use it to my advantage."

She listened in trembling silence as he went on. "Yes, they'll likely arrest me, perhaps even today. If not for one small twist of fate, they would have already done so. But it doesn't matter. They'll let me out again because they can't prove anything. There's no solid case against me, and there never will be. I give you my word on that. But I wanted you to know where things stand. I'll find a way to explain all of this to my mother and sister so they won't be too frightened. My sister's future is secure now, I believe, and I'll ensure my mother's is as well. That's all I wanted to say. Be cautious, Sonia."

He paused, a flicker of something softer crossing his face. "Will you come and see me in prison, if it comes to that?"

"Oh, I will, I will!" Sonia exclaimed, her voice shaking with emotion as she clutched at his sleeve.

For a long moment, they sat side by side, their expressions weighed down by despair and exhaustion. They seemed like two castaways washed up on a desolate shore, united by their shared misery yet utterly alone in their thoughts. As Raskolnikov looked at Sonia, he felt the full force of her love for him—a love so pure, so unconditional, that it suddenly seemed like a heavy burden. A strange, almost painful sensation welled up inside him, a feeling of unhappiness that he hadn't expected.

"Sonia," he said quietly, his tone subdued, "it might be better if you didn't come to see me in prison after all."

Sonia didn't respond immediately. Tears streamed down her face, and she simply sat there, crying softly. Several minutes passed in silence before she looked up at him.

"Do you have a cross?" she asked suddenly, her voice trembling but earnest.

Raskolnikov blinked, momentarily confused by the question. "No," he said after a pause. "Of course not."

"Here, take this one," Sonia said quickly, reaching into her pocket and pulling out a small cross made of cypress wood. Her hands trembled as she held it out to him. "I have another, a copper one that belonged to Lizaveta. We exchanged them once—I gave her my little ikon, and she gave me her cross. I'll wear Lizaveta's now, and you take this one. It's mine. It's precious to me. Please, take it. We'll go through this together, and we'll carry our cross together."

Raskolnikov hesitated, then extended his hand to take it, but he stopped short, pulling back at the last moment. "Not now, Sonia. Not yet," he said gently, trying to ease the disappointment on her face. "Later, when the time comes."

"Yes, later," she agreed, nodding quickly as if trying to convince herself. "When you go to face your suffering, I'll put it on you. We'll pray together, and then we'll go forward together."

At that moment, there was a sudden knock at the door—three sharp, deliberate taps. Both of them froze, and Sonia's eyes widened in alarm.

"Sofya Semyonovna, may I come in?" came a familiar and polite voice from the other side.

Sonia leapt to her feet, rushing to the door, her heart racing. When she opened it, the flaxen-haired figure of Mr. Lebeziatnikov appeared in the doorway, his expression both anxious and inquisitive.

Chapter 5

Lebeziatnikov appeared visibly unsettled as he entered, his movements hurried and his expression uneasy.

"I came looking for you, Sofya Semyonovna," he began, his voice carrying a mix of urgency and awkwardness. "Excuse me... I thought you'd be here," he added, briefly glancing at Raskolnikov. "Not that I intended to interrupt anything... I just thought..." His words faltered for a moment before he suddenly blurted out, "Katerina Ivanovna has gone out of her mind."

Sonia gasped sharply, her hand flying to her mouth as her eyes widened in alarm.

"At least it seems so," Lebeziatnikov continued hastily, his words spilling out in a disorganized rush. "We're not entirely sure what to do with her. She came back in such a state—she might have been turned out of somewhere, possibly even beaten... though I can't confirm it. Anyway, she went to your father's old superior, hoping for help, but he wasn't at home; he was dining with some other general. And can you imagine? She actually went to that general's residence, insisted on seeing him, and even managed to have him brought out from dinner. She's utterly relentless, you know. What happened next is what you'd expect: she was thrown out, naturally. But according to her, she hurled insults at him and even threw something in his direction before leaving. It's a wonder she wasn't arrested on the spot."

Sonia let out a small, horrified cry, but Lebeziatnikov, oblivious, pressed on.

"Now she's telling everyone about it, including Amalia Ivanovna, but she's completely incoherent—screaming, crying, flinging herself about. She keeps declaring that, since everyone has abandoned her, she'll take the children out onto the streets to beg. She's planning to perform with a barrel organ, make the children sing and dance, and go daily to that general's window to show off what she calls 'well-born children, whose father was an official.' She's even started beating the children in her hysteria, trying to teach them songs like 'My Village' and make them practice dancing. Poor Polenka and Lida are terrified. She's ripping apart what little clothes they have, fashioning costumes for them, and she's determined to carry a tin basin to rattle for money. She won't listen to reason—she's beyond control. It's sheer madness!"

Before Lebeziatnikov could continue, Sonia, who had been trembling with each word, sprang into action. She grabbed her cloak and hat, throwing them on as she bolted for the door.

"I must go!" she cried, her voice thick with desperation.

Raskolnikov followed her without hesitation, and Lebeziatnikov trailed behind, muttering anxiously as they hurried into the street.

"She's undoubtedly gone mad," Lebeziatnikov said to Raskolnikov, lowering his voice but still speaking with conviction. "I didn't want to alarm Sofya Semyonovna, so I said it 'seemed like it,' but there's no question about it. I've read that consumption can sometimes lead to mental disturbances, particularly when the disease progresses to the brain. It's a pity I don't have a stronger background in medicine—I tried to explain it to her, but, of course, she wouldn't listen."

"Did you actually try discussing the medical details with her?" Raskolnikov asked, his tone edged with disbelief.

"Well, not precisely about the tubercles themselves," Lebeziatnikov admitted. "She wouldn't have understood anyway. But logically speaking, if one convinces a person that they have no reason to cry, shouldn't they stop crying? That's how I see it. Don't you agree?"

"Life would be too simple if that were true," Raskolnikov replied dryly.

"Of course," Lebeziatnikov conceded. "It might be difficult for someone in Katerina Ivanovna's state to grasp such logic. Still, in Paris, they've been experimenting with treating insanity through reason alone. One professor even argued that insanity stems from logical errors rather than physical ailments. He believed you could cure a madman by pointing out their mistakes, though he also used cold water treatments, so it's unclear which method actually worked...."

But Raskolnikov had already stopped listening. As they reached his building, he nodded briefly to Lebeziatnikov and entered without a word. Lebeziatnikov, startled, stood for a moment, then hurried off.

Once inside his room, Raskolnikov stopped abruptly, standing in the center of the dim, oppressive space. He glanced around at the familiar surroundings: the peeling wallpaper, the dusty furniture, the dismal sofa. The stillness was punctuated by a repetitive, rhythmic knocking from the yard outside. He moved to the window, rising on tiptoe to peer out, but the yard was empty. His gaze wandered to the neighboring house, where limp geraniums sat in pots on the windowsills, and linens hung lifelessly out to dry. He turned away, retreating to the sofa and sinking onto it heavily.

Never before had he felt so utterly and terrifyingly alone.

He thought of Sonia and felt a pang of guilt mixed with an inexplicable bitterness. Why had he gone to her at all? To beg for her pity? To drag her into his torment? What right did he have to ruin her life, to burden her with his despair? The thought filled him with disgust for himself.

"I'll stay alone," he resolved, his voice barely a whisper. "She won't come to the prison."

But as the minutes ticked by, a strange idea surfaced in his mind, unexpected and unsettling. He sat up, a faint, almost sardonic smile curving his lips.

"Perhaps Siberia wouldn't be so bad after all," he thought.

He sat there in a fog of vague and chaotic thoughts, unable to discern how much time had passed, when suddenly the door creaked open. Startled, he looked up to see Dounia standing in the doorway. She hesitated for a moment, gazing at him with a mix of sorrow and determination, before stepping inside and taking a seat in the same chair she had occupied the day before. Her expression was soft, thoughtful, devoid of judgment.

"Don't be angry, brother," she said gently. "I've only come for a moment."

Her eyes, bright with emotion, met his, and in that instant, he understood—she had come to him with love.

Dounia's visit had left Raskolnikov in a whirlwind of conflicted emotions, but he barely had time to process them when he found himself swept into another maelstrom of chaos. As he wandered through the streets aimlessly, his mind heavy with the weight of despair and exhaustion, a familiar voice startled him from his brooding.

"Raskolnikov! There you are!" Lebeziatnikov came running up to him, his face flushed and his gestures frantic. "It's Katerina Ivanovna—she's completely lost her mind!"

Raskolnikov turned sharply toward him, his heart sinking at the words.

"What happened?" he asked, his voice low but urgent.

"She's carried out her wild plan!" Lebeziatnikov exclaimed breathlessly. "She's taken the children out into the streets, just as she threatened. We've been searching for them—Sofya Semyonovna and I—but now we've found them. She's out there clapping her hands like a madwoman, making the children sing and dance at the crossroads! They're crying, Raskolnikov, all of them, and a crowd of fools is gathering to watch. You must come at once!"

Without waiting for an explanation, Raskolnikov set off after Lebeziatnikov, his pace quickening with every step. The mention of Sonia's distress only heightened his sense of urgency.

"They're by the canal, near the bridge," Lebeziatnikov continued, hurrying alongside him. "It's chaos! Katerina Ivanovna is utterly deranged. She's shouting and coughing, trying to coax or force the children to perform. And the crowd—oh, the crowd! They're gawking at her as if it's some kind of spectacle. If this keeps up, the police will surely get involved."

When they reached the canal bank, Raskolnikov saw the scene that Lebeziatnikov had described. A small crowd of onlookers, mostly children and idlers, had gathered, drawn by the commotion. In the center of it all was Katerina Ivanovna, her gaunt figure moving with feverish energy. She wore the same tattered green shawl and the misshapen straw hat, now further crushed and askew, giving her a wild, almost tragic appearance. Her face, ravaged by illness and desperation, was flushed and glistening with sweat as she clapped her hands sharply, commanding the children to dance.

"Dance, Kolya! Sing, Lida!" she cried hoarsely, her voice breaking from exertion. "Polenka, sing louder! Let them all see what you're capable of! Stand up straight, Lida! Don't shuffle your feet, Kolya! You must look proper—show them your worth!"

The children, pale and terrified, stumbled through their steps. Kolya, dressed in a makeshift "Turkish" costume with a red and white turban, tripped over his oversized shoes, while Lida clutched the hem of her ragged dress, adorned with an old feather that seemed ready to fall off at any moment. Polenka, dressed as she always was, stood close to her mother, her wide eyes filled with tears as she looked from Katerina Ivanovna to the jeering crowd. Sonia stood nearby, her hands clasped in desperation, pleading with Katerina Ivanovna to stop.

"Please, Katerina Ivanovna, come home," Sonia begged, her voice trembling with emotion. "This isn't the way—it won't help. You're hurting yourself and the children!"

But Katerina Ivanovna was deaf to reason. She whirled around to face Sonia, her expression one of fierce determination and indignation.

"Home? Back to that German harpy's lair?" she spat, her voice rising with hysteria. "Never! I'll show them all! Let them see what they've done to us! An honorable man's family begging in the streets! I'll take the children to the Tsar himself—he is merciful, he will protect us! The whole city shall know of our suffering!"

As she spoke, she broke into a fit of coughing, doubling over and clutching her chest. Sonia rushed forward, but Katerina Ivanovna waved her off, her movements jerky and erratic.

Raskolnikov pushed through the crowd, finally catching Katerina Ivanovna's attention. Her face lit up with a mix of recognition and frantic relief.

"Rodion Romanovitch!" she cried, rushing to him and grasping his arm. "Tell this foolish girl that I'm right! Explain to her that we must show the world our plight! Even organ-grinders earn their keep, and we are of noble blood! These children—these poor, innocent children—must be seen! The Tsar will not turn away from us, you'll see. But these stupid children—oh, how will I make them understand?"

"Katerina Ivanovna, please," Raskolnikov said firmly, though his voice was tinged with compassion. "This isn't the way. The children are frightened. You're hurting them—and yourself."

She looked at him as though his words were incomprehensible, her face twisting with a mixture of defiance and despair.

"Hurting them? I'm saving them!" she shouted. "Saving them from starvation, from obscurity! They'll remember their father's name, they'll know his honor!"

As if on cue, Kolya began to sob, his small frame shaking as he clung to his sister. Lida buried her face in Polenka's skirt, and even Polenka, the most composed of them, looked ready to collapse from fear and exhaustion.

Sonia moved closer, her voice breaking with urgency and pain. "Katerina Ivanovna, please stop this. Think of the children. They need rest—they need you."

For a moment, Katerina Ivanovna faltered, her eyes darting between Sonia, Raskolnikov, and the weeping children. But the madness in her expression did not fade.

"No," she muttered, shaking her head. "No, we can't stop now. They must see us—they must see!"

Raskolnikov turned to Sonia, their eyes meeting in a shared understanding of the desperate fragility before them. Together, they stepped forward, ready to intervene before the situation spiraled further out of control.

Katerina Ivanovna, her thin, trembling hands gesturing wildly, barely paused for breath as she continued her torrent of words. Her voice, though strained and hoarse from her incessant coughing, carried a fierce determination. She pointed frantically at the crying children, her eyes glistening with both frustration and tears.

Raskolnikov stepped closer, attempting to reason with her. "Katerina Ivanovna," he said firmly but gently, "this is no way for you to be seen in public. You aspire to establish a boarding school—surely you see how inappropriate this is?"

At his words, Katerina Ivanovna erupted into a bitter laugh that quickly dissolved into a racking cough. "A boarding school? Ha! That dream has crumbled into dust, Rodion Romanovitch!" she cried, her voice breaking. "Everyone has abandoned us. Everyone! Even that despicable general—do you know what I did? I threw an inkpot at him! It was sitting there on his desk, just waiting for me. I signed my name, hurled it straight at him, and ran! Oh, the scoundrels, the vile scoundrels!"

She stopped, panting heavily, her hand pressed against her chest. For a moment, her expression softened as she glanced at Sonia. "But no matter. I'll take care of the children myself. I won't bow down to anyone anymore. Sonia has suffered enough for all of us."

She turned abruptly to Polenka, her frail figure trembling with a mixture of agitation and determination. "How much have you got, Polenka? Show me!" she demanded, her tone urgent. Polenka hesitated, then shyly held out her small hand, revealing only a few coins.

"Two farthings!" Katerina Ivanovna exclaimed in despair. "Two farthings? Is that all these wretches have given us? And yet they stand there, mocking us, sticking out their tongues!" She glared fiercely at a man in the crowd who dared to chuckle. "And you, Kolya," she snapped, rounding on the boy, "why must you be so stupid? You make everything so difficult!"

Turning back to Polenka, she straightened her shoulders and adopted a haughty tone. "Speak to me in French, Polenka! Parlez-moi français! Show them that you are not some common beggar child, but of good family, a well-bred young lady!"

Polenka looked nervously at her mother, then at the crowd. Tears welled up in her eyes as she struggled to form the words her mother expected of her.

Katerina Ivanovna waved a hand dismissively. "No matter," she muttered, her mind already racing ahead. "We must decide on a song. Something genteel, something that will prove we are not like ordinary street performers. 'My Village' won't do—everyone sings that. No, we need something refined."

Her eyes lit up suddenly as an idea struck her. "Ah! We'll sing in French! That will show them we are of noble blood. Polenka, do you remember 'Cinq sous'? I taught it to you. Yes, yes, that's perfect. And Kolya, put your hands on your hips! Stand properly, Lida, don't slouch! We must rehearse—this is only a practice run. Later, we'll go to Nevsky Prospect, where the refined people gather."

With that, she began clapping her hands rhythmically, her hoarse voice attempting to lead the children in song.

"Cinq sous, cinq sous, Pour monter notre ménage..." she sang, but her voice broke almost immediately, and she doubled over in a coughing fit. Gasping for air, she gestured impatiently at Polenka. "Straighten your dress! It's falling off your shoulders. I knew we should have cut the bodice longer—Sonia, this is your fault with your advice to make it shorter. Look at her now—completely deformed!"

The children, overwhelmed and trembling, could barely respond. Kolya's lip quivered as he glanced nervously at the crowd, while Lida clung to Polenka, her small face streaked with tears.

Just then, a policeman pushed his way through the crowd, his expression stern. Katerina Ivanovna stopped mid-sentence, her eyes narrowing as she noticed his approach. But before she could say anything, a gentleman in an overcoat stepped forward. He was middle-aged, with an air of quiet authority, and a medal glinted at his neck. Without a word, he extended a green three-rouble note to her.

Katerina Ivanovna's demeanor shifted instantly. She straightened up, her face lighting up with a mixture of gratitude and pride. Taking the money, she gave the man a dignified bow.

"Thank you, kind sir," she said with a lofty air. "You see, Polenka, there are still noble and honorable people in this world." She turned back to the gentleman. "These children, sir—they are of good family, left destitute by cruel misfortune. Their late father served faithfully and with distinction, and yet we find ourselves reduced to this!"

The policeman, however, interrupted her. "Madam, you're creating a disturbance. This isn't allowed in the streets."

"A disturbance?" Katerina Ivanovna shot back indignantly. "What difference is this from an organ grinder playing on the corner? I've seen far worse and never heard of a license being required for grief!"

"Madam, please calm yourself," the gentleman interjected gently. "Allow me to escort you home. This is no place for you or the children."

For a moment, Katerina Ivanovna looked ready to argue, but her breath caught in another violent cough, and her energy seemed to wane. Sonia rushed to her side, whispering softly and placing a steadying hand on her arm. At last, Katerina Ivanovna allowed herself to be led away, her steps faltering but her head still held high. Behind her, the crowd slowly began to disperse, murmuring about the strange and tragic spectacle they had just witnessed.

Katerina Ivanovna's cries filled the air as she turned frantically toward the gentleman who had intervened. Her voice, strained with both fear and despair, rose above the murmurs of the gathering crowd. "Honoured sir, you don't understand! We're going to the Nevsky! Sonia! Where is Sonia? She's crying again! What is happening to everyone? Kolya, Lida—where are they running off to now?" she called out, her tone trembling with panic as she noticed the children darting away.

Kolya and Lida, terrified by the tumultuous crowd and their mother's erratic behavior, clung to one another for courage. The sight of the policeman moving toward them only heightened their fear, and in an instant, they bolted, their small forms weaving through the legs of the onlookers.

"Stop them! Bring them back!" Katerina Ivanovna screamed, her frail body jolting into motion as she stumbled after them, her arms flailing. "Ungrateful, foolish children! It's all for you—everything I do is for you!" Her cries grew fainter as she struggled to keep pace, her energy waning with every step. Sonia and Polenka hurried after her, their faces pale with worry.

Then, it happened. Katerina Ivanovna tripped, her weakened legs giving way beneath her. She fell hard to the cobblestones, her hands catching against the pavement in an instinctive attempt to break her fall. Sonia reached her first, her voice breaking in a cry of alarm. "She's fallen! Oh, she's hurt! Katerina Ivanovna—there's blood!"

The crowd surged forward, a collective gasp rippling through the bystanders as they pressed closer, craning their necks to see. Raskolnikov and Lebeziatnikov pushed their way to the front, arriving just as Sonia bent over Katerina Ivanovna, her hands trembling as she tried to assess the injury. The blood wasn't from a scrape or a wound as Sonia had initially thought. Instead, it came from her chest—a dark, alarming stain spreading across her dress.

"It's her lungs," murmured the official who had been assisting. His tone was grave. "I've seen this before—consumption. The blood can come suddenly, and it's severe when it does. She's dying."

Katerina Ivanovna's breathing was shallow and erratic, her frail body trembling as her lips moved faintly, forming incoherent words. Sonia looked up, her wide, desperate eyes meeting those of the policeman. "Please, we must get her inside. I live nearby—just there!" She pointed to a modest house not far from where they stood. "Help me—help me get her there!"

With the official's guidance and the policeman's begrudging assistance, Katerina Ivanovna was carefully lifted and carried to Sonia's small, sparsely furnished room. The bed was hastily cleared, and Katerina Ivanovna was laid upon it, her head propped up with pillows as she coughed weakly, her face pale and damp with sweat. The bleeding had momentarily stopped, but her labored breathing and glassy eyes told a grim story.

Polenka, her arms wrapped protectively around Kolya and Lida, led the children into the room, their small bodies shaking with silent sobs. From the adjoining rooms, curious neighbors peered in—wide-eyed children and nervous adults who whispered among themselves but didn't step forward. Among them was Svidrigaïlov, who lingered in the doorway, his expression unreadable as he watched the unfolding scene.

Katerina Ivanovna's eyes fluttered open. Her gaze moved sluggishly across the room until it landed on Sonia, who knelt beside her, gently wiping her brow. A faint smile touched Katerina Ivanovna's lips, though it was tinged with both sadness and regret. "Sonia," she rasped, her voice so soft that those nearby had to lean closer to catch her words. "This is your room. I've never been here before."

Her gaze shifted to the children. "Polenka... Kolya... Lida... come here. My darlings, my little ones." They approached hesitantly, their faces streaked with tears. She reached out weakly, her trembling hands brushing over their heads. "Sonia, I leave them to you now. I've done all I could. I... I've failed them. The ball is over."

Her body convulsed with another coughing fit, and fresh blood appeared at the corners of her lips. Sonia cried out, gripping Katerina Ivanovna's hand tightly as though willing her to hold on. "No, no, you mustn't say that! Please, rest—don't talk."

But Katerina Ivanovna's delirium had taken hold. Her words grew scattered, her voice rising and falling as she spoke of forgotten songs, long-lost days of happiness, and fantastical plans that would never come to fruition. She muttered phrases in French, barked out commands for the children to dance, and then, in a hoarse, broken voice, attempted to sing.

"In the heat of midday... in the vale of Dagestan..." she gasped, her breath catching painfully. Her voice cracked, and she clutched at her chest, her eyes wide with terror. "With lead... in my breast..."

Sonia wrapped her arms around Katerina Ivanovna, holding her close as her words faded into silence. The room fell still except for the ragged sound of Katerina Ivanovna's breathing, which slowed with each passing moment. The children huddled together, their sobs muffled as they clung to Polenka's skirts.

It was Sonia who broke the silence, her voice trembling but resolute. "We need a priest," she whispered, looking around the room, her tear-streaked face filled with urgency. "Please, someone—fetch a priest."

Katerina Ivanovna suddenly cried out with a piercing, heart-wrenching wail that startled everyone in the room. "Your excellency!" she screamed, her voice trembling with desperation, her tears streaming uncontrollably. "Protect the orphans! You were their father's guest... you dined under his roof... you may even call it aristocratic hospitality!" Her words were punctuated by gasps for breath, as if she were pouring out every last ounce of her strength.

For a brief moment, a flicker of awareness seemed to return to her pale, sunken eyes. She looked around the room, bewildered, her gaze moving from face to face as though searching for something familiar. Then, with a start, her expression softened into one of recognition and fragile relief.

"Sonia... Sonia!" she murmured faintly, her tone filled with both wonder and tenderness. It was as though she had only just noticed Sonia's presence. "Sonia darling, you're here, too?" Her voice quivered, and a fleeting, fragile smile touched her lips.

They lifted her frail body slightly, trying to make her comfortable, but she suddenly cried out with a bitter despair that seemed to rise from the depths of her soul. "Enough! It's over! Farewell, poor thing! I am done for! Broken!" Her voice cracked, and her head fell back heavily onto the pillow as though the weight of her words had drained the last of her strength.

Once again, she slipped into unconsciousness, but this time it was different. The room seemed to grow heavier with silence as her breaths became labored and shallow. Her face, yellowed and gaunt, sank into the pillow. Her mouth fell slightly open, her body tensed for a brief moment, and her leg jerked in a final, spasmodic movement. Then came a deep, ragged sigh—a sigh that seemed to echo through the small, crowded room. And with that, she was gone.

Sonia flung herself onto the lifeless body, wrapping her thin arms tightly around Katerina Ivanovna as though trying to hold her soul in place. Her head rested against the woman's wasted chest, and she remained motionless, frozen in grief. Polenka fell to her knees at her mother's feet, clutching them with trembling hands and pressing desperate, tear-soaked kisses to the worn fabric of her dress. She wept violently, her small frame shaking with each sob.

Kolya and Lida, still dressed in their makeshift costumes, stood a few steps away. Though they could not fully grasp what had just occurred, the atmosphere of despair was enough to pierce their innocent hearts. They clung to one another, their tiny hands gripping each other's shoulders for comfort. Their eyes, wide with terror and confusion, locked as if searching for answers. Then, all at once, they both let out piercing cries, their wails joining the sorrowful cacophony that filled the room.

On the bed, beside Katerina Ivanovna's still form, lay an unexpected sight—a crumpled certificate of merit. Its presence there, so poignant and absurd, caught Raskolnikov's eye. The piece of paper, a symbol of faded pride and unfulfilled dreams, rested near her pillow as though mocking the life that had just ended. He turned away from the scene, unable to bear the sight any longer, and walked silently to the window.

Lebeziatnikov, who had been hovering uncertainly nearby, stepped forward. "She's gone," he said softly, his voice breaking the oppressive silence.

Raskolnikov nodded slightly but did not look back. At that moment, Svidrigaïlov approached, his expression calm but unreadable. "Rodion Romanovitch, may I have a word?" he said smoothly. His presence seemed out of place amid the grief, yet strangely fitting in its eeriness.

Lebeziatnikov, sensing the need for privacy, stepped aside. Svidrigaïlov gestured for Raskolnikov to move further from the bed, and the two men retreated to a quieter corner of the room.

"I will take care of everything," Svidrigaïlov said, his tone both casual and firm. "The funeral, the arrangements—it will all be managed. You know, money is no concern for me, as I've told you before. I will also see to it that these poor children—Polenka, Kolya, and Lida—are placed in a proper orphanage. I'll ensure they're provided for, with fifteen hundred roubles set aside for each of them when they come of age. Sofya Semyonovna will have no need to worry about them. And her, too—I'll help her rise out of this mess. She's a good soul, after all, isn't she?"

Raskolnikov frowned, his expression darkening. "What is your reason for such... generosity?" he asked, suspicion thick in his voice.

Svidrigaïlov chuckled, his tone light and amused. "Oh, you sceptic! Must there always be a motive beyond simple humanity? That poor woman over there," he said, nodding toward Katerina Ivanovna's body, "she wasn't just some worthless old pawnbroker, was she? And as for Polenka and the others—what would become of them without help? No, Rodion Romanovitch, I'm merely acting out of decency."

But his words sent a chill through Raskolnikov. There was something unsettling in the way Svidrigaïlov spoke, something that made Raskolnikov's stomach churn. The phrases he used, so eerily similar to those Raskolnikov himself had once uttered, seemed to echo back at him mockingly. His face turned pale, and he took an involuntary step back.

"How do you know?" Raskolnikov whispered, his voice barely audible, his breath catching in his throat.

Svidrigaïlov smiled—a sly, knowing smile. "I lodge here, on the other side of the wall. Madame Resslich is a dear old friend of mine. Through her, I've been... quite aware of certain conversations. You, Rodion Romanovitch, are a man of great interest to me."

Raskolnikov stared at him, his blood running cold. He felt as though the walls were closing in, as though the air in the room had grown too thin to breathe. Svidrigaïlov's gaze remained fixed on him, unyielding, as though daring him to respond.

Part 6

Chapter 1

A peculiar and heavy period began for Raskolnikov, one that felt as though he were enveloped in a thick, unyielding fog—a haze of isolation and confusion from which there seemed no escape. When he later recalled this time, he believed his mind had been clouded, occasionally slipping into a state of detachment, which lasted intermittently until the culmination of events that shattered his fragile equilibrium. He became convinced that he had misremembered or misinterpreted much of what had occurred, mixing up the sequence of events and attributing causes to circumstances that existed only in his imagination. It was as though he were grappling with a fragmented reality, trying to piece together the disjointed memories of those days.

During this period, he was plagued by relentless waves of unease, often bordering on panic. At other times, he experienced stretches of apathy, moments so devoid of feeling they resembled the eerie detachment of the dying. These phases of emptiness seemed to be a reaction to the sharp pangs of terror he experienced. It was as if his mind was deliberately shielding itself from the full weight of his predicament. Yet, certain pressing realities—facts that demanded immediate attention—gnawed at him with their urgency. He longed for relief from these responsibilities, knowing that neglecting them would only lead to inevitable ruin.

Among these concerns, the figure of Svidrigaïlov loomed largest in his thoughts. The memory of their unsettling encounter in Sonia's room, at the moment of Katerina Ivanovna's death, seemed to linger like a shadow, distorting the normal workings of Raskolnikov's mind. Those cryptic, menacing words from Svidrigaïlov haunted him. Yet, despite the unease they stirred, Raskolnikov felt no urgency to confront or understand them. Instead, he found himself slipping into moments of near-dissociation, only to be jolted back to reality by the recurring thought that he must address this enigmatic man's intentions.

He would often find himself in unfamiliar, desolate parts of the city, seated in a shabby tavern or wandering aimlessly. At times, he would suddenly become aware of a strange certainty that Svidrigaïlov was waiting for him somewhere, that they had arranged to meet, even though he knew this was not true. On one occasion, he awoke at dawn beneath a thicket of bushes outside the city, unable to recall how he had come to be there. These moments revealed the fractured state of his mind, caught between delusion and reluctant clarity.

In the days immediately following Katerina Ivanovna's death, Raskolnikov encountered Svidrigaïlov twice or thrice at Sonia's lodging. Each time, their interactions were brief and disjointed, as though they shared a tacit agreement to avoid discussing the pressing matters that connected them. Svidrigaïlov was preoccupied with organizing Katerina Ivanovna's funeral and making arrangements for her orphaned children. He informed Raskolnikov during one of these meetings that he had secured placements for the children in reputable institutions, leveraging his connections and the financial provisions he had set aside for them. This, he claimed, made their placement far more feasible than if they had been destitute. He also spoke vaguely about Sonia, hinting that he would return to discuss certain matters with Raskolnikov in more detail.

Their last conversation occurred on the stairs of Sonia's building, as Svidrigaïlov prepared to leave. He paused for a moment, scrutinizing Raskolnikov with a curious intensity. "Rodion Romanovitch," he said, his tone almost playful yet edged with something unnameable, "you don't seem yourself. You're listening, but it's as though you don't quite understand. Cheer up! We'll sort everything out. But what you need, more than anything, is fresh air... fresh air, my friend."

Before Raskolnikov could respond, Svidrigaïlov stepped aside to allow the priest and server to pass. They were ascending the stairs to conduct a requiem service for Katerina Ivanovna. Svidrigaïlov moved off without further comment, leaving Raskolnikov standing alone, his thoughts tangled. After a moment's hesitation, he followed the priest into Sonia's room, where the quiet, mournful chanting of the service had already begun.

The somber atmosphere inside the room struck a chord deep within Raskolnikov. From his earliest memories, the presence of death and the rituals surrounding it had always weighed heavily on him, filling him with a sense of oppressive mystery. The requiem service, long unheard by his ears, now felt both familiar and profoundly unsettling. But there was something else here, an element too awful and disquieting to ignore. His gaze shifted to the children kneeling solemnly by the coffin, their small faces wet with tears. Polenka wept openly, her shoulders shaking with quiet sobs, while Sonia stood just behind them, praying with a trembling voice, her own tears silently falling.

The scene was heart-wrenching, and yet, for Raskolnikov, it carried an almost unbearable weight. It was not just the sorrow of the moment, but something deeper—a recognition of the human cost of his actions, of the lives altered irrevocably by choices he could no longer undo. The chanting of the requiem, mournful and deliberate, seemed to echo this realization, pulling him further into the depths of his own torment.

The days following Katerina Ivanovna's funeral seemed to blend into one another for Raskolnikov, marked by a haze of unease and disconnected thoughts. He felt as if he were moving through a fog, one that separated him from the world while pressing down heavily on his spirit. Even Sonia's presence, her unfailing kindness, and her selfless gestures failed to pierce this shroud. When she rested her head on his shoulder after the requiem service and held his hands without a trace of judgment or hesitation, he was bewildered. Her lack of repulsion, her quiet acceptance, felt to him like the deepest act of self-sacrifice. But it left him more miserable than comforted, burdened by her love in ways he could not articulate.

Leaving the service, he pressed her hand briefly and retreated into the streets. An oppressive loneliness gripped him. Solitude was not new to Raskolnikov—he had been isolating himself for some time—but now, even in the most desolate places, he could not escape a pervasive feeling of being observed. It was not fear that troubled him, but a deep irritation at the sensation of an unseen presence, an unrelenting reminder of something unresolved within himself.

Seeking relief, he would immerse himself in the crowds, walking through bustling streets, frequenting taverns, and even listening to songs sung by strangers. These moments provided fleeting distractions, but they were inevitably followed by a gnawing unease. Once, while sitting in a dimly lit tavern at dusk, he found himself oddly comforted by the music. But just as suddenly, a voice in his mind scolded him: What are you doing here? Is this what you should be doing now? He felt that the question was not entirely about his presence in the tavern but about a deeper, unresolved decision—something that loomed over him, unclear but unavoidable.

He left the tavern abruptly, almost running, and his thoughts turned to Dounia and his mother. The thought of them filled him with a sense of dread and helplessness. That night, he woke shivering among the bushes on Krestovsky Island, feverish and disoriented. He stumbled back to his apartment, arriving just as dawn broke. After a few hours of restless sleep, the fever subsided, leaving him unusually calm but physically drained.

That afternoon, as he sat eating the food Nastasya brought him with an uncharacteristic appetite, Razumihin entered, his face etched with concern. He sat across from Raskolnikov, his tone filled with irritation but also a resolute determination.

"You're eating, so you're not dying, at least," Razumihin said bluntly, pulling up a chair. "That's something."

Raskolnikov said nothing, continuing to eat with an indifferent air.

Razumihin leaned forward. "Listen to me. I've had enough of this nonsense. I don't care what secrets you're hiding or what's going on in that twisted head of yours. Frankly, I don't even want to know. But I need to understand one thing—are you mad? Because, to be honest, that's what it looks like. Your behavior has been nothing short of monstrous, especially toward your mother and sister. No sane man treats his family like that."

"When did you last see them?" Raskolnikov asked, his voice subdued.

"Just now. Haven't you seen them? Do you even know what's going on? Your mother has been seriously ill since yesterday. She wanted to come and see you herself, but Avdotya Romanovna tried to stop her. 'If he's unwell, who can look after him better than his mother?' she said. So we all came here together. But you weren't here. She waited, sat quietly for ten minutes, then got up and said, 'If he's well enough to be out, then he's well enough to come and see his mother. And if he doesn't, it's clear he doesn't care about us.' She went home and took to her bed. She's burning with fever now. And she thinks—God knows why—that you're spending all your time with Sonia. She called her your... betrothed or your mistress. What a mess."

Razumihin paused, his frustration evident. "I went to Sonia's place to see for myself. What did I find? A coffin, crying children, Sonia trying to dress them in mourning clothes. And where were you? Nowhere to be found. I apologized, left, and told Dounia everything. So it's clear you don't have a girl or anything like that. Most likely, you're just mad. But here you sit, stuffing yourself with boiled beef like you haven't eaten in days. And you're not mad, are you? No, you're not insane. You're hiding something. Well, keep your secrets. I don't care. I came here to tell you off and be done with it."

Razumihin stood abruptly, his chair scraping against the floor.

"What will you do now?" Raskolnikov asked quietly.

"None of your business."

"You're going to drink."

Razumihin's eyes narrowed. "And how do you know that?"

Raskolnikov allowed himself the faintest smile. "It's obvious."

Razumihin stared at him for a moment, his anger mingled with a grudging concern. Then, without another word, he left, leaving Raskolnikov alone once more in the dim, suffocating stillness of his room.

Razumihin lingered for a moment, his face softening as he spoke with unexpected warmth. "You've always been a rational person. Not mad, not once. Never." He paused, then added with a touch of defiance, "And yes, you're right—I'll drink. Goodbye!"

He turned toward the door, but before stepping out, Raskolnikov's voice halted him. "I spoke with my sister the day before yesterday. We talked about you, Razumihin."

Razumihin froze, his hand on the doorframe. He turned slowly, his complexion paling slightly, as though his heart had momentarily ceased its rhythm. "You spoke with her? The day before yesterday? How?"

"She came here. Alone. She sat where you're sitting now, and we talked," Raskolnikov said calmly, though his words carried a deliberate weight.

"She... came here?" Razumihin repeated, his voice almost trembling.

"Yes," Raskolnikov affirmed.

"And... and what did you say to her about me?" Razumihin pressed, his face a mix of confusion and something close to dread.

"I told her what I believe to be true," Raskolnikov said, locking his gaze with Razumihin's. "That you are a good man. Honest, diligent, loyal. I didn't tell her you love her because that, I think, she already knows."

Razumihin's lips parted, but no sound came out. He stood as if rooted to the spot.

"You care for her deeply, and she sees that," Raskolnikov continued. "Whatever may happen to me, I trust you'll look after her—and our mother. I am leaving them in your care, Razumihin. I know you'll protect them, not because I ask it, but because you love her. And I believe she may already love you too. Now, think on that and decide whether you still need to drown yourself in drink."

For a moment, Razumihin could only stare, his emotions playing out in rapid succession across his face—shock, gratitude, disbelief. He shook his head and muttered, "Rodya... I... damn it all." He glanced at the door, then back at Raskolnikov. "But where are you going? What's next for you? I mean, if it's a secret, fine, but—"

"I'm going to see someone," Raskolnikov interjected, "someone who told me yesterday that what people need most is fresh air. I need to ask him exactly what he meant by that."

Razumihin studied him, his thoughts visibly racing. He looked almost as if he were piecing together a puzzle. "Fresh air... fresh air," he murmured, then stopped suddenly, his eyes narrowing. "You're meeting someone. And Dounia knows about it. That letter... that must have something to do with this too."

"What letter?" Raskolnikov asked sharply.

"She received one earlier today," Razumihin said, his tone shifting to something more serious. "It upset her. She was pale as a ghost. I mentioned you, and she practically begged me to stop. Then she said something strange—that soon we might all have to part ways. She thanked me... for something... and locked herself in her room."

Raskolnikov frowned. "A letter?" he repeated thoughtfully.

"Yes," Razumihin confirmed. "But you didn't know?"

Neither of them spoke for a moment. Finally, Razumihin sighed heavily, looking at Raskolnikov with an odd mixture of frustration and resignation. "Goodbye, Rodya. There was a time when I... Well, never mind. Goodbye. I'm not going to drink, after all. There's no need for it. Not anymore."

He opened the door and stepped out but suddenly turned back, hesitating. "Oh, by the way," he said, glancing to the side, "do you remember that murder? The old pawnbroker? The one Porfiry was so keen on?"

Raskolnikov's expression tightened, though he said nothing.

"Well, they've found the murderer," Razumihin continued, a hint of incredulity in his voice. "He's confessed. One of those workmen, the painter. Can you believe it? Porfiry explained everything. Apparently, the whole scene—the fighting, the laughing on the stairs—was all an act to throw off suspicion. The man's a genius of deception, they say. But it all fell apart, and he confessed."

Raskolnikov's composure faltered slightly. "Porfiry told you this?"

"Yes. Psychologically, he laid it all out for me, his usual style," Razumihin said. "Fascinating stuff. Anyway, I'll tell you about it another time. For now, I've got to go. And no, I'm not drinking. You've made me drunk enough just talking to you."

With that, Razumihin left, the door closing behind him. On the stairs, his thoughts continued to churn. "He's involved in something bigger," he muttered to himself. "Some conspiracy. And Dounia's caught up in it. That letter—what was in it? I'll figure it out. I have to."

As he descended, he shook his head. "God, what a tangle. And to think... I almost believed—no, never mind. Nikolay confessed, after all. But this letter... I need to find out more."

Raskolnikov's thoughts turned to Dounia, the weight of what he had just heard pressing against his chest. A sudden urgency overtook him, and his heart began to race as though it were trying to break free from the cage of his ribs. Without realizing it, he broke into a run, his footsteps echoing on the narrow staircase.

When Razumihin left, Raskolnikov remained standing for a moment, his eyes fixed on the door. Then, as though propelled by some unseen force, he turned toward the window, paced the length of the small room, then back again, his movements quick and jerky. The confined space felt suffocating, and he found himself longing for air, for release, for escape. He sank back onto the sofa, breathing heavily, but his thoughts were clearer than they had been in days.

"Yes," he whispered to himself, as though confirming an unspoken realization. "A way out has come at last."

The oppressive fog that had hung over him for days seemed to lift slightly. That crushing, paralyzing lethargy, which had gripped him since the moment Nikolay had confessed to the murder, now gave way to something sharper, something keener. His encounter with Sonia had left him raw, exposed. His words, his behavior—they had spiraled beyond his control, veering into realms he could not have predicted. He had been stripped bare, his strength eroded, and yet, within the depths of his despair, a kernel of resolve had taken root.

"Svidrigaïlov..." The name came unbidden to his lips, tinged with a mixture of unease and loathing. There was something about that man—something dangerous, something enigmatic. He posed a threat, no doubt, but also... an opportunity. Raskolnikov could feel it. If only he could decipher the puzzle that was Svidrigaïlov, he might yet find a way forward.

Porfiry, however, was another matter entirely. The thought of him sent a wave of bitterness coursing through Raskolnikov's veins. The man was relentless, calculating, always circling, always watching. And now, to hear that Porfiry had been feeding Razumihin lies about Nikolay's guilt, pretending to entertain the possibility, when Raskolnikov knew—knew—that Porfiry didn't believe it for a moment. It was maddening. Their earlier confrontation came flooding back to him, vivid and raw. The glances they had exchanged, the unspoken truths hanging between them—how could Porfiry now act as though none of it had happened?

The room felt even smaller now, the walls closing in. Raskolnikov grabbed his cap and left, his thoughts swirling chaotically. As he stepped onto the street, a sense of purpose began to take shape. "I need to deal with Svidrigaïlov," he thought. "And soon. He's waiting for me to make the first move, I can feel it."

Hatred simmered just below the surface, a hatred so intense it startled him. He clenched his fists, imagining—for a fleeting moment—what it might feel like to strike Porfiry, to silence Svidrigaïlov. His mind recoiled from the thought, but the visceral urge remained, bubbling like a poison in his blood.

"We'll see," he muttered under his breath. "We'll see."

But as he reached for the door handle to step outside, he found himself face-to-face with Porfiry Petrovitch. The man stood in the passage, his expression one of cheerful ease, though his eyes betrayed a sharper edge.

"Rodion Romanovitch," Porfiry said, his voice light and conversational, as though they were old friends. "You didn't expect me, did you? I've been meaning to drop by for ages. Just passing by, you know, and thought I'd pop in for five minutes. Are you going out? Oh, don't let me keep you. Just a quick chat. Let me have a cigarette, will you?"

Raskolnikov froze, his breath caught in his throat. For a brief, wild moment, he considered slamming the door in Porfiry's face. But then, to his own astonishment, he found himself smiling—genuinely smiling—and gesturing for Porfiry to sit.

"Come in, Porfiry Petrovitch," he said, his voice unnervingly calm. "Have a seat. Let's talk."

He motioned toward a chair and settled into one himself, positioning himself directly across from Porfiry. Their eyes locked, and for the first time in days, Raskolnikov felt a strange sense of clarity, as though all the noise in his head had suddenly quieted. Whatever was coming, it would end here, in this room. The final act was beginning.

Porfiry struck a match and lit his cigarette, his gaze never leaving Raskolnikov. The silence between them stretched, taut and electric.

"Well?" Raskolnikov thought, his heart pounding. "Speak. Why don't you speak?"

The moment hung in the air, suspended, and both men seemed to understand that nothing would ever be the same after this conversation.

Chapter 2

Porfiry Petrovitch exhaled a long stream of smoke, his gaze fixed somewhere in the vague distance as though he were meditating over some profound truth hidden within the wisp of smoke curling upward. "Ah, these cigarettes!" he exclaimed again, his voice tinged with both amusement and frustration. "Positively pernicious, don't you agree? And yet, I find myself utterly unable to give them up. You see, Rodion Romanovitch, I have a bit of a cowardly streak. I recently visited Dr. B——n, a very serious man, always takes at least half an hour with each patient. And do you know, he laughed at me! Laughed, yes! Told me my lungs are starting to show signs, warned me tobacco is no good for me. But what is one to do? What, I ask, is there to replace it? I don't drink, after all. He-he-he. That's the rub! Everything is relative, you see, my dear fellow. Everything!"

Raskolnikov, seated stiffly opposite him, felt an icy wave of irritation rise within him. He's performing again, he thought, his stomach churning with the same revulsion that had overtaken him during their previous encounters. The memory of that last interview came flooding back in vivid detail—every insinuation, every glance, every unspoken accusation—and he could feel himself teetering on the edge of the same volatile mixture of dread and fury.

Porfiry continued in his conversational tone, seemingly oblivious to Raskolnikov's growing discomfort. "I dropped by here the day before yesterday, you know," he said suddenly, as though recalling the fact with some amusement. "You didn't notice, of course. Your door was wide open, and I stepped inside—this very room. I stood here, looked about, waited a moment, and left again without leaving my name. Tell me, Rodion Romanovitch, do you always leave your door unlocked?"

Raskolnikov's face darkened further, the gloom settling like a shadow across his features. His thoughts raced. What was Porfiry's game? Was he probing, testing, or merely toying with him for his own amusement?

Porfiry seemed to sense his unease, for his tone shifted ever so slightly. Leaning forward, he lightly patted Raskolnikov's knee in a gesture that was both friendly and oddly condescending. "Now, now, my dear Rodion Romanovitch, no need for such a sour expression! I've come to clear the air between us, so to speak. I owe you an explanation, and I intend to give it to you. You and I, after all, are gentlemen. And as gentlemen, we must address the... ah... peculiarities of our prior interactions with candor and dignity."

There was something different in Porfiry's demeanor now. For the first time, Raskolnikov noticed a flicker of weariness in the man's eyes, a fleeting shadow of sadness that seemed wholly out of place. This was not the smug, self-assured investigator he had encountered before; there was an unfamiliar sincerity to Porfiry's words and gestures that left Raskolnikov both suspicious and strangely disarmed.

"Yes," Porfiry continued, his voice quieter now, almost reflective. "Our last meeting... it was a peculiar scene, wasn't it? And our first meeting as well—strange, very strange. But let us focus on the last. How it ended... well, that was far from decorous, wouldn't you agree? You were trembling; I was trembling. It was all very... ungentlemanly. Yet here we are, you and I, still gentlemen, no matter the circumstances."

Raskolnikov sat in stunned silence, his thoughts a tumult of confusion and apprehension. What is he playing at now? Does he truly believe I'm innocent? Or is this another one of his infernal traps?

Porfiry seemed almost to read his mind, for he suddenly shifted again, this time adopting a more earnest tone. "You see, Rodion

Romanovitch, I've decided that openness is the best course between us. There's no point in prolonging the misunderstandings that have plagued our interactions. That workman—Nikolay—his confession was a pivotal moment. It forced me to reconsider many things. And yet..." Porfiry paused, his eyes narrowing slightly as though wrestling with some unspoken thought. "And yet I must admit, I had hoped for a different kind of resolution."

He leaned back in his chair, studying Raskolnikov with a penetrating gaze. "Do you know, I had great hopes for you, Rodion Romanovitch. Yes, indeed. Your temperament—so fiery, so passionate—I thought, here is a man capable of extraordinary things. But your nerves... ah, your nerves are your undoing, my friend. I imagined, perhaps, that you might reach a breaking point, that you might... well... relieve me of the burden of proving anything."

Raskolnikov stiffened, his heart pounding in his chest. The room seemed to close in around him, the walls pressing ever tighter.

"But alas," Porfiry continued, a faint smile playing at the corners of his lips, "life is rarely so accommodating. And so here we are, two men with much to discuss and yet so much unspoken between us. I have wronged you, Rodion Romanovitch, and for that, I seek your forgiveness. Whatever else may come, let it not be said that I am without a conscience."

As Porfiry's words hung in the air, Raskolnikov felt a cold sweat break out across his brow. He could not decide which was worse— the possibility that Porfiry truly believed in his innocence or the chilling thought that this entire performance was merely the prelude to some final, devastating revelation.

Porfiry Petrovitch settled into his chair with a slow, deliberate motion, the cigarette between his fingers trailing a thin spiral of smoke. His eyes, half-lidded and thoughtful, rested on Raskolnikov, whose stiff, silent demeanor betrayed his growing tension. Porfiry's tone, conversational yet insidiously penetrating, continued its relentless flow.

"It seems unnecessary to recount every detail," he began, waving his hand slightly as though dismissing the very thought of minutiae. "Indeed, I doubt I could even attempt such a thing. Suffice it to say, there were rumors, as there always are. Who started them, how they reached me, or in what manner they evolved—well, those details are unimportant. What matters is the idea they planted in my mind. A curious accident, too—a chance occurrence, nothing more—served to corroborate those whispers. That accident, as trivial as it might have been, pointed to you. And so, Rodion Romanovitch, I found myself unable to look away. It was like a thread, fine but strong, that pulled me toward certain suspicions."

He paused, as if to gauge Raskolnikov's reaction. The latter's face, pale and strained, gave nothing away. Porfiry pressed on, his voice tinged with a faint amusement that made his words all the more unnerving.

"Ah, but what was it, you ask? That accident? Does it matter? Let us call it intuition, for lack of a better term. And then there was the business with the old woman's pledges—her little notebook, her receipts. Yet even there, nothing conclusive, nothing concrete. Your name, Rodion Romanovitch, was but one among a hundred. A mere shadow among shadows. And yet... the scene at the office, as it was described to me, painted a vivid picture. Quite vivid, I must say. It seemed to me, even then, that I could almost hear the tone of your voice, feel the heat of your indignation, and read the suppressed turmoil in your words. One detail after another, one brushstroke atop another—how could I not begin to see the outline of a figure, a shape?"

Porfiry leaned forward slightly, his eyes narrowing as though to pierce through Raskolnikov's defenses. "But let us not forget your article. Ah, yes, the infamous article. Do you remember our discussion about it during your first visit? I recall jeering at you then, deliberately, I admit. It was not malice, but rather... curiosity. You see, I recognized something in your writing, something familiar. The feverish passion, the restless fervor—it struck a chord, you see. There was something unmistakably youthful, raw, even desperate in it. And, my dear fellow, it was precisely that undertone of suppressed desperation that lingered with me. That kind of intensity—well, it's rare, but it's also... dangerous. Yes, dangerous."

He drew a long breath, allowing his words to sink in. Raskolnikov's hands tightened into fists on his knees, but he remained silent.

"That article," Porfiry continued, his tone turning almost wistful, "was like a piece of music played with too much force. The notes struck too sharply, the rhythm too erratic. And yet, there was something... compelling in its discord. I thought to myself, 'This man will not go the common way.' And so, when the rumors began to circle, when the accident pointed to you, when the pieces seemed to assemble themselves—it all seemed too perfect to ignore. And yet, I reminded myself: a hundred suspicions don't make proof. A lawyer must remain grounded, must he not?"

Porfiry leaned back now, smiling faintly. "Ah, but then there was that scene in the tavern. You remember, of course. Zametov told me all about it. Your bold declaration—'I killed her!'—what a move that was! Too daring, too reckless. And yet, in its recklessness, it betrayed... something. I thought, 'If this man is guilty, he is a dangerous opponent indeed.' And so, I waited. I spread my net wider, prodded at the edges, watched how the ripples moved. And, Rodion Romanovitch, you came to me, as I knew you would. Why wouldn't you? You were drawn to the flame, as they say."

His voice dropped to a near-whisper, his gaze sharpening. "And when you came, the way you laughed... oh, that laugh! Had I not been expecting you, it might have seemed ordinary. But I was expecting you, and so it was like a thunderclap in my ears. Every word you spoke, every gesture you made, seemed to carry double meanings. Even the smallest details—such as that mention of the stone in the garden where the stolen items might have been hidden—they lingered in my mind, like faint echoes of a melody half-heard."

Porfiry exhaled again, letting the cigarette burn down in his fingers. His tone shifted once more, now soft, almost coaxing. "But let us not dwell too much on psychology, as fascinating as it is. No, let us simply say that there are puzzles within puzzles, and sometimes the most intricate ones resolve themselves in the most unexpected ways. You, Rodion Romanovitch, are a puzzle. And I—well, I do love a good puzzle."

Porfiry Petrovitch leaned back slightly, letting out a contemplative sigh as though surveying a landscape only he could see. His tone remained conversational, yet it brimmed with the peculiar energy of a man unraveling a story whose threads had tangled even him.

"So, you see, Rodion Romanovitch," he began again, his voice almost musing, "I came to a point where I had to stop and ask myself what I was really doing. I had followed the threads as far as they could take me, reaching what felt like a dead end, a post against which I had knocked my own head. It was at that moment I told myself, 'Perhaps it can all be interpreted another way. Perhaps I'm forcing the narrative.' And, indeed, there was a far more natural explanation for much of what I had observed. I couldn't deny it. But you see, it bothered me— a nagging feeling that wouldn't let go. 'No,' I said to myself, 'I need something more, something tangible, a little fact, a morsel of evidence to hang my thoughts on.' And when I heard about that bell-ringing incident... ah, that was it. I felt my heart leap. 'Here is my little fact!' I thought."

He paused and glanced at Raskolnikov, whose pallor and rigid posture betrayed the storm within him. Porfiry smiled faintly, almost wistfully, and continued.

"Oh, how I would have given a thousand roubles to witness it myself—that moment when you walked beside the workman after he had accused you, called you a murderer outright to your face, and you didn't so much as question him. Not a single word. All the way, a hundred paces, and you said nothing. And then, of course, there was your trembling, your delirium, and that peculiar bell-ringing episode during your illness. How could I not be intrigued? How could I not follow the trail?"

He leaned forward slightly, his voice dropping to a conspiratorial whisper. "Can you really be surprised, Rodion Romanovitch, that I began to play these little games with you? The timing was almost too perfect. And then, as if the heavens themselves had conspired, you came to me of your own accord—at precisely the moment I least expected, yet most hoped for. Ah, what a twist! And just when Nikolay burst onto the scene with his wild confession... do you remember how that unfolded? A thunderbolt, if ever there was one! I didn't believe it for a second, of course. Not for a single second. You must have seen it on my face. But still, he presented his story with such earnestness, such unexpected plausibility on some points, that even I had to pause and wonder at his audacity."

Porfiry chuckled softly, shaking his head. "But I'll tell you this: Nikolay's confession never swayed me. How could it? I already knew where the truth lay, or so I thought. No, Nikolay was a diversion—a puzzle piece that didn't quite fit. And yet, there was something about him that piqued my curiosity. Would you like to know what kind of man he is, this Nikolay?"

He didn't wait for a response, launching into a detailed and colorful portrait. "To begin with, he's still a boy in many ways—a child, really. Not a coward, mind you, but sensitive, impressionable, and, I would dare say, something of an artist at heart. Oh, don't laugh! It's true. He's a dreamer, a storyteller, the kind of fellow who can make others laugh until they cry with his tales. He sings, he dances, and, when the mood strikes, he drinks himself into a stupor—not from vice, but like a child indulging in forbidden sweets. And he has a curious spiritual streak, too, steeped in the traditions of the Old Believers. Imagine him as a boy, guided by some elder in his village, praying fervently at night, reading the ancient texts with such devotion that he nearly drove himself mad. And then—ah, Petersburg! The city had its way with him: the women, the wine, the temptations of an artist's world. He lost himself in it, forgot his elder, his teachings, everything."

Porfiry's voice softened as he went on, weaving the tale with a storyteller's cadence. "And then, this incident. This crime. He panicked. Tried to hang himself, poor fellow. You see, Rodion Romanovitch, the mere thought of a trial can terrify men like him— turn their hearts to water. And in prison, his old beliefs crept back in. The word 'suffering' has a peculiar power over such people, you know. It's not that they suffer for a cause, but because suffering itself becomes a kind of salvation, a path to grace. Nikolay now believes that he must 'take his suffering,' and he's begun to lean on those old teachings, his elder's words, as a crutch. But mark my words: he'll come around. He'll take back his confession. He'll crumble. It's only a matter of time."

He sat back again, a faint, amused smile lingering on his lips. "Ah, but Nikolay is a fascinating study. I find myself almost liking the fellow, despite everything. He's a creature of contradictions, clever in some ways, hopelessly naïve in others. But tell me, Rodion Romanovitch, what do you think? Do you believe in such people—these fantastical, suffering souls? Or do you think I've let my imagination run away with me?"

Porfiry's gaze sharpened, his smile fading into an expression of curious intensity, as though daring Raskolnikov to answer.

Porfiry paused, drawing out his words, almost as if savoring the moment. "...because I see you are being crushed under the weight of it all, Rodion Romanovitch. You are not the sort of man to endure such strain for long. You're suffering, I can see it, and sooner or later it will break you. Why should I rush matters when it's only a matter of time? Besides," he added with a faint, almost imperceptible smile, "you're already punishing yourself more than anyone else ever could."

Raskolnikov shifted uncomfortably, his fingers gripping the edge of the table as though to steady himself. "What do you mean by that?" he demanded, his voice low but trembling with suppressed intensity. "Punishing myself? What nonsense! You think I've come to you to confess or to plead for forgiveness? You think I feel remorse?"

Porfiry waved a hand dismissively, as though brushing aside Raskolnikov's protestations. "No, no, don't misunderstand me. I'm not accusing you of remorse, at least not in the conventional sense. But you see, Rodion Romanovitch, a man like you cannot help but suffer when he has severed himself from his own humanity. You're too proud, too intelligent, too... idealistic, in a way, to live comfortably with such a burden. You committed the act, yes, but the why of it— ah, that's where the torment lies. The theory, the justification—it's all crumbling, isn't it? That's the true punishment, my friend. Not the fear of capture, not the threat of prison, but the slow realization that you are not the extraordinary man you thought yourself to be."

Raskolnikov's face darkened, his expression hardening into one of icy disdain. "You think you've got me all figured out, don't you, Porfiry Petrovitch? The all-knowing detective, weaving his little psychological traps. But you're wrong. I feel nothing, do you hear me? Nothing!"

Porfiry leaned forward, his gaze piercing yet almost tender. "Do you? Truly? Then why are we here, you and I, having this conversation? Why haven't you fled, escaped this city, this country? You're clever enough to have done it, resourceful enough. But no—you stay. You linger. Why? Because you are tied here, Rodion Romanovitch, not by the law, not by me, but by something far more unyielding: your own conscience."

Raskolnikov stood abruptly, pacing the small room like a caged animal. "And what if I do leave? What if I walk out of here right now and vanish? What then, Porfiry? Will you still sit there, smug and satisfied, waiting for me to crumble under the weight of your 'psychology'?"

Porfiry watched him with an almost paternal air, his voice calm but firm. "You won't leave. You can't. Not because I'll stop you, but because you've already condemned yourself to face this to the end. That's why I'm here—to make it clear to you, as clear as daylight, that I know, and you know, and there's no escaping it."

Raskolnikov stopped pacing, his chest heaving, his face pale and drawn. He turned to Porfiry with an expression that was equal parts defiance and despair. "And what now? What do you want from me? If you believe so firmly in my guilt, why not arrest me, end this charade?"

Porfiry stood as well, his demeanor suddenly grave, almost solemn. "Because it's not for me to end it, Rodion Romanovitch. This is your path, your choice. I've told you what I know, and I've given you time. What you do with that time—whether you confess, whether you run, whether you fight to the bitter end—that's up to you. But remember this: the truth has a way of surfacing, no matter how deeply it's buried. And when it does, you'll have to decide what kind of man you truly are."

With that, Porfiry stepped toward the door, pausing briefly as though to add something more. But instead, he simply nodded, a gesture of finality, and walked out, leaving Raskolnikov alone with his thoughts, the room heavy with an oppressive silence that seemed to echo with unspoken truths.

"Yes, yes, secondly?" Raskolnikov leaned forward, every nerve tense, his breath coming faster.

Porfiry Petrovitch adjusted himself in his chair, crossing one leg over the other with deliberate care. "Because, as I mentioned earlier, I owe you an explanation. I have no wish for you to think of me as a heartless tormentor. No, Rodion Romanovitch, that is not what I am. In truth, I have developed a genuine regard for you. You may take that as you will, whether you believe me or not, but I felt it important to make it clear."

He paused for a moment, as though allowing his words to settle in Raskolnikov's mind, then continued. "And thirdly, I have come here today with a direct and straightforward proposal. I am suggesting that you surrender yourself and confess. Yes, surrender voluntarily, Rodion Romanovitch. It will work to your advantage—and mine as well, for it will conclude this matter once and for all. Do you not find this approach... open?"

Raskolnikov leaned back slightly, narrowing his eyes as he studied Porfiry. He was quiet for a moment, his mind racing to grasp the implications of this unexpected turn. Then, with a bitter edge to his voice, he said, "Listen to me, Porfiry Petrovitch. You said yourself not long ago that all you have against me is psychological conjecture. Now you're telling me you've moved to facts—something solid, mathematical, you claim. So, what if you're wrong? What if this little fact of yours isn't as damning as you believe?"

Porfiry smiled faintly, shaking his head as though pitying Raskolnikov's attempt to find a foothold. "No, Rodion Romanovitch, I am not mistaken. And as for this fact, Providence saw fit to place it into my hands at just the right moment. It is small, yes, but significant. And no, I will not share it with you—not yet."

Raskolnikov stiffened, his jaw tightening. "And yet, despite your supposed certainty, you hesitate. You don't arrest me now. Why?"

Porfiry's expression grew more serious, his gaze steady and unwavering. "Because I'm giving you the chance to make the choice for yourself. You see, Rodion Romanovitch, it makes no difference to me whether you confess or not—I will carry out my duty either way. But it will matter to you. I speak for your sake. Believe me when I say, it would be better for you if you confessed willingly."

Raskolnikov responded with a twisted smile, one filled with defiance and resignation. "That's absurd—no, it's worse than absurd; it's shameless. Even if I were guilty, which I deny, what reason would I have to confess? Especially when you yourself suggest that prison might offer me safety. Why should I hand myself over?"

Porfiry sighed, leaning forward slightly as if trying to bridge the gap between them. "Ah, Rodion Romanovitch, don't take my words too literally. Prison may not be the safe haven I alluded to—it's only a theory, after all, and one can't trust theories too much, can they? But consider this: a confession made now, under these circumstances, will change the course of everything. You must see that. Another man has already tangled himself in this web, confused the case. If you confess now, you'll appear not as a cold-blooded murderer but as someone who lost his way—a victim of his own theories and inner turmoil."

"And you'll arrange all that for me, will you?" Raskolnikov said mockingly, though his tone lacked real force.

"Yes, I will," Porfiry replied without hesitation. "I swear it. I will present your confession in such a way that your crime appears not as one of malice but as a moment of madness, a tragic error born of an unbalanced mind. Because that's the truth, isn't it? I'm not your enemy, Rodion Romanovitch. I want to help you, not destroy you."

For a long moment, Raskolnikov said nothing. His head sank, his shoulders slumping as though weighed down by an invisible burden. He looked up at last, a sad, weary smile playing on his lips. "No, Porfiry Petrovitch," he said softly. "It's not worth it. I don't care about lessening the sentence."

Porfiry's face flickered with something that might have been regret, or perhaps understanding. "That's what I was afraid of," he said, his voice heavy with genuine concern. "That's exactly what I feared—that you would see no value in mitigation, that you would disdain the idea of mercy."

Raskolnikov met his gaze, his eyes tired but steady. "Life, you say. A great deal of it still lies ahead for me. But what kind of life are you talking about, Porfiry? What do you know of it, really? You speak as if you see something waiting for me that I cannot."

Porfiry's voice softened. "I see potential, Rodion Romanovitch. I see redemption. This might be your chance to find it. Do not throw that away. Seek and you shall find—so it is said. And though the road may seem bleak now, you cannot know what lies beyond."

Raskolnikov gave a faint, bitter laugh. "The time will be shortened, will it? That's what they always say."

"Why, is it the fear of bourgeois disgrace that holds you back? Maybe you're afraid of it without even realizing it, because you are still young and caught up in your pride. But that fear is baseless. There is no shame in giving yourself up and confessing," Porfiry Petrovitch said firmly, his voice calm yet insistent.

Raskolnikov turned his head slightly, a sneer twisting his lips. "Ach, hang it!" he muttered under his breath, his tone laced with loathing and contempt. It seemed as though he didn't even want to waste the effort of speaking aloud.

He stood abruptly, as if to leave, but then sank back into his chair, visibly defeated, his movements heavy with despair.

"Hang it, if you like!" Porfiry continued, undeterred. "You've lost your faith, and you think I'm just flattering you with hollow words. But tell me, how long has your life really been? How much have you truly understood? You constructed your grand theory, but when it crumbled under its own weight, you were ashamed—not because of the crime itself, but because it wasn't as original as you had imagined. Yes, it turned out to be something base, I grant you that. But you, Rodion Romanovitch, are not irredeemably base. Not by any means. At least you didn't deceive yourself for long. You went straight to the furthest point, in one bound."

Porfiry leaned forward, his gaze steady and penetrating. "Do you know how I see you? I see you as one of those rare individuals who would stand unflinching before their torturer, even as he cuts their entrails out, if only they had found faith or some higher purpose. Find it, Rodion Romanovitch, and you will live. You've long needed a change of air. And let me tell you, suffering isn't the curse you think it is. It can be a good thing—perhaps even a blessing. Maybe Nikolay is right in seeking suffering. You may scoff at this, but I urge you: fling yourself into life. Don't overthink it; don't hold back. The current will carry you to the shore and set you safely on your feet again."

He paused, as if measuring his words. "What shore, you ask? How can I tell you that? I only know this—you have a long life ahead of you, one filled with possibilities. You may not see it now, but someday you will. I'm sure you think I've rehearsed these words, that I'm delivering a prepared speech. Perhaps you're right. But even if you dismiss me now, I believe my words will stay with you. Perhaps they will help you when you need them most."

Porfiry's tone grew softer, almost reflective. "It's a blessing, you know, that your crime was limited to what it was. If you'd embraced another theory, who knows what you might have done? Something a thousand times more terrible, perhaps. Have you ever thought of that? Maybe God spared you for a reason. How do you know? Maybe He has a plan for you still. So take heart, and stop fearing the great expiation that lies before you. It would be shameful to shrink from it now. Since you've already crossed this line, you must harden your heart and face what comes. There's justice in that."

He leaned back slightly, as though giving Raskolnikov space to process his words. "You'll live it down in time. Believe me, life has a way of bringing you through, even when you can't see how. What you need right now is fresh air—fresh air, fresh air, and more fresh air!"

Raskolnikov jolted slightly, almost startled. He turned to Porfiry with a sudden intensity in his gaze. "But who are you? What prophet do you think you are, to proclaim all this with such authority? From what lofty place do you imagine you're speaking?"

Porfiry smiled faintly, his expression tinged with weariness. "Who am I? I'm a man who has nothing left to hope for, that's all. A man of feeling and sympathy, perhaps, maybe even of some understanding— but my time has passed. My day is over. But you, Rodion Romanovitch, you are a different story. Life is still waiting for you, no matter how bleak it seems now."

He shrugged slightly, his voice taking on a note of self-awareness. "Of course, who knows? Maybe your life will also pass in smoke and come to nothing. But does that really matter? You've stepped into a new realm, a new class of existence. It's not comfort you're mourning—it's something far deeper. And you have it within you to rise above this, to become something greater. Be the sun, Rodion Romanovitch. The sun doesn't lament its isolation; it simply shines, and all see it. Why are you smiling now? At my idealism, at my 'Schiller-like' ramblings? Perhaps I do sound like a romantic fool.

Maybe you think I'm trying to manipulate you with flattery. But that doesn't mean there isn't truth in what I'm saying."

Porfiry's tone shifted, becoming more pragmatic. "When will I arrest you? I'll give you another day or two. Use that time wisely— think it over and pray, if you can. It's in your best interest, believe me."

"And what if I run?" Raskolnikov asked suddenly, a strange smile curling his lips.

Porfiry chuckled softly, shaking his head. "No, you won't run. A peasant might run, or a weak soul desperate to escape. But you? No. You've already abandoned the very theory that brought you to this point. What would you run with now? What purpose would hiding serve? You'd only end up back here, back with yourself—and that's far worse than anything else. You can't live without resolution, without clarity. And if I do arrest you, if I put you in prison for a month, or two, or three—you'll find yourself confessing, perhaps even to your own surprise. It will happen when you least expect it."

Porfiry stood as Raskolnikov rose and took his cap. He looked at the younger man with a mix of pity and resolve. "Suffering, Rodion Romanovitch, is a great thing. There's wisdom in it, whether you believe me now or not. Nikolay understood that, and so will you in time. No, you won't run. You'll come to terms with this, sooner or later."

As they prepared to part, Porfiry glanced out the window. "Are you going for a walk? The evening promises to be fine, unless we get a storm. Though, perhaps a storm wouldn't be so bad—it would clear the air."

He picked up his own cap, ready to leave, his words lingering in the small room like the echo of a challenge.

"Porfiry Petrovitch, let me make one thing absolutely clear," Raskolnikov began, his voice low but filled with sullen determination. "Do not, under any circumstances, assume that I have confessed to you today. You're a peculiar man, and I've listened to you out of mere curiosity—nothing more. But I've admitted nothing. Remember that."

Porfiry leaned back slightly, his expression a mixture of patience and amusement. "Oh, I know, I'll remember," he said with a faint chuckle. "Look at you, though—you're trembling! Don't worry, my dear fellow, we'll have it your way. Walk about as much as you like, though I doubt you'll get very far."

His tone shifted slightly as he continued, lowering his voice to a confidential murmur. "There's something I must ask of you—a small request, but an important one. It might seem awkward, even absurd, but I hope you'll hear me out. Should you—though I hardly think it likely—be overcome in the next forty or fifty hours by some fantastic notion, some sudden urge to put an end to all this in... let's say, a drastic way, laying hands on yourself—well, do me this one courtesy. Leave behind a brief but clear note. Just two lines, no more. And mention the stone." He paused for a moment, his eyes steady on Raskolnikov. "That would be the more generous course. Think about it. Come now, until we meet again! May good thoughts and sound decisions find their way to you!"

Without waiting for a reply, Porfiry turned and made his way to the door, his posture slightly stooped, as though weighed down by some unspoken burden. He did not look back at Raskolnikov, his retreat deliberate and composed.

Raskolnikov remained motionless for a moment, his gaze fixed on the door that had just closed behind Porfiry. Then, almost mechanically, he turned and stepped to the window, his mind racing. He watched the street below, waiting, his impatience sharp and irritable. He calculated the time it would take for Porfiry to reach the street and move away, counting seconds in his mind as if measuring his own frayed resolve.

When he judged that Porfiry was gone, his tension burst into action. Without hesitation, he grabbed his cap, threw it on, and hurried out of the room, his steps quick and purposeful, as though driven by some new and unrelenting force.

Chapter 3

He hurried to Svidrigailov's place. He didn't know exactly what to expect from the man, but he felt Svidrigailov had some kind of hidden power over him. Once he realized this, he couldn't rest, and now the moment had come.

On the way there, one question troubled him deeply: had Svidrigailov gone to see Porfiry? From everything he could recall, he was almost certain that he hadn't. He kept replaying Porfiry's visit in his mind—no, Svidrigailov hadn't been there, he was sure of it. But if he hadn't gone yet, would he go soon? For now, Raskolnikov thought he wouldn't. Why was he so sure? He couldn't say, but even if he could explain it, he wouldn't have spent much time thinking about it at that moment. This whole situation frustrated him, yet he couldn't focus on it completely. Oddly enough, though no one would have believed it, he wasn't terribly anxious about his immediate future. What really tormented him was something deeper, something personal and far more pressing. At the same time, he was overwhelmed with a sense of moral exhaustion, though strangely, his mind seemed sharper that morning than it had been in a while.

After everything that had happened, was it even worth the effort to deal with these new, petty problems? Was it worth plotting to keep Svidrigailov away from Porfiry? Was it worth trying to uncover the truth or wasting energy on someone like Svidrigailov? Oh, how tired he was of it all! And yet here he was, rushing to see Svidrigailov. Was he hoping for something new—a piece of information or a way out? People will cling to anything when they're desperate! Was it fate pulling them together, or just some instinct? Maybe it was simply exhaustion or despair. Perhaps it wasn't Svidrigailov he needed at all, but someone else, and Svidrigailov just happened to be nearby. Sonia? Why should he go to her now? To make her cry again? He was afraid of Sonia too. She represented a kind of final judgment, an unchangeable truth. He had to choose either her path or his own. And at that moment, he didn't feel ready to face her. No, maybe it was better to try with Svidrigailov instead. Deep down, he had to admit he'd felt for a long time that he needed to meet with him, though he wasn't entirely sure why.

But what could they possibly have in common? Even their wrongdoing was entirely different. Svidrigailov was unpleasant, clearly corrupt, and undeniably clever and deceitful—maybe even dangerous. There were so many rumors about him. Sure, he had been helping Katerina Ivanovna's children, but who knew what his real motives were? The man always seemed to have some kind of hidden agenda, some scheme.

Another thought had been nagging at Raskolnikov for a while, one that caused him great discomfort. It was so troubling that he had to make an effort to push it out of his mind. He sometimes wondered if Svidrigailov was following him, watching his every move. He suspected that Svidrigailov knew his secret and might have some plan involving Dounia. What if he still did? It seemed almost certain that he did. And what if, now that he knew Raskolnikov's secret, he used it against Dounia as leverage?

This idea had haunted his dreams before, but it had never felt as vivid as it did now, on his way to Svidrigailov. The very thought filled him with dark anger. If it were true, everything would change—even his own position. He would have to confess his secret to Dounia immediately. Would he need to turn himself in to stop Dounia from making a reckless move? The letter? That morning, Dounia had received a letter. Who could be writing to her in Petersburg? Luzhin, maybe? It was true that Razumihin was there to look after her, but Razumihin didn't know the full situation. Should he tell Razumihin? The thought disgusted him.

In any case, he decided he had to see Svidrigailov as soon as possible. The specifics of their meeting didn't matter much, as long as he could uncover the truth. But if Svidrigailov really was scheming against Dounia—then what? Raskolnikov was so drained from everything he had been through that there seemed to be only one answer: "Then I'll kill him," he thought, with cold despair.

A sudden wave of anguish gripped him. He stopped in the middle of the street and looked around, trying to figure out where he was and where he was going. He found himself on X. Prospect, about thirty or forty steps from the Hay Market, which he had just walked through. The entire second floor of the building to his left was a tavern. All the windows were wide open, and the figures moving about inside made it clear the rooms were packed. He could hear music—singing, a clarinet, a violin, and the thumping of a Turkish drum. Women's laughter and shrieks echoed through the air. He was about to turn back, wondering why he had come to X. Prospect in the first place, when he suddenly spotted Svidrigailov. He was sitting by an open window at the far end, smoking a pipe and drinking tea.

Raskolnikov froze, startled and uneasy. Svidrigailov was watching him closely. What struck Raskolnikov immediately was the way Svidrigailov seemed ready to slip away unnoticed. Raskolnikov quickly pretended not to see him, looking absently in another direction while keeping an eye on him from the corner of his vision. His heart pounded in his chest. It was clear Svidrigailov didn't want to be noticed. He took the pipe out of his mouth and began to move his chair back, as if to hide. But as soon as he did, it was obvious that he realized Raskolnikov had seen him and was watching him. The moment reminded Raskolnikov of their first meeting in his room. A sly smile spread across Svidrigailov's face, growing wider and wider. Each man knew the other had seen and was observing him. Finally, Svidrigailov burst out laughing.

"Well, well, come in if you're looking for me. I'm right here!" he called out from the window.

Raskolnikov climbed the stairs into the tavern. He found Svidrigailov in a small back room connected to the main saloon. In the saloon, merchants, clerks, and people of all kinds were drinking tea at about twenty little tables, their conversation drowned out by a rowdy chorus of singers. In the distance, the sound of billiard balls clicking could be heard. On the table in front of Svidrigailov sat an open bottle of champagne and a half-filled glass. The room also held a boy with a small hand organ and a cheerful, rosy-cheeked girl about eighteen years old. She was wearing a striped skirt pulled up high and a Tyrolean hat with ribbons. Despite the loud singing in the other room, she was performing a servants' hall song in a husky contralto voice, accompanied by the boy's organ.

"Come now, that's enough," Svidrigailov said, cutting off the girl's song as soon as Raskolnikov entered the room. The girl immediately stopped singing, standing still with a respectful air, as though she had been performing for an audience far more important than the small gathering here. Her face was serious, her expression almost reverent, as if she regarded her rough, guttural song as something of significance.

"Philip, a glass!" Svidrigailov called out loudly, turning toward the waiter.

"I'm not drinking anything," Raskolnikov said firmly, shaking his head.

"As you wish. It wasn't meant for you, anyway," Svidrigailov replied casually, his tone light, almost dismissive. He turned to the girl. "Drink, Katia! I don't need anything more today. You can go after this." He poured her a full glass of wine and placed a bright yellow banknote on the table in front of her.

Katia drank the wine in a single continuous motion, not pausing even once to set the glass down. She gulped it down quickly, taking no more than twenty swallows to finish it. Then, with a strange mix of humility and gratitude, she picked up the note, leaned forward, and kissed Svidrigailov's hand. He allowed it, his demeanor strangely solemn, as though accepting the gesture as a matter of routine. She left the room without another word, the boy with the little hand organ trailing behind her. Both of them had been pulled in from the street, it seemed. Despite having been in Petersburg less than a week, Svidrigailov had already established an almost patriarchal presence wherever he went. The waiter, Philip, acted as though they were old friends, bending to his every request with an exaggerated show of deference.

The door to the saloon had a heavy lock, which seemed to suggest that this back room was more than just a casual retreat for Svidrigailov; it was a place he had made his own. It wasn't hard to imagine him spending entire days here, lounging in the dingy, third-rate tavern. The place was filthy, run-down, and not even worthy of being called second-rate, but Svidrigailov appeared entirely at home.

"I was looking for you," Raskolnikov began, his voice quiet but steady. "I was on my way to see you, but I don't know why I turned off the Hay Market onto X. Prospect just now. It's not a turn I usually take. I always go right at the Hay Market. And this isn't even the way to your place. I don't know why I turned, but here you are. It's... strange."

"Why not just call it a miracle?" Svidrigailov suggested with a smirk.

"Because it might just be chance," Raskolnikov replied, his tone flat.

"Oh, that's typical of people like you," Svidrigailov said with a laugh. "Even when you secretly believe it's a miracle, you refuse to admit it. Instead, you say it might only be chance. People around here are so terrified of having their own opinions, it's laughable. They'll deny anything just to avoid standing out. But not you, Rodion Romanovich. You've got your own mind, and you're not afraid to use it. That's what caught my attention about you."

"Is that the only reason?" Raskolnikov asked coldly.

"Well, it's enough, isn't it?" Svidrigailov replied, clearly in high spirits. He had only drunk half a glass of wine, but his mood seemed unusually light.

"I think you were interested in me long before you realized I had what you call 'my own mind,'" Raskolnikov observed, his voice tinged with skepticism.

"True enough. Everyone has their own reasons for what they do," Svidrigailov said with a shrug. "As for your so-called miracle, let me remind you that I told you about this tavern myself. There's no mystery in you finding your way here. I even explained how to get here and when you'd find me. Don't you remember?"

"I don't recall," Raskolnikov said, genuinely surprised.

"I believe you. But I told you twice. The address must have lodged itself in your memory, even if you weren't aware of it. You came here without thinking, guided by the directions I gave you. It's mechanical, that's all. But you give away too much, Rodion Romanovich. And another thing—I've noticed a lot of people here in Petersburg talk to themselves as they walk. This city is full of lunatics. If we had more scientists, philosophers, and doctors, they'd have endless material to study here. The city is a reflection of everything wrong with the human soul—climate, politics, ambition—it all leaves a mark. But that's beside the point. The real issue is this: I've been watching you."

"Watching me?" Raskolnikov asked, narrowing his eyes.

"Yes. I've seen you walk out of your house, head held high. But after a few steps, you let your head drop, fold your hands behind your back, and lose yourself in thought. You stop seeing the world around you. Then you start muttering to yourself, moving your lips as if having a conversation. Sometimes you even wave your hand, like you're arguing with someone. Then you stop in the middle of the road, oblivious to anyone watching. It's not a good habit. Someone might notice—and not just me."

"Do you know that someone's following me?" Raskolnikov asked sharply.

"No, I didn't know that," Svidrigailov replied, sounding genuinely surprised.

"Then leave me alone," Raskolnikov muttered, his voice low and tense.

"Very well, let's leave you alone," Svidrigailov said with a slight smile.

"But answer me this," Raskolnikov demanded. "If you wanted me to come here and even told me how to find you, why did you try to slip away when you saw me from the window? I saw you."

"And why," Svidrigailov countered smoothly, "did you lie on your sofa pretending to sleep, though you were wide awake when I stood in your doorway? I saw that too."

"I may have had my reasons," Raskolnikov said carefully. "And you know that."

"And I may have had mine," Svidrigailov replied, his tone equally measured.

Raskolnikov rested his elbow on the table, leaning his chin into his hand as he studied Svidrigailov's face. For a full minute, he scrutinized him intently. It was a striking face, almost like a mask—pale, with bright red lips and thick, flaxen hair that framed a handsome yet unsettling expression. His eyes, an unnatural shade of blue, were heavy and fixed, giving him an unnervingly intense look. He seemed far younger than his years, yet something about him was deeply unpleasant. He was dressed impeccably in light summer clothing, his linen spotless, and a large ring with a gleaming gemstone adorned his hand.

"Am I supposed to worry about you now too?" Raskolnikov asked abruptly, his voice laced with irritation. "You might be the most dangerous man I know, and yet I can't bring myself to care anymore. Let me make myself clear. If you still have any plans involving my sister—if you think you can gain anything from what's come to light recently—I'll kill you before you can turn me in. Count on it. You know I'll keep my word. And if you have something to tell me—because I've had the feeling this whole time that you do—then say it now. Time is running out."

"Why the rush?" Svidrigailov asked, tilting his head slightly as he regarded Raskolnikov with a mix of curiosity and amusement. His gaze lingered, as if he were trying to decipher the motivations that lay beneath Raskolnikov's terse demeanor.

"Everyone has their plans," Raskolnikov replied, his voice heavy with gloom and impatience. He spoke as though he had neither the energy nor the inclination to elaborate further.

"You urged me to be open and honest just a moment ago," Svidrigailov pointed out with a faint smile, "and yet, the first question I ask, you refuse to answer. You suspect I have my own hidden agendas, and I don't blame you—it's perfectly natural, given your circumstances. But let me assure you, while I might enjoy the idea of us being friends, I won't go out of my way to convince you of my sincerity. Frankly, it's not worth the effort. And for the record, I didn't call you here with any particular intention."

"Then what did you want with me?" Raskolnikov demanded, his tone sharp. "It was you, after all, who went out of your way to seek me out."

"Why, simply because I find you fascinating," Svidrigailov replied, leaning back in his chair with an air of satisfaction. "Your situation is so... extraordinary, so unusual, that I couldn't resist observing it up close. And besides," he added with a sly grin, "you're the brother of someone I've found deeply intriguing. I learned a great deal about you through her. From what she told me, it was clear you've had a significant influence on her life. Isn't that reason enough? Ha-ha! Still, your question is more complicated than it seems, and I admit it's not easy to answer fully. But let's turn the tables for a moment—you've come here with a purpose, haven't you? Surely you're not here by accident. Perhaps you're looking to hear something new from me. Isn't that it? Am I wrong?"

Svidrigailov's sly smile widened as he leaned forward, studying Raskolnikov's face with a glint of mischief in his eyes. "And if that's the case," he continued, "isn't it fair to think I might be expecting the same from you? On my way here, I thought to myself, 'Raskolnikov might tell me something new, something valuable.' You see, we're both richer than we think!"

"Rich? What profit could you possibly gain from me?" Raskolnikov shot back, his brows furrowing in skepticism.

"Ah, now that is the question, isn't it?" Svidrigailov said with a chuckle. "I couldn't say for sure. How should I know? Look at where I spend my time—a wretched little tavern like this. It's no paradise, but one needs a place to sit, doesn't one? Take that poor girl, Katia, for example—you saw her, didn't you? If I were the sort of man who found joy in fine dining or luxurious clubs, I'd hardly settle for this." He gestured toward a small table in the corner, where the remains of a dismal-looking beefsteak and a heap of cold potatoes sat on a battered tin dish. "This is what I've been eating. Have you eaten today, by the way? I've had enough, and I don't need anything more."

He waved dismissively at the idea of excess. "I don't drink much either. Champagne is the only thing I'll touch, and even then, no more than a single glass. Even that is enough to give me a headache. I only ordered some now to wind myself up. You see, I'm about to head somewhere, and my mind's in a peculiar state. That's why I tried to hide when I saw you earlier—I thought you might delay me. But now I see I can spare an hour after all." He pulled a pocket watch from his coat and checked the time. "It's only half-past four. If only I had some grand purpose—something to call my own—a career, a family, anything. But instead, here I am, floating through life with no specialty, no anchor. Sometimes, I get so bored, it's unbearable. I thought you might help with that, tell me something worth hearing."

"And what are you, exactly? Why are you even here?" Raskolnikov pressed, his irritation growing.

"Me? I'm a gentleman," Svidrigailov replied breezily. "I served in the cavalry for two years, then drifted around Petersburg for a while. After that, I married Marfa Petrovna and settled in the countryside. And there you have it—my life story in a nutshell!"

"You're a gambler, aren't you?" Raskolnikov asked sharply.

"Not a very good one," Svidrigailov admitted with a laugh. "A card-sharper at best, not a proper gambler."

"So you've cheated at cards?" Raskolnikov pressed further.

"Yes, I've done that too," Svidrigailov replied without hesitation.

"Did anyone ever beat you for it?"

"Oh, more than once," Svidrigailov said with a shrug. "Why does that surprise you?"

"You could have challenged them to a duel. I imagine life must have been lively for you."

"Lively? Perhaps. But what's the use of dwelling on it? I won't argue with you. Philosophy isn't my strong suit. To be honest, I came to Petersburg for one reason only—women."

"As soon as you buried Marfa Petrovna?" Raskolnikov asked bluntly.

"Exactly," Svidrigailov answered with disarming candor. "And why not? Does that shock you?"

"Do you even hear yourself?" Raskolnikov snapped. "You ask if I have a problem with vice?"

"Vice? Oh, so that's your issue! But I'll answer you anyway. Tell me, why should I restrain myself? If I have a passion for something, why deny it? It gives me purpose, at least."

"A purpose? You call that purpose?" Raskolnikov's voice was thick with disgust. "It's nothing more than a disease—a dangerous one at that."

"Ah, perhaps," Svidrigailov conceded, "but what isn't a disease in excess? Everyone goes too far in something. At least with this, there's an honesty to it. It's rooted in nature, not some fleeting fancy."

Raskolnikov leaned back, feeling the weight of the conversation pressing on him. The room, the man before him—it all felt stifling. "Why am I even here?" he muttered under his breath.

"Stay a little longer," Svidrigailov urged, suddenly eager. "I'll tell you something worthwhile—something about your sister, if you're willing to listen."

Chapter 4

"You might recall—or perhaps I mentioned it to you before," Svidrigailov began, his tone deliberately casual, "that I was once in the debtors' prison here, owing an enormous sum of money. I had no hope of paying it off. There's no need to bore you with all the details about how Marfa Petrovna managed to get me out of that wretched situation. But let me tell you this—do you know how far a woman's love can go? To what extremes it can drive her? Marfa Petrovna was, at her core, an honest woman, though uneducated, and very practical in her way. Yet her love for me bordered on madness, pure madness."

He paused, his expression thoughtful, as though reliving the memory. "You might find this hard to believe, but that virtuous and intensely jealous woman eventually agreed to what you might call a peculiar arrangement—a contract of sorts—that she adhered to throughout our married life. Imagine this: she was older than me by quite a bit, and, well, let's just say she had certain... habits. She was rarely without a clove or some other spice tucked in her mouth. But that didn't stop her from being both fiercely loyal and fiercely controlling."

Svidrigailov leaned back in his chair, folding his arms. "I won't deny it—there was a lot of filth in my soul, but there was a sort of honesty too. I told her outright, at the very beginning, that I couldn't be entirely faithful to her. My frankness drove her to hysterics at first, naturally, but strangely, she seemed to admire it in some twisted way. She took it as proof that I wouldn't deceive her—because, after all, I'd been upfront from the start. And for a jealous woman, that's a critical detail, you see."

He chuckled dryly. "So, after countless arguments, tears, and dramatic scenes, we established an unspoken agreement. First, I was to remain her husband and never abandon her. Second, I would never leave the house without her permission. Third, I was forbidden to maintain a long-term mistress. In return for these concessions, she granted me certain... liberties with the maidservants—but only with her knowledge and approval. Fourth, and most importantly, I was absolutely forbidden to fall in love with a woman of our own class. Should I ever—God forbid—find myself consumed by a genuine passion for someone, I was obligated to confess it to her immediately."

Svidrigailov gave a wry smile. "On that last point, Marfa Petrovna had little to worry about. She saw me as a dissolute man, incapable of real love. She was practical enough to understand that. But practicality and jealousy don't always go hand in hand, and therein lay the trouble. A sensible woman and a jealous one are rarely the same thing. To judge her fairly, though, one must abandon preconceived notions. I have no illusions about the absurdities and ridiculous quirks people attributed to her. Still, I feel genuine regret for the pain I caused her—pain I can't entirely dismiss, even now."

He waved his hand as though to brush away the sentiment. "But enough of that. Consider this a fitting eulogy for the most patient wife of the most charmingly flawed husband. When we quarreled, I made it a point to hold my tongue. I avoided provoking her further, and, strangely enough, that restraint seemed to impress her. There were moments when she even seemed proud of me—proud of my so-called gentlemanly conduct."

He leaned forward, his tone shifting slightly. "But your sister? Ah, she couldn't stand her. To this day, I can't quite fathom why Marfa Petrovna would risk bringing someone as beautiful and captivating as Avdotya Romanovna into our household. My guess? Marfa Petrovna was an emotional and impressionable woman, and she quite literally fell in love with your sister. Yes, fell in love! And honestly, who could blame her? Look at Avdotya Romanovna—she's extraordinary. From the very first moment, I recognized the danger. And do you know what I resolved to do? I decided not to look at her, not even once, for fear of the consequences. But would you believe it? Avdotya Romanovna made the first move."

Raskolnikov's eyes narrowed slightly, his expression hardening.

Svidrigailov laughed softly. "You don't believe me? Well, Marfa Petrovna, as you might imagine, was furious at my apparent indifference. She couldn't understand why I didn't react to her endless praises of Avdotya Romanovna. And, of course, Marfa Petrovna had the unfortunate habit of telling everyone about our family affairs. She couldn't resist confiding in her new friend—sharing all our secrets, all her grievances about me. What do you suppose they talked about most of the time? No doubt, me. And I wouldn't be surprised if your sister heard all the dark, salacious rumors people whispered about me. No doubt you've heard some of them yourself."

"I have," Raskolnikov said bluntly. "Luzhin accused you of causing the death of a child. Is that true?"

Svidrigailov's expression darkened. "Don't bring up such vulgar tales," he said sharply, his voice tinged with both irritation and disgust. "If you're determined to hear about all that nonsense, I'll tell you another time. But not now."

"I've also heard about a footman in your service," Raskolnikov pressed. "Apparently, you treated him rather cruelly."

Svidrigailov's patience visibly frayed. "I beg you to drop the subject," he said, his tone clipped.

"Was it that same footman who supposedly came to you after his death to light your pipe? You told me about that yourself," Raskolnikov said, his irritation clearly mounting.

Svidrigailov studied him intently for a long moment, his pale blue eyes glinting with a flash of something unreadable—spite, perhaps, or mockery. But when he finally spoke, his voice was measured, even polite.

"Yes, it's true," Svidrigailov admitted, a peculiar smile playing on his lips. "I can see that you're deeply curious about all this, and I suppose it's only fair to satisfy your interest at some point. Truly, I sometimes feel as though I've become a romantic figure in the eyes of certain people, and why not? Consider how much I owe to Marfa Petrovna for spreading such mysterious and tantalizing stories about me to Avdotya Romanovna. I dare not imagine what impression they made on her, but they certainly worked in my favor.

"Despite her natural aversion and my consistently grim, even repellent demeanor, she felt something for me—pity, no less. Yes, pity for a lost and damned soul. And let me tell you, Rodion Romanovich, when pity finds its way into a girl's heart, it's far more perilous than love itself. Pity leads to dreams of salvation, of noble rescues and reformations. She dreams of bringing the fallen man to his senses, lifting him up to some higher plane of existence, restoring him to new life, and making him useful once again. It's intoxicating, that feeling. I recognized it immediately—the bird was fluttering straight into the cage of its own accord. And naturally, I prepared myself accordingly."

Svidrigailov paused, watching Raskolnikov's expression. "Are you frowning, Rodion Romanovich? Don't worry, there's no need for alarm. As you know, it all amounted to nothing. It ended in smoke." He gestured toward his glass, smiling faintly. "Hang it all, I'm drinking far too much."

He leaned forward slightly, his tone taking on a wistful quality. "Do you know, I've often thought that Avdotya Romanovna was born out of her time. She should have lived in the second or third century A.D., perhaps as the daughter of a prince or a proconsul in some corner of Asia Minor. She would have made a perfect martyr—one of those who smiled even as they were branded with hot pincers. And she wouldn't have hesitated; she would have walked to her fate willingly, with her head held high. Or in the fourth or fifth century, she might have retreated into the Egyptian desert to live thirty years on roots and visions. She's the kind of woman who thirsts for suffering, for sacrifice. And if she can't find it, she might very well throw herself out of a window."

Svidrigailov chuckled softly. "I hear there's a fellow named Razumihin—someone sensible, by all accounts, and his name seems to suit him. Is he a divinity student, perhaps? He'd better look after your sister carefully. I flatter myself that I understand her in ways others cannot, and I take pride in that. But then again, when one first meets someone, one doesn't always act wisely. People are careless, impulsive. And honestly, who can blame me? Look at her—why must she be so beautiful? That's not my fault, is it? Of course, my initial interest in her was entirely... shall we say, physical. Her chastity, though, is something to marvel at—phenomenal, almost to the point of being unnatural. Believe me, I state it as a fact: she is almost morbidly chaste, despite her intelligence. And that chastity, Rodion Romanovich, is bound to cause her trouble.

"At the time, there was a girl in the house—a maid named Parasha. She had just come from another village, a simple creature, pretty enough, but dreadfully dim-witted. One day, after dinner, Avdotya Romanovna confronted me in the garden. Her eyes were flashing with indignation as she demanded that I leave poor Parasha alone. Can you imagine? That was the first time we spoke alone. Naturally, I agreed immediately, pretended to be embarrassed, and played my part as convincingly as I could. After that, there were more conversations— mysterious, earnest, full of entreaties and tears. Yes, tears, Rodion Romanovich! Imagine the passion for reform that drives a girl to such extremes. I played along, of course, casting myself as the wretched sinner desperate for enlightenment, thirsty for redemption. And then I employed the most reliable weapon of all—flattery.

"You see, flattery is infallible. Speaking the truth is fraught with risks—a single false note can create discord and ruin everything. But flattery? Even when it's entirely false, it's irresistible. It appeals to everyone, from the simplest peasant to the most virtuous vestal virgin. I've often laughed at the memory of how I once seduced a woman utterly devoted to her husband, children, and principles. It was almost too easy. All I had to do was prostrate myself before her supposed purity, flatter her shamelessly, and act as though every small favor she granted was a miraculous victory over my unworthiness. She remained convinced of her own virtue even as she yielded to me."

Svidrigailov laughed, but his tone turned rueful. "And poor Marfa Petrovna—she was hopelessly susceptible to flattery. If I'd cared to, I could have had her sign over all her property to me while she was still alive. But let's not dwell on that. As for your sister, I was beginning to have the same effect on her. I might have succeeded, but I was stupid—impatient. Worse, my eyes betrayed me. Avdotya Romanovna told me once that there was something in my gaze that frightened her. She said it grew stronger, more unguarded, until it became intolerable. And so we parted. I jeered at her efforts to reform me, mocked her noble aspirations, and turned back to Parasha—along with others. It was a mess.

"But ah, Rodion Romanovich, if only you could have seen her eyes when she was angry! Even now, her glance haunts my dreams. The sound of her footsteps, the rustle of her dress—it was enough to drive me mad. I truly believed I might become epileptic. But by then, reconciliation was impossible, and I—well, I acted in utter frenzy. Never act in a frenzy, Rodion Romanovich. It leads only to disaster."

He hesitated, then leaned closer, lowering his voice. "Imagine this: I resolved to offer her all my money—thirty thousand rubles—if she would run away with me to Petersburg. I would have promised her eternal love, devotion, anything she wanted. I was so consumed by passion that, if she had asked me to poison Marfa Petrovna or marry her on the spot, I would have done it without hesitation. But you know how it ended—a catastrophe. And when I learned that Marfa Petrovna had tried to match her with that scoundrel Luzhin, it was as though she had beaten me at my own game. Don't you think? Wouldn't you agree?"

He paused, noticing Raskolnikov's attentive gaze. "Ah, I see I've captured your interest, my fascinating young man."

Svidrigailov struck the table with his fist, the sound cutting through the room with a sharp finality. His face was flushed, and Raskolnikov observed that even the small amount of champagne Svidrigailov had consumed—a glass, perhaps a glass and a half—was beginning to affect him. He appeared to be losing his usual guarded composure, and Raskolnikov decided this was an opportunity he could not let slip. His distrust of Svidrigailov had only deepened, and now was the time to press him further.

"Well," Raskolnikov began, his tone deliberate and direct, "after everything you've said, I am fully convinced that you came to Petersburg with the intention of pursuing my sister."

Svidrigailov stirred as if snapping out of a daze, his expression sharpening slightly. "Oh, nonsense," he retorted, brushing the comment aside with a wave of his hand. "I've already told you—your sister can't stand me."

"Yes, I'm certain she despises you," Raskolnikov replied, his voice firm. "But that's not the point."

"Are you so sure she can't endure me?" Svidrigailov asked, his tone turning sly. He screwed up his eyes and smiled mockingly. "You're probably right—she doesn't love me. But let me remind you of something: no one can ever truly know what passes between two people—whether they're husband and wife or lovers. There's always a little corner of their relationship that remains hidden from the world, a private sanctuary only they understand. Can you swear, with absolute certainty, that Avdotya Romanovna looks at me with nothing but aversion?"

Raskolnikov leaned forward, his suspicion intensifying. "From the way you talk, it's clear to me that you still harbor designs on her—evil ones—and that you intend to act on them soon."

"Designs?" Svidrigailov repeated, feigning innocence. He looked genuinely surprised, even dismayed, as if the very suggestion were an affront. "What words have I let slip to give you that impression?"

"You're letting them slip even now," Raskolnikov replied coldly. "Why are you so on edge? What are you so afraid of?"

"Me? Afraid? Afraid of you?" Svidrigailov laughed, though there was a faint tension in his voice. "If anything, my dear friend, you're the one who should be afraid of me. But this is all nonsense... nonsense. I've clearly had too much to drink." He shook his head abruptly, then raised his voice. "Philip! Bring water!"

In a sudden gesture, Svidrigailov grabbed the champagne bottle and flung it out the window with little ceremony. The crash was audible, but he seemed unbothered. When Philip returned with water, Svidrigailov soaked a towel and pressed it to his flushed face. "There, that's better," he muttered. "But all this is nonsense. Let me put your suspicions to rest with one simple fact." He dropped the towel and looked directly at Raskolnikov. "Did you know that I'm getting married?"

"You told me so before," Raskolnikov said, his expression unreadable.

"Did I?" Svidrigailov looked momentarily surprised. "I must have forgotten. At the time, though, it wasn't definite. I hadn't even seen the girl yet. But now it's settled—I've met her, and we're engaged. If it weren't for some urgent business I need to attend to, I'd take you to meet her right this minute. I could even use your advice. But look!" He pulled out a watch and showed it to Raskolnikov. "Only ten minutes left. Still, it's quite an interesting story—this engagement of mine. Where are you going? Are you leaving?"

"No, I'm staying," Raskolnikov said curtly.

"Good. Very good. Let me tell you, the woman I'm lodging with, Madame Resslich, arranged the whole thing. You've heard of her, haven't you? Yes, she's the one people whisper about—the woman whose maid drowned herself in the winter. She told me I needed something to occupy myself, to fill my time, because, you know, I'm not a particularly cheerful person. Quite the opposite, in fact. Do you think I'm light-hearted? No, I'm gloomy—a depressive, even. I can sit in a corner for days without speaking a word. Anyway, Resslich, being the sly woman she is, decided to play matchmaker. She probably thinks I'll tire of the girl eventually, abandon her, and then she'll be able to use her for her own schemes—marrying her off to someone of our class or perhaps higher."

He laughed, the sound a mixture of amusement and bitterness. "She told me all about the family. The father's a retired official, paralyzed for three years and confined to a chair. The mother is practical but worn down by life. There's an older brother in the provinces who doesn't help them, and a married sister who never visits. Then there's the youngest daughter—just fifteen, almost sixteen—who they've pulled out of school so she can be married off."

Svidrigailov's voice grew animated as he described his visit. "So, I presented myself to them—a widower, a landowner, a man of means and connections. Never mind that I'm fifty and she's not yet sixteen—who cares about such trifles? You should have seen their faces! The girl herself came in, curtseying shyly in her short frock, blushing like a sunset. She's a picture of innocence—fair hair, tiny feet, soft, rosy lips. A little lamb! I spoke to the parents, of course, and made a good impression. The very next day, we were engaged. Now, when I visit, she sits on my knee, and I kiss her as often as I please. Her mother tells her it's her duty to accept my affection—this is her husband, after all! Isn't it fascinating?"

Raskolnikov's face darkened, but Svidrigailov continued unabated. "She's not just a pretty face, you know. She's intelligent, too. Sometimes she looks at me with an intensity that's almost frightening. Her eyes remind me of Raphael's Madonna—there's something otherworldly about them. Yesterday, she even flung her arms around my neck and promised to be the most devoted wife, asking for nothing in return but my respect. Imagine that—a declaration like that from an angel in a muslin dress! It's worth every penny of the fifteen hundred rubles I've spent on her gifts so far."

Svidrigailov leaned back, his expression turning sly. "And now, my dear friend, what do you think of my betrothed? Shall we go see her? No, not now—you'll have to wait."

Raskolnikov's voice was sharp when he finally spoke. "The difference in age and development between you is monstrous. This is nothing but an indulgence of your basest desires. Do you truly intend to go through with this marriage?"

"Of course I do," Svidrigailov replied with a laugh. "Why shouldn't I? Everyone lives for themselves, after all. The happiest people are those who are best at deceiving themselves. But tell me, why are you so concerned with virtue? Spare me your moralizing—I am, after all, just a sinful man. Ha-ha!"

"But you've provided for Katerina Ivanovna's children," Raskolnikov said, his tone laced with bitterness. "Though, of course, you had your own reasons for doing so... I understand it all now."

Svidrigailov laughed, a low, almost indulgent chuckle. "I've always been fond of children," he said lightly. "Very fond of them. In fact, I can tell you a rather curious story to illustrate the point. It happened the very first day I arrived here in Petersburg. After seven years in the country, I found myself rushing to reacquaint myself with certain... haunts." He smirked, a gleam of mischief in his eyes. "I've no great eagerness to renew ties with my old friends, mind you. I can do without them for as long as possible. But the places themselves? Ah, those I missed. You probably noticed it yourself—this city reeks of its peculiar atmosphere, the sort that never changes. And upon my arrival, I plunged headfirst into it."

He leaned back in his chair, gesturing expansively as he spoke. "While living with Marfa Petrovna, I often found myself haunted by memories of Petersburg—the vodka-soaked peasants, the educated young fools wasting themselves on impossible dreams and pointless theories, the Jews amassing fortunes, and the rest of them wallowing in debauchery. The moment I set foot in town, the air seemed to hum with its old, familiar odors. It was like stepping into a memory. Naturally, I ended up in some filthy dive—a dance hall of sorts, though it was little more than a cesspit."

He paused for effect, his smile widening as he gauged Raskolnikov's reaction. "There was a cancan, the likes of which I'd never seen in my day. Progress, you know. And there, in the midst of it all, was a little girl. No more than thirteen, dressed neatly, almost elegantly, but utterly out of place. She was dancing awkwardly with some seasoned performer—a true specialist in that grotesque art—with another one opposite her. Her mother sat nearby, a weary figure slumped against the wall.

"You can't imagine the scene," Svidrigailov continued, his voice tinged with mockery. "The girl was blushing furiously, clearly embarrassed, but she kept trying. Eventually, she began to cry. Her partner, of course, took no notice and began spinning her around wildly, performing exaggerated steps meant to humiliate her further. And the crowd—oh, your glorious crowd! They laughed, they jeered, shouting, 'Serves her right! Serves her right! Why bring a child here?' A logical sentiment, I suppose, though hardly comforting."

Raskolnikov's expression darkened, but Svidrigailov pressed on, his tone almost jovial. "I decided on a course of action right then and there. I approached the mother, sat beside her, and struck up a conversation. I told her I was a stranger in town, too, and that the people here were terribly ill-bred, incapable of recognizing decent folk. I hinted, of course, that I had plenty of money and offered to take them home in my carriage. Naturally, she agreed. They were living in some miserable little hole, having just arrived from the countryside on some legal business. The mother, poor thing, could hardly stop thanking me. She and her daughter considered my acquaintance an honor. Imagine that!"

He laughed again, shaking his head. "I offered to help with their affairs, to pay for the girl's education—French lessons, dancing, whatever they needed. They accepted with enthusiasm, seeing it as nothing short of a miracle. We're still on good terms, you know. If you'd like, I could introduce you to them—though perhaps not just now."

"Enough!" Raskolnikov snapped, his voice sharp with anger. "I've had enough of your vile, disgusting anecdotes. You're a depraved, base, and revolting man!"

"Ah, Schiller! My dear Rodion Romanovich, you're such a Schiller," Svidrigailov said, grinning broadly. "O la vertu va-t-elle se nicher? But I'll confess, I share these stories purely for the pleasure of hearing your indignant cries. It's delightful."

"You're mocking me," Raskolnikov muttered, his anger barely contained. "And yes, I'm aware I look ridiculous."

Svidrigailov burst into hearty laughter, his amusement echoing in the room. Finally, he signaled for Philip, paid his bill, and stood up.

"Enough talk. I must admit, I've had quite a bit to drink," he said, his words slightly slurred but still clear. "This has been... entertaining."

"Entertaining?" Raskolnikov stood as well, his face a mask of disdain. "For you, perhaps. A worn-out libertine reveling in his twisted tales, concocting monstrous schemes while sharing them with someone like me. I suppose it's stimulating."

Svidrigailov's smile faltered for a moment as he scrutinized Raskolnikov. Then, to Raskolnikov's surprise, he nodded, as if acknowledging some unspoken truth. "Well, if you put it that way," he said, his tone softer but still laced with irony, "I suppose I am a cynic. But then, so are you, my dear friend. A thorough cynic. You've lived enough, seen enough, to understand much more than most— and to do much more, too. But alas, our conversation must end. I do regret not having had more time to talk with you. Don't worry, though. I won't lose track of you."

With that, Svidrigailov turned and strode out of the restaurant, leaving Raskolnikov to follow at a distance. Outside, the fresh air seemed to sober Svidrigailov somewhat. His earlier joviality faded, replaced by a look of preoccupation. His brow furrowed, his stride purposeful yet tense. It was clear he was consumed by something— some urgent matter weighing heavily on his mind. His manner toward Raskolnikov had shifted as well, becoming increasingly curt and dismissive, as though he no longer saw the need to maintain the veneer of civility.

Raskolnikov noticed the change and felt his own unease growing. His suspicions about Svidrigailov deepened with each step. Whatever the man was planning, Raskolnikov was determined to find out. Without a word, he resolved to follow.

When they reached the pavement, Svidrigailov turned to him briefly, his smile returning but tinged with irony. "You go right, and I'll go left," he said lightly. "Or, if you prefer, the other way around. Adieu, mon plaisir. Until we meet again."

Without waiting for a reply, he turned and walked briskly toward the Hay Market, disappearing into the crowd.

Chapter 5

Raskolnikov followed Svidrigailov out of the building, his steps deliberate and unwavering.

"What's this?" Svidrigailov asked, spinning around abruptly. His expression was a mixture of irritation and amusement. "I thought I told you…"

"It means I'm not going to lose sight of you now," Raskolnikov interrupted, his tone cold and resolute.

"What?" Svidrigailov stared at him, his brows furrowing in confusion.

They stopped in the middle of the street, facing each other like two adversaries preparing for a duel. Their gazes locked, and for a moment, neither spoke. The air between them seemed to hum with unspoken tension.

"From your half-drunken ramblings," Raskolnikov said harshly, breaking the silence, "I am now certain that you haven't given up your designs on my sister. In fact, you seem more determined than ever. I know she received a letter this morning. And you—you've hardly been able to sit still. Perhaps you've managed to 'discover' a wife along the way, but that proves nothing. I intend to see for myself."

He couldn't have said precisely what he was looking for or what he hoped to confirm. The words came out in a rush, driven more by instinct than reason.

"Upon my word, I'll call the police!" Svidrigailov threatened, though his voice lacked real conviction.

"Go ahead, call them!" Raskolnikov shot back, unflinching.

Again, they stood in silence, measuring one another like boxers in the ring. At last, Svidrigailov's expression shifted. The mockery faded, replaced by something lighter—an almost friendly air, though the gleam in his eyes betrayed a hint of calculation.

"What a strange fellow you are," Svidrigailov said with a half-smile. "I've deliberately avoided bringing up your situation, though I confess I'm dying of curiosity. It's such a fantastical affair! But you—ha! You're enough to rouse the dead. Very well, come along if you must. But I'll warn you now: I'm only going home to fetch some money. After that, I'll lock up the flat, take a cab, and spend the evening at the Islands. What will you do then? Follow me all night?"

"I'm coming to your lodgings," Raskolnikov replied flatly. "Not to see you, but Sofya Semyonovna. I owe her an apology for not attending the funeral."

"Well, that's your choice. But I should warn you—Sofya Semyonovna isn't home. She's taken Katerina Ivanovna's three children to visit an old lady of some prominence, a patroness of orphanages, whom I happened to know years ago. I charmed the woman, of course, by depositing a sum of money for the children's future and subscribing to her institution. I also told her Sofya Semyonovna's story in its entirety, leaving out none of the sordid details. The effect was remarkable, to say the least. The lady was so moved that she insisted on meeting Sofya Semyonovna today at the X. Hotel, where she's staying temporarily."

"No matter," Raskolnikov said stiffly. "I'll come anyway."

"As you like," Svidrigailov said with a shrug. "It's no concern of mine. But I won't be accompanying you. And here we are—my lodgings."

As they climbed the stairs, Svidrigailov turned to Raskolnikov, his voice laced with irony. "You know, I suspect you've been watching me so closely because my discretion unnerves you. You can't understand why I've shown such delicacy—why I haven't bombarded you with questions. Admit it, that's what's bothering you! Well, let this be a lesson in the dangers of being too polite."

"And of eavesdropping at doors," Raskolnikov snapped.

"Ah, there it is!" Svidrigailov laughed, a genuine belly laugh that echoed in the narrow stairwell. "I'd have been surprised if you let that one go, given everything that's happened. But tell me—what exactly did you mean by it? I caught bits and pieces of your conversations with Sofya Semyonovna. Some of it sounded quite... imaginative. Perhaps I'm out of touch and need someone like you to explain the latest theories to me."

"You couldn't have heard anything," Raskolnikov said sharply. "You're making it up."

"Maybe," Svidrigailov replied with an infuriating smile. "But that's not what I meant. No, I'm talking about the way you've been sighing and groaning lately, as though the weight of the world rests on your shoulders. The Schiller in you is rebelling, isn't it? But if you're so troubled by the idea of listening at doors, perhaps you should march down to the police and confess everything—admit you made a mistake in your grand theory. Or better yet, run to America while you still can! I'll even pay for your fare."

"I'm not thinking about that at all," Raskolnikov retorted, his voice thick with disgust.

"I understand, I understand," Svidrigailov said quickly, waving a hand as if to dismiss the subject. "But don't strain yourself. Moral questions, duties as a citizen and a man—they're irrelevant to you now. You might say they don't belong to you anymore. Lay them aside; they'll only weigh you down."

"You're trying to provoke me into leaving," Raskolnikov observed, narrowing his eyes.

"What a strange young man you are," Svidrigailov said with a grin. "But come along. Here's Sofya Semyonovna's room—locked, as I told you. And Madame de Kapernaumov will confirm it. She's hard of hearing, though, so you may need to shout. Still don't believe me? Come to my room, then. Surely that's what you've been after all along."

Inside his flat, Svidrigailov moved with purpose. He opened a bureau, extracted a five-percent bond, and waved it in Raskolnikov's direction. "See? This one gets turned into cash today. I still have plenty more. Now, the bureau is locked, the flat is locked, and I'm off. Shall we take a cab together? No? Suit yourself. But I warn you—it might rain."

With that, Svidrigailov climbed into a carriage and disappeared down the street. Raskolnikov stood watching for a moment, then turned back toward the Hay Market. He did not see Svidrigailov exit the cab just a short distance away, dismiss the driver, and walk briskly in the opposite direction.

As Raskolnikov walked, his thoughts churned with bitterness and regret. "To think I could have even momentarily looked to that coarse, depraved man for help," he muttered. "What was I thinking?"

Yet even as he dismissed Svidrigailov as a vile, sensual brute, a nagging sense of intrigue lingered. There was something original, even mysterious, about him. But Raskolnikov pushed the thought aside— it was too exhausting to dwell on such things.

When Raskolnikov found himself alone, he had barely walked twenty paces before sinking into his familiar state of deep thought. His mind, as always, was a storm of conflicting emotions and endless questions. Reaching the bridge, he stopped by the railing and stared down at the water below, his gaze heavy with contemplation. He didn't notice that his sister, Dounia, was standing just a short distance away, watching him.

She had seen him as he approached the entrance to the bridge, but he passed by without acknowledging her, his eyes fixed ahead as though in a trance. Dounia had never encountered him like this, wandering the streets lost in thought, and the sight filled her with dismay. She stood rooted to the spot, torn between the urge to call out to him and the fear of disturbing whatever tumultuous thoughts consumed him.

Suddenly, she became aware of another presence. Svidrigailov was approaching from the direction of the Hay Market. His movements were calculated, almost cautious, as though he were deliberately trying to avoid Raskolnikov's notice. When he caught sight of Dounia, his expression shifted. For a moment, he stood still on the pavement, making subtle gestures in her direction. She understood his signals as an urgent request—not to approach her brother, but to come to him instead.

Hesitating only briefly, Dounia obeyed, slipping quietly past Raskolnikov without a word and making her way toward Svidrigailov.

"Let's move quickly," Svidrigailov whispered as she reached him. His voice was low but insistent. "I don't want Rodion Romanovich to see us. I must tell you, he sought me out earlier. We sat together in a restaurant nearby, and I had quite the ordeal shaking him off. He's discovered something about the letter I sent to you and is suspicious. I trust it wasn't you who told him?" He studied her face carefully, his eyes narrowing slightly. "If not you, then who?"

"We've turned the corner now," Dounia said, cutting him off. She glanced back briefly to confirm that her brother couldn't see them. "My brother won't notice us here. I'll hear what you have to say, but I'm not going any further with you. Speak now, in the street."

Svidrigailov frowned, his lips pressing into a thin line. "I can't explain here," he replied curtly. "First, you must hear Sofya Semyonovna as well. Second, I need to show you certain documents. If you refuse to come with me, I'll simply leave, and you'll get no explanation at all. But don't forget, Avdotya Romanovna, that I hold a rather significant secret about your beloved brother. A very curious one."

Dounia hesitated, her expression hardening. She fixed him with a piercing stare, searching his face for any trace of sincerity or deceit.

"What are you afraid of?" Svidrigailov asked quietly, though his tone carried a note of mockery. "This is the city, not the countryside. Besides, you've done me more harm than I've ever done to you, so what have you to fear?"

"Have you prepared Sofya Semyonovna for this meeting?" Dounia demanded, her voice sharp.

"No," Svidrigailov admitted, shrugging. "I've said nothing to her yet, and I'm not entirely sure she's home right now. But most likely she is—she buried her stepmother today, so I doubt she's out visiting anyone. For now, I'd prefer not to involve anyone else. To be honest, I half-regret speaking to you about this at all. Even the slightest indiscretion in matters like this can have disastrous consequences. But here we are. That building there is where I live. See the porter? He knows me well, as you can tell by the way he's bowing. I imagine he's already noticed your face too, which should put you at ease if you're still suspicious of me. But really, am I so terrible?"

His lips curved into a condescending smile, but his mood was anything but light. His chest rose and fell with quick, shallow breaths, and his hands trembled faintly at his sides. Svidrigailov's outward confidence was betrayed by a barely contained excitement—or perhaps something closer to desperation.

Dounia, however, was too irritated by his smug remark to notice the subtle signs of his unease. "Though I know you're not a man of honor," she said coldly, "I'm not afraid of you. Lead the way."

She spoke with an air of composure, but her face was pale, her lips tight.

Svidrigailov stopped at the door to Sofya Semyonovna's room. "Allow me to see if she's in," he said, stepping forward. After a moment, he turned back to Dounia. "She's not here. How unfortunate! But she might return soon. If you like, I can send her to you later today. In the meantime, let me show you something."

Dounia followed him reluctantly into his flat. His rooms were modestly furnished, though something about their arrangement made her uneasy. The space seemed deliberately chosen, tucked away between two nearly empty apartments. Unlocking a door in his bedroom, Svidrigailov gestured for her to look inside.

"See here," he said, pointing to a chair positioned near the door. "This is where I sat—two evenings in a row, for hours at a time— listening. Sofya Semyonovna's table is just on the other side. She sat there talking to Rodion Romanovich. Of course, I learned quite a bit. What do you think of that?"

"You listened?" Dounia asked, horrified.

"Yes, I did," Svidrigailov replied unapologetically. "Come back to the sitting room. We can't stay here."

Back in the main room, Svidrigailov sat across from her at the table. Though he maintained a polite distance, the intensity in his eyes unsettled her. She shuddered, glancing around the room, her discomfort evident despite her efforts to hide it.

Dounia drew a folded letter from her pocket and placed it on the table. "Is what you wrote here true?" she demanded. "You hinted at a crime committed by my brother. You were too clear in your insinuations to deny it now. I've already heard this ridiculous story before, and I don't believe a word of it. You promised proof—well, speak! But let me warn you, I don't believe you."

"If you don't believe me," Svidrigailov said, his voice calm but probing, "then why did you come here? Why take the risk of coming alone? Was it curiosity?"

"Don't torment me. Speak!" Dounia cried, her voice trembling.

Svidrigailov's smile widened. "You're braver than I expected, coming here without even asking Razumihin to escort you. That proves something—your loyalty to Rodion Romanovich, perhaps. But as for your brother, tell me: what did you think of him when you saw him today?"

"Surely that's not all you're basing this on?" she said, her voice wavering.

"No, of course not. I'm basing it on his own words. He confessed everything to Sofya Semyonovna—the murders, the theft, all of it. He killed the old pawnbroker and her sister, Lizaveta. He told her everything."

Dounia stared at him, her face pale, her breath coming in short gasps. "It's not true," she whispered. "It's a lie. It must be!"

"What... were the causes?" Dounia asked, her voice trembling, though she tried to maintain her composure.

Svidrigailov leaned back in his chair, his pale lips curling into a faint smile. "Ah, Avdotya Romanovna, it's a long story. Where shall I begin?" He paused, seemingly savoring the tension. "Let's call it a theory of sorts, the same kind of reasoning by which one might justify a single misdeed in the service of a greater good. You see, the idea is simple: one wrongdoing can pave the way for hundreds of noble deeds. A trade-off, if you will."

He gestured vaguely, as if outlining an abstract concept. "Imagine, for example, a young man, brimming with talent and ambition, who finds himself crushed by his circumstances. Suppose he lacks a mere three thousand rubles—the amount that would change everything for him, that would set his future on a completely different trajectory. Add to that the irritability born of hunger, the misery of living in a wretched hole, the constant humiliation of wearing rags, and the acute awareness of not only his own suffering but that of his mother and sister. And then," he added, his voice dropping, "layer on top of all that pride—yes, an overweening pride—and vanity. It's a volatile combination."

Svidrigailov leaned forward slightly, his gaze fixed on Dounia. "Understand, I'm not blaming him. Don't think that. I'm merely stating the facts. And then, of course, there was a theory—a particular little theory that appealed to him. It involved dividing humanity into two groups: the ordinary and the extraordinary. The ordinary people, you see, are bound by the law, while the extraordinary, by virtue of their superiority, are above it. They're the ones who make the laws, who guide the rest. To someone like your brother, this notion must have been intoxicating."

He let out a small laugh, shaking his head. "Napoleon, for instance, fascinated him. What drew him in was not just Napoleon's genius but the fact that men like him never hesitated to overstep boundaries, to break laws when it suited their purposes. And your brother, well, he fancied himself a genius too—or at least he was convinced of it for a time. But here's the tragedy: he's tormented by the realization that he lacked the resolve to truly overstep. To make the leap. And that, Avdotya Romanovna, is a bitter pill for a young man of pride to swallow."

"But remorse?" Dounia interjected, her voice trembling. "You speak of theories and pride, but what about his conscience? Are you saying he has none?"

Svidrigailov gave a small shrug. "Remorse? Conscience? Ah, my dear Avdotya Romanovna, everything is in chaos now. Though, to be fair, it's never been particularly orderly. Russians, in general, are broad in their thinking—broad like their land, and prone to the fantastic, the chaotic. But breadth without true genius? That's a curse."

He gave her a sidelong glance. "Do you remember those long talks we used to have, sitting on the terrace after supper? We spoke of these very things. Why, you used to accuse me of being too broad, too unstructured in my ideas! Who knows, perhaps we were discussing all this at the very moment your brother was lying somewhere, formulating his plan."

Dounia's face was pale, but she managed to meet his gaze. "I know about his theory," she said quietly. "Razumihin showed me his article—the one he wrote about men who believe all is permitted."

Svidrigailov raised his eyebrows. "Your brother published an article? I had no idea. But how intriguing! And yet, what an irony that those lofty ideas brought him to this." He studied her closely, noticing the slight tremor in her hands. "But where are you going now, Avdotya Romanovna? You seem restless."

"I need to see Sofya Semyonovna," Dounia said faintly. "Where is she? Is she home? I must speak with her—now."

"Sofya Semyonovna?" Svidrigailov repeated, feigning a thoughtful expression. "I'm afraid she won't be back until nightfall. At least, I believe so. She was supposed to return earlier, but if she's delayed, it will likely be quite late before she arrives."

Dounia's composure cracked. "You're lying!" she cried, her voice rising. "You've been lying all along. I don't believe you—I don't believe a word you say!"

Almost as if her strength had left her, she sank into a chair. Svidrigailov immediately sprang into action, pouring her a glass of water and sprinkling a few drops on her face. "Avdotya Romanovna, calm yourself," he said gently, though his own voice trembled slightly. "Here, drink this. You mustn't let yourself get so worked up."

She shuddered as the water touched her skin, her breath coming in short gasps.

"You see?" Svidrigailov muttered to himself, frowning. "It's affected her more than I expected. Avdotya Romanovna," he continued, his tone softening, "believe me when I say I want to help. He still has friends—people who can protect him. If you like, I'll take him abroad. I have money. I could arrange everything in just a few days. He can start a new life, do good deeds to make amends for his mistakes. Please, calm yourself."

"Cruel man!" Dounia exclaimed, tears in her eyes. "To speak of this as though it were a game. Let me go!"

"Go? Where would you go?" Svidrigailov asked, his voice growing colder. "To him? Do you even know where he is? And if you did, would you truly rush into his presence like this, in your current state?"

Dounia rose from her seat, her trembling hand reaching for the door handle. "Why is this door locked?" she demanded. "When did you lock it?"

Svidrigailov leaned against the wall, his face an unsettling mixture of calm and amusement. "We couldn't very well discuss such delicate matters with the door wide open," he said smoothly. "But come now, you're letting your imagination run wild. Let's sit and talk this through rationally."

Dounia ignored him, rushing to the far corner of the room and positioning a small table between them. She fixed her eyes on him, watching his every move with the intensity of a cornered animal.

Svidrigailov remained by the door, his pale face illuminated by a faint, mocking smile. "You spoke of outrage just now," he said quietly. "But let me assure you, I've taken precautions. No one is home. The landlady is gone. There are five locked rooms between us and the Kapernaumovs. You could scream, but who would hear you? And even if they did, who would believe you? A young woman, alone, visiting a man in his lodgings—it would raise questions, don't you think?"

"Scoundrel!" Dounia whispered, her voice trembling with indignation.

"As you like," Svidrigailov said softly, his tone smooth and calculated. "But let me remind you, I was speaking only in general terms. My personal conviction aligns entirely with yours—violence is detestable, abhorrent even. I only meant to show you that you need not feel any guilt or remorse if you decided to save your brother by your own choice, as I have proposed. You wouldn't be yielding to me; you'd be yielding to the force of circumstances, to violence itself—if we must call it that."

He paused for effect, studying her face as he continued. "Think about it, Avdotya Romanovna. Your brother's life, your mother's peace of mind—they are in your hands. Only you can decide their fate. As for me, I would be your slave... for life, if that's what you wished." He lowered himself onto the sofa, deliberately choosing a spot about eight paces away from her. "I will wait here."

Dounia's heart pounded in her chest. There was no mistaking the steely determination in his eyes. She knew him too well to doubt his resolve now. He was entirely serious, unyielding in his intentions. Her mind raced, searching for a way out, for some means of defending herself against his growing menace.

Then, without warning, she reached into her pocket and drew out a small revolver. With a sharp, deliberate motion, she cocked it and laid it on the table in front of her, her fingers never straying far from the trigger.

Svidrigailov leapt to his feet, startled by the sudden display. "Aha! So that's how it is?" he exclaimed, his surprise quickly morphing into a malicious smile. "Well, this changes everything, doesn't it? You've made things much simpler, Avdotya Romanovna. Wonderfully simpler. But tell me—where did you get that revolver? Was it Razumihin who armed you? No, wait—I recognize it. It's mine! An old friend, as it happens. How amusing. Do you remember the shooting lessons I gave you in the country? It seems they haven't gone to waste."

Dounia's voice was sharp and trembling with fury. "It is not your revolver! It belonged to Marfa Petrovna, whom you murdered, you vile creature! There was nothing of yours in her house, and I took this when I began to suspect what you were capable of. If you dare take one step closer, I swear I will kill you."

Svidrigailov froze, his smile thinning but not disappearing entirely. "And your brother?" he asked, tilting his head. "What will you do about him if you shoot me? I'm merely curious."

"Inform on him if you like!" Dounia spat. "Don't move! Don't come any closer! I'll shoot, I swear it. You poisoned your wife—I know it. You're a murderer!"

"Ah, so you're convinced I poisoned Marfa Petrovna?" His voice carried an edge of amusement, but his eyes betrayed a flicker of something darker.

"You did!" Dounia cried, her grip tightening on the revolver. "You hinted at it yourself. You spoke to me about poison. I know you had it ready. It was you—you were behind it all, you scoundrel!"

Svidrigailov sighed, spreading his hands in mock defeat. "Even if that were true, it would have been for you, Avdotya Romanovna. All for your sake. You would have been the cause."

"You're lying!" Dounia shouted, her voice breaking with rage. "I have always hated you—always!"

"Ah, but do you remember," he began, his tone turning sly, "how you softened toward me once, during those long evenings of 'propaganda'? I saw it in your eyes, Avdotya Romanovna. Do you remember that moonlit night? The nightingale was singing..."

"That's a lie!" Dounia's voice rose sharply, her eyes flashing with fury. "A disgusting, shameless lie!"

"A lie? Very well, if you say so," he said, shrugging with feigned indifference. "Let's call it a lie, then. Women don't like to be reminded of such things, after all." His smile returned, colder than ever. "But I know you'll shoot, you wild, beautiful creature. Go ahead. Shoot me."

Dounia raised the revolver, her hands trembling but her resolve unshaken. Her face was pale as death, her lower lip quivering, and her dark eyes burned with an intensity he had never seen before. In that moment, Svidrigailov thought she had never looked more stunning. Her fierce beauty struck him like a blow, and a pang of anguish passed through him.

He took a single step forward.

The gunshot rang out, sharp and deafening in the small room. The bullet grazed his head, tearing through his hair before embedding itself in the wall behind him. He froze, his hand instinctively reaching for his temple. A thin stream of blood trickled down his face.

"The wasp has stung me," he murmured, almost to himself. He pulled a handkerchief from his pocket and dabbed at the wound, still smiling faintly. "You aimed for my head. Impressive, really. What's this? Blood? So, you weren't bluffing after all."

Dounia lowered the revolver slightly, her expression shifting from fury to a kind of stunned disbelief. She seemed momentarily lost, as though unable to comprehend what she had just done.

"Well," Svidrigailov said softly, his voice thick with a strange mixture of amusement and resignation. "You missed. Go on—fire again. I'll wait."

His eyes locked onto hers, unblinking, unwavering. Slowly, Dounia raised the revolver once more, her trembling hands betraying her inner turmoil.

"Let me go," she whispered, her voice breaking. "I'll shoot again. I swear I'll kill you."

"At this range, you probably will," Svidrigailov replied calmly. He took another step forward, his gaze burning with an unholy intensity. "But if you hesitate, even for a second, I'll seize you before you can fire."

Desperate, Dounia cocked the pistol again and raised it higher. But when she pulled the trigger, the weapon failed to fire.

"You didn't load it properly," Svidrigailov said, his tone almost gentle. "No matter. You still have another charge. Take your time. I'll wait."

He stood just two paces away, his eyes wild with determination. His entire being radiated a feverish, stubborn resolve. Dounia realized in that moment that he would rather die than let her go. Her hands shook as she struggled to steady the revolver, her mind racing with dread and disbelief.

And then, all at once, something in her snapped. With a sudden cry of despair, she flung the revolver aside, the weapon clattering uselessly to the floor.

"She's dropped it," Svidrigailov murmured, his voice tinged with a mixture of surprise and disbelief. For a moment, he stood frozen, his breath catching in his throat. Then he exhaled deeply, the sound carrying an unmistakable weight, as though something oppressive had been lifted from his chest. It was not merely the relief of escaping death—perhaps he had never truly feared the revolver's aim. No, this was something darker, more profound, and more insidious. A feeling that had wrapped itself around his heart now seemed to loosen, though he could not have named it even if he tried.

Slowly, almost cautiously, he approached Dounia, his eyes fixed on her pale, trembling form. She stood motionless, like a fragile leaf caught in the wind, her wide, pleading eyes locked on his. Gently, he slipped an arm around her waist, his touch light and tentative, as though fearing she might shatter under the pressure. Dounia did not resist. She made no move to push him away, but her trembling only deepened, a visible manifestation of the fear and revulsion coursing through her.

Svidrigailov opened his mouth, attempting to speak, but no sound came. His lips moved in silence, his throat tightening as though strangled by the weight of unspoken words. The emotions surging within him—longing, despair, perhaps even a trace of shame— rendered him mute.

"Let me go," Dounia whispered at last, her voice quivering yet resolute. Her words pierced through him, slicing cleanly into the fragile veil of his composure.

He shuddered visibly at her plea, and for the first time, his arm fell away from her as though it had become unbearably heavy. Something in her voice—its gentleness, its firmness—struck a chord deep within him.

"Then... you don't love me?" he asked softly, his words trembling in the air like a fragile thread. There was no accusation in his tone, only a quiet, almost childlike yearning for reassurance.

Dounia shook her head, her gaze unwavering.

"And... and you can't? Never?" he whispered, his voice breaking as despair took hold.

"Never," she replied, her voice firm, final.

A moment of harrowing silence fell between them. The weight of the word hung in the air, vast and unyielding. In that instant, Svidrigailov's face contorted, his features shifting with the force of an internal battle too complex and too agonizing to articulate. He stared at her with a gaze that seemed to hold all the torment of a soul caught between resignation and yearning. His breathing grew shallow, and his hands clenched at his sides as though grasping for something to anchor him.

Suddenly, as though something within him had broken, Svidrigailov turned sharply away. He strode to the window and stood there, his back rigid, staring out at the world beyond. His shoulders rose and fell with the force of his breaths, but he made no sound. Another moment passed, heavy with unspoken emotions.

At last, he reached into the left pocket of his coat and withdrew a small, tarnished key. Without turning to face Dounia, he laid it on the table behind him, the motion slow and deliberate.

"Take it," he said, his voice low but commanding. "Make haste."

Dounia hesitated, her eyes flickering between him and the key.

"Make haste! Make haste!" he repeated, louder this time, though he still did not turn. There was a terrible urgency in his tone, as if each second carried some dire, unspoken consequence.

Understanding the unyielding finality in his voice, Dounia darted forward, snatched up the key, and rushed to the door. Her fingers fumbled for only an instant before the lock clicked open. Without sparing a glance back, she fled, her footsteps echoing sharply in the silence. Moments later, she burst out onto the canal bank, her breath coming in short, ragged gasps as she ran toward the X. Bridge, her mind racing as fast as her feet.

Inside the room, Svidrigailov remained motionless, still staring out the window. He did not turn, even as the sound of her retreating footsteps faded into the distance. For three long minutes, he stood there, his mind a storm of conflicting emotions. At last, he exhaled shakily, as though awakening from a terrible dream, and turned slowly to face the empty room.

His eyes swept over the disarray left in Dounia's wake, and his hand rose instinctively to his forehead. He wiped it with a trembling hand, as though trying to erase the memory of what had just occurred. A strange smile twisted his features—a smile that was pitiful, sad, and weak all at once. It was the smile of a man standing on the edge of despair, peering into an abyss he could neither escape nor comprehend.

As he lowered his hand, he noticed the dried blood smeared across his fingers. His expression darkened, and with a sudden flash of anger, he grabbed a towel, dampened it, and began scrubbing the wound at his temple. His movements were brisk, almost mechanical, as though attempting to distract himself from the turmoil within.

The revolver caught his eye then, lying discarded near the door where Dounia had flung it. He approached it slowly, bending down to pick it up. Turning it over in his hands, he examined it with detached curiosity. It was a small, old-fashioned pocket revolver with three barrels. Testing the mechanism, he noted that two charges and one capsule remained. It was still capable of firing.

He stood there for a moment, turning the revolver in his hands as though weighing its significance. Finally, he slipped it into his pocket, grabbed his hat, and stepped out into the evening air.

Chapter 6

Svidrigailov spent the evening wandering aimlessly from one dismal haunt to another, immersing himself in the city's most sordid corners. The hours passed in a haze of cheap entertainment and hollow diversions. At some point, Katia appeared, her presence as striking as it was predictable, and she launched into another one of her coarse songs. This time, it was a raucous tune about a "villain and tyrant" who "began kissing Katia," her exaggerated gestures drawing occasional laughter from the crowd.

Svidrigailov, playing the role of benevolent patron, treated Katia generously, as well as the organ-grinder accompanying her. He didn't stop there—he extended his largesse to a group of singers who had gathered, the waiters attending to them, and even two little clerks who had caught his attention. These clerks intrigued him not for their wit or charm but for their peculiar similarity: both had crooked noses, one bent sharply to the left, the other to the right. Their appearance amused him, and he spent the next hour in their company, drawn to their absurdity.

Eventually, the clerks invited him to a so-called pleasure garden, which Svidrigailov agreed to visit without hesitation. He paid for their entrance, finding a strange satisfaction in their delight. The garden, however, was a pitiful sight. It featured one scraggly pine tree, no more than three years old, and three scrappy bushes scattered across the barren space. At its center stood a makeshift "Vauxhall," which was little more than a dingy drinking-bar. Tea was served alongside stronger beverages, and a few green tables and mismatched chairs surrounded the establishment.

The entertainment at the garden was as lackluster as its appearance. A group of wretched singers croaked out a discordant chorus while a drunken German clown, his face flushed red and his nose even redder, stumbled through a dismal performance. The clown, reportedly from Munich, seemed more melancholic than amusing, his every movement betraying a sense of despair.

As the evening wore on, Svidrigailov found himself embroiled in a petty dispute between the two clerks and another group of clerks. Voices rose, tempers flared, and the argument threatened to escalate into a full-blown brawl. Svidrigailov, somewhat amused, was called upon to mediate. For a quarter of an hour, he listened as they shouted over one another, their accusations blending into an unintelligible din. The only detail he could discern was that one of the clerks had stolen something—a teaspoon, of all things. The theft had been quickly discovered, and the stolen spoon had even been sold on the spot to a

Jew. The argument stemmed from the thief's refusal to share the proceeds with his companion.

The situation soon became tiresome. Svidrigailov, eager to extricate himself, paid for the missing teaspoon, diffusing the quarrel before it could escalate further. He stood up abruptly, brushing off the clerks' thanks, and walked out of the garden. The time was approaching six o'clock.

Despite spending the evening in such surroundings, he had not consumed a single drop of alcohol. He had ordered tea earlier, but only for the sake of appearances. His mind was elsewhere, preoccupied with matters far more pressing than the dull chaos around him.

As night fell, the air grew heavy and oppressive. Thick storm clouds gathered overhead, their dark shapes casting a foreboding shadow over the city. By ten o'clock, the storm broke. A deafening clap of thunder shattered the silence, and rain began to pour in torrents. The downpour was relentless, each drop merging into streams that pelted the streets. Lightning illuminated the sky with startling regularity, each flash lingering long enough for one to count to five.

Svidrigailov trudged home through the storm, his clothes soaked through, clinging uncomfortably to his skin. He reached his lodging, locked the door behind him, and moved methodically to the bureau. From its depths, he retrieved all his money, carefully counting and organizing the bills. He tore up two or three papers, their contents seemingly of no further use to him.

Pocketing the money, he glanced at his sodden clothes and considered changing into something dry. But as another flash of lightning lit up the room, he stopped. The storm's ferocity seemed to call him out into the night. Resolutely, he put on his hat, left his room without locking the door, and stepped back into the rain.

His destination was clear. He made his way directly to Sonia's modest lodging. When she answered the door, she appeared surprised to see him standing there, dripping wet, water pooling at his feet. The four Kapernaumov children were with her, sitting around a small table where she had been serving them tea. At the sight of Svidrigailov, the children fled in terror, their footsteps echoing down the hall.

Sonia remained, her posture tense, her face a mixture of confusion and unease. She gestured for him to sit, and he took a seat at the table, motioning for her to do the same.

"I may be leaving for America, Sofya Semyonovna," he began without preamble. His tone was calm, almost detached. "Since this is likely the last time we'll see each other, I've come to settle a few matters."

Sonia blinked, her hands clasping nervously in her lap.

"Did you see the lady today?" he asked, though he waved off her response before she could speak. "I already know what she said to you; you don't need to tell me." Sonia shifted uncomfortably, her cheeks flushing with embarrassment. "Those sorts of people have their ways," he continued. "But as for your sisters and your brother, they're provided for. I've ensured the money assigned to them is safely kept, and I've received proper acknowledgments. Here—take these receipts. Keep them safe in case anything happens."

He placed the papers in front of her, his movements precise and deliberate. "Now, that's settled. Here are three five-percent bonds, amounting to three thousand rubles. These are for you, entirely for yourself. Let that remain strictly between us, no matter what you hear. You'll need the money, Sofya Semyonovna. Continuing to live as you have is no longer necessary, nor is it good for you."

Sonia's eyes widened, and she began to stammer. "I am so much indebted to you, and so are the children and my stepmother," she said hurriedly. "If I've said too little—please don't think..."

"That's enough," Svidrigailov interrupted firmly. "There's no need for thanks."

"But as for the money," she continued hesitantly, "I am truly grateful, but I don't need it now. I can always earn my own living.

Don't think me ungrateful, but if you are feeling charitable—then that money could—"

"It's for you, Sofya Semyonovna, and there's no need to waste words over it," Svidrigailov said firmly, his tone brooking no argument. "I haven't the time for long explanations. You'll need this money, whether you realize it now or not. Rodion Romanovitch has two paths before him: a bullet in the brain or Siberia."

At these words, Sonia's eyes widened with horror, and she instinctively recoiled. "Don't look so alarmed," he continued, waving a hand dismissively. "I know all about it—from him, no less. But don't worry, I'm not one to gossip. I won't breathe a word of it to anyone."

He paused, studying her reaction before pressing on. "It was good advice you gave him, urging him to confess and give himself up. It really would be better for him in the long run. If it comes to Siberia—and it likely will—you'll follow him there, won't you? That's your plan, isn't it? And if that's the case, you'll need money. You'll need it for him, for his sake. Giving it to you now is no different from giving it directly to him. Besides," he added with a slight smirk, "you made a promise to Amalia Ivanovna to pay the debt owed to her. I heard it myself."

Sonia blinked, startled that he was aware of such a detail.

"How can you take on such obligations so recklessly, Sofya Semyonovna?" Svidrigailov continued, his tone adopting an air of mock chiding. "It was Katerina Ivanovna's debt, not yours. You shouldn't have let that German woman intimidate you into taking it on. You can't navigate life like that—taking on everyone else's burdens as though they're your own. It will destroy you."

He stood up abruptly, signaling that the conversation was nearing its end. "If anyone questions you about me—whether tomorrow or in the days to come—don't say a word about this visit. Don't mention the money to anyone. And most importantly, don't let anyone see it." He leaned slightly toward her, his voice lowering conspiratorially. "Do you understand? Not a word."

Sonia stood as well, her anxiety evident in her trembling hands.

"One last piece of advice," he said, glancing at her. "For the time being, it might be best to leave the money with Mr. Razumihin. You know him, of course? Yes, you must. He's a decent enough fellow— trustworthy, even. Take it to him tomorrow, or when the right moment comes. Until then, hide it. Keep it safe."

Sonia wanted to respond, to ask a dozen questions that now swirled frantically in her mind, but the words caught in her throat. Her dismay and confusion rendered her silent for several moments. Finally, she managed to stammer, "How can you... how can you think of leaving now, in such rain?"

Svidrigailov chuckled, the sound light and strangely detached. "What kind of man would I be to let a little rain stop me when I'm bound for America?" he said, his lips curving into a sardonic smile. "No, Sofya Semyonovna, this storm won't delay me. Goodbye, my dear. Live long, and may your life be a blessing to others."

He turned toward the door, hesitating only briefly before adding, "Oh, and one last thing—send my regards to Mr. Razumihin. Tell him Arkady Ivanovitch Svidrigailov sends his greetings. Don't forget."

With that, he left. Sonia remained frozen in place, her emotions a chaotic mix of anxiety, gratitude, and vague, gnawing dread. She couldn't shake the feeling that there was something ominous about his parting words, something left unsaid.

Later that evening, at precisely twenty past eleven, Svidrigailov made another unexpected and baffling visit. The rain was still falling heavily, drenching him to the skin as he walked with measured steps to the modest flat where the family of his betrothed lived, on Third Street in Vassilyevsky Island.

It took several sharp knocks before the door was finally opened, and his sudden appearance caused a stir of apprehension among the inhabitants. The family's initial reaction was one of great alarm. The sight of him, soaked and disheveled, coupled with his unannounced arrival at such a late hour, led the sensible parents to conclude that he must have been drinking heavily and had lost his bearings.

But Svidrigailov, when he chose, could be exceedingly charming, and it didn't take long for him to put them at ease. His polite demeanor and well-practiced smile quickly dispelled their initial concerns. The mother, a tender and sensible woman, began her usual roundabout method of inquiry. She rarely asked direct questions, preferring instead to circle around the subject with irrelevant observations and polite chatter.

"How is Paris these days?" she began, clasping her hands with a nervous smile. "And the court life there, it must be dazzling! Ah, but such rain tonight! It must remind you of those grand European storms. And speaking of the weather, I hope the streets here are not too muddy for you."

This meandering prelude would, on any other occasion, have been an effective means of steering the conversation. But tonight, Svidrigailov seemed impatient, almost restless. He interrupted her tactful digressions with a curt request to see his betrothed immediately, despite being informed that she had already gone to bed.

The mother hesitated, but Svidrigailov's insistence left her with little choice. The decrepit father, confined to a wheelchair, was brought into the room to join them, though he offered little beyond a few grumbled remarks. At last, after some whispered deliberation, the girl was summoned. She entered the room hesitantly, her youthful features betraying a mix of shyness and confusion at being roused so abruptly.

Svidrigailov wasted no time once inside the modest flat. He immediately announced, in his usual composed and matter-of-fact tone, that urgent and important affairs were compelling him to leave Petersburg for a time. Without waiting for a response, he presented them with a bundle of fifteen thousand roubles, insisting they accept it as a token of his goodwill. "Consider it a trifling gift," he said with a faint smile, "one I've long intended to give before our wedding."

The sheer illogic of his gesture—its connection to his abrupt departure, and the inexplicable urgency of his visit in the midst of a torrential rainstorm at such a late hour—was left unaddressed. Yet, somehow, the presentation went over seamlessly. The family's initial surprise gave way to restrained exclamations of wonder and regret, while questions, which might have been awkward or even accusatory, remained remarkably few and mild.

The gratitude, however, was effusive. The sensible mother, moved by the unexpected generosity, shed tears of joy as she thanked him profusely. Svidrigailov bore it all with his usual air of detached patience. When the mother's emotional display seemed on the verge of becoming overwhelming, he laughed lightly, kissed his betrothed on the cheek, and gently patted her face, much like one would a child.

He lingered for a moment longer, noticing in the young girl's eyes a mixture of naive curiosity and an unspoken question—a kind of silent pleading to understand the man who had so suddenly and inexplicably turned their modest lives upside down. For a fleeting second, the earnestness of her gaze gave him pause, and he felt a flicker of something—was it anger? Resentment? He brushed it aside and kissed her again, a brief, impersonal gesture, before bidding them farewell.

Internally, however, a trace of bitterness lingered. He knew full well that his "trifling gift" would be promptly secured in the hands of the practical and ever-sensible mother. The thought irked him, though he couldn't quite articulate why. As he made his way to the door, he left them all in a state of hushed excitement and confusion, their whispered conversations already beginning before the door had closed behind him.

Once he had gone, the tender mother took charge of managing the family's speculation. In hushed but authoritative tones, she began to unravel the mystery of Svidrigailov's behavior for the benefit of her daughter and husband. Her explanation painted him as a man of vast wealth and even greater eccentricities, one accustomed to the unpredictable whims of the elite.

"A man like that," she concluded with a sage nod, "can do as he pleases. Why, he might hand out thousands of roubles one day and leave on a journey the next, all without a second thought. These people of high society, they're like that, you know. They don't care what anyone thinks. And coming in drenched to the skin? Perhaps it was deliberate—a statement of sorts. Perhaps he wanted to show that he's unafraid of anything."

She emphasized the need for discretion, instructing them all not to breathe a word about the visit to anyone, especially not to Madame Resslich, whose prying nature and loose tongue could not be trusted. The money, she declared, would be locked away securely that very night. They whispered and speculated until the small hours, while the young girl, amazed and inexplicably sorrowful, retired much earlier, her mind swimming with thoughts she could not fully grasp.

Meanwhile, precisely at midnight, Svidrigailov crossed the bridge on his way back to the mainland. The rain had finally ceased, but a roaring wind whipped through the city streets, chilling him to the bone. He paused briefly by the black waters of the Little Neva, his gaze fixed on the turbulent currents below. For a moment, his expression hardened with a strange intensity, as though searching for answers in the restless waves. But the cold quickly drove him onward, and he turned toward Y. Prospect.

He walked for nearly half an hour down the endless street, stumbling occasionally on the uneven wooden pavement. The dim light made it difficult to navigate, but he kept his focus on the right side of the street, searching for something he had noticed once before. Towards the end of the road, he recalled, there was a wooden hotel—a long, blackened structure that seemed out of place even in its forlorn surroundings. Its name, Adrianople, had stuck with him. At last, he spotted it, the building standing stark against the night with faint lights flickering in its windows.

Entering the hotel, Svidrigailov was greeted by a ragged man loitering in the corridor. Without preamble, he asked for a room. The man, sizing him up with suspicion, eventually led him to a cramped, airless room tucked beneath the stairs at the end of the hallway. "It's the only one available," he muttered.

Svidrigailov glanced around, unimpressed but indifferent. "Is there tea?" he asked.

"Yes, sir."

"And what else?"

"Veal, vodka, and some savouries."

"Bring me tea and veal," Svidrigailov said curtly, waving him off.

The ragged man hesitated, as though expecting further requests. "Nothing else?" he asked, his tone edged with surprise.

"Nothing," Svidrigailov replied sharply. "Just the tea and veal."

The man left, muttering under his breath, clearly disappointed.

Svidrigailov looked around the room with mild curiosity. It was oppressively small, its low ceiling just high enough for him to stand upright. A single window let in no light, and the furnishings—a dirty bed, a plain-stained chair, and a wobbly table—left little room to move. The walls were covered in peeling yellow wallpaper, so worn and dusty that its original pattern was all but invisible. One wall sloped awkwardly under the stairs, adding to the room's claustrophobic feel.

He set down the candle the man had provided and sat on the bed, sinking into thought. His introspection was soon interrupted by a persistent murmur from the adjacent room. The sound, a mixture of tearful scolding and muffled shouting, had been present since he entered the room. Now it grew louder, drawing his attention. He tilted his head, listening intently, but he could discern only one voice. Who was in there, and what drama was unfolding behind the thin walls?

For a moment, he considered knocking on the wall or opening the door to investigate. Instead, he leaned back against the bedframe, a faint smirk playing on his lips. "It must be an interesting place," he thought wryly. "How did I not know of it before?"

Svidrigailov stood abruptly, shading the dim candlelight with his hand as he moved closer to the wall. A faint beam of light filtered through a narrow crack, catching his attention. His curiosity piqued, he leaned in to peer through the gap. The adjacent room, slightly larger than his own, housed two occupants in a scene that seemed absurdly theatrical.

One of the men, a curly-headed individual with a face red and inflamed from drink, stood in a dramatic pose. Coatless and slightly unsteady, he planted his legs wide apart to maintain his balance, all the while smiting his chest as though delivering an impassioned sermon. His voice, loud and slurred, was filled with indignation as he berated the second man, who sat slumped in a chair nearby.

"You are nothing but a beggar," the orator bellowed, his gestures erratic. "No standing, no respect! I dragged you out of the gutter! Me! And I can throw you back there whenever I please. Only the hand of Providence sees it all."

The target of his tirade was a sullen, disheveled figure who sat with a bewildered, sheepish expression. His unfocused eyes turned toward the speaker from time to time, but it was clear he barely understood the words being hurled at him. He gave the impression of a man on the verge of sneezing but unable to follow through. The table between them was cluttered with the remnants of a pitiful feast: half-empty glasses of vodka, stale tea, a few slices of bread, and a lonely cucumber lying limp on the edge.

Svidrigailov watched the scene with mild interest, his sharp gaze absorbing every detail. But the absurdity of it all quickly lost its charm. With a faint shrug of indifference, he turned away and returned to his bed.

Soon after, the ragged attendant arrived, carefully balancing a tray with a steaming glass of tea and a plate of veal. He hesitated at the door, his curiosity getting the better of him. "Are you sure you don't want anything else, sir?" he ventured again, his tone almost hopeful.

"Nothing," Svidrigailov replied curtly, his irritation thinly veiled. The man sighed, his disappointment evident, and left without another word.

Svidrigailov drank the tea quickly, hoping it might warm him, but he barely touched the food. A feverish sensation was creeping over him, making his limbs heavy and his thoughts sluggish. He removed his coat, wrapped himself tightly in the coarse blanket, and lay down on the bed. The room, oppressively close and tinged with the faint odors of damp leather and mice, did little to improve his mood.

"Damn it all," he muttered under his breath, shifting uncomfortably. "It would have been better to feel well for this occasion."

The candle flickered weakly in its holder, casting restless shadows on the peeling walls. Outside, the wind howled with a ferocity that made the wooden structure creak. A faint scratching noise came from the corner, unmistakably the sound of a mouse. Svidrigailov's lips curled in annoyance. He tried to direct his thoughts elsewhere, to fix his imagination on something less mundane.

"There must be a garden under the window," he mused, straining to catch the rustling of tree branches amidst the storm. "I hate the sound of trees on nights like this. It stirs something... unpleasant."

His mind wandered back to Petrovsky Park, where the sight of the trees earlier that evening had left him with the same unsettling sensation. The memory brought with it the icy chill he had felt while standing on the bridge over the Little Neva. "I've never liked water," he thought, grimacing. "Not even in paintings."

A strange smile flickered across his face. "How ridiculous it all is. At a time like this, when none of it should matter, I find myself more particular than ever—like some animal carefully selecting its final resting place. I should have gone to Petrovsky Park. It seemed dark and cold, yes, but perhaps that was the point."

He noticed the candle burning low and blew it out abruptly. The sudden darkness felt oppressive, but he welcomed it. "They've gone to bed next door," he thought, noting the absence of light from the crack in the wall. "Well, now would be the perfect time, Marfa Petrovna, for you to appear. Dark, stormy, and just the right setting. But of course, now you won't come."

His mind flickered to Raskolnikov, and he allowed himself a bitter chuckle. "I really did suggest he trust Dounia to Razumihin, didn't I? Just as he thought—to torment myself. What a rogue he is, though. He's suffered, yes, but he has potential. With time, he might make a fine scoundrel. Too eager for life now, though. These young men— they're all the same. Contemptible."

He tried to sleep, but the effort was futile. His thoughts refused to quiet, darting back to Dounia. Her image rose unbidden, vivid and haunting. He shuddered involuntarily, attempting to push it away. "No," he muttered, "I must leave all that behind."

But the memory persisted. He saw her again as she had been that morning, revolver in hand, her terror mingled with defiance. He recalled the pang he'd felt when she lowered the gun, the momentary flash of pity. It had startled him then, and it startled him again now. "Damnation!" he growled, grinding his teeth. "I won't think about this anymore."

A faint scuttling under the blanket jolted him out of his reverie. He froze, feeling something small and quick dart over his leg. "A mouse," he muttered grimly, though he loathed the idea of uncovering himself to deal with it. Another movement, this time on his arm, forced his hand. He flung the blanket aside and lit the candle, shivering in the damp chill of the room.

He bent to inspect the bed, but the mouse darted away before he could catch it, zigzagging frantically across the sheets. It finally disappeared beneath the pillow. He threw the pillow aside, only to feel something dart across his chest and down his back. Shivering violently, he awoke with a start.

The room was dark again, the candle extinguished. The wind howled under the window, rattling the fragile panes. "Disgusting," he muttered, sitting up and wrapping the blanket around himself. "I might as well not sleep at all."

But sleep eluded him still. His mind wandered, conjuring images of serene gardens and fragrant flowers. He imagined a bright day, a country cottage surrounded by roses, and an air of tranquility so vivid it felt real. Yet in the heart of this imagined paradise lay a coffin, stark and cold. Inside, a young girl rested, her fair hair adorned with a wreath of roses. Her face, pale and rigid, bore an expression of unchildish sorrow. Svidrigailov recognized her, and the realization sent a chill through him. She was only fourteen. Her angelic purity had been shattered, her despair brutally ignored.

The vision dissolved into the darkness, leaving him alone with the storm.

Svidrigailov stirred, rousing himself from the restless state that had plagued him all night. He got up from the bed, his limbs heavy, and shuffled to the window. His fingers fumbled for the latch, and as he pushed it open, a sharp gust of wind whipped into the room, carrying with it a biting chill that stung his exposed face and chest. He stood there in his thin shirt, shivering but resolute, leaning on the windowsill as the cold air clawed at him like icy fingers.

Below the window, he could make out the faint outline of what seemed to be a garden, likely a small pleasure garden with tea tables and music during the day. Now, in the dead of night, it was drowned in darkness, and the trees and bushes were barely discernible, reduced to vague, shifting blurs against the blackness. Droplets of rain, carried by the wind, spattered his face and the wooden floor beneath the window.

For five minutes, Svidrigailov remained in this position, bent over the windowsill, gazing into the void. The desolate night seemed endless, its silence broken only by the distant groan of the wind. Then, suddenly, a deep boom echoed through the air, followed shortly by another. The sound, heavy and foreboding, seemed to roll out from some distant point across the city.

"The signal," he murmured to himself, his voice barely audible. "The river must be overflowing." His mind painted a vivid picture: by morning, the water would surge through the lower streets, flooding basements and cellars. Rats would swim desperately for higher ground, and drenched men would haul their belongings upstairs, cursing the relentless rain and wind. "What time is it?" he wondered aloud, and as if in answer, a nearby clock struck three with a hurried, almost frantic rhythm.

Svidrigailov straightened, shaking off the chill that had settled into his bones. "It will be light in an hour," he mused. "Why wait? I might as well leave now." He smiled faintly, a strange mix of humor and resignation tugging at the corners of his mouth. "Yes, I'll go to the park. Find a bush there, one soaked with rain, so that when I brush against it, millions of droplets will cascade down my head and shoulders."

He shut the window with a firm hand and relit the candle, its flickering flame casting a faint glow over the room's grimy walls. Moving with purpose, he put on his waistcoat, overcoat, and hat, then picked up the candle and headed into the corridor to find the ragged attendant. The man, no doubt dozing somewhere amid heaps of rubbish and burnt-out candle stubs, needed to be paid before he could leave the dreary hotel. "Now's the best moment," he muttered to himself. "I couldn't choose a better one."

The narrow corridor stretched before him, dark and claustrophobic. He walked for several minutes, his candle barely illuminating the way, but found no sign of the attendant. Just as he was about to call out, his eye caught a peculiar sight in a shadowed corner between an old cupboard and a door. Something was there—a small, trembling figure that seemed almost alive.

Bending down, he held the candle close, its dim light revealing a child. She couldn't have been more than five years old, her soaked clothes clinging to her frail frame like a sodden rag. Her pale, tear-streaked face was framed by damp, matted hair, and her large, black eyes gazed up at him with a mixture of blank astonishment and exhaustion. She sobbed intermittently, the hiccupping cries of a child too worn out to shed more tears, yet still caught in the throes of fear.

"How did you get here?" Svidrigailov asked, his voice uncharacteristically soft. The little girl stirred at his words and, as if encouraged, began to chatter in broken, childish sentences. Between sobs, she muttered about her "mammy," who would surely beat her for breaking a cup. Piece by piece, Svidrigailov pieced together her story. She was the neglected child of a hotel cook, most likely a drunken and abusive woman. The girl had broken something precious and, terrified of the inevitable punishment, fled into the night. She had wandered outside in the rain before finally slipping into the corridor and curling up in the dark corner where he had found her.

Moved by a vague, inexplicable impulse, Svidrigailov scooped her up and carried her back to his room. He set her gently on the bed and began removing her soaked shoes, noting how her tiny feet, bare and reddened from the cold, trembled against his hands. He wrapped her in the blanket, tucking it securely around her small frame. The child relaxed almost instantly, her eyes fluttering shut as sleep overtook her.

He stood over her for a moment, watching the rise and fall of her chest. Her pale cheeks had taken on a flush of warmth, though it was unnaturally bright, more akin to the heat of a fever than the healthy glow of childhood. Her crimson lips seemed to burn, vivid and startling against the pallor of her face.

But then, something changed. Her long, dark lashes quivered as if her eyes were about to open. A faint smile began to tug at the corners of her lips, and Svidrigailov felt a chill that had nothing to do with the cold. The expression on her face was no longer innocent; it was sly, almost knowing. Her lips curled further, widening into a grin that was unmistakably adult in its shamelessness. He recoiled, horrified, as her eyes snapped open, glimmering with a mocking, provocative light.

"No," he muttered, his voice trembling. "This... this isn't right." The child's small arms reached out to him, her face alight with a grotesque mixture of invitation and mockery. It was obscene, unnatural—a depravity that shattered every boundary of innocence.

"Accursed child!" he cried, his hand raised as if to strike her. But in that instant, he woke up.

He was back in the dim room, wrapped in his blanket. The candle had gone out, and pale daylight was filtering in through the grimy window. The storm outside had abated, leaving only the faint sound of dripping rain. He sat up slowly, his heart pounding, and glanced toward the bed. It was empty, the blanket undisturbed. The child had been nothing more than a nightmare, but the lingering sense of dread refused to leave him.

Svidrigailov rubbed his temples, trying to shake off the memory. "How disgusting," he muttered under his breath, his voice thick with self-loathing. But the unease remained, pressing down on him like the weight of the storm itself.

"I've been plagued by nightmares all night!" Svidrigailov muttered with irritation as he swung his legs off the bed. He stood up abruptly, his entire body feeling as though it had been pummeled in his sleep. His joints ached, and there was a stiffness in his limbs that only deepened his foul mood. The room seemed oppressive in the dim morning light. Outside, a thick, soupy mist blanketed the town, obscuring everything beyond the window. It was nearly five o'clock, and he realized with annoyance that he had overslept.

He began dressing hurriedly, throwing on his still damp jacket and overcoat. As he reached into the coat's pocket, his fingers brushed against the cold metal of the revolver. Taking it out, he examined it briefly, then set it on the table. Sitting down, he reached into another pocket and pulled out a small notebook. With deliberate care, he opened it to the first page and wrote a few lines in large, bold letters, making sure they stood out conspicuously. After reading over the words, he paused, resting his elbows on the table and his chin on his hands. His expression darkened as his thoughts wandered. The revolver and the notebook lay untouched beside him.

The stillness of the room was broken only by the faint buzzing of flies. They had woken with the first light of dawn and now hovered greedily over the untouched veal still sitting on the table. Svidrigailov watched them absently, his mind elsewhere. Eventually, without really thinking, he reached out with his right hand and began swatting at one of the flies. The tiny insect dodged and darted out of reach, eluding his grasp again and again. He continued this aimless pursuit until he suddenly became aware of what he was doing. Startled by his own distraction, he pushed back his chair and stood up resolutely. Without a backward glance, he left the room and stepped out into the street.

The air outside was cold and damp, the kind of chill that seeped into the bones and lingered. A dense, milky mist had settled over the town, muting the colors of the world and making everything seem distant and dreamlike. Svidrigailov began walking along the slippery, dirty wooden pavement that led toward the Little Neva. The image of the swollen river filled his mind: the rushing waters from the night's storm, the drenched paths and glistening trees on Petrovsky Island, and the dripping bushes that seemed to beckon to him. He pictured it all vividly but found the thoughts irritating. To distract himself, he focused instead on his surroundings.

The street was eerily empty. There wasn't a single cabman or pedestrian in sight. The bright yellow wooden houses lining the road appeared grim and dejected, their shutters closed tightly as though to shut out the bleakness of the day. The cold and wetness seemed to penetrate his very soul, and he pulled his coat tighter around himself as he shivered. His eyes wandered to shop signs, reading each one carefully as though searching for some hidden meaning in their mundane lettering.

At the end of the wooden pavement, the street gave way to a larger, more imposing stone building. Just then, a mangy, shivering dog crossed his path, its tail tucked so low it nearly brushed the ground. Nearby, a man lay sprawled face down on the pavement, his greatcoat soaked through. He was clearly dead drunk. Svidrigailov cast a fleeting glance at the pitiful figure and walked on without stopping.

Ahead, a high tower loomed on the left, its silhouette faintly visible through the mist. He paused, a sudden thought crossing his mind. "Why Petrovsky?" he muttered under his breath, almost laughing at himself. "This will do just as well. At least there will be a witness here—official, even."

A grim smile flickered across his face at the irony of the thought as he turned toward the street leading to the tower. Before long, he reached the gates of the imposing building. A small, hunched figure stood leaning against them, wrapped in a coarse grey soldier's coat and wearing a battered copper helmet that gleamed faintly in the dull light. The man's face, unmistakably of Jewish descent, bore a perpetually sour and dejected expression, one that seemed etched there by years of hardship and resignation.

For a moment, Svidrigailov and the man stared at each other in silence, their gazes locked in mutual scrutiny. Finally, the man, whom Svidrigailov mentally nicknamed Achilles because of his helmet, seemed to find the silence irregular. Straightening slightly, he addressed the stranger.

"What do you want here?" Achilles asked, his tone flat and indifferent.

"Nothing, brother. Good morning," Svidrigailov replied, a faint smile playing on his lips.

"This isn't the place."

"I'm going to foreign parts," Svidrigailov said casually, as though announcing a trivial errand.

"Foreign parts?" Achilles repeated skeptically.

"Yes. To America."

"America," Achilles echoed, still eyeing him warily.

Without further comment, Svidrigailov pulled the revolver from his pocket and calmly cocked it. Achilles' eyes widened, his expression shifting from indifference to alarm.

"I say, this is not the place for such jokes!" Achilles exclaimed, his voice rising slightly.

"Why not?" Svidrigailov asked, tilting his head as though genuinely curious.

"Because it isn't," Achilles insisted, his tone growing more urgent.

"Well, brother, it's a fine place to me," Svidrigailov replied evenly. "When they ask you, just say I was going to America."

With that, he raised the revolver to his right temple. Achilles' face contorted with panic as he took a step forward.

"You can't do it here! It's not the place!" Achilles cried, his voice cracking.

But Svidrigailov, unmoved, pulled the trigger.

Chapter 7

That same day, around seven in the evening, Raskolnikov made his way to the lodging Razumihin had secured for his mother and sister in Bakaleyev's house. The narrow stairs leading up from the street seemed steeper than he remembered, and he ascended them with sluggish, hesitant steps. It was as though he were dragging some invisible weight behind him, his uncertainty growing with each step. He paused at the top, debating whether to turn back, but the resolution he had wrestled with all day held firm.

"It doesn't matter anymore," he murmured to himself as he took the final step to the door. "They don't know anything yet. Besides, they've always thought of me as peculiar. Why should this be any different?"

His appearance was nothing short of appalling. His clothes were a disgrace—torn, stained, and still damp from the relentless rain of the night before. His face bore the unmistakable marks of exhaustion: pale, gaunt, and lined with the strain of sleepless nights and an unrelenting inner torment. For twenty-four hours, he had wandered aimlessly through the city, wrestling with demons no one else could see, but now, at least, he had reached a decision.

He knocked on the door, and a moment later, it was opened by his mother. Pulcheria Alexandrovna's face lit up in astonished joy as she saw him standing there. She was momentarily speechless, overwhelmed by a mixture of surprise and relief. Without a word, she grabbed his hand and gently pulled him inside.

"My boy! You're here!" she exclaimed, her voice trembling with emotion. Her joy was so intense that it spilled out in tears. "Oh, Rodya, don't be angry with me for crying—it's just that I'm so happy! Look at me, weeping like a fool. No, no, I'm not crying. These are happy tears. You mustn't think I'm sad!"

Her words tumbled over one another, and she laughed nervously through her tears. "I've been like this ever since your father passed. I cry at the slightest thing now—it's become a habit, I suppose. But come in, sit down. You must be so tired. Look at you, though— muddy and soaked! What have you been doing?"

"I was caught in the rain yesterday, Mother," Raskolnikov said quietly, brushing off her concern.

Pulcheria Alexandrovna waved her hands dismissively, cutting him off before he could say more. "No, no, don't worry. I won't bombard you with questions like I used to, pestering you for answers. I've learned better since I came here. I understand now that you have your own plans, your own concerns, and it's not for me to interfere. God only knows what you're working on, but whatever it is, I'm sure it's important. I'll stop prattling now—I'm making a spectacle of myself."

She paused, glancing at him with a mixture of pride and affection. "Did you know, Rodya, I've been reading your article? Dmitri Prokofitch brought it to me. I've read it three times already. When I first saw it, I thought, 'There's the answer! That's what he's been so busy with!' And I felt so foolish for not understanding sooner. It's wonderful, Rodya. I didn't understand everything, of course, but how could I? It's meant for people far more learned than me."

Raskolnikov reached for the magazine she handed him and glanced at the article. For a brief moment, he felt a strange flicker of pride—a bitter-sweet sensation that every author feels the first time they see their words in print. But the feeling was fleeting. As he read the lines, memories of the months of turmoil and doubt that had plagued him while writing it came rushing back. Disgusted, he tossed the magazine onto the table.

"Rodya," Pulcheria Alexandrovna began hesitantly, "I know I'm not clever enough to grasp everything in your writing, but I do know this—you are destined for greatness. I can see it so clearly. You'll be one of the most brilliant minds in Russia, if not the whole world. And to think some people dared to question your sanity! Imagine that! Even Dounia was almost persuaded at one point. Can you believe it?"

Raskolnikov interrupted her, his tone heavy. "Is Dounia not home, Mother?"

"No, my dear, she isn't," Pulcheria Alexandrovna replied, her face clouding briefly. "She's been going out a lot lately. Dmitri Prokofitch comes to see me often, though. He's such a good man, always speaking so highly of you. Dounia... well, she has her own way of doing things. She seems to have her secrets these days. But don't worry, I'm not upset. I know she loves us both dearly. Still, I can't help but wonder what's weighing on her mind."

She paused, studying her son's face. "But you've come to see me now, haven't you? That's all that matters. You've made me so happy just by being here."

Moved by her words, Raskolnikov reached out and took her hands in his. His voice trembled as he spoke, as though the words were spilling out of him unbidden. "Mother, listen to me. Whatever happens—whatever you hear about me, no matter how terrible it may be—promise me you'll always love me. Promise me you'll never stop loving me."

Pulcheria Alexandrovna stared at him, bewildered by the intensity in his voice. "Rodya," she whispered, "what are you saying? Of course I'll always love you. How could you think otherwise?"

Tears welled in her eyes again as she reached up to touch his face. "You're my son, my dear boy. Whatever happens, I will love you just as much as I do now, if not more."

Raskolnikov looked away, unable to meet her gaze. His heart felt heavy, as though it were being crushed under the weight of her unconditional love. For a fleeting moment, he wished he could stay there forever, basking in the warmth of her faith in him. But deep down, he knew that moment was already slipping through his fingers.

"Rodya, Rodya, what is the matter? How can you ask me such a thing?" Pulcheria Alexandrovna's voice broke with anguish as she clutched his hands in hers, her eyes wide with disbelief. "Who could ever tell me anything about you that would make me stop loving you? And even if they tried, do you think I would believe them? I wouldn't listen for a second, my son."

Her unwavering love struck a deep chord in Raskolnikov's heart, and he continued, compelled by an inexplicable urge to speak, his voice trembling with the intensity of his feelings. "Mother, I came here today to tell you something I've wanted to say for so long. I needed to assure you—no matter what happens—that I have always loved you. More than anything, I wanted you to know that, even if you've doubted it. And I'm glad we're alone right now; I'm even glad Dounia isn't here. I want you to know that whatever you might feel in the days ahead, no matter how hard it becomes for you, you must believe this: your son loves you more than he loves himself."

His voice wavered, but he pressed on, his words tumbling out in a rush. "Everything you thought about me—that I was cruel, that I didn't care—it was all wrong, Mother. I've loved you deeply all along, but I never knew how to show it. Please, believe me. I needed to tell you this before anything else, to make sure you know."

Pulcheria Alexandrovna, unable to speak, pulled him into a silent embrace. Her tears flowed freely as she pressed him to her chest, the way she had done when he was a child. The tenderness in her touch broke something inside him, and for the first time in months, his defenses began to crumble.

After a long silence, she finally spoke, her voice soft and tremulous. "I don't understand what's wrong, Rodya, but I've known—oh, I've known for so long that something terrible was weighing on your soul. I thought it was just us, that we were burdening you. But now I see it's far worse than I imagined. There's a great sorrow in store for you, isn't there? Something dreadful is coming. I've felt it in my heart for weeks, like a shadow looming over us. Forgive me for speaking of it, but I can't help it. I lie awake at night, thinking, praying."

Her voice broke again, and she wiped her eyes before continuing. "Even Dounia—last night, she talked in her sleep, and it was all about you. I couldn't make sense of it, but it left me with such a terrible feeling. And now, here you are, and I know. I know the moment has come. Rodya, where are you going? You're leaving us, aren't you?"

"Yes," Raskolnikov whispered, the single word heavy with resignation.

She straightened, her face a mix of determination and desperation. "Then I'll come with you. Wherever you need to go, I'll follow. And Dounia will come too—she loves you so much. We'll all go together, even Sofya Semyonovna, if you like. Dmitri Prokofitch will help us. We'll find a way. Just tell me—where are you going?"

He shook his head, a faint, sorrowful smile on his lips. "Goodbye, Mother."

"What? Today?" she cried, clutching his arm as though she could physically keep him from leaving. "You can't mean that! Not today! Don't leave me now."

"I have to," he said softly, avoiding her gaze. "I can't stay."

"But why? Why can't I come with you? At least let me—"

"No," he interrupted gently. "But kneel down, Mother. Pray for me. Your prayers might reach Him."

Her eyes widened in disbelief, but she obeyed. She knelt before him, her trembling hands raised as though to bless him. "Let me sign you with the cross," she whispered. "That's right, that's right. Oh God, what are we doing? What is happening to us?"

Raskolnikov's resolve broke entirely. He dropped to his knees in front of her, tears streaming down his face as he clung to her hands. "Mother," he murmured, "my dear mother." They wept together, their arms wrapped around each other in a silent, desperate embrace.

For a moment, it was as if they had been transported back in time. Pulcheria Alexandrovna stroked his hair, her voice filled with a mother's infinite tenderness. "My darling, my firstborn. Just like when you were a little boy. You'd run to me like this, throw your arms around me, and tell me everything would be all right. Even when we were so poor, even when your father and I had nothing, your smile made everything bearable. And when he died, how we wept together at his grave! Do you remember?"

He nodded, unable to speak.

"And now," she continued, her voice breaking, "I've felt it again— that same shadow of sorrow. The day I arrived here and saw you for the first time, I saw it in your eyes, Rodya. My heart sank then, and today, when you walked through that door, I knew. The hour had come. But you're not leaving us forever, are you? Tell me you'll come back."

"No," he said firmly, though his voice cracked. "Not forever."

"You'll come again?"

"Yes," he said, his tone quieter now. "I'll come back."

"Is it far where you're going?" she asked, her voice trembling with dread.

"Very far," he replied simply.

"And what will you find there? A new life, perhaps? A career?"

"What God sends," he answered softly. "Just pray for me."

He turned to leave, but she clung to him, her eyes wide with terror. "Not forever, Rodya! Tell me it's not forever. Promise me you'll come tomorrow."

"I will," he whispered, his heart breaking as he tore himself from her grasp. "Goodbye, Mother."

Outside, the evening was warm and clear, a sharp contrast to the storm raging in his soul. He made his way back to his lodgings with hurried steps, desperate to finish everything before the sun set. He didn't want to see anyone—not yet.

Ascending the stairs, he noticed Nastasya peering at him curiously from the samovar, her eyes following him intently. A fleeting thought crossed his mind: Has someone come for me? But he dismissed it, suppressing the unwelcome image of Porfiry. When he opened his door, however, he was startled to find Dounia waiting for him. She stood alone, her face pale and drawn, her eyes filled with grief and fear.

He froze in the doorway. "Am I to come in or leave?" he asked uncertainly.

She rose slowly, her movements heavy with sorrow. "I've been waiting all day," she said, her voice low. "Sofya Semyonovna and I— we both thought you'd come to her."

He stepped inside and sank into a chair, utterly exhausted. "I feel weak, Dounia," he murmured. "I should have liked to be stronger for this moment."

Her gaze did not waver. "Where were you all night?" she asked.

"I don't remember clearly," he admitted. "I wandered by the Neva, trying to make a decision. I thought about ending it all, but... I couldn't."

Dounia's shoulders sagged in relief. "Thank God. That's what we feared most—Sofya Semyonovna and I. You still have faith in life, then?"

He smiled bitterly. "Faith? No. But I wept in Mother's arms today. I asked her to pray for me. I don't understand it, Dounia. I don't understand anything anymore."

"Have you been to see Mother? Have you told her?" Dounia asked, her voice filled with alarm and horror. Her wide, fearful eyes searched his face for any hint of what he might have done. "Surely you haven't done that?"

"No," Raskolnikov said quickly, shaking his head, though his tone betrayed a faint tremor of regret. "No, I didn't tell her outright... not in words. But she understood a great deal, Dounia. You were talking in your sleep last night, and she overheard some of it. I think she already half understands the truth, even if she doesn't want to admit it to herself." He paused and ran a hand through his hair, his expression heavy with self-reproach. "Perhaps I did wrong in going to her. I don't even know why I did. I'm a contemptible person, Dounia."

Dounia stepped closer, her face softening, though her distress remained evident. "A contemptible person?" she repeated, her voice trembling. "But you're ready to face suffering, aren't you? You're willing to endure it, to stand by your decision?"

"Yes, I'm going," he said, his tone resolute. "At once. I've made up my mind." He hesitated briefly, then confessed, "I even thought about drowning myself, Dounia. Last night, as I walked by the Neva, I stared into the water and seriously considered it. But then, as I stood there, I thought that if I've always considered myself strong, then I shouldn't be afraid of disgrace. And that thought stopped me."

"It's pride, Rodya," Dounia murmured, her voice tinged with sadness.

"Yes," he admitted, a flicker of fire igniting in his otherwise weary eyes. "It's pride, Dounia." For a brief moment, his face seemed to regain some of its vitality, and his lips curled into a faint, sardonic smile. "You don't think," he added, looking directly into her eyes, "that I was simply afraid of the water, do you?"

"Rodya, please, hush!" Dounia cried out, her voice breaking with anguish. She turned away, unable to look at him for a moment. Silence fell between them, stretching for what felt like an eternity. He sat motionless, staring at the floor, while she stood at the far end of the table, her hands gripping the edge as though for support. At last, Raskolnikov rose to his feet.

"It's late," he said abruptly. "It's time to go. I'm going at once to give myself up." He paused, then added with a bitter edge, "But I don't even know why I'm doing it."

Dounia's eyes filled with tears, and they began to spill over, tracing silent paths down her cheeks. "You're crying," he observed softly. "But can you—can you still hold out your hand to me?"

Her response was immediate. "Did you ever doubt it?" she asked, her voice firm despite her tears. In an instant, she closed the distance between them and threw her arms around him, holding him tightly. "Aren't you already half expiating your crime by choosing to face the suffering?" she whispered through her sobs, pressing her lips to his temple in a gesture of desperate love.

"Crime? What crime?" Raskolnikov exclaimed, his voice suddenly sharp and defiant. He pulled away from her embrace, his face contorted with a wild mixture of emotions. "Do you mean that I killed a vile, useless insect—a wretched old pawnbroker who contributed nothing to the world? Killing her was atonement for a hundred sins! She leeched the life out of desperate people. Was that a crime?" His voice rose as he continued, his words tumbling out in a torrent. "I don't think of it as a crime, and I don't feel the need to expiate it! Why does everyone keep throwing that word at me? 'Crime! Crime!' Only now do I see clearly how absurd my cowardice has been. I've decided to face this ridiculous disgrace because I am weak—because I am contemptible! And perhaps, as Porfiry suggested, I'm even doing this for my own advantage!"

"Rodya, stop!" Dounia cried, her voice breaking with despair. "You shed blood—you took a life!"

"Blood?" he retorted with almost frenzied intensity. "What blood? Blood flows everywhere! It has always flowed, in streams, in rivers! Men shed blood and are crowned in the Capitol for it—called saviors and benefactors of mankind. I wanted to do good too! I would have done countless good deeds to make up for one single act of stupidity. And it wasn't even stupidity—it was clumsiness! The idea itself was not stupid; it only seems that way now because I failed. Failure makes everything seem foolish. But if I had succeeded, I would have been praised and glorified. Instead, I'm trapped, and all anyone sees is failure."

"Rodya," Dounia pleaded, her voice trembling, "that's not true. You're wrong—don't say such things!"

He laughed bitterly, shaking his head. "It's not aesthetically pleasing, is it? That's what bothers people. It's not picturesque. But what makes regular war, with its bombarding and sieges, any more honorable? This obsession with appearances—it's a sign of weakness. And never have I understood that more clearly than I do now. I've never been more certain of my actions, never been more convinced of my strength, than in this moment."

But as his eyes met Dounia's, he faltered. Her expression—an anguished mixture of sorrow and love—pierced through his defiance. He saw in her face the pain he had caused, the weight of his actions on those who loved him most. His voice softened. "Dounia... if I'm guilty, forgive me," he whispered, his tone raw and unguarded. "Though I know forgiveness is impossible. Good-bye. Let's not argue anymore. It's time—I must go."

"No!" she cried, clinging to him. "Don't leave yet!"

"I have to," he insisted, his voice firmer now. "But don't follow me. Go to Mother. Stay with her—she needs you more than ever now. It's my last request of you, Dounia. Please, stay by her side. She's not well, and I left her in such a state of anxiety. She'll die of worry if you're not there to comfort her. Razumihin will help you. I've already spoken with him."

He gently loosened her grip and stepped back. "Don't cry for me. I'll try to live honestly, to be manly, even if I'm a murderer. Maybe one day I'll make a name for myself—something that won't disgrace you. You'll see."

"Rodya," she began, but he cut her off.

"Goodbye, Dounia. This isn't forever. We'll see each other again. Ah, wait—there's something I almost forgot!"

And with that, he turned, searching for something he couldn't name, while Dounia stood frozen, her tears still falling.

He moved to the table with slow, deliberate steps, as though every motion carried a weight. From a thick, dusty book that had been lying untouched for some time, he withdrew a small, delicate watercolour portrait painted on ivory. It was a likeness of his landlady's daughter, the frail and enigmatic girl who had died of fever—a girl whose strange ambitions of becoming a nun had often bewildered and intrigued him. For a long moment, he stood there gazing at her delicate, almost ethereal features, captured so vividly in the portrait. Her face seemed to hold a quiet serenity, a tragic understanding, as though she had foreseen the life and death awaiting her.

Gently, almost reverently, he pressed his lips to the portrait before extending it toward Dounia. "Take it," he said quietly, his voice tinged with a kind of bitter thoughtfulness. "I used to speak to her a great deal—more than I ever spoke to anyone else. She alone knew many of my thoughts, my fears, and my plans... plans that have since become so hideously real." He paused, his gaze distant, his mind reaching back to those moments of intimacy and confession. "But don't worry," he added, turning his attention back to Dounia, "she was as much against it all as you are. Perhaps it's better—no, I'm sure it's better—that she's gone now. She doesn't have to see what I've become."

He ran a trembling hand through his hair, his composure faltering as his thoughts shifted abruptly. "The great thing," he said, his voice rising with sudden fervor, "is that all of it—everything—is about to change. It's all going to be broken, shattered into pieces." But just as suddenly, his energy dissipated, and he slumped into a familiar dejection. "Everything will change, and yet, am I truly ready for it? Do I even want it? They say suffering is necessary. Necessary!" He spat the word with disdain. "But what's the purpose of this senseless suffering? What will it teach me, in the end? Will I understand anything better when I'm crushed under the weight of hardships, weakened by years of penal servitude, stripped of everything human until I'm no more than a broken, aging man?"

His voice grew quieter, almost reflective, though the bitterness never left. "And when those years are done, what then? What will there be to live for? Why am I even agreeing to this life now? Oh, I knew I was contemptible, standing there by the Neva at daybreak this morning," he murmured, his voice dropping to a whisper.

At last, the two of them walked out together. It was agonizing for Dounia to leave him like this, to let him go knowing the pain he carried within, but her love for her brother was unshakable. As she walked away, her steps heavy with sorrow, she turned to look back at him after fifty paces. He was still standing there, watching her, his expression unreadable. At the corner, he, too, turned to glance back at her, and their eyes met one final time. But when he saw that she was looking at him, he waved her away with a sharp, impatient gesture, almost as if her concern irritated him, and then abruptly turned the corner and disappeared.

"I'm wicked," he thought to himself as he hurried on, a pang of regret already welling up within him. The memory of his gesture toward Dounia stung him, and he felt ashamed of his own impatience. "But why do they love me so much when I don't deserve it? Why do they care for someone like me?" His thoughts grew darker as he continued walking. "If only I were truly alone—if no one loved me, and if I had never loved anyone—none of this would have happened. There would be no guilt, no suffering."

And yet, a deeper bitterness began to creep into his musings. "But what will become of me in those fifteen or twenty years? Will they grind me down so thoroughly that I become meek, that I'll kneel before them all and grovel, confessing my guilt at every turn? Is that what they want from me? That's it, isn't it? That's exactly why they're sending me there. They want to break me, to see me humbled."

His mind wandered to the people he had so often seen on the streets—the indifferent crowds bustling about, their faces hard and self-absorbed. "Look at them," he thought, his lip curling in disdain. "Running to and fro like ants, every one of them a scoundrel at heart, no better than me. Worse, even—because they don't have the courage to admit it. And yet, if someone tried to save me now, to stop me from going, they'd be the first to howl with righteous indignation. How I hate them all!"

He walked on, consumed by these thoughts, his mind circling endlessly around the same questions. How could he bear the humiliation of being humbled before such people? What would it take to break his pride and make him bow his head? And yet, deep down, he knew it was inevitable. "Twenty years of chains, twenty years of being treated like an animal... it will wear me down. Water wears away stone. I'll be nothing but a shell by the end of it." He shivered at the thought. "And why? Why should I even live through that? Why am I choosing this now when I already know how it will end?"

It was not the first time he had asked himself these questions. It was not even the hundredth. But despite all his doubts, all his despair, his feet carried him forward. He was still going.

Chapter 8

When Raskolnikov entered Sonia's room, the evening shadows were already thickening. The day had been long and oppressive for her, filled with agonizing anticipation. Sonia had been waiting for him with a kind of dread she could hardly articulate. Dounia had spent much of the day with her. She had come early in the morning, her thoughts burdened by Svidrigaïlov's ominous assertion that Sonia knew the truth about her brother.

The meeting of the two women, though deeply emotional, brought them closer in a way neither had anticipated. Their conversation had been full of tears and mutual understanding, though no words could truly convey the weight of what they both felt. Dounia, at least, found some solace in the encounter—her brother would not be alone. He had sought Sonia first with his confession, had trusted her with his torment. She saw in Sonia a quiet but steadfast strength, the kind of devotion that would carry him through whatever fate awaited him. Though Dounia didn't explicitly ask, she understood implicitly that Sonia would follow Raskolnikov wherever his path led. This realization brought a mixture of reverence and sorrow, and at times, Dounia's gaze almost overwhelmed Sonia with its intensity.

For her part, Sonia felt unworthy of such respect. Dounia's graciousness, her composure, and the quiet dignity with which she had first greeted Sonia in Raskolnikov's room seemed to elevate her to a plane Sonia could hardly comprehend. That moment had remained in Sonia's memory as a vision of impossible grace, a reflection of everything she wished she could be.

Later in the day, Dounia, unable to sit still, decided to wait for her brother at his lodging. She was convinced he would return there first. Alone now, Sonia's anxiety surged. The idea of Raskolnikov taking his own life loomed large in her mind, and despite Dounia's earlier reassurances, the fear gnawed at her. Dounia, too, had shared this dread, though both women had spent hours trying to convince each other otherwise. Together, they managed to stave off their fears, but apart, the silence became unbearable, allowing their darkest thoughts to surface. Sonia could not stop replaying Svidrigaïlov's chilling assertion in her mind—Raskolnikov had two choices: Siberia or...

As the sun began its descent, Sonia stood at her window, staring blankly at the unpainted wall of the building opposite. The oppressive stillness pressed down on her, and her despair deepened. Just when she had begun to lose hope, he appeared.

The sight of him filled her with an involuntary cry of joy, but as her eyes met his, her heart sank. His face, pale and strained, bore an expression she couldn't quite decipher.

"Yes," Raskolnikov said with a faint, almost bitter smile. "I've come for your cross, Sonia. You told me to go to the crossroads, and now, here I am. Why are you frightened now that it's come to this?"

Sonia looked at him, bewildered and stricken. His tone, his words—they felt alien to her, as though he was hiding behind them. A shiver ran through her, and she realized he was masking something deeper, something he could not or would not say outright. His eyes avoided hers, darting away as though afraid of what they might reveal.

"You see, Sonia, I've made up my mind," he continued, his voice detached, as though rehearsing a speech. "There's no need to explain the reasons—they're not important now. What annoys me is the thought of all those dull, brutish faces gawking at me, pestering me with their idiotic questions. I can already see them pointing their fingers and whispering. Tfoo!" He spat the word with disdain. "I'm not going to Porfiry—I've had enough of him. No, I think I'll go to my good friend, the Explosive Lieutenant. Can you imagine the sensation I'll cause? I must keep my composure, though. Lately, I've been far too irritable. I almost shook my fist at my sister today just because she turned back for one last look at me. What have I become? Anyway, where are the crosses?"

He rambled on incoherently, his words rushing out in a chaotic torrent. Sonia watched him with growing concern. His hands trembled, and his movements were restless, as though his mind couldn't settle on any one thought.

Without a word, she went to her drawer and took out two crosses—one of cypress wood and one of copper. She made the sign of the cross over herself, then over him, and gently placed the wooden cross around his neck.

"This is the symbol of taking up the cross, isn't it?" he said with a hollow laugh. "As if I haven't suffered enough already! The wooden one is the peasant's cross, and the copper one—you'll wear it yourself, won't you? It was Lizaveta's, wasn't it? She wore it... at that moment. I remember now. Two things like these—a silver cross and a little ikon—I threw them back on the old woman's neck. How appropriate they would be now. But I'm rambling again. You see, I came to warn you, Sonia, so you'd know. That's all. That's all I came for."

He paused, as if searching for something more to say, but then waved his hand dismissively. "You wanted this, didn't you? You wanted me to go. Well, I'm going. What are you crying for? Oh, I hate all this!"

Despite his harsh words, his heart ached as he looked at her. "Why is she crying?" he wondered. "What am I to her? Why does she care for me like this? Like my mother, like Dounia... she'll follow me, won't she?"

"Cross yourself," Sonia pleaded softly, her voice breaking. "Say at least one prayer."

"Oh, certainly," he replied with forced enthusiasm, crossing himself several times. "As many as you like, Sonia. Sincerely, of course."

But his mind was elsewhere. He noticed her draping her shawl over her head—the same green shawl that had belonged to her family, a relic of her late father's memory. The sight of it stirred something in him, but he didn't ask about it. He was too distracted, too unsettled. Suddenly, he realized what she intended.

"Wait! What are you doing? You're not coming with me!" he exclaimed, his voice rising in irritation. "Stay here! I'll go alone. There's no need for a procession."

He turned toward the door, muttering to himself, "What's the point of all this ceremony?" Without so much as a goodbye, he left, leaving Sonia standing alone in the center of the room, her green shawl still draped over her head, her eyes filled with silent sorrow.

As he descended the stairs, a storm of conflicting emotions surged within him. He stopped briefly, realizing he hadn't even said goodbye to her, hadn't thanked her, hadn't acknowledged her pain. But before he could turn back, another thought struck him—a thought that had been lurking at the edges of his mind, waiting for this exact moment to make itself known.

Raskolnikov trudged forward along the canal bank, the weight of his thoughts bearing down on him like an oppressive mist. His steps were slow, hesitant, as if his body resisted moving closer to the inevitable. His mind whirled with questions, recriminations, and half-formed justifications.

"Why did I go to her just now?" he asked himself bitterly. "I told her it was for business, but what business could I possibly have? There was no reason, no purpose. I only wanted to see her, to witness her terror, to feel her pain. I am despicable. I am a coward who clings to others' suffering to delay my own." He winced at the thought and gritted his teeth. "I wanted her tears, her fear... something, anything to hold me back for a moment longer. And I drove her away like a dog."

His mind churned, and he quickened his pace as if to outdistance his thoughts. Before long, he reached the bridge. But instead of crossing it, he veered off and turned toward the Hay Market, drawn almost instinctively to the throng of humanity bustling there.

The sights and sounds of the market flooded over him, jarring his senses. He stared intently at every sign, every face, yet nothing seemed to register. "In another week, or perhaps a month, I'll cross this bridge in a prison van," he thought suddenly. The vision sprang unbidden into his mind: the canal waters glinting below as the cart rumbled forward, the iron bars separating him from the world. "What will I feel then, looking out over the water? Will I even remember this moment?" His eyes darted to a sign on a shop. "Campany," he read, misinterpreting the faded letters. "That letter 'a'... how trivial it all seems, and yet how vital. I should remember this. How will I see it when I'm dragged through here in chains?"

He glanced at the people around him—the peasant woman with a baby begging at the corner, the stout German man who bumped into him without apology. Each one seemed a fragment of a world he no longer belonged to. His hand brushed his pocket and found a five-kopeck coin. He hesitated, then handed it to the peasant woman.

"Take it," he said brusquely. The woman blessed him tearfully, her voice thick with gratitude.

The market teemed with life—noisy, chaotic, indifferent. Raskolnikov hated the crowd, yet he remained in its midst, almost as if he needed the human closeness to push against his isolation. A drunkard stumbled nearby, attempting to dance but repeatedly falling. A ring of spectators jeered and laughed. Raskolnikov pressed forward to watch, but his attention quickly waned. The drunkard, the crowd, the noise—all of it blurred into a meaningless haze.

He wandered aimlessly into the square, his thoughts darkening with every step. Suddenly, Sonia's words surged into his mind with searing clarity: "Go to the crossroads. Bow down to the people. Kiss the earth, for you have sinned against it. Say aloud, 'I am a murderer.'"

The memory struck him like a blow. The weight of those words, the raw honesty of her plea, broke something inside him. His chest heaved, and his vision blurred with tears. He felt the misery of the past weeks and months crash over him in an overwhelming wave, and in that moment, he surrendered to it.

Without thinking, he fell to his knees in the center of the square. The cold, filthy ground pressed against him as he bent down and kissed it with trembling lips. He rose unsteadily, then knelt again, bowing his head to the earth as though begging its forgiveness.

Laughter erupted around him.

"He's drunk!" shouted a young man nearby.

"Must be saying goodbye to the city before he heads to Jerusalem!" another jeered.

"Quite the show he's putting on," added a slightly tipsy workman, grinning as he raised a bottle. "Kissing the earth and everything. Must be a real gentleman to be so dramatic."

Raskolnikov heard their mocking, felt their scorn like a dozen daggers in his back, but he remained motionless. The words "I am a murderer" hovered on his lips, but they would not come.

When he finally rose, he glanced around—and froze. Among the sea of jeering faces, he saw her. Sonia stood fifty paces away, partially concealed by a wooden stall, her eyes fixed on him with unwavering devotion. She had followed him, shadowed him in his torment. Her presence struck him like a lightning bolt.

"She'll follow me anywhere," he thought, his chest tightening. "No matter what happens, no matter where I go, she'll be there. She's bound herself to me forever." A pang of guilt shot through him. He wanted to hate her for it, to drive her away again, but all he felt was a deep, aching tenderness.

Turning, he walked toward the police station, his steps heavy with finality. The yard loomed ahead, and he entered it resolutely, though each step felt like an eternity. He climbed the staircase slowly, the weight of his guilt pressing harder with every step.

The smells of unwashed stairwells and stale air assaulted him, memories from that other fateful day flooding back. The eggshells, the grimy walls, the cracked tiles—every detail screamed at him. His legs threatened to give way, but he pressed on, gripping the bannister tightly. "The more revolting, the better," he thought grimly. "Let it all be as vile as possible. If I am to drink the cup, I'll drain it to the dregs."

He reached the third floor at last and paused, breathless. The familiar vision of Ilya Petrovitch, the "explosive lieutenant," rose in his mind. Was he truly about to confront that man? Would it not be better to turn back, to go to Nikodim Fomitch instead, to speak quietly, privately?

"No," he told himself, shaking his head. "Let it be public. Let the disgrace be complete."

Steeling himself, he pushed open the office door. The room was almost empty—a house porter lounged in a corner, and a lone clerk sat at a bureau scribbling away. The air felt stagnant, lifeless. Raskolnikov stepped inside, his heart pounding. This was it—the moment he had both dreaded and longed for. But even now, standing on the precipice, he felt the doubt clawing at him again. Could he still turn back? Could he still escape?

The clerk looked up briefly but said nothing. Somewhere deep inside, Raskolnikov felt the faintest flicker of hope that he might yet hold his silence. But he stepped forward anyway, his fate sealed by the very act of walking into that room.

The sudden exclamation hit Raskolnikov like a thunderclap, freezing him in place. He stared at Ilya Petrovitch with wide, unblinking eyes. The room seemed to tilt slightly, and he had to grip the back of a chair to steady himself. The name echoed in his mind, reverberating against his swirling thoughts: Svidrigaïlov... has shot himself?

"What, do you know Svidrigaïlov?" Ilya Petrovitch repeated, his tone a curious blend of surprise and casual inquiry. His words seemed distant, as though coming from the other end of a long tunnel.

"Yes," Raskolnikov managed to reply hoarsely after a pause. "Yes, I knew him. But... what happened?"

The officer leaned back, waving his hand dismissively as though the matter were already old news. "Well, what usually happens with such fellows? One moment, they're full of grand plans, and the next, they're driven to despair. He shot himself early this morning at the 'Adrianople,' that dingy hotel near the Little Neva. Left quite a mess, as I hear."

Raskolnikov's heart seemed to stop for a moment before resuming its heavy, uneven rhythm. He could vividly picture the scene—the decrepit hotel, the sordid room, the murky waters outside. He tried to speak, but his throat felt dry, and he could only manage a faint whisper. "How... how did it happen?"

"Ah, well," Ilya Petrovitch said, now fully absorbed in recounting the event, "it seems he was a peculiar man, even in his last moments. He paid his bill before doing it, as if settling a mundane matter. Witnesses said he stood calmly in the yard, had some words with the watchman—told him he was going to America, of all things—and then, bang! Right there, in front of everyone."

Raskolnikov's grip on the chair tightened as he felt the air being sucked from his lungs. He could see it so vividly: Svidrigaïlov's measured steps, his final words, the flash of the revolver. It was as if he were there, watching the entire scene unfold.

"A strange man, that Svidrigaïlov," continued Ilya Petrovitch, oblivious to the effect his words were having on his listener. "Not quite right in the head, if you ask me. Always had that look—haunted, you might say. I've met his sort before—sly, calculating, but beneath it all, deeply troubled. And then, of course, there were his... peculiar entanglements. Rumours about the women in his life, you know. But it seems he finally reached the end of his rope."

Raskolnikov forced himself to breathe, though each breath felt shallow and insufficient. He struggled to hold himself together, nodding mechanically as Ilya Petrovitch prattled on. The officer's voice seemed to fade in and out, as though the room itself were spinning.

"And to think," Ilya Petrovitch added, chuckling at his own wit, "he told the watchman he was heading to America. Well, he certainly took a one-way trip, didn't he?"

A sick feeling churned in Raskolnikov's stomach. He felt the weight of Svidrigaïlov's final moments pressing heavily upon him, like a shadow that refused to be shaken. The man's cryptic words from their last encounter came rushing back—his strange, resigned demeanor, his veiled remarks about life and death. It all seemed to converge now into a singular, dreadful realization.

"He... left nothing else? No note, no... explanation?" Raskolnikov asked suddenly, his voice barely above a whisper.

Ilya Petrovitch shrugged, seemingly unbothered by the question. "Who knows? These fellows don't always bother with such things. Besides, what could he possibly explain? Some debts here, some misdeeds there. Perhaps he thought silence would be more poetic."

Raskolnikov remained silent, his thoughts racing faster than he could contain them. A crushing sense of inevitability filled his chest, mingled with a strange, inexplicable sorrow. The news of Svidrigaïlov's death had not just startled him—it had pierced something deeper, something he had not yet fully understood.

"Well," Ilya Petrovitch said, clapping his hands together as if to signify the end of the topic, "it's a grim story, but not an uncommon one. The city eats people alive, doesn't it? Anyway, what was it you came for? You mentioned Zametov?"

Raskolnikov shook his head faintly, his thoughts too scattered to focus on the question. "No... nothing. It's not important anymore."

Ilya Petrovitch gave him a curious look, his good humor momentarily tempered by confusion. "Not important? Well, suit yourself. But don't hesitate if you've got business to discuss. We're here to serve, you know."

Without another word, Raskolnikov turned and walked out of the office, his steps unsteady. The weight of Svidrigaïlov's death seemed to follow him, clinging to him like a phantom. As he descended the stairs, the world outside felt strangely distant, its noises muffled, its colors muted. He stepped into the street, the air cold against his face, and began to walk aimlessly, his mind a storm of memories, regrets, and questions he could not yet articulate.

Svidrigaïlov's final act had left a mark, one that Raskolnikov could not yet fully comprehend but knew he would carry with him, perhaps forever.

"Yes... I knew him..." Raskolnikov replied faintly, his voice trembling as though the words themselves were a burden. "He hadn't been here long."

"Ah, indeed," said Ilya Petrovitch, nodding sagely. "A tragic end, and in such a dreadful manner. A reckless man, they say. He had lost his wife and, just like that, decided to shoot himself. He even left a note—a peculiar one. Claimed he was in full possession of his faculties and made it clear that no one was to blame for his death. Odd, isn't it?

They say he had money, too. And you—how did you come to know him?"

Raskolnikov struggled to steady his voice, each word feeling like an ordeal. "I... was acquainted with him. My sister... she was a governess in his family."

"Ah, bah-bah-bah!" Ilya Petrovitch exclaimed, his interest piqued. "Then surely you can tell us something about him! Did you notice anything unusual? Had you any inkling?"

"I saw him yesterday," Raskolnikov said, his words coming haltingly. "He... he was drinking wine. I had no idea... nothing."

A weight seemed to press upon Raskolnikov's chest, tightening with every breath. He felt as though the air in the room had grown thick, suffocating him. He could barely focus on Ilya Petrovitch's words, though their cadence rang faintly in his ears.

"You've turned pale again," the officer remarked, squinting at him with concern. "It's awfully stuffy in here, I know. Are you unwell?"

"Yes... I must go," Raskolnikov muttered, his voice barely audible. He stumbled over his words, his mind racing. "Excuse me... for troubling you."

"Oh, not at all, not at all!" Ilya Petrovitch said warmly, rising slightly from his chair. "As often as you like. Always a pleasure to see you. And let me say, you're welcome here anytime."

He extended his hand, but Raskolnikov barely registered the gesture. "I only wanted... I came to see Zametov."

"Yes, yes, I understand," Ilya Petrovitch replied, shaking his head and smiling. "Do come again."

"I... am very glad..." Raskolnikov forced a smile that looked more like a grimace. "Good-bye."

He turned and made his way toward the door, but his legs felt unsteady beneath him, as though the ground might give way at any moment. His head spun, and his vision blurred. He clung to the wall for support as he descended the stairs, his hand trailing along its rough surface. The world around him seemed distant and distorted. He thought he saw a porter rushing past him, a dog barking furiously on a lower floor, a woman shouting angrily and throwing something—a rolling pin?—but it was all a haze.

When he finally stepped out into the yard, he froze. Sonia stood there, pale as a ghost, her wide, terror-stricken eyes fixed on him. Her hands were clasped tightly, as though in silent prayer, and her whole being seemed to tremble with fear and sorrow. For a moment, they stared at each other, the silence between them heavy with unspeakable despair.

Raskolnikov's lips twisted into a strange, grotesque smile, but it was empty, meaningless. He lingered for a moment longer, then abruptly turned back and re-entered the police office, leaving Sonia standing in the yard like a statue.

Ilya Petrovitch was at his desk again, sifting through a pile of papers. A peasant, the same man who had brushed past Raskolnikov on the stairs, stood before him, speaking in low, muffled tones.

"Hullo! Back again?" Ilya Petrovitch exclaimed, looking up in surprise. "What's this? Have you left something behind? What's the matter?"

Raskolnikov staggered into the room, his face as white as a sheet, his eyes wide and staring. He moved toward the desk, his steps slow and heavy, like a man wading through a dream. He leaned on the edge of the table for support, his trembling hand gripping it tightly.

"I..." he began, but the words caught in his throat. He tried again, but all that came out was an incoherent murmur.

"Sit down, man! You're ill!" Ilya Petrovitch cried, jumping up and motioning for a chair. "Some water here—quickly!"

Raskolnikov sank into the chair but didn't drink the water that was offered. His gaze remained fixed on Ilya Petrovitch, who now looked thoroughly alarmed. A minute passed, the room tense with anticipation. Finally, in a soft but distinct voice, Raskolnikov said:

"It was I... I killed the old pawnbroker woman and her sister Lizaveta with an axe... and robbed them."

The words hung in the air like a thunderclap. Ilya Petrovitch's mouth fell open, his face frozen in shock. The peasant gasped audibly. From nearby rooms, people began to gather, their faces a mixture of astonishment and disbelief.

Raskolnikov repeated the confession, his voice steady but devoid of emotion. The weight that had been crushing him for so long now seemed to lift, leaving in its place an empty, hollow relief. All around him, the room buzzed with a sudden commotion, but he sat motionless, staring at the floor, as though he had finally been released from the chains of his torment.

EPILOGUE

Chapter 1

Siberia. Along the desolate banks of a wide, lonely river stood a remote town, one of the many administrative outposts of the vast Russian Empire. Within this town, a somber fortress rose as a grim reminder of authority and punishment. Inside the fortress, hidden behind thick, impenetrable walls, was a prison, and in that prison, for the past nine months, Rodion Raskolnikov—now officially known as a second-class convict—served his sentence. It had been nearly a year and a half since the terrible crime that changed his life forever.

The trial that followed his arrest unfolded without much complication or dramatic contention. From the beginning, Raskolnikov adhered strictly and unwaveringly to his confession, recounting the events of his crime with unsettling precision. He neither sought to obscure the facts nor to present them in a light favorable to himself. Every detail, no matter how small, was laid bare: how he had struck the old pawnbroker, Alyona Ivanovna, with an axe; how Lizaveta had walked in unexpectedly, forcing him to kill her as well; how he had stolen the keys, rummaged through the chest, and hidden the stolen items under a stone in a yard off Voznesensky Prospect. He described the piece of wood with the metal strip in the pawnbroker's hand, the knocking on the door by Koch and the student, his desperate flight down the stairs, and his frantic concealment in an empty apartment. He even confessed his precise thoughts and fears in those harrowing moments.

The clarity and detail of his account left little room for doubt. He directed authorities to the stone where the stolen purse and trinkets were hidden, items he had never once used. The purse, when opened, was found to contain precisely three hundred and seventeen roubles and sixty copecks. Some of the topmost banknotes, dampened by prolonged exposure under the stone, had begun to deteriorate. But what shocked everyone most was Raskolnikov's admission that he had never even looked inside the purse. He didn't know how much money it contained, nor could he recall the nature of the trinkets he had stolen.

This peculiar lack of interest in his loot baffled everyone involved in the case. At first, it seemed implausible, even absurd, and some suggested he might be lying about this detail. But as more evidence of his peculiar state of mind surfaced, legal experts and psychologists began to entertain the possibility that his crime had been committed not out of greed but during a moment of psychological derangement. They argued that this was a case of temporary insanity, a theory increasingly fashionable in criminal cases of the era.

Many testimonies supported this perspective. Dr. Zossimov, his former classmates, his landlady, and even her servant all attested to his erratic behavior and melancholic disposition in the months leading up to the crime. Witnesses described him as a man teetering on the brink of mental collapse, haunted by poverty, hunger, and an unbearable sense of failure. His actions, they argued, were not those of a typical murderer or robber but of a man consumed by an inner torment he could not fully understand or control.

What confounded his observers further was his reluctance to offer any defense. When asked about his motive, Raskolnikov responded bluntly: his miserable circumstances, his poverty, and his desperate hope to secure three thousand roubles to begin anew. He spoke with disarming candor, describing his own character as cowardly and shallow, exasperated by his failures and privations. When pressed on why he ultimately confessed, his answer was simple: heartfelt repentance. There was no attempt to justify, romanticize, or excuse his actions, and his stark honesty bordered on the coarse.

The court, taking into account the unusual circumstances, handed down a sentence that was unexpectedly lenient: penal servitude in the second class for eight years. The confession, given at a time when the case was hopelessly entangled by the false testimony of Nikolay, weighed heavily in his favor. Additionally, Porfiry Petrovitch had honored his promise, keeping certain incriminating suspicions out of the public eye until Raskolnikov had come forward voluntarily.

Other factors worked in his favor as well. Razumihin unearthed several incidents from Raskolnikov's past that painted a picture of a man capable of compassion and selflessness. He had once supported a consumptive fellow student with his own meager resources and had even arranged for the care and burial of the student's father after his death. Witnesses also confirmed that Raskolnikov had saved two children from a house fire years earlier, sustaining burns in the process. These acts of kindness and bravery softened the perception of his character and lent weight to the argument that his crime was an aberration, not a reflection of his true nature.

The trial's aftermath brought profound sorrow to his family. Pulcheria Alexandrovna, Raskolnikov's mother, fell gravely ill as soon as the proceedings began. Her condition, a nervous affliction that gradually clouded her mind, worsened with each passing day. Dounia and Razumihin, who had become steadfastly devoted to one another, took her away from Petersburg to a quieter town along the railway. Razumihin stayed close to the city to monitor the trial and visit Dounia regularly, their bond growing stronger under the weight of shared grief.

For Raskolnikov, the journey to Siberia marked the beginning of a new, harsh chapter—a path laden with suffering, reflection, and the faint hope of redemption. Though the weight of his crime would never fully lift, the strange, winding path that led him there seemed, in some inexplicable way, to promise transformation. Yet, as he stared at the vast expanse of the river and the stark walls of the prison, he could not help but wonder whether that promise was real—or merely another illusion born of his tormented mind.

When Dounia returned from her final meeting with her brother, she found their mother already stricken with illness, feverish and caught in the grip of delirium. That very evening, Dounia and Razumihin deliberated over how to answer Pulcheria Alexandrovna's inevitable questions about Raskolnikov. They fabricated a detailed story, claiming that he had been sent on a significant business commission to a distant region of Russia—a venture that would ultimately bring him both wealth and recognition.

Yet, to their astonishment, Pulcheria Alexandrovna did not ask any questions about her son's sudden departure, either then or in the days that followed. Instead, she seemed to possess her own version of events. Tearfully, she confided to them her belief that Raskolnikov had been forced into hiding due to powerful enemies working against him. She hinted at mysterious knowledge that only she was privy to, and with unwavering conviction, she assured Razumihin and Dounia that her son's future would be brilliant once these malevolent influences were neutralized. She often pointed to his article as evidence of his extraordinary talent and bright destiny, reading it over and over again, even aloud, and sometimes clutching it as though it were a talisman. Strangely, though she immersed herself in these fantasies, she rarely inquired about his whereabouts, even when their evasiveness on the subject should have aroused her suspicions.

Dounia and Razumihin grew increasingly uneasy with Pulcheria Alexandrovna's peculiar silence on certain matters. She never once expressed concern over the absence of letters from Raskolnikov, a stark contrast to her earlier years when she had lived for every word he sent. This absence of inquiry unsettled Dounia deeply. She began to suspect that her mother harbored unspoken fears, that she had guessed something dreadful about Raskolnikov's situation but was too terrified to seek confirmation. Over time, Dounia could no longer avoid the conclusion that their mother's mental faculties were not entirely sound.

There were moments, however, when Pulcheria Alexandrovna maneuvered conversations so deftly that avoiding the truth became almost impossible. When she received vague or evasive answers, she would lapse into prolonged periods of silence, her mood dark and brooding. Dounia realized that trying to deceive her was futile and potentially harmful. At times, Pulcheria Alexandrovna's suspicions seemed to surface in bursts of anxiety, only to be buried again beneath fits of hysterical energy, during which she would speak endlessly of Raskolnikov's promising future. She imagined scenarios so peculiar and elaborate that Dounia and Razumihin could do nothing but humor her, even as they feared these fantasies betrayed her inner turmoil.

Five months after Raskolnikov's confession, he was sentenced to penal servitude. During that time, Sonia and Razumihin visited him in prison as frequently as they could. When the day of his departure for Siberia came, it was an emotional and painful farewell. Dounia and Razumihin vowed that the separation would not be permanent. Razumihin, with his characteristic determination, promised to secure a stable livelihood within a few years and save enough money to join Raskolnikov in Siberia. He envisioned a future where they could all begin anew, building a life together in the very town where Raskolnikov was imprisoned. This vision offered some solace, though the parting was marked by tears and anguish.

In the days leading up to his departure, Raskolnikov was unusually quiet and introspective. He seemed haunted by thoughts of their mother, frequently inquiring about her condition. The news of her worsening health darkened his already somber mood. With Sonia, he remained reserved, though it was tacitly understood that she would follow him to Siberia. Thanks to the inheritance left to her by Svidrigaïlov, Sonia had long since prepared for this journey. The subject was never openly discussed between them, yet their mutual understanding was clear.

When the moment of separation arrived, Raskolnikov met his sister's and Razumihin's optimistic visions of the future with a strange, bittersweet smile. Their hopes seemed to him like a distant dream, something intangible and unreachable. Privately, he predicted that Pulcheria Alexandrovna's illness would soon claim her life, a thought that added another layer of sorrow to the already grim departure. Finally, accompanied by Sonia, he began his journey to Siberia.

Two months later, Dounia and Razumihin were married. The ceremony was modest and tinged with melancholy. Porfiry Petrovitch and Dr. Zossimov attended, their presence a quiet reminder of the connections that bound them all. During this time, Razumihin devoted himself entirely to his plans for the future. He resumed his university studies with the aim of earning his degree and laying a foundation for their eventual emigration to Siberia. Dounia placed complete faith in his resolve, drawing strength from his unwavering will and shared vision of a new beginning.

Meanwhile, Pulcheria Alexandrovna's mental state continued to deteriorate. Though she gave her blessing to Dounia's marriage, she became increasingly restless and melancholic afterward. Razumihin's stories of Raskolnikov's past acts of kindness—his support of a sick student and his bravery in rescuing two children from a fire—stirred her imagination to a feverish pitch. She spoke of these events with anyone who would listen, often recounting them to strangers in public places, much to Dounia's alarm. The danger of such public discussions, given the notoriety of Raskolnikov's trial, was ever-present.

Her erratic behavior escalated. One day, she became convinced that Raskolnikov would return imminently, based on an imagined timeline from their last goodbye. She threw herself into preparing his room, cleaning and redecorating with a manic energy. Dounia, though deeply concerned, chose not to contradict her and instead helped with the preparations. After one such exhausting day, Pulcheria

Alexandrovna fell gravely ill. Her fever worsened, and within two weeks, she succumbed to brain fever. In her delirium, she let slip fragments of knowledge that revealed she had understood far more about Raskolnikov's fate than anyone had realized.

Raskolnikov, already in Siberia, remained unaware of his mother's death for a considerable time. Correspondence with him was maintained through Sonia, who wrote to Dounia and Razumihin monthly and received their replies in return. Initially, her letters seemed distant, devoid of emotion, but they soon came to appreciate their precision. Sonia's accounts painted a vivid and detailed picture of Raskolnikov's life as a convict. She refrained from speculating on his state of mind or future, focusing solely on factual updates—his health, his requests, and his day-to-day life. Through her meticulous letters, Dounia and Razumihin were able to piece together the reality of their brother's existence in exile, though the weight of that knowledge did little to ease their pain.

Dounia and Razumihin found little solace in the updates they received from Sonia, especially in the beginning. Sonia's letters described Raskolnikov as withdrawn and uncommunicative, immersed in a sullen silence that he rarely broke. He seemed uninterested in the news she relayed from their letters, and although he occasionally asked about his mother, it was clear to Sonia that he already suspected the truth. When she finally told him about his mother's death, expecting an emotional response, she was surprised and even disheartened by his outward indifference. He exhibited no visible reaction, as though the news barely touched him.

In her letters, Sonia painted a picture of a man who appeared to accept his new life with a dispassionate resignation. He understood his circumstances clearly, harbored no false hopes of reprieve, and adjusted to the harsh realities of prison life without resistance or complaint. He seemed neither shocked nor particularly dismayed by the stark differences between his new existence and his former life. His health, she reported, was holding steady, and he carried out his assigned labor dutifully, neither shirking his tasks nor seeking additional work. His attitude toward food was similarly indifferent. Although he initially refused any special provisions, the poor quality of the prison meals eventually led him to accept Sonia's offer of money to buy tea, which he drank daily. Yet even this gesture of care seemed to irritate him; he implored Sonia not to make any further efforts on his behalf, insisting that such attentions only troubled him.

Sonia also described the bleak conditions of the prison. Raskolnikov lived in a crowded, poorly ventilated barrack shared with other convicts. Though she had not seen the inside herself, she inferred from others that it was miserable and unhealthy. He slept on a bare plank bed with only a thin rug for comfort, but Sonia emphasized that his rough and spartan way of living was not deliberate or principled—it was simply the result of his pervasive indifference to everything.

At first, Raskolnikov seemed resentful of Sonia's visits. He greeted her presence with irritation and reluctance, unwilling to converse and, at times, outright rude. Her persistence, however, gradually wore down his initial hostility. Over time, her visits became a fixture in his routine, something he came to depend on almost unconsciously. When Sonia fell ill and was unable to visit for several days, he showed visible distress at her absence. These visits, brief as they were, took place on holidays at the prison gates or in the guardroom, where he was allowed to meet her for a few minutes. On working days, she would seek him out at his labor—whether in the workshops, at the brick kilns, or along the banks of the Irtish River, where the convicts toiled.

Sonia also shared details about her own life in the town near the prison. She had begun to build a small circle of acquaintances and found work as a seamstress. With few skilled dressmakers in the area, she quickly became indispensable to many households. Yet Sonia refrained from mentioning a critical aspect of her efforts: through her quiet perseverance, she had gained the interest and favor of local authorities, who, in turn, ensured that Raskolnikov's workload was lighter than it might otherwise have been. These small interventions, unspoken but deliberate, were her way of easing his burden without drawing attention to her sacrifices.

As the months passed, however, the tone of Sonia's letters began to shift. Dounia, who had become attuned to every nuance in Sonia's writing, noticed growing hints of alarm and unease. Sonia reported that Raskolnikov was withdrawing even further into himself. He had begun to hold himself apart from the other prisoners, rarely speaking to anyone and showing little inclination to form bonds or camaraderie. This aloofness did not go unnoticed by his fellow convicts, many of whom resented his silence and peculiar demeanor. He would go days without speaking, and Sonia observed with growing concern that his complexion was becoming increasingly pale, his already fragile health showing signs of deterioration.

The ominous tone in Sonia's updates culminated in the most troubling news yet. In her last letter, she revealed that Raskolnikov had fallen gravely ill and had been moved to the convict ward of the hospital. The news struck Dounia and Razumihin like a thunderclap. Sonia's earlier letters had hinted at this possibility, but neither of them had been prepared for the reality of his condition. For Dounia, the thought of her brother lying in a grim, overcrowded hospital ward, far from home and surrounded by strangers, was almost unbearable. Sonia's brief descriptions of the situation only deepened their sense of helplessness, as they could do nothing but wait for her next letter, hoping against hope for a sign of recovery.

Chapter 2

He fell ill for a long time, but his sickness was not caused by the harshness of prison life itself. The exhausting labor, the meager meals, the shaven head, and the coarse, patched clothing—none of these outward hardships truly weighed on him. In fact, he almost welcomed the physical toil because it granted him a few precious hours of unbroken sleep each night. The thin cabbage soup, even with beetles floating in it, hardly bothered him; during his years as a student, he had often gone without even that. His coarse prison garments were warm and adequate for his surroundings, and he barely noticed the weight of his fetters. There was no one from whom he needed to hide his shame—certainly not Sonia, who, though devoted, seemed to fear him more than ever. And yet, it was precisely in Sonia's presence that his shame burned the brightest. But it was not shame for his appearance or the visible signs of his punishment—it was his pride that had been wounded, and this wound went far deeper.

His pride was stung to the core, and it was this inner torment that made him ill. If only he could have blamed himself fully, he might have found some solace in his suffering. If he could have seen his crime as unambiguously evil, he might have borne the accompanying disgrace with a measure of dignity. But he could not. Instead, his relentless introspection led him to see his crime as nothing more than an error—a tragic miscalculation that could have happened to anyone. And for this blunder, he now had to endure the humiliation of submitting to what he saw as the absurdity of his sentence. This submission felt like an act of forced obedience to a fate he neither understood nor accepted.

In the present, he was consumed by a vague and aimless anxiety; in the future, he saw nothing but an endless series of sacrifices leading nowhere. The idea that he might eventually be freed—that at thirty-two he could begin life anew—held no comfort for him. What was there to live for? What purpose could he possibly serve? Why should he struggle merely to exist, when existence without meaning had always been intolerable to him? Even before his crime, he had been willing to give up life entirely for the sake of an idea, a vision, or even a fleeting dream. Mere survival had never satisfied him; he had always demanded more. Perhaps it was this very intensity of his desires that had led him to believe he was entitled to more than others—to believe he was a man for whom ordinary rules did not apply.

If only repentance had come to him—true, searing repentance that might have shattered his pride and kept him awake at night with its agony! He would have welcomed such torment, for at least it would have felt like life. Tears of remorse and moments of unbearable anguish might have been a kind of salvation. But no such repentance came. He did not grieve for his crime. He could not even find comfort in raging against his own stupidity, as he had in the immediate aftermath of his arrest. When he revisited the events in his mind, he no longer saw his actions as grotesque or foolish. They seemed, if anything, logical—part of a coherent plan that had simply failed.

"What made my theory so much worse than the others that have clashed and collided since the beginning of time?" he asked himself bitterly. If one were to step back and consider the idea objectively, without the influence of convention, it would not seem so outrageous. He mocked the skeptics and petty philosophers who condemned him without fully understanding his reasoning. "Why does my crime shock them so deeply?" he wondered. "Is it merely because it was illegal? Very well, I broke the law and shed blood—punish me for that. But what about those great men who seized power for themselves, breaking laws and shedding blood along the way? They succeeded, so they were justified. I failed, so I was not."

This was the only fault he acknowledged: his failure. He admitted no guilt beyond that. And yet, another torment gnawed at him: why had he not ended his own life when he had the chance? Why had he stood on the riverbank, staring into the water, only to turn away and confess? Was his will to live so strong, or was it sheer cowardice? Svidrigaïlov had found the courage to end his life, despite his fear of death—why couldn't he? He wrestled with this question, unable to see that, even in that moment of despair, a faint glimmer of self-awareness had held him back. Somewhere deep within, he had sensed the falsity of his beliefs and the emptiness of his convictions. This dim awareness, though he could not name it, was the first stirrings of a potential transformation—a hint that his life might yet hold something worth living for.

He began to notice things about his fellow prisoners that puzzled him. Despite the appalling hardships they endured, they clung to life with a fierce tenacity. Many of them—especially the tramps—seemed to treasure memories of the simplest pleasures: a hidden spring in a forest, the feel of sunlight on their faces, the sound of a bird's song. It baffled him that they could endure such suffering yet still find joy in such small things. At first, he tried to dismiss these observations, but they lingered in his mind, slowly eroding his cynicism.

Yet the greatest source of his anguish was the unbridgeable gulf between himself and the other prisoners. They seemed like an entirely different species, and he could feel their distrust and hostility toward him growing with each passing day. He understood the reasons for this separation—his crime, his demeanor, his pride—but he had not realized until now just how deep those reasons ran. Among the prisoners were some political exiles who looked down on the others as uneducated brutes, but Raskolnikov could not share their scorn. He saw wisdom in those "brutes" that the exiles failed to recognize. Still, his own sense of superiority and his refusal to conform made him an outcast. The other convicts mocked him, even despised him. They laughed at his crime, saying, "You're a gentleman; hacking away with an axe isn't work for your kind."

As time went on, the isolation grew more unbearable. He was avoided, even hated. One day, during the second week of Lent, he went to take the sacrament with the rest of his group. A quarrel broke out—he never learned how it started—but soon all the prisoners turned on him with a furious intensity.

"You don't believe in God!" they shouted. "You're an infidel! You deserve to die!"

Raskolnikov had never spoken to the other convicts about God or his beliefs, yet they singled him out as an infidel, as though this alone were reason enough to hate him. The hostility was palpable, and one day it boiled over. A prisoner, gripped by a wild frenzy, lunged at him with murderous intent. Raskolnikov stood his ground, calm and silent, his face a mask of unflinching composure. His gaze betrayed neither fear nor anger. If the guard had not intervened in time, blood would surely have been spilled.

But his isolation went deeper than their scorn. Another mystery gnawed at him: why did these hardened men hold Sonia in such high regard? She had made no effort to endear herself to them; she rarely saw them, except for fleeting moments when she came to visit him at work. And yet everyone knew who she was and what she had done—how she had followed him to this remote place, how she lived humbly and worked tirelessly. She never gave them money, nor did she perform any great service for them. Once, at Christmas, she had sent some rolls and pies to the prisoners, but that was all. Over time, though, she became a figure of quiet reverence among them.

Sonia wrote and posted letters for them, delivering messages to their families. Visitors from the convicts' homes brought gifts and entrusted them to her for safekeeping. The wives and sweethearts of the prisoners began visiting her, drawn by some unspoken bond. When Sonia passed by, whether at the work site or on the road, the convicts would take off their caps and call out to her with affection: "Little mother Sofya Semyonovna, you are our good, dear little mother." They admired everything about her—her small, frail frame, her gentle smile, even the way she walked. They turned to her in their illnesses, as though her mere presence could ease their suffering.

Raskolnikov watched all of this from the periphery, his thoughts muddled by fever and delirium during his long stay in the hospital, which began in the middle of Lent and stretched past Easter. While he was ill, strange dreams haunted him. One recurring vision troubled him deeply: the entire world had fallen victim to a catastrophic plague that originated in the depths of Asia. This was no ordinary disease; it was caused by intelligent, willful microbes that attacked the minds of men as well as their bodies. Those infected became deranged, consumed by a conviction of their own intellectual and moral infallibility. Villages, towns, entire nations descended into chaos. Each person believed themselves the sole bearer of truth, and this certainty drove them to madness.

People could no longer distinguish between good and evil, right and wrong. They argued endlessly, accusing one another, yet finding no resolution. Communities fractured; even armies, gathered for mutual defense, turned on themselves in senseless violence. Society collapsed under the weight of its collective delusions. Amid the chaos, only a small, unseen group of "pure" individuals—the chosen few— survived. They were destined to rebuild the world, but no one had seen them or heard their voices. Raskolnikov awoke from this dream time and again, shaken and deeply disturbed by its vividness. Even after the fever passed, the memory of it lingered, haunting him like a shadow.

By the second week after Easter, the weather turned warm and bright. The hospital windows were open to the fresh spring air, and the sounds of life drifted in from outside. Sonia, though limited in her visits by the difficulty of obtaining permission, often came to the hospital yard in the evenings, standing silently beneath the windows. One evening, as he was nearly recovered, Raskolnikov saw her waiting at the gate. The sight of her struck him with an inexplicable pang, and he turned away, retreating into his thoughts. For several days afterward, she did not appear, and he found himself growing restless and uneasy, surprised at the intensity of his anticipation.

When he finally returned to the prison, he learned from the other convicts that Sonia had fallen ill. Her condition was not serious, but she was confined to her home. His anxiety only deepened when she sent him a note in her shaky handwriting, assuring him that she was recovering and would visit him soon. The sight of her words made his heart ache in a way he could not explain.

One bright morning, he was sent to work by the riverbank, helping to prepare alabaster. The vast expanse of the river stretched before him, its waters shimmering in the sunlight. In the distance, he could see the dark shapes of nomadic tents scattered across the steppe. The scene spoke of freedom, of a life untouched by the harsh realities of the prison. Lost in a haze of daydreams, he sat on a pile of logs, staring out at the tranquil landscape. For once, his mind was still, his thoughts suspended in a strange, restless calm.

And then, without warning, Sonia appeared beside him. She had come up silently, her slight frame wrapped in her familiar green shawl. Her face was pale, still marked by the signs of recent illness, but she smiled at him with a quiet joy. She held out her hand timidly, as though unsure whether he would take it. For once, he did not hesitate. Their hands met and remained clasped.

He glanced at her briefly, his eyes filled with something unspoken, then lowered his gaze to the ground. No words passed between them. They sat there together, alone on the riverbank, unnoticed by the others. For the first time, he felt a faint stirring of something he could not name—a flicker of warmth, fragile and unfamiliar, but undeniable. The silence between them was not empty; it was alive, full of unspoken understanding. The guard, for a moment, had turned away, and they were left in peace.

How it happened, Raskolnikov could never explain, even to himself. One moment, he was sitting beside her, staring at the ground, lost in a haze of thoughts and emotions. The next, something invisible, something overwhelming, seemed to take hold of him, pulling him forward as if by an unstoppable force. Before he knew it, he had flung himself at her feet, clasping her knees in an outpouring of raw, unfiltered emotion. Tears streamed down his face, unbidden and uncontrollable, and he buried his head against her as though seeking refuge from everything that had ever tormented him.

For an instant, Sonia froze in terror. She grew pale, her thin, fragile frame trembling as she looked down at him. The suddenness of his action shocked her, and she did not know what it meant. But almost as quickly as fear had seized her, understanding dawned in her eyes. She saw through the tears, through the desperate gesture, through the weight of everything unsaid—and she knew. A light of boundless joy illuminated her pale features, softening her expression into something that could only be described as radiant. She understood, without the need for words, that he loved her. It was not a fleeting affection, nor an obligation born of guilt or gratitude. It was love in its purest, most profound form—a love that had been buried under layers of torment and despair but had finally found its way to the surface. She knew, too, that the moment she had waited for, had dared to hope for, had come at last.

Both of them tried to speak, but no words came. Their voices were caught in their throats, choked by the intensity of their emotions. Tears filled their eyes, reflecting the same feelings, the same unspoken promises. They were both frail and worn, their faces marked by suffering and exhaustion, yet those pale, sickly faces seemed luminous now, transformed by the dawning of a new life. It was as though a veil had been lifted, revealing a future that, while still distant, was filled with infinite promise. They were no longer the broken, lost souls they had been mere moments before. Love had breathed new life into them, and in their hearts, they carried a wellspring of hope and strength. Each found in the other an endless reservoir of renewal, a source of vitality that would sustain them through the trials yet to come.

Together, they resolved to wait, to endure, to persevere. Seven long years lay before them, years that would bring untold hardship but also untold joy. The road ahead was arduous, but they faced it with a shared determination. He had risen again, and in the depths of his being, he felt the stirrings of a resurrection—an awakening to a life that held meaning and purpose. And Sonia—Sonia lived only in his life, her happiness intertwined with his in a bond that could not be broken.

That evening, after the barracks were locked and the prisoners lay in their assigned places, Raskolnikov lay on his plank bed, staring at the ceiling, lost in thought. His mind kept returning to her, to Sonia, to the way her face had lit up with joy when she understood his unspoken feelings. He even recalled, with a faint sense of wonder, how the convicts who had once despised him now seemed to regard him differently. There had been a subtle change in their attitudes, a softening of the hostility that had once surrounded him. Some had even exchanged a few friendly words with him, something unthinkable not long ago. He felt it was inevitable—that everything around him, everything within him, was beginning to change.

His thoughts lingered on Sonia. He remembered how often he had hurt her, how cruel and dismissive he had been, even when she had done nothing but offer him her love and support. Her pale, thin face, her quiet, unwavering patience—these images filled him with a mixture of sorrow and a newfound resolve. He would make it right. He would repay her for every moment of suffering he had caused, not out of obligation but out of the infinite love that now filled his heart. The pain of the past, even his crime and his imprisonment, seemed to fade into insignificance. It was as though those events belonged to someone else, to a life that no longer felt like his own.

Under his thin pillow lay a small, worn copy of the New Testament. He had taken it from Sonia, though she had never pressed it upon him or spoken to him of religion. She had simply handed it to him without a word when he asked for it before his illness. Now, as he held the book in his hands, he did not open it but let his fingers trace its edges. A single thought flickered through his mind: Could her faith, her convictions, become his as well? Could her aspirations, her unwavering belief in goodness and redemption, become the guiding light he so desperately needed?

Sonia, too, had been deeply moved that day. The intensity of her happiness was almost too much to bear, and by nightfall, she had fallen ill again. Yet even in her weakened state, she was filled with a quiet joy that frightened her with its unexpectedness. Seven years, she thought—only seven years. In the first flush of their shared happiness, those years felt like nothing, like days that would pass in the blink of an eye. But she did not know, could not know, how much those years would demand of them. She did not yet see the struggles he would face, the battles he would have to fight within himself, nor did he fully grasp it.

Theirs was the beginning of a new story—a story of gradual renewal, of transformation, of a man's journey from one world into another. It was the story of his slow but inevitable regeneration, of his awakening to a life he had never imagined. That story was yet to be written, but the story that had brought him to this moment had reached its end.

Notes From the Underground

(1864)

Fyodor Dostoyevsky

Part 1 - Underground

Chapter 1

I am a sick man. A spiteful man. An unattractive man. My liver, I believe, is diseased. Yet, I know nothing definitive about my condition, nor do I know precisely what ails me. I avoid consulting doctors. Not because I distrust medicine—on the contrary, I respect the field and its practitioners, though my respect is oddly intertwined with superstition. Yes, I am superstitious, despite my education, which should have eradicated such tendencies. But no, my refusal to see a doctor stems not from logic, but from sheer spite. A concept you may find difficult to grasp, yet one I understand all too well.

Who am I punishing by this stubbornness? Certainly not the doctors, for they remain unaffected by my refusal. I am perfectly aware that I injure no one but myself. And yet, in spite of knowing this, I persist. My liver is bad, you say? Let it deteriorate further, I respond. This perverse resolve has governed me for years—two decades, to be exact. Now I am forty. Once, I served in the government, but that chapter of my life has long since closed. Back then, I was a spiteful official, deriving pleasure from my rudeness. I never accepted bribes, so I compensated by indulging in malice. A poor jest, perhaps, but I'll let it stand—I am too self-aware to erase it now. I see clearly that even this attempt at humor reeks of self-importance and pettiness, and yet I let it linger, an unpolished fragment of my nature.

When petitioners approached my desk seeking assistance, I ground my teeth at them, savoring my ability to make their lives miserable. My pleasure was heightened by their timidity, though I reserved a special hatred for those who dared to challenge my authority. One officer, in particular, incensed me with his arrogant clank of a sword. Our silent battle over that infernal sword lasted eighteen months. Eventually, I triumphed—he ceased clanking it. A hollow victory, but one I savored in my youth.

And yet, at the core of my spite lay something much more contemptible: shame. For even in my most venomous moments, I was painfully aware of my own charade. I knew I was neither truly spiteful nor genuinely embittered. I was merely playing a part, frightening sparrows for my amusement. I could rage and fume, but hand me a doll to play with, or offer me a cup of tea sweetened with sugar, and my anger would dissolve. In fact, I might even find myself touched by the smallest kindness, though I would later curse my own weakness, lying awake at night consumed by shame.

I lied earlier when I called myself a spiteful official. That was another petty amusement, born of the same spite I pretend to condemn. In truth, I was incapable of genuine spitefulness. My inner life was a cacophony of contradictions—opposite impulses swarmed within me, clamoring for release. I felt their presence every moment, these forces I refused to acknowledge or unleash. They tormented me, gnawed at my conscience, until I could no longer bear them. And yet, I held them back, refusing to act, wallowing in the misery they caused. Their constant churning drove me to sickness, both of body and soul.

Do you think I am asking for your forgiveness, perhaps confessing my guilt? I can almost see the thought forming in your mind. But let me assure you: I do not care. Believe what you like—it makes no difference to me.

It is not just that I failed to become spiteful; I failed to become anything at all. Neither cruel nor kind, neither villain nor hero, neither honest man nor scoundrel—I remained suspended in a void of indecision and purposelessness. My life is a lamentable existence spent in a corner, taunting myself with the idea that an intelligent man can never truly be anything of significance. To achieve such a state, one must be simple, limited, even foolish. Yes, I firmly believe that in this modern age, a man of intellect must, by necessity, be devoid of character, while men of action—those decisive, purposeful individuals—are nothing more than narrow-minded brutes.

Forty years! It is a lifetime, a span that borders on senility. To live beyond forty is vulgar, even immoral. Who are the wretches that persist past this age? Fools and mediocrities, without exception. I tell this to the world, to every venerable elder who parades his silver hair and stoops beneath the weight of his years. I proclaim it boldly because I, too, will outlive my conviction. Yes, I will continue—past forty, past fifty, past sixty. I will persist, clinging to this miserable existence, extending my life into an unseemly longevity. Seventy, perhaps eighty—who can say? But let me catch my breath. This tirade, even against myself, is exhausting. Let me pause, just for a moment...

You might think, gentlemen, that I aim to entertain you. If so, you are mistaken. I am far from the kind of person to conjure up amusement for anyone's benefit. Perhaps you imagine me a jovial fellow, someone who thrives on wit and humor—but you would be wrong about that, too. In fact, I am neither light-hearted nor entertaining, as you seem inclined to believe. And yet, irritated by my rambling discourse, which I suspect has begun to grate on your nerves, you are tempted to ask who I am. Fine, I will answer: I am a collegiate assessor.

I entered the service not out of ambition or duty, but simply to ensure I had something to eat, and that alone. For years, I toiled with that singular goal in mind—sustenance. But fortune, or rather a distant relation, saw fit to intervene. Last year, I inherited six thousand roubles upon his death. The moment I came into this modest windfall, I abandoned my post and retreated to my corner of the world. It's not a new corner—I have lived there before—but now, I am firmly ensconced in it, for better or worse.

This corner I speak of is no sanctuary, no haven of peace or comfort. It is a grim, miserable little room, tucked away in the outskirts of the city. The very walls seem to emanate a kind of oppressive dreariness. My servant, an old and perpetually cross countrywoman, is a constant source of annoyance. Her ill nature stems from sheer stupidity, and as if that were not enough, she carries with her a foul, lingering smell that permeates the air around her. My neighbors, my so-called friends, and various advisors—all self-proclaimed sages— are fond of reminding me that Petersburg's climate is ill-suited to my constitution. They warn me that, with my meager inheritance, life here is both impractical and unnecessarily costly.

Do they think I don't know this? Do they imagine I haven't already weighed these considerations a thousand times over? Let me assure you, I understand my circumstances far better than these well-meaning busybodies ever could. Yet I remain here, stubbornly fixed in Petersburg. Why? Why do I choose to stay in this city, when all logic and advice point to the contrary? I'll tell you why: because it doesn't matter. That's all. It doesn't matter in the least whether I leave or stay. My presence or absence is utterly insignificant. I could uproot myself and disappear, or stay put for the rest of my days—it would make no difference to the world, nor, I suspect, to myself.

You may wonder what drives a man like me to speak at all, especially when I claim that so little in life truly matters. What can a decent man—if I may dare to call myself decent—discuss with genuine pleasure? Is there any topic that can animate such a man, stir him from his apathy? The answer is simple: himself. Yes, of all the subjects under the sun, a man finds the most pleasure in speaking about his own life, his own thoughts, his own peculiarities.

And so, I will oblige. I will talk about myself.

Chapter 2

I wish now to explain to you, gentlemen, whether you care to hear it or not, why I could not even degrade myself to the level of an insect. I assure you, I have made several attempts—earnest, deliberate attempts—to become an insect, but I have always fallen short. I swear to you, with all the solemnity I can muster, that being overly conscious is itself a form of illness—an all-consuming, relentless disease. For the needs of everyday life, the average human consciousness—basic, unburdened, and unexamined—would suffice. A mere fraction of the overdeveloped consciousness we, unfortunate denizens of the nineteenth century, are cursed with would be more than enough, especially for those of us unlucky enough to live in Petersburg—a city that seems to exist not by accident but by design, the most deliberate, theoretical, and artificial of places on the entire planet.

There are, after all, cities that are "intentional" and those that are "unintentional," and Petersburg falls squarely in the former category. It is no place for those burdened by excessive thought, and yet here I am, doomed to suffer under the weight of my hyper-awareness. I know what you must be thinking—that I am merely trying to be clever, mocking the so-called men of action and their simple-minded directness. Perhaps you think I am posturing, clanking my metaphorical sword like some self-important officer. But who among us, truly, would take pride in their afflictions and parade them about as a badge of honor? And yet, isn't that precisely what we all do? Do we not boast, in our own peculiar ways, about our misfortunes? Perhaps I am more guilty of this than anyone. I will not deny it. Still, I insist on my claim: too much consciousness, any kind of excess in consciousness, is a disease.

But let me set that aside for a moment. Let me pose a question instead: why is it that in the very moments when I am most attuned to all that is noble and sublime—when I am most capable of appreciating beauty, goodness, and the finer things of life—I am simultaneously compelled to engage in the ugliest, most degrading acts? Why is it that in those moments, I seem almost designed to sink into the depths of my own filth, as though it were my natural state? And what's worse, this depravity does not feel accidental or temporary; it feels intrinsic to my very being. It feels as though it belongs to me, as though it is me. Over time, I have lost even the desire to fight against it. At some point, I nearly convinced myself—perhaps I truly believed—that this state of moral and emotional degradation was my true condition.

But it wasn't always like this. In the beginning, I struggled. Oh, how I struggled! I tormented myself endlessly, convinced that no one else could possibly share in this secret shame of mine. I hid it from everyone, burying it deep within myself. I was so ashamed of the conflict, so appalled by the wretched duality of my nature. And yet, over time, I began to derive a twisted kind of pleasure from my self-loathing. I would return to my miserable corner on those wretched Petersburg nights, acutely aware of my most recent moral failure, knowing that what was done could never be undone. I would gnaw at myself internally, tearing at my soul, until the bitterness of my shame transformed into something else—something grotesque and accursed, but undeniably real: a kind of pleasure. Yes, pleasure! I swear it! There was a sick, perverse joy in that consciousness of my own degradation.

And here is the crux of it: this pleasure arose not from the degradation itself, but from the heightened awareness of it. It came from the knowledge that I had reached the limits of despair, that there was no escape, and that I had become trapped in a state of utter hopelessness. And yet, in that very hopelessness, there was a strange sweetness. There was a kind of freedom in realizing that I could never change—that even if the possibility of redemption or transformation remained, I would not seize it. And even if I wished to seize it, I would likely do nothing about it, because in the end, perhaps there was nothing to be done. Perhaps there was no better version of myself to transform into.

What is most insidious, though, is that all of this feels entirely natural, as though it conforms to some fundamental law of consciousness. And because it feels natural, it carries with it a crushing inertia—a sense that change is not only impossible but irrelevant. And yet, this understanding brings no comfort. To know that one's actions are dictated by some inexorable law of nature is no solace to the scoundrel who must live with himself. On the contrary, it makes the burden even heavier to bear.

Do I sound like I'm rambling? Perhaps I am. I have said a great deal, and yet I feel as though I've explained nothing at all. But I will get to the bottom of this, I swear. That is why I have taken up my pen today—to try to make sense of this torment, to put it into words. Let me give you an example, if I may. I have always been painfully sensitive, quick to take offense, as defensive as a dwarf or a hunchback. And yet, there have been moments when I would almost welcome a slap in the face. Yes, you heard me correctly. I would find a peculiar sort of joy in being humiliated, in being reduced to nothing. There is a strange, intoxicating pleasure in despair, especially when one is fully aware of the hopelessness of their condition.

But no matter how I look at it, I always come to the same humiliating conclusion: I am the one to blame. Always, I am to blame. And the most galling part of it is that my culpability seems to stem not from any particular fault of my own, but from the very nature of my existence. It is as though the laws of nature themselves have conspired to make me this way. I have always considered myself cleverer than those around me, and yet I have been ashamed of this cleverness, as though it were a deformity. I have turned my eyes away from people all my life, unable to meet their gaze. Even if I had been capable of acts of great magnanimity, they would have brought me no solace. For what good is magnanimity in a world governed by such cruel and indifferent laws?

And yet, even in my desire for revenge, I am powerless. I lack the resolve to act, even when I feel I must. Why? Why is it that I can never bring myself to do anything? That is the question I wish to address next.

Chapter 3

When it comes to people who know how to get back at others or stand up for themselves, how do they handle it? Imagine someone consumed by the feeling of revenge. In that moment, nothing else matters to them. They charge toward their goal like an angry bull with its horns down, stopping only if they hit a wall. (By the way: when such people face a wall, they are genuinely baffled. For direct, action-oriented people, a wall isn't something they interpret as an escape route like we overthinkers do. For us, a wall can be a handy excuse to turn away, even though deep down we know it's not a valid one. But for them, a wall is calming, even reassuring—it feels final, maybe even a little mysterious. More on the wall later.)

I see this kind of direct person as the true, normal human being, just as nature intended when she brought them into existence. Honestly, I'm jealous of such people—it makes me green with envy. Sure, they might be a little stupid, but maybe that's how the normal person is supposed to be. Who's to say that isn't beautiful in its own way? I'm even more convinced of this when I think about the opposite of the normal man: the person with extreme self-awareness. Such a person wasn't born naturally but seems more like they were created in a laboratory. (This might sound mystical, but I'm suspicious it's true.) This overly conscious person can feel so inferior compared to the straightforward type that they start thinking of themselves as a mouse rather than a person. Sure, it's a mouse with high self-awareness, but still—a mouse. Meanwhile, the straightforward person is undoubtedly human, and the difference is painfully clear. Worse yet, the self-aware person willingly accepts this label as a mouse. No one forces it on them, and that's a crucial detail.

Now let's observe this "mouse" in action. Suppose it feels insulted—it almost always does—and wants revenge. It might carry even more bitterness than the straightforward "man of nature and truth." The nasty, burning desire to get back at its attacker eats away at it. But unlike the straightforward person, who sees revenge as simple justice thanks to their natural ignorance, the mouse doesn't believe in the justice of its actions. When it comes time to actually take revenge, the mouse doesn't just act. Instead, it gets lost in endless doubts, questions, and second-guessing. These swirling thoughts create a toxic, messy storm made up of its uncertainties and emotions. To make things worse, the straightforward people—those direct, action-oriented types—watch from the sidelines and laugh at the mouse, mocking it with healthy, hearty laughter. The poor mouse has no choice but to pretend it doesn't care. It waves it off with a fake smile, though it doesn't even believe in that smile, and slinks away into its little mouse-hole.

Once there, in its dark, smelly underground lair, the mouse lets its humiliation and bitterness fester. It stews in its cold, relentless spite for decades, replaying the insult over and over in its mind, adding more humiliating details each time. The mouse knows it's tormenting itself with these thoughts, and it's even ashamed of its own imagination, but it still can't let go. It remembers every tiny detail of the insult, invents new ones to make it worse, and refuses to forgive anything. Sometimes, it might attempt revenge—but only in sneaky, petty ways, from the shadows, without any confidence in its right to act or belief that it will succeed. In fact, the mouse knows it will suffer far more from its attempts at revenge than the person it targets, who likely won't even notice or care.

Even on its deathbed, the mouse will relive the insult, remembering every petty detail and nursing its bitterness one last time, adding up all the years of resentment like interest on a debt. And that's how it ends for the mouse.

But it is precisely in that cold and dreadful state—a mix of despair and faint belief—that the peculiar essence of this strange enjoyment lies. It is the conscious act of burying oneself alive in grief, retreating into an internal underworld for decades, knowingly stepping into a state of hopelessness that feels both undeniable and yet oddly uncertain. It is a hell filled with unfulfilled desires, turned inward to fester, with feverish swings between bold resolutions that feel final and immediate regret the very next moment. This is the essence of that strange and bitter pleasure I speak of. The flavor of it is so subtle, so intricately woven, that it defies easy analysis. Those with a simpler outlook on life—or even those with merely strong nerves—cannot comprehend even the smallest fragment of it.

You might grin and think to yourself, "Well, perhaps people who've never experienced a slap in the face would struggle to understand this." You'd likely be insinuating, in your own polite way, that I must have been on the receiving end of such a slap and speak from personal experience. I can see you thinking it! But let me assure you, gentlemen, that no such indignity has been inflicted upon me. Frankly, it doesn't matter to me in the slightest what you believe about that. If anything, I sometimes regret that I haven't dealt out more slaps myself during my life. But let's move on from that topic, which I'm sure is of great fascination to you.

Let's return to the subject of those sturdy, practical types who cannot grasp the subtler nuances of this enjoyment. While these men, in certain circumstances, may roar with indignation and strength like raging bulls—let's agree this is to their credit—they quickly retreat when faced with something impossible. For them, the impossible means the stone wall. What stone wall, you ask? The stone wall of reality itself: the immutable laws of nature, the deductions of science, the logic of mathematics. If someone proves to them, for example, that humanity evolved from monkeys, they won't argue; they'll just accept it as fact. If they're told that one drop of their own fat matters more to them than the well-being of a hundred thousand others—and that this truth underpins all so-called virtues and moral duties—they bow to the logic. After all, they reason, twice two equals four. Try as they might, they cannot refute it.

These types will shout at you with certainty, "It's pointless to argue! This is twice two equals four—it's a law of mathematics!" Nature, they'll insist, doesn't care about your opinions or desires. It doesn't ask for your permission or concern itself with your preferences. You are compelled to accept its unyielding rules, like it or not. "A wall is a wall," they'll say, smugly. "You can't change that."

But, merciful heavens! What do I care for the laws of nature or arithmetic when, for some reason, I detest them? Why should I be forced to love the fact that twice two equals four just because it is undeniably true? Certainly, I can't break through the stone wall by bashing my head against it if I lack the strength, but I refuse to simply accept it as a comfort because it stands there immovably. Why should its existence, its impenetrability, provide me with solace?

As though this stone wall could ever offer real comfort or consolation! As though it contains some hidden message of peace, simply because it embodies an unshakable truth like twice two equals four. What nonsense! How much better it is to understand it all fully, to recognize the wall's permanence, its impossibility, and still refuse to reconcile with it if it disgusts you. How much better to follow the inevitable logic to its most revolting conclusions—acknowledging that even in the face of the stone wall, you somehow feel responsible for its existence, though it is entirely clear you are not to blame. And yet, with this awareness comes the grinding of teeth in silent frustration, sinking into a kind of luxurious inertia. You sit there, stewing in the knowledge that there is no one to blame, no target for your spite, and perhaps there never will be.

It's maddening! You realize it's all a sleight of hand, a cruel trick, a game rigged by some card-sharp who remains invisible. It's all a meaningless jumble—no one to blame, no one to hold accountable— and yet the ache persists. And the less you understand about its origins or resolution, the sharper the ache becomes. It grows in proportion to the very confusion and uncertainty you feel, feeding on your inability to resolve it, consuming you in its merciless grip.

Chapter 4

"Ha, ha, ha! Next, you'll be saying people enjoy toothache," you exclaim with a laugh.

"Well, even in toothache there is a certain enjoyment," I reply. I say this because I've had toothache for an entire month, so I know it's true. In such cases, people don't merely suffer in silence—they moan. But those moans aren't innocent or straightforward; they're filled with spite, and that's precisely the point. The enjoyment of the sufferer reveals itself through those very moans. If there were no twisted pleasure in them, people wouldn't moan at all. This is a useful example, gentlemen, so let me elaborate.

Those moans, in their own way, express the sheer absurdity of your pain—its cruel aimlessness. They capture how humiliating it feels to your consciousness to endure such suffering. You despise the rigid laws of nature that govern this misery. You may scoff at nature, spitting on its so-called justice, but even as you rebel, you're still at its mercy. Nature, indifferent to your plight, carries on without any suffering of her own. The moans also express the bitter knowledge that you have no enemy to strike back at, no one to blame for your pain—only the unyielding reality of the ache itself.

In that moment, you're acutely aware of your helplessness, knowing you are utterly enslaved to your own teeth. You realize that if some invisible force decides to relieve the pain, it will end, and if not, it will torment you for months on end. What's left for you then?

If you refuse to resign yourself to this fate and insist on rebelling, all you can do is thrash about, perhaps hitting a wall with your fist in frustration. And yet, even in this hopeless scenario—this mocking, invisible assault—there emerges a peculiar kind of enjoyment, one that sometimes crescendos into an almost intoxicating pleasure.

Think about it: listen closely to the moans of an educated man of the modern age who is suffering from toothache. By the second or third day of his agony, his moaning changes. It is no longer the primal, honest moaning of the first day, when the pain was new and unfiltered. No, by the second or third day, he moans differently, not like a simple, uneducated peasant might, but like a man shaped by progress, by European civilization, by all the supposed sophistication of modernity.

His moans become vile and deliberate—almost artistic in their nastiness. They drag on for hours, for entire nights, and they take on a malicious quality, as though he is savoring his suffering and weaponizing it against anyone unfortunate enough to hear. Of course, he knows perfectly well that his moaning does him no good. He understands better than anyone that he is only making himself, and everyone around him, miserable for no reason. He knows that his family, his captive audience, listens to his dramatic wailing with disgust and pity. They can see through his theatrical flourishes, recognizing that he could moan more simply, more honestly, without all the exaggerated trills and embellishments.

And yet, this awareness doesn't stop him. In fact, it fuels his enjoyment. He seems to say through his moans: "Look at me! I am torturing you all! I am disturbing your peace, tearing at your hearts, keeping you awake with my relentless cries. Feel my pain as I feel it! I no longer pretend to be a hero in your eyes. I don't care if you see me as weak, irritating, even despicable. Yes, I'm an impostor—so be it! If my suffering makes you uncomfortable, good! I'll add another flourish to these moans, just for you, just to make it worse."

Do you still not understand, gentlemen? No? It seems that our development and understanding must advance even further to truly grasp all the complexities of this bizarre pleasure. You laugh?

Excellent! Laughter is welcome here. But yes, I must admit that my humor is crude, awkward, and full of insecurity. It lacks grace because, frankly, I don't respect myself. And why should I? Can a man who sees the world as it truly is ever really respect himself?

Chapter 5

Can a man who actively seeks enjoyment in his own degradation truly possess even a shred of self-respect? I doubt it. And I don't say this out of some pathetic sense of regret or guilt. No, that isn't it. In fact, I've always found it unbearable to grovel or say things like, "Forgive me, I won't do it again, I promise." It's not because I'm incapable of saying such words; it's quite the opposite. I've been entirely too capable of saying them—and in the most despicable ways imaginable. Time and again, I'd find myself in situations where I wasn't even at fault, and yet I would still end up apologizing profusely, as though on purpose. That, right there, was the most detestable part of it.

What made it worse was how genuine I felt in those moments. I wasn't pretending. I was truly overcome by emotion and remorse, sometimes even to the point of tears. And yet, all the while, I was lying to myself without even realizing it. It wasn't a calculated performance, and yet it was false, entirely false. Deep down, I knew it, and the knowledge left a sick feeling in my chest. But what could I do? It wasn't nature's laws at fault here—no, this one was all on me. And nature, as much as it has offended me throughout my life, was innocent in this case. Still, it's nauseating to remember these episodes. It was just as nauseating when they were happening, too.

Moments later, of course, I would come to my senses and feel a wave of anger at myself. I'd recognize how revolting, how utterly fake all that penitence had been. My tears, my emotions, my promises to do better—it was all an elaborate lie. And yet, even knowing that, I couldn't stop. Why did I put myself through such humiliating antics? Simply because I was bored. That's the answer. Sitting idly with my hands folded was unbearable to me, so I would manufacture drama, invent scenarios, just to give myself something to do.

Think about it. How often have I deliberately taken offense at nothing, just to stir up trouble? I would know, even as I was doing it, that there was no real insult, nothing to be offended by. But I would force myself to feel offended anyway, and eventually, I would convince myself it was real. It became a habit, a compulsion, one I couldn't control. More than once, I even tried to fall in love—not because I truly felt anything, but because I wanted to feel something. I suffered through the whole ordeal, too, with all the passion and jealousy of a man deeply in love. But in the back of my mind, there was always a faint trace of mockery, as though some part of me was laughing at the absurdity of it all.

Why did I do this? Because of boredom, gentlemen. Pure, unrelenting ennui. Inertia consumed me. You know as well as I do that the natural outcome of heightened consciousness is inertia. The more you reflect, the less you act. I've mentioned this before, and I'll repeat it here: all direct, action-oriented people are active because they are, frankly, stupid and narrow-minded. Their limited understanding allows them to take superficial causes for ultimate truths. They find comfort in this, persuading themselves that they've discovered an unshakable foundation for their actions.

And that, gentlemen, is the key. To act, one must first be at peace with one's mind, free of doubt. But how can I ever be at peace? Where are these so-called ultimate causes on which I'm supposed to build my life? The more I reflect, the more I question, and every cause I identify leads to another deeper, more fundamental one. It's an endless chain. That is the curse of consciousness. Reflection only multiplies the causes until you're left with infinity.

Take vengeance, for instance. When a man seeks revenge, he believes in the justice of it. That belief becomes his foundation, his ultimate cause, and he acts decisively. He finds peace in his certainty, which allows him to carry out his revenge with confidence. But I find no such certainty. I see no justice in revenge, no virtue, no inherent value. So if I were to seek revenge, it would be out of pure spite.

Spite, I suppose, could suffice as a driving force, replacing the need for a cause. But what happens when even spite dissolves under the weight of reflection? In my case, anger disintegrates. It evaporates like mist under the scrutiny of thought. The target of my anger fades, the reasons vanish, and the so-called crime becomes a phantom. It's like toothache—a source of pain for which no one is to blame. And once again, I'm left with the same impotent response: to pound my fist against the wall in frustration.

But let's say I try to silence my consciousness for a moment and let myself be carried away by blind emotions—love or hate, anything to escape the paralysis of thought. It might work briefly. But by the next day, I'll despise myself for it. I'll see through my own self-deception, and what will I be left with? A soap bubble and inertia.

Ah, gentlemen, do you know what I suspect? Perhaps I consider myself intelligent only because I have never been able to truly begin or finish anything in my life. Yes, I am a babbler, a harmless, vexing babbler—just like the rest of us. But what else can I do? Babbling, after all, is the sole vocation of the intelligent man. It is the deliberate act of pouring water through a sieve, knowing full well it will never be filled.

Chapter 6

Oh, if only I had done nothing in life purely out of laziness! What a remarkable thing that would have been! Heavens, I would have respected myself so deeply for it. Imagine it—a life of deliberate laziness! I would have respected myself because I would have shown that I was at least capable of being truly, magnificently lazy. That would have been a quality in me, a defining characteristic, something tangible, even positive, to which I could cling. People could ask, "What is he?" And the answer would come: "A sluggard." How delightful it would have been to hear that said about me!

To be defined so simply, so clearly—what a relief that would be. It would have meant there was something solid and real to say about me, something that gave me a purpose. "Sluggard"—a title, a calling, even a career! Don't laugh; I'm quite serious. There would have been no shame in it. I would have belonged, by right, to a prestigious club of the truly idle, and my occupation would have been nothing less than the relentless and satisfying act of respecting myself. I once knew a man who spent his entire life taking pride in being a connoisseur of fine wine, particularly Lafitte. He considered this his one true virtue, his defining quality, and he never doubted himself for a moment. When he died, it was not merely with a peaceful conscience, but with a triumphant one. And he was absolutely correct to do so.

If I had chosen my own career path, it would have been something similar. I would have been a sluggard, yes, but not an ordinary one. I would have added to my laziness a cultivated appreciation for all things sublime and beautiful. Imagine it! A life spent lounging in the pursuit of everything lofty and magnificent, my days filled with admiring art, literature, and the grandeur of existence, all while doing nothing of substance. What could have been more satisfying?

I have dreamed of such a life many times. At forty, the weight of that ideal—of the sublime and the beautiful—still presses heavily on me. But back then, oh, back then, it would have been glorious! I would have found a way to make this aesthetic idleness my sole occupation, a purpose unto itself. I would have spent my days drinking to the health of all that is sublime and beautiful. Every glass raised would have been accompanied by a heartfelt tear shed for the majesty of it all.

I would have turned even the most mundane, even the most dreadful, into something sublime and beautiful. In the ugliest, most meaningless things, I would have sought out some kernel of grandeur, some fleeting spark of beauty. And oh, how I would have wept! I would have shed tears as readily as a soaked sponge squeezes out water. If an artist painted a dreadful, kitschy picture, I would raise my glass to him without hesitation. "To the artist!" I'd say, "For even this kitsch contains something sublime and beautiful!" If an author wrote a play titled As You Will, I'd toast the health of "whoever you will," for I would find beauty even in that.

I would demand respect for this noble pursuit, and I would hound anyone who failed to give it to me. My life would be one of ease and comfort, and when the time came, I would die with great dignity, full of purpose. What could be more charming? Perfectly charming!

And think of what I would have become! I would have grown a good, round belly, the kind of belly that speaks of indulgence and satisfaction. My chin would have multiplied—one, two, perhaps even three chins—each more dignified than the last. My nose would have taken on the rich, ruby hue of a man who truly appreciates life's pleasures. People would look at me and say, "Now there's a man of substance! Here is someone solid and real!"

And isn't that what we all crave, in this age of emptiness and negation? To be seen as something real, something that undeniably exists? Say what you like, but there is something deeply satisfying about hearing such things said about oneself. It's a rare gift, a kind of immortality in the eyes of others. Yes, a life of laziness, of deliberate idleness and cultivated appreciation, would have been nothing short of magnificent.

Chapter 7

But these are nothing more than golden dreams, fanciful illusions of an ideal that could never exist. Tell me, who was it that first proclaimed—who was it that boldly declared—that man behaves badly only because he does not know his true interests? And further, that if man were enlightened, if his eyes were opened to his real, normal interests, he would immediately stop doing nasty things? That he would suddenly transform into a noble, good, virtuous being, acting always in accordance with his best advantage, simply because he would see that his own benefit lies in doing good and nothing else? After all, we are told that no man, when truly conscious of his own interests, could ever act against them. It is said that this awareness would compel him, almost by necessity, to pursue goodness.

Oh, what a sweet, innocent belief! What a naïve, childlike assumption! But let us look back—when in all the thousands of years of human history has there ever been a time when man acted solely from his own interest? What about the countless examples that prove the opposite? What about the millions of cases where men, fully aware of their true interests, deliberately ignored them? How often have they knowingly set aside their advantage to rush headlong down a perilous path? Compelled by no external force, guided by no necessity, they have rejected the safer, easier road simply because they disliked its predictability. Instead, they stubbornly and willfully chose the harder, more absurd way, seeking it almost blindly, as though it held some inexplicable appeal.

And what does this tell us? That perhaps the sheer perversity of such a choice—the obstinate rejection of one's own advantage—was more pleasurable to them than the advantage itself. But what, then, is this "advantage"? Can we even define it? And who among us can claim to know, with perfect certainty, what truly constitutes the advantage of man? What if, in some cases, a person's advantage lies not in what benefits him but in what harms him? What if there are situations where a man's desire compels him toward what is harmful, even destructive? And if such cases exist, then doesn't the entire principle of enlightened self-interest crumble into dust?

You laugh, of course. Go ahead and laugh. But I ask you: can we really claim to have identified and cataloged all of man's advantages? Are there not some that elude classification entirely—some that defy inclusion in any neat list or register? Your modern thinkers, with their statistical averages and economic formulas, would have us believe that human advantages consist solely of prosperity, wealth, freedom, and peace. These, they say, are the primary markers of human progress. But what of the man who knowingly and openly rejects all of these? What of the one who, with full awareness, chooses a path in direct opposition to wealth, freedom, or peace? By your logic—and, admittedly, by mine as well—such a man must be either an obscurantist or a madman.

And yet, isn't it remarkable how your statisticians, philosophers, and humanitarians always seem to overlook one critical advantage?

They fail even to consider it in the proper form, though everything depends upon it. It would be so simple to include it, to acknowledge this strange and elusive advantage—but they cannot. For this peculiar advantage defies all systems, all logic, all attempts at classification. It doesn't fit into their lists, and that is precisely the problem.

Let me give you an example. I have a friend—a friend of yours as well, I'm sure, for he seems to be a friend to everyone. This man, whenever he embarks on any endeavor, begins by eloquently and passionately explaining how he must act in accordance with reason and truth. He'll lay out, with perfect clarity, the true and normal interests of man. He'll ridicule the short-sighted fools who fail to understand their own interests or the deeper significance of virtue. And yet, within minutes, without any external provocation, he'll abandon his carefully reasoned principles entirely. He'll act in direct opposition to everything he just claimed to believe—against reason, against his own advantage, against every law of logic and decency.

What drives him to do this? It isn't external pressure or necessity; it's something internal, something stronger than all his rational interests. This is why I say my friend is a compound personality, a microcosm of humanity itself, and thus difficult to blame as an individual. For what this reveals is that there is something within us, something deeper and more fundamental than any rational calculation of advantage. There exists an "advantage" that is so profound, so intrinsic, that it overrides all others.

You might argue that this mysterious advantage is still an advantage, in its own way. But I disagree. This advantage is unique precisely because it destroys all classifications, shatters every system constructed by philosophers and humanitarians. It undermines the entire framework of enlightened self-interest, rendering it obsolete.

Before I reveal what this advantage is, let me first admit something openly: I find all these grand theories about human regeneration through rational self-interest to be nothing more than intellectual exercises. Yes, mere logical gymnastics. To claim that mankind can be reformed simply by understanding and pursuing his own advantage is, in my opinion, as naïve as believing that civilization makes us gentler and less bloodthirsty.

Consider this: we are told that as civilization advances, humanity becomes less inclined toward violence. But look around you. Blood flows more freely than ever, and it flows not out of necessity but as if for sport. Take the 19th century as an example—Buckle's own era. Look at Napoleon, both the Great and the lesser one. Look at the wars in America, the eternal conflict of Schleswig-Holstein. Has civilization softened us?

On the contrary, it seems to have made us more vile in our bloodshed. In the past, men justified violence as a form of justice. They killed with a clear conscience, believing their actions to be righteous. But now, we condemn violence even as we commit it with greater fervor than ever before. Civilization has given us a greater capacity for experiencing complex sensations, but this has only made us more adept at finding pleasure in cruelty. The most civilized men are often the most skilled and subtle murderers, far surpassing the likes of Attila or Stenka Razin in their ingenuity.

Civilization has not made us less bloodthirsty; it has made us more insidious in our thirst for blood. And so, the dream of a rational, enlightened humanity remains just that—a dream.

Which is worse? I leave that for you to decide. Take, for example, Cleopatra (excuse a reference to Roman history), who was reportedly fond of piercing her slave-girls' breasts with gold pins, delighting in their screams and writhing. You might dismiss this as a relic of comparatively barbarous times, but are these times truly so different? Even now, metaphorical pins are still being driven into people, though perhaps in subtler, more refined ways. Man may have learned to see more clearly than in the days of Cleopatra, but has he truly learned to act in accordance with reason or the dictates of science?

You believe, of course, that he will learn. Once man sheds his old bad habits and is fully re-educated by common sense and scientific principles, you are convinced that human nature will turn in a new, rational direction. You are confident that, when this enlightenment comes, man will cease to err intentionally. He will no longer rebel against his own best interests and will be, so to speak, compelled to align his will with reason and logic.

But that is not all. You claim that science itself will one day prove to man—though I personally find this notion superfluous—that he has never really had free will at all. According to this theory, man is nothing more than a mechanism, like the key of a piano or the stop of an organ, responding only to the immutable laws of nature. Everything he does, then, is not truly his doing but rather the inevitable result of these natural laws. Once these laws are fully discovered and understood, man will no longer bear responsibility for his actions. Life will become blissfully simple.

Human behavior will be cataloged, you imagine, with mathematical precision, like logarithmic tables extending to 108,000, and recorded in vast indices. Or perhaps encyclopedic lexicons will be published, with every possible human action and reaction explained, calculated, and categorized. In such a world, there will be no more surprises, no more unexpected adventures. Every question will have a ready-made answer, every decision an optimal solution.

Then, you say, new economic systems will emerge—pre-designed, mathematically exact, and universally beneficial. In this utopia, all social and moral dilemmas will vanish like smoke, for every answer will be predetermined and irrefutable. Humanity will build its so-called "Palace of Crystal," a shimmering monument to reason and logic. Those will be halcyon days, you assure us, a time of unparalleled harmony and order.

And yet, I cannot help but ask: what guarantee is there that such a world will not be insufferably dull? What will man do in a world where everything is calculated, tabulated, and resolved? Boredom, after all, is a dangerous thing. It is boredom, I dare say, that drove Cleopatra to stick golden pins into her slaves. But even if boredom doesn't lead to such cruelty, what's truly alarming is that, in this hypothetical future, people might actually come to thank others for their metaphorical golden pins.

Why? Because man is phenomenally stupid—or, rather, he is not stupid at all but so ungrateful that his behavior defies comprehension. Imagine this: in the midst of this rational paradise, where every need is met and every question answered, a man with a cynical expression and a mocking smile might suddenly rise and declare, "Gentlemen, why don't we just tear this whole thing down? Scatter all this rationalism to the winds! Send these logarithms straight to hell and live once again as we please, with all the sweet foolishness of free will!"

This alone would be shocking enough, but what's worse is that he would almost certainly find followers. People would join him, driven not by necessity but by the sheer perversity of human nature. And what would be their reason? A reason so foolish, so absurd, that it hardly seems worth mentioning: simply that man, throughout history, has preferred to act as he chooses rather than as reason or logic dictate.

Man will even choose what is contrary to his own interests. Sometimes, he must choose against his advantage, precisely because it is his choice. This is what I believe. Independent choice, no matter how irrational, how costly, or how destructive it may be, is what man truly desires. His own free will, his caprice, his fanciful whims—even when they border on madness—are the ultimate advantage. This is the "most advantageous advantage" that has been overlooked, the one that defies all systems and classifications, shattering every theory designed to contain it.

How do these so-called sages and philosophers know that man desires a virtuous, rational choice? What evidence is there to suggest that man wants a life defined by reason and utility? What man truly craves is freedom—the freedom to choose, no matter the cost, no matter the consequences. He wants independence, even if that independence leads him to ruin.

And what choice will he make? Who can say? The devil himself wouldn't dare predict it. Man's choice is his alone, as wild, irrational, and unpredictable as the very nature of his soul.

Chapter 8

"Ha! ha! ha! But you know, there is no such thing as choice in reality, say what you like," you will interrupt, chuckling to yourself. "Science has already peeled back the layers of human behavior so thoroughly that we now know choice and what we call free will are nothing more than—"

Wait a moment, gentlemen, let me stop you there. I had intended to begin with that very point myself. I admit, I was hesitant at first, even afraid. I was about to say that only the devil knows what choice truly depends on, and that maybe it's better that way, but then I remembered the lessons of science and quickly held my tongue. And now here you are, taking up the topic on your own.

Indeed, if someday science discovers a formula for all our desires and whims—a precise, mathematical explanation for why we feel what we feel, how these emotions develop, what goals they aim for in one case or another—if such a formula were ever devised, then most likely man would lose the ability to desire entirely. For who would want to desire according to a predetermined rule? The moment desire becomes an equation, man will cease to be man; he will transform into something else entirely—a mechanical instrument, an organ stop, a lifeless cog in the machinery of nature. And what is a man without desire, without the freedom to choose, if not precisely that—a soulless organ stop?

But let us consider: could such a thing ever come to pass? Let us weigh the possibilities.

"Hmm," you might muse. "Our choices are usually mistaken because we misunderstand our true advantage. Often, we choose nonsense because we foolishly see in that nonsense an easier path to some imagined benefit. But once these tendencies are fully understood, written down, and worked out on paper—once the laws of human behavior are deciphered—then, certainly, desires as we know them will vanish. After all, if a desire contradicts reason, we will choose reason, won't we? It would be impossible for a rational person to knowingly choose something harmful over something beneficial, wouldn't it?"

And thus, you suggest, with the help of these formulas, all human choices will one day be calculable. There might even be a table of rules—something akin to logarithmic charts—that outlines every possible human action, including why and how it will occur. Perhaps I'll wake up one day, look at such a table, and discover that every decision I've ever made was inevitable, that every gesture, every impulse was predetermined by the laws of nature. If, for instance, I learn that I once stuck out my tongue at someone not because I chose to, but because some law dictated it, then what freedom remains for me?

You imagine that if these laws are uncovered, people could calculate their entire lives in advance, decades at a time. Perhaps they'd even predict precisely how they'll act in any given moment thirty years from now. In such a world, life would lose its unpredictability, its spontaneity. All events would unfold according to natural laws, and man would be forced to accept this truth. We would have no choice but to resign ourselves to nature's terms and abandon our fantasies of bending her to our will.

Some of you might see this as progress, the inevitable result of reason's triumph over chaos. You might even believe that this rationalization of life is something to aspire to, something that will elevate humanity to new heights of enlightenment. But here, I hesitate. Gentlemen, you must forgive me if I seem overly philosophical; these are the musings of a man who has spent forty years in solitude, turning over such ideas in the dark. Permit me this indulgence.

Reason, as I see it, is indeed a marvelous thing. No one disputes that. But reason is only reason. It serves the rational side of man, yes, but man is not just a creature of reason. Man's will is something greater; it is a manifestation of his entire being—reason included, but also every irrational impulse, every instinct, every inexplicable yearning.

Even when man's life is messy, flawed, or downright destructive, it is still life, and that is what matters. Life, in all its chaotic entirety, is more than just the extraction of square roots or the solution of equations. Take me, for instance. I don't want to live merely to satisfy my rational capacities. I want to live fully, to experience everything life has to offer, not just one narrow slice of it.

And yet, you look at me with pity, as though I were some relic of a less enlightened time. You tell me that in the future, man will no longer desire anything irrational or harmful. You insist that this can be mathematically proven, and I don't argue with you. I agree—it can be. But even so, I tell you this: there is one scenario, one exception, where man will deliberately, consciously choose something stupid, something harmful, something downright self-destructive.

Why? Simply to assert his right to choose. Simply to prove, if only to himself, that he is not bound by reason alone. This irrational, capricious desire—this need to act against one's own interests—is, paradoxically, one of the most advantageous things man can experience. It is his way of rejecting the tyranny of reason, of asserting his independence in a world that seeks to confine him to predictable patterns.

You see, gentlemen, it is not about logic. It is not about advantage in the conventional sense. Man desires freedom, even if that freedom leads him to ruin. And sometimes, that ruin is the only true advantage he can claim.

And indeed, this so-called advantage, this freedom of choice, may be more valuable than any other advantage, even when it causes obvious harm or contradicts the clearest conclusions of reason. Why? Because it preserves something that is most precious to us—our individuality, our personality. Some argue that this individuality is, in fact, the highest good for mankind. Choice, they say, can align with reason when it chooses to do so, and in such cases, it can be beneficial and even admirable, provided it is exercised within certain bounds.

But here's the strange thing: more often than not, choice defies reason entirely. It stands stubbornly opposed to logic, and yet—believe it or not—even that can be beneficial, sometimes even praiseworthy. Gentlemen, let us suppose for a moment that man is not stupid. Surely, we must assume that, if for no other reason than this: if man is stupid, then who or what is wise? But if we grant that man is not stupid, we must also acknowledge that he is monstrously ungrateful—phenomenally so. In fact, I would argue that the best definition of man is this: the ungrateful biped.

But ingratitude is not even his worst trait. No, his greatest flaw is his perpetual moral perversity, a defect that has plagued him from the earliest days of history, from the time of the Flood right through to the Schleswig-Holstein question. This moral perversity breeds a persistent lack of good sense, for it has long been established that poor judgment stems from moral corruption. Consider the history of mankind—cast your eyes upon it and tell me, what do you see? Is it a grand spectacle? Yes, perhaps it is. Take the Colossus of Rhodes, for instance—a wonder of the ancient world. As Mr. Anaevsky remarked, some claim it was crafted by human hands, while others insist it was shaped by nature itself.

Is history colorful? Perhaps it is. Look at the uniforms of all the armies and officials throughout the ages, their bright colors and elaborate designs. That alone is enough to fill volumes. And yet, if you consider the "undress uniforms"—the less glamorous, everyday lives of people—you will find so much monotony that no historian could ever hope to catalog it all. Is history monotonous? Certainly. It's nothing but endless fighting, war after war. From the beginning to the end, mankind has fought.

In short, you can say anything about human history—anything your imagination can conceive, no matter how wild or disordered—but the one thing you cannot say is that it is rational. The very word seems to choke in your throat when applied to the actions of humanity. And here is the paradox: in every age, moral and rational men—sages, lovers of humanity—have dedicated their lives to demonstrating that it is possible to live both rationally and morally. They strive to be shining examples for their fellow men, showing them how life should be lived. And yet, inevitably, these same paragons of virtue end up betraying their ideals, committing strange and often disgraceful acts.

Now, tell me, what can we expect of mankind, given that he is such a peculiar creature? Shower him with every earthly blessing, drown him in a sea of happiness, so that nothing but bubbles of bliss rise to the surface. Give him economic prosperity so complete that he has nothing to do but sleep, eat cakes, and procreate. And what will he do? Out of sheer ingratitude—out of sheer spite—he will deliberately disrupt this paradise. He will risk losing his cakes and deliberately choose chaos, absurdity, and suffering, just to inject some madness into the monotony of reason.

Why? Simply to prove to himself that he is still a man, not a piano key. He will crave his foolish dreams, his vulgar follies, for no other reason than to assert his humanity. He will desire freedom—the kind of freedom that allows him to choose the irrational, the destructive, and the nonsensical. Even if science were to prove, beyond a shadow of a doubt, that man is nothing more than a piano key or an organ stop, functioning entirely according to natural laws, man would still rebel. He would intentionally act against reason, simply to assert his independence.

And if he cannot find a means to rebel, he will invent one. He will conjure chaos, suffering, and destruction out of thin air, simply to prove his point. He will curse the universe—not just out of anger, but as an act of defiance. For only man can curse; it is his unique privilege, his distinction from all other animals. And through his curse, he will achieve his goal: he will convince himself that he is a man, not a mechanism.

If you argue that even this rebellion, this chaos, could eventually be calculated, that reason and science could reduce even madness to a formula, man would go one step further. He would deliberately descend into madness itself, rejecting reason entirely, just to escape the straitjacket of logic. I believe this wholeheartedly. The entire history of humanity seems to be nothing more than an ongoing effort to prove, again and again, that man is not merely a machine, not merely a creature of reason.

He will go to any lengths to assert this truth—even if it costs him his comfort, his happiness, or his very life. He will tear himself apart, engage in the most barbaric acts—even cannibalism—if that is what it takes to reaffirm his humanity. And so, I find myself strangely comforted by the fact that this grand rational utopia has not yet come to pass, that human desires remain mysterious and untamed.

You might argue, of course, that no one is truly trying to take away my free will. You might insist that the goal is simply for my will to align naturally with my best interests, with reason, with the laws of nature and arithmetic. But I ask you, what kind of free will is left when everything is reduced to a formula? When life becomes nothing more than a calculation, when twice two makes four is the ultimate truth, where is freedom in that? Twice two makes four, no matter what I will. As if free will could ever mean that.

Chapter 9

Gentlemen, let me begin by saying that I am jesting, and I know my jokes lack brilliance. Still, one can view everything as a joke, can't one? Perhaps my humor is awkward and forced, but isn't it often the case that the deepest questions are posed under the guise of jesting? I, too, am tormented by questions—questions I ask of you, though I doubt you have any satisfying answers for me. For instance, you wish to reform man, to cure him of his old habits and reshape his will according to the dictates of science and reason. But tell me, how do you know that it is even possible to reform man in this way, let alone that it is desirable? What makes you so certain that man's inclinations are in need of reform?

Let us get to the heart of the matter: why are you so utterly convinced that acting in accordance with what reason and arithmetic define as man's "real" and "normal" interests is always beneficial? How do you know that this must always be a law for mankind? So far, this is merely your supposition—a theory dressed up as inevitability. It may be the law of logic, but it is not necessarily the law of humanity. Perhaps you think me mad for questioning these things, but allow me to defend myself.

I agree with you on one point: man is a creative creature by nature. He is designed, it seems, to strive consciously toward a goal, to engage in what you might call "engineering"—constantly building, constantly forging new paths. But have you ever considered that the very reason man sometimes veers off course, seemingly without purpose, is because he is destined to make the road itself? Perhaps the road, not the destination, is what matters most to him. Even the most practical man, no matter how straightforward or narrow his thinking, must occasionally wonder whether the process of creating the road is far more meaningful than reaching wherever it may lead. After all, if we begin to despise the act of engineering itself, we might succumb to idleness—and, as we all know, idleness is the mother of every vice.

Yes, man loves to create, to build; this is indisputable. But why, then, does he also seem to love destruction and chaos with equal passion? How do you explain this paradox? I would venture to say that it's because man fears the finality of achieving his goals. He dreads completing the structures he builds, instinctively aware that the moment an edifice is finished, the act of creation ends. Perhaps he only loves his work from a distance, loving the act of building but not the completed structure itself.

Once the edifice is complete, he might leave it to the ants or other "respectable" creatures who appreciate order and permanence. Ants, for example, have their perfect ant-heaps—marvels of engineering that endure unchanged for generations. The ants began with the ant-heap, and they will end with it, a testament to their perseverance and practical good sense. But man is not an ant. Man is a frivolous, contradictory creature. Like a chess player, he may love the intricacies of the game, the strategies and movements, more than the final checkmate.

Who can say, with absolute certainty, what humanity's ultimate goal might be? Perhaps the goal is not an endpoint at all but the process itself—the striving, the endless act of reaching. Life, in other words, not the final destination. And what is the final destination, anyway? It must always be expressed as a formula, as something as clear and undeniable as twice two makes four. But twice two makes four is not life. It is the beginning of death.

Man has always been afraid of mathematical certainty, and I am afraid of it too. Yes, we strive for it; we cross oceans, scale mountains, and even risk our lives in pursuit of it. But when we finally approach it, we recoil. We sense that with such certainty comes the end of striving, and without striving, what remains? When the work is finished, when the task is complete, what does man do? A workman, at least, receives his pay, visits the tavern, perhaps spends a week in the police station—these are occupations of a sort. But where can man go when all striving has ceased?

Observe him closely when he reaches his goal. There is an awkwardness about him, a restlessness. He loves the process of attaining, but he is uneasy with attainment itself. This is absurd, of course. Man is a comical creature, a jest of nature, and yet it is a jest that should not be dismissed lightly. For mathematical certainty, despite its brilliance, is ultimately insufferable. Twice two makes four may be a truth, but it is an insolent one. It stands there like a smug bureaucrat, arms akimbo, barring your path and spitting in your face. I admit, twice two makes four is an excellent thing. But I also say this: sometimes, twice two makes five is a far more delightful possibility.

And why are you so convinced that only the rational, the normal, the positive—what we commonly think of as well-being—is truly advantageous for man? What if reason itself is mistaken about what constitutes "advantage"? Does man not, perhaps, crave something beyond well-being? Might he love suffering just as passionately as he loves comfort? It is a fact that man sometimes seeks out suffering, embraces it with extraordinary fervor. You need only look within yourself to see it; there is no need to consult history.

To care solely for well-being strikes me as vulgar, almost uncivilized. There is a certain pleasure in smashing things, in embracing destruction, for no other reason than that it asserts one's freedom to act. I do not advocate suffering, nor do I advocate well-being. What I stand for is caprice—the right to choose, even if that choice is absurd or harmful.

Suffering, after all, has no place in your "Palace of Crystal," that utopia of reason and order. Suffering introduces doubt and negation, and doubt has no role in a world built on perfect certainty. But I believe that man will never willingly renounce suffering, for destruction and chaos are integral to his nature. Suffering is the sole origin of consciousness. Though I have said before that consciousness is mankind's greatest misfortune, I also know that man values it above all else. He treasures consciousness, even when it brings pain, because it reminds him that he is alive.

Mathematical certainty offers no such reminder. Once you have twice two makes four, there is nothing left to do, nothing left to question or understand. Consciousness, on the other hand, allows man to rebel, to doubt, to flog himself if necessary—anything to break the monotony of certainty. Reactionary as it may seem, even self-inflicted suffering is better than the lifeless contemplation that mathematical certainty demands. For in suffering, in chaos, in the freedom to destroy, man finds proof that he is not merely a machine, not a piano key, but a living, breathing being. And that, gentlemen, is something no formula can ever take away.

Chapter 10

You believe in the "palace of crystal," an indestructible edifice of perfection where no one could dare to stick out their tongue or make a mocking gesture, even in secret. And perhaps it is precisely this invulnerability, this absolute rigidity of the crystal palace, that fills me with dread. It is not the grandeur of the idea that frightens me, but the thought that it is so perfect, so unyielding, so complete, that it leaves no room for defiance, no space for even the smallest rebellion, not even a sly, playful mockery.

If it were not a palace of crystal but something humble, like a henhouse, then perhaps I could accept it for what it is. I might crawl into it to avoid getting wet in a storm, but I would not deceive myself into calling it a palace simply out of gratitude for keeping me dry. You may laugh and argue that in a storm, when one needs shelter, a henhouse is as good as a mansion. To that, I would reply: yes, if the sole purpose of living were simply to keep out of the rain.

But what if I reject that as the sole aim of life? What if I insist that life must aspire to something higher, something grander? What if I believe that, if one is to live at all, one ought to live in a mansion, not a henhouse? That is my desire, my preference, and no amount of argument can change it unless you first change me, my ideals, my very nature. You would need to present me with another vision, something better, something that could genuinely replace the desires that already consume me. Until you do that, I refuse to accept a henhouse as a palace.

The crystal palace may be nothing more than a fantasy, a dream that defies the laws of nature and reason. Perhaps it is nothing but the foolish product of my outdated, irrational ways of thinking. Yet, does that make it any less real to me? Does its impossibility diminish its power as an ideal? It exists in my desires, and as long as my desires exist, so too does the vision of the palace.

You may laugh at this, mock my stubbornness. Go ahead; I will endure your mockery. What I will not endure is pretending to be satisfied when I am still hungry. I will not let myself be pacified by compromises, by half-measures that offer nothing but a recurring cycle of mediocrity and resignation. I will not accept a "practical" solution—a block of buildings crammed with tenants, topped with a dentist's signboard, leased out for a thousand years—as the ultimate expression of my desires.

Destroy my desires, if you can. Eradicate my ideals and replace them with something better, something truer, and I will follow you. But until then, I refuse. You may tell me it isn't worth the effort to persuade me, to appeal to my stubbornness. If that's the case, I'll simply respond in kind: it isn't worth my effort to entertain your world of compromises. We are speaking of serious matters here, but if you refuse to engage with me seriously, then I have no choice but to withdraw. I will retreat into my underground hole and leave you to your edifices.

But as long as I live and have desires, I would sooner let my hand wither than lay a single brick for such a structure. Do not mistake me: my rejection of the crystal palace is not driven by some childish delight in sticking out my tongue. No, I do not reject it because I revel in mockery. Perhaps, in fact, my deepest grievance is that none of the edifices humanity has built thus far have ever been so perfect that one could not stick out their tongue at them. If there were such a structure, so ideal, so complete, that it could quell my desire to mock, I would offer my gratitude—even if that meant letting my tongue be cut out to silence it.

But that is not the world we live in. Things cannot be arranged so perfectly, and I cannot pretend otherwise. So, why am I burdened with such desires? Why am I constructed in such a way as to hunger for something that seems unattainable? Can it really be that I was made only to discover that my very nature is a fraud, that my existence is nothing but a cosmic jest? I cannot believe that.

Do you know what I think? I believe that those of us who live underground—those who dwell in this shadowy world of dissatisfaction and rebellion—should be kept in check. We may sit quietly for years, brooding in silence, but when we finally emerge, we do not simply step into the light. We erupt. We break out in a torrent of words, of grievances, of unrelenting questions and arguments. And we talk, and talk, and talk... endlessly. It seems, perhaps, that this is all we know how to do. But even this endless talking is better, I think, than the silence of complacency. At least in our talking, we assert that we are still alive, still yearning, still unwilling to settle for less than what we desire, no matter how foolish those desires may seem to others.

Chapter 11

The long and the short of it, gentlemen, is that it is better to do nothing. Better to embrace conscious inertia, to deliberately surrender to inactivity. So, hurrah for the underground! Yet even as I say this, I must admit that I am conflicted. I envy the normal man with every ounce of my being, down to the very last drop of bile in my body. I envy him, yet I cannot bear the thought of being him—not as he is now, at least. I will never stop envying him, but neither will I stop rejecting his existence. No, no, I say! Life in the underground, for all its misery and contradictions, is still more advantageous. At least there, one can...

Ah, but even now I am lying. Yes, I admit it—I am lying because I know, deep down, that life in the underground is not better at all. What I truly yearn for is something entirely different, something I cannot even name or find. Damn the underground! Damn this shadowy existence!

Let me confess something else: it would be better still if I believed even a single word of what I have written. I swear to you, gentlemen, that I do not truly believe a single line of it—not one word. Or rather, perhaps I do believe it in some way, but at the same time, I feel as though I am lying like a cobbler, stitching together half-truths and pretense.

"Then why have you written all of this?" you might ask. "Why not bury yourself underground for forty years, do absolutely nothing, and see what happens? Wouldn't that suit you perfectly? How could a man live for forty years with nothing to do?"

You might even wag your heads at me in contempt, scoffing, "Isn't this shameful? Isn't this humiliating? You claim to thirst for life, and yet you try to resolve the questions of life with meaningless, convoluted logic. Your arguments are both insolent and desperate, full of audacity yet riddled with fear. You talk nonsense and seem pleased with it; you say impudent things yet immediately try to excuse yourself. You claim to fear nothing, yet you constantly seek our approval. You gnash your teeth in rebellion, yet you try to amuse us with your wit, even when you know your jokes are weak and your literary style is mediocre. You may have suffered, but you show no respect for your suffering. You may have sincerity, but it is tainted by vanity, as you parade your inner struggles for public spectacle. You seem to have something important to say, yet you hide the essence of it, too cowardly to speak your final word outright. You boast of your self-awareness, but your heart is corrupt, and without a pure heart, your consciousness is incomplete. Lies, lies, lies!"

And yet, all these accusations—every last one—I have invented myself. No one has said these things to me. I've imagined them while listening through the cracks of the floorboards during my long years underground. I've created these criticisms because, frankly, there was nothing else for me to create. I've repeated them to myself so many times that I've memorized them, and now they have taken on a kind of literary shape.

But do you really think I would publish all of this and offer it to you to read? And why, I ask myself, do I even address you as "gentlemen," as though you were real readers? Such confessions are not meant to be printed or shared. They are private things, meant to remain hidden. I am not strong enough to expose them to the world, and I don't see why I should be. Yet, an odd fancy has gripped me, and I feel compelled to see it through, no matter the cost.

Let me explain. Every man has memories that he would share only with close friends. Beyond that, he has other thoughts, more private still, that he keeps locked away, shared with no one but himself. And deeper still, there are secrets that a man is afraid even to admit to himself, thoughts so troubling that he buries them in the darkest corners of his mind. The more decent and respectable the man, the more of these hidden thoughts he possesses.

For years, I have avoided confronting my own memories, skirting them with unease. But now, for reasons I cannot fully explain, I have decided to recall them—and not just to recall them, but to write them down. I want to see if it is possible to be completely honest with myself, to confront the entire truth without flinching. Heine once said that a true autobiography is almost impossible because a man is bound to lie about himself. He believed that Rousseau lied in his confessions, and not accidentally, but out of vanity. I think Heine was right; I can easily imagine how vanity could lead one to exaggerate even one's worst traits.

But Heine spoke of those who write for an audience. I write only for myself, and if I address you as though you were my readers, it is only because it is easier for me to write in that form. It is nothing more than a literary device, an empty framework. I have no real readers and never will.

I do not want to burden myself with any restrictions as I write these notes. I will not attempt to impose order or system on them; I will jot things down as they come to me, in whatever form they arise.

But I can hear you objecting already. "If you don't expect readers," you'll ask, "then why do you explain yourself at every turn? Why do you make such elaborate excuses, justifying your lack of method and apologizing for your disorganized thoughts?"

To that, I can only reply: it is what it is. There is a whole psychology behind it, no doubt. Perhaps I am a coward. Or perhaps I imagine an audience to give myself the illusion of dignity as I write. There may be thousands of reasons, none of which I can fully articulate.

And why am I writing at all? If I have no readers, why not simply recall these memories in silence, in the privacy of my own mind? Perhaps because writing them down feels more substantial. There is something about committing them to paper that makes them more real, more weighty. Writing allows me to scrutinize myself more thoroughly, to refine my thoughts and perhaps even my style.

And then, of course, there is boredom. I have nothing else to do. They say that work ennobles a man, that it fosters kindness and honesty. Well, perhaps this will serve as my work.

Today, for instance, I am haunted by a memory from my past. It has clung to me for days, like a stubborn tune I cannot shake. I believe that if I write it down, I might finally free myself from it. Why not try?

The snow is falling again today, wet and yellowed, the same as it has for days. Perhaps it is the snow that brought this memory back to me, reminding me of something long buried. And so, let this be a story prompted by the falling snow.

Part 2 - À Propos of The Wet Snow

When, from the grip of deep confusion and error,
My passionate words of encouragement
Lifted your struggling spirit into freedom;
And as you lay, tormented and broken,
You cursed the vices that had consumed you,
The very chains that had held you captive—
And when the smoldering fire of your conscience,
Awakened by the sting of sharp memories,
Began to burn within, exposing the terrible truths
Of the life you had lived before I came to you;
And then, when I saw you suddenly falter,
Tears streaming as you covered your face in agony,
Shaken by disgust, overwhelmed and horrified,
Haunted by the shame of what you had endured.

Chapter 1

At that time, I was only twenty-four. My life was bleak, chaotic, and isolated—almost as solitary as that of a wild animal. I had no friends, nor did I seek any. In fact, I deliberately avoided speaking to people, retreating further into my shell, burying myself deeper and deeper in my self-made underground. At work, I avoided eye contact with anyone, fully aware that my colleagues viewed me as peculiar, possibly even repulsive. I often imagined they looked at me with something beyond mere disdain—something approaching loathing. I couldn't understand why no one else seemed to feel this way about themselves.

One clerk, for instance, had a hideous, pockmarked face that looked almost villainous. I was convinced that if I had such a grotesque appearance, I wouldn't have been able to bear anyone's gaze. Another clerk wore a filthy, threadbare uniform that reeked, and yet he appeared entirely unconcerned about the stench or his appearance. Neither of them seemed to notice or care that they might be viewed with disgust by others. They carried on with a carefree indifference, so long as their superiors didn't express any disapproval.

Looking back, I see now that my feelings were rooted in my excessive vanity and the impossibly high standards I held for myself. This vanity made me judge myself harshly, with a loathing that I projected onto everyone around me. I hated my own face, for instance, considering it repulsive. I even suspected that there was something inherently base in my expression. Every day as I walked into the office, I tried to adopt a haughty demeanor, striving to appear independent, proud, and above reproach. "Let them think my face is ugly," I thought, "but let it also be intelligent, lofty, and expressive."

But deep down, I knew this was impossible. I was painfully certain that my face could never convey those qualities. Worse still, I thought it looked outright stupid. I would have been content with just looking intelligent—even if that intelligence was paired with a base, unattractive appearance.

Of course, I hated my colleagues, every single one of them. I despised them, yet at the same time, I feared them. Oddly enough, there were moments when I thought more highly of them than I did of myself. My feelings would swing suddenly and dramatically—I would despise them one moment and feel inferior to them the next. A cultured, respectable man cannot be vain without setting impossible standards for himself and, in turn, despising himself for failing to meet them. This self-hatred then leads him to despise others or, paradoxically, to elevate them above himself.

Whenever I encountered someone at work, I would avert my eyes. Even if I resolved to meet their gaze, I was always the first to look away. This inability to hold someone's gaze tormented me. I constantly feared appearing ridiculous and developed a slavish attachment to conventionality in all outward appearances. I clung to the safe, well-trodden path, terrified of any eccentricity in myself. But how could I possibly live up to this? I was hypersensitive, as every man of our age should be.

And yet, they were all so dull, so ordinary, like a flock of sheep. Perhaps I was the only one who realized I was a coward and a slave. But it wasn't merely a suspicion; it was the truth. I was a coward and a slave, and I say this without the slightest embarrassment. Every decent man of our time is a coward and a slave—that is simply the natural condition of such men. I am firmly convinced of this.

This cowardice and servility are not mere products of our era or circumstance; they are universal and eternal traits of "decent" men. Even if one of these men happens to act bravely in a specific instance, he shouldn't be too proud, for he will surely cower before some other challenge. This is how it always ends. Only stubborn fools or mules show courage, and even they are only brave when they're cornered with no way out. They're not worth paying attention to; they're inconsequential.

Another thought gnawed at me during those days: the idea that I was utterly unlike anyone else, and that no one resembled me. "I am alone, and they are everyone," I thought repeatedly. This belief consumed me, further isolating me from those around me. In hindsight, it's clear that this line of thinking was proof of my youth and inexperience.

Yet at other times, the opposite occurred. There were moments when going to the office was so unbearable that I would return home physically ill. But then, without warning, a phase of indifference would take hold (everything in my life happened in phases). I would laugh at my own intolerance and call myself foolishly romantic. One day I couldn't bear to speak to anyone, while the next I would find myself not only talking but actually contemplating friendship. My feelings of fastidiousness and disdain would disappear entirely, as though they had never existed.

Who knows? Perhaps that disdain wasn't even real. Perhaps it was all an affectation, something I had picked up from books. I still haven't resolved that question. Once, I even went so far as to befriend my colleagues. I visited their homes, played cards, drank vodka, and joined in discussions about promotions. But here, I must digress.

We Russians, speaking broadly, have never been prone to those foolishly transcendental "romantics" of the German or, even more so, French variety—those unshakable types who seem unaffected by anything. Even if the world were crumbling beneath their feet, even if France itself were falling at the barricades, they would remain unchanged, serenely singing their lofty songs to the bitter end, oblivious to reality. Such people are fools. We, in Russia, do not have such fools; that much is widely acknowledged. It is, in fact, one of the key traits that distinguishes us from other nations. Consequently, the pure, transcendental romantic as seen in Europe does not exist among us.

The notion that such figures might be found in Russia stems not from reality but from the misrepresentations of our "realistic" journalists and critics of that era. They were always on the lookout for caricatures—Uncle Pyotr Ivanitchs or Kostanzhoglos—and often mistook these exaggerated figures for our ideal, thereby slandering our romantics. They falsely equated them with the transcendental types of Germany or France. But in truth, the Russian "romantic" is entirely different, bearing no resemblance to the European mold. On the contrary, the traits of our romantics are directly opposed to those of their European counterparts, rendering any foreign standard useless for understanding them.

(Allow me, if you will, to use the term "romantic" here. It is an old-fashioned word, but one that carries weight and familiarity, and it serves my purpose.)

The hallmark of our romantics is their capacity to see everything, to understand everything with an acuity that often surpasses even the sharpest of realistic minds. They accept nothing, trust no one, yet somehow manage to avoid outright contempt. They yield when it serves their interests but always with an eye on practical benefits, whether that means rent-free quarters, a government pension, or some honorary decoration. Amidst their poetic enthusiasms and proclamations of the "sublime and beautiful," they never lose sight of these practical objectives. They carry their ideals—their "precious jewel"—carefully wrapped in metaphorical cotton wool, preserving both their dreams and themselves with astonishing skill, as though safeguarding a treasure meant not for the world but for their own satisfaction.

Our romantic is a man of vast breadth and, quite honestly, the most cunning of rogues. I assure you of this from experience. But, of course, he is a rogue only if he is intelligent—and our romantics are always intelligent. Even when they fall into folly, it is only because, in the bloom of their youth, they succumbed to the allure of German sentimentalism. To protect their "precious jewel" with greater comfort, such men often settled abroad, in places like Weimar or the Black Forest, where they could indulge their ideals in peace.

Take myself, for instance. I genuinely despised my official work, though I refrained from openly criticizing it. Why? Because I was part of it and received a salary for it. Even so, I never openly condemned it—that is the mark of a true Russian romantic. A Russian romantic would sooner lose his sanity—though this rarely happens—than risk openly denouncing his circumstances, unless he had a secure alternative path. He would not be dismissed outright. At worst, he might end up in an asylum, fancifully styling himself "the King of Spain." And even then, it is only the pale, thin ones among us who are prone to such madness.

Many romantics, in fact, achieve considerable rank later in life. Their adaptability is remarkable. They are capable of embracing the most contradictory impulses, navigating them with a fluidity that leaves their superiors and peers in stunned admiration. This versatility, this "broadness of nature," is unique to us Russians. It allows even the most depraved individual to retain an unshaken reverence for their original ideal, even as they descend into dishonesty and corruption. A Russian romantic can be both a consummate rogue and an intensely honest man, holding both qualities simultaneously without contradiction.

I repeat, our romantics frequently rise to astonishing heights of practicality and realism, displaying an unflinching sense of reality that confounds all expectations. Their sheer versatility defies prediction, and who knows what such a nature might achieve in the future? This is not idle patriotism. It is the truth. Yet I suspect you think I am either joking or deadly serious. Either way, I take it as a compliment.

Forgive me for this digression, gentlemen. Let me return to myself. I did not maintain friendly relations with my colleagues at the office. In my youthful arrogance, I even stopped bowing to them entirely, as though severing all ties. That phase, however, was brief. For the most part, I was always alone.

Much of my time was spent at home, reading. I tried to quell the restless turmoil within me through the distractions of external impressions, and reading was my primary escape. Books gave me fleeting relief, filling my mind with both pleasure and pain. Yet, at times, even reading bored me to tears. No matter how hard I tried, I craved movement, action—something that reading alone could not provide. This craving often drove me into dark, sordid habits, the smallest and most shameful of vices.

My emotions were sharp and raw, my irritability constant. I experienced hysterical outbursts, often accompanied by tears and convulsions. I was a man entirely out of harmony with my surroundings. There was nothing in my environment that I could respect, nothing that inspired me. Overwhelmed by depression and an insatiable desire for contrast, for incongruity, I descended into vice— not out of pleasure, but out of sheer desperation.

I am not sharing this to justify myself—no, that would be a lie. I realize now that part of me did want to justify myself, and I admit this observation for my own benefit. I have vowed not to lie to myself in these confessions.

And so, I indulged in vice furtively, timidly, and always alone. At night, under the cover of darkness, I sought out the filthiest of pleasures, all the while plagued by a shame that never left me—not even in my most depraved moments. This shame was so profound that it nearly drove me to curse myself. Even then, I carried my underground world within me, a hidden realm of misery and contradiction.

I was consumed by a paralyzing fear of being seen or recognized. I avoided familiar places, visiting only the most obscure and disreputable haunts where I could remain unnoticed. My actions were drenched in self-loathing, yet I could not stop myself. This was the life I lived, driven by forces I barely understood, always at odds with the world and with myself.

One night, as I walked past a tavern, I caught sight of a scene through one of its glowing windows. A group of men was fighting, brandishing billiard cues as weapons, and I even saw one of them thrown unceremoniously out of the window. Normally, such a sight would have filled me with disgust, but I was in such a wretched state of mind at the time that I actually found myself envying the man who had been hurled out. Yes, envying him so much that I resolved to step inside the tavern and enter the billiard room.

"Perhaps," I thought, "I might provoke a fight myself and get thrown out of the window, too." The absurdity of the thought did not deter me. I was not drunk, but depression, that insidious force, can drive a man to the edge of hysteria. However, nothing came of it. It turned out that I was not even worthy of being tossed out of a window. No fight occurred, no insults were exchanged. I left the tavern as I had entered, invisible and insignificant, my humiliation deepened.

An officer made sure of that from the moment I arrived. Standing by the billiard table in my ignorance, I unknowingly blocked his path. Without a word of explanation or even the courtesy of a glance, he grabbed me by the shoulders, shifted me aside as if I were a piece of furniture, and continued on his way, never once acknowledging my presence.

Had he struck me, I might have forgiven him. But this? This complete disregard, this treatment as though I were nothing at all, stung more deeply than any physical blow could have. I was treated like a fly, brushed aside without thought or care. He was over six feet tall, a towering figure, while I was nothing but a thin, unremarkable man. Still, the quarrel had been in my hands—I could have protested, could have demanded satisfaction. Surely, if I had made a scene, I would have been thrown out of the window as I'd hoped.

But I didn't. I swallowed my pride and slinked away, defeated. I left the tavern confused, my thoughts in turmoil, and returned home. Yet the humiliation didn't stop me. The very next night, I went out again with the same pathetic intentions, furtive and miserable, practically on the verge of tears.

Don't mistake this retreat for cowardice. I assure you, I have never been a coward in spirit, though I admit I have always been one in action. There is a difference, and I beg you not to laugh—I can explain it.

Had the officer been the sort of man who would consent to a duel, things might have turned out differently. But no, he was one of those types—long extinct, alas—who preferred to settle matters in cruder ways, with billiard cues or, like Gogol's Lieutenant Pirogov, by involving the authorities. A duel with a civilian like me would have seemed absurd to him, an unspeakable breach of decorum, not to mention a display of dangerous, French-style free-thinking. Such men were bullies, especially when their towering height gave them a natural advantage.

No, my retreat wasn't born of fear but of vanity—a vanity so overpowering that it paralyzed me. I wasn't afraid of his height, his strength, or even the physical pain he might inflict. I wasn't afraid of being thrown out of the window. No, what I feared most was the scorn of the onlookers. I feared the jeering laughter of everyone in the room, from the insolent billiard marker to the greasy, pimply clerk loitering in the corner. I dreaded their ridicule, their inability to understand me when I inevitably protested in the language of honor— a language that, in our society, can only be spoken in literary terms.

Imagine me, standing there, speaking of point d'honneur while they howled with laughter. The officer wouldn't simply beat me; he would mock me, kick me around the billiard table, and only then, perhaps, throw me out of the window. It wasn't the physical humiliation I feared but the utter obliteration of my dignity.

Of course, this trivial incident didn't end there. It festered within me, growing into an obsession. I began noticing that officer everywhere. I wasn't sure if he recognized me—he likely didn't—but I scrutinized him whenever I saw him, my gaze filled with spite and hatred. This continued for years.

Eventually, I started making discreet inquiries about him, though this was difficult since I had no acquaintances. One day, by chance, I overheard someone call out his surname in the street while I was following him from a distance, as though bound to him by an invisible chain. Another time, I followed him to his apartment building and, for ten kopecks, bribed the porter to tell me everything: his name, his floor, whether he lived alone or with others.

In my desperation for revenge, I conceived a new idea. Though I had no experience with writing, it occurred to me to compose a satirical novel about him. In it, I would expose his villainy, magnifying his faults and unmasking him for what he truly was. I wrote the story with great enthusiasm, relishing every detail. At first, I disguised his name so that it could be easily recognized, but later I changed it entirely. I sent the manuscript to Otetchestvenniya Zapiski, hoping for publication.

But satire was not in vogue at the time, and my story was rejected. The failure was a crushing blow, and my resentment burned hotter than ever.

At last, I resolved to challenge him to a duel. I drafted a letter, carefully worded, imploring him to apologize for his insult and subtly hinting at the prospect of a duel should he refuse. The letter was a masterpiece of tact and persuasion, written so elegantly that, had the officer possessed even the slightest appreciation for the sublime and the beautiful, he would have been moved to embrace me as a friend. In my mind, I imagined how we would reconcile, how he would shield me with his rank, and how I, in turn, would elevate him with my culture and ideas. Together, we would achieve great things.

But, of course, this was all a fantasy. By the time I considered sending the letter, two years had passed since the incident—a ridiculous length of time for such a challenge. No amount of eloquence could disguise the absurdity of it.

Thank God, I never sent that letter. To this day, I shudder at the thought of what might have happened if I had. Cold shivers run down my spine when I recall the humiliation I narrowly avoided.

And suddenly, as if by a stroke of genius, I found the simplest way to take my revenge! A brilliant idea dawned on me, filling me with an exhilarating sense of triumph. It all began on one of those holidays when I used to walk along the sunny side of Nevsky Prospect at around four in the afternoon. Though "walk" is perhaps the wrong word—it was more of a series of torturous encounters, endless humiliations, and seething resentments. Yet somehow, this was precisely what drew me there.

I would slink along like an eel, constantly shifting out of the way for generals, officers of the guards, elegant ladies, and haughty hussars. Each time I stepped aside, a sharp, stabbing pang would shoot through my chest, and a wave of heat would crawl down my spine as I became hyper-aware of my own shabby appearance. My scrawny figure, darting nervously about, felt wretched and insignificant amidst the splendor of Nevsky.

This daily humiliation was a kind of ritual, an unending torment that reminded me, over and over, that I was nothing more than a fly to the grand world around me—a vile, irritating fly. True, I considered myself more intelligent, more refined than the people who brushed me aside, but that only made the sting of their indifference worse. Why did I subject myself to this? Why did I return to the Nevsky again and again, knowing what awaited me? I couldn't say. Something deep inside me pulled me there, as though I were irresistibly drawn to my own suffering.

After my first encounter with the officer, the one who had moved me aside without a word, I began frequenting the Nevsky even more often. It became a kind of obsession, as if I were looking for him, yearning to see him again. And I did see him—many times. Like me, he seemed to favor the Nevsky on holidays. But while I twisted and turned to avoid others, making way for generals and dignitaries, he did no such thing. He moved straight ahead, striding boldly as though the path before him were his by right.

To those of higher rank, he would yield, of course, but to men like me—or even to those better dressed—he would walk directly toward them, forcing them to move aside as if they were invisible. He treated them, and me, as though we were nothing but air, nonentities in his world. I watched him with a mixture of fascination and fury, seething with resentment but always yielding to his stride. Each time I stepped aside, my rage deepened. It infuriated me that even in the chaos of the street, I couldn't be his equal.

"Why is it always you who steps aside?" I would scream internally, often waking in the middle of the night, my thoughts racing. "Why is it you and not him? There's no law, no regulation demanding it! Why can't the respect be mutual? Why can't he move halfway and I move halfway?" But that never happened. Each time, it was I who yielded, and each time, he passed without so much as noticing me.

And then, like a thunderbolt, an audacious thought struck me: what if I didn't move aside? What if I stood my ground, refused to yield, and allowed us to collide? The idea thrilled me and took root in my mind, growing stronger with each passing day. It consumed me, replaying itself in endless variations. "I'll run into him," I thought, "not violently, just enough for us to brush shoulders. I won't push him deliberately—just enough to meet him on equal terms, just enough to assert myself."

The idea became an obsession. I dreamed about it, fantasized about it, and began visiting the Nevsky more often, rehearsing the moment in my mind. It seemed more and more possible, even inevitable. But I realized that if I were to carry out my plan, I would need to look presentable. The Nevsky was not just any street; it was the center of society, a place frequented by countesses, princes, and literary figures. If a scandal arose, I couldn't afford to look shabby.

Appearance was everything—it would signal respectability and place me on equal footing with him in the eyes of onlookers.

With this in mind, I requested an advance on my salary and set about improving my attire. I purchased a pair of black gloves at Tchurkin's, deeming them more elegant and understated than the lemon-colored pair I had initially considered. Lemon-colored gloves seemed too ostentatious, too attention-seeking. The black ones felt dignified, refined, a symbol of quiet strength.

Next, I readied my best shirt, complete with white bone studs. My hat, too, was newly purchased, a respectable and well-fitted choice. My overcoat, however, presented a challenge. It was warm and serviceable, but the wadded material and raccoon collar were unmistakably vulgar. Such a collar, I realized, would never do for my purpose. It had to go.

After much deliberation, I decided to replace the collar with a beaver one—just like those worn by officers. Beaver collars were the epitome of elegance, and though genuine beaver was far beyond my means, I found a suitable German imitation at the Gostiny Dvor. True, it wouldn't last long, but it would look splendid for the occasion.

Even so, the expense was too great. I resolved to sell my raccoon collar and borrow the remaining money from my superior, Anton Antonitch Syetotchkin. Anton Antonitch was a serious and judicious man who rarely lent money, but he had been told by an influential figure to "look after me" when I joined the service. The thought of borrowing money from him filled me with dread; it seemed monstrous, humiliating. I agonized over it, losing sleep for several nights as I wrestled with my pride.

Finally, trembling with nervous energy, I approached him. At first, he was surprised, then he frowned and hesitated. But, to my immense relief, he agreed. He lent me the money, but only after I signed a written authorization allowing him to deduct the sum from my salary two weeks later.

With the loan secured, I began preparing in earnest. Each piece of my ensemble was carefully chosen, every detail planned to perfection.

Soon, I would be ready to confront the officer. Soon, I would meet him not as a cowering, scurrying figure, but as his equal. The thought filled me with a strange, exhilarating joy, though I couldn't yet foresee the full weight of what I had set in motion.

At last, everything was ready. The shabby raccoon collar had been replaced with the elegant beaver one, transforming my overcoat into something much more respectable. Each detail of my appearance had been carefully tended to, and I finally felt equipped for the confrontation. But I knew better than to act hastily. This was not the sort of plan to execute recklessly or on impulse. It required precision, patience, and just the right moment.

I began putting my plan into motion, venturing out to the Nevsky more often, with purpose in every step. Yet, to my dismay, nothing seemed to work. Time after time, I saw the officer approaching, my resolve hardening with each step, and just as we were about to cross paths—just when I thought I would finally stand my ground—I instinctively stepped aside, yielding to him as I always had. He would pass me by, utterly oblivious to my presence, and I would be left humiliated, burning with rage at my own weakness.

I even prayed for strength. As I walked toward him, I silently pleaded with God to grant me the courage to stand firm, to not flinch or falter. Once, I was certain I would succeed. My determination was absolute, my heart pounding as I drew nearer and nearer. But when I was only a few inches away, my nerve deserted me. In a moment of panic, I stumbled and fell, landing clumsily at his feet. Without so much as a glance, he calmly stepped over me and continued on his way, while I rolled to the side like a discarded ball.

That night, I was consumed by fever and delirium. My failure haunted me, replaying over and over in my mind. It seemed as though my humiliation was complete, that I would never escape the shadow of this man or my own inadequacy.

And yet, just as I was about to abandon the entire scheme, fate took an unexpected turn. The night before, I had resolved to give it all up. I decided I would go to the Nevsky one final time, not to confront the officer, but simply to bid farewell to my foolish plan. It was meant to be a gesture of surrender, a way of letting go of the resentment that had consumed me for so long.

But then, as I walked down the Nevsky, I saw him. He was only a few paces away, striding confidently toward me. Without warning, something inside me shifted. In an instant, all my hesitation, all my doubts, melted away. I clenched my fists, closed my eyes, and walked straight ahead.

And then it happened. We collided—shoulder to shoulder, with the full force of our strides. I didn't yield, not an inch. For the first time, I stood my ground. We passed one another as equals.

He didn't stop. He didn't look back. He pretended not to notice, of course—but I am certain he felt it. To this day, I am convinced that he knew exactly what had happened and chose to ignore it, as if nothing had occurred. But it didn't matter. What mattered was that I had done it. I had finally achieved my goal.

Of course, I got the worst of it. He was taller, broader, and far stronger than me, and the impact sent a sharp pain shooting through my shoulder. But that was irrelevant. What mattered was that I had preserved my dignity. I had refused to yield, and in doing so, I had placed myself on an equal footing with him—not just in my own eyes, but in the eyes of the world.

I walked home that night feeling triumphant, my heart soaring with victory. I had avenged every slight, every humiliation. My chest swelled with pride, and I even found myself singing Italian arias as I paced my room, exulting in my newfound sense of power and self-worth.

What happened three days later, of course, is not something I need to explain here. If you've read the earlier chapters of my story, you can easily guess. Let's just say the euphoria didn't last.

As for the officer, he was transferred shortly after that incident, and I haven't seen him in fourteen years. I sometimes wonder what became of him. Where is he now? Who is he walking over these days, with that same unyielding stride? It's strange to think how much he once occupied my thoughts, and how little he must have cared or even noticed. But I suppose that, too, was part of the lesson.

Chapter 2

After each period of indulgence, I would always feel terribly sick, as if my very soul had been poisoned. What followed was a wave of remorse, which I would try in vain to push away. The weight of my actions left me too drained to resist. But, over time, I grew accustomed to this cycle. Or perhaps it's better to say that I resigned myself to enduring it. I found solace in a peculiar escape that seemed to reconcile everything—my retreat into "the sublime and the beautiful," a refuge found in dreams. I was an inveterate dreamer, capable of losing myself in fantasies for months on end, secluded in my corner as if the real world didn't exist.

In those moments, I became someone entirely unrecognizable from the man who, out of cowardice and shame, had adorned his coat with a collar of German beaver. In my dreams, I transformed into a hero of the highest order. I imagined myself so elevated that I wouldn't even deign to acknowledge the six-foot lieutenant if he dared to visit me. He simply didn't exist in the luminous world of my imagination.

What exactly were these dreams, and how could they satisfy me so completely? It's hard to say now. Yet, at the time, they filled me with a sense of purpose and fulfillment. And even now, I must admit that part of me still finds some satisfaction in recalling them. These dreams were especially vivid and intoxicating after a period of debauchery. They arrived hand in hand with my remorse, often bringing tears and a tempest of emotions. Within those dreams, I experienced moments of unadulterated happiness, so profound that not a hint of irony could touch them. I believed in them entirely, with a faith so pure that I could almost feel hope and love coursing through me.

During those times, I clung to the belief that, through some miraculous twist of fate, everything in my life would suddenly fall into place. I imagined a perfect opportunity arising—a moment of beneficent action, noble and righteous, appearing fully formed and ready for me to seize. What kind of action this might be, I never knew, but the details seemed unimportant. What mattered was that it would elevate me, pulling me into the light of day as though I were riding a white horse, crowned with laurel. In these dreams, anything less than the foremost position in life was inconceivable to me.

And yet, in reality, I was content to occupy the lowest depths. That, in itself, was my undoing. For when I was mired in disgrace, I comforted myself with the thought of my imagined heroics. I believed that the hero within me somehow excused my baser actions. An ordinary man might feel ashamed to wallow in the mud, but a hero was above such shame. A hero, I thought, was too exalted to be truly defiled, even by the filthiest of sins.

What is worth noting is that these bursts of "the sublime and the beautiful" did not occur after dissipation alone. They also intruded during those very moments when I was sinking to my lowest. They came in fleeting, unexpected waves, as though to remind me of their existence. Strangely, their presence did not interrupt my vices. On the contrary, they seemed to heighten the experience, serving as a sharp and flavorful contrast. These dreams became a kind of seasoning, a tantalizing sauce that lent my debauchery a peculiar depth of meaning.

This "sauce" was composed of contradictions—suffering mixed with agonizing self-reflection. The constant pricking of my conscience and the painful internal analysis gave my indulgence an almost artistic quality. Without this layer of complexity, I doubt I could have endured the sheer vulgarity of it all. After all, what could possibly have drawn me to such filth, sending me out into the streets night after night? No, it wasn't the depravity itself but the loftier, more intricate way I processed it that kept me enthralled.

Oh, and the love I felt in those dreams—what boundless, intoxicating love! It was an ethereal, fantastical love, one that never translated into anything tangible or real. Yet there was so much of it, so overwhelming a flood, that I never felt the need to apply it to real life. It seemed unnecessary to bring it into the waking world when it worked so beautifully in my imagination. Everything from those dreams flowed seamlessly into the realm of art, manifesting in the refined, poetic forms of life that I had pieced together from poets and novelists.

In these fantasies, I always triumphed. My enemies, of course, lay humiliated in the dust, forced to acknowledge my undeniable superiority. And I, in my infinite magnanimity, forgave them all. I was a poet, a nobleman, and a man of immense fortune—fortunes that I immediately devoted to the betterment of humanity. At the same time, I publicly confessed my sins, revealing not just their shameful nature but the deeper elements of "the sublime and the beautiful" embedded within them, something akin to the grandeur of Byron's Manfred.

Everyone wept as they listened to my confession, overcome by their admiration and remorse. Naturally, they kissed my hands and begged for forgiveness. Then, in an act of self-denial, I would walk barefoot and hungry, preaching revolutionary ideas and leading heroic battles against ignorance and oppression. My victories would echo through the ages, accompanied by grand marches and declarations of universal amnesty. The Pope himself would abdicate and retreat to Brazil, while Italy celebrated with a grand ball at the Villa Borghese. And as for Lake Como? Naturally, it would be relocated to Rome for the occasion, where it would provide the perfect setting for a romantic interlude in the bushes.

Oh, how ridiculous it all sounds now. You might say it's vulgar and shameful to reveal these fantasies after admitting to the tears and passion they once inspired in me. And you would be right. It is vulgar. It is shameful.

Yet, even so, I feel no embarrassment. Do you think this was somehow worse or more foolish than anything you've dreamed of, gentlemen? I doubt it. Besides, some of these imaginings were crafted with genuine care and artistry. They didn't all involve Lake Como.

Still, you are correct. It's contemptible. Perhaps the most contemptible part is that I feel the need to justify myself to you now.

And even worse is the fact that I am fully aware of how contemptible it is, yet I continue to do it anyway. But enough. If I don't stop here, I'll only sink further, each step becoming more disgraceful than the last.

I could never go more than three months of living in my dreams before feeling an overwhelming urge to interact with other people. For me, "interacting with society" meant visiting my superior at work, Anton Antonitch Syetotchkin. He was the only real acquaintance I ever had in my life, something I find rather astonishing when I think about it now. But even then, I only went to see him when I was in a particular mood—when my fantasies had reached such heights that I felt an irresistible need to embrace all of humanity. Of course, to embrace humanity, I needed at least one actual person, and that person was Anton Antonitch. However, I could only call on him on Tuesdays, which was his designated at-home day. Because of this, I had to carefully time my bursts of enthusiasm for mankind so they would coincide with a Tuesday.

Anton Antonitch lived on the fourth floor of a building in the Five Corners neighborhood. His home consisted of four small, low-ceilinged rooms, each more cramped and modest than the last. The place had a pale, worn-out look about it. He lived with two daughters and their aunt, who always poured the tea. His daughters, aged thirteen and fourteen, both had upturned noses and a habit of whispering and giggling together. Their constant whispers made me terribly self-conscious, and I felt so shy around them that I tried to avoid their glances altogether.

Anton Antonitch himself usually sat in his study on a leather couch near a table, chatting with another gentleman, often one of his colleagues from the office or someone from another department. There were never more than two or three visitors at a time, and they were always the same people. Their conversations revolved around the same topics: taxes, senate business, salaries, promotions, and the best ways to win favor with His Excellency. I had no idea what to say during these gatherings and never dared to open my mouth. I simply sat there for hours like a fool, quietly sweating and feeling paralyzed. Despite how stifling the experience was, I found it oddly comforting. Somehow, after spending those hours in their company, my intense desire to embrace all of humanity would subside for a while.

I did have another acquaintance of sorts, a man named Simonov, who had been one of my schoolmates. In fact, there were several former classmates of mine living in Petersburg, but I had no connection with them. I had even stopped acknowledging them in the street. If I'm honest, I think I deliberately chose my current department at work just to avoid running into any of them and to sever all ties to my miserable school years. I loathed that school and all the memories it carried—those years felt like a form of punishment. As soon as I entered adulthood, I cut myself off from my former classmates entirely. Out of all of them, Simonov was the only one I still occasionally nodded to in passing.

Simonov wasn't a particularly remarkable person at school. He had a calm and steady temperament, and I had to admit there was a certain honesty and independence about him. He wasn't particularly bright, but he wasn't stupid either. At one time, I had shared a few meaningful conversations with him, moments of what I considered genuine connection. But those moments had been brief and soon gave way to an awkward tension. It always seemed as though he was uncomfortable with me, as if he were afraid I might try to rekindle that deeper tone of conversation. I suspected he didn't like me, but I couldn't be sure. For some reason, I continued to visit him now and then, unable to fully convince myself of his dislike.

One evening, when I couldn't stand the suffocating loneliness any longer and knew that Anton Antonitch wouldn't be receiving visitors because it was Thursday, I decided to visit Simonov instead. As I climbed the stairs to his fourth-floor apartment, doubts crept into my mind. I couldn't shake the feeling that Simonov didn't want to see me and that visiting him was a mistake. But, as was so often the case with me, these very thoughts only seemed to push me toward making the mistake. And so, despite my misgivings, I knocked on his door.

It had been almost a year since I last saw him.

Chapter 3

When I arrived, I found two of my old schoolmates with Simonov. They were deep in a serious conversation and hardly acknowledged my presence, which felt strange considering we hadn't seen each other in years. Their dismissiveness was palpable; it was as if they regarded me as no more significant than a fly. Even back in school, though I'd been hated by most of them, I hadn't been treated with such blatant disregard. Now, it was clear to me that they despised me for my lack of success, for the way I had let myself decline—my shabby clothing and overall appearance, which to them symbolized my incompetence and insignificance. But still, I had not expected such open contempt.

Simonov himself seemed genuinely surprised to see me. He had always looked surprised whenever I visited, even in the old days. The reception threw me off balance, and I sank into a chair feeling small and out of place, listening to their conversation without a word.

They were discussing plans for a farewell dinner to be held the next day for one of their comrades, Zverkov, an army officer who was about to leave for a distant province. Zverkov had been in school with me as well, and my dislike for him had grown over the years. In the lower grades, he was just a cheerful, good-looking boy whom everyone seemed to like. But even then, I had hated him precisely for being so cheerful and good-looking.

As we got older, my hatred only deepened. He was never a good student and only got worse with time, yet he managed to leave school with a glowing certificate, thanks to his influential connections. During our last year, he inherited an estate with two hundred serfs, and since most of us were poor, this inheritance elevated his status among our peers. He took on an air of arrogance, but even so, he was annoyingly good-natured, which made his swaggering behavior all the more infuriating.

Despite his obvious vulgarity and his shallow ideas of honor and dignity, nearly everyone fawned over him. The more he boasted and postured, the more they adored him—not out of self-interest, but simply because he was blessed with good looks and natural charm. It was an unspoken rule among us that Zverkov possessed unmatched tact and social grace, and this particular assumption infuriated me the most.

I loathed the self-assured tone of his voice, the way he admired his own jokes, which were often painfully stupid. I despised his handsome but vacant face—though, secretly, I would have traded my so-called intelligence for his looks without a second thought. I hated his casual military demeanor, which was all the rage in the 1840s. His boasts about future conquests of women made my skin crawl, especially since he hadn't dared approach women until he became an officer and wore his epaulettes. He looked forward to those conquests with unbearable impatience, as though they were his birthright.

I remember a particular instance when he bragged about his plans for the women on his estate. He spoke with unrestrained arrogance, claiming he wouldn't spare a single village girl and that it was his droit de seigneur. If the peasants dared to complain, he said, he would have them flogged and double their taxes for their insolence. This declaration enraged me—not out of compassion for the girls or their fathers, but because our spineless group of classmates cheered for him. Their servile applause for such a wretched creature filled me with fury. I confronted him, and for once, I bested him in our argument.

But Zverkov, though undeniably stupid, had a quick wit and a carefree boldness that made him immune to humiliation. He laughed off the whole encounter, turning it into a joke, and the rest of the group joined in his laughter. My small victory was hollow, and in the end, the joke was on me.

After that, there were other clashes between us. He often got the better of me, though never maliciously. He treated me with casual amusement, as though I were beneath his notice. I grew bitter and silent, refusing to respond to his provocations. When we left school, he tried to maintain some kind of friendship with me, and I, flattered by his attention, did not push him away. But our association didn't last long, and we naturally drifted apart.

Years later, I heard about his successes as a lieutenant and his reckless lifestyle. Stories of his popularity and rapid rise in the military trickled back to me. By then, he had taken to ignoring me in public, as though acknowledging me might damage his reputation. I once saw him at the theater, seated in one of the upper-tier boxes. He was charming an old general's daughters with his polished manners. He was still handsome and nimble, though it was clear he had begun to age prematurely. I could see he would likely grow stout and coarse by the time he reached thirty.

And now, it was this same Zverkov for whom my former classmates were organizing a farewell dinner. Despite maintaining their connection to him over the years, I could tell that deep down, they didn't see themselves as his equals. I was certain of it.

Simonov had two visitors with him. One was Ferfitchkin, a Russianized German—a short man with a face like a monkey. He was a fool who loved mocking others, and he had been one of my fiercest enemies back in school. Ferfitchkin was vulgar, loud, and full of himself, always pretending to have a strong sense of personal honor, though deep down he was nothing but a coward. He was one of Zverkov's most devoted admirers, constantly sucking up to him for favors and even borrowing money from him. The other visitor, Trudolyubov, was an unremarkable man—a tall young officer with a cold expression. He was fairly honest but obsessed with success and promotions. He admired anyone who seemed to be doing well in life. Though he wasn't particularly rude to me, he clearly thought I was insignificant and treated me accordingly. He was a distant relative of Zverkov's, and while that connection wasn't much, it gave him a certain standing among us.

"Well, seven roubles each," Trudolyubov said. "That makes twenty-one roubles between the three of us. That should be enough for a decent dinner. Zverkov, of course, won't pay anything."

"Of course not. We're the ones inviting him," Simonov agreed.

"Can you imagine," Ferfitchkin interrupted, puffing himself up like an arrogant servant bragging about his master's achievements, "can you imagine Zverkov letting us pay for everything? He'll accept out of politeness, of course, but he'll order half a dozen bottles of champagne."

"Do we really need six bottles for just the four of us?" Trudolyubov asked, ignoring everything except the mention of the champagne.

"So, the three of us, plus Zverkov as the fourth, twenty-one roubles. Tomorrow at five o'clock at the Hôtel de Paris," Simonov concluded, since he was in charge of making the arrangements.

"How twenty-one roubles?" I asked, unable to hide my agitation and pretending to be offended. "If you include me, it won't be twenty-one roubles—it will be twenty-eight."

I thought inviting myself so boldly would seem charming and that they'd immediately respect me for it.

"You want to join us?" Simonov asked, clearly unenthusiastic and avoiding eye contact. He knew me too well, and his reaction made me furious.

"Why not? I went to school with Zverkov too, didn't I? And to be honest, I feel hurt that you didn't include me," I said, my anger boiling over again.

"And how were we supposed to find you?" Ferfitchkin asked rudely.

"You never got along with Zverkov," Trudolyubov added, frowning.

But once I'd grabbed hold of the idea, I wasn't about to let it go.

"Doesn't that give me even more reason to want to join now?" I replied, my voice trembling as though I were defending something monumental. "Maybe it's precisely because we weren't on good terms before that I want to go now."

"Oh, there's no making sense of you and your weird justifications," Trudolyubov said mockingly.

"We'll add your name," Simonov finally said, addressing me directly. "Tomorrow, five o'clock at the Hôtel de Paris."

"What about the money?" Ferfitchkin muttered to Simonov, glancing at me, but he stopped mid-sentence, perhaps realizing that even Simonov was embarrassed.

"That's enough," Trudolyubov said, standing up. "If he wants to come so badly, let him."

"But this was supposed to be just us friends," Ferfitchkin grumbled as he picked up his hat. "It wasn't meant to be some public gathering."

"Not that we wanted to invite him at all," he muttered under his breath.

They left shortly after. Ferfitchkin didn't even glance in my direction, and Trudolyubov gave me only the faintest nod. Simonov and I were left alone, and he looked at me with a mix of irritation and awkwardness. He didn't sit back down, nor did he invite me to stay.

"Well... yes... tomorrow, then. Will you pay your share now? I'm only asking so I know," he said hesitantly, clearly uncomfortable.

I felt my face flush with embarrassment. As I reached into my pocket, I suddenly remembered that I still owed Simonov fifteen roubles—a debt I hadn't forgotten but had conveniently ignored.

"Simonov, you must understand—I couldn't have known I'd be coming here today. I'm really sorry I didn't bring the money with me," I said, my voice faltering.

"It's fine, it's fine. Don't worry about it. You can pay tomorrow after the dinner," he said quickly, trying to dismiss the topic. "I just wanted to check... that's all."

He trailed off and began pacing the room, clearly more frustrated than before. As he walked, he stamped his heels against the floor.

"Am I keeping you?" I asked after an awkward silence.

"Oh!" he said, startled. "Well, actually... yes. I do have to go see someone nearby," he added apologetically, looking slightly ashamed.

"For heaven's sake, why didn't you say so sooner?" I exclaimed, grabbing my cap and pretending to be far more casual and confident than I felt.

"It's not far—just a short walk," Simonov repeated, escorting me to the door with an unusual fussiness that didn't suit him at all. "So, five o'clock tomorrow, don't forget," he called out as I descended the stairs. It was obvious he was relieved to see me go.

I left in a fury. "What was I thinking, forcing myself into their plans like that?" I muttered through clenched teeth as I stomped down the street. "And for what? To spend time with a scoundrel like Zverkov?"

Of course, I told myself I wouldn't go. I'd just write Simonov a note and back out of the whole thing. But deep down, I knew the truth. I would go. No matter how awkward, how inappropriate it would be, I would make a point of going. The more absurd it was for me to show up, the more determined I became.

At that time, I had a serious obstacle to attending the dinner: I didn't have enough money. I only had nine roubles, and out of that, I owed seven to my servant, Apollon, as his monthly wages. That was all I paid him, and he had to manage his own expenses with it. Not paying him was practically impossible given his personality, which I'll explain another time. Still, I knew I would go to the dinner and would delay paying his wages.

That night, I had terrible dreams, no doubt because I'd been haunted all evening by memories of my miserable school days. I couldn't shake them off. Distant relatives who supported me had sent me to that school, but I never heard from them again. They sent me off as a lonely, quiet boy, already weighed down by their criticisms, full of doubt, and looking at everyone around me with suspicion. My classmates greeted me with cruel jokes and relentless taunts, simply because I was different from them. I refused to endure their mockery or lower myself to fit in as they did with each other. From the very start, I hated them and withdrew into myself, nursing a fragile pride that was both wounded and out of proportion. Their rudeness and cruelty disgusted me.

They mocked my face and my awkward appearance, even though their own faces were no better. In fact, it seemed as though the boys at our school became uglier and dumber over time. Many arrived as good-looking boys, but after a few years, they became repulsive. By the time I was sixteen, I viewed them with a brooding disgust. Their shallow thoughts, stupid interests, and meaningless conversations stood out to me. They cared nothing for truly important matters, and I couldn't help but see them as inferior. It wasn't just my wounded ego—don't assume I was merely a dreamer while they were grounded in reality. That wasn't the case. They understood nothing about real life, and their blind respect for superficial success infuriated me.

They worshipped rank as if it were intelligence. By sixteen, many were already fixated on finding comfortable jobs. Their stupidity and the poor influences they'd grown up with shaped their depravity. Much of it was superficial—an act of cynicism—but even their youthful innocence was tainted, appearing in the form of cheap rebellion. I hated them deeply, though I might have been even worse than they were. They hated me just as much and made no effort to hide it. By then, I didn't want their friendship; instead, I craved their humiliation. To escape their scorn, I threw myself into my studies and climbed to the top of the class. This earned me a begrudging respect. They began to realize that I read books they couldn't understand and knew things far beyond our curriculum. This impressed the teachers as well, which silenced the mockery but didn't end the hostility. A cold, strained distance settled between me and the others.

Eventually, I grew tired of being so isolated. As the years passed, I began to yearn for friendship. I tried to build connections with my classmates, but every attempt failed. My relationships with them always felt forced and fell apart quickly. Once, I had a close friend, but

I became a tyrant in the friendship. I wanted to control him completely, to fill him with disdain for everyone else and make him reject the world around him. My intense affection overwhelmed him and drove him to tears. He was a simple and loyal person, but as soon as he gave himself entirely to me, I began to despise him. It seemed that all I wanted was to dominate him, and once I achieved that, I had no use for him. Yet I couldn't dominate the others. My friend was nothing like them—he was an exception.

When I finished school, I immediately abandoned the career path that had been planned for me. I wanted to sever all ties with my past, curse it, and move on. And yet, despite all of this, I still found myself heading to Simonov's house!

The next morning, I woke up feeling restless and excited, as though something monumental was about to happen. I convinced myself that this day would bring a dramatic change to my life. Any event, no matter how small, had the power to make me feel this way because such moments were so rare. I went to the office as usual but left early to prepare for the evening. I decided that arriving first at the dinner would make me seem overly eager, so I carefully planned my timing. Every tiny detail consumed me, overwhelming me with anxiety. I polished my boots twice myself because Apollon, my servant, refused to clean them more than once a day, insisting it was beyond his duties. I stole the brushes from the hallway and made sure he didn't see me, fearing his scorn.

As I inspected my clothes, I realized how shabby and worn everything looked. My uniform was presentable, but it wasn't suitable for dinner. The worst part was a large yellow stain on the knee of my trousers. I felt certain this stain would ruin nine-tenths of my dignity. I knew it was ridiculous to think that, but I couldn't help it. My heart sank as I imagined Zverkov greeting me with cold disdain, Trudolyubov looking down on me with unshakable contempt, and Ferfitchkin mocking me to win Zverkov's favor. Simonov would see through it all and despise me for my pathetic vanity. Worst of all, the entire scene would feel ordinary, boring, and painfully unremarkable.

Of course, the best decision would have been not to go at all. But that was impossible. If I had backed out, I would have hated myself forever, mocking myself with the thought: "You were too scared! You chickened out!" On the contrary, I burned with the desire to prove to that group that I wasn't as weak and insignificant as I seemed. Even in my feverish panic, I fantasized about triumphing over them, dazzling them with my wit and brilliance. In my mind, they would abandon Zverkov, leaving him humiliated and silent, while I would win them over. We would reconcile and toast to eternal friendship. Yet, deep down, I knew I didn't truly want any of this. I didn't care about impressing them or earning their approval. I wasn't sure what I wanted at all.

Desperate for time to pass, I gazed out the window at the snow falling thickly in the darkness. When the clock finally struck five, I grabbed my hat, careful to avoid Apollon's gaze. He had been waiting all day for his wages but stubbornly refused to bring it up. Slipping past him, I spent my last half-rouble on a fancy sledge and arrived at the Hôtel de Paris in style.

Chapter 4

I was certain the day before that I would be the first to arrive. However, it wasn't just about being early—I found myself confused when I couldn't even locate our room. To make matters worse, the table hadn't even been set. What was going on? After pestering the waiters with questions, I found out the dinner was actually scheduled for six o'clock, not five as I had been told. The buffet staff confirmed this too. I felt humiliated just asking about it. It was only twenty-five minutes past five. If they had decided to change the time, they could have at least informed me—that's what letters or notes are for. Instead, I was left looking ridiculous, not only in my own eyes but also in front of the waiters.

I sat down, and the servant began laying the table. Somehow, this simple act made me feel even more embarrassed. By the time they brought in the candles at six, although the room already had lamps, it didn't occur to anyone to set the atmosphere earlier, even when I was there. In a nearby room, two grim-looking men were silently eating at separate tables. From farther away, I could hear loud laughter and shrill, irritating voices in French. There were women at that dinner, adding to the racket. The whole situation made me miserable. When they finally arrived, right on the dot at six, I actually felt relieved to see them. I was so glad that I forgot I was supposed to be upset with them.

Zverkov led the group in, clearly the center of attention. They were all laughing, but when Zverkov saw me, he adjusted his posture slightly and walked toward me with a deliberate, almost smug air. He shook my hand with a courtesy that felt both polite and distant, like the formal gesture of a general. It was as if he was trying to keep me at arm's length, even while greeting me. I had expected him to immediately break into his usual loud, obnoxious laughter and throw out his shallow, silly jokes. I had been bracing myself for that ever since the day before. But this restrained, self-important manner was unexpected. It hit me—he genuinely believed himself to be superior to me in every way. The thought made me burn with anger.

"I was surprised to hear you wanted to join us," he said, speaking slowly and deliberately in a new, affected tone. "You and I haven't seen much of each other. You avoid us, don't you? You shouldn't. We're not as terrible as you might think. Anyway, I'm glad to reconnect." He placed his hat on the windowsill casually and turned away from me.

"Have you been waiting long?" Trudolyubov asked.

"I arrived at five, as you told me yesterday," I replied, my voice sharp with irritation.

"Didn't you let him know about the time change?" Trudolyubov asked Simonov.

"No, I forgot," Simonov replied indifferently. He didn't even apologize but instead walked off to order the appetizers.

"So you've been here an entire hour? Poor fellow!" Zverkov exclaimed mockingly. To him, this was the height of comedy. Ferfitchkin snickered along with him, like an annoying little puppy.

"It's not funny!" I snapped at Ferfitchkin, feeling my anger rise. "It wasn't my fault—it was someone else's mistake. It was ... it was ... just absurd."

"It's more than absurd. It's downright rude," Trudolyubov muttered, surprisingly taking my side. "And Simonov should have handled it better."

"If that had happened to me," Ferfitchkin began smugly, "I would have—"

"You should have just ordered dinner for yourself," Zverkov interrupted smoothly. "Why wait for us?"

"I could have done that without asking your permission," I shot back angrily. "If I waited, it was—"

"Let's sit down, gentlemen," Simonov interrupted, returning to the room. "Everything's ready. The champagne is perfectly chilled." He glanced at me briefly. "I didn't know your address, so where could I have sent word?" His tone was defensive, and he avoided looking directly at me. Clearly, he still resented what had happened the day before.

We all sat down. The table was round, with Trudolyubov on my left and Simonov on my right. Across from me sat Zverkov, with Ferfitchkin next to him between him and Trudolyubov.

"Are you in a government office now?" Zverkov asked, addressing me directly. He seemed to think I needed encouragement and was trying, in his way, to be friendly.

"Does he want me to throw a bottle at him?" I thought, already seething with irritation. Everything about this setting put me on edge.

"Yes, in the N—— office," I answered curtly, keeping my eyes fixed on my plate.

"And do you have a good position there? Why did you leave your previous post?" he continued in a drawling tone.

"I left because I wanted to," I replied, mimicking his affected manner and barely containing my anger. Ferfitchkin burst into laughter, while Simonov smirked sarcastically. Trudolyubov stopped eating and stared at me curiously.

Zverkov flinched at my response but tried to appear unfazed. "And what about the salary?"

"What about it?" I snapped.

"I mean, how much do you earn?" he pressed.

"Why are you interrogating me?" Despite my frustration, I told him my salary. As I spoke, I could feel my face flush red with embarrassment.

"With that income, it's no surprise you can't afford to eat at cafés," Ferfitchkin said, his tone sharp and mocking.

"In my opinion, that salary is quite inadequate," Trudolyubov added seriously.

"And look how thin you've become! You've really changed," Zverkov chimed in, his voice carrying a faint note of malice as he looked me over from head to toe with a smug air of pity.

"Oh, leave him be, spare him the embarrassment," Ferfitchkin teased, letting out a snide chuckle.

"My dear sir, let me assure you I am not embarrassed," I finally snapped, raising my voice. "Do you hear me? I'm dining here at this café at my own expense—not at someone else's, mind you. Make a note of that, Mr. Ferfitchkin."

"What? Isn't everyone here paying for themselves?" Ferfitchkin shot back, his face flushing bright red, his anger visible as he glared at me. "You sound like—"

"That's enough," I interrupted, realizing I might have gone too far. "I think it would be better if we discussed something more intelligent."

"Oh, so now you're trying to show us how smart you are?"

"Not at all," I said dryly. "I'm just suggesting that this conversation is getting tiresome."

"Why are you running your mouth like that? Have you lost your mind working at your office?" he spat.

"Enough of this, gentlemen, enough!" Zverkov intervened in a tone of authority, trying to restore order.

"This is ridiculous," Simonov muttered under his breath, clearly irritated.

"It's not just ridiculous—it's downright inappropriate," Trudolyubov declared, looking directly at me with a disapproving frown. "We came here as friends to give a farewell dinner for a comrade, and now you're disrupting everything. You invited yourself here, so at least don't ruin the mood."

"That's enough!" Zverkov said firmly. "Let's move on, gentlemen. I've got a story for you about how I almost got married the day before yesterday."

Zverkov launched into an exaggerated tale, supposedly about nearly getting married, though it was less about the wedding and more about the prominent generals, colonels, and court officials he had rubbed shoulders with. He made himself out to be a central figure among these high-ranking individuals. His story was met with laughter and applause. Ferfitchkin squealed with delight, as though it were the funniest thing he'd ever heard.

No one paid the slightest attention to me. I sat there, crushed and humiliated.

"Good heavens," I thought, "these are not my kind of people. What a fool I've made of myself in front of them! I let Ferfitchkin insult me too much, and they probably think they're doing me a favor by letting me sit at their table. They don't realize it's an honor for them, not for me! And Zverkov noticed everything—the yellow stain on my trousers, my shabby appearance. Damn it all! What's the point of staying here? I should get up right now, grab my hat, and leave without saying a word. Tomorrow, I'll send a challenge. Let them see who I am! As if I care about the seven roubles—they can keep them. I'll walk out with my dignity intact!"

But of course, I stayed. I drank glass after glass of sherry and Lafitte, trying to drown my discomfort. Unaccustomed to alcohol, I quickly felt its effects, and my irritation only grew. The wine stirred up a reckless urge in me—to insult them all, spectacularly, and then storm out. I imagined myself seizing the moment, making a scene so dramatic and cutting that they'd have no choice but to admit, "He's sharp, even if he's absurd." I wanted to prove something, even if only to myself. And yet, as the thought burned in my mind, all I could do was sit there and seethe.

I scanned them all with a bold and insolent gaze, though my eyes were heavy and tired. They seemed to have completely forgotten my presence. They were loud, cheerful, and completely engrossed in their conversation. Zverkov, as usual, was dominating the discussion. I started to listen. He was boasting about some lively woman who had finally confessed her love for him (an obvious lie) and how his friend, a certain Prince Kolya, an officer in the hussars who owned three thousand serfs, had helped him in his conquest.

"And yet this Prince Kolya, with all his three thousand serfs, hasn't even shown up tonight to bid you farewell," I cut in abruptly.

For a moment, everyone fell silent.

"You're already drunk," Trudolyubov said at last, throwing me a disdainful glance. Zverkov, without a word, looked me over like I was some kind of insect. I dropped my eyes, humiliated. Simonov quickly began refilling glasses with champagne.

Trudolyubov raised his glass, and everyone except me followed suit.

"To your health and good fortune on your journey!" he said loudly to Zverkov. "To old times and the future—cheers!"

They all drained their glasses and crowded around Zverkov to embrace him. I remained still, my glass untouched before me.

"What, you're not drinking?" Trudolyubov growled, losing patience as he turned toward me threateningly.

"I have a separate toast to make, on my own," I said, my voice trembling with irritation, "and then I'll drink it."

"Spiteful fool," Simonov muttered under his breath.

I straightened in my chair, gripping my glass tightly, preparing for something dramatic—though I had no idea what I was going to say.

"Silence!" shouted Ferfitchkin mockingly. "Let's hear his brilliant speech!"

Zverkov watched me with a serious expression, fully aware of what was coming.

"Lieutenant Zverkov," I began, "let me first say that I despise empty phrases, empty talkers, and men who wear corsets. That's my first point, and there's a second one."

The room stirred uncomfortably.

"Second, I despise vulgarity and vulgar people—especially vulgar people. And third, I value justice, truth, and honesty above all else." My voice wavered slightly as I spoke; I was starting to feel horrified at my own words, unsure why I was even saying them. "I love deep thought, Monsieur Zverkov. I love genuine camaraderie on equal terms. But ... well ... I'll drink to you anyway, Mr. Zverkov. Here's to your health! Seduce all the Circassian girls you want, shoot the enemies of the fatherland, and ... and ... to your health, Monsieur Zverkov!"

Zverkov stood up slowly, bowing slightly toward me. His face had gone pale with offense.

"Thank you very much," he said coldly.

"Damn him!" shouted Trudolyubov, slamming his fist on the table.

"He deserves to be punched for that!" squealed Ferfitchkin.

"We should kick him out," muttered Simonov angrily.

"Not a word, gentlemen, no action!" Zverkov declared solemnly, silencing their outrage. "Thank you, but I can show him myself how little his words mean to me."

"Mr. Ferfitchkin," I said loudly, turning toward him with a strained dignity, "you will give me satisfaction tomorrow for the insult you've just delivered."

"A duel, you mean? Of course," Ferfitchkin answered with a sneer. But it was clear my challenge was so absurd, given my appearance, that the entire table erupted in laughter, including Ferfitchkin himself.

"Leave him alone. He's drunk," Trudolyubov said with open disgust.

"I'll never forgive myself for letting him join us," Simonov muttered once again.

"Now's the time to throw a bottle at their heads," I thought bitterly. I grabbed the bottle in front of me but ended up pouring myself another glass instead. "No, I'll stay to the end," I resolved. "They'd be thrilled if I walked out now. Nothing will make me leave. I'll sit here drinking to prove I don't care about them at all. This is a public place, after all, and I've paid to be here. I'll sit, drink, and maybe even sing if I feel like it. Yes, sing! I have the right to sing if I want to…"

But I didn't sing. Instead, I kept my eyes down, trying not to look at anyone. I forced myself to act indifferent and waited for them to speak to me first. But they didn't. Oh, how I wished at that moment they would say something—anything—to break the silence.

The clock struck eight, then nine. They moved from the table to the sofa, leaving me behind. Zverkov stretched out lazily on a lounge chair, placing one foot on the round table in front of him. He ordered three bottles of wine for the group—on his own tab, of course. Naturally, I wasn't invited to join them. They sat around him on the sofa, listening to him speak with almost reverent attention. It was obvious they adored him.

"Why?" I wondered to myself. "What do they see in him?"

From time to time, their drunken excitement bubbled over, and they kissed each other in fits of camaraderie. They discussed the Caucasus, debated the meaning of true passion, bragged about cozy government jobs, and marveled at the wealth of a hussar named Podharzhevsky—someone none of them had ever actually met. They even admired the supposed beauty of a Princess D., though none of them had seen her in person. Eventually, the conversation turned to the immortality of Shakespeare.

I smiled with contempt and started pacing back and forth across the room, deliberately on the opposite side from the sofa where they all sat. I moved from the table to the stove and back again, trying my best to show them I didn't need their attention. I made as much noise as possible with my boots, stomping my heels against the floor, hoping they would notice. But it was pointless. They completely ignored me.

For three long hours, from eight o'clock until eleven, I walked back and forth in that small space, stubbornly pacing from the table to the stove. I told myself, "I'm walking because I want to, and no one can stop me." A waiter came into the room occasionally and would pause to watch me as if I were some spectacle. The constant turning made me dizzy, and at times I felt like I was in a fever dream. Throughout those three hours, I was drenched in sweat, dried off, and soaked again three separate times.

As I paced, an agonizing thought pierced me: ten years, twenty years, forty years could pass, and I would still look back on this moment with shame and disgust. I would always remember it as one of the most humiliating, pathetic, and ridiculous times of my life. I was painfully aware of how much I had degraded myself, yet I continued pacing from the table to the stove, unable to stop. "If only you knew how intelligent and cultured I truly am," I thought, silently addressing the sofa where my so-called enemies lounged. But they acted like I wasn't even in the room.

Only once during those hours did they seem to acknowledge me. It was when Zverkov was talking about Shakespeare, and I suddenly let out a sarcastic laugh. It was forced and unpleasant, even to me.

They all paused, turning toward me and watching silently as I continued my pacing for two whole minutes. For a brief moment, I thought something might happen. But nothing did. They quickly returned to their conversation, ignoring me once more.

By the time the clock struck eleven, Zverkov jumped up from the sofa.

"Friends," he announced, "let's head out now, shall we?"

"Absolutely," the others agreed, immediately following his lead.

In that moment, I couldn't hold back any longer. Exhausted, humiliated, and desperate, I turned sharply to Zverkov. My body was drenched in sweat, my hair clung to my forehead, and I felt like I might collapse at any second.

"Zverkov, I owe you an apology," I said, my voice resolute but shaky. "And you too, Ferfitchkin. In fact, I apologize to all of you. I insulted you all."

"Aha! So a duel isn't really your thing, is it?" Ferfitchkin sneered, his voice dripping with venom.

The words cut deeply, like a knife.

"No, Ferfitchkin, I'm not afraid of a duel!" I shot back. "I'll prove it to you tomorrow. After we reconcile, I'll challenge you to a duel. You'll shoot first, and I'll fire into the air to show I'm not afraid."

"He's trying to console himself," Simonov said coldly.

"He's just rambling nonsense now," added Trudolyubov.

"Move aside! Why are you blocking our way? What do you want from us?" Zverkov demanded with a tone of disdain.

Their faces were flushed, their eyes bright from all the wine they had consumed.

"I want your friendship, Zverkov," I said, my voice trembling. "I insulted you earlier, but I want to make amends."

"Insult me?" Zverkov responded with a sneer. "Understand this: you could never, under any circumstances, insult me."

"And that's the end of it. Now, get out of the way," Trudolyubov added, his tone dismissive.

"Olympia is mine, friends, agreed?" Zverkov declared, already turning away from me.

"No argument from us! She's all yours," the others replied, laughing as they followed him out.

I stood there, feeling completely humiliated, as if I had been spat on. The group left the room loudly, laughing and joking. Trudolyubov started singing some ridiculous song as they walked out. Simonov stayed behind briefly to tip the waiters. Without thinking, I suddenly approached him.

"Simonov, lend me six roubles!" I demanded with desperate determination.

He stared at me in shock, his eyes blank and uncomprehending. He was clearly drunk too.

"You're not serious about coming with us, are you?" he asked, his tone sharp.

"Yes, I am," I replied.

"I don't have any money," he said dismissively, letting out a scornful laugh before turning to leave.

I grabbed his coat in desperation, refusing to let him go. The whole moment felt like a horrible nightmare.

"Simonov, I saw you had money!" I pleaded. "Why are you denying me? Do you think I'm a scoundrel? Don't refuse me—if you only knew why I need it! My whole future, everything I've planned, depends on this!"

Simonov sighed, pulled out the money, and practically threw it at me.

"Take it, if you have no shame," he said coldly, his words cutting like a knife. Then, without waiting for a response, he hurried to catch up with the others.

For a moment, I was left alone in the room. It was a mess—dirty dishes from the dinner, a broken wine glass on the floor, spilled wine staining the tablecloth, cigarette butts scattered everywhere. The air was heavy with the smell of alcohol, and my head spun from the chaos and humiliation. Misery weighed down on my heart like a stone. Even the waiter, who had witnessed everything, stood nearby, staring at me with a curious expression.

"I'm going!" I shouted suddenly, my voice trembling with emotion. "Either they'll all get down on their knees and beg for my friendship, or I'll slap Zverkov in the face!"

Chapter 5

I stumbled down the stairs, muttering to myself, "So this is it, real life at last." I felt an almost sarcastic comparison in my head. "This is nothing like imagining the Pope leaving Rome for Brazil or some elegant ball on Lake Como!"

"You're a coward if you laugh at this moment," a voice in my mind accused me.

"No matter!" I shouted back at myself. "Everything's ruined now!"

The group was nowhere to be seen, but that didn't bother me—I already knew where they had gone. Outside, a lone sled driver stood waiting, wrapped in a rough peasant coat dusted with wet, heavy snow that kept falling in clumps. The air was hot and steamy, almost suffocating. His little piebald horse was also covered in snow, coughing now and then—a detail I remember vividly. I lunged toward the shabby sled but froze as soon as I lifted my foot to climb in. The memory of Simonov giving me six roubles slammed into me, filling me with shame. I collapsed into the sled as if I were nothing more than a sack of potatoes.

"No! I have to make up for everything," I shouted aloud. "I'll fix it all tonight or die trying. Drive!"

The sled jerked forward, the reins snapping tight, and my thoughts began spinning out of control.

"They won't beg for my friendship—that's just a pathetic illusion, some stupid, romantic fantasy, like the Lake Como nonsense. No, I have to slap Zverkov's face. That's my duty now. It's settled—I'm flying there to slap him. Faster!"

The driver urged the horse onward, its hooves crunching through the snow.

"When I get there, I'll walk straight in and slap him. Should I say something first? No, no speeches. I'll just walk in and do it. They'll all be sitting in the drawing room, and Zverkov will be on the sofa with Olympia. That awful Olympia! She once laughed at my looks and turned me down. Maybe I'll pull her hair too—or yank Zverkov's ear! No, just one ear—that'll be enough. I'll drag him around the room by it."

My thoughts spiraled further into chaos.

"Of course, they'll probably gang up on me and beat me senseless. Trudolyubov will hit the hardest—he's the strongest. Ferfitchkin will grab at my hair like the coward he is. But none of that matters! I'll get the first move; I'll land the slap. That's what counts. By the rules of honor, the slap will mark him forever. He'll have no choice but to fight me. They can beat me up all they want—let them! At least they'll have to see the tragic hero I've become!"

I yelled at the driver to hurry. Startled, he snapped the reins again and flicked his whip.

"We'll fight at dawn. It's already decided. I'm done with the office anyway—Ferfitchkin mocked me about it earlier. But wait—where will I get pistols? My salary? I'll take an advance and buy them. What about powder and bullets? That's the second's job. But who'll be my second? I don't have friends. No, no, that doesn't matter! The first person I find on the street will have to do it. People are bound to help, like pulling a drowning man out of the water. Strange things happen all the time. Maybe I'll even ask the director to be my second—he'd have to agree out of honor, wouldn't he? Yes, Anton Antonitch!"

Even as these wild ideas consumed me, a darker realization crept in. I knew—more clearly than anything—that my entire plan was absurd. It was ridiculous, shameful even. But I kept going, whipping my mind into a frenzy.

"Faster, you fool! Get going!" I screamed at the driver.

"Alright, alright, sir," he muttered, his voice tired as he pushed the little horse onward.

A sudden chill ran through me. Should I just go home instead? My God, why did I invite myself to this dinner? But no, I can't turn back now. All those hours I spent pacing back and forth from the table to the stove—they must pay for that humiliation! They have to make up for this disgrace. Drive on!

But what if they call the authorities? No, they wouldn't dare. They'd be too scared of causing a scene. And what if Zverkov is so arrogant that he refuses to fight a duel? He probably will. If that happens, I'll show them all! I'll follow him to the post station tomorrow when he's leaving. I'll grab his leg as he's getting into the carriage, pull his coat off, bite his hand if I have to. "See how far you've pushed a desperate man!" I'll shout. Even if they hit me and throw me to the ground, I'll yell to the crowd, "Look at this coward, running off to chase Circassian girls after letting me spit in his face!"

Of course, that will ruin everything for me. My job will be gone; I'll be fired, arrested, and sent to Siberia. But even that doesn't matter. Fifteen years later, when I'm released, I'll track him down. I'll find him living happily in some small town, married with a grown-up daughter. I'll stand before him, a broken man in rags, and say, "Look at me! See what you've done! I've lost my career, my happiness, my dreams, and even love—all because of you. Here are the pistols. I've come to end this once and for all. But instead, I forgive you." Then I'll fire into the air and disappear from his life forever.

Tears welled up in my eyes as I imagined this, even though I knew I was acting out a scene straight from Pushkin's Silvio or Lermontov's Masquerade. Suddenly, shame washed over me. I stopped the sled, jumped out, and stood still in the snow, right there in the middle of the street. The driver looked at me, sighing, confused.

What was I supposed to do now? I couldn't keep going—that would be foolish. But I couldn't just leave things unfinished either. That would look like cowardice. How could I walk away after being insulted like this? "No!" I shouted, climbing back into the sled. "It's meant to be! It's fate! Drive on, now!"

In my frustration, I punched the driver lightly on the back of the neck.

"What are you doing? Why are you hitting me?" he shouted, but he whipped the horse, making it trot faster.

The wet snow kept falling in heavy flakes. I unbuttoned my coat, not caring about the cold. I didn't care about anything else now because I had made up my mind. The slap was going to happen. I felt it deep inside me, terrifying and unstoppable, like it was fated. The dim streetlamps flickered through the snowy darkness, glowing like funeral torches. The snow crept under my coat and scarf, melting against my skin. I didn't bother to button up again. It didn't matter anymore. Everything was already lost.

Finally, we arrived. I stumbled out of the sled, barely aware of myself, and rushed up the steps, pounding and kicking at the door. My whole body felt weak, especially my legs, which seemed ready to give out under me. The door opened quickly, as if they had been expecting me. Simonov must have warned them that another guest might show up. This was one of those so-called "millinery establishments," which the police had shut down long ago. By day, it operated as a shop, but at night, if you had the right connections, you could visit it for other purposes.

I walked quickly through the dark shop into the familiar drawing room. Only one candle was burning, casting dim light across the space, and I stopped in surprise. The room was empty. "Where are they?" I asked someone nearby. But of course, they had already gone their separate ways. Standing before me was the madam herself, wearing a dull smile. She recognized me from previous visits. A moment later, another person entered the room.

Ignoring everyone, I began pacing around, muttering to myself. I felt as though I had just been saved from something terrible, like escaping death at the last moment, and the realization filled me with a strange, almost joyous relief. I would have done it—I would have slapped him! I was certain of it. But now they were gone, and everything felt different, like the tension had evaporated into thin air.

I glanced around, trying to process what had just happened. My thoughts were still scattered. Mechanically, my eyes fell on the girl who had just entered. She had a pale face, straight dark eyebrows, and serious eyes that seemed thoughtful, almost questioning. Something about her gaze pulled me in immediately. I knew I would have hated her if she had been smiling. Slowly, I focused on her, forcing myself to look at her more closely. My mind was still a mess, and I was trying to make sense of it all.

Her face had a certain simplicity, an honest and kind expression, but it was overshadowed by a solemn gravity that didn't belong in a place like this. It must have made her stand out, and yet I was sure none of the other fools here had noticed her. She wasn't exactly beautiful, but she was tall, strong, and carried herself with a quiet strength. Her outfit was plain, but it suited her. Something dark stirred inside me as I looked at her. Without hesitation, I walked straight toward her.

As I moved, my reflection in a nearby mirror caught my eye. My face looked terrible—pale, exhausted, and twisted with anger and shame. My hair was messy, adding to my pitiful appearance. I stared at my reflection and felt repulsed, but instead of feeling ashamed, I found myself thinking, "Good. I'm glad I look awful. I want her to find me disgusting. I like that."

Chapter 6

Somewhere behind a screen, a clock let out a wheezing sound, like it was struggling, as if someone were choking it. The wheezing dragged on unnaturally long before it was followed by a sharp, unpleasant chime, as though someone had leapt forward unexpectedly. It struck two. I came to, though I hadn't really been asleep—just lying in a half-conscious daze.

The narrow, cramped room felt even more suffocating in the dim light. It was packed with an enormous wardrobe, piles of cardboard boxes, and all kinds of useless clutter. A tiny candle stub on the table flickered weakly, struggling to stay lit, and I knew it wouldn't last much longer. Soon, the room would be completely dark.

I quickly regained full awareness, and everything from the day before came flooding back to me instantly, as though it had been lying in wait. Even while I'd been half-conscious, one thought had stayed anchored in my mind, around which my hazy dreams had swirled. Strangely, everything that had happened earlier now felt like it belonged to a distant past, as though I had lived it years ago and left it behind.

My head felt heavy, clouded. Something seemed to hover over me, stirring up my thoughts and agitating me. Misery and bitterness churned inside me, looking for a way out. Then, suddenly, I noticed a pair of wide-open eyes staring at me. They were cold, detached, and utterly distant, scrutinizing me in a way that felt oppressive.

A dark thought crept over me, chilling me to my core, like the feeling of stepping into a damp, moldy cellar. There was something unnatural in those eyes, something unsettling about how they had begun to focus on me only now. I realized, with a shudder, that I hadn't spoken a single word to this person during the past two hours. I hadn't even thought it necessary. In fact, the silence had somehow pleased me. But now, an ugly, crawling thought came over me—like a spider scuttling across my mind. I was struck by the loathsome idea of vice, of a connection without love, starting with what love itself considers its purest expression.

For a long while, we just stared at each other. Her eyes didn't look away, nor did her expression change, until eventually, I began to feel uncomfortable.

"What's your name?" I asked abruptly, hoping to break the tension.

"Liza," she answered softly, almost in a whisper, but without any warmth. She turned her gaze away.

I didn't say anything for a moment.

"What awful weather," I muttered, more to myself than to her, as I rested my arm beneath my head and stared at the ceiling. "The snow… it's disgusting."

She didn't respond. Her silence was unbearable.

"Have you always lived in Petersburg?" I asked after a pause, my tone sharper now, as if annoyed.

"No."

"Where are you from?"

"Riga," she replied curtly.

"Are you German?"

"No, Russian."

"How long have you been here?"

"Where?"

"In this house."

"Two weeks."

Her answers grew shorter and more clipped. The candle flickered one last time and went out, plunging the room into darkness. I could no longer see her face.

"Do you have parents?" I asked.

"Yes… no… I do."

"Where are they?"

"In Riga."

"What do they do?"

"Nothing."

"Nothing? What kind of people are they?"

"Tradespeople."

"Did you live with them?"

"Yes."

"How old are you?"

"Twenty."

"Why did you leave them?"

"No reason."

That answer felt like a plea: "Leave me alone. I feel sick and sad."

We sat in silence again.

For some reason, I couldn't bring myself to leave. I felt a growing heaviness in my chest, a sense of sickness and gloom. Memories of the previous day started to flash through my mind, jumbled and disorganized. Suddenly, I remembered something I had seen that morning while rushing anxiously to the office.

"I saw them carrying a coffin yesterday, and they almost dropped it," I said aloud, without really meaning to start a conversation.

"A coffin?"

"Yes, in the Haymarket. They were bringing it up from a basement."

"A basement?"

"Well, not exactly a basement, but a place below street level... you know, from a filthy house. It was disgusting. The ground around it was covered in trash, eggshells, and reeking garbage. The smell was unbearable."

She didn't respond. The silence stretched on.

"It was an awful day for a burial," I said, trying again to fill the quiet.

"Why awful?" she asked after a pause.

"The snow. The slush," I said, yawning.

"It doesn't matter," she said after another brief silence.

"It's terrible," I replied, yawning again. "The gravediggers must have cursed about working in the freezing wet snow. The grave must have been filled with water."

"Why would there be water in the grave?" she asked, her tone sharp and curious.

Her harshness provoked me.

"Because there's always water at the bottom of the graves in Volkovo Cemetery. You can't dig a dry one there."

"Why?"

"Why? Because the ground there is waterlogged. It's practically a swamp. So, they bury people in water. I've seen it myself... plenty of times."

(That wasn't true; I had never been to Volkovo Cemetery. I'd only heard about it.)

"Do you mean you don't care about how you'll die?" I asked.

"Why should I die?" she said defensively.

"Well, someday you'll die, just like that woman did. She was a girl like you. She died of consumption."

"A wench would have died in a hospital..." she muttered, as if she already knew how things worked. She didn't say "girl" but "wench."

"She owed money to her madam," I replied, irritated by her tone. "She kept working for her even though she was sick with consumption. Some sledge-drivers were talking about it outside, joking with a couple of soldiers. They said she worked until the very end, and then laughed about it. They were planning to meet later in a tavern to drink to her memory."

A lot of this was something I'd made up on the spot. Silence followed, a heavy, oppressive silence. She didn't move.

"And do you think it's better to die in a hospital?" I asked.

"Isn't it the same?" she shot back. "Besides, why should I die?"

"If not now, then a little later," I said.

"Why later?"

"Why not? You're young now, pretty, fresh. You fetch a high price. But in a year? Things will be different. You'll change."

"In a year?"

"Yes. A year from now, you'll be worth less," I said, my voice growing cruel. "You'll leave this place and end up in a worse one. A year after that, you'll go somewhere even lower, and in seven years, you'll end up in some basement in the Haymarket. That's if you're lucky. It could be worse. Maybe you'll get sick—consumption, perhaps—or catch a chill. In your line of work, illnesses don't go away easily. You might not recover. And then, you'd die."

"Fine, then I'll die," she snapped, her voice sharp with anger. She shifted suddenly, as if to dismiss me.

"But isn't it sad?"

"Sad for who?"

"Sad for life," I said. Silence stretched between us.

"Have you ever been engaged?" I asked suddenly. "Huh?"

"What's it to you?"

"Oh, I'm not interrogating you," I said, frustrated. "It's none of my business. Why are you so upset? I just thought… maybe you've had your share of hardships. What's it to me? I only felt sorry."

"Sorry for who?"

"Sorry for you."

"There's no need," she whispered so softly it was barely audible. She shifted again, just slightly.

Her indifference made me angry. What? I'd been so patient, and yet she...

"Do you really think this is the right path for you?" I asked.

"I don't think anything."

"That's the problem—you don't think. You need to realize it while there's still time. There's still time for you. You're young, you're beautiful. You could fall in love, get married, and be happy…"

"Not all married women are happy," she snapped, her tone sharp and abrupt like before.

"Not all, of course," I replied, "but it's still so much better than the life here—infinitely better. With love, you can live even without happiness. Even in sorrow, life can be sweet; it's still life. But here? What do you have here except filth and misery? It's disgusting!" I turned away in revulsion. I wasn't speaking rationally anymore. My emotions were taking over, and I felt heated as I spoke. It was as though I'd been waiting for an opportunity to share these thoughts I had brooded over in my isolation. Suddenly, I felt a purpose—an audience for my words.

"Don't pay attention to the fact that I'm here," I continued. "I'm not an example for you to follow. I might even be worse than you. I was drunk when I came here, though," I quickly added in my defense. "Besides, it's not the same for a man as it is for a woman. I might degrade myself, but I'm not enslaved to anyone. I can leave whenever I want, and that's the end of it. I can shake it off and move on. But for you, it's slavery from the start. Yes, slavery! You give up everything—your freedom, your choices. If you try to escape later, you won't be able to. The chains will only get tighter. It's a cursed life. I know what I'm talking about."

I paused, but she said nothing, only stared at me silently, deeply engrossed. "And I won't even talk about everything else, since you might not understand. But tell me—are you in debt to your madam? See?" I said, even though she didn't answer. "That's what slavery is. You'll never buy your freedom. They'll make sure of that. It's like selling your soul to the devil. And maybe I'm no better off. Maybe I wallow in the mud out of despair, just like you. People drink to drown their sorrows; maybe I'm here for the same reason."

I stopped pacing and looked directly at her. "Tell me, what good is there in this place? Look at what just happened with us. We were together, but we didn't say a single word to each other the whole time. Only afterward did you start staring at me like some wild animal, and I stared back at you. Was that love? Is that how one human being is supposed to connect with another? It's disgusting—that's what it is."

"Yes," she said quickly and firmly, almost cutting me off.

Her immediate agreement surprised me. I hadn't expected such a prompt response. Could she have been thinking the same thing when she was staring at me earlier? Maybe she was capable of deeper thoughts after all. A thrill of interest stirred in me—this was a connection, a point of understanding! And, truthfully, the idea of influencing her, of exerting some power over her, was irresistible.

She leaned slightly closer, and I thought I could see her propping herself up on her arm in the dim light. Perhaps she was studying me carefully. I wished desperately that I could see her eyes. Her deep, steady breathing filled the silence.

"Why did you come here?" I asked her, my tone growing firmer, almost commanding.

"I don't know," she replied flatly.

"But wouldn't it be so much better to live at home with your father? It's warm there, and it's your own place."

"What if it's worse than this?" she shot back.

Her answer gave me pause. "I need to strike the right tone," I thought. "Sentimentality won't work." But the thought passed quickly. She intrigued me, and my curiosity about her was genuine. Besides, I was tired and emotional, and sometimes feeling and cunning go hand in hand.

"Anything is possible," I said quickly, trying to keep her engaged. "I'm sure someone has wronged you. You're more a victim of circumstances than anything else. I don't know your story, but it's hard to imagine a girl like you coming to a place like this willingly."

"A girl like me?" she whispered softly. I could barely hear her, but the words reached me.

I hesitated. Was I flattering her? Maybe I was, but perhaps it wasn't a bad thing. She didn't respond further.

"Listen, Liza," I said, leaning forward slightly. "If I'd had a home as a child, I wouldn't be the person I am now. I think about that often. No matter how bad things are at home, at least you have parents. They're not strangers or enemies. Once in a while, they show you love. At least you know you belong somewhere. I grew up without a home, and maybe that's why I've become so... cold."

I waited for her to say something, but she stayed silent. "Maybe she doesn't understand me," I thought. "Maybe this is all pointless, just moralizing."

"If I were a father and had a daughter," I said, changing tack and speaking more casually, "I think I'd love her more than my sons."

"Why?" she asked, her interest piqued.

So she was listening! Encouraged, I continued, "I don't know, Liza. I knew a man once, a strict and serious father, but when it came to his daughter, he would kneel before her and kiss her hands and feet. He adored her. When she danced at parties, he would stand and watch her for hours without moving. He loved her so much that nothing else mattered. She was his everything."

I paused, letting the image sink in. "He wore old, shabby clothes and was stingy with everyone else, but he'd spend his last penny to buy her expensive gifts, just to see her smile. Fathers always love their daughters more than their mothers do. Some girls live happily at home, Liza. That's what I believe."

"And you wouldn't let your daughter marry?" she asked, a faint smile on her lips.

"Probably not," I admitted with a laugh. "I'd be too jealous. The thought of her kissing someone else, loving a stranger more than her own father... it would break my heart. Of course, I'd have to let her marry eventually. But I'd spend every moment worrying, finding faults in all her suitors. And yet, in the end, I'd let her marry the one she truly loved. Funny thing is, the man she loved would probably seem like the worst choice to me. That's how it always is. So many family troubles come from that."

"Some people would rather sell their daughters than marry them off honorably."

Ah, so that's what she thought!

"Liza, that kind of thing happens in cursed families where there's no love and no faith," I said passionately. "Without love, there's no reason or sense. Yes, such families exist, but I'm not talking about them. You must have seen something terrible in your own family to think this way. Truly, you've been unlucky. Hm... that kind of thing often comes from poverty."

"And do you think it's any better among the rich? Even poor, honest people live happily."

"Yes, maybe you're right. But listen, Liza, people love to count their troubles but rarely count their joys. If they did, they'd see that every life has its share of happiness. What if a family is blessed? What if the husband is good, loves you, cares for you, and never leaves? There's happiness in such a family! Even amidst sorrow, happiness can be found—because sorrow exists everywhere. If you marry, you'll understand this yourself. Think of those early years of marriage with someone you love. What joy, what happiness there can be! In those days, even arguments with your husband end sweetly. I once knew a woman who would start fights with her husband just to show how much she loved him afterward. It was her way of saying, 'I love you so much that I'll make you feel it, even if it's through a little torment.' Women do that sometimes—they torment a man just to love him even more afterward. It's their way of showing devotion."

I paused and leaned forward slightly. "And imagine, Liza, how the whole house would light up because of you—happy, cheerful, peaceful, and respected by everyone. That's what happens when love is in a home. Though some women get jealous. I knew one who couldn't stand it if her husband went out. She'd wake up at night and sneak after him to see if he was with another woman. It's sad, but she couldn't help herself. Even though she knew it was wrong and it tore her apart, she did it because she loved him."

"And the best part," I continued, warming to my thoughts, "is making up after a fight. To admit you were wrong or to forgive him— it's so sweet. Suddenly, you're both happier than ever, as if you're starting fresh, like newlyweds all over again. That's the beauty of love—keeping it private and sacred, shared only between husband and wife. No one else needs to know what happens between you, not even your own parents. Love is a sacred bond, and keeping it hidden makes it stronger. Respect grows from that, and respect is the foundation of so much."

I paused again to let the words sink in. "And if there was love to begin with, why should it ever disappear? True love doesn't have to fade. The first rush of love might pass, yes, but then it deepens into something even more beautiful. It becomes a bond between two souls. You share everything—no secrets, no barriers. And when you have children, even the hardest times feel happy. When there's love and courage, even struggles can bring joy. You'll work hard for your children, maybe even go without, but it won't feel like a sacrifice. Your children will love you for it someday, and you'll see that you're building something for the future."

I looked at her closely now, my voice soft but firm. "When your children grow up, you'll see yourself in them. They'll carry your thoughts and values, and they'll even look like you. That's a great responsibility, Liza—a duty that brings parents closer together. People say having children is hard, but who says that? It's one of life's greatest joys! Do you like children, Liza? I love them. Imagine a little rosy baby boy in your arms, looking up at you. How can a father's heart not melt when he sees his wife nursing their child?"

I smiled faintly, lost in the image I was painting. "Picture it—a plump, rosy baby with tiny hands and feet, so small and perfect it makes you laugh. And its little eyes, as if it understands everything. While it nurses, it grabs at you with its little hands, plays, and laughs when its father comes close. It might even bite a little when its teeth are coming in, but it'll look at you as if to say, 'See, I'm teasing you!' Isn't that happiness? A family—husband, wife, and child—together. Those moments make everything worthwhile. You can forgive so much for the sake of love and those fleeting, precious times."

I leaned back, letting my voice soften, but keeping the same seriousness. "Liza, you need to learn how to truly live before you judge others. That's the most important thing."

"It's through pictures, pictures like this, that I can reach her," I thought to myself, even though I was speaking from the heart. All at once, though, my face flushed bright red. "What if she suddenly bursts out laughing? What would I do then?" The thought filled me with anger. Towards the end of my speech, I had felt genuinely moved, but now my pride had been pricked. The silence that followed felt unbearable. I almost nudged her to say something.

"Why are you—" she started but didn't finish. Yet, I understood what she meant. There was a tremor in her voice, different from before. It wasn't abrupt or harsh anymore; instead, it was soft and uncertain, almost shy. The change in her tone made me feel a sudden wave of shame and guilt.

"What is it?" I asked gently, curious but careful.

"Why, you..." she began again but hesitated.

"What?" I prompted.

"Why, you... speak as if you were reading from a book," she finally said. Her voice carried a faint trace of irony again.

Her words hit me like a blow. They were the last thing I expected.

What I didn't understand was that she was trying to hide her real feelings behind her sarcasm. For people like her—those with a modest and guarded soul—irony is often the final shield they use when someone gets too close to their innermost thoughts. Their pride won't let them reveal their emotions right away, and they shrink from baring their heart in front of others. I should have realized this from the hesitant way she had approached her sarcasm earlier. Each time, she had seemed to hold back before finally letting it out, almost as if it cost her an effort to say it. But I didn't recognize the truth, and instead, an unpleasant, bitter feeling crept over me.

"Just wait," I thought.

Chapter 7

I leaned back and lowered my voice, but it remained firm. "Oh, Liza, how can you talk about being like a book when even I, an outsider, feel sick thinking about it? And I'm not even an outsider, because this cuts straight to my heart. How can you not feel disgusted being here? It seems that habit really can work miracles. Who knows what it can do to a person? Do you seriously believe you'll stay young forever, that you'll always be beautiful, and that they'll keep you here as long as you want? I won't even speak about the filth of this life, but I'll say this—right now, you're young, lovely, full of soul and feelings, but even so, the moment I came to my senses earlier, I felt sick at being here with you. This is the kind of place a man only comes to when he's drunk.

But if you were somewhere else, living like a decent person, I might fall for you. I'd be happy just to see you, to get a single word from you. I'd wait by your door, kneel before you, and consider it an honor if you accepted me as your fiancé. I wouldn't even dare to have an unclean thought about you. But here, it's different. Here, I only have to whistle, and you have to come, whether you like it or not. Your wishes don't matter, only mine. Even the lowest laborer can choose to leave his job, but you? When are you ever free? Think about what you're giving up here. You're not just a slave with your body— you've given up your soul. You've sold it, and no one has the right to do that. You let anyone, even the most worthless drunkard, take your love and throw it away.

Do you even realize how precious love is? It's like a priceless diamond. It's a treasure. Men would give up their very souls to earn true love. But what does your love mean now? You're completely sold—body and soul—and no one needs love from you when they can have everything without it. That's the biggest insult to a woman. Do you understand? And yet they trick you here, telling you that you can have a lover of your own. But you know that's a joke, right? It's all fake. They're mocking you, and you fall for it. Do you think he really loves you? How could he, knowing you can be taken away from him at any moment? No man who respects himself would love under those circumstances. He probably just uses you, maybe even steals from you. If he doesn't beat you, consider yourself lucky. Ask him if he'll marry you—he'd probably laugh in your face. Maybe he'd even hit you. And for what? For a little bit of comfort, for some meals they give you? Do you think that's worth ruining your life over?

Even the food they give you comes with a price. A decent girl couldn't stomach it, knowing why she's being fed. You're in debt here, and you'll stay in debt. That's how they keep you. And eventually, even the men who come here will start to look down on you. That won't take long. Time passes quickly in a place like this. Soon, you'll be thrown out, not just quietly either. The madam will start yelling at you, blaming you as if you've ruined her, when it's you who's sacrificed everything for her. And don't expect your coworkers to stand up for you—they'll turn on you to gain favor with her. Everyone here is trapped. They've lost their conscience, their pity, everything.

And what are you giving up here? Everything. Your youth, your health, your beauty, your hope. By the time you're twenty-two, you'll look like you're thirty-five. If you're lucky, you won't be sick. Pray for that. Right now, you think this is an easy life, don't you? No work to do, nothing to worry about. But this is the hardest, most degrading work in the world. Even your heart will wear out from all the tears. And when the time comes that they kick you out, you won't even be able to say a word. You'll leave as if you're the one to blame. Then you'll move to another house, then another, and eventually, you'll end up in the Haymarket. There, you'll be beaten regularly because that's just how they treat women there. You don't believe it? Go see for yourself.

Once, on New Year's Day, I saw a woman outside. They'd thrown her out as a joke into the freezing cold because she'd been crying too much. She was drunk by nine in the morning, half-naked, with bruises all over her. Her face was powdered, but she had a black eye, and her teeth were bleeding. A cabman had just beaten her up. She was sitting on some steps, holding a salt fish in her hand, wailing about her bad luck, and banging the fish on the steps. Drunken soldiers and cab drivers were standing around laughing at her. Do you think that could never happen to you? Maybe it couldn't. But what if, ten years ago, that very same woman had been like you? Maybe she came here, fresh-faced and innocent, thinking she'd never end up like the others. And yet, look where she ended up.

And what if, even as she sat there on those filthy steps, she remembered the time she lived with her family? Back when she'd go to school, and the boy next door would wait for her, saying he'd love her forever. What if she recalled all of that, only to realize what she'd lost?

No, Liza. It would almost be better if you died young, in some corner or basement. Maybe in a hospital, if they'll even take you. But do you think the madam will let you go so easily? No, not as long as you're useful to her. Consumption doesn't take you quickly; it lets you hope until the very end. That's exactly what she counts on. But when you're dying and can't give her anything anymore, then everyone will turn away from you. No one will give you a drink of water without cursing you first, saying, 'When will you finally die, you wretch? You're making us sick with your moaning.'"

I have heard things like that myself, and they're true. When you're dying, they'll shove you into some filthy corner of a damp, dark cellar. What will you think about, lying there all alone? When you die, strangers will prepare your body with impatience, annoyed by the task. No one will bless you, no one will mourn you. All they'll care about is getting rid of you quickly. They'll buy a cheap coffin, take you to the grave like they did with that poor woman today, and then they'll celebrate your memory by drinking at the tavern.

At the cemetery, there will be sleet, wet snow, and filth. No one will go out of their way to care. "Lower her down, Vanuha; she's unlucky, even in death—she's gone headfirst into the grave, the poor fool." "Shorten the rope, you idiot." "It's fine as it is." "Fine? Look, she's lying on her side! She was a human being, after all. Oh, never mind, just throw the dirt on her." They won't waste much time arguing about it. They'll toss the wet blue clay on the coffin as fast as possible and head straight to the tavern. And that will be the end of your memory on earth. Other women have children to visit their graves, or husbands, or parents to cry for them. But you? Not a single tear, not a single sigh, not a single memory. No one in the entire world will ever visit you. Your name will vanish as if you had never existed, as if you had never been born at all.

Even if you were to pound on your coffin lid in the night, screaming, "Let me out, kind people, let me live again in the light of day! My life wasn't a life at all. It was wasted, thrown away like trash, drunk away in the taverns of the Haymarket. Let me out, kind people, let me live!"—no one would hear you.

I was so worked up that I could feel a lump rising in my throat. Then, all at once, I stopped, sat upright, and bent forward, straining to listen. My heart was pounding, and for good reason—I felt uneasy.

I knew I was tearing apart her soul and breaking her heart, and the more certain I became of it, the more desperately I wanted to finish what I had started. I was caught up in the thrill of it—caught up in the power of my words—but it wasn't just a game.

I was aware that my words sounded stiff, even forced, as though I were reciting from a book. But I didn't care. I knew she would understand. I even thought that the formal tone might help me. But now that I had achieved my goal, panic suddenly overwhelmed me. I had never seen despair like this before.

She was lying face down, pressing her face into the pillow, clutching it with both hands as if holding on for dear life. Her whole body shook, as if in convulsions. Suppressed sobs burst from her chest, growing into wails. Then she buried her face deeper into the pillow, trying to hide her anguish, trying to keep anyone from hearing her cry. She bit the pillow, even her own hand until it bled (I noticed that later). Sometimes, she gripped her tangled hair with trembling fingers, holding her breath and clenching her teeth to keep her emotions in check.

I tried saying something to comfort her, to calm her, but my words felt wrong, and I didn't dare continue. A cold chill ran through me, almost like fear. In the dim light, I fumbled to get dressed as quickly as I could. But the room was too dark, and I kept stumbling. My hands finally found a box of matches and a candlestick with an unlit candle. When I struck the match and the room lit up, Liza suddenly sat up in bed. Her face was twisted with a strange, almost crazed smile, her eyes wide and wild.

I sat down next to her and took her hands in mine. She seemed to snap out of her daze and leaned slightly toward me, as if she wanted to hold me but didn't dare. Instead, she bowed her head, her fingers clutching mine tightly.

"Liza, I'm sorry. I was wrong. Forgive me," I said softly, but her grip only tightened, as if my words weren't enough. I fell silent, unsure of what to say.

"This is my address, Liza," I said finally, handing her a slip of paper. "Come find me."

"I will," she said firmly, her head still bowed.

"But I have to go now. Goodbye... until we meet again."

I stood up. She stood too, her face flushing bright red. She gave a small shiver, grabbed a shawl from a nearby chair, and wrapped it tightly around herself up to her chin. She tried to smile but it looked forced, almost painful. Her strange, embarrassed expression made me feel even worse.

I couldn't stand it any longer. I had to leave. I had to disappear.

"Wait a moment," she said suddenly, stopping me in the hallway just as I was about to leave. Her hand rested on my overcoat. She quickly put down the candle she was holding and ran off, as though she had just remembered something important or wanted to show me something. Her face flushed, her eyes sparkled, and there was a faint smile on her lips—what could that mean? Against my better judgment, I waited. A minute later, she returned, her expression soft and apologetic. It was as if she sought forgiveness for something. Her face was entirely different from the night before—no longer sullen, mistrustful, or stubborn. Her eyes, now warm and gentle, carried a timid but trusting look, the kind of gaze children reserve for those they love and hope to please. Her light hazel eyes were full of life, capable of both love and deep resentment.

Without saying a word, as though expecting me to understand everything without explanation, she handed me a piece of paper. Her face lit up with a naive, almost childlike triumph. I unfolded the paper. It was a letter, written by a medical student or someone similar. The letter was filled with dramatic, overly poetic language, yet it was deeply respectful. Though I no longer remember the exact words, I recall how genuine the feelings behind them seemed—something that could not have been faked. As I finished reading, I looked up to find her glowing eyes fixed intently on me, eager and impatient, waiting for my reaction.

In a hurried but joyful voice, tinged with pride, she explained the story. She had been to a dance at a private home hosted by a "very nice family who didn't know anything" about her situation. It was all still new to her, and she hadn't made up her mind to stay where she was. She insisted she planned to leave as soon as she paid off her debts. At the party, she had met the student, who danced with her the entire evening. They talked and discovered that they had known each other as children in Riga. He had even known her parents. Of course, he had no idea about her current circumstances. The day after the dance—three days ago—he sent her that letter through the friend who had brought her to the party. That was the whole story.

When she finished, she lowered her bright, shining eyes, almost shyly.

The poor girl had treasured that student's letter, likely her most precious possession. She had run to fetch it, desperate for me to see that she, too, was loved honestly and sincerely. She wanted me to know that someone had treated her with respect. She must have realized that the letter might never lead to anything, that it would stay in her box and remain just a memory. But even so, she would probably cherish it for the rest of her life, as proof of her worth and dignity. At that moment, she brought it to me with naive pride, hoping to raise herself in my eyes, to make me think well of her.

I said nothing. I simply pressed her hand and left. I wanted nothing more than to get away.

I walked all the way home, even though the heavy, wet snow continued to fall. I felt drained, both physically and emotionally. My mind was in chaos, but deep down, beneath the confusion, I already saw the truth—the vile, undeniable truth.

Chapter 8

When I woke up the next morning after a few hours of heavy, dreamless sleep, the events of the previous day came flooding back to me. I couldn't believe how sentimental I had been with Liza—those "outbursts of pity and horror." Disgusted with myself, I thought,

"What a ridiculous attack of hysterics, like some overly emotional woman! Pah!" I also wondered why I had given her my address. What if she came? Let her come—it didn't matter. But even that wasn't my main concern now. What truly mattered was saving my reputation with Zverkov and Simonov as soon as possible. That was my top priority, and I became so focused on it that I completely forgot about Liza for the rest of the morning.

My first step was to repay the money I had borrowed from Simonov the day before. I decided on a bold plan: I would borrow fifteen roubles from Anton Antonitch. Luckily, he was in an excellent mood that morning and gave me the money right away, without hesitation. I was so relieved and happy that, as I signed the IOU with a confident flourish, I casually mentioned, "Last night, I was out with some friends at the Hôtel de Paris. We were throwing a farewell party for an old comrade—actually, an old childhood friend. He's quite the character, you know—a bit of a wild one, spoiled rotten. Of course, he comes from a good family, has plenty of money, and a brilliant future ahead of him. He's witty, charming, a real ladies' man—you get the idea. We ended up having an extra half-dozen bottles of wine…"

I delivered this little speech effortlessly, with just the right mix of ease and self-satisfaction, and it went over perfectly.

When I got home, I immediately sat down to write a letter to Simonov. Even now, I can't help but admire the gentlemanly, good-natured tone I achieved in that letter. It was polite and tactful, without any unnecessary explanations. I apologized sincerely for everything that had happened. To defend myself (if I could even be allowed to defend myself, as I put it), I explained that I was completely unaccustomed to drinking and had already been tipsy after just one glass, which I had consumed while waiting for them at the Hôtel de Paris between five and six o'clock. I specifically apologized to Simonov and asked him to share my explanation with the others, especially Zverkov, whom, as I vaguely recalled "as though in a dream," I had insulted. I added that I would have gone to apologize in person, but I had a headache and couldn't bring myself to face them.

What pleased me most about the letter was its light, almost carefree tone, which was still respectful and well-mannered. It subtly conveyed that I didn't take the previous night's events as seriously as they might think. Far from being crushed or humiliated, I was treating the whole matter as any self-respecting gentleman would. "A young hero's past is never held against him," I thought with satisfaction as I reread the letter.

"There's something almost aristocratic about this tone," I told myself proudly. "It's all because I'm a cultured and educated man. Anyone else in my situation would have been lost, but I've managed to navigate this smoothly and come out unscathed. It's because I'm a 'man of intellect,' an 'educated person of our time.'" Then I began to wonder whether the wine really was to blame for my behavior the night before. After all, I hadn't had anything to drink between five and six while waiting for them. I had lied to Simonov—blatantly, shamelessly lied. And yet, even as I realized this, I wasn't the least bit ashamed.

But none of that mattered. The important thing was that I had dealt with the situation and put it behind me.

I put six roubles into the letter, sealed it, and handed it to Apollon, asking him to deliver it to Simonov. When he realized there was money inside, his attitude shifted, and he became more respectful, agreeing to take it. That evening, I went out for a walk. My head still ached, and I felt lightheaded from the events of the previous day. As the evening deepened and the twilight thickened, my thoughts and emotions became increasingly chaotic and hard to understand. Something deep inside me wouldn't let go, a restless unease in my heart and conscience that refused to die. It weighed on me, leaving me feeling deeply unsettled.

I wandered aimlessly through the busiest streets—Myeshtchansky Street, Sadovy Street, and Yusupov Garden—places always teeming with people at dusk. I'd always been drawn to these streets during this time, observing the crowds of workers heading home, their faces marked by weariness and worry. There was something oddly appealing about the raw, unvarnished reality of it all, the gritty, everyday bustle. But this time, the crowds and noise only irritated me. I couldn't figure out what was wrong with me. Something inside kept rising up, gnawing at my soul, and I couldn't make sense of it. I came home completely distraught, as though a terrible guilt or crime was pressing down on me.

The thought of Liza coming kept nagging at me. It was strange that out of everything that had happened the day before, her potential arrival seemed to haunt me the most, as if it existed apart from all my other memories. By evening, I had managed to forget everything else. I was even pleased with the letter I'd written to Simonov, but I couldn't shake this feeling of unease about Liza. "What if she comes?" I kept thinking. "Well, so what if she does? Let her come! But… it's awful to think of her seeing how I live." Yesterday, I had appeared almost heroic to her, but now? It would be humiliating for her to see my shabby room, the sofa with stuffing poking out, my tattered dressing gown, and even Apollon, who would surely insult her just to antagonize me. I could already see myself panicking, trying to act polite and cheerful, pulling my dressing gown around me, smiling nervously, and lying to cover my embarrassment. The thought disgusted me. But it wasn't just the embarrassment—it was something deeper, something more vile.

Then I stopped myself. "Why vile? Why dishonest?" I thought angrily. "I was sincere last night. I genuinely wanted to stir something noble in her. Her crying was good—it will do her some good." Yet the discomfort wouldn't leave me. Even when nine o'clock came and I convinced myself that it was too late for her to show up, she still lingered in my mind. Worse, the image that haunted me most vividly was her pale, tortured face when I struck the match last night. That unnatural, pitiful smile stuck with me. I didn't realize then that, even fifteen years later, I would still see her in my mind with that same heartbreaking, twisted smile.

The next day, I dismissed everything as foolishness, just an overreaction from my overly sensitive nerves. I was always aware of my tendency to exaggerate and worried about it. "I blow everything out of proportion—that's my problem," I told myself repeatedly. But despite these rationalizations, the thought that Liza might come wouldn't leave me. I grew restless, even angry at the possibility. "She'll come—she's bound to come!" I muttered, pacing the room. "If not today, then tomorrow. She'll find me out! Damn this romantic nonsense about pure hearts. How pathetic—how stupid!" Yet when I reached this point, I would stop short, feeling embarrassed and confused.

Occasionally, I toyed with the idea of going to see her myself—to explain everything and beg her not to visit me. But this thought filled me with such fury that I imagined if she were standing in front of me at that moment, I would insult her, throw her out, or worse.

As the days passed and she didn't come, I began to calm down. By nine o'clock each evening, I even felt bold and cheerful. I started daydreaming—sweet fantasies where I became her savior simply by talking to her. In these dreams, I educated her, guided her, and eventually noticed that she had fallen deeply in love with me. At first, I pretended not to understand her feelings—just for dramatic effect, I suppose. Finally, overcome with emotion, she would confess her love, calling me her savior and saying she loved me more than anything.

In my fantasy, I would act surprised. "Liza," I'd say, "do you think I didn't notice your love? I saw it all, but I didn't approach you because I didn't want you to feel obligated. I didn't want to pressure you into loving me out of gratitude. That wouldn't be right. It wouldn't be fair." Then, overcome with joy, I would declare her my noble wife, my creation, my pure and redeemed partner. Together, we would start a new life, perhaps travel abroad, and so on. But as I daydreamed, it all began to feel ridiculous, even to me. I caught myself sticking out my tongue at my own absurd imagination.

I kept thinking that they wouldn't let her leave—"that girl!" I thought bitterly. They don't let them go out easily, especially not in the evening. For some reason, I imagined she'd come in the evening, precisely at seven o'clock. Though she had said she wasn't completely enslaved there and still had certain freedoms, I couldn't shake the feeling. Damn it, I thought, she will come. She's sure to come!

It was fortunate, in a way, that Apollon distracted me with his rudeness during this time. He drove me past the limits of my patience. He was like a curse on my life, sent by Providence itself. We had been bickering constantly for years, and I hated him. My God, how I hated him! I don't think I had ever hated anyone in my life as much as I hated him, especially in certain moments.

Apollon was an older, dignified man who worked part-time as a tailor. For some reason I couldn't fathom, he despised me completely and treated me with unbearable disdain. Though, in truth, he seemed to look down on everyone. Even glancing at his neatly combed flaxen hair, with that tuft slicked back on his forehead using sunflower oil, or the way his thin lips formed into a self-assured "V," was enough to tell you this was a man who had never doubted himself. He was the greatest pedant I had ever met, utterly precise in every detail of his life. His vanity could have rivaled Alexander the Great's; he seemed infatuated with every button on his coat, every fingernail on his hand, and it showed in the way he carried himself.

When it came to me, he was nothing short of a tyrant. He barely spoke to me, but when he did, it was with a cold, ironical gaze that drove me mad. He worked for me as though doing me a great favor, and yet, in truth, he hardly did anything at all. He didn't even consider himself obligated to do much. It was painfully clear that he thought me the biggest fool on earth, and the only reason he stayed was for the seven roubles a month I paid him. For those seven roubles, he would barely lift a finger for me. My hatred for him reached such heights that even the sound of his footsteps sometimes sent me into fits of rage.

What irritated me most was his lisp. It wasn't severe, but it seemed as though his tongue was slightly too long, which caused him to lisp. He seemed oddly proud of it, as if it added to his dignity. He spoke in a slow, deliberate tone, with his hands behind his back and his gaze fixed on the ground. His habit of reading psalms aloud in the evenings, in a dreary, sing-song voice like a funeral chant, was a particular source of annoyance for me. I had waged countless arguments with him over this habit, yet it continued. Later in life, he even took to reading psalms over the dead for hire, while also killing rats and making shoe polish on the side.

At the time, though, I couldn't get rid of him. It was as if he were chemically bound to my existence. Even if I'd wanted to dismiss him, he would never have left. My small flat, shabby as it was, was my sanctuary, my cave, my place to hide from the world. For some strange reason, Apollon felt like an inseparable part of that space. For seven years, I couldn't bring myself to send him away.

Being even two or three days late with his wages was unthinkable. If I ever delayed payment, he would cause such a scene that I wouldn't know where to hide. Yet, during those days of irritation and frustration, I decided to take some small revenge. I resolved not to pay him for two whole weeks, just to teach him a lesson and remind him who was in charge. I had been considering doing this for two years, and now I was finally going to act on it. I wanted to see him squirm, to make him be the one to speak up first about his wages.

I imagined how I would respond. I would take the seven roubles from the drawer, show him that I had the money set aside, but refuse to pay him. I wouldn't hand it over simply because I didn't want to— because I was the master here, and I decided when and if he got paid. He had been rude and disrespectful to me for too long, and this was my way of putting him in his place. Perhaps, if he humbled himself and asked politely, I might give him the money. But if not, he could wait another fortnight—or even three weeks, or a whole month. It would all depend on me.

I was furious, but he still got the better of me. I couldn't hold out for even four days. He began his usual routine, the same tactics he'd used before, which I knew all too well. First, he'd fix me with a stern, relentless stare, holding it for several minutes, especially when we crossed paths or when I was leaving the house. If I ignored him and pretended not to notice, he'd escalate.

Next, he would silently walk into my room while I was pacing or reading, stand in the doorway with one hand behind his back and the other foot tucked neatly behind the other, and glare at me with even greater contempt. If I asked what he wanted, he wouldn't reply, just keep staring for a few more seconds before turning around deliberately and leaving. Two hours later, he'd do the same thing again. Sometimes I'd grow so furious that I wouldn't even ask what he wanted. Instead, I'd snap my head up and stare back at him, glaring furiously. We would lock eyes for a solid two minutes before he finally turned away, just as composed and deliberate as before.

If none of this worked and I still didn't give in, he'd start sighing deeply as though measuring my moral failure with each breath. Inevitably, this wore me down. I'd yell and rage, but in the end, I'd have to do whatever he wanted.

This time, I lost my temper almost immediately. The moment he began his usual staring routine, I snapped. I was already on edge.

"Stop right there!" I shouted as he began to turn back toward his room, his hands folded behind his back. "Come back! I said come back!" My voice was so loud and unnatural that he paused, even looking slightly surprised. But he said nothing, and his silence only made me angrier.

"What gives you the right to come here and stare at me like that without being called? Answer me!" I demanded.

He calmly watched me for a few seconds, then began to turn around again.

"Stop!" I roared, rushing toward him. "Don't move! Tell me— what are you here for? What do you want?"

"If you have any orders for me, it's my duty to carry them out," he replied slowly, in his infuriatingly measured tone, lisping as always. He raised his eyebrows and tilted his head, as though he were the one who should feel exasperated.

"That's not what I'm asking, you miserable tyrant!" I shouted, my face hot with anger. "I know exactly why you're here—you want your wages! But you're too proud to ask for them. So you're trying to punish me with your stupid, silent stares. It's childish! Stupid, stupid, stupid!"

He started to turn away again, but I grabbed him.

"Listen to me!" I yelled. "Here's the money! See it? Here it is!" I yanked the seven roubles out of the drawer. "But you're not getting it—not until you bow your head and respectfully apologize to me. Do you hear me?"

"That's not going to happen," he replied, calm as ever, his confidence maddening.

"It will happen," I insisted. "I swear it will!"

"And I have nothing to apologize for," he said, as though my outburst didn't matter at all. "Besides, you just called me a 'tyrant.' I could report you to the police for insulting me."

"Go ahead, report me!" I screamed. "Do it right now! You're still a tyrant!"

But he only gave me a cold look, then turned and walked away, ignoring my shouts. His footsteps were slow, steady, and deliberate, each one more infuriating than the last.

"This is all because of Liza," I thought bitterly. "None of this would have happened if it weren't for her."

After a moment, I decided to follow him. My heart was pounding, but I forced myself to walk into his room with as much dignity as I could muster.

"Apollon," I said firmly, though I was out of breath, "go and fetch the police immediately."

He was sitting at his table, threading a needle with his usual composure. Hearing my order, he burst into laughter.

"Right now," I insisted. "Go, or you won't believe what I'll do next."

"You've lost your mind," he said, not even bothering to look up. His tone was as slow and deliberate as ever. "Who calls the police on themselves? You're making a fuss over nothing."

"Go!" I screamed, grabbing him by the shoulder. I was ready to hit him.

At that moment, I noticed the door to the passage slowly opening. A figure stepped inside and stopped, staring at us in confusion. When I turned and saw who it was, shame washed over me. I bolted back to my room, clutching my head in both hands. Leaning against the wall, I stood motionless, humiliated and furious.

Two minutes later, I heard Apollon's calm footsteps approaching.

"There's a woman asking for you," he said, his tone more severe than usual. Then he stepped aside and let Liza into the room. He didn't leave, though. He stood there, staring at us with a sarcastic look on his face.

"Leave! Get out of here!" I shouted desperately.

At that moment, the clock began to whirr and chime. It struck seven.

Chapter 9

I stood in front of her, completely defeated and embarrassed, awkwardly fumbling with the ragged edges of my old dressing gown, trying to wrap it around myself. It was exactly as I had imagined it would be during one of my earlier fits of despair. After staring at us for what felt like an eternity, Apollon finally left the room, but his departure didn't make me feel any more comfortable. In fact, it only made things worse. She was just as uneasy as I was, maybe even more so, which surprised me. She looked flustered, clearly uncomfortable at the sight of me.

"Sit down," I said automatically, pulling out a chair for her. I sat down on the sofa. She immediately obeyed, sitting stiffly and looking at me with wide, expectant eyes, as though she was waiting for me to say something meaningful. That look—so trusting, so naïve—infuriated me, though I did my best to hold back my anger.

She should have pretended not to notice anything unusual, acted as if everything were perfectly normal. But instead, she sat there like that, making it impossible for me to ignore her presence. I could feel myself thinking that she'd pay for this awkwardness somehow.

"You've caught me in a strange situation, Liza," I began hesitantly, knowing even as I spoke that it was a terrible way to start. "No, no, don't get the wrong idea," I quickly added, seeing her face flush. "I'm not ashamed of my poverty. On the contrary, I take pride in it. I may be poor, but I'm honorable. You can be poor and still be honorable," I mumbled, my voice trailing off. "Would you like some tea?"

"No," she began softly.

"Wait a moment."

I jumped up and rushed out to find Apollon. I couldn't stay in the room a second longer.

"Apollon," I whispered urgently, slamming the seven roubles down in front of him, the same ones I'd been clutching tightly in my fist. "Here's your pay. Take it. But I need your help—bring me some tea and a dozen rusks from the restaurant. If you don't, I'll be ruined! You don't understand what's at stake here. This woman—she's everything! You're probably thinking something awful, but you don't know—she's everything!"

Apollon, seated calmly at his table with his spectacles on, didn't even glance at the money at first. Slowly, he looked at it out of the corner of his eye but said nothing. He kept fiddling with his needle, which he still hadn't threaded. I stood there for three agonizing minutes, arms crossed like Napoleon, my temples damp with sweat. I could feel the color draining from my face. Finally, after what felt like an eternity, he must have taken pity on me. With excruciating deliberation, he threaded his needle, set it down, rose from his chair, adjusted his spectacles, and counted the money.

"Should I get a whole portion?" he asked over his shoulder, his tone infuriatingly indifferent. Then, still moving deliberately, he walked out of the room.

As I made my way back to Liza, a wild thought crossed my mind: Should I run away? Just bolt out the door in my dressing gown and disappear? Anything to escape this situation.

I sat down again. She was watching me uneasily, and for a few moments, neither of us spoke.

"I'll kill him!" I suddenly shouted, slamming my fist on the table so hard that ink splattered out of the inkwell.

"What are you saying?" she gasped, startled.

"I'll kill him! I'll kill him!" I shrieked, pounding the table in a fit of rage. At the same time, I was completely aware of how ridiculous I looked, but I couldn't stop myself. "You don't understand, Liza. That man is my tormentor! He's torturing me! He's gone now to fetch rusks, but he..."

Before I could finish, I burst into tears. It was an uncontrollable, hysterical breakdown. Even as I sobbed, I felt a deep shame, but I couldn't hold back.

Liza was clearly frightened.

"What's wrong? What's happening?" she asked, moving closer to me.

"Water... bring me water, it's over there," I muttered weakly, though deep down, I knew I didn't need water at all. I was putting on a show, trying to save face even in the middle of a genuine breakdown.

She brought me a glass of water, her face filled with confusion. At that moment, Apollon returned with the tea. The sight of the mundane teapot and rusks felt almost comical after the drama of the last few moments. The sheer normality of it embarrassed me, and I felt my face burn with shame. Liza looked at Apollon as though he were some kind of threat. He didn't even glance at either of us before leaving the room.

"Liza, do you despise me?" I asked suddenly, staring at her intently. I was trembling, desperate to know what was going through her mind.

She seemed flustered, unsure of how to answer.

"Drink your tea," I said harshly, my voice full of anger. Though I was furious with myself, it was she who had to endure it. A sudden, overwhelming bitterness toward her welled up in my chest; I felt as though I could have hurt her. I silently swore to myself not to say a single word to her the entire time she was here, as if punishing her could somehow soothe my rage. "This is all her fault," I thought to myself.

We sat in silence for five long minutes. The tea sat untouched on the table between us. I made a deliberate choice not to speak first, relishing her discomfort, wanting her to feel awkward for not knowing how to break the silence. She glanced at me a few times, her expression a mix of sadness and confusion. But I refused to speak, even as my own behavior filled me with shame. Deep down, I knew how petty and cruel I was being, but I couldn't stop myself.

"I want to leave that place for good," she said quietly, breaking the silence. Her voice trembled, as though she was testing the waters. Poor girl—she couldn't have picked a worse moment to say something like that, especially to someone as spiteful and pathetic as I was at that moment. Her honesty and vulnerability only made me angrier, as if her words were an attack on me. My heart briefly ached for her, but my nastiness snuffed out any compassion I might have felt.

Another five minutes passed.

"Maybe I'm bothering you," she said timidly, her voice barely a whisper, as she made a move to stand up.

But the moment I saw her trying to leave, her quiet dignity struck a nerve, and my bitterness exploded. I trembled with anger and lashed out.

"Why did you come here?" I demanded, my voice shaking. "Tell me! Why are you here?"

I was barely able to catch my breath, and my words tumbled out in a chaotic rush, as if I was trying to release everything at once. "You want to know why you came? I'll tell you why! You came here because of all that sentimental nonsense I said to you. Now you're soft and eager to hear more of those pretty words. But guess what? I was laughing at you then, and I'm laughing at you now! Why are you flinching? Yes, I was laughing at you! You think I came to save you? Is that what you thought? Well, let me tell you the truth—I came to you because I was furious! I'd been humiliated by the others at dinner, and I wanted to take it out on someone. I couldn't find the person I wanted to hit, so I found you instead. You were convenient, so I used you. That's all it was. I wanted power. I wanted to humiliate someone, anyone, just so I could feel like I wasn't powerless. And you thought I came to save you? Is that what you believed?"

Her face went pale as a sheet. She looked like she'd been struck. She tried to say something, her lips moving soundlessly, but she couldn't form the words. Finally, she collapsed onto a chair like someone who had been physically attacked. Her lips parted slightly, and her eyes widened in horror as she stared at me, trembling as though she couldn't process the cruelty of my words. But she understood. She understood everything.

"Save you?" I continued, my voice rising. I jumped up and began pacing the room like a madman. "Save you from what? Do you think I'm better than you? I'm worse! I wanted power, that's all. I wanted the satisfaction of seeing you cry, of watching you break down. That's what I wanted! I gave you my address in a moment of stupidity, and the moment I did, I hated you for it. I cursed you for making me feel guilty, for making me feel anything at all! You don't know me—I'm not some noble hero. I'm selfish. I just want peace. I don't care about anyone or anything, as long as I have my tea. Did you know that? Did you?"

I laughed bitterly and kept going, my voice filled with venom. "I'm a liar, a coward, a selfish little worm. I was terrified you'd come here and see me like this, in this torn, filthy dressing gown, and now here you are! And I hate you for it! I hate you for seeing me like this. I hate you for being here when I lost control and cried in front of you. I hate you for listening to me now, for standing there silently while I spill all of this! And what's worse is that I hate myself even more! Do you hear me?"

She sat frozen, still trembling. Her face was pale, her expression blank as though she didn't know what to do. I could feel the weight of her gaze on me, but I couldn't stop.

"Why are you still here?" I yelled. "Why don't you leave? Why are you just sitting there, staring at me? Don't you understand? I hate you for being here, and I'll hate you even more once you're gone! So why don't you just go?"

Something unexpected happened. I was so used to imagining the world as I had read about it in books or dreamed it up in my mind, that I couldn't immediately grasp the strange reality in front of me. What happened was this: Liza, whom I had insulted and humiliated, understood far more than I ever expected. She realized something that a woman in love often understands first—that I was deeply unhappy.

At first, her expression, full of fear and hurt, shifted into one of sorrowful confusion. When I started calling myself a scoundrel and a wretch, with tears running down my face as I ranted, her face twisted in pain. She looked like she was about to stand up and stop me. But when I ended my tirade by shouting, "Why are you here? Why don't you leave?" she didn't respond to the words themselves. Instead, she saw how much it hurt me to say them. Poor Liza—she was so crushed and considered herself so far beneath me that she couldn't feel anger or resentment. Suddenly, with a burst of emotion, she jumped up from her chair, reaching her hands toward me, though she was still timid and unsure.

At that moment, something changed in my heart, too. Then she rushed toward me, threw her arms around me, and began to sob. I couldn't hold back anymore either, and I cried as I never had before. "They won't let me… I can't be good!" I managed to say, brokenly. Then I stumbled to the sofa, fell face down onto it, and sobbed uncontrollably for what must have been fifteen minutes. Genuine hysterics.

Liza stayed by me, wrapping her arms around me and holding me tightly. She didn't move. But the tears couldn't go on forever, and eventually (this is the awful truth), as I lay with my face buried in that shabby leather pillow, I began to feel something else. Slowly, almost against my will, a thought crept into my mind. I started to feel embarrassed—embarrassed to lift my head and meet Liza's eyes. Why was I ashamed? I don't know. But I was. And another thought entered my mind: our roles had reversed. Now she was the strong one, the heroine, while I was the humiliated, broken one—just as she had been when we first met a few nights ago.

As I lay there, the realization sank in, and I wondered, my God, could I be jealous of her? To this day, I don't know for sure. At the time, I certainly couldn't figure out what I was feeling. I've always had a need to dominate, to control someone. But reasoning about these things never gets you anywhere—it's pointless to even try.

Eventually, I forced myself to raise my head. I had to; I couldn't lie there forever. And I'm certain now that it was because I felt too ashamed to look at her that another feeling suddenly flared up inside me. A feeling of power and ownership. My eyes burned with passion, and I gripped her hands tightly. In that moment, I hated her and wanted her more than ever. The two feelings fed off each other, each one making the other stronger. It felt almost like revenge.

At first, her face showed surprise—maybe even fear—but it lasted only a moment. Then she wrapped her arms around me warmly, with complete and unreserved affection.

Chapter 10

Fifteen minutes later, I was pacing back and forth across the room in a frenzy of impatience. Every few moments, I would peek through the crack in the screen to look at Liza. She was sitting on the floor with her head resting against the bed, and it seemed like she had been crying. But she wasn't leaving, and that irritated me even more. This time, she understood everything. I had insulted her in the worst way, but there's no need to go into details. She realized that my sudden outburst of passion had been nothing but revenge—a fresh humiliation. She must have sensed that my earlier, almost groundless hatred had now turned personal, born from envy.

I don't claim she understood all of this clearly, but she certainly grasped the most important truth—that I was a despicable man and, even worse, completely incapable of loving her.

You might think this is unbelievable, but I tell you it's not. What's hard to believe is how spiteful and foolish I was. Some might find it strange that I didn't love her or at least value her love. But why would that be strange? By then, I wasn't capable of love. For me, love always meant having power over someone, showing my moral superiority. That was the only kind of love I could imagine. In fact, I often think now that love, at its core, is about having the right—freely given by the other person—to control them.

Even in my fantasies, love was always a struggle. It started with hatred and ended with me triumphing over the other person. But after I "won," I never knew what to do with them. Looking back, it's no wonder I behaved the way I did. I had corrupted myself so completely and had become so detached from real life that I actually felt justified in blaming her, even shaming her, for coming to me seeking "beautiful words." And I didn't even realize that she hadn't come for words. She had come because she wanted to love me. For a woman, all redemption, renewal, and salvation often begin and end with love.

Still, as I stormed around the room and spied on her through the screen, I didn't hate her as much as I hated her presence. Her being there suffocated me. I wanted her gone. I wanted peace, to be left alone in my miserable underground world. Real life was too overwhelming for me—it was so unfamiliar, it felt like I couldn't even breathe.

Several minutes passed, and still, she didn't move. She sat there as if she were in a trance. Shamelessly, I tapped softly on the screen, trying to remind her to leave. She flinched, then jumped up and hurried to gather her things—her scarf, her hat, her coat—as though she were trying to escape. Two minutes later, she stepped out from behind the screen, her eyes heavy with sorrow.

I forced a cruel grin, mostly for show, and turned away to avoid meeting her gaze.

"Goodbye," she said quietly, heading toward the door.

I rushed over to her, grabbed her hand, pried it open, and placed something inside before quickly running to the other corner of the room, too ashamed to look at her.

A moment ago, I almost lied about this. I almost wrote that I had done it without thinking, as if in a moment of foolishness. But I won't lie. I'll admit the truth: I put the money in her hand out of sheer spite. As I had paced back and forth earlier, the idea had come to me. And although it was cruel, it didn't come from my heart—it came from my bitter, twisted mind. This act of cruelty was deliberate, calculated, and artificial. It came from the same dark place as all the books and fantasies I used to build my warped understanding of life.

But even after doing it, I couldn't stand myself. I immediately ran to the far corner, ashamed and in despair. A second later, I bolted out the door after her, shouting, "Liza! Liza!" as I reached the stairs. My voice was low at first, timid. There was no reply, but I thought I heard footsteps echoing below.

"Liza!" I called again, louder this time.

Still no answer. Then, I heard the heavy outer door creak open and slam shut with a loud bang that echoed up the stairwell. She was gone.

I hesitated for a moment before going back to my room. The weight in my chest felt unbearable. I stood there by the table, staring at the chair where she had been sitting, my mind blank. After a minute, I noticed something on the table.

There, crumpled up, was the blue five-rouble note I had thrust into her hand. It was the same one—there was no mistaking it. Somehow, in the moment I had turned away, she had managed to throw it back onto the table without me noticing.

Well, I should have expected this. Should I? No, I couldn't have. I was so selfish, so blind to other people's dignity, that I hadn't even considered she might do such a thing. The realization was too much for me.

A moment later, like a madman, I began throwing on my clothes. I didn't care what I wore—I just needed to go after her. She couldn't have gone far. She must have only been a few steps ahead when I burst out into the street.

The night was still, and the snow fell steadily, blanketing the pavement and the empty streets like a thick, soft pillow. The street was silent, completely deserted, and the dim streetlights gave off a weak, pointless glow. I ran about two hundred paces to the crossroads and stopped abruptly.

Where had she gone? And why was I chasing after her?

Why? To fall to my knees before her, to sob and beg her forgiveness, to kiss her feet. That was what I longed to do. My heart felt like it was being torn apart, and even now, I can't think of that moment without feeling overwhelmed. But then I stopped to ask myself—what would come of it? Would I not, perhaps even by tomorrow, start to hate her simply because I had kissed her feet today? Would I truly bring her any happiness? I already knew, for the hundredth time, what I was capable of. Wouldn't I just hurt her again?

I stood there in the snow, staring into the darkness, my thoughts churning.

"Would it not be better," I mused later, sitting at home and trying to smother the pain in my heart with fantasies, "if she kept the bitterness of this insult forever? Bitterness—it's purifying, even though it stings. Tomorrow, I would only corrupt her spirit and drain her heart. But now, the memory of this insult might linger in her soul, making her stronger, elevating her—perhaps even purifying her—through hatred or maybe even forgiveness. But will that make her life easier?"

And here I pause to ask, not just for her sake but for my own: what's better? A cheap happiness or profound suffering? Which one is more worthwhile?

That evening, as I sat at home, nearly crushed by the weight of my sorrow, this question tormented me. I had never experienced such deep regret or anguish. And yet, could there have been any doubt that I would turn back halfway as soon as I ran out of my apartment? I never saw Liza again, nor did I hear anything about her. For a long time, though, I clung to that phrase about resentment and hatred being a form of purification, even though I nearly made myself ill with misery.

Now, after so many years, this memory still feels like an ugly scar. I have many such scars, but perhaps it's better to stop here. I think I made a mistake even starting to write these "Notes." The whole time I've been writing, I've felt nothing but shame. This isn't literature—it feels more like punishment. Why should anyone want to read a long story about how I ruined my life, how I wasted away in bitterness, shut away from real life, festering in my underground world? It's not interesting. A story needs a hero, and I am no hero. In fact, all the traits of an anti-hero are laid out here, and what's worse, they leave an unpleasant aftertaste.

We are all disconnected from life. We're all crippled, every one of us, to some extent. We've grown so detached that we recoil from real life, finding it distasteful, even burdensome. We prefer the version of life we find in books. And yet, we complain and demand something different. But what is it we want? We don't even know ourselves. If our impatient demands were granted, we'd be the first to regret it. Take away the restraints that bind us, give us freedom and independence, and what would we do? I'm sure most of us would beg to have the chains back, to be told what to do.

You might argue with me and say, "Speak for yourself! Don't include us in your miserable underground existence." Fine, I'm not speaking for everyone. But as for me, I've simply taken things to an extreme, whereas you, perhaps, have only gone halfway and called your restraint "good sense." You comfort yourselves with lies. So maybe there is more life in me than in you. Think about that!

We no longer even know what it means to live. Leave us without books, and we'd be utterly lost. We wouldn't know where to turn, what to hold onto, what to love or hate, what to respect or despise. We are ashamed of being real, flesh-and-blood people, and instead, we try to be some abstract, generalized version of humanity. We've become lifeless, and for generations, we've been brought into this world by nothing but empty ideas, not by living people. And we've grown to like it that way. Soon enough, we'll find a way to be born entirely from abstract ideas.

But that's enough. I don't want to write anymore from my "Underground."

Translated by Tim Zengerink

Thank You for Reading

Dear Reader,

We hope this timeless classic has sparked your imagination and enriched your literary journey. Now that you've turned the final page, we want to share a vision for the future of reading—one where every classic you've ever wanted to explore is at your fingertips, in a format that best suits your life.

We'd like to invite you to gain immediate, unlimited digital & audiobook access to hundreds of the most treasured literary classics ever written—along with the option to secure deluxe paperback, hardcover & box set editions at printing cost. Together, we can spark a new global literary renaissance alongside our small, independent publishing house called "The Library of Alexandria."

Thousands of years ago, the Library of Alexandria stood as a beacon of knowledge—until it was lost to history. We aim to reignite that spirit of preservation and discovery right now, in the modern age—only this time, it's accessible to all, in every language and every format.

Picture a world where every timeless classic, novel, poem, or philosophical treatise is not only available to read but also updated for today's readers—modernized, translated into any language or dialect, and ready to enjoy in any format you choose, whether that is in an eBook, audiobook, paperback, or deluxe hardcover & box set version a printing cost.

By joining our movement to rebuild the modern Library of Alexandria, you become part of an unprecedented mission to offer:

- **Unlimited Audiobook & eBook Access to the Greatest Classics of All Time**

  Instantly explore thousands of legendary works, from Plato and Shakespeare to Jane Austen and Leo Tolstoy. All are instantly ready to read or listen to, giving you a complete literary universe at your fingertips.

- **Paperback & Deluxe Editions at Printing Costs:**

Purchase any title in a paperback, deluxe hardbound, or deluxe boxset edition at printing costs, shipped right to your doorstep. Curate your personal library of Alexandria with editions worthy of display—crafted to last, designed to captivate, and delivered straight to your door.

- **Modern translations for Contemporary Readers in all languages and dialects**

Discover a vast selection of classics reimagined in clear, current language—no more struggling with outdated phrases or obscure references. Next to the original versions, we aim to offer translations in as many languages and dialects as possible.

As we continue our translation efforts and add new languages, readers everywhere can connect with these works as if they were written today. By bridging linguistic divides, you're contributing to ensuring that these timeless stories become more meaningful, accessible, and inspiring for people across the globe.

- **Your Personal Library of Alexandria:**

Over the months and years, you'll curate a unique physical archive of classics—each volume a testament to your taste, curiosity, and love of knowledge. It's not just about owning books—it's about curating a cultural legacy you'll cherish and pass down for generations to come.

- **Join a Global Literary Renaissance:**

Your support fuels an ongoing mission: allowing us to reinvest in offering deluxe print editions (including special boxsets) at their true cost, broaden the range of available formats and translations, and extend the reach of these works to new audiences worldwide. By joining today, you're not just preserving a legacy of masterpieces; you set in motion a powerful wave of literary accessibility.

We are more than a publisher—we're a movement, and we can't do it alone. Your support lets us scale our mission, preserving and reimagining history's greatest works for tomorrow's readers.

Become a Torchbearer of knowledge.

Thank you for picking up this book and allowing us into your literary journey. As you turn the pages, know that you're part of something larger: a global effort to keep these stories alive, share their wisdom across borders and generations, and spark a true cultural revival for the modern era.

If this resonates with you—please consider taking the next step by visiting:

www.libraryofalexandria.com

With gratitude and a shared love of knowledge,

The Modern Library of Alexandria Team

Visit:

www.libraryofalexandria.com

Or scan the code below: